Gog and *Magog*

Yawm al-Qiyamah, Yawm al-Din
The Day of Judgment

Carl Douglass

Neurosurgeon Turned Author Writes with Gripping Realism

Publication Since 1978
Consultants

PO Box 221974 Anchorage, Alaska 99522-1974
books@publicationconsultants.com—www.publicationconsultants.com

ISBN 978-1-59433-379-8
eBook ISBN 978-1-59433-380-4
Library of Congress Catalog Card Number: 2013940673

Manufactured in the United States of America.

Gog *and* Magog

Yawm al-Qiyamah, Yawm al-Din
The Day of Judgment

A Novel by Carl Douglass

DEDICATION

GOG AND MAGOG is dedicated to all those American and Israeli martyrs to the systematic evil of terrorism and to all of those who have fought against terrorism for civilization and liberty.

DISCLAIMER

This is a work of fiction. Except for a few place names and oblique references to well-known individuals, organizations, or events that play only a very limited role in this novel, everything is fictional. Any resemblance to any real person—living or dead—or any real event is purely coincidental, accidental, and un-intended.

For I will no more pity the inhabitants of the land, saith the Lord; but, lo, I will deliver the men every one into his neighbour's hand, and into the hand of his king; and they shall smite the land, and out of their hand, I will not deliver thee.
Holy Bible, Zechariah 11:6

And I will shew wonders in the heavens and in the earth, blood, and fire, and pillars of smoke. The sun shall be turned into darkness, and the moon into blood...
Holy Bible, Joel 2:30-31

That day is a day of wrath, a day of trouble and distress, a day of wasteness and desolation, a day of darkness and gloominess, a day of clouds and thick darkness.
Holy Bible, Zephaniah 1:15

And the earth with the mountains shall be lifted up and crushed with one crash. Then on that day will the Event befall.
Holy Qur'an, 6:33

When the heavens shall be rent asunder,
And when the stars shall be dispersed...
Again, what will teach thee what the Day of Judgment is?
It is a Day when no soul will avail aught for another soul...
Holy Qur'an, 82:1-19

CHAPTER ONE

OCTOBER, 2001

The Great Satan and the Little Satan were nicked, but not maimed, annoyed, but not ignited. The members of the Council of Leaders of Islam were collectively frustrated that thirty years of effort by Freedom Fighters had produced so little at so great a cost.

The chairman told them, "I am well aware of your good intentions, your dedication, and your piety. What I do not see is your patience. It is a fool who blunders into martyrdom for the sake of The Prophet, may God's blessings be upon his Messenger, and for Allah. We are making progress; we are coming to know our enemies well enough to find their weaknesses, but we do not yet know enough. It will be a short time, let me assure you, and then we will know enough, and Allah will grant us all that we require for the last day. I have spent enough time among the infidels to know that they cannot hold their blasphemous tongues. Our people know much of their plans; they know nothing of ours. Mark this, brothers, the plan is well under way. The forces of God, and the fools he provides us from the enemy camp, are bringing our strategic and tactical plans to the brink of execution. I have just come from their United Nations Security Council where I kept quiet and listened and learned.

"There is a Western book that describes our situation nicely. It is called *The Lion in Winter*, written by a man named James Goldman. Never mind that he is an accursed Jew; there is wisdom in the vignette he relates. The young, trusting, and inexperienced king of France, Philip II, met with the older and more cunning Henry II of Great Britain before they entered into a great

European war against each other. Young Philip perceived that their conversation had just begun when Henry abruptly rose to leave. Philip asked why, and Henry responded with the comment that 'winning is very satisfactory.' Philip denied that Henry had won anything. Henry paused and explained, 'I've found out the way your mind works and the kind of man you are. I know your plans and expectations. You have burbled every bit of strategy you've got. I know exactly what you will do and exactly what you won't. And I've told you exactly nothing. To these aged eyes, boy, that's what winning looks like. *Dormez bien.*'"

Prince Ahmed Wahhab ibn Saud, the Chairman, looked down at the Council members for a moment. Their attention was rapt as it always was when this son of both great Saudi Arabian families—the religiously powerful Wahabis, and the secularly powerful Saudis—chose to convey his thoughts to an audience. One of more than 5000 Saudi princes, the man was almost unknown in the Western world and was a shadowy figure in the Muslim world, but he wielded more power than the all the princes and presidents on the council combined. He was their appointed absolute leader for the final struggle.

Prince ibn Saud was an imposingly large man, tall, heavy boned, and portly. He had the face of a desert hawk with an aquiline nose, large straight white teeth, and piercing brown eyes. The prince never smiled, a price of leadership. He wore an elaborate Van Dyke beard that his servant carefully groomed every day. His skin was light because he had never allowed it to be exposed to direct sunlight, a factor of leadership his father had taught him. Light skinned men ruled the world, his princely father had told him from childhood, and Ahmed never forgot it.

The prince cared little for the affectations of the West and almost never wore Western clothing. The flowing white thobe he wore was made of subtly woven Egyptian cotton and white Thai silk, and was hemmed with gold thread. He wore a red and white patterned *smagh* shawl head cover held in place by a comfortable adjustable Bedouin style *Egal* head band and Moroccan leather slippers with upturned toes, which set him apart as a man who had never been obliged to stoop to manual labor. On a handsome red leather belt around his waist, tooled with inscriptions from the *Qur'an*, he carried a razor sharp ornate curved Omani kunja dagger with a handle of black rhinoceros horn. His mode of dress, like his carefully maintained body size, and his imperious face were the physical hallmarks of leadership in his world.

The prince gazed at the assembled men—the cream of Islam—his men. God's men. He had known them all for years, and every one of them was willing to die for Islam, and more importantly, to kill for God's Holy Religion. He never lost his sense of wonder at God's work in which he was engaged or his deep-seated love for the brothers looking up at him for direction. More than his wives, his children, or his biological brothers; he looked upon these men as family.

He paused to reflect a few moments on how he had arrived at this pinnacle and about how he would wield the immense power he had been granted. He had to smile at himself; he had been born with a figurative gold spoon in his mouth, at the top of the social stratosphere, and had worked his way upward from there. Ahmed's father was a Saudi prince who occupied what would have appeared to be a minor role as a functionary in the Kingdom: he was the Minister of the Interior. However, to those who mattered, even foreigners and *kaffirs* [unbelievers] from the diplomatic and business world, Prince Abdullah Mohammed ibn Saud was the ruler of Saudi Arabia in everything but title.

Ahmed grew up in a household where his father currently had four wives, an uncertain number of concubines, and fifty-two children. Over the course of Abdullah's life of fifty-eight years, he had had seventy-one wives, many divorces, a few deaths, and more than 150 children, some of whom were dead from disease or battle, some from infanticide—a father's prerogative—and the rest were engaged in the family businesses. Abdullah was what his associates called a *mizwaj* [a man who likes to wed often].

Ahmed was the first son of Abdullah's first wife; so, he started his life's social race in front of the pack of most favored children. His father's revered wife, Ahmed's mother, was Adria, the adored daughter of Farrukh Hassan Al-Wahhab, the recognized and deferred to eldest brother of the pre-eminent family in the kingdom's clerical hierarchy. Prince Abdullah was a strict constructionist of the strict Wahhabi sect of Sunni Islam. The Wahhabi variation was the legal religion of the state; Abdullah was the confidant of the Wahhabi family, and served his Saudi king unflinchingly. Unlike many polygamous Arab patriarchs, Prince Abdullah insisted on gathering all of his wives and concubines into a compound. Each wife had her own house and kept her own children with her in near autonomy. However, the education of the boys was the exclusive purview of the grand patriarch of the nuclear and extended family. The compound in which young Ahmed lived had been built by the fabulously wealthy and favored bin Ladens—the work directed personally by Muhammad bin Oud bin Laden, himself.

Prince Abdullah had known Muhammad practically from the time that the man was nothing more than a porter on the Jeddah docks. The prince had recognized the illiterate young man's genius with figures and his razor sharp mind. He gave him a job, cultivated Muhammad's budding genius as an engineer—and greatest of all—introduced him to King Saud. The old king was in a wheel chair, and the clever Muhammad, now the head of a small construction company, personally built a ramp from the first to the second floor of the palace thereby gaining for the commoner entrance into the favor and the houses of the royal family. When Muhammad built a road full of hairpin curves up a sheer cliff that shortened the royal family's commute to the summer palace in at Taif, he was rewarded by the early construction contracts that ensured that he and his family would be among the truly rich of the world for as far in the future as they could foresee. bin Laden never forgot that string of favors, and the two families grew to be trusted friends.

Muhammad's seventeenth son of fifty children—the boy Usama—was the child of the patriarch and a foreign born Syrian concubine, said to be a favored consort among all his women. Although the bin Ladens steadfastly denied that it was so, Usama was stigmatized by the foreignness of his mother and her reduced status; she was not a wife, and even under the law, the responsibility to her and the status she occupied made it impossible for her or one of her children ever to rise to the same level as the offspring of the four wives. Actually, Muhammad had eleven wives during his lifetime—only four at a time—the limit required by the Sharia [Islamic law].

As a result of his limited status in the family, Usama became quiet, introspective, and somewhat reclusive. He was not fully included in the childhood society of his half brothers and sisters and cousins. Even in adulthood, Usama was never granted any significant position in the bin Laden family multi-billion dollar business. The boy Usama brooded over the subtle slights that came his way from his family and because he was not treated with the same deference as his half-brothers by the royal family. He was soft and non-confrontational, a kind and overly solicitous child who began—at an early age—to ponder the deep meaning of the Holy Religion.

He was described as a sad boy according to his family because he and his half brothers all had different fathers. This smacked peripherally of immorality to Usama, a small drip of acid that soured his character as he matured. One of his few friends was Prince Ahmed Wahhab ibn Saud, the scion of the pre-eminent Saud family, and this was largely due to an accident of birth. Both boys had been born in 1955 within a day of each other, and they were regularly placed together as playmates because of their parents' wishes that the inter-familial bonds between the families of Muhammad bin Laden and Abdullah ibn Saud should be strengthened even into the next generation.

Prince Ahmed and Usama were placed in the same prestigious primary school in Jeddah where the bin Ladens lived due to the school's reputation for building men and leaders. The Saudi educational system is divided: segregated by sex and by religious choice. Usama and his parents decided for him that he would pursue a secular education, and Prince Ahmed's parents—knowing the greatness that lay in his future as a first tier prince in the royal family—chose the traditional Islamic education for him. That educational track trains boys to become members of the Ulema [religious clergy] with the process eventually leading to membership in the High Judiciary of the Sharia. It was crucial for the boy, Ahmed, to have both the background and the credentials for him to assume an august role in the future of *Al-Mamlaka al Arabiya as-Saudiya* [the Kingdom of Saudi Arabia].

It was crucial to the bin Laden family that their sons—including Usama—become proficient in mathematics, science, business, and engineering. Ahmed and Usama sat side by side at their desks and shared dreams and secrets. They both learned Arabic, art education, geography, history, mathematics and physical education; but Ahmed's education, as determined by the administrators of education—Imam Muhammad bin Saud Islamic University—steadily increased focus on Arabic and Islamic studies. Both boys excelled in primary school and easily earned their *Shahadat Al Madaaris Al Ibtiba a'iyyah* [leaving elementary school certificate], and their life's paths began to diverge slowly but inexorably.

When Prince Ahmed and Usama turned ten and were presumed to have reached the age of accountability by the religious establishment, they were introduced to a life changing experience. Prince Abdullah and Muhammad bin Laden took their sons aside and began to explain the real world to them. It was time, the fathers declared, that they demonstrate their true allegiance to the Holy Religion and come to its defense against its enemies. The principle enemy, they were told, was not the foreign kaffirs, who should be regarded as useful fools, but the *Rafida* [rejectionists of religion], the unholy Shi'a. The pubescent prince and the wealthy construction mogul's son were given books published by secular government agencies, official religious books, and compilations of decrees from government religious agencies that clearly proved to them that the Shi'a constituted an unlawful Jewish conspiracy against Holy Islam, and deserved to be demeaned, insulted, and finally eradicated—all five percent of the population that were of the accursed Shi'a—to cleanse the kingdom of nonMuslims.

The reasons were clear and compelling. Shi'a, they learned, was an infringement on Islam, a distortion of real Islam—they were *Mushriks* [polytheists]. Under Allah—said the Wahhabis—there could be no righteous harmony between Sunnis and Jews or Christians or the Shi'a.

Prince Abdullah told his son flatly, "You may never eat their food, marry their women, or allow the atheists to bury their dead in a Saudi graveyard. We have been successful in preventing the establishment of any Shi'a girls' private schools in the Rafida majority areas; we have prevented their whore mothers from finding day care centers to permit them to take the jobs of good Sunnis; and to date there is not a single Rafida principle in a girl's school in the Kingdom. It is all but unthinkable to have a Shi'a teacher of good Sunni boys. The day of cleansing will come. I will include you, my son, when it does; and on that day you will become a man."

That day did come, and not more than three months away. It was March; cold winds swept over the desert from the north. Madmen in the majority Shi'a areas of Qateet, Saihat, and Safwa in the Eastern Province around the oases of Al Hasa and Al Qatīf, decided that the Saudi rulers had become soft enough to permit the observance of their most revered holiday—an outlawed public expression of their filthy dissidence—the festival of Ashura or Moharram,

Saudi newspapers carried the shocking stories. *Al Madina* described in detail the offense to the true religion by the spectacle of hundreds of men and boys marching towards the principle city of the region—Al Huffuf—flagellating themselves with short knotted whips, drawing blood for that most mournful of Shi'a holidays that, if permitted, would take place on the tenth of every Islamic year. The penitential bleeding emulated the pain and suffering of Imam Hussain, grandson of the Prophet, may Allah bless and keep his Messenger, during Hassan's martyrdom—suffering that his loyal followers had failed to prevent, and for which failing they would forever feel shame.

His father offered Ahmed a steaming cup of extremely hot, cinnamon scented tea. They sat quietly as they slowly nursed down the scalding liquid. When their cups were empty, the *pater familias* turned soberly to his son.

"My favored boy," Prince Abdullah intoned, "the day I foresaw is upon us. You and I will join the faithful and partake in God's holy jihad. We will go with our brethren of the true religion and will make war on the atheists. Come with me to prayer."

14

Young Prince Ahmed and Usama bin Laden were excited beyond control to be included in the jihad, to be able to march with the army of God.

"Maybe we will even become Holy Martyrs," enthused Ahmed. "Think of it, Usama, my friend."

"I somehow think it is better for me to fight and to survive to fulfill my destiny, whatever that may be. But *Inshallah* [As God wills]."

The prince and his family joined the bin Ladens, Wahhabis, some five hundred enthusiastic Saudi princes, and a very large contingent of the *Mutawwa'in* [enforcers of the Committee to Prevent Vice and Promote Virtue] and boarded Saudi army trucks bound for the east. For the boys, it was a festive occasion. They rubbed shoulders with hardened, profane soldiers—real men. They absorbed the rhetoric of the common men with their ingrained hatred of all things foreign and learned first-hand the bigotry against the lowest socio-economic class in their country—the despised Shi'a.

Eventually, hungry, dusty, thirsty, and tired, the military convoy came within sight of small straggler groups of Shi'a flagellates. The forlorn looking religious zealots were a pathetic lot. They were scarcely able to walk as they shambled along with bleeding backs, a few with enough remaining strength to bash their foreheads with jagged rocks in an orgy of suffering and penitence.

The senior *Mutawwa'in [Religious and moral police]* ordered the Wahhabi convoy to halt. He was the designated combat leader, and even the princes and the moguls gave him strict obedience.

"Out, brothers," his carrying voice shouted. "Unsheathe your swords. This is not a day for guns or bullets or other Western infringements. This is a day for God, for the cleansing sword. *Allahu akbar!*"

Excited men, imbued with heretofore unexpressed religious fervor alighted from the trucks and faced the pathetic Shi'a men limping towards Al Huffuf and communion with their ecstatic brethren.

Prince Abdullah and Muhammad bin Laden drew specially crafted light but toughened steel swords from ornate carrying boxes and presented them to their sons.

"Follow close at my side, my son," each father said to his son, each bursting with pride in his offspring. "Use your sword like one of the Prophet's warriors, may God bless his *Rasuli* [Messenger]."

The overheated Sunnis fell upon the unsuspecting Shi'ites hacking and slashing. Gouts of blood spurted everywhere, and every man was bespattered with another's blood. The Shi'a men could not even fight back; they were too exhausted from their religious castigations to have energy for their own defense. None of them were armed.

Prince Ahmed was a natural. What he lacked in size and training, he made up for in enthusiasm. He was a wolverine. He swung his sword as one of God's elite cleansers and had an adrenaline rush like a nascent sexual charge every time his blade met sinew or bone. He came upon a wounded man staggering from several deep slashes. Ahmed thrust his sword deep into the man's chest, administering the *coup de grace*. He could all but feel the hand of God guiding him. For him it was an epiphany. In an illuminating instant, he saw his life's mission. He would be one of God's purifying angels.

Usama was more reticent. He silently cried when he cut deep into the upper arm of his first victim. He turned to look at Ahmed and spoke quietly as the slaughter around them drew towards a close.

"I thank God, Ahmed, that I could serve Allah and his Holy Religion today, but I am not sure that I am up to this. Is that cowardly of me?"

"No, my friend, just practical," Ahmed reassured him. "You will have much to give to the cause of Islam without being the man who holds the sword. Besides, who knows? We are only boys, after all. There are many battles to come."

Prince Ahmed Wahhab ibn Saud, standing in the great hall gazing at his soldiers—the elite of the Islamic world—ventured a smile at his boyish wonder at the experience he and Usama had taken part in and witnessed. It had been heady stuff then; and thirty-six years later, the prince had scarcely lost a heartbeat of the fervor although he had learned to control himself far better since that seminal day.

It was not over. The *Mutawwa'in* ordered the still blood thirsty men back into the trucks. Boys of ten and twelve, covered with dust and blood, were accepted as men; and Prince Ahmed and Usama basked in the acceptance of their battle experienced companions. The convoy moved out and drove to the first Shi'a village along the road. The rutted dusty streets and pitiful houses appeared empty and devoid of life and activity. The leader halted the trucks and ordered the recently blooded soldiers of the Holy Religion out of the trucks.

"We are the *muwahhidun, the ahlal-tawhid* [Unitarians, the people who promote unity]; do your duty to eradicate these unclean vessels. Unify all

Arabia under the green banner of Islam. There is no God but God, and Mohammed is His Messenger! Unify this place under the true Islam!"

He rushed forward with his blood smeared sword glinting in the bright spring sun. The throng of ardent co-religionists burst from the trucks and raced each other into the streets and alleyways of the small village. They looked like avenging angels, covered with the blood of the evil doers. Soon screams of women and the cries of children and the death shouts of old men began to fill the air. Uncovered women were dragged into the streets, one and sometimes more from each hut, and there they were ravished and put to the sword. Fetuses were slashed from the swollen bellies of pregnant women; suckling babies were torn from their mother's breasts and decapitated. Old men and boys too young to join their older brothers and fathers in the wailing trek of the flagellants were slashed, some castrated, some decapitated. The open trench sewer ditches ran with blood. In less than quarter of an hour it was over, and God's army rushed on to the next village and to the next. They obliterated every Shi'a person, shrine, mosque, and holy site they could find. They only stopped when they were too worn out to lift their sword arms again.

Ahmed, Usama, their fathers, and their brothers in the Holy Religion left the Eastern Province after a two day orgy of slaughter confident that the evil of Shiism was gone from their beloved land. They were deeply moved at the workings of God that they had witnessed.

The Shi'a, it turned out, were more resistant than the attackers supposed. They went into hiding, publicly denied their membership in their accursed sect, and over years, utilized their custom of a very high birth rate to swell their ranks of believers. Nothing was written of such pogroms; and less than a generation later, the cleansing was required anew. The pogroms took place four times in disparate places in the kingdom during the school years of Ahmed and Usama, reinforcing their brotherhood and commitment to their religious life—their involvement in the true work of God.

Even approaching middle-age Prince Ahmed ibn Saud never lost his fervor for reformation of the world into an Islamic paradise, and Usama bin Laden gradually deepened his conviction to a degree that nearly matched the Prince's. Prince ibn Saud wondered how many of the men he surveyed today would have the same fire when God called them to the final solution and how many would shrink, would become shirkers.

———————

The two boys attended different intermediate schools owing to Prince Ahmed's more religious bent and Usama's growing business interest, acumen, and expectation of taking his rightful position at the top of the BinLaden Group. They both added English and science to the extension of the primary school curriculum that constituted intermediate school and both obtained their *Shahadat Al-Kafa'at Al-Mutawassita* [intermediate school certificate] with honors. Religious studies occupied a greater portion of Prince ibn Saud's time and energy, and he recognized that he had found his true calling. Business was uninteresting and unnecessary for him because of his family's immense inherited wealth. It was everything for Usama. They often talked of the difficulty of such choices in their young lives and assured each other that they were moving in the direction for which they were best suited to make their contribution to the eventual righteous world ruled by the Sharia and with the philosophy of the *Qur'an*.

Prince Ahmed earned his certificate of leaving secondary school a year early at age 17 from his religious high school. His *Shahadat Al Thanawiyyah Al'Aama lil Ma'aahid Al llmiyya* [religious certificate] set his course in stone, or so it seemed to the ardent young man. With that certificate he was guaranteed to be able to go on to university level study, but he could only be admitted for studies in the humanities and social science. That suited him perfectly well. Usama's religious education would be somewhat curtailed; but his horizons could expand in the study of English, the sciences, technology, and business. Occasionally both young men would suffer a pang of question about whether or not he had made the right choice. They both knew that they had little choice; their fathers had determined their life's courses.

Prince ibn Saud graduated with high honors from Umm Al-Qur'a Islamic University in *Makkah* [Mecca] in the shadow of the Holy Mosque, the most revered place in Islam. He was awarded a judgeship by the High Judiciary Institute. The first goal of his young life—that of becoming a judge of the Shariah—was realized. Still, somehow that fell short of the mark of greatness in the world of Islam he had set for himself. The rest of his life would be spent in pursuit of the grand goal. It was not until he went to America that he crystallized exactly what the nature of that goal would be.

Usama went on to obtain degrees in civil engineering, public administration, and economics from King Abdul-Aziz University in Jeddah. He changed from a gangly boy with an awkward smile, unsure of himself, completely disinterested in rock music, fashion, and indeed all things Western into a tall, soft spoken capable businessman, scholar, and intensely religious man. He married young—age seventeen—to a Syrian girl—a relative—to protect himself from the sexual corruption he saw around him. He would have four wives and fifteen children compared to his princely friend's three wives and eight children.

Prince ibn Saud did not marry until he was fully mature, until after his life changing stay in America. The decision to go there came as a response to a call to duty. While at the university, he, like almost all of his fellow students joined the World Association of Muslim Youth (WAMY) and became politically active in promulgating Wahhabism. The leaders found him to be a gifted persuader and organizer; and, shortly after graduation, they came to him with a proposal.

"Brother, our religion is just beginning to take hold in the corrupt Western world and needs the help of our best men to see that it grows strongly and correctly. We must control that growth; we must prevent any successes by weak and immoral Sunnis, or, God forbid, the Shi'a heresy. We need you to go to America and assist in building Allah's kingdom there among the infidels. Will you heed God's call, brother?"

Of course, he would. It was the calling that he had envisioned years ago during those marvelous days in the Eastern Province. He sought and was given a sabbatical from the High Judiciary Institute and the blessing of his father. He was saddened that his friend, Usama, could not accompany him, but the young bin Laden was clawing his way into the family business with no more than a modicum of success at this early point in his career. It was particularly sad that Usama had lost his father in a plane crash in 1967 when Usama was only eleven. With the loss of his father, Usama grew up a lonely boy under the thumb of his elder brother, Salem, and became convinced that he must excel beyond all of his brothers in order ever to be included in the upper echelon of the BinLaden Group.

Prince Ahmed arrived in New York City in 1995 and was met by the leaders of the local chapter of the Muslim Student Association (MSA). The ostensible collegiate student organization was established to foster Islamic principles, purity of moral conduct, and to further the true Islamic religion in a country where African-American converts were patterning their religion in their own way—an admixture of holy-roller Christianity, African militancy, and Islam based on gurus who were ignorant of the *Qur'an*, Egyptians with all of their additions, and finally with some contamination by the Shi'a. The charter of the MSA attests to the benign, pro-American, pro-democracy, benevolent nonpolitical intent of the movement.

"Greetings, brother. We are thankful that you have arrived in safety."

"*Il-hamdouLilah* [thanks be to God]," Ahmed said.

"We will give you rest for a few days, then we have great need for you to go to the places of sin in this forsaken country. We have arranged for you to go to Los Angeles where Shaytan rules through their movie industry. They have need of our true religion before any more heresy creeps in."

The MSA was established in 1963 with a direct link to WAMY and to the Muslim World League (MWL), all directly sponsored by Wahhabi Saudis. The MSA is headquartered in Northern Virginia, has 150 chapters throughout the United States; and, contrary to its charter and mission statement, has very active political action task forces. The rhetoric in chapter meetings throughout the United States is virulently anti-Israel: its message to the largely Saudi student members of the organization regarding America is: This is the Great Satan; topple it. MSA chapters—generously funded by private and governmental Saudi agencies—contributes significantly to Muslim charities such as the Holy Land Foundation, Global Relief, and the Benevolence Foundation, all of which would eventually be accused by the Federal Bureau of Investigation for links to terrorism, prior to the events of September 11, 2001 that resulted in the deaths of some 3063 people.

That was the message Prince Ahmed Wahhab ibn Saud delivered to and successfully promulgated throughout California. There, he made contact with the most activist fundamentalist Muslims and through them with such unlikely friends as the Black Panthers, communists, the Weathermen, and truly fringe people like the Symbionese Liberation Army—the leftovers of the left. He forged partnerships intent on the destruction of the United States with the Masjid Bilal Islamic Center as his base of operations. Ahmed curried the favor of the mosque and its Muslims by procuring vast sums of money for the Bilal Islamic Primary and Secondary School. The school was completed in 1999, the year that the Prince returned to his homeland. It was with considerable satisfaction in a later year—2003—that he learned that one of his students—one Hassan Akbar—while serving as an American soldier in America's dastardly attack on Iraq, killed several of his fellow soldiers in Kuwait.

Ahmed was God's instrument in procuring funding for the Wahhabi mosque complex in Los Angeles—the Ibn Taymiyyah—named for the forerunner of Wahhabism, the Omer Bin Al-Khattab Mosque in western Los Angeles, the Los Angeles Islamic Center, the Fresno mosque, and set the example for similar expansions of the holy cause in Washington D.C., Denver, Harrison, New York City, and the Islamic Center in Northern Virginia. The contributions from his fellow Saudis averaged out to one million dollars per mosque for a total of $324 million.

The leftover left and the radical Islamic students were the quintessence of impatience.

"The weak and wicked rulers of this country, and the fools they govern are sleep walkers approaching the precipice. They are no longer capable of avoiding the coming disaster brought on by their wicked ways. It is time to strike decisive blows against this evil regime, these infidels who are an affront to all that is holy," became the mantra from the imams in their Friday sermons and among the student radicals over their expressos.

They hatched plans for attacks, feverishly arranged demonstrations, and plotted incessantly, all without direction or guidance from the well-founded and sensible Wahhabis. As much as anything, it became Prince Ahmed's task to bring the feverish young colts to the bridle bit.

His mantra was, "Patience, patience and planning, patience to be able to prepare for the great blow and not to rise to the attention of the daunting police services of America. It was a frustrating task dealing with the nearly ungovernable American youth who seemed bent on infecting the good Muslims who came to America. Prince ibn Saud forged alliances and established networks with men he could trust. He came to a realization that the United States was the most important enemy of the True God, and he developed a deep and abiding hatred for everything the Great Satan believed and stood for. He became utterly convinced that long term planning must be developed to bring down eventually the terrible monster that opposed Islam. Most important, the Saudi prince learned patience for himself. He would prevail, but only with infinite patience.

———————

He thought of those lessons as he steadied himself for the tasks of the day. He had more work to do to ready these brothers of his for the final battle.

The Prince continued, "Let us get down to work. The committees will report to me separately; you will all be informed in due time on a need-to-know basis. I do not need to remind you that what is said and done here, stays here. And the retribution of Allah is swift and terrible for any one who reveals our work, even by accident. First, President Farouk, let us retire to the rear office, and you can give me the Egyptian report."

CHAPTER TWO

1992

DBC Purgatory, Elizabeth Leavitt Rowan, walked into the admitting room of Purgatory, the federal prison in the barren desert one hundred miles outside Yuma, Arizona. Mrs. Rowan hoped that her insecurities were not showing on her first day as Director of the Bureau of Corrections, Purgatory Maximum Security Corrections facility. The concept of a single most secure and strictest facility to house the worst of the worst American criminals was hers. She had been a federal prosecutor troubled by the violence, escapes, and danger to the corrections' staffs and prisoners in the nation's prisons for several years. Privatization had worked fairly successfully at the state level for minor and medium offenders, but not for the incorrigibly violent offenders.

Fed up with the litany of failing attempts to correct the situation by brutish wardens, permissive socially conscious judges and parole boards, and federal inattention, she had researched the feasibility of creating a new prison system for the Worst of the Worst (the "WOWs")—one in which the public was protected from criminals, and the more petty and less violent criminals were safe from arrogant rapacious prison war lords. She submitted her long studied and detailed plan to the attorney general; and to her surprise, he passed it on to the FBI, the judicial system, and the president. She was included in the planning and construction process; and her reward was to be the director of the most secure facility in the country, built with the best and most modern construction, monitored by the ultimate in smart wiring and surveillance equipment, with the most sensitive alarm systems, the most rapid lockdown capability;

and best of all, she had had her choice of corrections officers who now owed her complete loyalty. That was because she had persuaded the powers that be to increase their salaries by half to work with the most dangerous men in the country; and also because she was strictly fair, nonpolitical, and nondiscriminating. She was able to hire a United Nations of ethnic, social, racial, religious, and law enforcement background officers and had trained them into a proud and efficient paramilitary organization. The facility itself and the earned devotion of her subordinates was the great achievement of her life and career thus far, and the diminutive commandant had no real ambition for anything greater.

Elizabeth Rowan was small—only five feet two inches tall—and weighed one hundred pounds. Her spare frame was wiry and her thin limbs were made of clearly defined muscles, the product of her near religious devotion to her sport—Brazilian Jiu Jitsu. Elizabeth was one of ten black belts in the country and the only woman. She had earned the title by mastering the art and in unforgiving combat with her peers. She had short but feminine blond hair, the same hairdo she had worn for her entire adult life. Her face reflected her age—thirty-eight—and her avocation. Her nose had a very slight deviation, the result of a fracture that left her with a look not quite the same as before. Her left ear had a thickening, a minor post traumatic cauliflower appearance; the ear and the nose gave her face an interesting asymmetrical look—a look that made one pause before considering violence.

She was not unattractive, but would not be described as beautiful or even pretty. Her greatest admirers described her face as vibrant, or more accurately, intense. Elizabeth smiled and laughed often, priding herself on a self-deprecating sense of humor. That humor left her with smile lines by her lips and her eyes that softened the intensity of her strong face. The strongest, most intense, and the most captivating feature of her face was her eyes. She had light blue-silver grey irises that seemed nearly iridescent, especially if they were fixed on someone who fell well short of her exacting expectations of them.

The new prison director wore a standard navy blue uniform pant suit, starched white long sleeved blouse with a regulation blue and red lady's cravat, her name tag—last name only—and a single star on her epaulets, the designation of her rank, whenever she was at work—which was most of the time. At home—the only place she would ever be seen in casual dress—she wore old tee shirts, worn blue jeans, and brilliantly colored and patterned espadrilles.

Mrs. Rowan never wore jewelry, not even a wedding band. She disdained makeup. She was divorced and never spoke of her husband, of any children, of her hobbies or preferences, of her political or religious preferences, or of any personal information for that matter. To every one who knew her—and no one claimed to know her well—Elizabeth Leavitt Rowan was all business, a professional's professional, and enigmatic. Her enduring reputation was that she got things done and done well. She did not curry favor otherwise from those above her in rank, and she did not abuse those of lesser rank. She told all of them the truth and let the consequences fall as they would.

Mrs. Rowan was about to meet the first half dozen men to enter Purgatory, the first to be caged in her new prison—not coddled, catered to, feared, or rehabilitated—caged. Her voice was low and quiet indicative of an adamant unyielding personality. She did not suffer fools, slackers, or toadies with any frequency, and she did not suffer the dishonest or liars ever. Her officers—like the construction men in the building phase—came to know her as a hard, fair task master unforgiving of mistakes, but full of praise and rewards for work well done.

The director strode purposefully into the pink walled room—the color chosen for its calming effect. She walked in ahead of three impressively large and taciturn faced guards and made a sharp military left face so that she could fix her steely eyes on the scowling shackled prisoners. An additional three guards flanked the prisoners from behind and on both sides. Each guard had been hand-picked by the new director for their competence and for their imposing size and ramrod stiff posture, designed quite frankly to intimidate; and all of them were African-Americans. This batch of prisoners was all Caucasian. Mrs. Rowan had selected the powerful black men as guards to feed on the innate fears of vulnerable men of one race when confronted by a cadre of disciplined giants of another race. In the afternoon a busload of black men would arrive and would be met by an equally imposing coterie of white corrections officers. Every new inmate had both hands cuffed to a belt ring behind his back and was further shackled above the knees and at the ankles so that he could move no more than at an awkward *marche á petits pas* shuffle.

"Inmates, I am the director, the only woman you will encounter among the corrections officers. I am the law here. You were told on the bus on the way in to abandon all hope when you entered this building—all hope of escape, of intimidating officers, of terrorizing fellow inmates, of legal appeal or of eventual release. Every one of you is an incorrigible, violent criminal, a lifer. None of you will ever again see the outside world. You will be prevented from committing suicide. You have proved your inability to live in society—even the society of ordinary prisons—and this is the ultimate place for men like you. There is no escape; this is the most secure facility ever built. The walls are higher and thicker and stronger than any other prison in the world. The technologies employed here are the products of the best minds and the greatest resources in our country. Even the most flagrant liberals in our government have agreed that you must spend your lives here and that I must have full control of you. Do not think to appeal the ACLU; they are on board. Do not think to fake illness; I will decide if you are ill.

"There are very few privileges here. If you misbehave, you will lose a privilege, and once lost it can never be regained. Do not address any corrections officer without first being given permission by raising your hand. Do not presume to call any officer by name ever. Do not make eye contact. All officers are to be called 'officer.' Use a derogatory term like 'bull' or 'pig', and you will permanently lose another privilege. You will be given a number. Do not forget it. You will never again be addressed by your name. That is another privilege you lost by earning your place here. You will all be fed the same thing at two meals each day. Do not ask for different food or more food. In other prisons, you have been led to believe that such regulations are demeaning, even dehumanizing. That is intentionally true here, and it is a policy etched in stone.

"You will be alone in your cells 24 hours a day, seven days a week except for a single weekly exercise period for fifteen minutes, no more, no less. You will have limited book privileges and a black and white television featuring four local stations. There are no telephone rights. Because you are subject to transfer to a different cell or cell block at any time without warning, you will not be permitted to keep personal items of any kind in your cells. Misbehave and you will lose any or all of those privileges. It is your responsibility to keep your cell clean. Failure to do so will result in loss of privileges. You will receive a single change of clothing once a week at the time of your exercise period and the shower and delousing that is required at that time. You may receive one visitor per month from a list of 12 people you may designate. They will be vetted, and no one with a criminal background need apply. This, also, is a revocable privilege.

"You will wear clothing made of paper, eat from paper dishes with your fingers, and drink from flimsy disposable paper cups. You will never have metal or glass or plastic. You have no springs under your mattress which lies on the floor. There is nothing in your bedding out of which you can make a weapon. Each of you will be given a prison manual to memorize. It is simple and lays out the rules and regulations clearly. Even if you cannot read, you will be bound by that manual. You are informed now and only this once that you may be subject to corporal punishment, lock…"

A powerfully built prison inmate body builder covered with black newspaper ink tattoos spoke up from his position facing the director.

"Listen, lady, we heard it all. We'll run the place just like we did in the last place; so, give it a rest. My ears are sore. Besides, I gotta take a leak."

Mrs. Rowan nodded to the two flanking guards. The men moved with remarkable quickness for their size. The first pounded the end of his baton into the solar plexus of the unruly prisoner, and the second struck the man simultaneously behind his knees. He crumpled to the ground with a gurgled moan. The guards duct taped his mouth in a swift practiced action. When he attempted to rise, the guards pushed his shoulders so that he remained kneeling.

The director allowed herself a brief hint of a smile of satisfaction noting the success of the weeks of drills that resulted in precision control with minimum force with which the unruly prisoner was handled.

"I was telling you that you are subject to the prison manual and may well experience corporal punishment, lock down, random search and seizure, solitary confinement, as well as loss of the few privileges you are permitted to start with here. All reading material will be censored and general categories of pornography, violence including weaponry, hate literature, information subversive to the United States or any other government, and manuals for making weapons will be excluded from the prison before entrance. There will be a short authorized list of magazines and periodicals permitted. All mail will be censored. There will be no gatherings in this prison, including religious. A poet named Dante long ago described the sign over the gates of hell:

'Before me things create were none, save things
eternal, and eternal I endure.
All hope abandon, ye who enter here."

She paused for effect and was gratified to see the cowed expressions on the face of these remorseless murderers, rapists, arsonists, and career criminals. Even if they did not fully understand the classical reference, the DBC Purgatory's tone was clear—icy clear. The object lesson vividly portrayed by the coughing prisoner on his knees was not lost on the new inmates, men who respected only strength and force. No one had gone to the uncomfortable man's aid.

"Finally, what you do here will determine how easy or how hard it goes for you. You are responsible. You will be safe here; you can expect fairness and justice, but no mercy. You can expect very exact adherence to the rules by the corrections officers and me, and you can count on swift punishment for even the slightest infraction of the rules on your part.

"You are dismissed. Take them to their cells."

At her signal, two guards entered from the far door and took the first man with them into the steel lined corridor leading to the cell blocks. Two more guards stepped in and escorted the second man, and two more took the arms of the third angry lifer until all of the new inmates were secured in their cells.

The afternoon batch of prisoners were more uncooperative with two jail house lawyers reciting their rights and a litany of abuses suffered by themselves and their black brethren at the hands of the colonialist whiteys. They ended up kneeling, short of breath, and with duct-taped mouths. By the end of the day twelve prisoners had been admitted to their cells, and be the end of the week eighty-four men had been distributed to six of the twelve available cell blocks. Mrs. Rowan knew it was a tedious process but believed it to be a necessary one for every new prisoner to undergo in order that they'd never have questions later.

Mrs. Rowan was pleased with the efficiency with which the prison transfers had gone in this test period. She e-mailed her counterparts in two dozen prisons across the United States, and set in motion a program to admit twenty-four men per group of new inmates in four groups a day, six days a week. She gave her entrance speech unerringly after half a dozen repetitions. The prison was filled to eighty-five percent capacity in its first ten months without a single violent incident. The director was pleased with the smoothness of the transition, but was concerned that there had been no opportunity for a real-life exercise to control a violent reaction to the rigid regime in the prison. Her officers were thoroughly drilled but untested.

She need not have concerned herself on that account. The first incident occurred during the eleventh month of the prison's existence. Prisoner 88296-092 decided to test the system. He waited until the second meal of the day, a pleasant boneless pork chop with potatoes au gratin and a chopped lettuce and tomato salad.

"Guard, I got a gut ache. I gotta have somethin' more bland. I got ulcers."

"Nothing wrong with this food, 88296-092. This is it for the day. Like it or lump it," the corrections officer said. "And you will address me as 'officer.'"

88296-092 crumpled up the food on his paper plate and hurled it at the opening in his cell door through which the officer was communicating. He balled up the paper plate and cup and threw them at the opening as well. He gave the officer the finger and cursed him with a life time of practice on prison vocabulary. His snarling face would have given a gorilla a moment of pause. The inmate was a Neanderthal with craggy acne scarred face, bald head, and a super heavyweight's physique.

The unintimidated corrections officer touched the red button on his communicator. Then, he stood quietly outside the cell while the inmate ranted. In forty-five seconds seven guards marched up to the cell door and joined the first officer on the scene. They formed a human wedge, and the lead man spoke into his communicator. The door opened electronically, and the flying wedge of burly officers burst into the cell armed with truncheons and small round shields. Two men dropped and took one of the massive inmate's squat muscled legs each and swept him off his feet. Four men pummeled the supine prisoner with their truncheons until he raised his arms to his face and in supplication. He no longer cursed. He now pled. The remaining two men positioned themselves to place shackles on his wrists and ankles. The officers glanced briefly at one another, nodded and ceased the pummeling. The lead officer produced duct tape and slapped a patch over the prisoner's eyes and one over his mouth. Two officers on each arm dragged the now completely unresisting inmate out onto the cell block walkway.

Hearing the commotion, nearby inmates began yelling, cursing, and throwing their food as they had done in their previous prisons. The disturbance spread in both directions up and down the cell block and onto the tiers above and below the one first involved. The lead officer dispatched the four officers to drag the defeated inmate to solitary confinement. He then tapped the speaker button on his communicator three times in rapid succession.

Two officers entered the cell blocks on each tier from both entrances. The officers manned fire hoses and systematically blasted high pressure water into the cells one at a time until the cell's occupant was gasping and flopping about on the floor moaning in pain from the near cutting force of the water pressure. In five minutes there was not a sound except whimpering coming from the cells.

The captain of the guard called Director Rowan.

"Ma'am, we have had a disturbance on 12-A."

"Is it handled?"

"Yes."

"Efficiently?"

"Very. You will have my full report in half an hour. All the hours of drilling paid off in spades. The men did great."

"Splendid."

"Any orders?"

"Yes. Move every man on all of the involved tiers to another cell block chosen at random. Not one of those men is to be on the same block as any other perp. And, Mr. Denis, order the cooks to place the next meal, and all subsequent ones, in a grinder and serve the glop of food in a single ball on a small paper plate."

"It'll be a little difficult logistically to keep track of which inmates get the glop and which don't since they will be scattered throughout the population."

"No difficulty at all, Captain Denis. The order applies to the entire population. By the way, have the facts—all of them—printed in the next edition of the monthly prisoner information bulletin. Include prisoner numbers."

"Ooh, okay, ma'am, that ought to increase our popularity."

"Not our popularity. Mine. Attribute the orders to me. Refer to officers in the plural."

"Aye, aye, ma'am."

Purgatory was a quiet and subdued place for the next few weeks. Several prisoners told their visitors about the incident and got them to contact the ACLU and PIN. The local director of the civil liberties group, Angie Buchanan, and the chairman of the board of directors of the Prisoner Information Network, Jacob Stein—with whom the corrections officers were familiar—were accompanied by Ms Buchanan's superior from the Arizona state office, Emily Horowitz, and by the Washington D.C. based national director, Rachel Levy, when they came to Purgatory to investigate.

Ms Levy announced to her cohort as they entered the first security station, "We will leave here with fundamental rights restored. We will see full freedom of speech, and that means any and all periodicals and books will enter uncensored. We will have kosher diets for our Jewish unfortunates incarcerated here, Muslim diets, vegan fare, Atkins diets, and whatever these men request."

And, not to be outdone, Stein stated emphatically that, "every man here will have access to PIN and to full privacy in his use of the network."

Rachel Levy was small, dark, and intense with crooked teeth and thick glasses. She took pride in wearing cheap, ill-fitting, and drab dresses and orthopedic shoes like her icon, Bella Abzug. In contrast, the chairman of the Prisoner Information Network was a dapper, Hollywood clone—moussed blond hair, teeth capped so that every one of them was perfectly uniform, no Chiclet thick teeth for him. He was tall, broad shouldered, and tanned. He grinned all of the time. He wore a $1200 tan double breasted Armani afternoon suit, a silk shirt of exactly the same color, and a black and tan paisley tie. His Gucci tasseled loafers were mirror shined.

Ms. Buchanan recognized the shift captain—number two in the institution—when he entered the security area.

"Hello, captain," she greeted cheerily.

"Hello, Ms. Buchanan. I presume you are ready to enter the lockdown area?

"Yes, sir."

Captain Denis escorted the ACLU and PIN officials down a cell block corridor where they were scrutinized by surly, but silent, prisoners. He tapped on Director Rowan's outer office door.

"Remind me that the gray drabness of the walls and floors will have to go," announced Ms. Levy *soto voce* to her companions.

"Who seeks entrance?" came the crisp bass voice from inside the armored office door.

"Shift Captain, Denis, ACLU investigation team, Angie Buchanan, Emily Horowitz, and Rachel Levy, and Jacob Stein of PIN."

"Enter."

The heavy door slid along its railing into the wall. A uniformed officer saluted the captain and directed the four visitors to the director's inner office door. He placed his left hand on a gel pad and stated his name and rank. The door opened electronically as had the outer door.

"Welcome, ladies and gentleman," the prison director said. "Please find a seat. I'm Elizabeth Rowan."

She walked out from behind her desk and took a seat from among the circle of standard institution metal chairs. The delegation and Captain Denis sat around her.

"How can we help you in your investigation?"

"We need to see the complainants and the men involved in the actual disturbance. We need to see each of them alone and without monitors," the National Director said without preliminary chit chat.

"These men are too dangerous for you to see them entirely alone. Each of them will have to be shackled to a table with his hands fixed to the table top. We will have to watch them through a two-way mirror, but we can turn off the sound. One of you can monitor our compliance."

"I don't think so. We are here to help these men. We have been in these situations before without a problem. We insist on complete privacy," replied Rachel Levy.

Then Emily Horowitz said, "Hey, wait a minute, Rachel, Director Rowan is right. These guys are the worst and most violent people we will ever encounter. I, for one, am not going in alone and unprotected with any one of these guys. Let's get real. I have known Mrs. Rowan to be a person of her word. How about a compromise?"

Angie shifted her body in the direction of her state director.

"I'm with Emily. Rachel, we can do this safely and still get the information we need. Frankly, I'm scared of these guys. They're hardly human."

"That statement is no more than I might have expected from people who make judgments about the character of inmates. They are individuals. Each one of these men is some mother's son. They are entitled to respect and the maintenance of their dignity," said Stein hotly.

"I don't want to hear any more of that kind of characterization of the men. But, I will bow to the majority opinion. We'll do it your way, Madam Director," Ms. Levy said reluctantly.

"Before we begin, I have a demand," said Stein. "You are directed to give me all reports from the National Adult Inmate Management System regarding the choice of placement from every inmate on the complainant list."

"I have two comments on your request, Mr. Stein. To make things perfectly clear to you, no one makes demands here except me and my superiors in the Federal Bureau of Prisons. Secondly, we have no reports from the Inmate Management System because it does not apply here. Every man fits into one category: most aggressive and violent. Every man occupies a cell by himself. There is no public area and no general population of inmates here."

"Oh," said Stein quietly.

"Good. We can start now. Captain Denis, arrange for the inmates on the list to be brought to interrogation room D one at a time. Station two guards outside with no sound reception. If these investigators want to see anyone else, accommodate them."

She turned to the National Director.

"Rachel, I hope I can call you by your first name. Please call me Elizabeth. I know that it is done differently elsewhere in your experience, but here we require that none of you give your names and that you refer to the inmate only by number. I assure you, that you can only be safe if you go along with this request. Please don't touch the men or get close enough for any of them to touch you. Do not, under any circumstances, give any man any thing—no paper, no pencils, no little treats. It will go much better for you and for them if you don't. If they have to sign something, signal the guards; and they will supervise the signing and provide innocuous writing materials. Thank you in advance for you cooperation. However, if you decide not to comply and attempt to pass something to the prisoners, you will be arrested."

"Your pugnacious attitude is duly noted. We will have our report to you within the week."

"Thank you. Now, you have a lot to do. Let's get you to work."

The interviews took more than three hours. The four investigators were sobered and quiet after their encounters with the most dangerous men in the United States. Despite their innate distrust of governmental authorities, the ACLU representatives and even the PIN chairman had to admit among themselves that the corrections officers were intimidating and controlling but not abusive. The facility was immaculate and gave every evidence of being impregnable. Their post-visit conversation took less than an hour.

On the sixth day after the inspection, a formal letter arrived from the Washington office.

Madam Director:

The fact finding investigation team from the American Civil Liberties Union and the Prison Information Network has concluded its evaluation of the evidence regarding claims of cruel and unusual methods and punishments in the Purgatory Federal Maximum Security Prison in Arizona. We interviewed every individual involved—inmates and corrections officers. We find that there is no actionable cause. No cruel or unusual punishment or unfair treatment was found to have occurred. We evaluated the food being received by the prisoners. It is of high quality, fresh, nutritious, and of sufficient quantity. That it is served in a single ground ball does not alter the adequacy of the diet, and the complaints of the inmates are adjudged to be unfounded.

Yours respectfully,
Rachel A. Levy, National Director of the American Civil Liberties Union
Jacob J. Stein, Chairman, Board of Directors of The Prisoner Information Network

———————

1997

The junior Senator from California, Hollings Braithwaite, stared gloomily out the window. His moment of depression was occasioned by the fact that today was his forty-third birthday. Vilate Apflebaum, the senator's administrative assistant, entered his office without knocking and hailed her boss with her usual annoying effervescence.

"Hey, chief, why the long face, like the barkeep said to the horse?"

"Hello, Vilate. Do you have to exude all that cheeriness today? It's my forty-third birthday. By this age JFK was already the president. I am scarcely making headway towards a national constituency."

"You'll get there, Sir. And you will do it without the help of the mafia."

"What's on my agenda that's worth the effort of getting up?"

"You meet with the Liberal Caucus at nine and the Democratic majority leaders at one. The rest of the day you see constituents from LA and Fresno, go to a Girl Scout cookie sale startup, cast a mandatory vote for the new director of the federal prison system, and meet with Justin Blackley about the Central California Water Project."

"When's that?"

"Eleven thirty?"

"Any chance I can get out of the rest of the drivel?"

"Nope, you already cancelled the Girl Scouts and one group from Fresno. They were not happy, said you treated Fresno like they didn't exist just like everybody else does. You can't afford to offend another delegation. And the leadership wants this prison person. She is a nobody, and they want to show that they are nice even handed guys because they are going to stonewall every judgeship the Republicans nominate."

"Heavy sigh. Okay, I'll take dope and get myself prepared."

"Hey, Chief, brighten up. The bigwigs want to give you a chairmanship, something they wrestled out of those nefarious Republicans."

"Yeah, yeah, we'll see. Get me some coffee, okay?"

"Yessah, massa, comin' right up."

Hollings Braithwaite was every inch a Southern Californian. He looked like he had stepped out of a slick page advertising magazine for Orange County. The forty-two year old junior Democratic senator from Anaheim was six foot four and carried his two hundred pounds on an enviably slender frame which made him the perfect clothes horse. His past occupations had, in fact, included a stint as a male evening clothes model during his undergraduate years at UCLA. He had the mandatory golden brown real sun tan, wavy dark blond razor cut hair that neatly combed back over his ears and stayed that way thanks to weekly $200 hair treatments. Braithwaite was movie star handsome without the need for plastic surgery. His face was perfect—even set eyes, high cheek bones, full lips, large even white teeth, even a lady killer cleft chin. His smile dazzled with pearly teeth and deep dimples in his cheeks and carefully trained smile lines around his deep blue eyes. He was wearing a dark blue three button suit and elevator shoes to emphasize his imposing height. His shirt was light blue silk and his $400 broad silk tie was the same color and cut from the same cloth. His shoes were custom made in Italy at $1,800 each; his $3,000 suits came from his exclusive Saville Row tailor.

The up-and-coming unapologetic liberal senator was a Protestant of no particular denomination, a Rotarian, a pro-abortion advocate, an opponent of the death penalty, a leader in the fight against the rights of the red necks to have guns, a defender of gays and their right to marry, and a Democrat with impeccable ratings from conservationists, unionists, and minorities, all of whom he had assiduously courted. He was a below par golfer, good enough at tennis to be a pro at any fashionable club in California, and could still catch a wave with the best surfer dudes. He was unmarried and had no children and made no bones about the fact that he had a significant other, who was a past president of NOW.

The meeting with the Democratic minority leader and her deputy and the senators from Maine, Vermont, and New York, the institutional liberals and most influential members of the largely submerged liberal senatorial group, started with juice and a fruit and vegetable plate. The senior Senator from California and minority leader was a granola and refused to allow meat or coffee or soda pop and certainly no liquor at any meeting she controlled. It was as bad as having a Mormon in charge.

Margaret Puncher—Braithwaite's nominal senior—announced, "Let's come to order, ladies and gentlemen. We're here to strategize—to make ourselves a future. We need to get Senator Braithwaite into the chair at Foreign Relations. Matt Denning traded our spot on interstate commerce for that plum. We need a liberal in that seat of influence; so, we won't go off into another stupid Republican war. They keep rumbling about the Mid-East terrorists and doing something about them. They refuse to see the Palestinian or the Arab side, and we've got to get our guy in a position to blunt their one-sided approach."

"Here, here," chorused the assembled senators as they ignored the health food, hoping the meeting would be short enough to let them get out in time for a trip to McDonalds.

"Senator Braithwaite, I didn't mean to talk about you as if you weren't here. What do you say, Hollings? You up to challenging the tiger in his lair?"

"I'd be honored, Margaret. I guess I can tolerate rejection and confrontation as well as the next guy. Sure, I'll accept. I want to keep my place on the Rules and Regulations and the Appropriations committees, though. I've worked long and hard to carve out a niche for us there."

"Any objections?"

"None," said the senator from Vermont. "If we don't watch this guy, he'll be making the news; and next thing we know, he'll be a presidential candidate."

They all laughed politely, but each secretly held half a thought that there was more than a little truth to that facetious speculation. Braithwaite would not be such a bad choice if they could bring him up right over the next few years.

The confirmation hearing was perfunctual. Every Senator and aide was preoccupied with weightier matters and needed to get through this non-controversial appointment and on to things that mattered.

"Order, order," said the president pro tempore, acting as he commonly did when the vice-president was off on one junket or another. "Have we a quorum?"

He glanced at the administrative assistant who nodded yes.

"We have before us the President's nomination for the post of director of the Federal Prison System, Elizabeth Leavitt Rowan. Mrs. Rowan has been the director of the nation's most secure prison for five years and in that time as run it like a well disciplined military garrison. Remember, these inmates are the worst that the criminal element of our fine nation can produce. She has turned them into pussy cats. Over the course of that five years in response to infractions, privileges for television viewing were revoked; library books were reduced to nonfiction, nonviolent tracts on a variety of unemotional subjects; and the exercise... each week and; best of all, food is now served in a ground up ball."

An appreciative laughter circled the Senate Chamber.

"Director Rowan introduced a program for inmates to be taken one at a time to witness the twice daily exercise, martial arts training, and tactical control drills by the corrections officers. The prisoners were appropriately impressed—since the corrections officers in her prison are definitely impressive. She's a black-belt herself, in case you didn't know. The next series of disturbances involved only single individuals who received prescribed punishments, and the general population of the prison lost nothing in the way of privileges. During that five year period, there was not a single incidence of inmate versus inmate or inmate versus officer violence; no one escaped or attempted to do so, and there were no suicides. A total of ninety-two dollars of government property was destroyed by prisoners. Four investigations by the ACLU and the Justice Department returned non-culpatory judgments and the federal investigators went so far as to write a letter of commendation for the prison—the equivalent of a military unit efficiency award. Upon the recommendation of the outgoing Republican attorney general, Elizabeth Leavitt Rowan was selected to be the director of the Federal Prison System. Her appointment should be approved unanimously by the Senate."

Braithwaite signaled that he had a question.

"Her program sounds harsh. I did not hear anything about rehabilitation for these unfortunate prisoners. Perhaps we should be considering someone with a little compassion and understanding, some appreciation of the root causes of their dysfunctional behaviors."

"Thank you, Senator," said the president pro temp. "Let me refresh your memory. The men chosen to spend the rest of their lives in Purgatory Federal Penitentiary—the name was well chosen, I think—are the most hardened criminals we have. To get there, you have to be incorrigible, a career criminal, and adjudged by the prison system panel to be beyond rehabilitation. They are, without exception, violent and the majority of them are murderers; in fact, most of them have committed murder *while* in prison. Part of the perceived need for this prison was to protect the other, less violent, less dangerous inmates. We debated this arrangement ad nauseum when the concept of best security was first propounded. Incidentally, the plan came from our nominee. We agreed—virtually unanimously—that we would not back off from this plan as it was drafted by the nonpartisan, nongovernmental committee. As you no doubt further recall, Senator, the committee was selected to save each of us from having to go through any political heat. And frankly, Senator Braithwaite, with all due respect, this office is not one of those we allow to be politicized."

Braithwaite silently cursed Vilate for failing to brief him on the history of the prison system.

"What do we know about the nominee, Mr. President Pro Tem?" he asked, more meekly.

"Mrs. Rowan was born in a little town in Utah…Heber City, my notes say, and lived all over the country because her father was career military. Forty-three years old. She is a divorcee of twelve years, no children, not a religious fanatic, transparently non political. So far as our investigators can determine, she has no party affiliation although she does vote. She is not associated with any organizations outside those involved with her professional obligations. Bio indicates that she got her B.A. in physics at Princeton. She is an attorney—graduated cum laude from Stanford Law—and has served as a federal prosecutor before assuming the directorship at Purgatory.

"She is presently up for promotion to DDIO-Director of the Division of Institutional Operations for the prison system complex in Florence, Colorado and is uniformly considered to be a shoo-in for the position. For all of that, she has not committed any of the conservative sins you and yours deem unpardonable; she's not even an advocate of the death penalty. As a sop to you conservatives, I tell you that Mrs. Rowan has never marched in a demonstration—no history of being an activist. The FBI did not find a scintilla of scandal, no problematical writings—in fact, she has been silent outside her professional journals. For our peace of mind, she seems to have no social life, certainly nothing that has ever made the news. She appears to be bright and dedicated and no threat to either party. She is not running for president."

Another circle of amused laughter ran through the assembled senators.

"If there are no further questions or discussion, let us proceed to the vote."

The vote for approval was unanimous, the first such acclamation for the current administration and remarkable because the candidate was leapfrogged over her next career step and in front of longer serving, more politically connected candidates. Elizabeth Leavitt Rowan was named the Director of the United States Federal Prison Bureau. That fact was announced in the *Washington Post* on page D-13. No other paper—and none of the media—considered it to be newsworthy.

The following week, Hollings Braithwaite was named chairman of the Senate Foreign Affairs Committee. He held his first meeting that same day, and unwilling to play the shrinking violet, proceeded to ram through a proposal to equalize military appropriations for the Palestinians and Israel, notwithstanding the inevitable floor fight and probable failure the measure would engender.

CHAPTER THREE

1997

Each year the government of Iran holds a gathering, something of a festival, for radical Islamic fundamentalists, Sunni and Shi'ite, to which the leaders of the world's terrorist/freedom fighter/soldiers-of-God groups, even non-Muslim, are formally invited. The visiting brass are treated with class: Upon arrival at Mehrabad Airport they are fetched by limousine from the airport west of the city over the Mohammed Baqer-e Sadr Highway, the entrance to Tehran and to Azadi Square. The meeting in 1997, as in the two decades preceding, was held in the luxurious surroundings of the Five Star Azadi Grand Hotel in Cross Chamran, Evin, Tehran.

President Muhammad Ali Hashemi chaired the gathering and gave the keynote address. Prince Ahmed Wahhab ibn Saud was bored with the rhetoric, substantially unchanged during the past forty years.

"My Islamic friends and guests from around the world, *as-Salaamu-alaykum*. I greet you as brothers during an occasion when we can all gather, set aside our differences, and pursue the blessed work of Allah, His Jihad against the decadent Great Satan and its running dog, Little Satan. We have made progress around the world. The so-called peace process with the occupiers of Palestine is a sham and shall not come to pass. Hezbollah—under the dedicated and capable soldier of God, Imam Hadi Abolhassan Rajavi—has exacted a toll of retribution against the occupiers that has caused them to appeal shrilly to their new protector, the fool, Clinton, in Washington. We see that as a measure of our success—the shriller, the better. To our surprise, the U.S. president seems powerless or better, unwilling, to speak out against us without, at the same time, condemning Little Satan. The PLO has been handled masterfully by our comrade-in-arms, Yasir Arafat. He as been able to befuddle the Western media by uttering in English the platitudes he wishes for them to hear, and at the same time, exhorting his oppressed brethren to great acts of holy martyrdom in the beloved tongue of God and our Prophet Muhammad, blessed be his name.

"I compliment *Jaish-i-Muhammad* and the *Laskar-i-taiba Pakistani* for keeping the polytheists worried for these many years, 1997 being no exception. We all applaud *Abu Sayyaf* and the Moro Islamic Liberation Front for the destabilization of the unholy Catholic democracy in the Philippine Islands, may they soon accomplish the establishment of their separate Islamic state. I do not need to acknowledge the contributions of al Qaeda and their brother fighters in Indonesia, Thailand, Singapore, and Australia—the *Jemaah Islamiyah*—whose representatives occupy a place of honor on our podium and will chair several of our working gatherings this next week. We all salute our brother, Usama, a living *wali* [saint], whose jihad in Afghanistan prevents his attendance here."

Prince Wahhab ibn Saud closed his eyes and allowed the speeches to wash over him. He prided himself in being a doer rather than an orator—there had been enough of talk about rooting out the evils of the West and not nearly enough action. With the exception of the actions of the *wali*—Usama bin Laden, may Allah continue to keep him—precious little would have been done on a world scale. He had humiliated the ungodly Soviet occupiers in Afghanistan, and Prince Wahhab ibn Saud intended to make his own mark by bringing Europe and America to their knees one day, but that would take time. The Prince was working on his personal *jihad* to learn to be patient.

He smiled enigmatically. How pompous of him. He was not a doer; he was a planner. No great battle had been won by him or his forces, just annoyances to his enemies. Allah alone would decide whether or not his life's plans would come to fruition. This week, he had to get full participation from his chosen lieutenants or his plan would dwindle away into the nothingness that all former grand schemes of the Muslims for final domination of the unholy world abroad. His mind was on his own critical meeting this afternoon and not on President Ali Hashemi's remarks.

"...*Hamas*, the Muslim Brotherhood, *Tanzim*, Force 17, the Taliban, our US Muslim charity contributors, indeed, our brothers throughout the world, have made life intolerable for the leash dog Occupiers of Palestine and have kept their wicked puppet masters' teeth on edge.

"We have succeeded beyond expectations in the transportation of our school curricula for the children of Islam. Our Wahhabi brothers have been able to erase the Occupier country from the maps and from the texts of the school books and have inserts on the holy jihad interspersed throughout the texts to enlighten and to enliven our youngsters' minds. The Saudi textbook for ninth graders has been utilized all over the world. Allow me to quote just one successful passage. It is from The Prophet, may Allah's blessings be upon his Messenger. 'The hour—and here The Prophet, may he live in the bosom of Abraham and Jesus, means the day of judgment—will not arrive until Muslims fight Jews; and Muslims will kill Jews until the Jew hides behind a tree or a stone. A Jew will hide behind a rock or a tree, and the rock or tree will call upon the Muslim: 'O Muslim, O slave of Allah! There is a Jew behind me, come and kill him.'

"Our Saudi brothers, from the man on the street to the Imam in the mosque to the prince in the government palace have aggressively campaigned to export and to further the message. From time to time the decadent and foolish Western intruders complain, and then our brothers make cosmetic changes, but nothing has changed in the spirit of the messages. The ignorant Westerners know nothing of the language of God; so, we are able to tell them in English what they want to hear and to continue with the true education in the madrassahs and in the secular schools as Allah would have us do."

The prince endured the remainder of the morning's sermons on the only subject the speakers and invitees seemed to know, and the one they never tired of hearing. At noon he signaled his two aides; and they quietly exited through the servants' entrance and passed down the hallway to the third meeting room named Hasan, after the son of the fourth Caliph, Ali. Abdullah Kaswari—the prince's chief of security—met the three men as they entered the room.

"The room has been swept thoroughly, my prince. There are no listening devices. As an added precaution, we have installed our own jamming equipment. You can speak freely here."

"Thank you, Abdullah, nothing quite succeeds like excess."

Kaswari smiled or at least his thin lips turned up. It may have been a grimace.

"Place two men in resort dress outside the door and make sure they do not draw attention to themselves or their weapons. I want six more seated among the participants, and four obvious and well and visibly armed to stand in the corners of the room."

"Already done, prince."

"Good. I don't know why I even bother to remind you—but so much is at stake."

"I know. My men and I are ready to die for the cause of Islam—the cause you are heading; you can count on us."

"I'm grateful. These are treacherous times."

Kaswari was an immensely powerful man who worked out seven days a week, fought full contact karate bouts with able opponents twice a week, and ran four miles a day. He was an expert at hand to hand combat, the use of small weapons, light arms, and persuasive ways to obtain information he desired. He was an ugly man; and, after a depressing childhood with respect to interaction with the opposite gender, he was only too happy to swear an oath of celibacy for the cause of Islam. He was squat, hirsute, and snaggle toothed. His nose was a large bent hook and his close set black eyes were the definition of cruelty.

Kaswari wore a grey-green *Salwar Kamees* devoid of embroidery and loose fitting enough to conceal his weapons underneath, black nylon pajama pants, black soft soled lace-up combat boots, and perched a white embroidered cotton *Kufi* cap—one size fits all—over the growing bald spot on the back of his head. As a security chief he was perfect; he was not really intelligent, but was, instead, street-wise, a more useful attribute of a thug. Besides his forbidding presence, he was utterly devoid of the milk of human kindness and every man or woman whom he detained or challenged was soon aware of the grim reputation of the prince's shadow, as he was known behind his back.

Prince Ahmed Wahhab ibn Saud and his two aides, President Mohammed Yahya Farouk of Egypt and his trusted colleagues, Muhammad Mohfouz, head of *Salafiya*, Abduh Ajami of *Jamal al-Din al Afgani* Pan Islamic Movement, and Walid Patel of *Jemaah Islamiyah* took their places on the dignitaries' stand. In short order the representatives of freedom fighting groups from around the Islamic world and the Western democracies filed in. Each entrant was subjected to an x-ray and manual body search for weapons and recording devices before being admitted. They promptly found their assigned seats and sat in taciturn silence.

Prince ibn Saud stood quietly surveying the greatest assemblage of freedom fighting dedication, expertise, finance, and brain power ever congregated in a single location. When the security officers closed and barred the doors, the prince began to speak.

"This will not be a speech. You will hear enough of that this week to last you until next year. I have a brief announcement—two of them, in fact. The first is positive—our meetings with the French engineers and metallurgists and with the Chinese scientists and party officials and with the Russian technology crews have proved fruitful. As of this day, I can tell you that we will be ready in five years with all we need to accomplish the final solution. As a body, we will then debate timing and placement."

Munir Radwan, the second ranking *Fatah* representative, stood in front of his chair and rudely interrupted.

"Five years! You sound like the old ladies in the Saudi government. Why not now? Must we take down the Saud family to get anything done? Our Palestinian Freedom Fighters are being martyred every day. I have been in communication with the German al Qaeda cell. We can hijack fifteen US cargo planes and dismantle three power line intersections and shut down power in all of the Eastern US and Canada for a month. I hear promises and see no action from you, Prince."

If Prince ibn Saud was affected by the outburst, his aquiline face and obsidian eyes did not betray it.

He said, "Brother Radwan, thank you for your willingness to question and to challenge. You deserve an answer, but permit me to speak to you in private. I will allay all of your concerns."

"I demand a public statement, and I demand it now," the impetuous PLO representative hoarsely shouted.

Radwan was tall, and he stood well above his seated Muslim brethren. His lean face was intense, and he riveted his close-set eyes on the prince. He was dressed in an old style Arab suit, now threadbare and shiny, with wide lapels, three buttons—one missing—and sleeves and trouser legs too long. His beard was excessive—even by the freedom fighter standards in the room—which gave him the look of a rebel Berber Rif transplanted into unaccustomed Western surroundings. His countenance matched his defiant tone.

"Then you shall have your answer. The Leadership Council is well aware of your communications with the cell in Munich. You met with three Pakistanis on March twenty-second this year for thirty-five minutes in a seedy hotel—the *Neue Putsche*—on *Alten Bruederen Strasse*. Your conversation was doubly recorded. Our agents made one copy, and the three members of the Pakistani Intelligence Service each made a copy of their own. Unfortunately, one of those copies was sent directly to the CIA. Fortunately, the other two Pakistanis met with fatal accidents before they could further spread the information your flapping tongue revealed. You may not recall, but you did some name dropping…"

Radwan blanched visibly and reached out to steady himself on his chair back.

"But, brother, you meant well; you were just hasty. I understand."

The prince gave the quavering Palestinian a benign avuncular smile.

"Now, perhaps you will accord me the courtesy of speaking with you in private."

Radwan nodded wanly, looking at his shoe toes extending beyond the seedy, worn cuffs of the trousers of his suit that were mismatched with his suit jacket.

Prince ibn Saud stepped down from the dais and walked along the aisle nearest Munir Radwan's seat. He gestured in a friendly manner for the bearded brown man to follow him. Radwan moved quickly and obediently to the rear of the conference room and joined the prince there. Prince ibn Saud smiled again, a friendly, forgiving smile.

But his black eagle's eyes did not smile.

"Brother, how is it that you have come to esteem me to be your enemy?"

Radwan flinched back involuntarily. All eyes in the room were on the pair, and the prince had spoken just loud enough to be heard on the rear rows of the room.

"I bear you no ill will, my friend. I acknowledge your many contributions to our cause. You know, of course, that we cannot permit the slightest, even unintentional, slips of the tongue that could reach our many enemies."

"I know that. I would cut out my own tongue before I would knowingly give up a secret," Radwan said softly trying to keep any note of pleading out of his voice.

"I am sure of your sincerity, brother, but your days in our organization are finished. Chairman Arafat will have to select another in your place. To show you that there is no ill will on my part or on the part of the Leadership Council, I am going to give you a copy of the preliminary plans for our great coup. I do this to bind you to us—you will be privy to the greatest secret in military history. I know you will never betray us."

"I am honored, but I beg you to keep me. I can help. I have contacts, influence, my own militia. Please, my prince, grant me this favor as I publicly repent."

He looked about the room at row upon row of unforgiving eyes.

"Here, my friend. Your wish I cannot grant. But I have this final parting gift."

Prince ibn Saud reached into the pocket of his dark suit jacket. The edge of a thick envelope appeared and all around them envious prying eyes saw the envelope full of documents that their leader was about to hand over to the man most of them considered a fool and a miscreant for his failure of security and more so for his public admission, to say nothing of publicly crossing the most powerful man in Islam.

The prince fumbled with the envelope for a moment and it disappeared back into his suit. In a lightening fast movement the prince's hand swept from his pocket holding a tiny .22 caliber revolver. He pointed the small gun at Radwan's forehead and fired twice with .22 shorts at a distance of less than half a meter. The first entered the center of the man's forehead and the second passed through Munir Radwan's left eye. Both bullets traversed Radwan's brain stem. The sound was less than that of a child's cap pistol. Radwan was a dead man standing. He crumpled to the floor and did not so much as twitch.

The prince gave a curt nod to his security men, and they moved swiftly to wrap a kaffieyh around the tiny bullet holes preventing any blood from soiling the carpet. They carried the body to a side entrance and left the room. The remaining men in the room were silent. They were wiser than they had been when they arrived.

After the meeting, the prince and his lieutenants took one of the hotel's limousines to the Rah Ahan Sofrekheneh Restaurant on Vali-e-Asr Avenue in Rah Ahan Square. They enjoyed carefully prepared and poison tester tasted Chelo Kabab and joujeh Kebab. There was no mention of the passing of unfortunate *akh* [brother] Munir.

CHAPTER FOUR

2000

The Senate Liberal Caucus met in dejection. The election had been stolen from them; Al Gore had proved to be an inadequate match for the usurper—George W. Bush—and the reactionary Republican packed Supreme Court. It appeared inevitable that the bubbas and wild eyed evangelists of the country would sweep the federal offices and probably the states, both elected and appointed, as well. President Clinton had narrowly avoided senatorial conviction after the House impeached him, and the debate in their ranks was whether their icon was to be heralded as a victim and used to whip up flagging enthusiasm from his African-American, soccer mom, and Latino constituencies hereafter, or whether they should cut their losses and keep a tight rein on the outgoing president. The galling prospect of chafing under a Republican administration and a de facto Republican Congress cast a pall over the gathering.

Chairman, Senator Richard Cleveland Longbough of Connecticut, stood glumly looking out over the drooping heads. The chairman had a shock of snow white hair and a tanned and wrinkled face that showed all of his seventy-seven years. He no longer had the stamina to work up an enthusiastic bit of oratorical flourish to enliven the flagging liberal spirit in the room. He wanted to, and he knew he should; but it was no longer in him. He had been up all night considering his decision and what he could say to the men and women whose passions he shared and whom he loved sincerely after a decade of being their leader.

He steeled himself. As he began to speak, even his voice had a noticeable quaver of age. He despised the bit by bit losses being inflicted on him by his advancing years.

"Greetings. I want to give you a pep talk, but I don't feel like it. I, like you, cannot conceive of how we could have sunk to this point. Our principles are right; our cause is just; our contributions to the poor and to the minorities and the working people are legion. What happened, other than the obvious theft by a conservative packed Supreme Court? I guess it is a time to assess. Not to lament, not to hang our heads, and certainly not to give up. But we must take stock if we are to come back up in the 2002 mid-terms and get ourselves ready for the 2004 presidential year.

"I have given a great deal of sobering thought as to why we are in the condition we now are and why we face such an uphill battle. I confess that I do not know what we did so poorly that we were not able to get our message out to the public. It was a dismal result, and I admit that I do not have an answer. *Mea culpa*. If I were a Roman, I suppose I could just fall on my sword, but being no more than an American senator, I will do the even more painful thing. Today, I am resigning from my position as chairman of this august organization. I am not going to exercise the temerity even to suggest a successor. As my final act in office, I turn the time to you, my friends, to elect a new chairperson. May God have mercy on him or her."

The assembled senators were shocked into silence.

Finally, Margaret Puncher, the senior senator from California, stood up and said, "I'd like to have the caucus give a standing ovation for Richard. He has been—like our beloved President Clinton, a beacon for us—a light flickering in the darkness of conservative cold-heartedness for these past eight years. We owe him a great deal for staying the course with us until now. No one can blame him for wanting a rest now that the Bushies are in. Let's hear it!"

She raised her hands from her waist to well above her shoulders, and her fellow liberal senators stood awkwardly up and watched Puncher's face. She led them in a cheer.

"Hip, hip, hooray! Hip hip hooray! Hip, hip, hooray!"

The senator from New Hampshire, proud of his fine baritone singing voice started in with, "For he's a jolly good fellow, for he's a jolly good fellow…", and the senators all joined in a hearty round for Senator Longbough.

Everyone sat down with spirits raised, and a touch of their old enthusiasm having returned. Shortly, the men and women began looking across at one another and an awkward silence ensued. Finally, Roxanne Fuller, Oregon's junior senator, stood up.

"Nobody elected or appointed me anything, but I can't just sit here like a bump on a log while we have a Quaker meeting. Forgive me for being forward, but can I suggest that we take nominations for a new caucus chairman?"

Relief surged through the group. Someone was doing something, and that seemed symbolic of the needs of the caucus, maybe even a harbinger of better times.

Cliff Assure, the junior senator from Nevada, and the only man in the Senate with perfect liberal credentials, stood up. He was young—the minimum age to be a senator—and with his chubby face and pink tinged cheeks and red hair, he looked like a college freshman. He was comfortably identified with his Generation X constituency in his faded button down blue shirt, tweedy jacket, stone tossed blue jeans and hiking shoes. His eyes twinkled with enthusiasm, mirth, and rebellion. He was a life long spark plug, full of ideas and causes. Cliff was a joker and a wisecracker, a gaminerie who irritated as many of his Senate colleagues as he charmed.

"Look, you guys, like we need to get on with the life of our caucus. We used to say in the Sierra Club that if we didn't do what was good for the country, the rapacious Repubs and their corporations would take it away from us and there wouldn't be anything left to protect. I say that we should look alive. Let's elect a chair and vice-chair and let's come out swinging. There's no way we'll let the Bushies steal another election. We can't let them cut down all of the forests, kill all of the endangered animals, arm every redneck, beat up on the gays, overthrow Roe v. Wade, or keep that accursed death penalty on the books. Let's look alive. I nominate Senator Hollings Braithwaite to be chairman and his senior from the great state of California, Senator Margaret Puncher, to be his vice."

Laughter rippled through the room.

"*What*?" Assure asked archly.

Senator Braithwaite stood and chuckled.

"I can imagine Margaret being my 'vice', but perhaps we should not let it become public. You know how the rumor mill works in this town."

There was a brief appreciative laugh. The ice was broken.

"Anyone here have a better suggestion?" Cliff Assure asked, his voice sounding a little petulant.

He liked making jokes but was not fond of being the butt of jokes; he had been the goat on more than enough occasions since his election; and he was determined to be taken seriously.

Carl Washington Aviard—the longest serving Senator currently in office and the grand old man of Senate protocol—took the occasion to rise. Everyone quieted in deference. The man had brought more money in for his state, had prevented more land from being freed up for greedy Western ranchers, had seen to it that more animals made it onto the endangered species list, and had gotten more legislation passed for women and for affirmative action, and had retarded or prevented the appointment of more Republican judges than all the rest of the caucus put together. When he talked—which was infrequent— he had something worthwhile to say, and everyone stopped to listen.

"My fellow Americans, my fellow liberal senators. I, for one, am proud to be a liberal. Liberals stopped lynching in the South, stopped discrimination against minorities and women, have saved the jobs and the nest eggs of countless humble American workers; and we can all be proud to be labeled with that frightening "L" word. I have been in the Senate long enough to know that our turn will come. Speaking frankly, I think it will be another cliff hangar in 2004, and I think we need to get to work to see to it that the scales tilt to us then. We need a foundation, deep and solid. We need an activist who is young enough now to be able to last out until 2004 or even 2008. I am not a betting man; but if I were, I would risk the farm that we will be back on top by 2008 at the latest. I've been watching Senator Braithwaite for a long time. Right now, I'm ready to pin my own hopes and those of the world's liberals on him to bring us back from the hole we're stuck in at the moment. In fact, let's elect him and Senator Puncher by acclamation. What do you say?"

The senators all stood up and cheered.

"Second the motion," someone yelled.

"Third it!" a zealot echoed.

Everyone laughed.

"All in favor, shout 'aye'," yelled Senator Assure over the general din.

There was a thunderous 'AYE', remarkable for the small size of the caucus.

Assure called out, "The 'ayes' have it by acclamation. The 'nays' can go join up with the born-agains."

Afterwards, in the hallway, Margaret Puncher caught up with Senator Braithwaite.

"So, Hollings, what cats are we going to pull out of the hat?"

"Let's get the San Rafael Swell National Park set aside this week, keep Francisco Gonzales from becoming a federal judge next week, and get started on a constitutional amendment protecting gays including their right to marry. Then, we can look towards the 2002 midterm liberal landslide," he said with a disarming wry smile.

"And the election of President Braithwaite in '04."

He laughed and said, "To get real, we ought to work on '08. Frankly, I think that's the liberals' best year. No matter who gets elected in '04, the country is not ready to become generous, pacific, and socially responsive by then, and it will be more or less business as usual. We have our work cut out for us. How about lunch this Thursday?"

Senator Puncher nodded.

"*This guy's the comer everyone says he is,*" the plump and dowdy matriarch of nearly half a century of union fights said to herself.

Elizabeth Leavitt Rowan woke up and grumped at her alarm for sounding a cheery chorus of bells at six in the morning. She felt like she was too old to be getting up like a farm wife. She cleared her head with a brief severe set of calisthenics, showered, dressed, and promised herself that she would get something from the Congressional cafeteria. She was due to testify in the appropriations hearing today, and the effective life of her bureau depended on her persuasiveness. Senator Braithwaite was the leader of the Congressional and Senatorial Bicameral Budget committee, noted to be a staunch fiscal conservative, for all of his liberal credentials when it came to capital improvements, the Justice and Law Enforcement Agencies—and presumably—prisons. It was one of those days when Elizabeth wished that someone else was the director, and she could go back to being a warden. She had had some freedom of maneuver then.

Elizabeth berated herself as she drove to the Justice Building for having failed to heed the advice of her predecessors and her mentors in Justice to make some friends. She was leery—it was more than a joke when people said that if you wanted to have a friend in Washington, you should get a dog. Still, she realized that she was pretty much a loner in this appropriations business, and she was going to have to find a rabbi somewhere in the governmental apparatus to go to bat for her. Maybe next year.

She was scheduled to be sworn by the committee at nine. She was waiting in the antechamber at eight; at least, she remembered to bring her laptop to get some work done. Elizabeth shook her head at her excessive zeal for punctuality; it was probably true that she had been potty trained too early.

The doors to the committee chamber opened at ten thirty, and the room quickly filled with staffers. The first senator arrived at nine-ten sharp, and a quorum was achieved at nine fifty.

"Good thing I'm not busy," Elizabeth groused to herself.

The committee was called to order by the master-at-arms, and Senator Braithwaite tapped his microphone and asked in general if the witnesses and their staffs were present and accounted for.

"Yes, sir," the master-at-arms declared.

"We'll get started then," Braithwaite said. "Who's the first witness?"

"The director of the Federal Prison Bureau."

"Who's he?

"It's a she, Mr. Chairman. Elizabeth L. Rowan."

"Director Rowan, please take your seat. Have your staff and attorneys fill in beside you."

"There's just me, Mr. Chairman."

He raised an eyebrow. Maybe this day was not going to drag on as long as he had feared.

"Are you an accountant, Director?"

"No, I'm an attorney by education, but our accountants and attorneys have checked out our proposal and find it to be completely realistic. I'll say two things about our budget proposal. First, it is not inflated. This is what we need, and without it, we will not be able to provide the essential services we are charged by statute to provide; and second, while I have been conservative in our budget estimates; and it is on the low side, next year, we are going to have to propose serious capital improvement expenditures. Finally, I needed our people back in their offices doing the people's work. I will take responsibility for the proposal including its details. I am hoping that we will be able to conclude this business today."

"That would be a refreshing change," Senator Christensen of Minnesota said. "Do we have copies of the proposed budget?"

"On your desk, Senator," the administrative assistant said quietly from behind the row of seated congressmen.

"I presume you have all read Mrs. Rowan's document, ladies and gentlemen," Senator Braithwaite said.

A silent chorus of mildly sheepish smiles answered him.

"So what do the GAO and the bicameral accounting office have to say? Where do we use the hatchet and where the scalpel?" asked Senator Braithwaite.

All heads turned to the small cluster of staffers to the right and behind the row of congressmen. A bespectacled youngish African-American man wearing a regulation blue blazer, a starched button-down collared blue shirt, a red bow tie, charcoal grey trousers with a newly sharpened crease, and gleaming wing-tips cleared his throat.

"Mr. Chairman, ladies and gentlemen. We work for you and have put in our due diligence on this one because the presentation is complete, which is unheard of, clear, concise, and for the first time in our experience, not a wish list but a practical and workable budget. Let me point out that it is only a thousand dollars more than last year's. I know this is going to sound strange from the Scrooges you have hired to yield the hatchet, but we are actually going to recommend that the budget be increased by five hundred thousand dollars for fiscal '03 to include a novel new rehabilitation program suggested by the honorable senior senator from California. Otherwise, we recommend its adoption *in toto*."

He sat down, gestured to the administrative assistant and handed her a stack of papers delineating the additions. Each member of the committee took time to peruse the rehabilitation proposal.

The senior senator from Nebraska, and the foremost conservative voice on the committee that was heavy on conservatives and light on liberals, gestured for the floor.

Senator Braithwaite nodded to him.

"Esteemed colleagues, this is just another tax-and-spend liberal program, this rehab for criminals idea, that is being recycled for the umpteenth time. No, it isn't a great deal of money; but our constituents are crying out for tax relief. Rehab has proved to be useless in the past and there is no reason to expect anything different in the future. I'm against it. This little lady has given us a piece of good work, and I say let's approve it as is without amendments."

"And keep on caging the unfortunates and minorities, and keep on recy-cling them through the criminal justice system, never changing the recidivism rate, never giving these young people a real chance to be part of the American dream?" broke in the senator from New Hampshire.

"Hear, hear," chorused the five liberals of the committee.

"I have to admit that it seems counterproductive to warehouse these people and to hope against realistic hope that they will be able to find honest work and become productive citizens without at least some effort to improve their educations and prospects," said the conservative junior senator from Utah, a man of sixty-eight.

"Let's hear from Director…" Senator Braithwaite fumbled for her name.

"Rowan," Elizabeth said. "Well, this comes as a surprise. The prevailing thinking among corrections officials and students of the criminal justice system is that it *is* a waste of money to try and rehabilitate hardened criminals. The great preponderance of evidence verifies that pessimism. However, I would like to be so bold as to recommend to this committee that a compromise approach be taken. Budget the money for rehabilitation and let me find a committee of well informed prison officials and students of the subject to come up with a workable plan. Basically, I would like to concentrate on the first time offenders who are young enough to be vulnerable to change for the better. I would like to provide some isolation from the hardened population to allow them enough peace and safety to pursue some education. That will cost something, and perhaps the extra half a million might prove to be well spent. Maybe we *can* make a difference."

The committee members all nodded their heads. If there was anything they liked better than a compromise, it was an opportunity to get out to an early lunch. There was schmoozing to be done.

"All right, Mrs. Rowan, we'll vote on tentative approval. If you can have a workable program in my hands by the end of the week, we will give you a final answer. Now, ladies and gentlemen, let's vote," announced Senator Braithwaite.

The vote was along party lines except that two conservative Republicans broke ranks and voted for approval along with the liberals. That produced a tie vote that was broken by the vote of the chair, Senator Braithwaite, in favor of the proposed budget and the amendment.

In the prescribed four days, Elizabeth Rowan arrived at Senator Braithwaite's office for her appointment with the committee chair. She was fifteen minutes early.

"The senator had a cancellation and can see you now, Madam Director. Thank you for coming early," Vilate Apflebaum, Braithwaite's secretary, temple door guard, and essential administrative assistant, said.

"Don't mention it."

"Come on in, Mrs. Rowan. Thanks for e-mailing me your proposal. I like it," said Senator Braithwaite who was waiting by the door of his inner office. "I especially like the chutzpah you include of recruiting volunteer well-vetted non-government university professors and grad students, people from all walks of community life, and, of course, that that idea adds almost nothing to the overall cost. By golly, I think you might just be able to pull this off."

"I hope to be given the chance, Senator."

"Well, anyway, I will recommend approval. I don't foresee any real obstacle. Congratulations. I have gotten a good report on your work at the bureau. If there is any way I can be of assistance, feel free to call me."

"Thanks very much. That is generous of you. I might just take you up on your offer one day."

"Please do. And, by the way, I have an idea that might just be useful to you. May I ask, are you a liberal or a conservative, a Democrat or a Republican?"

"No."

The senator laughed.

"Good answer. And, actually, it is the one I wanted to hear. Let me suggest that you join with a rather casually organized but important think tank group of young upwardly mobile government officials called the Independents. Their accent is on thorough study of important issues irrespective of party affiliation or political or social or cultural bias. It is an anything-can-be-studied-or-questioned sort of organization. It couldn't hurt to make some contacts among the rising stars in your level of the government, Mrs. Rowan; want me to put in a good word?"

"I would be pleased if you would, senator. I suppose I have been a bit of a loner, even reclusive, to date. I guess I am going to have to learn to play the game better if I am going to be able to function optimally."

"Just a note, Mrs. Rowan. Try not to get jaded and to look at all of this as 'playing the game.' The reason I like this group I'm recommending, is that they are very capable people in their respective positions; but to a person, they eschew the very idea of 'game playing.' I think you are that kind of person. I am; and I will tell you up front that first, last, and always, I will be a liberal."

"Thanks, senator. You're right. I didn't mean to come across as flip or—as you put it—'jaded.' I have no high ambitions, but I know I need to do some networking to be able to get anything done. I have a lot to learn. Hopefully, these people will be what I need."

It was three hours until darkness and the close of the day's fast. Ramadan seemed to be coming around more quickly each year, and Prince ibn Saud was finding the fast and especially the sexual abstinence during the day to be a little more onerous every year. He had no complaints. It was one of only five things Allah asked of the Believers; he could scarcely complain when he considered the bounties of life he enjoyed; and the success that was mounting towards the realization of his life's dream. He would be able to announce to the Council next Ramadan that all of the pieces were in place—*Inshallah* [God willing].

The prince was almost shaking with anticipation. The single most significant transaction of the entire plan thus far was to be negotiated during the next hour. He knew he was about to do business with the world's most ancient hagglers—the Chinese. Hang Li Po—the deputy director of the PRC nuclear program, and presumably, an even more senior intelligence officer— was striding up the path towards the opening of the prince's tent. They had agreed to meet after one of the prince's obligatory days of arbitration when any and every man of Saudi citizenry was free to come to the acknowledged regional leader and present his claim for service or redress and have a fair hearing from the leader.

As usual, Prince ibn Saud had heard the drivel of stolen sheep, unfair weights in the *souk*, unrequited efforts at arranged marriages, applications from men who wished to take a second or third wife—only Allah could understand why—and today, a request to divert some oil from the pipeline going from the east towards Syria to supply a thriving, but fuel challenged, trading route crossroads city. In truth, he enjoyed the company of these real men. His real roots were here, and all that he did was for them and for men like them. But an entire day of dispensing wisdom, mediation, and justice was wearing. The Prince took a deeply satisfying pleasure in the knowledge that he would make them all princes of the world, if he could carry off his ambitious plan. *When* he could do so. *Inshallah*.

Hang Li Po was escorted into the prince's tent. The formalities of body searching were avoided—Prince ibn Saud could not afford the slightest affront to this man; he had to demonstrate his trust in the People's Republic of China which had been insulted as atheists recently by fundamentalists throughout the Muslim world.

"Greetings, my friend, *Ahlan wa sahlan, ahlan wa salan* [my house is your house]. Enter in peace. You are, no doubt, hot, dry, and thirsty. May I get you anything, some tea, fruit perhaps?"

"*Alaykum as salaam.* [Hello] *Shukran.* [Thank you]. *Wahad, burtaqal* [Please, an orange]?"

Deputy Hang seemed somewhat strained using Arabic; so, the prince switched to English.

"I will have my people prepare a light meal, but will get you a cup of our tea and a nice orange for now."

He gave a slight nod of his head, and two servants appeared from the tent folds behind the men bearing a tray for each of them. They talked about conditions in China, and Prince ibn Saud expressed his sympathy for the sufferings of the people of Xian during the recent earthquake. Deputy Hang spoke at some length about the Arabian drought. Each of them offered assistance to the other's country.

After a suitable time, Prince ibn Saud thought it was at last apropos to broach the subject for which the two men had met.

"Deputy Hang, the Council of The Leaders of Islam is most appreciative of the difficulties attending your journey here. We recognize that more than just distance and terrain were involved. We know that it has been difficult for you to maintain secrecy, that some in your government might be opposed to your visit; and that this cannot be regarded as official."

"You are wise to acknowledge these difficulties. What we do in the future will be tempered by these obstacles. I hope you know that."

"Of course. However, we are both men of good faith; and this is both good business and will benefit each of our peoples in the future."

"I would not be here if I did not think so, prince."

"Now, Deputy Hang, can you tell me how much of the precious ore you can provide us? All of our activities hinge on that number."

"It is negotiable to a certain extent."

"We will take all that you can spare and can ship without coming to the attention of your government or to the attention of the accursed Western intelligence services."

"And you can meet our price?"

"We can. What do you require?"

"In money terms, a little over ten billion US dollars. Logistically, we must be able to have full documentation for our planes to deliver irrigation equipment weighing over seventy tons into the Saudi port or city of your choice. We can never appear to have been involved; it would be better for us if the material were to be dumped in the ocean than for our part to be known."

It went against the prince's grain not to haggle, but he was afraid of alienating this somber Chinese officer. He had to swallow his pride. This was what it was like to have to do business with the uncivilized and atheistic infidels. He fretted inwardly about the precariousness of having to trust these people who were not of his faith—even accursed outright atheists. It would not always be like this. He kept his face unreadable.

"Agreed," he said. "We must work out the full details; but for now, the point of arrival of your shipment will most likely be at a small airport of mine near Dhahran. It is part of the Samba Financial Group complex. They are not only the major financial group for OPEC, but they manage our funds; and we are perfectly secure with them."

"I believe that concludes our business."

"Yes, and I look forward to our further communications."

The servants appeared again, this time with small meals of *shorba, hummous, zayton, jibneh*, and *tabbouleh* [soup, pureed chickpeas, olives, white cheese, and cracked wheat salad with parsley and lemon]. The second course was cardamom spiced coffee, spiced lamb, and rice. The men ate in silence.

CHAPTER FIVE

JUNE, 2001

"Mrs. Rowan, as my last act as chair of the Independents' Club, I announce your elevation to the chairmanship. I know it is merely your turn in the rotation; but still, you certainly merit the position," said Perry Ralston, the Acting Deputy Secretary of Defense.

"Thanks, Perry. I thought a bit about what we should discuss today. We have pretty well covered the economy what with Secretary of Labor, Hinton's presentation and AFL/CIO President Larry Packer's rebuttal. We have heard both sides of Roe v. Wade and appreciate Justice O'Conner's incisive talk with us. We have begun a study of gay marriage, AIDS treatment in Third World Countries, and prescription drugs for Medicare recipients. I would like to turn to a more international subject—that of terrorism—recognizing that one person's terrorist is another one's freedom fighter. In our next several sessions I am going to bring in the best minds we can discover to brief us objectively on the nuances that distinguish between legitimate nationalist efforts and terrorism. We will cover the Israeli/Palestinian question, the issue of Muslim Fundamentalism—is it really a threat to world stability? And, is it true that the Muslim World hates us; and if so, why, what can we do or should we do about it; and does it really matter?"

"Good choices, Elizabeth. Have at it."

"I will start off with a bit on terrorism that I have gleaned from my investigations. I have had conversations with the FBI, CIA, and several of the nation's police chiefs, including the chief in Washington and the New York

Commissioner of Police. They are all of the opinion that we have been naïve about the threat: Arab terrorists and their cohorts in the murky world of armed quasi-political malcontents from the Greens in Germany to the Tamil Tigers in Sri Lanka to the Path of Light in Peru are becoming ever more emboldened and homicidal.

One particular individual who has gotten scant coverage is a Saudi Arabian multi-millionaire living in Sudan or Afghanistan, named Usama bin Laden. The best evidence from the CIA is that he runs sophisticated and well funded terrorist training camps in the hinterlands of Afghanistan to arm, equip, indoctrinate, and to turn into a united albeit multi-celled, disparately based world-wide terrorist complex. He hates the Western World with a passion and the United States as what he calls the Great Satan. They are convinced that he means to pull off a grand attack that will cripple us or our interests. The State Department, on the other hand, thinks he is little more than a crack-pot; and that his activities are for the most part confined to his own region. They view the more credible sponsor of terrorism and the spread of weapons of mass destruction to be Saddam Hussein in Iraq.

"Let's review some classified documentary information then I want us to hear that originates from Mike Jeffery from the NSC who was one of the co-founders of the Independents' Club. I think you will be surprised at the wealth of information we have, and the widespread ignorance among the people in the government to say nothing of the general public."

Mrs. Rowan spent the next forty-five minutes giving a timeline summary of events in the modern history of terrorism, a brief description of the known groups around the world, an in-depth study of American groups allied with terrorist networks—including pseudo-charity organizations—and an outline of the Israeli-Palestinian hostilities and their consequences for the United States.

"When we complete the more social aspects of the series, we will turn our attention to the weapons of terrorism, from crude homemade bombs made of ammonium nitrate fertilizer plus diesel fuel to suitcase size dirty nuclear bombs."

The well-prepared summary was appreciated by the Independents, and Rowan was comfortable with the realization that she was accepted as an equal among her colleagues. She was pleased with the thought that she could act as a cabinet officer for any one of her colleagues if he or she were to become president; and that she, herself, was becoming familiar enough with the inner workings of the government and with the people who make it run to be able to name several entirely competent combinations of cabinet members and leaders throughout the federal government. Her only inadequacy in that regard was her unfamiliarity with the military hierarchy. She was embarrassed to have to admit to herself that her best source to this point was Tom Clancy's collection of military fiction and nonfiction, and she meant to rectify that deficit soon.

JULY, 2001

Islam Yasyn drove his ancient Ford truck to the top of the road overlooking the large Dabencheng wind farm. He left the gravel road and drove along the crest of the low hill looking down into the shallow basin of the wind farm. He calculated the approximate location of the center of the collection of large electricity producing white windmills and drove there. It was a bumpy trip with numerous unexpected jolts because Islam did not dare to turn on his head lights. When he arrived at his planned stopping place, Islam alighted from his truck and began laying electrical cord from a central control box to the bases of nearly two dozen of the expensive metal windmills. He gingerly molded home-made gelignite plastic explosives to each support and connected a fuse into the dangerous plastic material.

The night was clouded, and there was not so much as a star to light his way; so, Islam followed his last cord hand-over-hand back to the central control box. He set a crude timer for forty-five minutes, then hurriedly got back into his truck and retraced his route back to the gravel road as best he could in the dark. He made such good time on his way back to Hotan that he was too far away from the Dabencheng wind farm to hear the two dozen near simultaneous explosions.

Islam Yasyn was an ethnic Turkic Uighur, the majority culture of the Autonomous Region of Xinjiang, a twenty year old engineering student at Xinjiang University in the capital city of UrUmqi, a clandestine member of the separatist group—the East Turkestan Islamic Movement—and a deep cover operative of al Qaeda. The main aim of the ETIM was to gain nationhood status for their beloved East Turkestan—the land most Uighurs regarded as their country while they considered China and the Chinese to be foreign.

In the past ten years, the movement became infiltrated with Islamic Fundamentalists whose world view cared little for separatism or Uighur aspirations. Ethnic violence for them was a means to their deeply coveted end—the destruction from within of the atheist communist Chinese and destabilization of relations with the Great Satan. Al Qaeda found ETIM to be fertile ground for infiltration of its hard-core cell. Islam Yasyn was recruited from among the malcontent Muslim students at the university after he daringly expressed in public his disdain for ethnic Uighurs who spied on their brothers for the godless ones and because he was a very promising engineer.

Islam was a handsome young man with a flat brown face and almond eyes set wide apart. The marked medial epicanthal folds of his eyes—like his height of five feet ten inches—set him somewhat apart from his fellow Uighurs, but his fierce nationalism and his perpetually determined facial expression and unsmiling full lips dissuaded any but his nearest associates to venture any suggestion of his having a hint of Chineseness. Islam was poor; and his clothing differed little from his classmates and the citizens of his native city of Hotan—ill fitting and poorly matched four dollar suits, flip-flop sandals, and white shirts turned grey with age and too many ironings.

The young student took himself seriously and was not above a little vanity. One of the reasons he almost never smiled was that his teeth were grey and decayed from poor hygiene, poorer nutrition, and his enjoying the common habit of smoking cheap cheroots and chewing tobacco laced beetle nut. He cultivated a wispy mustache that he thought made him look older and more serious.

UrUmqi—Xinjiang's capital—is a fairly prosperous Chinese city with its blocky but functional quasi-modern architecture and bustling traffic. There is a hum of capitalist enterprise emanating out of every shop, office building, and up from the streets. Islam had only to drive a short distance south from the capital city to enter the ancient East Turkistan countryside. Here, everything is as unChinese as the cautious ethnic majority can make it.

The time zone observed by locals is two hours different from the official Beijing time, which is roundly ignored. The roads are rutted dirt lanes—the best of which are gravel covered—in contrast to the asphalted streets of UrUmqi; and the modern thoroughfares of the principle cities of the People's Republic of China. The people obstinately refrain from learning Mandarin, choosing to continue to speak a tongue more similar to that ancient language spoken in Turkmenistan—three countries away—or in close-by Turkey. There is little resemblance between the regional indigenous costume worn by men, women, and children and the westernized and varied wardrobes of the sophisticated Han Chinese in UrUmqi. Hotan is 2,300 miles and a century away from Beijing. The two cities might as well have been on different continents.

Islam made his way into Hotan, the principle town south of the capital. The outskirts of the city consisted of scattered mud-hut villages interlinked by serpentine tracks and roads more similar to Kandahar, Afghanistan than to Beijing. Very little of the city proper resembled the bustling international metropolis of Shanghai.

Islam drove to the heart of the city and parked near the bazaar. He made his way among the cramped alleys of the main bazaar paying no attention to the hawkers of flat discs of bread roasting in the small cone-shaped coal ovens, or fresh melons, or aromatic spices—especially cumin—from donkey carts. The people looked pretty much like him—small, dark-skinned, rather more Mongolian than Han—and every man in a Muslim skull cap. He looked about but saw no police presence which dominated UrUmqi. The Uighurs all said that there was no need for visibility of the police because Uighur traitors spied on their neighbors in a vast network that reported any dissident activity to the Chinese authorities.

The al Qaeda operative and resistance fighter slipped carefully into a belt makers shop, and, seeing that there were no customers, swept aside a handsome hanging hand knotted carpet to reveal a hidden door which he entered without knocking.

He was greeting in Turkic by the lone occupant of the cluttered room.

"Greetings, brother."

The man was short and barrel-shaped with a tough scarred face, a small mustache, and the cruelest eyes Islam had ever seen. He wore the ample bloused silk trousers and vested shirt of an Ottoman Turk and upturned toe slippers, none of which was any too clean.

"May the peace of Allah be upon you and your house, my brother," responded Islam.

"Report," said Ujimamadi Rahman, leader of Islam's al Qaeda cell.

Islam told of his night's activities without missing a detail and totally without embellishment. He stated that he had not heard the explosion; so, he could not be certain whether or not he had succeeded.

"Good," Ujimamadi said. "Have some *chai*."

Islam gratefully accepted the steaming cup of tea from his leader. The extremely strong mixture of green tea, goat's milk, cinnamon, and sugar served near boiling caused the young man's eyes to water. He nursed it for nearly thirty minutes as it cooled. The two men sat in silence until they had finished their cups.

"You must get back to your classes, brother. You must not be missed. I will contact you in the usual way when your services are next needed. *Thawra, thawra, hat al-nasr-revolution.* [Arabic-Revolution until victory].

AUGUST, 2001

Muhammad Khattab was proud to be a distant nephew of the late hero of the Chechen resistance. Muhammad's grand-parents had been deported to the Central Asian republic of Kazakhstan by Josef Stalin during World War II because of their religion and for fear that they would collaborate with the Nazis. The grand-parents starved to death along with tens of thousands of other Chechens. His parents were survivors who were allowed to return to their devastated homeland only after Stalin's death in 1953. Hatred of the Russians was as much a part of the religion of the Khattab home as was strict observance of the restrictions of Ramadan as far back as Muhammad could remember.

The young Khattab joined the Chechen resistance while he was still in grammar school. He killed his first Russians—a farm family of seven, the Kharkovs—when he was ten years old. He was especially proud of the fact that the Kharkov family—nuclear and extended—were outspoken atheists and unrepentant adherents to the late Josef Stalin. When he turned twenty, he became a blooded member of the nationalist resistance group—the Riyadus Salakhin Reconnaissance and Sabotage Battalion of Chechen Martyrs—and a recruiter at the university for al Qaeda backed rebels.

Muhammad was summoned to a meeting with a man he knew only as Abdul-Bari [Servant of the Creator]. It was quietly speculated that the leader was none other than the legendary Shamil Basayev, but no one in the al Qaeda cell dared breathe the man's name. Muhammad and Abdul-Bari sat at adjacent tables in the New Europe Café on Moussaoui Street in Grozny. After a careful interlude—during which each man glanced surreptitiously around the café and the street—Abdul-Bari spoke to the young man sitting at the nearby table.

"Nice day, no, my friend?"

"It is. A good day."

"Have you been following the news?"

"I have. I was particularly interested to hear of the opening of the Muscovy Arcade in the suburbs of Moscow. It was reputed in the news to be the world's largest—even grander than some of those in the United States."

"I also have heard of the opening. What a magnificent place it must be. Have you heard if all plans for the opening are finalized?"

"I was assured that they were."

"Most interesting. I wish that we could prolong our chat; but, unfortunately, I must get back to work."

Abdul-Bari rose slowly and stepped towards Muhammad's chair. He dropped his keys and knelt down to pick them up. As he did, he spoke rapidly in a voice hardly above a whisper.

"I am leaving an envelope here on the floor. It contains the payments for your operatives and instructions for you to pick up a load of hashish brought in from Turkey. You are to sell it and meet me here in one week to transfer the proceeds to Allah's cause."

He stood up, stretched his back somewhat theatrically to remove a kink, and moved with dispatch out of the café and up Moussaoui Street towards the train station.

The following day, Muhammad took pleasure in the CNN World News report that mentioned that a tremendous bomb had been detonated in the center of the newest and largest shopping mall—the Muscovy—in all of Russia, perhaps in all of the world, if Russian claims were to be believed. 172 men, women, and children had been killed and as many as 700 more were severely injured and upwards of 1000 people were unaccounted for. The shopping center was demolished. No organization had taken credit, but it was widely speculated by Russian citizens and officials—according to CNN— that the bomb was a terrorist attack by Chechen separatist rebels. President Putin was due to speak on national Russian television within the hour.

CHAPTER SIX

SEPTEMBER 11, 2001

Elizabeth Rowan awakened early as was her habit. Her internal clock was pushed by the discomfort of the muggy heat in her motel room in Florence, Colorado. The Mile-High State, or was that the descriptor applied to the city of Denver, was not supposed to be this hot, she thought irritably. Her first meeting with the Board of Directors for the Federal Correctional Complex in Florence was not until ten; that gave her four hours to kill. She got up and stretched, did a few deep knee bends and touched her toes a dozen times but was hampered by her nightgown. She washed the worst of the night's accumulation off her teeth and put on her shorts, tee shirt, and running shoes. She left the Super 8 and ran up a narrow winding dirt path that took her over a seven mile course through trees and sagebrush hillsides.

Elizabeth was back in her room at half past eight. As she disrobed for her shower, she clicked the channel changer on and surfed for CNN. She was walking away towards the bathroom when she heard horrific news. The twin towers of the New York Trade Center had been bombed. No, not bombed, but attacked by hijacked passenger airlines used like human guided bombs. The videos on the TV screen showed a chaotic white dusted world where New York had once been. Wall Street was shown; it was like a scene drawn from *On the Beach*. The images were repeated endlessly to drill home the horror, the devastation, and the death. Elizabeth sat on her bed for a few moments, then put her hands on her eyes and lay back to try and understand what had, what was, happening.

"There may be as many as twenty thousand dead," exclaimed the news. "Islamic fundamentalists are suspected but don't forget the federal building bombing in Oklahoma. The first thought then was that Arab terrorists were behind it."

Elizabeth shook her head. The news anchorwoman was right; who could know? Maybe they would never know. That made Elizabeth even more depressed. She felt like crying, but tears would not come for some reason. She decided that she was too angry to feel sad enough to cry.

"Get those emergency measures underway and save as many as we can. Then, let's go find the monsters that did this and make perfectly sure that they are never *able* to do anything like this again." Elizabeth muttered between clutched teeth.

She felt impotent, that her country had been attacked, emasculated. She looked at the TV again, unable to tear herself away. The scene was from BBC coverage from the Middle-East. The prime minister of Israel, looking genuinely distraught, conveyed his condolences to his friends—the American people. Then the cameras panned in on a scene of absolute jubilation in a crowd of Arabs on a main street in Gaza City. Very much the same scene was repeated in Riyadh, in Tehran, and in Cairo. Arabs in the forty-four Muslim dominated and Muslim population majority nations were having a festival expressing their surpassing joy in the streets of the entire Muslim world.

The BBC reporter spoke to a Hezbollah chieftain.

"What can you tell us about the mood here in Hebron? I mean, thousands of Americans have been killed, innocent people. What is the significance of this apparently senseless act?"

"My friend, you have jumped to the very conclusion that the Satanic Zionist Occupiers want you to. Can't you see that the Zionists perpetrated this? They will blame it on the PLO or Hezbollah or Hamas as usual; and given the tilt of the US towards the Occupiers, the U.S. media will sell this pack of lies that Arabs did this. That is not only a preposterous lie, but absurd. We are peaceful people; the *Qur'an* teaches us that. We have nothing to gain. Look to the Zionist Entity. I have it on good authority that the Jews were informed beforehand and stayed away today. If the truth is ever allowed to be known, you will see for yourself that not a single dirty Jew died in that attack."

"Thank you, Mr. Haddad, I am sure your opinion has considerable support in this region."

Elizabeth rolled her eyes.

WAFA, the Palestinian News Agency, presented documentary evidence of the involvement of the Israelis in the plot, citing instructions to world wide Jewry to avoid the Twin Towers on this day and noting that not a single Jew was even in the vicinity of the destruction.

Elizabeth gritted her teeth.

The members of the Liberal Caucus instinctively moved to their usual meeting place. Senator Braithwaite was there to greet and to soothe the pale and distraught members.

"How could they?"

"Why do they hate us so?"

"We have been making such strides for peace. They must know that there are some decent people in this country that don't agree with the obvious bias that our government has demonstrated against the Palestinians."

"We have been so generous to them. How could they?"

"Hold on," Braithwaite cautioned. "First of all, we don't know who *they* are. I heard an authoritative report just a couple of minutes ago that this may well have been perpetrated by the Israelis to place blame on the Palestinians to inflame American public opinion. Let's calm down and try and sort this out."

"And, I have it on good authority that anti-government American survivalists did it. Remember the Oklahoma City terrorist bomb attack on the Alfred P. Murrah Federal Building in Downtown Oklahoma City on April 19, 1995. Remember Timothy McVeigh; he was about as Muslim as the Reverend Al Sharpton."

"And even if it was by Islamists, we must remember that they are not the same as the true peace-loving Muslims. We'll have our work cut out defending them!"

"If it was done by Islamic fundamentalists, this could set back our peace-making efforts for a decade or more," Senator Assure said dejectedly.

"You have hit on my greatest fear, Cliff. I certainly hope that this is the worst the murderers have to do against us right now. If they do, my real fear will be that Bush will have his right wing day and will launch a military blunder; and we will have to appear to support him. This is just what that McCarthyite needs—a foil for his conservative cronies that will take the place of the ridiculous communism scare during the Cold War."

"Is that how you think it will play out, Hollings?"

"In the short run, yes. We are not helpless, however. We can shape public opinion; we have the mainstream media with us; and we will make certain that our message prevails. Cliff, you have to get through to CNBC this morning. We will emphasize the need for a united America to deal with this on-the-ground emergency and gradually attack the war hysteria for what it is. We can get some op-ed pieces in our newspapers, the *Washington Post*, the *New York Times*, and the *Los Angeles Times* that will sway the masses back our way. Peace and prosperity with decent jobs, a vigorous appreciation of cultural diversity—that's what we really need. We can rehabilitate the Muslims by pulling the heart strings of the decent caring people in the country. We will point out the unfairness on the part of the U.S. towards the members of that venerable world religion.

"We can show images of the poor and desperate refugees in the Palestinian camps. We can see to it that NPR is filled with charitable speakers who ponder why they hate us so and show that they are the real victims, and we are the real bullies. It'll take time though. Be patient. The great unwashed out there in Kansas will call us traitors when they first hear us; but if Bush makes the mistake of embroiling us in some kind of long lasting military fiasco, even the Kansans will come around. We'll have to tough it out for a while, and then I think this is going to be a boon for our cause. I think the economy is going to go into the toilet as well, and we will have two unbeatable issues for the 2002 and even the 2004 campaign."

E-mails filled up the computers throughout the Middle-East. From Cairo to Tehran; from Baghdad to Gaza, and from Istanbul to Kabul to Fez, they filled up the ethernet with near hysterical jubilation. The members of the Council of the Leaders of Islam—usually grandly taciturn—were unable to maintain complete dignity. The cheers, the hurriedly passing jokes, and the predictions that this was the end of the Great Satan even warmed the cockles of their cautious hearts.

In the afternoon, they met in Benghazi, Libya in a pleasant out of the way hotel overlooking the Gulf of Sidra. Prince ibn Saud signaled to his Council that they needed to begin. His serious face captured their attention.

"Brothers, this is a great day. The Great Satan has been dealt a severe blow that will set back their economy and will have a severe lasting psychological effect. Our Islamic brother, Usama's, name is rightfully on every good man's lips today. His plan and its execution were audacious and effective. His name will live among the blessed."

He paused to allow that show of comradeship with the august leader of al Qaeda to register fully because he wanted no suggestion of envy or competition to be perceived. There was too much work to be done, and the need for absolute loyalty was too critical to allow for distractions.

"But, brothers, know this. Usama's feat—however brilliant and wounding— is not a lethal one. He has angered and aroused the *jinn*—America. Even their liberals will not be able to control the vengeance that will come. I fear for Afghanistan and for Usama and his al Qaeda network. Mark my words; our Taliban brothers will see Americans on their soil very shortly. We will have to do our work more slowly and ever more carefully while the firestorm blows over us. Let us cease our celebrating and get on with the work planned before this great day. Follow your sub-chiefs to your appointed rooms. I will bring your individual assignments to your section meeting rooms."

Prince ibn Saud's chosen lieutenants—some of the luminaries of the Islamic World—stood world, stood on cue and walked out to their assigned rooms. Every room had been swept for spy devices in the last hour. Every entrance and exit to the hotel, every access to every floor, on every elevator and stairway, and at each meeting room were world class technical surveillance devices and competent human guards provided by the prince's personal security service. Ali Abdullah Kaswari, the prince's security chief, reported that it was safe to proceed.

Prince ibn Saud intentionally divided the several contingents of Muslim leaders to keep the grand strategy a secret known only to him and everyone else operating on a need-to-know basis. The first room he visited was that headed by Egyptian President, Mohammed Yahya Farouk.

The Egyptian delegation stood as a gesture of respect.

"Please be seated around the working table. I have a packet for each of you which outlines your assignments. President Farouk will necessarily have details not given to any of you."

He handed each member an envelope.

"Do not share your information with anyone else in or outside this room. The Council's full security will be in force."

Anwar el-Meshad opened his envelope and found the following instructions in Arabic:

> *Meet a Frenchman, whose identity will be made known to you later, in room 1128 in the Hotel de Crillon on October 29, 2001. The room will be registered to one Karic Singh, a British citizen. Present the Frenchman*

the information which will be given to you beforehand by a man you will recognize. The man whom you will recognize will also give you your cover papers. You are authorized to offer up to one hundred twelve million US dollars, no more, for the equipment and up to two billion dollars for the weapon ready plutonium and an additional one hundred million dollars yearly for enough plutonium for twenty bombs. Report to President Farouk on the evening of October 30 at 2322. Use frequency Q-LCoC 01.

Saad Makram el-Deen received a fat manila envelope containing a list of four hundred seven pieces of equipment including exact specifications. The envelope contained a recent photograph of Pierre de Gastogne-la Croix, the Deputy Director of the CEA—the *Commissariat à l'Énergie Atomique*—an authentic British passport in the name of Karic Singh, and the location of a safe house in the outskirts of Paris in case of trouble. Also included was a Paris telephone number to be used only in the most dire emergency.

Naguib Eddin Moheiddin was given an envelope with the name of Liechenstein Credite Mutual Bank, and a number 997A-Q-LCoC 01-GP. The brief instructions told him to give the envelope to the man he was to meet in the Hotel de Crillon, room 1128, on the early evening of October 29, 2001. He was to leave Paris by the midnight flight to London and to leave London the following morning. Two passports were included in the envelope, the first, a British passport in the name of Matthew B. Carleton-Fiske, and the second, an Israeli passport in the name of Abraham Levy. He was instructed which to use on which flight, even though it was obvious, and to destroy the passports as soon as they had been used. Three airplane tickets in his three cover identities were included as were two passports and two airline tickets for the recipient of the envelope in Paris. He was told to call President Farouk's chief of intelligence, Gamal Monem, after meeting his contact in Paris and to give a brief report. He was to make certain that he was using a secure line. The telephone number was included and the code, Q-LCoI 01, provided for identification.

Yahya Mohammed Ali received an envelope instructing him to travel to Brussels tomorrow morning—September 12, 2001—using the passport provided. There he would be met at the airport by a man he would recognize and together they would go to a pre-assigned rendezvous with a small group of men. The men would receive further instructions later in the day.

Colonel Hosni Esmet Badr was given instructions to leave that night from Tunis to arrive in Brussels at 0710. Proper cover passports were included in his packet for himself—three different ones—and for the man he would meet in the airport arrival hall—two different ones. He was given an address and told to wait in front of the airport departure entrance, and he and the other man would be met by a taxicab which would take him and his companion to the address in the instructions.

The taxi driver, however, was under instructions to take the two men to a different address despite instructions from Col. Badr.

Prince ibn Saud next went to the room where the Pakistani Intelligence Service men were waiting. Seven packets of instructions were distributed to the men including cut-outs, location and telephone numbers for safe houses in Kiev, Tbilisi, and Moscow, identification documents, and instructions on whom to meet and where in Kiev, and in Murmansk in northwest Russia. No man was to know the identity or mission of anyone else in his cell.

Code words, "Muhammad, blessed be the Messenger, applauds your work," were given to all of the men.

Ali Abdullah Kaswari accompanied his Prince to the Iranian room. He did not trust the volatile Shi'ites.

"Greetings, brothers. Ayatollah Ali Velayati Mossadeq, I salute you," Kaswari said in Turkic, the Ayatollah's native tongue. Then to the others he spoke Farsi. "Thank you for making this journey. Remember that we are all brothers in Islam, not Sunnis, nor Shi'ites, Sufis, or Wahhabis. We are not Egyptians or Iranians or Saudis. We are Muslims entrusted with a sacred mission."

The hard faced men in black robes nodded unenthusiastically.

Kaswari handed out the envelopes. Each of the sets of instructions indicated that the men had been chosen because of their fluency in English and because they had relatives in the United States. They were to enter the territory of the Great Satan over the porous border from Canada and to contact their family members where they would stay. All but one were instructed to make collections from the Islamic charity front organizations, send a wire deposit to a Grand Cayman bank, and to leave after being in the country for no more than three days. The fourth man received instructions to contact Mullah Ali Hussein Mercooi of the Benevolence International Foundation in Columbus, Ohio. Mercooi would give him a series of under ten thousand dollar cashiers cheques for deposit in the People's Republic of China Bank in Hong Kong. The mullah would also get him to a safe house in Peoria, Illinois where he would meet five trusted operatives to whom he would give instructions. He would obtain he would those instructions in a chance meeting on Queen Street by a man he would recognize. The instructions would relate to the five men's responsibility for gathering unmarked vans, mapping out locations, providing safe houses, and mapping escape routes in ten major cities. He was to instruct those men to convey their information over the charity's internet server to Ayatollah Ali Mazdi Sekhavatal al-Muderasi, Director of the MOIS—the Ministry of Intelligence and Security.

The Syrian contingent received similar instructions for visits to Holland; the Libyans were given instructions relating to their activities in South Africa. Each of these men, like their brothers from Egypt, Pakistan, and Iran were impressed by the thoroughness of the prince. No threats were necessary, they already knew the price of failure and the dreadful fate of traitors and careless men. A few of them had been in attendance at the Council meeting when Munir Radwan had received his lesson, and the rest had heard about the unfortunate PLO operative from reliable sources.

Prince ibn Saud's last meeting was with the al Qaeda cell from Saudi Arabia. He warned them that it was their responsibility to see to it that there was control in their orchestrated attacks on the Saudi royal family; it was critical to the Council's plan that no major upheaval such as a coup happen before the day of execution of the Council's plan. They must be patient because that day was years away, they were told. The al Qaeda operatives grudgingly acquiesced.

SEPTEMBER 28, 2001

Zhiang Ho Peng, Assistant Deputy Foreign Minister of the People's Republic China, took his seat opposite his counterpart, David Yu-en Lee, Assistant Deputy Secretary of State for the United States of America. The two men had been classmates at Yale and had competed on the same crew team.

Zhiang greeted his old friend, "I personally regret the atrocious crime committed against your country, David. I convey the formal condolences of Minister Ling on behalf of the Chinese government and people."

"Thank you, Peng. I know you are sincere, and I will convey the sentiments of your government to Secretary Powell."

"Your administrative assistant told me how busy you are today, and much as I would prefer to chat with you, I will come right to the point."

"Don't feel that you are at all discourteous, Peng, or that my need for a brief meeting in any way reflects on our friendship or on my government's friendly intentions towards China."

The two men bowed to each other slightly.

Assistant Deputy Minister, Zhiang, a tall, handsome man with quick eyes and a quicker mind, came directly to the purpose of his visit.

"In past, our governments have disagreed on the definition of a separatist fighter and a terrorist. I am afraid that you are now beginning to experience what we have suffered from the rebel factions in Xinjiang."

"The East Turkestan Islamic Movement?"

"As always. Let me recap for you, David. My government has incontrovertible evidence of well over 200 separate acts of out-and-out terrorism perpetrated by the ETIM. Their tactics have included bombs, arson, assassinations, tortures, rapes, and extortion. More than 300 deaths and 500 injuries have been inflicted. The financial losses exceed $100M USD. Our intelligence service has proof that foreign interventionists from Kyrgyzistan with al Qaeda financing have been directing this so-called separatist movement."

"What can we do for you, Peng?"

"Allow me to be frank, David. In past your government has been critical of mine for any and all attempts to reign in this terrorism network. David, that is what it is. You are well aware that wherever a Muslim country or majority abuts a nonMuslim country or people, the Muslim fundamentalists foment terrorism. Our country is no different than yours. We wish to defend ourselves in a significant way without interference. In fact we wish to have your help with intelligence and promise a two-way information street about the al Qaeda networks we encounter."

David replied succinctly, "I will not return to our former conversations about the excesses my government believes have been a part of your government's responses to the ETIM. Instead, I will tell you that I am empowered to offer complete cooperation with your efforts. We will officially assign the ETIM terrorist status; we will freeze their assets in this country and will urge our European, Canadian and South American friends to do the same. Our intelligence services will await contact from yours, and I can assure you that there will be a level of unprecedented cooperation on our part. This decision comes officially from the resident."

"I will convey your good will and cooperative sentiments and actions to my government, David. This is the dawning of a new age for both of our countries."

"Thank you for coming, Peng. Enjoy your stay in Washington."

"I will, my friend. My auntie lives in Sterling and I plan to stay with family while I am here."

———————

David Yu-en Lee was having a busy day—an important day. Two hours after his meeting with the Chinese deputy, he walked into the same conference room and sat across the same highly polished oak table. This time he was meeting Assistant Deputy Foreign Minister, Basil Sergeivich Skevar of Russia. Unlike Zhiang Ho Peng, David had never met the Russian.

"Good afternoon, Minister. I am happy to be able finally to meet my counterpart from the Russian Republic."

David was mildly annoyed with himself for having been in such a rush that a thin sheen of sweat glistened on his forehead and his bald pate. The U.S. assistant deputy foreign secretary was afraid that the Russian would regard that as a sign of nervousness.

"The pleasure is mine, Mr. Lee. I am very strongly hopeful that our business today will prove fruitful and that we can conduct many more successful conferences. Such outcomes could not hurt our personal careers and more importantly may be of material benefit to each of our countries."

"Indeed, a worthy hope. You asked for this meeting, Mr. Skevar. I await your pleasure."

"My department and my government again wish to convey our condolences for the recent despicable terrorist attack on your great city. We wish to work with you to reduce such incidents in the future. I am empowered to offer the resources of our intelligence services for your—for *our*—war on terrorism. I am to be the liaison for our two governments, and I trust that we will be working together."

"Thank you, Mr. Skevar."

"Please, call me Basil. May I call you David?"

"Of course. Now, Basil, is there anything that we can do to show our cooperation with you?"

"There is. I will be blunt. We need a free hand in Chechnya. We need your government to acknowledge that those so-called 'separatists' and 'freedom fighters' are no better than the monsters who blew up the Twin Towers of the World Trade Center. They are Muslim fundamentalist terrorists pure and simple, and we have no choice but to deal with them for the threat that they are. Just last week, two women bribed their way onto a Sibir Airline flight from Novosibirsk to Ekaterinburg and a Pulkovo Airline flight from St. Petersburg to Moscow. A Chechen man bribed his way onto a Transaero flight from Novosibirsk to Kamchatka. They thereby avoided detection of their forged papers. They set off suicide bombs destroying three planes and killing a total of three hundred twelve people. We ask that your government cease its rhetoric favoring those terrorists and discontinue suggesting that we Russians are acting like neo-Stalinists. We need the Chechens to be branded as terrorists and to share the intelligence you have as we will share ours with you. Have I an agreement?"

"It will be a hard sell to our liberal establishment since they are absolutely convinced that the Chechens have a just cause."

"They also prattle on about the evils of your own government and its uneven treatment of the Palestinians."

"True. I tell you now that my president has given me authority to grant your request, and our secretary and your minister can formalize the agreement in the very near future. He does require that we go a bit slow and keep our support muted for the public early on. And, I am under orders to convey our request that you use restraint so that we can gain public support for what will undoubtedly be an unpopular agreement."

"I will do my best to convince my superiors, but you and I both know that we are but small cogs in a large machine; and neither of us can predict what our leaders will do, let alone what the terrorists will inflict or what changes their actions may provoke."

"Completely true. I would like to shake your hand, Basil. Let us hope for the best."

"Let us drink to it. Can a man get good chilled Stoly in this town?"

"I know just the place."

They shook hands and left together.

CHAPTER SEVEN

SEPTEMBER 21, 2002

Anwar el-Meshad, using a cover name and documents identifying him as
an Israeli Christian Arab, Yasir Atef Nusseibeh, thoroughly enjoyed his Air
France flight from Tunis, Tunisia to Paris with a stopover in Rome. Flying was
the one chance he got to sneak a few drops of alcohol. He needed to do so as
part of his cover. He decided that he liked undercover work. The flight was
smooth; the service by the French girls was impeccable; they were all blonds
and easy to look at with too much form revealed in their fitted uniforms;
and the landing was scarcely noticeable. The only thing difficult about the
entire short journey was going through passport control at *Aéroport d' Orly*—
Charles de Gaulle Airport. He watched dozens of Arabs pass quickly and
with a minimum of questioning. His status as an Israeli caused him no end of
inconvenience including an item by item search of his luggage. He filled out
twelve sheets of information about himself, his business in France, and his
itinerary. He would have laughed if he were not in cover.

His airport cabbie was a little less surly once he learned that his passenger
was on his way to the Hotel de Crillon. El-Meshad was aware that he was
being taken on a round-about route to drive up the fare, but he did not
care. He was on the Council's expense account. His whole being felt lighter
and less stressed there on French soil. The French were so civilized and Arab
friendly. Along the way, they passed a small old Jewish cemetery. There were
conspicuous swastikas defacing the cemetery walls and several of the visible
tombstones. It was enough to warm the heart of a man of God.

At the hotel, he tipped the cabbie. The man continued to hold out his hand to el-Meshad. The Arab gave him a few more francs. The cabbie looked at his hand as if el-Meshad had spat on it. El-Meshad peeled off five more francs, placed them firmly in the man's impudent hand and turned on his heel and marched into the safety of the elegant hotel's marbled lobby.

The check-in process went too fast and was too complicated for el-Meshad. It was the main thing he disliked about the West. Everything was too fast, too automated, too computer driven. The condescending clerk tired quickly of explaining each step of the process to el-Meshad and reached out to take his credit card and passport and proceeded to complete the formalities without further input from El-Meshad. Karic Singh, British Sikh citizen's reservation was found, and he was duly registered, all with an unbroken smile for the blushing Arab. El-Meshad kept his facial expression bland, but vowed that he would one day return to see the smug smile gone from this infidel's face.

He was aware of the body odor of stress induced sweat emanating from his armpits despite the hair having been so carefully plucked only the day before. He quickly undressed, showered, and applied a thick coat of deodorant and extra drops of Arabian Nights essential oil. The shower relaxed him, and he was able to take a short nap before his telephone rang and awakened him.

"Hello, Singh here."

"Hello, Mr. Singh. This is the front desk. Sorry to disturb you. But there is a gentleman asking to see you. Would you like to have me put him on the line, or would it be all right for him to come to your room."

"Send him up. It's fine."

"Thank you, Mr. Singh. Please let us know at the front desk if there is anything we can do for you."

Ten minutes later there was a soft knock on his door.

He peered through the safety peep-hole and recognized his fellow council member, Saad Makram el-Deen. It was a relief to see a familiar face.

He undid the safety chain latches and opened the door.

"Come in, Saad. I'm glad to see you."

El-Deen shook his head.

"No names."

He walked into el-Meshad's room, and said, "Muhammad, blessed be the Messenger, applauds your work."

"As I applaud yours. Sorry about the slip."

At least he had remembered the pass code, if a bit late.

"No problem. Here is the envelope you were promised."

He handed el-Meshad a thin white envelope with the name of Karic Singh typed on the front.

"Any other instructions?"

"No, only that we are not to have a conversation. As the Western spies are fond of saying, 'even the walls have ears.'"

El-Meshad nodded. El-Deen shook his hand, then turned and left.

El-Meshad quickly opened the envelope and digested the contents. He hid the new sets of documentation for himself in secret pockets in his new Western suit. There was no indication of the hidden passports; he was satisfied.

Forty-five minutes later another knock came on his hotel door.

Ever cautious, El-Meshad peered out and saw an immaculately suited European standing in front of his door.

El-Meshad admitted the man, a patrician gentleman with long grey hair, an unmistakable Frankish nose, and pursed full lips. He had on an expensive grey afternoon suit, and monochromatically matching silk shirt and tie. He wore a Rolex and a diamond ring on his fifth finger. His shoes were maroon Gucci loafers.

"Are you from the Council?" he asked.

"Yes."

"I am Pierre de Gastogne-le Croix," he said. "I believe that you are expecting me."

El-Meshad said, "I am sorry, Monsieur, but I hope you will understand, I need to verify your identity."

"I don't mind at all. In fact, I insist on such a mutual protection."

He showed El-Meshad his identity papers, and the Egyptian did the same.

"Monsieur le Croix, before we go any further, I must ask you for the agreed upon code," el Meshad requested somewhat sheepishly.

"Of course, I should have used it when I walked into the room. It is, 'Muhammad, blessed be the Messenger, applauds your work.'"

"Thank you, sir. I just had to be certain."

De Gastogne-le Croix then said, "I hope you will understand, but there is one more security measure my government requires. You know of the murders of diplomats when the Iraqis came seeking nuclear materials."

"Of course."

"Then, for our mutual safety, I have arranged for the hotel to provide us with a private steam room. There neither of us will be obliged to hide anything."

El-Meshad smiled his acquiescence. To do so meant that he had to overcome his innate sense of ill-at-ease at the exposure of his flabby pink, almost hairless body and the sense of violation of the modesty rules of his religion.

He had male pattern baldness which he endeavored to conceal by growing the hair on the right side of his head extremely long and winding it around the large posterior bald spot. The spiral of hair was brilliantined in place like an organic skull cap. To accomplish the aims of the Council, El-Meshad was willing to suffer almost any indignity or to make any sacrifice.

In the sauna the Egyptian and the tall, handsome, well proportioned, lean, and muscular Frenchman talked to one another with frankness equal to their physical nakedness. El-Meshad presented the requests from the Council.

"These items are the minimum we seek. We are willing to pay a full two billion dollars and to arrange for the immediate delivery of the Mirages, Pluton, and Crotale Missiles, and for two exact copies of the French Osiris plant in Saclay. This must be *une copie conforme* [authentic] and with the full upgrades to produce plutonium. I have the exact specifications in the documents in my room. We will further pay one hundred million U.S. dollars a year to have you supply us with weapons grade plutonium and UF6 capable of making twenty bombs per year.

"Finally, the Council will agree to grant you most favored nation status for our oil; and you will be guaranteed to be able to purchase twelve percent of your national needs from Iraq and as much as five percent more from the Kingdom even in the event of a repeat of 1973. However, we will no longer be patient with delays. I am authorized to tell you that you must give me an answer now. If that answer is no, we will not do business with you again; and the nations that serve my cause with me will follow suit."

De Gastogne le-Croix had been on the negotiating team that came close to supplying the Iraqis with bomb making capacity only to be frightened off by the United Nations' International Atomic Energy Agency [IAEA] when he had been summoned to IAEA headquarters in Vienna. He remembered the anger from the Iraqi thugs, and the murders that they had blamed on the Israelis. He shivered a little at the memory even in that steamy room.

"I would be a fool to have come here if I thought that there was any chance of a repeat of our failed negotiations with the Iraqis. You know that the IAEA watched us very closely when we were talking with members of the Islamic nuclear fraternity before. We cannot sell you these materials outright; the U.S. would never stand for it. The Israelis will not let it happen. If even a hint of this gets out, they will make a pre-emptive strike. This is my plan to deliver the goods to you, and you and your people must assist us to have a deniable cover."

De Gastogne le-Croix presented the pertinent material succinctly and with a remarkable feat of memory. He did not so much as carry a business card with him that day.

CHAPTER EIGHT

SEPTEMBER 21, 2002

Pakistani Vice President Walid Shamma Atallah offered Prince ibn Saud the greetings and well-wishes of his president and the loyalty of the Pakistani Muslim people. He had arrived in Baghdad the evening before and had been driven to the secure villa in Tikrit provided by President Hussein in the early hours of the August morning. The selection of the hottest time of the year in Iraq discouraged crowds from leaving their homes until the last moment when they had to be about their day's activities. The location was unimposing but as secure as any presidential palace in the country. Their privacy was assured.

"I know you have been most careful, my leader," Atallah said, "but my president requires that I use our own technicians to verify that there are no monitoring devices in our meeting place. I am sure you understand that I do not have the slightest concerns about you, but I do confess some uneasiness regarding our host."

"I have no problem with any security measures you think necessary. Perhaps we could sit outside in the shade of the palms and talk of innocuous matters until your people complete their investigation."

"Thank you for your understanding, prince. What I have to convey to you is worth the inconvenience."

The two men and their discrete body guards lounged in the garden listening to the burbling artificial brook and sipping sugary scalding tea. The plump Saudi prince in his immaculate thobe contrasted with the slight and wiry Pakistani in his general officer uniform; but they both exhibited their fine minds and copious worldly knowledge as they debated, without enthusiasm, the question of the Arab world's handling of the Palestinian versus the Zionist Occupiers confrontation.

Prince Ahmed Wahhab ibn Saud summed up the conclusions of the Council of The Leaders of Islam, "As noisy and troublesome as the affair seems, it is the next best thing to having the Zionists obliterated—a result not attainable thus far. The conflict results in only a few casualties among our people, and the Palestinians, who are of no consequence, bear the brunt of the Occupiers' anger. Relative peace reigns throughout the forty-four nation Muslim world otherwise. We could accommodate the Palestinians' desires in a week. All we would have to do is to set aside a piece of desert in one of our countries and move them there, and that would be the end of the conflict. Since it suits our purposes for the conflict to continue, we can utilize the time and the diversion to further our own, much more important plans. The Little Satan is a flea on the camel's nose in the long run. We will take care of that annoyance in due time."

The Pakistani technicians pronounced the rooms for the meeting to be clean, and the two men and their guards returned inside to enjoy the air conditioned comfort and silk brocade lounging pillows of the small, well-appointed room. The prince observed the Pakistani official as they enjoyed a large, frosted mug of iced *maramiya* [sage tea] and *qatayif* [cake with a layer of mild soft cheese served hot with *teen*—fig syrup]. The man was nervous and intense. His nut brown falcon face betrayed his sense of ill-at-ease. He was small, muscular, and dressed in a carefully tailored olive drab uniform.

Atallah's only striking feature was a huge, old-fashioned man-of-the-desert handlebar mustache. Like his hair, the mustache was inky black and did not have a single grey hair. With that facial adornment Atallah might have seemed a mildly comic figure were it not for his black eyes that were as cold as pieces of coal. The prince knew from the man's history; he was not a man with whom one trifled. Atallah's mission was the stuff that changes history, and he knew it. It was enough to make a man nervous.

"I am on a very tight schedule, Leader. Forgive me if I have not the time to enjoy your company fully, but I must make appearances in Damascus in a time frame that makes my entire trip to Iraq deniable."

"I understand fully, my friend. Please give me your news. I confess to a measure of excitement."

His placid face gave no hint of such an emotion.

"We have a fully operational nuclear explosive device—several, in fact. We are willing to share one device and all of the technical expertise behind it to shortcut your own work and to further the cause. We have an expert—a metallurgist—who has been with our program from the beginning, and we can share his information. Unfortunately, he is a businessman and will require a certain price."

"A.Q. Khan?"

"Yes. I presume you have already had dealings with our eminent scientist?"

The prince nodded. Prince ibn Saud already knew of the secret Pakistani break through, and his intelligence network had given him precise details of the Pakistani program and its small stockpile.

"I am astounded at what you have accomplished", he said. "I have heard rumors, of course, but to know that it is a fact from the very mouth of men who would not lie is almost overwhelming. I cannot tell you how well your offer to share is received. May God be with you and your Muslim brothers."

"I am pleased to be of assistance. There are two obvious requirements for our bequest: First, the Americans—our current great friends—must never be able to find the slightest hint of our involvement. Even if key people must die to keep this secret, we must consider it the will of Allah. Second, the costs of producing this weapon system have been prohibitive. Much as we would like to present this mighty act of Allah to you gratis, we cannot. Our price must be four billion dollars."

The prince raised an eyebrow and then furrowed his brow in concerned contemplation. He was serious as he spoke.

"Brother, the greatness of your accomplishment is beyond measure and your willingness to share almost renders me speechless. But, you know that we cannot afford such a price. We could not raise such money, certainly not with the degree of secrecy required; and even if we could, we would not be able to pursue any other facet of our program in the foreseeable future. I wonder if your expenses in the past were not more on the level of three-quarters of a billion U.S. dollars. We could afford…say…one billion, and even that would render our treasury very anemic."

That was a lie, but there was no hint of that in the Leader's expression. He knew that the Pakistani program had cost between one and a quarter and one and a half billion dollars but was prepared to go as high as three to obtain the treasure.

"My government and the mullahs have allowed me some leeway, my Leader; not much, but some wiggle room. I believe that I might persuade them to come down to three billion, but no less."

"I have confidence in your powers of persuasion, Mr. Vice-President. I truly believe that you could make this thing happen for two billion which would further our cause considerably. And, it has come to my attention that you have been a faithful and productive contributor to your country's well-being and to the cause of Islam without thought of personal reward. Allah is pleased with you; but even His Messenger, the Prophet, may Allah's blessings be upon him, had no aversion to the accumulation of wealth by righteous followers."

"I have never sought personal position or reward; it is true. My wife points out that our children will soon be of age to go to university. I confess to be at a loss to see how that can be accomplished on the meager salary of a lowly government official. But that is an aside. I would be willing to try to bring the price down, but it will be most difficult. Two billion exceeds the level I have been authorized."

"Let me be frank, brother. We need you and men like you. You can not function in a state of pecuniary. I ask nothing of you in return for a gift I wish to give you. I have a fine estate near Aleppo from which there is a beautiful view of the valley and of the citadel. It produces more than an adequate living for the owner. I would like you to have it as a token of my esteem and friendship."

"I am overwhelmed by your generosity. You understand that there could be no strings attached. I can only promise that I will act in friendship and try to convince my superiors of the wisdom of your end."

"That is all a friend could ask."

Two months later the complex real estate transfer was accomplished with the title to the Aleppo estate coming into the possession of one Awad Musa Ishteyyeh, nephew of Walid Shamma Atallah on his wife's side. Prince Ahmed Wahhab ibn Saud concluded a most secret contract with the Pakistani Nuclear Energy Commission to purchase a nuclear device for one billion eight hundred million dollars with the costs of transportation to be borne by the Council of the Leaders of Islam. Vice-president Atallah acted as broker and was compensated with two hundred million dollars from the prince—quite unknowingly on the part of the prince or the Pakistanis, since the prince's copy of the contract indicated a two billion dollar price tag. It was a most satisfactory negotiation for all parties.

"Now, to the problem of manufacture of capable missiles and obtaining the necessary components. I will be obliged to travel to Paris and to Kiev without being detected, and I will have to speak more than once to the duplicitous French. Such an inconvenience, but necessary, I fear," Prince ibn Saud mused.

CHAPTER NINE

SEPTEMBER 22, 2002

While the Frenchman's instructions were still fresh in his mind, Anwar el-Meshad found a pay phone booth on Rue Fontaine, a narrow slum street faced on both sides by warehouses. There was no traffic at that time of night. The call went through immediately.

"This is a secure line. Give your frequency code."

"Q-LCoC 01"

He heard a faint humming noise interspersed with regular periodic low pitched beeping sounds as the code he had given was translated into numbers, and the scrambler was activated. He waited three minutes.

"Line secure, go ahead."

El-Meshad unfolded his conversation with Pierre Gastogne-de Croix to President Mohammed Yahya Farouk. Only the sound of his breathing let El-Meshad know that his president was on the line. The president heard the entire story before speaking.

"Good," he said. "Tell me again when all of this must happen."

"Eight days."

"Gamal Monem will see you in person at the Paris safe house tomorrow."

The line went dead. Even the mention of Monem—the chief of Egyptian Intelligence's name—provoked a slight shiver in the corpulent Egyptian. He checked out of the Hotel de Crillon, took a series of four taxis, and arrived at dawn at the safe house on Rue Marie Curie. They were expecting him.

El-Meshad showered off the stress sweat of the long day and collapsed into his bed.

It was close to noon when El-Meshad suddenly awakened, disoriented by the strange bed and room. His pulse went up, and he shook his head. His mind cleared the cobwebs of deep sleep, and he took a hurried look at the bedside radio clock. He rushed out of bed and through a quick shower. He was seated at a simple breakfast of coffee and cold cereal when Gamal Monem was ushered into the breakfast room.

El-Mashed stood out of deference to the intelligence chief. Monem bade him sit with a dismissive gesture.

"I am pleased to see you up and ready for the day's work, Anwar."

"I am at your disposal, sir," El-Meshad responded, adding to himself, *"ilham-douLilah,"* [thank God] for for his having not been found as a slug-a-bed.

"Good. On the way in from the airport, our people have been filling me in on trustworthy allies in the jihad and on ships and schedules. Please pack a small bag, and we will leave for Marseilles."

"I am ready now."

The two men were taken to a trucking company warehouse on the outskirts of Paris by a Yemeni taxi driver. There they found a decrepit appearing unmarked van whose engine purred like a Masarati. Monem drove evasively for nearly an hour through Parisian suburbs before finally feeling safe enough to move on directly to Marseilles. They parked in the side lot of a rundown bar two streets off the water front. They went into the empty bar and crossed to the rear stairway leading to the second floor. They found bottled water, chicken and lettuce croissants, and French chocolates sitting on a low table along side a pair of *Qur'ans.* The two men settled in for a long wait. El Meshad fidgeted while the ramrod stiff Col. Monem seemed oblivious to the boredom.

At the same time, a tractor trailer semi backed into the loading dock of the Belgonucleaire—parent company of Société Générale de Belgique. It bore the clear logo of the Belgium company and all required outward designations as a carrier of nuclear materials. Already inside the compartments of the truck was a heavy cargo of nuclear plant materiel including clearly marked highly specialized high-vacuum valves from Vakuum Apparat Technik that were shipped to the Électricité de France plant outside Lyon. There, the shipment joined crates of automatic controls manufactured by Comsip and a complete, dissembled extraction/reprocessing plant manufactured by the specialty engineering firm, The Saint-Gobain Techniques Nouvelles, capable of producing two hundred kilograms of plutonium from thirty tons of used reactor fuel.

At the dock, workers in white coveralls quickly moved the component parts of four radiochemistry laboratories onto the truck. The lab had been shipped to Belgonnucleaire the previous day from the Comitato Nazionale per l'Energia Nucleare buildings in Rome. The Italian nuclear agency had facilitated a rush order from SNIA Viscosa. The load was a heavy one including lead-shielded hot cells with glove boxes for remote manipulation and Pyrex Micromiser-settlers with Tygon and Teflon tubes for the easy handling of radioactive substances. The necessary chemicals for dissolving irradiated uranium oxide from spent nuclear fuel rods and for extracting and reprocessing plutonium were included.

Into the center of the trailer, workers gingerly moved a wooden crate lined inside with a thick sheathing of lead. Inside the box, fixed in place in two foot thick Styrofoam encasement was a perfectly spherical metal ball about the size of a soccer ball. The metal's finish gleamed with a polish that was dust free down to the nanometer microscopic levels of smoothness. The white clad workers quickly moved away from the deadly material. This box was marked: REPLACEMENT MACHINE PARTS FOR CHEMICAL CENTRIFUGES-Verenigde Machine-Fabreiken, Netherlands.

The box was identical to another box that indeed contained finely machined high-strength alloy steel P-2 superultra centrifuges—instruments capable of spinning a gas of uranium hexafluoride to 100,000 revolutions per minute and 5000 supermagnets for uranium enrichment. The invoices did not note that such centrifuges and magnets were present let alone that they were illegal everywhere in the world. The irony of the shipping invoice and box markings on that container was that the description read: LOW GRADE URANIUM FOR REPLACEMENT OF POWER PLANT RODS and listed the manufacturer as a plant in Almelo, Holland, gave the plant's IAEA approval number, and on all sides posted radiation symbols.

A perfectly legal set of documents with the stamp of approval of the International Atomic Energy Agency attested to the guarantee that all of the materials were for peaceful uses only and the buyers—the nation of Umm al Qaiwain of the United Arab Emirates—had passed all requirements to ensure the peacetime uses of the materials. The only items missing from the manifest invoices were the spherical ball of plutonium, the magnets, and the P-2 centrifuges in the mislabeled boxes.

The heavily laden truck set out for the docks of Marseilles and arrived there without incident three days later. The Egyptians—Col. Gamal Monem and Anwar El-Meshad—were on a rusty old cargo ship, the *Signor di Constantini,* under Italian registry, sitting in the Bay of Marseilles, when the truck and trailer arrived. Longshoreman's union representatives mobilized their men, and the precious cargo was passed efficiently and without inspection into the bowels of the old ship. The destination manifest indicating off-loading points in Milano and Amsterdam; and the compliance with safety regulations for handling of radioactive materials were certified by the harbor master, the union representative, and the chief of the Gendarmerie for the city. Everything was in order and completely open and above board, with the minor exception of the unlisted assiduously polished and lethal metal ball, the custom built, highly sophisticated magnets, and the world's most advanced nuclear centrifuges now nestled deep in the *Signor di Constantini's* hold.

Only after the ship's captain and the shipping company's agent had signed the manifests and clearance was given for departure, and the longshoremen and port authorities had left the ship; did Monem and el-Meshad come up on deck. They smiled a knowing smile of relief at the seamless acquisition and shipment of the precious equipment and materials to this point. The most critical phase of the operation was yet to take place, and the two Muslims still showed the signs of low-grade stress that had blanketed them since they had arrived in the port city.

Monem and el-Meshad left the ship and arranged separate flights—Monem to Aden, Yemen and el-Meshad to Cairo—each using an assumed identity.

The *Signore Pietro di Constantini* steamed into the Mediterranean. In an unusual gesture of international good will and as a reward for a job well and efficiently done by the crew, Capitano Piscetelli broke out bottles of brandy and good Scotch. The crew had been hired off the docks and hurriedly signed into the dockworkers union with a hefty financial incentive given to the union steward to move the process along with dispatch. They came from more than a dozen countries and the most difficult aspect of personnel management had been to deal with the Babel of native tongues spoken by the motley assortment of seamen. The union steward had wondered at the gross ineptitude in the selection of the crew, especially when there were perfectly capable French merchantmen abounding in Marseilles. But it was not his place to question; the extra money he pocketed would keep his two sons in the expensive private school they attended for another semester.

The sea was calm, and a thick fog shrouded the plodding ship. At four bells, it was pitch dark all over the ship; and the only sounds were the comforting creaking of the rusty old metal parts moving as they had done for twenty years and of the gentle sea lapping at the hull. The captain and first mate were the only men awake or sober on the ship; the rest of the crew—including the junior officers—was snoring softly in their hammocks and beds below.

Capitano Piscetelli studied the glowing numbers on his digital watch face. At exactly four o'clock, he tapped First Mate Figuerello's shoulder. The mate nodded wordlessly; and the two men stepped out of the wheelhouse, crossed the deck, and lowered the ship's dingy into the black waters. They climbed down the hull ladder and rowed into the fog.

Precisely ten minutes later two fast boats pulled up along side the ship and were tethered to the port and starboard sides. In complete silence ten men from each boat climbed up onto the deck. Each man carried an Uzi, two magazines of ammunition, a roll of duct tape, and a wicked notched combat knife. Their faces were blackened, and their black Israeli Defense Forces uniforms made them all but invisible. They synchronized their watches for the third time in an hour then spread throughout the ship. Each man took his assigned place and counted down with the LED lighted numbers on his watch.

At four fifteen precisely, the commandos struck with deadly swift efficiency on the crew lying anesthetized in their bunks. The sleeping men were so far narcotized that it was unnecessary for a single shot to be fired. In less than ten minutes all but one crewmember was dead without a struggle. The survivor, a terrified Portuguese cabin boy—fourteen years old—was frog marched to the rail. He heard his captors speaking in what he presumed to be Hebrew, having crewed with a few Israelis in the past. The uniforms were new to him, but he was bright enough to come to the conclusion that the men were wearing Israeli navy uniforms. He was given a life jacket and thrown over the side. He watched as the ship disappeared into the mists of the night.

The ship's officers and the cabin boy were picked out of the water two days later by an Italian naval patrol boat and returned to Marseilles. Each of them recounted how the men in black—presumably IDF naval uniforms—blackened faces and speaking Hebrew had hijacked their ship and had needlessly slaughtered the defenseless crew. Capitano Piscetelli was distraught at the loss of such a fine international crew. The incident was reported to Eurotom, and Eurotom protested to the United Nations who agreed to discuss the issue in the Security Council. UN sources leaked the news that the international body was considering sanctions against Israel as a rogue nation. The leftist Paris daily, *Libération* and less socialist papers *France Soir*, *Le Point*, and *Var Matin République* united in an unusual headline, front page coverage, and editorial opinion agreement: Piratical Israelis had hijacked a ship carrying nuclear materials and equipment on the high seas. What could the Western world—

let alone the Arab world—expect next from the murderous Zionist Occupiers? The story played equally well in the Cairo daily, *Akhbar al-Yawm*, the London *Al Hayat*, the Saudi *Al-Madina*, Tehran's *Etelaa* and *Mardomsalarit*, the *O Estado do Sao Paulo* in Brazil, and in the *New York Times*.

The *Signore Pietro di Constantini* made a brief stop in the night along side a Yemeni freighter—the *Lady Fatima*—whose crew swiftly and crudely covered over the *di Constantini's* name on the side of the old ship. The two ships sailed separately into the Port of Aden, and the newly named *Jacques Chirac* was towed by a tug boat to an obscure birth in the nearby small port at Shaqra. Its cargo was expertly transferred onto a sleek white cruise ship—the *Leonidas of Lakedaimon*. The handsome cruise ship had left from the port of Piraeus flying Greek colors. In addition to the cargo from the *Jacques Chirac*, nee *Signore Pietro di Constantini*, the *Leonidas* took on a shipment of vacuum pumps, gas purification equipment, and twenty thousand small precisely welded aluminum parts. This equipment had come in the previous day on the German ship, *Das Mere Meister*, with the parts originating from the firm of Leybold Heraeus. The heavily loaded cruise ship moved into the port of Aden during the night and left with full tourist fanfare the next evening. Had one bothered to take notice, it might have struck him odd that so few tourists were on deck to wave to the natives.

The rusty old *Jacques Chirac*—nee *Signore Pietro di Constantini*—left port in the middle of the night with a skeleton crew. They towed a speed boat from the after deck. When the vessel was well away from land into the Gulf of Aden; and no shipping was in sight, the three men on board climbed down into the speed boat and roared away towards the Yemeni coast. One hundred yards from the old ship, one of the men—Said Mohammed Sisi—pressed the red button on the remote control device in his hand, and the old ship erupted in a brief pyrotechnic cataclysm and disappeared quickly into the sea. As the three men rushed towards land, Sisi casually threw the remote control device overboard.

Sisi and his assistants sailed up the coast to Ash Shihr and spent the night on cots in a private hangar in the small airport. The following morning they boarded a Council jet that took them across the barren north of Yemen and the Ar Rub'al Khali of Saudi Arabia and on to Abadan, Iran. The next morning Iranian army drivers in a vegetable truck took the three men south and across the Shatt al-Arab to the tip of Iraq where they were housed in an old barracks outside of Al Faw across from Umm Qasr.

The Greek tourist cruise ship—the *Leonidas of Lakedaimon*—left the port of Aden and sailed north and east up the Gulf of Aden to the Arabian Sea. At

Muscat, Oman the ship took on one hundred thirty-five German tourists on an archeological adventure. The sleek cruise ship turned northwest into the Gulf of Oman. The *Leonidas* sailed calmly through the Straits of Hormuz; and at Abu Dhabi, the crew boarded an additional eighty five tourists who were part of a larger group that would meet in Kuwait for an industrial exposition. The *Leonidas* and its crew wined, dined, and entertained the small complement of cruise tourists through the Persian Gulf and disembarked the happy, slightly inebriated band of revelers at Umm Qasr. The tourists were taken by luxury buses to Basra and arrived in the wee hours exhausted. Their guides told them all about the next day's plans to have them travel in a convoy of well guarded Range Rovers to Kuwait, but none of them was coherent enough to pay attention.

As soon as the token group of tourists was out of sight, the *Leonidas* was joined by a South African freighter—*The Free Boer*. From the cargo hold of that ship, seven hundred sealed oil drums marked as containing liquid soap, water softeners, and decontaminates were off loaded onto semis bound for Shiraz, Iran. Not listed was the actual cargo: high grade yellow mash uranium from South Africa. The crew of the *Leonidas* was joined by a disciplined coterie of workmen from Iran. Despite their work-a-day attire, the men had unmistakable military bearing. The South African crew and its officers were taken into Basra for two days of bird shooting and picnicking in the desert while the Iranian work crew and the men from the *Leonidas* saw to the transfer of the cargoes into the convoy of trucks.

Said Mohammed Sisi and his two assistants were joined by Ali Abdullah Kaswari and Gamel Monem, and the five serious men watched the hectic activity from the docks while avoiding being observed by anyone from the ships or trucks. The officers of the *Leonidas* were brought to the Al Arabe restaurant to join the five Arab Council officials. The Council men were affable and generous. The officers of the cruise ship were given an all expense paid vacation in Basra for two days before they were permitted to return to their ship. The men from the Council explained that there would be some necessary changes in the crew. At the rate the officers and the cruise line were being paid, who were they to complain?

The five Council men followed the convoy of trucks at a discrete distance as it wound its way to Shiraz and observed as the precious cargo was transferred into a Royal Saudi Air Force C-130. The handpicked RSAF crew was kept under guard in a hotel five miles from their plane as it was loaded, and one of Sisi's men stayed with them when they returned to the cockpit to ensure that they did not allow their curiosity about the cargo of industrial machine parts to lead them to an unwarranted investigation. The huge C-130 left Shiraz the following morning and deposited its heavy cargo on a large ranch outside Aleppo, Syria—land once owned by Prince Ahmed Wahhab ibn Saud and now in the legal possession by Awad Musa Ishteyyeh, nephew of Walid Shamma Atallah of Pakistan. Again the crew of the air craft was taken away—this time into Aleppo—where they were treated to a lengthy personalized tour of the Citadel, a sumptuous seven course meal, and a much deserved nap.

The equipment and raw materials were offloaded with forklifts and transported to the farthest northern corner of the huge parcel of land where it joined a small city sized collection of sophisticated equipment and carefully husbanded raw materials sent to Ishteyyeh's land from Tikrit, Iraq in the waning days of 2002 when President Hussein began to feel that the threats of invasion by the Great Satan might just have substance.

Mohammed Sisi with his remaining assistant, Gamel Monem, and Ali Abdullah Kaswari joined the Iranian workmen in Shariz and boarded tourist buses along with the crew of the *Leonidas of Lakedaimon* whose officers were enjoying all the sweets that exotic Basra could provide. Some of the Greek crewmen good naturedly complained that the officers got all the perquisites while they—the poor working stiffs—would just finish one job and start another without so much as a good meal.

Ali Abdullah Kaswari laughed and replied to the griping, "We have not forgotten you, my friends. In fact, we have a great surprise for you. You will never forget your stay in Iran and Iraq."

He laughed out loud and gave the men a knowing wink.

The crew of the *Leonidas*, the Iranians, and the four Council officials traveled in swift air-conditioned comfort from Shiraz to Kazarun and then north towards Dow Gonbadan.

Half of the way to the oil fields, Kaswari stood up in the bus and announced, "Look to your left, my friends. Tell me what you see."

"Desert," grumped the Greek crew boss.

"Look harder."

"Look ahead, Dimitri," called out one of the cooks who had been commandeered into the heavy labor job, "there's a huge tent."

Dimitri Evangelis Karamanli squinted into the sun.

"All right, I see the tent. I see trucks and a couple of backhoes, a plow, and a bunch of cooks."

"And with a little imagination, you can see the *dolmadhés*, the *Saganaki*, the *tsatzíki*..."

"And the lamb from the *psistariá*,"

"And the *souvláki*,"

There was not a man who imagined that they had as their surprise a thoroughly Greek meal and a classical greeting.

As the buses turned onto a dirt track leading to the tent and the trucks that indeed were catering vehicles, one of the Greeks called out raucously, "and the *oúzo*!"

The men all laughed with surprise and anticipation.

When they stepped off the buses, they were greeted with the melancholy strains of rembétika music, and the romantic Greeks felt at home. They scrambled out of the buses and took seats under the large white tent. Around the assembled crewmen stood a dozen bus boys and waiters with covered platters. Ali Abdullah Kaswari, Gamal Monem, Said Mohammed Sisi and his assistant, and the Iranian work crew quietly took places at the four corners of the tent.

Kaswari called for their attention. "Here is your surprise! Praise be to Allah!"

All eyes of the crew turned towards the security chief. They could not fathom the next two seconds of action. Kaswari, Monem, Sisi, and his assistant opened their coats and pulled out short Heckler and Koch submachine guns and with lightening efficiency and accuracy sprayed the horrified Greeks with a withering cross fire. At the close of the two second interval, there were a few faint moans. With a nod from Sisi, his assistant was sent to dispatch the few mortally wounded survivors with a practiced shot in the back of the head. Two hundred seventy-eight men and women were dead.

"Unavoidable casualties," Gamal Monem commented tersely to Kaswari who nodded in agreement.

The Iranian cooks turned about face and headed out of the tent and mounted the earthmoving equipment standing at the ready. Backhoes dug a trench one hundred yards long and eight feet deep. The Iranian work crew brought in pickup trucks and the still warm Greek bodies were thrown into the trucks and driven to the trench where they were unceremoniously dumped all along its length. The cooks plowed desert sand over the bodies and tamped it down to avoid leaving a tell-tale depression in the earth. The Iranian crewmen and cooks then took down the tent, packed it in a truck, and then drove away in all of the vehicles used in the ruse and for the disposal of the potential informers.

Gamal Monem dialed his cell phone.

"Did the materials arrive safely?" he asked.

He listened, then said laconically, "Good."

The man on the other end of the call asked, "Should we remove the RSAF crew?"

"No, let them fly back to Riyadh."

He turned the cell to 'off' and replaced it in his pocket. The device used SIM technology that made it nearly impossible to identify the purchaser which therefore made it a use-and-jettison phone. He would throw it away in the desert as they moved on.

"Let's go," he said.

The four men traveled back to where the *Leonidas* was anchored and greeted the cruise ship's officers, "Your new crew will arrive in a little more than an hour. Why don't you board and rest. You must have had a busy couple of days."

The captain nodded and signaled to his officers to follow him aboard. A crew of local Iraqis and Iranian seamen arrived by bus and were directed to board the ship. The *Leonidas of Lakedaimon* sailed away—bound for Athens—just before sunset.

Ali Abdullah Kaswari dialed a secure number, and when prompted, punched in a long series of numbers, then paused.

"Yes?"

Kaswari recognized his master's voice.

"It is done. All equipment accounted for and in place. All nonparticipants have been neutralized."

"*Mabrouk*, [Congratulations]. Come home," replied Prince Ahmed Wahhab ibn Saud with a rare dollop of praise.

NOVEMBER 30, 2002

The mid-term elections went even worse for the Democrats than had the previous presidential elections and much of the blame fell on the liberals. The liberal caucus licked their collective wounds. Hollings Braithwaite was re-elected to his Senate seat by the closest margin of his career; the sting was made all the worse because his opponent had been a ranting conservative from Palmdale who had not been given a ghost of a chance at the beginning of the campaign. The meeting of the Senate Liberal Caucus started with an acrimonious debate.

"Senator Braithwaite, I really must be heard," demanded Nevada Senator Assure. "My wing of the caucus has had its voice stifled for too long. It is time for a more vigorous voice to be raised against the Hitlerian/McCarthyite entity in the White House and throughout the government."

"Feel free, senator. Your opinions are as welcome as anyone's here."

"Hmmph. Our voice has been suppressed throughout Fascist American history. McCarthy—that thug—put an innocent patriot—Alger Hiss—in prison for most of his adult life because he was an enlightened and educated Eastern liberal—a Yale man. The Republican conservative juggernaut rammed through the appointment of Clarence Thomas to the Supreme Court. Our government—or I should say, their Fascist tyranny—supports Israeli aggression against innocent Arab people and occupation of the Palestinian Homeland simply because those people, incidentally—the rightful possessors of the land Israel usurped—are brown skinned and have a different religion."

"There are several others waiting to be heard, Mr. Assure. Is there a point with relevancy to our current problems in your communication?"

"Indeed there is. I am going to propose several specific plans of attack with your indulgence."

"Go ahead."

"All right. The 2004 elections are not that far away. I propose first of all that we let the wannabes in the party exhaust themselves in a divisive campaign and not directly support any of them, not even Al Sharpton who best typifies our cause. I'm sure he is going to throw his hat in the ring. Instead, we should pick apart every action the Repubs propose or institute and find the flaw, expose it through our press and PACs, and undermine as best we can. Our candidate will—in all probability—be a sacrificial lamb.

"Secondly, I propose that we select the candidate for the 2008 election and begin a more subtle campaign now to make him or her appear presidential and to be able to articulate our patriotic American program that is unflinchingly liberal. Thirdly, I believe, right now, that we should look to making Hollis Braithwaite our new president in 2008. We will all have to sublimate our personal agendas to make this happen. The plan will have to be carefully and thoughtfully pushed in the media—and I have been assured by the *New York Times* that they will lend every asset they can muster for the plan—and selflessly carried out. I will sit down now. Let me hear your thoughts. This is a crusade that is bigger than any of us. We have to line up with the downtrodden of our country, the workers, the people who stand up for the little guys against the medical establishment, the corporations, the NRA, and the born-agains."

"Thank you for the call to arms, Senator. I'm flattered at your suggestion, of course. From the forest of hands, I can tell that this is going to be a hot topic. I can think of nothing more fitting for us to brainstorm about today and no better time than now. The floor recognizes Elijah Muhammad White, the senior senator from New Jersey."

CHAPTER TEN

JUNE, 2005

Margaret Puncher was defeated in the previous November elections in California. Hollings Braithwaite was now the senior senator from California, and he was enduring a tongue lashing from the president of the AFL-CIO of California. Senator Braithwaite did not like to be criticized—let alone berated—and if his long-term plans had not included another election or two to the Senate and a run for the presidency in 2008, he would have shared his colorful vocabulary with the pin-head. Maybe he could just haul off and punch him out. There would never again be anything so satisfying—or catastrophic—for him, he knew; and so, he held himself in a toothsome grin at each escalating insult.

"You have sat in this chair where I put you for the past twelve years, and you haven't done diddly for our union people. You pass gas up here and let the Republican Nazis pick our pockets year after year. You ashamed of yourself, Mr. Senior Senator?"

"I'm not the president, and I am not even a member of the majority party in Congress. In case you haven't noticed, Bush got re-elected and carried a huge majority of Republicans with him. What can I do?"

"Get off your dime and work for us. Get us a few of the plums. We're hurtin' out there where real people live, where people get their hands dirty—somethin' you wouldn't know nothing about."

"C'mon, Ed, I have been busting my butt up on the hill for as long as I can remember. The Bushies control the government—the jobs, the taxes, the pork, everything."

"Listen, Braithwaite, you better do something and fast; or I swear that me and the boys will find us a new worker-bee here inside the beltway."

"Every time we have one of these nice little chats, Ed, I find out that you have a very particular something you want from me. Is that the gist of it this time?"

"Now that you mention it, there is a little favor we need over at the AFL-CIO hall."

"You could knock me over with a feather."

Ed Franklin allowed a small roguish smile to crease the severe countenance of his porcine face. He was caught and glad of it. He knew as well as everyone else that the conservative juggernaut had been unstoppable and that another election cycle would be necessary before the working guys of the country would get their chance. He also knew that Hollings Braithwaite—for all his prissy upscale Ivy League ways and his blather about his liberal activisms—was the only real hope the Democrats and—therefore, the unions—would have in the next decade.

He paused to light up a cigar, a habit he knew Senator Braithwaite despised.

"Look, Hollings, I have to give you a hard time. But I do have a real thing that needs to get done."

"Um hmmh."

"Okay, so you know Marty Ivers pretty well?"

"For twenty-five years is all. What does he want?"

"You know he don't ask for hardly nothin', and he works for us all the time. He sits in the assembly kissin' it up and makin' compromises with the devil to get our guys a little somethin' year after year."

"And what does the esteemed leader of the California assembly have in mind?"

"Maybe you don't know it, but his wife's sister's kid is the local president of the Corrections Officers Union out of San Francisco. He's an up and comer. Marty wants he should get a little boost up, like somethin' juicy in the federal system."

"And, even though I don't know Marty's nephew—Carlos Sanchez, and his wife Maria Innocenta and their six children—all that well, maybe I heard a touch of grapevine gossip that there has been a little woman trouble in the union; and it wouldn't be a bad thing if Marty's friends found young Carlos a change of venue"

"Don't be such a smart fart. I shoulda known that you were up on all the stuff that matters. To be straight, we can't have that little creep around anymore; the women just won't have him; and in this day and age you gotta listen to them."

Ed patted his rotund belly under his old fashioned vest, complete with a locomotive engineer's pocket watch on an ornate chain.

"Anything you have in mind, Ed? I can't come up with any job that would fit him right off-hand."

"Matter of fact I do. Been studyin' the problem. My people here tell me that there's a broad runnin' the federal prison system that is about as bright and useful as they come. I'm told that she is long overdue for a step up. You followin' me?"

"Part of the way. Tell me exactly what that has to do with Marty's nephew?"

"Exactly, she gets bumped upstairs, and he gets the prison director job."

"Care to give me a little of what you're smoking, Ed? He couldn't direct a Little League team. What does he know about running a prison, to say nothing about being the director of the biggest prison system in the country—in the world? I can't just get the present director fired. As you so accurately suggested, she's everybody's poster girl for the best civil servant in the country. The Republicans won't even talk to me about that."

"I didn't suggest that you get her fired. Promoted was what I said."

"To what!? Have you got any idea how many of our fair citizens want federal jobs since there are no more plums in California? The Republicans have a pretty big say there, too, if you haven't already noticed. At this late day in the game, everything worth giving to our folks has been distributed. I would love to help out, but my hands are tied. You should have come to me last December."

"But the problem with Carlos wasn't there last December, and the solution didn't present itself until two weeks ago," Ed said with a 'gotcha' grin.

He squirmed on his seat for a more comfortable purchase. His legs were too short to reach the floor flatfootedly, and they got the jitters when he sat too long in one position.

"Stop playing around, Ed. I'm busy. Out with it. Obviously you know something I don't. Let's get down to brass tacks."

Ed blew a precise smoke ring from his cigar that Hollings presumed must have been made from choice Virginia street sweepings. He smacked his full lips with enjoyment of the good smoke and the senator's discomfiture.

"As a matter of fact, I do know the solution. Over in Justice, the chief deputy attorney general has just come down with a brain tumor. He was operated on two weeks ago and can't talk or move his right side, and it don't look like he's ever gonna be able to tie his own shoes. The common folk over there talk. And the talk is that there is a lot of unpleasantness over who's gonna take his place. Things are so heated that there's talk of quittings and firings. Some little birdie whispered in my ear that they was about ready to look around for a compromise candidate. Now, are you getting' my drift?"

"I do know a little something that may make a difference, Ed, now that you jog my memory. The federal prison director—her name is Elizabeth Rowan—is a member of a kind of club of which Craig Wirthlin—the brain tumor victim—is the current president. Mrs. Rowan is taking his place as acting president. Behind the scenes, these people are considered the best and the brightest. I think you may be onto something, my friend."

"You'll give it a push?"

"If you'll promise to get off my back."

"No problem."

Franklin stood up and smiled at the senator.

"Until the next favor I need."

He pantomimed jauntily tipping a bowler hat.

"I'll be waiting. And I'll let you know. Your number is in my little black book."

When Ed Franklin left—without closing the door to Senator Braithwaite's office and leaving behind the foul reminder of his cigar habit—the senator stroked his chin for a moment. He checked his electronic address book, scrolled to Justice, highlighted a name, and punched the call button.

"Fiske," the brusque voice of the new attorney general answered.

"Henry, this is Hollings. Hollings Braithwaite."

"Yes, how can I be of service, Senator?"

"How about remembering that you and I are still Hollings and Henry, my friend?"

"Touché. How're things?"

"Aside from being in the party that looks from the outside in, I guess things are about as good as I can expect."

"I can't help that you decided to be a flaming liberal and to join up with the pinkos and defeatists. We all have to pay the consequences of our follies."

"The righteous and generous will win out in the end, and you fascists will be just a footnote in history."

The old friends shared a laugh at their running joke. Neither man ever seriously criticized the other's heartfelt political philosophy.

"What can I do for you, Hollings?"

"I think maybe it's what I can do for you. One of my little birdies told me that your Craig Wirthlin has been laid low by a terrible brain tumor. I'm truly sorry to hear that and hope you'll let his wife and family know that I feel bad about it. He's a good man. I've heard that his incapacity comes at a time when you haven't been able to get the troops to settle in with you as boss."

"Well, all of that's true. I'm sure you didn't call to gloat. What are you suggesting?"

"The number three and four guys at your place are at each other's throats over who's going to get Wirthlin's job. His body's not even cold yet."

"You sound surprised. Welcome to Washington. This your first day here?" Hollings laughed.

"Not exactly. What if you could find a really competent and wholly acceptable outsider to appoint as an ambush for your two infighters? Then they could go back to doing their jobs which they do very well when they aren't playing our game of politics at which they aren't very good."

"I have been so focused on those two and trying to decide between them that I didn't have the creativity to think outside the envelope. Do you have someone in mind? Please don't try and foist off one of your blatant or latent Bush haters on me. You know that will never fly, and I'll just lose face; and you'll lose your marker."

"In all honesty..."

"Uh, oh, here comes a lie."

Hollings laughed.

"Hear me out. This is an honest suggestion, and I think a good one."

"Shoot."

"Do you know Elizabeth Leavitt Rowan, the director of the Federal Prison system?"

"Not directly, but, as a matter of fact, I have been hearing nothing but good stuff about her. Is she the compromise?"

"She's more than that. She's good people—nobody's patsy and nobody's fool. She gets things done. I've been watching her. She is efficient and frugal and as near as anyone can be in this mean town, she's apolitical. You know that she is a member of Craig Wirthlin's Independents' Club?"

"Ah, that's where I heard of her. Wasn't she a prosecutor some time ago?"

"Federal. That gives you something to investigate. I don't think you'll find any skeletons. She's about as straight as they come. You ought to think about getting the fibbies to look into her."

"Much as I hate to admit it, I think you have a real face-saving solution for me. It seems rude to ask, but is there a quid pro quo?"

"A small one. I want one of the lesser lights from the prison system in California to get the nod for Mrs. Rowan's job if she moves over to your shop."

"What's his name, and is he any good at all?"

"Carlos Sanchez. He's not all that great, but the unions will back him all the way and will throw any weight they have to help. He's Marty Iver's nephew. Between him and the unions, I think Carlos can become an asset. I would owe you a marker if you'd do it and get Ed Franklin off my case."

"Promise me he's not a closet queer, or a pedophile or a junkie, Hollings. The powers-that-be will hamstring me if he turns out to be a closet Clintonite or something close to that dreadful. You know the climate here."

"He is a little too friendly with the girls, but no real trouble, I've been told. Get the fibbies to look into him. Marty will give them the straight skinny; you know him."

"I'll give it a go. Can we still do business if Mrs. Rowan gets in and Carlos the Lech can't?"

"Of course, we have always gone on good faith, however different our politics may be. I'll give you a ring, and I expect you and Ruth to come to our spring soirée."

"Wouldn't miss it. Have a good day, as you say out there on the left coast."

"You, too."

Both men spent the next half hour on the telephone and on-line to make the proposed governmental changes happen. It was Hollings Braithwaite's modus operandi to complete every task possible before letting it get lost in the swamp of distractions he and his office encountered. By the close of business that day, he was able to call Ed Franklin and tell him that Mrs. Leavitt was a shoo-in and that she was ready for a change. It was going to be a little tougher to get Carlos into her job, but it did not look impossible. With the wheels turning without any further need for his intervention, the senator forgot about the situation and turned his attention to the Senate appropriations bill that had just left his committee. He had to get it passed before October, and he had plans to insert a few line items for his constituents before it went to the president, may he suffer a pox.

CHAPTER ELEVEN

SEPTEMBER, 2005

The Kola Peninsula in the Russian arctic is home to Saami tribesmen, coast dwelling Russian Pomor people, a variety of hardy wildlife, and reportedly a Yeti, who lives near Seidozero. It is among the most polluted portions of the world and is inarguably the most radioactive place on earth. Nearly twenty percent of the world's nuclear reactors are there in the densest concentration of such facilities anywhere. 120 retired submarines with their still active nuclear reactors—some with two—lie slowly rotting in the waterways. In September the capital city of Murmansk is cold and bleak with clouds scudding in to extinguish the fewer and fewer hours of daylight available to the four hundred thousand residents. Soon, it will be necessary to take all of the school children to special rooms in their schools to expose them to ultraviolet light for fifteen minutes a day to prevent them from developing rickets from vitamin D deficiency. To worry about skin cancer from too much sun exposure is more of a concern of southern climes and the Western world than for Murmansk, given the circumstances.

Nikel is a pathetic village less than forty kilometers from the Norwegian border. Radioactive nuclear materials have been stored in and around the town for nearly thirty years. The materials come from some of the more than one hundred retired Soviet submarines from the Cold War Era, and they are stored in perilously decrepit buildings secured only by padlocks that could be picked by any locksmith in the world and protected by intermittent patrols of elderly pensioners who believe that it is a sacred trust to protect these stores for Rodin, the Motherland. Two men could easily carry out a successful attack on any of those facilities and make off with sufficient nuclear material to make a dozen dirty bombs.

If the attackers were enterprising enough to have good transportation, it would be no great feat to carry away plenty of refined nuclear material to make a Hiroshima or Nagasaki size bomb. Given time—and more than one trip—enterprising nuclear smugglers could provide interested parties with uranium stockpiles adequate to make the conversion to plutonium and effect annihilation of whole major cities. The piers at Murmansk and at Nikel are lined with the decaying carcasses of nuclear submarines—some so deteriorated that no one dares enter or move them for fear of setting off an atomic explosion. The region has been described as a "Chernobyl in slow motion" by a neighboring Norwegian nuclear physicist, Nils Bohmer.

In Murmansk there is a semblance of security—a police force, a garrison of the Russian Army, and long time public servants who as regularly as possible get around to evaluate the stores and to ascertain if intruders have been at work. In Nikel the presence of the nuclear material is almost equally plentiful, but real security does not exist. Other than for the years of dumping spent radioactive materials into the ocean and the resultant elevation in the ambient radioactivity, the dangers of exposure are minimally acceptable in the small village.

The most dangerous problem in Nikel in September, 2005 was that the people of the Russian outpost were starving, enduring yet another terrible potato harvest. People who starve—who have experienced nine months of unpaid wages, and see shops with no consumer goods or even food—are not likely to be overly finicky about business niceties while surrounded by a veritable treasure trove. In Nikel the locals guarded their potatoes more vigorously than they did the nuclear wastes.

Walid Shamma Atallah, the vice president of Pakistan, was by education a nuclear physicist, and by profession—prior to his ascension to his political position—one of the directors of the Pakistani nuclear weapons manufacturing program. He knew about Nikel's predicament, and he knew a gift from Allah when he saw it.

Atallah sent three Algerians to reconnoiter and report—Algerians so that no trace could find a trail back to Pakistan. Abderrazak Abdul-Hamid di-France was selected because he was an especially resourceful adventurer completely loyal to the Council of Leaders of Islam and its cause and completely devoid of human compassion. Tawfik Rafi-Rafiq was included because he had been a communist until it was no longer healthy in Algeria. He was educated at Patrice Lummumba University in Moscow and was completely fluent in the Russian language and customs. Habeeba Junah, was a double PhD in nuclear physics and atomic energy manufacturing. She was a zealot in the cause of fundamentalist Islam without peer. Even in the company of revolutionaries, she wore a long flowing coal black jilbab and gave a withering look to any man who stared over long at her hands, feet, or face, the only parts of her person that were exposed. There was nothing she did not know about making atomic bombs, and nothing she would not do to provide the Council with the means to attack the decadent West.

Atallah made arrangements for the three emissaries to meet with Yevgeny Ataulla Bayazitov, the provisional governor of the Nikel region and of the nearby small islands. Atallah was persuasive; he was willing to send a shipload of food and plastic sheeting enough to cover the leaking ships in Andreeva Bay and the *Lepse*—a service ship containing almost six hundred fifty spent nuclear fuel assemblies—that had been forced into containers with sledge-hammers by uneducated, poorly fed, and woefully underpaid employees so that the entire area was a seething boil of radioactivity. Furthermore, Atallah offered to provide work for the local populace to deliver the food and to do the work of covering the leaking vessels to prevent further dispersion into the surrounding waterways. The best part of his offer was that it could all be done in secrecy so that Bayazitov would not have to answer to his employers as to why he was exposing the beloved Motherland to criticism from outsiders for its inability to manage its own problem.

di-France, Rafi-Rafiq, and Dr. Junah flew on separate Aeroflot flights from Moscow's Domodov and Sheremetyevo airports into Murmansk—and although they considered themselves to be brave freedom fighters—all of them were shaken by the obviously slovenly maintenance of their planes, the callous indifference on the part of their crews, and the total disregard for the published schedule.

"*Il-hamdouLilah,*" each of the Muslims muttered when their planes bounced in for their landings, each more than two and a half hours late.

The three freedom fighters stayed overnight in the Polyarnie Zori Hotel in the city center. They paid extra for a view of Kola Bay. In the morning, they were met by an ancient seven seater 1971 Zil 117 driven by a surly *babushka* who ferried them in silence to the provisional governor's humble residence. The three Algerians took note of the fact that they did not pass any where near the governor's office. The stout woman, clad in her best dress—she was able to save enough to buy a new one each year—opened the automobile's doors for her passengers which surprised them. The reasons for her apparent courtesy were two: first, it was required of her in her job description—not that that was particularly important to her—and second, because the door latches did not function properly and could not be opened from the inside. She grunted and made a gesture towards the house then clambered back into her vehicle which lumbered into motion and made a few asthmatic coughs as it disappeared down the white birch tree lined gravel road.

The three Algerians knocked on the front door of the house. A hand pointed to their right and waved them in that direction. They made their way along a trash strewn path to the rear door and found Yevgeny Ataulla Bayazitov waiting for them.

To their surprise and pleasure he greeted them with, "*Salam alekum*" [Peace be unto you].

The Algerians automatically responded in chorus, "*Wa alekum es Salam,*" [And upon you be peace].

"*Ahlan wa sahlan.*" [Welcome].

"*Ahlan bekum,*" they responded.

Once inside the humble house, Bayazitov told them that he was a Muslim and moreover that he was Wahhabi. He had divined their mission.

"I am willing to do all I can to further the cause, my brothers and sister. I believe I can obtain everything you need and that we can do this thing in such a way as to leave no record."

"Tell us what you can do, brother," di France said.

"With enough money, I can bring some trusted brothers into the region to do all of the work of moving the materials you need in the amounts you desire whenever you need to have it done. Kola Bay never freezes; so, we can even work in the winter if you want. By the way, the chance of being detected is much lower then. The citizens stay indoors, and the inspectors stay in the bars. With a little money spread in the right places many heads can be turned away, and eyes made not to see."

di France studied this earnest oriental looking man. He and the other Algerians had expected a prolonged beating about the bush and annoying negotiations over money.

"How much money would be needed?" he asked.

"We must be very careful in matters of the exchange of money. You have seen the poverty here. It would not do for the Russians or the Pomors to become rich all of a sudden. In all, I think you would need to infuse something on the order of one hundred million dollars spread out over about five years. We will need to invent an ongoing cover story that would allow you to bring in ships a few times of year carrying innocuous clean-up supplies and to leave with a cargo hold full of the magic material."

di France distrusted Bayazitov instinctively as he did everyone who did not look like his family. This one looked more like an Eskimo than a Muslim. He smelled like one, too. Bayazitov smiled conspiratorially.

"That does not seem unreasonable to me," di France said. "What do you think Dr. Junah?"

"I have a question. Mr. Bayazitov, your country exacts a fifty percent tax on all clean-up materials brought into the country. Does your price include that tax?"

"I cannot be certain, Doctor. There will be hidden costs like the tax and the corruption in our society runs from the street sweeper to the president. That will cost as well. We are likely to encounter overruns."

"You are probably a master of understatement, brother. Nevertheless, the costs do not seem especially unreasonable or prohibitive. I think we can accept them, Abderrazak."

rafi-Rafiq, the third Algerian, had been quiet. His was an untrusting nature even regarding his family because in his world—from his youth until now, treachery had been the order of the day; friends betrayed friends—and all too many of his compatriots had had their throats cut as they slept in the Algerian desert because they had chosen to trust.

"I am interested to learn that you are a Believer, Mr. Bayazitov. How is it that you came to embrace the true faith, and how is it that a Believer lives in this cold northern place?"

"I am from Nizhny Novgorod in the Privolzhsky Federal District. That is where the Russian state first met with Islam, and I was born into a family of Believers. I was educated in Azerbaijan in the Muslim school where I joined *Jamiat-i-Watan* [Patriotic Front]. I attended the conference of Muslims held in Saratov arranged by the Tajikistani Islamic Renaissance Party. The talk there was of secession, but I met there a man you may know from the ISI [Pakistan Inter-Services Intelligence organization], by the name of Ikram Khalid Atallah. He cautioned me to stay out of trouble and arranged for me to have money for bribes so that I could find civil service work on the Kola Peninsula. He told me that one day my services for Allah and our religion would be required. A week ago, Ikram's father called me and told me to expect you and to offer any service I could provide."

rafi-Rafiq nodded, not unpleasantly, which was as much as could pass for acceptance or trust by the man with the government inflicted burn scars on his back and buttocks. The name of Atallah was the clincher.

The next flight out of Murmansk to Moscow was not for two days—weather permitting. The three Algerians and Bayazitov took the oriental Muslim's *Pobeda, GAZ-20* [Victory] on a light hearted tour of the Murmansk fjord and sight-seeing around the tundra, the waterfalls and salmon rivers. The Algerians endured another Aeroflot flight to Moscow then flew in comfort on Air France to Paris. The two men partook of the small delights offered by the attractive French flight attendants. Dr. Junah abstained and visibly disapproved of the consumption of alcohol, but held her tongue since she was only a woman.

The three went their separate ways back to Algiers and Touggourt—their bases of operation in the eternal fratricide that was Algeria. Before he left Paris, di France went to the Pakistani Embassy and made a secure call to Karachi.

Vice-President Atallah was summoned by his aide-de-camp.

"What is it?" he asked brusquely.

"My friends and I have completed a pleasant trip to the ski areas and found the accommodations to be in order and promising. We recommend a cruise for your clients. I am sure they will be enchanted by the place."

"Thank you. I will expect a full report this week. I will be in Luxor at the end of the week. Would that be convenient?"

"I will be there."

The meeting in the ancient Egyptian city in the Winter Palace was friendly and productive. Plans were laid for a return to the Kola Peninsula in force in two years.

MAY, 2007

With pre-arrangement through the unflagging efforts of Yevgeny Ataulla Bayazitov, a large sturdy freighter under Panamanian colors was sent through the Norwegian Sea and to the Barents Sea and docked in the Port of Murmansk.

After clearance through customs—and by the Russian Atomic Energy Commission officials who confirmed that all movement of radioactive materials would be in accordance with international rules and the settling of all taxes and gratuities—tons of plastic sheeting and strapping equipment, lead lined barrels, ship repair tools, and tools for the dismantling of the daunting number of rotting submarines were taken from the holds and transferred to trucks. The truck drivers and loaders required pay in advance, having learned the Russian system of promises and disappointments all too well. The trucks deposited supplies along the fjord and near the dangerous submarine, the— *Lepse*—where a small army of workmen in hazmat clothing began to assemble the first effort to gain control of that disaster waiting to happen.

More of the trucks made the arduous journey to Nikel where they offloaded a veritable city of equipment to tackle the project of sealing off the dangerous radioactive leak points. The city of Murmansk and the village of Nikel erupted into a two day long drunken party, and no work was possible. Many families enjoyed a little inebriation and saw meat for the first time in a year.

The fleet of empty trucks gathered in a large forest glen outside of the village as the Kola Peninsula enjoyed its small period of celebration of hope. Hard faced Muslims from the peninsula and from the southern autonomous provinces had been assembled and waiting camped along the eastern coasts of the White Sea. Bayazitov communicated with the tribal headmen when he learned the exact time for the gathering in the forest. He arranged for the men to move almost entirely unnoticed through the wild country until they were gathered in the glen ready to work for the True Religion.

Vice President Atallah—ever security minded—had sent a coterie of Moroccans to complete the transfer of the precious atomic energy materials and equipment to its righteous place under the watchful eye of Allah and his mullahs and imams. Abdelghani Labied was the leader of the men appointed by the Council, and he ruled with an iron hand—the discipline of God. He was assisted by Mounir Binalshibh, Abderrazak el Motassadeq, Mohammed Jarrah, and Marwan Ramzi. These officers commanded two dozen hardened freedom fighters, and all of them knew how important their mission was if not its precise particulars.

Labied and Bayazitov met and worked out the details of the work to be done over the next two weeks. Like the workings of a Swiss clock—and unlike typical Arab work habits—the project moved forward with alacrity and care. Tons of enriched uranium enclosed in new safe sealed lead lined drums, whole reactors, testing equipment, ultracentrifuges, instruction manuals in Cryllic, and eighty-two fully operational nuclear warheads were secreted aboard the Panamanian vessel. Bayazitov was delighted with the response he received from the Moroccans. They were ecstatic about the unfathomable treasure they were loading, and Bayazitov was particularly relieved by the complete lack of interest they were stirring among the populace. The locals were busy doing the work of sealing off and protecting the dreadful leaking submarines and getting paid for it. Like good Russians throughout the huge nation, they were not paid to make observations or to ask questions.

Bayazitov held one surprise until the last two days of the loading of the clandestine materials. He led Labied deep into the birch forest and into a clearing which was served by an excellent road. There he showed the Moroccan his trump. There were twelve fully operational, albeit somewhat rusty SS-21 missiles, thirty-one medium and short range nuclear weapons and a neatly housed stack of well-protected nuclear warheads. The greatest prizes were four 8K-74 ICBMs maintained in mint condition, newly painted to remove all Russian markings.

"Tell me about these monsters," Labied said.

Bayazitov was something of an expert.

He said, "They were made by the best missile makers in the country, the S.P. Kordev Rocket and Space Corporation Energia. Missiles from this same lot were fired from the Baikonur Cosmodrome with 300 kilogram warheads. They have a proven range of 12,000 kilometers and can deliver a payload of almost 5500 kilos including a warhead weighing 2.9 metric tons. This is the Flying Sword of Allah."

Labied frowned.

"It will be some feat to get these huge things onto our ship. Did you think of that, my brother?"

Bayazitov grinned.

"I did. And it is easy. We have mobile missile trucks all over the place going unused and plenty of cranes to load even this cargo onto the trucks. They will be here at four this afternoon."

"I am impressed, Yevgeny. I am impressed."

Labied's soul soared. He would be a hero when he delivered these implements of the True God's vengeance on the Great Satan to the Council. Labied could see the end of the corrupt Western world in his mind's eye as he put a loving hand on the cold metal of the ICBM lying next to him.

The project of lifting and transporting the huge missiles proved to be more than Bayazitov had thought. It required bringing in cranes from all around the peninsula. The bribery required for work and silence ran the bills required of the Moroccans to a third again as much as the original price agreed upon. Labied grumbled but fairly good-naturedly since he was going to bring home a cargo of inestimable value to the cause of Islam. From the ship's safe he was able to produce twenty-two million dollars and gave it to Bayazitov along with a promise of another fourteen million when the ship was back in an Islamic port. Bayazitov had no reason to mistrust these—his co-religionists—who had been so efficient and generous to this point. He agreed without hesitation.

Finally, the cargo was ensconced in the gargantuan hold of the freighter and hidden under coverings with uninteresting markings—soap, fuel oil, iron ore, and crude petroleum.

Labied, Ramzi, Jarrah, Binalshibh, and el Motassedeq approached Yevgeny Bayazitov on the dock in Murmansk on the evening they were to set sail. Labied gestured to Binalshibh who reached behind him and produced a handsome box four and a half feet long.

Labied said, "My friend and brother, my countrymen and I, we have but one more task to perform here. Your service to our cause and to the service of the One God and his chosen servants has been of the greatest value and will never be forgotten. Unfortunately, of course, until the great day of the return of the great prophet, Jesus, to set the world right for Islam and to usher in the time of eternal peace and reward for all of the freedom fighters and holy martyrs, your service must remain a secret."

"I would rather have my tongue cut out than to utter a careless word about Allah's work," Yevgeny said fervently.

Abdelghani embraced his Russian brother and quickly kissed his cheeks three times.

"Is there a private place where we can unveil the token of appreciation sent with us by the Council, my true *akh*?"

"Even here in little Nikel the walls have ears. Perhaps it would be best if we went into Allah's forest."

"I like that," Abdelghani Labied said, and his fellow Moroccans nodded their pleasure with the arrangement as well.

Yevgeny led his four new friends and brothers to a small clearing near his house. He was almost beside himself with excitement, suspecting what lay within the long box.

"I believe we will be safe here, brothers. I have not detected any prying eyes, no spies. I can hide the precious honor under the floorboards of my basement, and none will ever be the wiser."

He was almost pleading. His narrow oriental eyes were glistening.

Labied gestured, and Binalshibh produced the box.

"Sit here, *akh*, on this stump. You will need to be seated when we show you the token of the Council's esteem."

Mounir Binalshibh handed the ornate box to Yevgeny, and the other men crowded around him as he worked with shaking fingers to open his treasure. The lid opened and a magnificent Damascus curved saber lying on black velvet was revealed.

"Can I touch it?"

"Of course. It is yours—for your sons and for their sons as long as men produce offspring for the Blessed One," intoned Labied solemnly. "Read the note."

Yevgeny opened the parchment envelope and read:

> *For conspicuous service rendered to the follower of the Prophet, Allah's blessings be upon him and a true servant of the One God, the Merciful, this great sword made with the love of brothers is presented to Yevgeny Ataulla Bayazitov.*

Bayazitov stared at the note and back to the sword. He was speechless.

Ramzi crowded closer and shot the Russian in the back of the head. Labied whisked the sword away so that it would not be defiled with blood. Jarrah took out his cigarette lighter and incinerated the note. The Moroccans dragged Bayazitov's body deep into the trees and brambles and left him there. They returned to the dock and gave orders to the Moroccans they had left armed and waiting.

"Go to their camp, and see to it that no one escapes being a martyr," Labied ordered.

The Moroccan freedom fighters drove away into the night in a Mockvich pickup and three Zil-150 trucks. They were well trained for night assassinations, and they were particularly efficient that night. It took more than five hours to kill the Muslim men with whom they had worked shoulder to shoulder for the past two weeks. They were remorseless men, and it was *Masha'allah* [God's will].

The freighter's crew had a half day of near panic as they left the Norwegian Sea and headed south through the North Atlantic past England. American warships tailed them from first light until nearly noon. It turned out that the ships were returning to London and were preparing to ship out for the United States, and the captain and his crew were feeling warm and friendly. They flag-signaled their greetings, and the freighter responded with a friendly, "Go save the world, we have work to do!"

When the Panamanian freighter docked in Lisbon for refueling—its last port before entering the Straits of Gibraltar and on into the Mediterranean—

Labied left the ship and took a cab to the Libyan embassy. There, he was expected and given carte blanche to make his communications. He made one call.

"This is the Norseman," he said as soon as he was connected.

"Intahal?" [Finished?].

"Mafeeish muskkhkilla." [No problem], he said; and that was the end of the conversation.

Three weeks later on October 13, a consignment clearly marked as pipeline equipment made its way from Tripoli to Aleppo by a series of ship transfers, overland truck convoys, and air transport on RSAF C-130Js—the latest and best military cargo airplane the United States could produce and sell at a bargain basement price to its Saudi friends. Syrian military maneuvers were conducted all around Aleppo requiring the cordoning off of the area near the large tract of land owned by Awad Musa Ishteyyeh. Not even the military battalions moving about the ancient city knew that a maturing nuclear research and manufacturing complex was blossoming in the fertile valley south and west of the city.

CHAPTER TWELVE

APRIL, 2008

The Braithwaite campaign started for real in July, 2007 with a meeting of the leadership of the Senate Liberal Caucus. Hollings Braithwaite stood up to chair the meeting.

"Let's come to order, please. Does anyone want the minutes from last month's meeting to be read?"

The answer was a murmured chorus of groans.

"I'll take that as a no. Can we have a motion to accept the minutes as written on the handout you all have before you?

"I respectively move that the minutes of June 6 be accepted without alteration," spoke up the senior Senator from Massachusetts.

Coming from him, it sounded like the beginning of a major televised policy announcement.

"Second."

"Any discussion?"

"No," came from everyone in the room.

"All in favor say, 'aye.'"

"Aye."

Every voice in the place concurred.

"All opposed say, 'no.'"

Silence.

"The ayes have it. Let's get to the first item on the agenda..."

Senator Clint Assure stood up and without waiting to be recognized by the chair, interrupted, "I want to introduce a motion that should be taken up immediately and, although it is not on the agenda, should take precedence."

"It is out of order, Senator," said Martin Bendrammen from West Virginia, the longest serving senator, and the Senate's parliamentarian.

"Let him make his motion."

"I want to hear what the Senator from the great state of Nevada has to say."

"I know what he wants to say, and so will every one else. Let's get to it."

Senator Assure and Senator Braithwaite both smiled.

"I guess you and I and the rules of order have been overruled, Senator Bendrammen. Okay with you?"

"I'll yield to this popular uprising. I must say that we have become altogether too loose in this body in the last few years."

"All right, Senator Assure, you have the floor."

"I move that our chairman, Senator Braithwaite absent himself during the next portion of this meeting. He should not be a party to or even hear the discussion."

The men and women of the caucus who mattered were already well aware of where Assure was headed with his motion.

"Second the motion," yelled Michael McGovern Pelosi from New Jersey.

"All in favor?"

"Aye."

"Senator Braithwaite, would you please make yourself scarce for the next half hour or so? We'll send someone out after you. We won't forget you."

Good natured laughter rippled through the room.

"Just a moment. I did not hear a call for those opposed," interjected Bendrammen.

"Oh, yes, let's hear from the nay sayers in deference to Sir Martin—the guardian of the Senate—" Cliff Assure said, grinning and giving the venerable old watchdog a deferential nod.

There were no 'nos.'

Senator Braithwaite and his aides left the room and went to the cafeteria. He treated them to carrot juice cocktails, and they all dutifully oohed and aahed.

"I'll get to the point immediately," said Senator Assure as soon as the door closed behind the chairman. "We have done miserably over the last eight years of bad government by Bush and his Nazis. The people were blinded in the last presidential and mid-term elections, but it is an entirely new ball game this go-around. Every poll I see suggests that this should be our year—not just the Democrat year—but the Liberal year. Not just in the presidential race, but in the Congress, in the gubernatorial contests, and in the state assemblies. We have practiced party hamstring self-destructive politics for too long. We cannot do it again this election cycle, or we may be finished as a party. Bear in mind that progressives and left leaning people and peace loving people's parties have come and gone in the past. We need to unite now behind a candidate who can win and who can articulate and get our liberal agendas through."

"For instance?" called out Carol Amman, Senator from Oregon.

"Have I been obtuse?" Assure responded. "Then, by all means, let me be direct. We need to convince Hollings Braithwaite to run for the nomination. Then we need to elect him as our candidate for the national election. And we need to elect him our next president. I know there are those among us who have aspirations, even some who tried last go around and feel that they have national name recognition. I'll be blunt. You lost, and we cannot afford to appear to be running another slate of people destined to lose. We need a man who is unequivocally a liberal and can stand up to the fascist offerings that the Republicans are bound to present. We need to sublimate our own ambitions for this cycle; and we all came to the Senate because we want to be resident, let's not be coy. We have to get behind Hollings Braithwaite early and hard and get our man elected for a change. What do you say?"

For a full three minutes no one spoke. It was quiet enough in the room to have heard the mental cog-wheels turning if they made sounds.

Senator Bendrammen stood up.

"I would like to have the floor, if I may, Mr. Acting Chairman," he said.

"We would value your input, sir."

"I have no aspirations to be president and, frankly, I can not understand how anyone would want to subject himself or herself to the attendant abuse. But, know that our chamber seethes with ambition and that fractionated ambition has led to our downfall in the past six or eight elections. I love the democratic process, but I would like to see us win even more than I would care to watch another rough and tumble and divisive Democratic primary campaign. I will support both the concept of getting behind a single candidate early-on and the choice of Hollings Braithwaite. I have watched him for years. He is the only one of us who has a strong likelihood of winning. Let's set aside our ambitions and differences and get Senator Braithwaite elected president and bring in a liberal Congress on his coat tails."

Sporadic but controlled applause began to echo around the room.

Donovan O'Laughlin from Massachusetts took a microphone and began to speak.

"I'll be frank. I want to run for president in 2008. I am going to seek support from this caucus and from the House. I am going to reach out across the aisle and get a campaign committee to run on a centrist platform. I do not...I will not be a part of this fast train that does not make any of the regular stops."

"Hear, hear," shouted his friend and vice-presidential hopeful, Gaylord Stratford from Pennsylvania.

The show of support was not lost on Senator O'Laughlin.

"Any other aspirants?" asked Senator Assure unable to keep the disappointment out of his voice.

"I can't speak for her, but one of our members who could not be with us today, will surely have something to say when she gets back from the front lines in the Sudan. We should give her due respect and wait until her intentions are known," offered the junior senator from Washington on behalf of his fellow Democrat from that great state.

"I did not intend to ignore the senior senator from Washington. I talked with her for better than three hours last night. She graciously agreed to bow to the will of the caucus and the party but insisted that a secret poll be done among party leaders—including a roll call by name—to ascertain the will of the party and especially our wing."

"That sounds fair," admitted Senator Williams a bit dubiously. "I would like to add the caveat that we keep her in the wings as a dark horse if we can't make the kind of progress we need to with Hollings."

"Let's hear the feelings of the group."

Quiet discussions were held around the room for several minutes, some of them quite heated. Finally, Sharon Hulme, from Colorado called for a vote.

"Let me put the vote this way and include everything I think I am hearing," said Cliff Assure. "First of all, we vote on whether or not we can go along with supporting one candidate. Secondly, if we can agree on Hollings Braithwaite. Thirdly, we vote on whether we can agree to hold a dark horse place for Senator Clivener as a fully prepared plan B."

The caucus members nodded in ascent in varying degrees of enthusiasm. Only Senator O'Laughlin conspicuously shook his head in the negative.

"Let's vote. But this time, make it a secret ballot. Mark your card yes or no for the one candidate idea, yes or no on whether it should be Braithwaite, even if you are opposed to the one candidate plan—rather like the election for governor of California back in 2003—and finally, yes or no on plan B. And let's make it a simple majority to carry. Any questions or further comment?"

He looked around the room. No one had a question or ventured a demurrer.

"The staffers are passing out the three by five card ballots—only one to the customer, please; this isn't Chicago."

Everyone laughed.

The results were uncomfortably close, only a ten vote margin carried the measure. Assure and his committee realized that they had an uphill battle on their hands. Senator Braithwaite was recalled and graciously expressed surprise and humbly accepted the choice of his caucus.

The quiet struggles within the party took place throughout the country. For once, the Democrats were able to keep a lid on their negotiations. It was not lost on anyone that there was a desperate need to win this election if the Democratic Party was to survive. Clarence Maddox—three term governor from Missouri and the most influential governmental voice speaking for the nation's unions—was given the back room nod for the vice-presidential spot along side Braithwaite. He was black—militantly so—liberal, knew the location of several party skeletons, and could carry the African-American vote with ease.

The Congressional delegations from New Jersey, New York, Pennsylvania, and Ohio were promised the right to get their people into the top posts on the cabinet, except for secretary of State. That post had to go to O'Laughlin from Massachusetts as a sop for bowing out early in the race, after the February primaries in Arizona, Delaware, Mississippi, New Mexico, North Dakota, Oklahoma, and South Carolina. He was also given the plums in the Appropriations Committee and Defense for his people. Representative Daniel Yamamoto from Hawaii agreed to carry on his efforts for the nomination until the primaries in Colorado and Pennsylvania in April and then throw his support to Braithwaite after the twenty-seventh. It cost the presumptive nominee's campaign four federal judgeships, half a dozen appointments to state appellate courts, and control of the Departments of Commerce and Transportation. Braithwaite and his campaign had to admit that Yamamoto drove the best bargain for himself and grudgingly admired his chutzpah. More than one of his senior campaigners wished that they could have him in the place of O'Laughlin at State.

Rosie Canardy—the chief advisor—even suggested that Clarence Maddox had some questionable areas in his business back-ground and that they should find some pretext to dump him along about the middle of next

May. Braithwaite was content to give the devil his due—the several devils—and take a win with any help he could get, and he knew that orchestrating Machiavellian intrigues was not his forte.

The press began to question how one candidate could so dominate the primaries so early, but could not come up with any real evidence of collusion to print a story. Besides, the *New York Times, LA Times, Boston Globe, Time, The Nation, and Newsweek Magazines* and the smaller establishment liberal voices all came out with ringing endorsements after Braithwaite's strong wins in Iowa and New Hampshire. Braithwaite was labeled the front-runner by every media outlet in the country—in the world—by the night of March 20 when he had taken Maine, Tennessee, Virginia, Washington D.C., Wisconsin, Hawaii, Idaho, California, Georgia, Maryland, Massachusetts, New York, Ohio, Rhode Island, Vermont, Illinois, Pennsylvania, and Colorado. His only losses—narrow ones at that—were in Alabama, Guam, Wyoming, Kansas, and Nevada. A recount was underway in Nevada, and the outlook for a reversal was looking better by the day.

Senator Helen Clivener called just before midnight on the twenty-seventh.

"Congratulations, Hollings," she began.

"Thanks, Helen, I couldn't have done it without you."

"Not true, but nice of you to think me useful. Tomorrow morning, I will drop out of my constantly hinted at dark-horse run and give you an enthusiastic endorsement."

"I can't tell you how crucial that will be, Helen. It will unite the party like nothing else. Now, we can be practical about this. How could I reward you? I know you are not asking for anything, but such loyalty should bear fruit."

"I want nothing more than to serve in the Senate; maybe my time will come after your second term."

She had to bite her lip to say it; however, her own polls had shown that the past distaste for her heavy-handed attempts to socialize medicine over the protests of her Democratic colleagues had alienated the moderates of the party; and she was considered anathema by the Republicans for her appearances in the Islamic capitals, Pyongyang, Paris, and Bonn and for her courageous attacks on U.S. policy throughout the Asian and Middle Eastern regions. Her use of the pejoratives Nazi and fascist, terrorist, and bully, had resonated with the left wing of her own party but had guaranteed eternal enmity from the Republicans and not a few of the moderate Democrats. There would be no serious hope of cross-overs to her in the 2008 election. Her admission was no more than bowing to the inevitable.

Helen Clivener was a dish water blond live wire, the estranged wife of a philandering multimillionaire publisher whose penance was to support Helen's political career. Helen was of medium height, weight, and build with big hips and small breasts that she hid in dressy pant suits or long skirts. She did not like the soft hanging flesh of her upper arms; so, she almost always wore long sleeves. She had a round, disingenuous face—which belied a steely personality—and light blue-pewter colored eyes. She had more energy than a cheer leader and more stamina than a marathoner. She worked her staff to the point of exhaustion then put in more hours than they did. She could drink the best man under the table. Helen Clivener knew all the ins and outs of Washington and exercised her senatorial office with efficiency and occasional brutality. Everyone recognized that the woman was a climber and would probably be president some day.

"I admire your dedication as I do your courage, you know that, Helen. I am confident that we can get you the majority leader spot, and you can name your own whip. There are a few judgeships left and the ambassadorships of France and England will be kept open for your people."

"That's more than generous, Mr. President. Thanks."

"Not quite yet, but the title does have a certain ring, doesn't it?"

"And a very real chance of becoming a reality, Hollings. I can't tell you what a giant step forward it will be to have a genuine unabashed liberal in the most powerful office in the world. Our people everywhere will have a renaissance; the Europeans are waiting with baited breath and will be ecstatic when you win. I can tell you from my talks with the Arab leaders that they will be ready to enter into a constructive dialogue with you. I assured them that you are nothing like that red-handed murderer—Bush, and his *Eminence Gris,* Cheney—and that you understand their pain, the reasons for their freedom fighting struggles, and their needs to see our bullying country put in its place. I will support you all the way. Maybe in the next eight years we can get fully out of the hegemony business."

"I will consider all of those issues as priorities—as holy quests—Helen. I expect your help all the way."

"You will have it, Hollings. We are going to create a new world, one with world peace based on justice and full international cooperation free of American dictatorship, one that recognizes and appreciates diversity."

"Indeed, we will, my friend."

"Good night, Hollings. May the Mother Earth bless you."

Hollings Braithwaite was elected the Democratic nominee on the first ballot taken on Wednesday of the August convention in Los Angeles. He waited until the next day to name his running mate in order to create a little suspense and excitement in the otherwise obvious and unexciting convention. Clarence Maddox and his wife, Anita, gave solid—if uninspiring, speeches at eight o'clock—and Hollings Braithwaite and Darlene MacIntosh—his long-time companion and the woman likely to be the only unmarried first lady in history—occupied the remainder of the prime time on the last evening of the convention.

He outlined his platform—identical to the party platform because his team had written it word for word. She told the party and the world that she would take as her two causes the eradication of HIV/AIDS, and she would work to set up free health clinics for anyone with an income less than thirty-eight thousand dollars a year. Her second most cherished aim was to see to it that same-sex marriages were legalized across the land; she compared that quest to the granting of freedom to the blacks and universal suffrage. Her first task in that project would be to defeat the one woman-one man concept of marriage. If anything, Ms. MacIntosh received a louder and longer ovation than her significant other. She was a willowy buxom blond—ten years younger than her man and glowed with fresh movie star brilliance. He was considered charismatic; she was idolized in the press as "the gorgeous and modern-day Eleanor Roosevelt".

Darlene MacIntosh was not an Eleanor Roosevelt. Where Mrs. Roosevelt was wise and kind, Darlene was cunning and self-serving and relied on her charismatic appearance to cover her multitude of nonegalitarian sins. Where Mrs. Roosevelt was genuinely interested in her fellow human beings, Darlene was brusque, had no time for the little people, and was self-absorbed. Eleanor Roosevelt was at home with down and out coal miners and people in bread lines. Darlene MacIntosh believed that Washington D.C. was beneath her, and she intended to spend as little time as possible in the archaic and uncomfortable White House. She had four houses of her own—two from each of her late, great, and rich husbands. Mrs. Roosevelt was the exemplar of family unity and marital loyalty; Ms. MacIntosh had had enough of marriage since she had ended up a billionaire from hers and had no intention of getting legally involved again, not even with the President of the United States. She preferred the lofty society of New York City and had met men there who pulled the strings on the presidential puppet. Mrs. Roosevelt stood by her man; Darlene used her men, many men. She openly espoused free love, gay marriage, polyandry, and group marriage.

But she was tall, willowy, buxom, blond, witty, beautiful, and chummed with the glitterati. That trumped all of Eleanor Roosevelt's virtues in American society in 2008.

On the first Tuesday in November, 2008, Hollings Braithwaite was elected president by a fifty-two percent margin in the popular vote and by a sixty-eight percent margin in the Electoral College. He set in motion the change-over in administrations with the full and gracious assistance of the outgoing Bush administration. Braithwaite kept all of his patronage promises despite the fact that some of them set his teeth on edge. One appointment he proffered was applauded by outgoing Republicans and incoming Democrats alike. He nominated Elizabeth Leavitt Rowan to be attorney general. On a drizzly overhung January twentieth, Braithwaite was inaugurated as the forty-eighth president of the United States and by late afternoon, he set into motion a sea change in United States foreign and domestic policy.

CHAPTER THIRTEEN

MAY, 2009

Dr. Abrar A'mal Bint Farouk obtained her doctorate in nuclear physics from the University of California at Berkeley and did a post-doctoral fellowship at the research facility in Alamagordo, New Mexico for an additional three years. Upon completion of her fellowship, she applied for a place on the staff at the Nuclear Materials and Equipment Corporation (Numec) in Apollo, Pennsylvania, the foremost U.S. fuel fabrication plant. The position she sought required a top-secret clearance rating; and because she was Egyptian—born and educated in Cairo—the vetting process by the FBI, CIA, NSA, and U.S. and IAEA Regulatory Agencies took nearly two years. She passed with the highest recommendations from all of the agencies. It did not hurt her standing that she was the niece of Mohammed Yahya Farouk, President of Egypt. After nine years in the United States, she applied for and was granted full U.S. citizenship. During the tenth year of her residence in America, she was accepted for the position at Apollo.

Dr. Farouk was brilliant and proved to be a considerable asset to the United States Nuclear Weapons program during the four years of her employment. She was widely considered to be next in line for the position of head of the United States Atomic Energy Commission. Dr. Farouk had as much power over the development of nuclear weapons and control over the dispersement of nuclear materials, research, and equipment as any one in the world. She was to all intents and purposes a progressive or even nominal Muslim, an exemplary soccer mom—the mother of four rambunctious children, and the president of the PTA for her eldest son's middle school. She was quiet, obviously dedicated to her work, apolitical, and perfectly assimilated into the culture of yuppie America.

And Abrar [Devoted to God] Farouk was a long standing member of the Arabian Peninsula Women's Information Bureau—an Al Qaeda front—and a lieutenant in the Pennsylvania cell of Al Qaeda. She had been recruited by Usama himself and had trained in al-Farooq Training Camp outside Kandahar, Afghanistan during the last two summers of her high school and during a vacation visit back home after her freshman year at Berkeley.

Usama bin Laden had visited the Egyptian Presidential Palace on Abrar's last day in Egypt. She had begged the exalted Islamic leader in the presence of her father and mother and President Farouk to be allowed to become a holy martyr of Islam. Usama—in his soft avuncular voice and manner—told her gently but firmly that women were not yet permitted to be intentional martyrs, but that one day her unique opportunities in America would be used against the Great Satan and that she must be patient. Prince Ahmed Wahhab ibn Saud was also visiting. He promised Abrar that he would personally see to it that one day she would be given a chance to prove herself. He enjoined her to silence and outlined her cover for her upcoming years in the United States. Periodically in the intervening years he had sent emissaries to meet with her and to reinforce the potential value she represented for the world of Islam. As she matured, Abrar came to realize that, indeed, she could make a substantial contribution; and she chaffed as she waited for that day.

The day came on August 17, 2010. Abrar turned over her children to her husband, Omar, and left the house for her long daily jog in the dark. She felt safer and surer of protecting her modesty running when and where she would not be seen, and she varied her route every day. Abrar was well aware that her dark exotic beauty made her attractive, and she resented that some men admired her youthful good looks more than they did her brains. Men were generally fools, she had concluded many years earlier. Dr. Farouk had gone three miles at an average speed of eight minutes per mile and was feeling unusually tired. Suddenly from a darkened rural road at right angles to her chosen route, a black mini-van pulled out in front of her and caused her to lurch to a stop to avoid a collision. Her first thought was that she was about to be robbed. Her second was that she was about to be raped, an unpardonable sin for a good Muslim woman. She cursed herself for not having covered better. And her third and more rational thought was that she was about to be kidnapped and her nuclear secrets extorted from her.

She whirled to the left and ran at her top speed towards the safety of the forest lining the roadway. Her top speed was not enough. A totally black clad commando ran her down in less than half a minute and swept her up in his powerful arms. She started to scream, but her cry was cut off by a leather gloved hand.

"Abrar," the commando said in a commanding voice. "Dr. Farouk."

"What do you want?" she gasped, completely out of breath.

He was barely puffing.

"We come from the Council Leader. Do you know who I mean?"

"Maybe."

"I am going to let you down. You must promise not to run or to fight me. I can't risk you being hurt. Will you listen?"

"Okay."

"The prince, himself, sent us. It is time for you to do the work of Allah."

"What is wanted?"

"Come back to the van. We can talk like civilized people, my *akht* [sister]."

"How do I know that you are who you say you are?"

"Because of this," he said and handed her a small beige envelope.

He flashed his Mag-Lite beam on it while she tore it open.

It said: I am *Bashshar* [Bringer of Good Greetings]. You know who I am. Obey the man who presents this to you. Accept the discipline of our holy leader and serve even unto death.

Dr. Farouk had never actually met Bashshar to her knowledge, and she knew that the word had nothing to do with his real name. However, his name or title was the most secret piece of information she possessed, and seeing it on the paper given her by this stranger was all she required.

"Destroy the message," she said.

He burned it with his cigarette lighter, and the two of them made their way back to the van. The three other people in the van and her message bringer never removed their face coverings. The man sitting in the front passenger seat turned his head towards Abrar.

"*Akht*, the Council requires that you supply four hundred pounds of highly enriched uranium to us by the end of the week. I am sure that you know that it is critical that no one ever knows who obtained this material. It is probably best that no one ever realizes that it is missing. But, it may become known despite all of your efforts and ours. In that case, you must obscure the paperwork to exclude any suggestion of our involvement or of yours. Can you do this thing?"

"Certainly. I have to know how the material is to be transported; so, we can be certain of timing and secrecy."

The conspirators hurriedly agreed on arrangements so that Dr. Farouk could get back to her house before her family's suspicions were aroused.

Six days later, a large black delivery van bearing the official seal of the Embassy of Israel on the driver's side door entered the northern most warehouse of the Apollo complex. An eight hundred pound wooden crate was placed carefully into the van's rear compartment from which the chairs had been removed. The fork-lift driver was the only representative of the nuclear corporation present. The authentic documentation for the transfer of the highly purified nuclear material was signed by the deputy ambassador of Israel, then he and his body-guard drove away. The entire transaction took less than ten minutes.

Thirty minutes later, the black van drove into a metal salvage yard. The box was transferred to a forest green Suburban, and the van was driven to the metal crushing presses and reduced to the size of a foot locker. The Suburban was driven to Boston where the heavy box was placed on a cargo ship bound for Bahrain. Six weeks later, the contents of the eight hundred pound box— four hundred pounds of enriched uranium—arrived in Aleppo, Syria in the middle of the night.

The sparse documentation was in compliance with the policies and laws of the U.S. Atomic Energy Commission and the IAEA although the signatures authorizing the transfer of the sensitive materials were blurred beyond recognition by a coffee stain. The orders fully annotated the material's origins and future. The two sheets of paper were properly filed with the other millions of papers in Apollo's files. Only years later, when the IAEA demanded that an investigation be done to find out how it came to be that four hundred pounds of uranium could be lost, did the papers again see the light of day.

The investigators from the National Nuclear Security Administration and the Department of Energy's office of Safety Performance Assessment determined that the nation of Israel was the on-paper recipient of the radioactive material, but the small commission of inspectors could not find out who had authorized the removal of the material from Apollo despite subpoenas, interrogations, and threats. There was never any proof that the material had reached Israel, and the government of the United States required complete secrecy about the potential nuclear scandal. As was the case in the matter of missing classified electronic discs from Los Alamos Laboratory investigated by the NNSA at about the same time, the public never learned of the incident.

CHAPTER FOURTEEN

EARLY JUNE, 2009

Oval Office, 1400

"Good to see you, Hank," said the president who had arisen from his swivel chair to greet the president of the American Trial Lawyers Association. "Once again, I want to thank all of your members for the stalwart help during the election. We wouldn't be where we are today without your help."

He extended his hand and took a firm grip on the soft manicured hand of Henry Dayton Lithgow who had brought in nearly $200M for Braithwaite and the democrats during the long and arduous campaign, which had started even before the previous chief executive had taken office. The response from Lythgoe was not as enthusiastic as the president had expected.

"Mr. President, thank you for seeing me on relatively short notice."

He was chaffing from having had to wait two days to see the nation's chief executive. Braithwaite was probably the only person in the world that he would tolerate being made to cool his heels.

"Have a seat, my friend. What can I do for you?"

"Can your attorney general."

The president paused a moment to be sure whether or not the richly dressed gentleman was joking. It was clear from the man's facial expression that he was not.

"Please explain, Hank. General Rowan is very highly regarded around here—on both sides of the aisle, I might add."

"That may well be, but she is the worst enemy that your largest single contributing group has ever faced. She has to go."

"I still haven't heard an explanation," said the president who was allergic to visitors to the Oval Office who issued ultimatums

"You familiar with the pending case of U.S v. Bagell, Tomlinson, and Negev Tort Consortium?"

"Vaguely. Something about perjury and criminal involvement in a scheme to influence the public in order to mount a huge tort case against essentially all of the pharmaceutical companies who manufacture vaccines."

"That's pretty much the gist of it. In all candor, Mr. President, Bagell, et. al. might just be guilty—maybe it should be civil, but it is not frivolous to see it as criminal. That notwithstanding, it could just go away if it weren't for an overzealous attorney general. I'm sure you recognize that huge sums of money are involved and that this is shaping up to be a major attack on tort lawyers in general, not just Bagell. I don't need to tell you, I'm sure, that the ugly head of tort reform will get a great big boost if that Nazi over at the DOJ doesn't get her wings clipped."

"I really can't see what I can do about it, Hank. Other than firing the woman without cause—which would be a political disaster—I cannot interfere with her independence. Neither party nor the American public would stand for that. You know I'm right."

"You can talk to her, get her to listen to reason. So, maybe Bagell needs a bit of a slap on the wrist—or at the outside—a little fine; but Rowan is talking jail time, prohibition of tort practice by Bagell and maybe some others, and a fine that would fund the highway system. The tort legal industry would be decimated, and it would take us years to recover. We would cease to be a force for the Democrats."

There, he had said it. He looked at the president without blinking.

"I'll see what I can do to soften things, but I'll have to walk on egg shells. For a sitting president to seek to influence an ongoing criminal case because a major contributor's interests were at stake could bring down the administration."

"Don't forget the power of both the force of persuasion and the political war chest that the ATLA controls."

"That wouldn't be a threat, now would it, Hank? Presidents have never liked to be threatened. I'll look into the case, and I will talk to General Rowan. Beyond that, I cannot go."

With a hard look, Henry Lythgoe rose from his chair as the president returned his attention to the stack of folders on his desk. Lythgoe did not like being dismissed. He was the one who did the dismissing. He had considered Braithwaite to be his boy; but for the first time, the ATLA president was not so sure of the man's reliability.

Two hours later, Attorney General Rowan joined President Braithwaite in the White House for brunch. Nothing was said of business until the light vegetarian meal was cleared.

"Elizabeth, I have a problem that is ticklish and political. It involves you, and I would like to discuss it with you as much as you think is proper."

"Yes, sir, Mr. President," General Rowan said expectantly.

"I'll get right to it. I had a not entirely friendly visit from Henry Lythgoe of the ATLA this morning. He brought up the case of U.S v. Bagell."

"And he wanted you to get it quashed. That about it, Mr. President?"

"More like lost in the mountain of paperwork somewhere in the bowels of the Justice Department subbasement, I think."

"The case is rock solid, sir. It is not an arcane bit of business. People are dead. Children are dead, and we have the whole consortium and their employees dead-to-rights. We are considering attaching RICO sanctions, assessing a half billion in fines, and insist on jail time for the big-shots, at least."

"That seems to put those lawyers on a par with Charlie Manson or Jeffery Dahmer, doesn't it? Seems pretty harsh."

"The tort lawyers have been getting away with murder for decades, Mr. President. They regularly suborn witnesses to perjury, bribe them, and black-mail them. It is time for those practices to be brought under control. In this case, the lawyers themselves set in motion such a heinous plan that—in the end—kids were allowed to catch terrible diseases and to die. We cannot let it pass."

Her intensity was daunting. His choices reduced down to firing her and accepting the fallout from the Congress, Justice Department, and the American public or trying to influence her.

"Elizabeth, you might consider giving the American Tort Lawyer Group a talk on the subject to see if there can be a compromise or a face-saving solu-tion. Will you do that?"

"I'll give it a try, sir, but there is very little wiggle room. It may well come down to how well I can persuade them, and they are highly resistant to persuasion. They are—after all—the great persuaders; and in this case, the client is themselves."

"Please try."

On June 20, Elizabeth Rowan stood nervously before the assembled and wholly hostile roomful of attorneys whose livelihoods she threatened. She made a strong effort not to appear to be nervous or unsure of herself or of her case. She collected herself in a pause that brought silence to the room.

"Ladies and gentlemen, I will not waste your time with dodging the subject that we all know is uppermost in all of our minds today. This is the government's class-action suit against the tort law conglomerate, Bagell, Tomlinson, and Negev and all of their subordinate contributing law firms. I will give the details as the government sees them very briefly. For years, people have been deathly afraid that autism is caused by the chemicals in various vaccines and is probably an immune reaction. As a result millions of children around the world were not immunized over the last two years, and the CDC has seen a marked upsurge in cases of whooping cough, measles, tetanus, and typhoid and several hundred more children have died of these diseases in those two years than at any time in the past twenty.

"The reason parents came to doubt the vaccines is because of a very influential scientific study published in a prominent British medical journal two years ago by a group of scientists whose credentials and reputations were considered to be above reproach, and—more's to the point for today—due to the unprecedented marketing blitz by the legal consortium. Questions were raised by other medical researchers about the reliability of the study done in England. The journal decided to go back and review every one of the 224 cases of apparent adverse reaction and death deemed to have been the fault of the vaccines. The results of that study were stunning.

The journal—one of the most reputable in the world—discovered that every one of the 224 cases was faked in a subtle and clever scheme, but blatantly falsified results were reported that incriminated the vaccines. The medical histories were misrepresented or altered; cases were invented whole cloth; and statistics were fabricated. M.D. and PhD researchers, lab companies, pediatricians, family physicians, and nurses were corrupted and suborned to perjury. The journal retracted its article with a stinging editorial which excoriated the entire class action tort industry. More than two thousand defendants have been identified. Frankly, most of those lesser-involved individuals will get off because we don't have the funds to prosecute the case on such an enormous scale. However, the adverse press will be catastrophic for your industry if we even start down that road.

"Our real interest and the major focus of our efforts is in seeing that Bagell, Tomlinson, and Negev Tort Consortium goes down for their blatantly and unconscionable criminal acts. We have incontrovertible evidence from Scotland Yard, Interpol, and the FBI that the lawyers involved not only corrupted a major government funded study, but they paid a huge bribe to the lead researcher to the tune of just over £550,000. There is not an ounce of doubt now that the FBI's findings are complete, that the man and his associates did it. They did it to corrupt results so as to give a strong basis for the class action lawyers to pursue a case against the pharmaceutical companies for the spurious claim that vaccines cause autism—a terrifying prospect to parents all over the world. The study was a fraud; the results were proved to be bogus; the financial transactions amounted to bribery and a criminal conspiracy that resulted in mass perjury, injury and death to children, and a terrible loss of confidence by people around the world in the efficacy and safety of life preserving treatments."

She paused to take a swallow of water.

"Scientists are just people, no better and no worse than the general people. They make mistakes. They might be faulted for producing a poorly conceived and badly executed study, but that is not what happened here. This was a criminal conspiracy, and the perpetrators are going down. The public of two dozen nations will settle for nothing less. The only question before you today is: how wide will this net spread? How many attorneys and their firms will waste a fortune in their own defense, in fines, and in loss of reputation?

"I will leave it to you as an association to ponder my question. I will make an offer to you one time and only today. If you will not use your tremendous power to influence government and the public to have this case emasculated or improperly quashed, the DOJ will limit the prosecutions to those already fully investigated. There is a growing movement in the DOJ to make this into a RICO case against your organization. At this point we do not have enough evidence to go all the way there; but given time and resources, we could make it a priority.

If we should see cooperation by the officers of the court—as all of you are—to get to a speedy and fair trial of the established defendants, then our cost versus risk in the prosecution would likely seem defensible without further litigation. We will be on the watch for undue influence by any attorney group on any governmental employee or department. We will not take such influence lightly. This problem can pass if the defendants are brought to trial. I leave it up to you as to how many defendants there are in the final analysis."

General Rowan did not take questions. She smiled at her grim-faced audience in an affable manner and exited the podium.

Whether or not the attorney general was bluffing, the American Trial Lawyers Association and the American Class Action Tort Lawyers Group came down hard on Bagell, et. al. and helped to move them swiftly along into federal court and assisted in the conviction of nearly 200 defendants, acting as amicus curiae. There was no government assisted program of leaks directed against the ATLA and no prejudicial media interviews that impugned lawyers in general. In fact, attorney general Rowan and the president both gave news conferences commending America's attorneys for cleaning their own house. The president did not hear from Henry Lythgoe again on the subject, and he did not forget the part Elizabeth Rowan played in extracting his administration from the political quicksand.

CHAPTER FIFTEEN

JULY, 2009

The courtroom in the E. Barrett Prettyman Federal Courthouse at 333 Constitution Avenue N.W. in Judiciary Square, Washington D.C. was filled to overflowing with vitally interested onlookers for what should have been a ho-hum case. On the contrary, U.S. v Hallweather Corporation had been front page news in the nation's newspapers and the lead story on the networks for a year. Two conference rooms in the building had been set up with two hundred chairs each leaving inadequate leg room. The ardent media personnel lucky to have drawn out for a seat did not complain about such minor considerations as pain. Live closed circuit television monitors with up-to-the-minute text captioning were strategically located. The men and women of the national and local media were in their places in the adjunct courtrooms forty-five minutes early. The main courtroom's limited seating was reserved for the defense contractor's corporate executives and their army of attorneys, the federal prosecutors and their investigators and staffers, and selected ranking governmental officials on a strict rotational basis. Outside the courthouse building, inside its halls, and inside the courtroom itself, security was omnipresent and daunting.

Elizabeth Leavitt Rowan, Attorney General of the United States, stood before the federal jury and Judge Joseph Patrick Aloysius McGee to make her opening statements. Her appearance of icy calm was matched by her inner sense of quiet. She knew what was at stake; she knew that this was a make/break case for her career; and all of that tended to calm her and to intensify her focus and to quicken her mind. It was a most useful trait for a person in the cat bird seat, and Mrs. Rowan had matured in her office to the point that she actually liked being in that advantageous position. The tinder sensitive nature of the case the United States was prosecuting was why the president and the secretary of Commerce had demanded that she take personal lead in the courtroom.

Rowan addressed the thirteen women and one man who constituted the jury and alternates:

"Ladies and gentlemen of the jury. I am Elizabeth Rowan. I am the attorney for the people of the United States in the case of the United States versus Hallweather Corporation and the five executives listed in the indictment. Those people have names, and they committed crimes against the taxpayers of our country. In the course of this trial, my deputies and I will prove that assertion bit by bit until we will paint you a detailed picture that proves beyond a reasonable doubt that Anton Forsum, CEO, Quentin Rice Anderson, CFO, Mary Elizabeth Murphy, President, and Hyrum Prentiss Maddox, Vice-President, knowingly and feloniously conspired to defraud the United States."

At the mention of the brother of the sitting vice-president of the United States, and the secretary of Commerce—Ms. Murphy—from the previous administration, a soft murmur skittered through the courtroom spectators. This earned a soft rap of Judge Joseph P.A. McGee's gavel, and silence resumed.

"The government of the People will prove that a cumulative sixty-eight million dollars were misappropriated by fraudulent means including fictitious cost overruns, income tax evasion, undue influence from and with government officials, and outright fabrication of defense projects.

"In fact, ladies and gentlemen of the jury, this is a rather simple case. We will—of necessity—have to present a great deal of factual material involving accounting mathematics, but the case can be reduced to a simple paper trail showing theft, deception, and betrayal of the American people. We will present forensic accountancy experts who will show you diagrams that will help you to understand the otherwise complex bookkeeping used here—in terms you can fully appreciate—cooked books, double accounts with one set of books as phony as a three dollar bill. This evidence will identify the character and magnitude of the crime. We will present testimony from witnesses who will identify governmental officials from the current and past administrations who accepted bribes and wielded undue legislative influence, finger print and voice print experts, telephone logs and wire tap and video evidence and finally, a confession, that will show you in perfectly obvious terms who committed what crimes. We will show how deeply our government—on a truly bipartisan basis—was corrupted. I might add that we have incontrovertible evidence that our service men and women have been injured, and some of them have died as a result of these nefarious crimes."

At the statement that the government prosecutors had a confession, Oscar Sugarman, chief defense counsel, blanched. He was about to rise to object because he had been ambushed. The wall of silence he had required of his clients had obviously been breached, and the fact of the betrayal came as a hammer blow surprise to him. He thought better of his impulse, and instead, wrote on his yellow legal pad, "Who?" in letters just big enough for his assistant to read. Jeremy Witherspoon shrugged his shoulders.

"Our first witness for your consideration will be Katherine Tatsuo Yokomatsu, a current employee of Hallweather. She is—as the media likes to dub such people—a 'whistle-blower.' Ms. Yokomatsu is a naturalized American citizen who loves her adoptive country passionately, and what she saw and heard and was required to do in the course of her duties at Hallweather sickened her. She collected a mountain of documentation of criminal activity over a three year period and agreed to work with the Federal Bureau of Investigation for the past six months. I am sure you will find Ms Yokomatsu and her documents compelling.

"Our second witness is one of the defendants—Quentin Rice Anderson— the Chief Financial Officer of Hallweather Corporation—a man intimately involved in the day-to-day business of the company and privy to every dirty little secret. Mr. Anderson and his attorney—Mr. Dimato—contacted my staff at five o'clock this morning and agreed to testify for partial immunity. That immunity was granted, and Mr. Anderson has agreed to testify in full detail about his own and his co-executives' complicity in the felonies that we will outline. He has agreed that he will tell the whole truth and will not spare himself. In return he will be allowed to plead guilty to the crimes listed in the indictment and will receive a five year prison sentence with four years of that sentence to be served under court supervised community arrest, and will do five thousand hours of community service as directed and monitored by the court."

The attorney general took twenty more minutes to list all of her witnesses and the gist of the testimony that would be given by each. Sugerman did not listen to the remainder of her opening because he was thoroughly familiar with all of her evidence and had prepared for it. Besides, the world had stopped for him at the announcement that that snake—Q. Anderson—had rolled over.

"…and, ladies and gentleman, that concludes the summary of the evidence and the case that will be presented by the People of the United States against this corporation and these defendants. Thank you for your attention."

She strode confidently to her seat. The courtroom was absolutely silent. It was as if there would be a judicial hanging in that very room that very day.

Judge McGee looked at the defense table and said, "Your opening statement, Mr. Sugarman."

Oscar Sugarman rose to his full six and a half feet trying not to look stunned or dizzy despite being both. He stood for a moment to make sure he would have full control of his voice, thought of Judge McGee's reputation as a hanging judge, and of the damning evidence Rowan had just described.

He said, "Your honor, the defense requests a side bar."

"Before your opening?"

"Yes, your honor."

"Approach."

Attorney General Rowan and defense counselor, Sugarman, walked briskly to the right side of Judge McGee's tall desk. He looked over his pince-nez glasses at the combatant attorneys.

"It's your nickel, Mr. Sugarman, shoot."

"Judge, my clients have just been ambushed. You cannot admit Anderson's testimony. We had absolutely no inkling that this was happening."

"What about that Madam Attorney General?"

"I learned about it less than five hours ago. I had my office try every means to contact Mr. Sugarman or anyone on the defense team. Mr. Sugarman had sequestered his team and would not allow any calls in or out of their hotel quarters from yesterday night at ten until this morning in the courtroom. I could not let him know."

Sugerman groaned, hoist by his own petard. He knew that and had no defense. About all he could do is to whine, and he would not be reduced to that.

Judge McGee said softly, "Oscar, how about you and the lady attorney general have a sit down? Would you be amenable to such a proposal, Ms. Rowan?"

"I would be willing, your Honor," the attorney general said without enthusiasm.

"And you, Oscar? Sounds like a reasonable approach at this point since I am going to deny your objection to Mr. Anderson's testimony."

"Well sprung ambush, Madam Attorney General. I don't suppose I have anything to lose by talking."

"We're agreed, then?"

The two attorneys nodded their acquiescence.

"Step back, then."

"Ladies and gentlemen of the jury, we will adjourn for the day. It's been a long session."

Judge McGee smiled at his humor—the court had been in session less than an hour. The courtroom assemblage laughed quietly.

"You are not to speculate on developments; and you are bound by your oath not to discuss this case with anyone at this point, not even your fellow jurors. I am going to sequester the jury overnight. I regret that, but we cannot have this case leaked to the press; we have had more than enough involvement with the media thus far. Bailiff, make necessary arrangements. You are excused until ten o'clock tomorrow."

DCIA Patterson Wrenn approached the Oval Office for his daily briefing with President Braithwaite with foreboding. The new president had little enough use for the summaries Wrenn was required to give and no interest in or patience for the raw data that backed up the agency's conclusions. Wrenn's credentials were impeccable, and his long involvement with the NSA's liaison group working with the CIA had made him seem the ideal professional to head the giant spy agency when he was first nominated. His poker-faced refusal to be drawn into taking sides in the overtly political wrangle that surrounded his final selection might have served another president well, but this one found his style concrete and boring and his conclusions too critical of the left in Europe and the misunderstood fundamentalists in the Middle-East.

President Braithwaite obtained most of his information and accepted almost of the counsel that mattered on areas of the world that concerned his administration from Daniel Y. Ajami—his National Security Advisor—who came into government directly from his position as Adlai E. Stevenson Professor of International Politics at Columbia University. It was galling to Wrenn to be given short-shrift personally by the president in favor of the absolutist antiwar, anti-military, anti-U.S. nationalism, anti-U.S. leverage one-worlder from the cloisters of the Ivy League; but more importantly, Wrenn was finding it to be more and more difficult to convey to the chief executive any of the factual information and conclusions he and his agency found to be alarming. Today's briefing was likely to prove to be the most disturbing yet, particularly since Patterson Wrenn had decided to put his career on the line and insist on a full hearing on the part of the president regarding the latest developments in the

Middle-East. He had strongly requested that Ajami be present; so, the air could be cleared once and for all.

Ms. Apflebaum, the president's secretary, showed the DCIA into the Oval Office. President Braithwaite and Ajami were seated close to one another on a couch and were in deep conversation. The president gestured to Wrenn to sit.

"Daniel", the president was saying, "I am adamant on that. The Joint Chiefs will have to come to grips with the fact—the *fact*—that there will be no discrimination in the military anywhere. The "no-ask-no-tell policy" is done. I do not want to have to give a repeat speech. My comments at the Air Force Academy were clear—thank you—and final. Tell those Neanderthals again. And tell them—for good measure—that the subject of equal roles for women—including combat, is law—and that comes from the Commander-in-Chief."

"Your speech to the academy was seminal. It was as crucial as the integration of African-Americans into the military. I think that you are going to have to accept a few resignations as an example to make it clear. They are hide bound to tradition, and only a strong show on your part will effect a change, if I may be so direct."

Ajami smiled warmly at the president. He was a small, nattily dressed fourth generation Egyptian/American with a pencil mustache. His red, white, and blue bow tie went well with his blue button-down collar shirt but was out of place with his rumpled tweed jacket—the Ivy League look. His black hair was slicked back in a pompadour. He barely glanced at Wrenn, whom he considered an intruder. Wrenn hated the little sycophant.

"Of course, Daniel, the president continued, "This administration won't abide 'yes' men. I respect your views. I want you to come up with some names, and we'll make it happen."

Ajami smiled briefly, then he and the president acknowledged the DCIA for the first time. It had become the rule rather than the exception for rudeness to be directed towards him and his agency in this room of late, Wrenn thought sourly to himself.

"The briefing, Mr. Director," ordered the president without bothering with pleasantries.

"Yes, sir. First, let me spread some Def 10 satellite photos of Aleppo, Syria for your review."

Wrenn was a tall, craggy Westerner who insisted on wearing black lizard skin boots and a cowboy style sport coat and string tie that was a source of humor in the president's inner circle. His tanned, lined face was serious today. He seldom smiled because he had crooked teeth in a world where straight ivory-white teeth were the rule. Today, he felt nothing to smile about. He quickly rose and placed twelve photos on the coffee table in front of the president.

"I am in a bit of a time-crunch today, Patterson. Could you summarize the findings and leave the photos with Daniel, here? He can give me the straight skinny."

"With respect, sir, I'd rather you looked at the raw data while we discuss the matter. Our people at the agency think this is a matter of some real concern."

"Of some delicacy," the national security advisor interjected.

"Well said, Daniel," added the president.

Wrenn went doggedly forward, knowing he was on thin ice.

"The top row of photos was taken by Def 10 two years ago. Actually, the first picture is seven years old. It shows an area of bare farm land. The others show the rapid build-up of an industrial complex. They have been confirmed by the National Geospatial Intelligence Agency, and thoroughly evaluated by the ODCI, my chief of staff, and the DCI's National Intelligence Council."

The president looked at his national security advisor.

"A peace time nuclear power reactor and electrical lines leading out to serve the nation."

The president nodded his agreement.

Wrenn continued as if he had not been interrupted, and the findings of his Office of the Director of Intelligence and the Council had not been ignored, "The bottom six photos were taken yesterday. If you notice, here, you are looking at a fully mature nuclear energy plant almost exactly like the Isis type reactor complex called Tammuz II sold by the French to the Iraqis in the 90s but ten times as large. This building here contains a huge reactor and adjunct equipment capable of separating U-238 into ninety-three percent pure U-235 and then bombarding it to make plutonium. The out-pouchings here are reprocessing cells to hold the carefully shielded very hot plutonium. The conclusion is that the Syrians either have a thermonuclear explosive device or are on the very verge of having one."

Ajami rolled his eyes and sighed.

"Mr. President, we have been over all of this before. The Syrians have every right to make their own cheap power. The U.S. has no right—none at all—to contravene the rulings of the IAEA which has had inspectors verify the peaceful purposes of this very plant."

"Again, with respect, sir. Unlike the experience of the IAEA inspectors, our agents have been able to look inside—at considerable personal risk, I might add—and they have submitted drawings that have been confirmed by our best research scientists to be weapons manufacturing layouts and machinery and not peaceful energy producers. I, personally, believe that this evidence is incontrovertible, and we cannot afford to have that dictatorship control weapons of mass destruction that could cause a conflagration in the region given their manifest hatred for the State of Israel."

Ajami started to speak, but the president laid his hand on his advisor's arm.

The president asked Wrenn, "Were the agents who made the drawings nuclear scientists at any level?"

"No, sir," admitted Wrenn.

"Have you any idea of the delicate nature of negotiations between us, the Palestinians, the Israelis, and the Syrians, sir?"

"I do. I think most of what the Syrians are saying is a sham. In fact, I know it is because they say one thing in Arabic and publish abroad in English an entirely different, more peace-seeking lip service pablum."

Braithwaite looked at Ajami.

"Mr. Director, I will take your evidence under advisement, but I think it best that important political decisions be left to the politicians and the diplomats, don't you?"

Wrenn controlled his mounting anger with growing difficulty. He had sworn to his deputy that he would not get angry and ruin his last chance to convince the administration of what they both felt was a growing and very real danger to the security of the United States.

"What else do you have for us?" the president requested with exaggerated courtesy and calm.

Wrenn took out a second dossier from his battered brief case. He moved the first set of photos aside and spread a second set of twelve satellite photographs.

"These images are of a point latitude 17 degrees and longitude 53 degrees."

"The first photo has essentially nothing in it. What's the relevance?" asked Ajami.

"Good observation, Security Advisor. This image was obtained last year—in fact—one year to the day. It is of the Ar-Rab' al-Khali."

"Empty Quarter, Saudi Arabia," Ajami told the president helpfully.

"I know about the Empty Quarter, Daniel. Give me some credit," Braithwaite said, not quite as sacchrine as before.

"Yes, Mr. President, the DCIA went on, "empty in the photos of a year ago, nothing but arrangements of sand in drifts, elongate sand seas called *nefuds*, and low hills called *hamadas*, maybe 50 meters high. The next eleven photos show sequentially the building of a road that becomes a major asphalted highway leading into the Quarter from Qasr Hamam—the nearest previous road. Then we see a massive excavation, something like building in the ocean using caissons. Our experts estimate that the structure you see being completed in the last two frames is twenty stories deep and is made of steel and reinforced concrete."

"And what is that line coming in from the north?" the president asked and traced it with his pen.

"A water pipe-line—an off-shoot from the great pipe-line from the Tigris-Euphrates confluence," Wrenn answered.

"Called The Waters of Babylon Project," Ajami added. "The Saudis were able to work out a contract with Iraq to permit the transfer of water from those two great rivers and their aquifers into the Kingdom. It was their great coup in the most recent Fourth World Water Forum. Their water minister described the need to solve the issues surrounding water in the region as a religious, national, and developmental duty to deal once and for all with the most precious resource in their desert."

"Thank you, Daniel. So it is nothing nefarious we are seeing."

"Not that I can see, Mr. President."

Ajami smiled at the president.

"Mr. Wrenn?"

"I have a different take. Let's start with the pipeline. It is the only branch going into the Empty Quarter. What is it that is so important that it has a dedicated water source coming into the driest place in the world?"

"A major water project to begin irrigation in a nation that desperately needs to expand its agricultural production," said Braithwaite almost mockingly.

"Hardly, Sir. This is a hardened silo; actually, there appears to be a series of them being built. These are going to house ICBMs," Wrenn insisted vigorously.

"What!!?" exclaimed Ajami. "What on earth would the Kingdom want with astronomically expensive military hardware. They can hit any country in the Middle-East with the medium range nuclear war-head armed CSS-2 missiles they purchased from China, the PAC-2 versions of our Patriot Missile Defenses, or even with the updated As Samoud 2s they bought from the left over stockpiles from the Iraqis after the new Iraq coalition government gave their approval. They have no need for long range weapons; and so far as we know, they don't have any."

"*This* is evidence to the contrary, sir," Wrenn said looking pointedly at the president. "It is public knowledge or nearly so that we allowed them to buy the plans for the LGM-118A Peacekeeper Intercontinental Ballistic Missile from Boeing, Martin Marietta, and Denver Aerospace after Congress voted down funding the missile due to survivability issues. Their contract was for forty billion dollars for research and development and infrastructure and five hundred million for each operational missile. They will have American know-how for maintenance, trouble-shooting, testing, and materials and equipment acquisition. These satellite images are proof-positive that the Peacekeeper project is underway for real so far as the agency is concerned. Let me remind you that it has the capability of delivering MIRVs, all nuclear warheads."

"Multiple independently targetable reentry vehicles," Ajami said for his president's benefit.

The president declaimed, "I don't think so, Director Wrenn. The Saudis are eminently sensible people. They have expensive personal habits, but they are frugal in their military and domestic outlays. It doesn't jibe. I want you to look at this some more. I don't need to remind that you are tarring our friends."

"You said you don't want 'yes' men in your administration; so, here goes. I cannot in good conscience brush this under the rug. There can only be one logical conclusion as to what target they intend. I'll spell it out so there can be no misconception. They are pointing their nuclear armed ICBMs at the United States of America, sir. We must act now, or it will be too late."

"You've gotten yourself all worked up, been listening to those wacko hawks over at Defense. Some of them will have to go. Can you imagine the reaction of the Saudis if I even hinted at what you have just said? Fifty years of diplomacy would go down the drain. We would lose them as an oil source. They would inflame the Muslim world against us. They are our oldest and dearest friends in the Middle-East. As a matter-of-fact, they are probably our best friends in the world since the Bush administration has so poisoned the international well for us. No sir, we are not going to 'act now' as you suggest. We are going to pursue our careful diplomacy with our friends as we have always done. And you are going to keep this information to yourself, are we understood?"

"I understand perfectly, Mr. President. However, I have a responsibility to the people of the United States to protect the Constitution and them. I must insist that this evidence regarding the Saudis and the Syrians be given due and concerned attention and some appropriate action pursued, or I will be forced to tender my resignation."

The president paused for a moment. He did not like the man personally and considered him a dinosaur from the old ready, fire, aim era of Bush; but he had a good mind and ran a tight ship. It was unfortunate that Wrenn's political savvy was nil, and his attitudes were antiquarian. But, the president could not allow himself to be challenged by a subordinate; and he could not jeopardize the critical Saudi/American relationship. During his entire career as an executive, Braithwaite had learned to consider it a rule that if a subordinate threatened to resign for any reason, he could not be kept on. He would forever be a liability. The president drew in a breath.

"I accept your resignation with regret, Mr. Director. It will be effective immediately. Please have a copy of the letter on my desk by this afternoon. It is customary for people with secrets to be escorted out of sensitive locations. I'm sure you understand. Mr. Ajami, will you take care of that?'

"Yes, sir. Ajami strained not to gloat.

A CIA security officer came to the Oval Office door and escorted the outgoing DCIA from the White House, supervised the removal of personal items from his desk and the transfer of codes and keys to his deputy and saw him to his car in the Langley building parking lot.

"I need a suggestion for Wrenn's replacement," the president said to Ajami as soon as Wrenn departed the Oval Office.

"I have just the person—Angelina Davis. She is a dynamic liberal, African-American, has an impeccable record and a superlative education. She is currently occupies the Alger Hiss Chair of International Politics at Bard College. I have known her for thirty-five years and can vouch for her without the slightest hesitation."

"Make it so, Scotty," the president said.

Angelina Davis was waiting for Ajami's call. He had let her know that he was sure that Wrenn would overstep today because he was passionate about an area that ran counter to the president's opinion and had hinted that he would even consider offering his resignation if the president would not take what he considered the necessary steps to correct a bad situation.

Ms Davis had every liberal credential; she was a lesbian and gay rights activist, a published feminist, an event organizer and speaker who was avidly in favor of a woman's right to choose, the ACLU, contraceptive and masturbation education in the nation's high schools, the right to protest, especially flag burning, and affirmative action. She was anti-death penalty, gun ownership, war, large families, racial profiling and discrimination, global warming, and big business. She regularly presented briefs to the ninth circuit court to prevent school prayer and to keep the mention of God and church out of public institutions. She had never married, because she disagreed with the institution, but lived rather prominently with her long-term same-sex partner in a civil contract arrangement.

The prospective new director of the Central Intelligence Agency was a middle-aged, severe faced, almost combative appearing, African-American with crooked teeth that were a badge of her disdain for the petty interests of the bourgeoisie. She wore her hair in corn rows, and her choice of clothing for public appearances was modified men's suits complete with tie and cufflinks. She liked her suits tailored with a generous cut to cover her somewhat corpulent figure, especially her large behind. It was cheaper and easier than going to the gym which she considered a waste of her valuable time.

Her nod to femininity was to wear graceful black high heeled shoes. Her suit coat had the requisite ribbons for acknowledgement of her support for homophilia and breast cancer. She never carried a purse, but did carry a backpack slung over one shoulder. Angelina Davis had been a communist when it was the thing to do, and now was a very vocal supporter of the Palestinian cause and for the need for our country to do away with its tilt toward Israel in its dealings with the improperly maligned Arab world. Though she belonged to no formal religious organization, she was publicly on record as being a student of Islam. Angelina Davis saw the post of director of Central Intelligence as a bully pulpit and a stepping stone to higher things.

Former DCIA Patterson Wrenn sat dejected and lonely in his Georgetown Tudor house, moping since his dismissal for speaking his piece. He felt humiliated and badly used personally; but he had a genuine fear for his country and for the world, for that matter. He was certain that the Braithwaite administration was blinding itself to reality, and succumbing to the drug of wanting to believe, wanting to have peace at all costs. Alone with his thoughts, the man who knew more about the current world than anyone else alive remembered the profound passage from Homer's *Odyssey*. Odysseus, while returning from his travels encountered a North African island people living where the most prevalent flora were lotus plants. The lotus fruits and flowers were the staple food of the islanders. The lotuses contained a narcotic, which caused the islanders to fall into a sleep of peaceful apathy. Homer then had Odysseus describe his concerns for his crew:

"When they had eaten and drunk I sent two of my company to see what manner of men the people of the place might be, and they had a third man under them. They started at once, and went about

among the Lotus-eaters, who did them no hurt, but gave them to eat of the lotus, which was so delicious that those who ate of it left off caring about home, and did not even want to go back and say what had happened to them, but were for staying and munching lotus with the Lotus-eaters without thinking further of their return…"
-Homer, *Odyssey* IX

"*How apropos of the world view and myopic thinking of the Braithwaite administration,*" he thought, "*and how dangerous it is to go about blind to the events gathering around the White House.*"

CHAPTER SIXTEEN

LATE JULY, 2009

The Council of the Leaders of Islam met in Riyadh Marriott Hotel on Al Mather Street. After the call to order, Prince Ahmed Wahhab ibn Saud turned to the first order of the day.

"As a body, we must hear what our Shi'a *akh*, Ayatollah Ali Mazdi Sekhavatal al-Muderasi, has for us."

The black robed cleric stood in unsmiling dignity. Even the Sunnis respected the man's intelligence and knowledge of the things of importance in their world. He was a noted scriptorian, Islamic jurist, historian of the outrages perpetrated by the Zionists, and linguist; he spoke all four of the major Iranian languages—Farsi, Turkic, Kurdish, and Arabic—with the fluency of a native speaker. He had a rich, reedy, well-modulated voice. Although he always spoke with the soft dulcet tones of a seasoned cleric, the people listened to him as if he were shouting. The ayatollah was physically powerful in appearance—a bear of a man—and wore a overgrown thick black beard. His eyebrows were very bushy; his frontal hairline was low; and his scalp hair was thick. As a result, al-Mudarasi showed scant facial skin. This gave him an air of mystery and menace; he was imposing and gave every indication that he was a man that should be reckoned with—as he certainly was.

"The Islamic Republic of Iran has a thermonuclear device—several in fact. In a just world we would be able to deliver them to the Great Satan without difficulty, but the world conspires against us." He shrugged. *"Allah alim.* [God knows best]. We ask the Council to provide us with the intercontinental ballistic missiles to deliver our warheads to save us precious resources and time. Ours is not as wealthy a country as our Sunni neighbor."

"I see a problem. We have no more of the Peacekeeper missiles. Can we make this happen soon, brothers?" Prince ibn Saud asked from his seat on the dais.

"We can ask the Americans for more," Abdu Ajami of the Egyptian delegation suggested in a tone of voice that suggested that he intended his idea to be taken tongue in cheek.

He smiled at the assemblage.

"I believe that *can* be accomplished with the new regime in Washington that is more favorable towards us," Walid Patel—the Indonesian Jemaah Islamiyah Leader—offered.

"You do not think that would stretch the credulity of those fools too far? And mightn't it tip our hand?" the prince queried.

Patel said, "It will take subtlety and a great deal of patience. We will have to make short-term and temporary concessions; but, yes, I believe that they will fawn over us to have the chance if we do it correctly."

"What do you suggest we offer as the 'short-term and temporary concessions' to which you refer? Bear in mind that we will have to convince our zealous brothers and many of our governments to accomplish any change," the prince said, dubious of the suggestion.

"It is an opportune time, prince. The new Washington regime prides itself on its diplomatic skills and its progressive ideas. We will respond to them in a way that will give them a success early in their administration—the honeymoon of which they speak so fondly. Thereby, we can strengthen their position which is a good thing for our cause. Allah forbid that we do anything that would nudge the Great Satan to want to elect another crusader like the former president named Bush. My specific suggestion is that we first propose to back an unconditional cease-fire between Little Satan and the Palestinians and force it upon the PLO, *al-Qassam Izzedine—the* military wing of Hamas—and Hezbollah unilaterally.

"The U.S. will force the Occupiers to go along. That will weaken the Zionist-Crusader alliance. Then we—and I mean all of the nations of the Islamic world—will make a formal offer to the U.S. and the UN to broker a peace settlement. Shortly thereafter we can propose a new homeland for the Palestinians in the Sinai or in Saudi Arabia, or Syria, or Yemen, or the Sudan—wherever we can agree. This will be the ultimate sacrifice on the part of Islam. We will agree to recognize Israel, and to give the Occupiers everything they want. The Palestinians will get what they want, just not where they want it. It will appear to be sincere, real, just, and generous, even sacrificing. And we can credit the diplomatic efforts of the U.S. and the UK for the break-through."

"Will not the actions of the holy martyrs and freedom fighters throughout the world appear to be at serious odds with your proposal, Mr. Patel?" asked Muhammad Mohfouz, head of Salafiya.

"Yes. You have hit on the most thorny problem we must face in order to appear not only willing, but capable of uniting and carrying out our proposal. We suffer from a lack of unity and every freedom fighting group operates semi-autonomously. If we are going to accomplish such an apparently huge change in Islamic policy, we must appear to have made a similarly huge change in action. This time I think words will not be sufficient."

"All of this so that the Iranians can get a MIRV carrying missile?" Ayatollah al-Mudarasi asked with pragmatic skepticism.

"Allow me to answer that, *akh*," interjected Prince ibn Saud. "It is more strategic than tactical. We can do all of this, make all of these temporary sacrifices and adjustments and get the missiles; and incidentally, we must not make our actions and the acquisition of the nuclear ICBMs seem to be linked; but also we can lull the Great Satan to sleep. When acts of war against them and the Occupiers come to a halt; and their evil concept of peace without the True God's plan appear to be implemented, they will relax their guard against us. The more I listen to him, the more I come to believe that *akh* Patel's plan has great merit; and we should exert all of our influence to make it happen. I also believe it will hasten the day when we can reach the final solution and usher in Allah's new world."

President Mohammed Yahya Farouk of Egypt spoke for his country, "We will give our full cooperation. We receive as much military aid from the Great Satan as do the usurpers of Palestine. We can request parity with the Saudis—who have been allowed to purchase the up-to-the-minute ICBMs—and we can ask it as an outright gift. We can obtain several of the missiles which we will ask for as status symbols and as an equalizer against the massive arsenal the U.S. gives and sells to the usurpers."

"I will commit my country to the project even to reigning in Hamas and Hezbollah," said Iranian President Muhammad Ali Hashemi after receiving an agreeing nod from Ayatollah al-Mudarasi.

"I offer an additional suggestion," said the delegate from Libya, Abdul Idris al-Megrahi. "Once the plan of *akh* Patel has gained serious momentum, we can offer to do away with our weaponry of mass destruction. We can do it in one of our countries at a time to keep feeding their news services and keep our peaceful intentions in the eye of their fickle and gullible American public for many months. We can feed anything we want to *Al Jazeera, Qatar Watch;* and the Western media will gobble it up."

"Is it not inconsistent with the upgrading in weapons we are seeking, *akh*?" asked the Yemeni delegate—Shafiq Mosed—an ultra conservative Audhali tribesman.

He felt for his Gambia—the straight hilt Yemeni knife all real men in his country carried. It made him ill at ease not to have the comfort of its presence, but he recognized that it had served the greater good for all weapons to be taken during the conference. Its absence made him fidget.

"The disarmament offer will come as a separate phase as soon as the cease-fire phase has been implemented and appreciated by those fools in the West, *akh*."

"Are we all agreed, my brothers?" asked Prince ibn Saud.

There was a murmur of discussion, some groupings for argument, and a few vigorous negative head shakes, especially from the representatives of al-Qaeda.

The prince gave them a few minutes to work out their differences. He was going to have his way, but he wanted the positive declaration to come voluntarily from all of the parties in the room. Genuine concurrence would make his work much easier and would hasten the end greatly.

Khalid Antranik Ayoub stood in the congregation after the hubbub died down.

He said, "I cannot speak for *akh* Usama—our hero and icon—but I will try and persuade him and our cells around the world to go along. We must be assured that it is only temporary and that the sacrifice will be rewarded with a victory as great as our coup of September 11, 2001. It will take time to get word to Usama in the northwest of Pakistan. I presume that this plan cannot go forward without his blessing. Is that a reasonable assumption?"

It galled the prince to have to say so, but he was willing to concede this much to his countryman, whom he considered to be a self-seeking megalomaniac in the Islamic cause. Self-seeking megalomaniacs had their uses.

"Of course, *akh* Ayoub. Though it will require the patience your name implies, we will await Usama's blessing," he announced.

"I can clear the way into the province," Walid Shamma Atallah offered. "I will have to have the permission from my president. This is a delicate matter since it could potentially interfere with our special but temporary relationship with the Americans."

"Please see to it that lines of communication are facilitated, Mr. Vice-President," asked the prince. "And let us have a vote on this issue. Who will support this program with all of its pitfalls and sacrifices as part of our *jihad*?"

Phrased that way, it was evident how much stock Prince ibn Saud and the leaders of the Council now put into this ambitious plan. The delegates all voted aye; some with more enthusiasm than others. The real work of making it happen began that afternoon with secret emissaries carrying Prince ibn Saud's personal request that the anti-Jewish anti-American rhetoric be curbed immediately. The messengers told of a meeting with the Council Leaders in the very near future.

CHAPTER SEVENTEEN

LATE JULY, 2009

Vice-President Clarence Maddox took the call on his secure line despite his personal vow never to mix his private business with the government, not even to using the same telephone. But, he was tired and out of sorts; and the secure line was so much more convenient than disguising himself and going out to find a pay phone—not that anyone would take a second notice of the Vice-President or of any other black man in D.C.—using a pay phone, if he could find one still working.

"I presume this is important. I told you that I cannot take a call from you here."

"This is Lepke. Look, Clarence; this is important; and besides, this is your secure line. You're safe. The feds—the FBI—were over at the distribution center this morning."

"Everything's covered and has been for the whole fifteen years we have been in business. So, what's the fuss today?"

"They made me get my attorney—you know, *our* attorney, if the truth were told—and meet with them and the assistant federal prosecutor and to produce all of our records. The federal prosecutor said point blank that I am a target for arrest, and they are preparing their case."

"But, I'm not involved, Phil—no paperwork or money leads to my door—I have to say that I think you are taking all of this too seriously."

"Yeah? And thanks for caring, my long-time friend. I made millions for you under the table while you were still the governor of Missouri. Maybe you don't recall, but it was me and my wife who set you up with the account in Vanuatu. And nobody—but nobody—can connect us; so, don't get self-defensive."

"I acknowledge that you did, Phil. Don't think I'm not appreciative. I am. I would be stuck in this dead-end job and pretty much broke if you hadn't gotten me into the business. It's always been risky; but I think we have covered our tracks so far; and I don't think the FBI agents have anything on you. I think they're just bluffing. Hang in there. This will blow over, and I'll see if I can use a little pull to get them to move their attention to some real criminals."

"I think a little reality check is in order, Clarence. Look, this business we're in is a scam, a felony; and we both went into it eyes wide open. We need to get together and work out a plan to deal with the feds. It's a mistake to think they're any kind of dummies"

"Of course I know it's technically illegal. But, you know as well as I do that this is just the way business is done in today's America."

"Well, I'm here to report that the FBI and the prosecutor used that particular distasteful phrase—ponzi scheme—a dozen times at least in our conversations. I'm scared, Clarence, I don't mind admitting it."

"Keep a lid on, Phil. A few mil came our way from big money guys—insurance companies, unions, retirement funds, and the Trial Lawyers Association Fund—not from a bunch of grandmas or orphans. We were consultants."

"Clarence, wake up. The SAC who sat me down knows all about the bribes and under the table stuff. Jeez, you should see the piles of documents they have on us."

"Did my name come up?" Maddox's voice had taken on an edge of concern now.

"Of course not. Do you think I'm completely stupid? The people we bribed were as greedy as us and perfectly willing to rake in the bucks from the folks they brought in. No one is going to feel any sympathy for the likes of them. And our attorney friend assured us that there was not a chance of any forensic accountant tracking the money back to either of us. We have legit books, you know. And that's what I gave them to fulfill the demand for records."

"I suppose our books are in a safe place, like never to see the light of day?" Maddox queried.

"Oh, yeah, the safest. I moved them to the Hickory House Inn in Vermont. It's the little place where we first did business with the Iranians. I liked the place so much that I bought it."

"In your name?"

"Give me more credit. I used your name."

"Don't even joke about something like than."

"And you shouldn't lose your sense of humor, Clarence. No, I paid off a college kid to let us use his moniker."

"I hope those books are out of sight from a nosy burglar or anyone making a police investigation."

"I have a safe in a cutout in the garage floor; you don't have to worry your pretty bald little head on account of any of our books."

"I always count on you, Phil. Keep me posted, but not on a government line; I don't trust any of them."

"I'll have Aldo talk you up at the Greek embassy party first of next week. He will be up to date, and he is as close mouthed as they come for anybody who isn't supposed to be in the know."

"Thanks Phil."

Vice-President Maddox hung up the receiver and put his fingers on his temples and rubbed. While he rubbed he thought. He considered himself the ultimate pragmatist; that's how he had gotten as far as he had come. He had plenty of money squirreled away—not as much as he had expected to retire on—but enough to live decently. It was time to cut his losses. He picked up the phone.

"Gracie, get me Tom Falderman, please."

"Yes, Mr. Vice-President."

Maddox busied himself shuffling papers related to the dozens of scheduled photo-ops with folks from around the country, the bane to his existence. He had nothing worthwhile to do because of the prima donna in the White House who treated him like a leper ever since the inauguration.

His phone rang.

"It's Mr. Falderman, Mr. Vice-President."

"I'll take it, Gracie."

"Hello, Tom."

"Mr. Vice-President."

"There's a little job that needs doing."

"A little quiet job? I trust it's a legal job."

"Let's just say that it's legal enough. The other party will never complain."

"You sure?"

"Certain. I want you to take your latest significant-other up to a little place in Vermont. Have a nice stay in the Hickory House Inn. While you are not the center of attention—like in the middle of the night—go out into the garage and look for a safe hidden in the floor. Bring me its contents."

"In a plain paper bag, as they say?"

"You've got the general idea, We'll have lunch at that Indian place in Tyson's Corner. You can give it to me then. Let's say, Friday."

"Do my best."

"That's always good enough for me."

Vice-President Maddox and Tom Falderman hung up at the same time.

The FBI agent who had been recording the vice-president's conversations for the past week signaled to his technician to cut it off.

"Make me a copy as soon as possible. I'll need it for my routine meeting with the director this afternoon, and he will enjoy having it for his meeting with President Braithwaite first of next week."

"Piece of cake," the technician said.

Special Agent Morrison turned to the man sitting next to him.

"Mr. Lepke, you done splendid, as Casey Stengel used to say. I'm assuming that Maddox's man will pick up your records in the next couple of days. We'll be there to help him. The last part of our deal is that you have to be willing to testify to every detail of your deals with Maddox over the years, and you better be able to back all of it up. This is a big fish we're going to fry, and we are not going to have any mishaps along the way. If you do, the director will have my job; and I will come and visit you in prison from time to time. We clear?"

"And I skate, if my stuff pans out."

"Free as a bird."

"You got a piece of paper attesting to that which we both sign, and we each get a copy of our very own?"

"Right here."

Morrison produced the document, two originals. The men signed it and shook hands.

Morrison called in the news to his boss. He listened to instructions from the director of the Federal Bureau of Investigation then signaled his partner. He turned his attention back to Philip Lepke.

"Mr. Lepke, we are going to give you a rent-free place with a great security system until this affair is over. We're going out to Fort Meade. They have a fine apartment for folks like you."

"A jail? That wasn't part of the deal!" Lepke exclaimed.

"Not at all. Trust me. You are going to be staying in the same place that half a dozen Mafiosos have been protected while they waited to sing about the Dandy Don some years ago."

"I heard about that. Not too bad a place, I heard."

"I wouldn't want to annoy my star witness, Phil. You can trust me. But this is a mutual trust thing. You can go into the Witness Protection Program if you want. You might want to think about that. Do me right, and I'll take care of you. Do me wrong, and I am the proverbial five-hundred pound gorilla."

"I'm your guy."

At seven in the morning on day two of the Hallweather trial, Attorney General Elizabeth Leavitt Rowan called Judge McGee.

"Your honor, Mr. Sugarman and I have worked out a plea bargain. We'd like to run the details of it past you in chambers."

There was a short pause on Judge McGee's end.

"I'll postpone the resumption of the trial on Thursday until two. I have a full docket otherwise. I know that we could all skip a power lunch in favor of pastrami on rye that day to put this mess behind us. Let's meet at ten."

"Can you get your administrative assistant to inform Mr. Sugarman's office?"

"Consider it done."

At the appointed hour, Attorney General Rowan and Oscar Sugarman arrived at Judge McGee's chambers at the same time. Sugarman held the door for Rowan, and they greeted the judge's administrative assistant.

"We're expected, I presume, Mrs. Dixon," Sugarman said.

"I'll let the judge know you're here."

She pressed a button on the console on her desk.

"The attorney general and Mr. Sugarman are here, your honor."

"Send them in, please, Alice."

Alice Dixon—an elderly white haired overweight indispensable African-American woman—pushed her way out of her swivel chair and led the two attorneys to the judge's inner chamber.

"Thanks for being right on time. It's a very hectic day around here," Judge McGee said.

He rose and walked to the front of his large Honduran mahogany desk and shook each of their hands. He nodded to them to sit, and he took a seat on a sofa facing them.

"So, at long last, we are going to come to the end of this media circus masquerading as a legal drama," he said and smiled hopefully.

"We have an agreement, your honor. I am dubious about the minimal punishment to be meted out to the defendants, but the plea bargain best serves the people," the attorney general said.

"I'll lay out the details; they are simple; and if you agree with them, we can make the formal announcement in the next session of court," said Oscar Sugarman. "I am not going to characterize the deal except to say that I have thought all along that much too much was made of the case, and I can speak for a whole host of people who will be glad to have this one over with. I predict that the news will last no more than a single news cycle."

"Let us pray," Judge McGee said. "Give me the short version."

Rowan nodded to Sugarman who laid out the deal.

"The defendants will receive ten year probated sentences except for a thirteen month stay in the D.C. jail. They will pay restitution of sixty-eight million dollars to the government for direct repayment, an additional one hundred million in fines and court costs; and they will set up and run a permanent education service for corporate executives and for potential government defense contractors. They agree to lose their licenses for five years and Hallweather will agree not to bid on government contracts for the same period. In return the government will drop all charges against the family members of the principles. They agree not to fire or to seek any type of reprisal against the whistle blower."

"A most generous offer on the government's part, given the perfect case we have," thought Elizabeth.

What she had not told Sugarman was that the president and the vice-president had called late last night and all but ordered her to come up with a reasonable sentence.

As President Braithwaite had put it, "The country cannot afford to kill off Hallweather." And Vice-President Maddox had put it more crassly, "We can't afford to prolong this scandal that reaches into the very heart of this administration and the previous one."

Judge McGee shook his head. "It's for the best, I suppose. I hope that I have the two of you pitted against each other in any case in which I am a defendant."

"And it wouldn't hurt to have the world's political press trumpeting every action and the federal government placed in such an embarrassing position that anything would be better than a trial in which all of the sordid details would be aired," the attorney general said.

"It's that kind of world," said Judge McGee.

"Always has been, your honor. Who are we to make revolutionary changes?" asked Sugarman rhetorically.

The three legal experts breathed a sigh of relief that would be echoed in their several bailiwicks over the next few days before they all settled into new rounds of accusations, motions, deals, and compromises that would bring each of them a few steps closer to burn-out.

Tom and Camilla Falderman found the late dinner at the Hickory Inn's Northeast Room more than passable. Tom paid the check with the Visa card in the name of Mordecai Gottesman and left a generous tip. He made a point of turning in early because he had to get back to the city for an eight o-clock appointment. He and Camilla waved to the crowd in the dining room before ascending the stairs to their room. When they left, two men in gray suits pushed back from their table, paid their bill, and left the restaurant through its main entrance.

Camilla turned on CNN and started watching the multiple repetitions of the day's news. Tom stripped out of his dress clothing. Camilla winked at him. Even after all those years of marriage, she still fancied him. He was medium height with large well defined muscles, like a wrestler. He was cue-ball bald, deeply tanned, and had a remarkably hairy chest, abdomen, and back. His face was pleasant enough, and Camilla thought it intelligent. Not intelligent, exactly, but more on the order of cunning. Tom slipped into his black coveralls, picked up the stylish leather carrying case that held his tools, and made his way quietly down the back stairs. He found the tape on the door latch just as he had left it earlier in the day and was in the unlocked garage in less than a minute.

Tom scanned the floor with his MagLite and saw nothing indicative of a false floor. The floor was dusty and greasy rags and old cardboard boxes were strewn around. He doused his light for a minute and watched the outside perimeter of the garage through its grimy windows. Nothing moved; nothing aroused anxiety. He turned on the flashlight again, found a push broom and began to sweep the dirty floor methodically one quadrant at a time. In the corner by the large tool box, he saw some streaking and drag marks in the dust. The clutter seemed formidable, perhaps too much so. The tool cabinet appeared to be extremely heavy; but when he pushed on it, the cabinet moved with surprising ease. It was mounted on wheels and when moved, Tom found that it overlay a square door in the floor. There were finger holes on one end. Tom lifted the door that proved to be mounted on springs and opened easily.

He squatted down and shined his light into the opening. There was a heavy metal box with a hinge lid fastened with a reinforced steel padlock. Tom opened his leather case and extracted his picklock set. He stepped into the compartment, squatted on the lid, bent over and deftly picked the lock—a task that took less than five seconds. He stepped back out, opened the lid, and saw a neat row of accounting ledgers—fifteen of them. He sighed at the work that he would have to do, rolled up his sleeves and removed all of the ledgers from the compartment and set them on the floor. He closed the lid and locked it and lowered the floor hatch door and replaced the tool cabinet. He bent over and picked up three of the heavy ledgers for the first trip to his car and made his way to the garage's side door using his teeth to hold the flashlight.

In a blinding flash of light, six large halogen flashlights came on and trapped him like a deer in headlights. He was stunned.

"Thomas Falderman! Halt! Keep your hands where they are. We are the FBI, and you are under arrest for theft of accounts ledgers that are evidence in a federal corruption case."

"I'm Mordecai Schwartz," Tom said feebly.

"Skip it, Falderman," snapped Special Agent Morrison. "Set the books down very slowly and keep your hands in plain sight."

Falderman was sure that his very influential boss would make quick work of getting him freed from custody; so, he complied promptly and carefully. Two agents approached him with guns drawn and stood in the standard leg forward FBI shooting position. Falderman knew that these guys meant business. He was only too happy to allow them to handcuff him and do a thorough pat-down. The agents removed the gun from his ankle holster. He patiently heard out the complete recitation of his Miranda rights—a litany he knew by heart from previous experience.

The officers gently pressed his head over; so, he could get into the FBI car comfortably and generally treated him with courtesy. On the way to the plane, Special Agent Morrison broke the silence.

"Tom?"

"Yeah?"

"May I call you Tom?"

"Sure. Say, could someone tell my wife; so, she doesn't think I just disappeared. You hear about a lot of weirdos in the neighborhood, you know."

"She's in custody as your accomplice."

"She had nothing to do with this. Just let her go."

"And what would we get in return, Tom?"

"I'll cooperate, won't give you any grief."

"We'll need more than that, Tom, quite a lot more. Let me lay it out for you very simply. You are on parole for your second felony. Tonight you were arrested in the commission of a felony burglary, and you were carrying a firearm in direct violation of the conditions of your parole. No doubt you are aware of the 'three strikes and you are in' laws, aren't you, Tom?"

"I'm familiar. I didn't do nothing. How come you are coming down so hard on me?"

"You haven't heard me out, Tom. You face the certainty of life in prison; there's not a chance that you will skate on this one. We have night vision videos of you in the commission of your crime, and we have a certified recording of your conversation with the vice-president."

Tom saw clearly where this was going.

"But, Tom, there is hope for you. You are a punk, a petty career criminal. We could use your help in making our case for bigger fish. You help us fully and freely, and we can maybe put in a good word at your trial."

"A good word!? That's it? I don't act the good soldier like Oliver North and his type, and instead give you all the gory details and in return you give me a little promise. With a promise and a fifty cent piece I could buy a cup of coffee!"

"What would you think would be more fair, Tom?" Morrison asked reasonably.

Tom thought for a moment desperately. He frowned and gritted his teeth. He decided to go for everything; he had nothing to lose.

"Okay, I'll tell you. I have dirt on Maddox that goes back more than fifteen years. I have a photographic mind; I keep meticulous records, and I have photocopies of everything I ever touched on the man's orders. I have tape recordings, videos, and a couple of eye witnesses I could direct you to. Here's the deal: I give you all of that and agree to testify when, where, and however often you want. You let my wife go as soon as you have the goods and don't charge her. You protect me; I want to have me and my wife put in the WPP. You drop all charges against me—give me complete immunity—and you stop all this talk about the third strike business. You fail on any of those, and I take the rap, and you get zip. Whatta you say?"

"I'll run it past my superiors, Tom. I rather think they will agree with me that the tradeoff is reasonable as long as you can deliver."

"So make a few calls, and then watch me."

Special Agent Morrison took out his cell phone and made a series of three calls. Falderman listened to Morrison's end of the laconic conversations and grinned broadly when the FBI agent finished. Morrison was singing silent Hallelujahs himself.

The principle call had been to the Director of the Federal Bureau of Investigation, Leland Marques, who was a veteran of a lifetime of political infighting to get to and to remain in his position in the Bureau. He knew a treacherous windfall when he saw one. This high profile case would look great for the Bureau and for himself if it was handled right. He had every confidence in Morrison and knew that he would be backing a winner when he assented.

Marques was very tall and had once been a bench warmer in the NBA. He had seen that he was never going to be star material; so, he got a law degree from NYU and immediately entered the FBI academy with the help of his influential father, the New York City district attorney. Now in his early fifties, Marques looked every bit the Washington official and consummate insider, both of which were accurate descriptions. He always wore three piece dark grey suits, custom made white shirts, and power ties. He always wore an enigmatic half smile that betrayed nothing. He had thick black hair graying at the temples that he had cut in an expensive salon in Tyson's Corner. His fingernails were professionally manicured; his shoes shined daily by the funny little man in the lobby of the J. Edgar Hoover building—and he had a small American flag pin on the left suit coat pocket of every one of his thirty suits.

He was carefully prepared for the surprise encounter with someone from the press at any time. Marques appeared affable with a pleasant demeanor that he studiously presented to the public. In fact, he was a hard task master and a hard boss for the men and women who worked under him. He was scrupulously fair, nondiscriminating on racial, age, or gender bases, and a perfectionist for himself and his subordinates when it came to the gathering of evidence for high profile cases. He did not suffer fools in the least. This case against the vice-president would be made without the slightest flaw. The director intended to see to it himself every step of the way.

CHAPTER EIGHTEEN

NOVEMBER 1, 2009

Secretary of State, Donovan O'Laughlin, was surprised, astounded even, at the diplomatic request that was sitting on his desk. A formal letter from the Saudi Palace and an identical one from Tehran seemed to glow, to have a life force. The King of Saudi Arabia, His Majesty, Abdullah Said bin Saud, and the Grand Ayatollah of Iran, Hussein Aliyy Bilal, both requested an audience with the president at the same time and in Washington on the subject of a new peace plan for the Middle East. The letters were polite, even more; they were conciliatory on the subject, offering heretofore unthinkable concessions. Donovan called the president.

"Mr. President. I have some remarkable news—news that I have to convey in person. I think it is a priority and urgent."

"All right, Secretary O'Laughlin, I'll have Ms. Apflebaum fit you in. Can you come over now?"

"As soon as we hang up. Good-bye, Mr. President."

"Good-bye Mr. Secretary."

Vilate Apflebaum showed Secretary O'Laughlin into the Oval Office, and he presented the electrifying documents to President Braithwaite and his National Security Advisor, Daniel Ajami. Braithwaite was exultant.

"Five presidents have labored for this chance," he said. "I knew that a more amicable, more constructive approach, would work finally. It looks like we are over the legacy of the American Nazi, Dubya, a whole lot sooner than anyone could have predicted. Bring those two Arabs on,"

"To be technical, Mr. President, the Iranians are not Arabs; and both of these two leaders would bristle at the suggestion. I'll get you a protocol summary and a synopsis of the history of the Palestinian versus Israeli conflict; so, you can be up to date. I will make an appointment for a summit or a secret meeting, whichever the two great leaders want. I think we shouldn't rush it too much, appear too anxious, what do you think?"

"Throw caution to the winds. This is a celebration; let's let them know how thrilled we are to have this historical breakthrough. I'll tell you frankly, Daniel, this may well define my presidency, and I think it will guarantee my place in history."

"I hope it pans out, Mr. President. With your guiding hand getting this to come to pass, I believe your historical position will be right up there with Lincoln and FDR."

"That's a bit much, Daniel, but thanks for the vote of confidence. You know I couldn't do any of this without you."

"Should we inform or try to include the Israelis?"

"Absolutely not! I can think of nothing that would put the kibosh on this initiative faster or more completely than even mentioning the inclusion of those irrational, unreasonable hotheads from Tel Aviv—the Zionist Terrorists."

"I agree. We will keep them in the dark until we have to bring them in. I'll get to work."

Donovan nodded his agreement.

"Give me a report as soon as you have any information. I can't overstress that this cannot be leaked. We need the political punch that we will gain from a surprise announcement that real peace in the Middle-East is about to become a reality."

———————

Secretary of State O'Laughlin telephoned his counterpart in the Saudi foreign ministry, and the prince quickly put him into direct contact with the king.

"Your Majesty, I am honored that you would speak directly with me."

"I wanted to be direct, Mr. Secretary. I was the author of the letter, and I want you to understand that this is a first priority for our country. As you might imagine, extensive negotiations were held with the Grand Ayatollah before we agreed to send identical letters. We are both fully behind the plan suggested in the letters."

"I think that your historical initiative will change the scope of international relations and will lead to peace with the Israelis. We are very optimistic."

"A note of caution, Mr. Secretary. I greatly appreciate that you have had the wisdom not to confer with the Jewish Entity."

"Thank you, sir, I ordered that caution personally."

The king continued, "Word of this proposal must not leak out before we work out a logistical plan, one acceptable to all three of our countries. My very reign would be in frank jeopardy if we were known to colluding on a plan to stop the jihad against the Occupiers. There would be rioting in Iran—and I think, bloodshed—in both our countries."

"We will exercise the most stringent precautions, Your Majesty. I would foresee having a U.S. C130 military transport specially fitted for yours and the grand ayatollah's comfort to bring the two of you at the same time to Washington. It would be too risky to gamble on bringing each of you separately. Do you think you and the grand ayatollah will be able to set aside your differences to make that trip together?"

"We have already done so, Mr. Secretary. We are ready to come as soon as you can make the final arrangements. I would look toward having us arriving in Western business attire at night at Andrews Air Force base and meeting the president and you on the base. If we come to a firm agreement, I see no reason why we cannot make a formal public announcement within days. I believe we can have the leaders of the PLO, the king of Jordan, and the presidents of Syria, Iraq, Libya, and Egypt on the same podium if the agreement is ironclad. It will take some persuading, as you might well imagine."

"Your Majesty, I can commit my country to virtually any measure to help that does not actually compromise our national security. Consider us to be at your service."

The arrangements were finalized in the utmost secrecy. No one from the media had even the slightest hint, and no provisions were made even to record the historic meeting for fear that the delicate deal making would be compromised. King bin Saud and Grand Ayatollah Bilals' C130 set down on the Andrews tarmac in the middle of the night and in a complete blackout, and the two dignitaries were shuttled by military vehicles to the conference room where the president was waiting.

"Greetings, Your Majesty, and greetings to you, Grand Ayatollah. It gives me great pleasure to welcome you to our country. I'm sure you are tired and would like a rest before we begin. We have some refreshments."

The grand ayatollah shook his head and looked over to the king, who was a majestic figure with his dark skin and carefully maintained beard. Although he only rarely wore Western attire, his two thousand dollar suit, perfectly tailored by his personal English tailor, his gleaming white shirt made to his specifications in Hong Kong, and his magnificent, one-of-a-kind Islamic green Egyptian silk tie patterned with an ornate arrangement of tiny crescents made a fashion statement that could be the envy of any movie or sports celebrity or any king.

"Mr. President, we had a most comfortable and restful flight thanks to you. We would like to get right down to business, if that would be all right with you," the grand ayatollah said.

"Of course. I am one who likes to get things done as well. Let's take a seat."

The king of Saudi Arabia spoke first on the substantive reason for the epochal visit.

"Mr. President, we have long observed the intifada against the Occupiers with concern and together with our Syrian, Egyptian, Jordanian, Libyan, and Iraqi friends, we find the seemingly endless cycle of violence to be deplorable. To demonstrate our good faith, we have already managed to ring serious concessions from all of the Muslim leaders to achieve a true and lasting peace."

"Our plan, Mr. President, is sweeping but actually very simple," the grand ayatollah added. "We propose that you chair a secret summit meeting between the heads of state of every Muslim country, the Zionist entity, and the heads of state of France, Germany, the United Kingdom, Canada, Australia, the United Nations, and your own great country to hear a unilateral Middle-East peace proposal proffered by the grand ayatollah and king. We will propose a plan that can be implemented by the members attending, and we will use every measure of influence to accomplish in advance the necessary actions on the part of the Islamic Nations.

"We will exert as much pressure as it takes to reign in the individuals and organizations that launch freedom fighters for the cause of Islam. We ask that you and your allies cease and desist from arresting, detaining, and engaging in hostilities with the fundamentalists and persuade the Zionist Entity of our sincerity so that they will stop their predations against the Palestinians and others who give assistance to Occupied Palestine.

"We will provide an Arab sanctuary in the Sinai for the Palestinians and together with you and the United Nations will assist in the orderly transferal of the Palestinian people to that area. We ask your financial assistance in achieving this monumental and historical dislocation of a people. We ask that you involve the Zionist Entity in the financial obligation. We ask that you recognize a Palestinian State as soon as the transferal is complete, the infrastructure is in place, and a stable government is functioning. We believe this can be accomplished in five years time. In that same time period, we will see to it that every Muslim country gives formal and functional recognition of the State of Israel and ask that you ensure that the Zionist Entity reciprocates. Only the United States can influence the Occupiers to remove its prejudicial barriers to movement of laborers and commerce with its Muslim neighbors. This condition should be established before the mutual recognition of states process is ratified.

"We ask that you grant blanket amnesty for those individuals and organizations that you currently label as terrorist organizations after one year of complete freedom, world-wide, from acts of provocation. We, of course, cannot control separatist movements, but we will use our not inconsequential powers to see to it that separatists confine their activities to their own countries. If acts of cross-border provocation or attacks occur on Western officials or entities after one year, then we pledge our complete support—including the full cooperation of our intelligence services—to apprehend and neutralize the individuals and their sponsoring organizations.

"We pledge that we will not again use an oil embargo such as occurred in 1973 and '74 and ask in return that you not pursue your old plan of developing a national petroleum stockpile.

"We offer to enter into good-faith negotiations with you and the Zionist Entity to achieve international control over the use of nuclear devices in our region and will seek to have an over-sight committee with real power to ensure Middle-East peace and mutual security."

President Braithwaite was quiet and contemplative for a few minutes. He sat rubbing the bridge of his nose with his steepled fingers before finally speaking.

"I am most impressed; I might even say amazed at the generosity of your offer, Your Majesty. I am compelled to ask the grand ayatollah directly if he and his nation concur fully. The scope and importance of this proposal is too great to leave anything to chance," the president said.

He turned his attention to the grand ayatollah who met his intent gaze with a look of quiet and guileless resolve. Grand Ayatollah Hussein Aliyy Bilal could have been a physical clone of his hero, the legendary Grand Ayatollah Ruhallah Al-Musavi Al-Khomenei—the same fierce and commanding facial expression, the same penetrating and unforgiving eyes, the unruly salt and pepper beard, and the same simple clothing. His grey-black robe reached the ground, and not even his hands were exposed. He wore an impeccably clean turban wrapped around his imposing head, and his earnest bodily posture would give an unsuspecting member of the faithful a moment of nostalgic pause.

The Iranian cleric said simply, "With the help of Allah, the All Powerful, the Muslims of Iran will grant all these concessions and will live up to the promises made."

The grand ayatollah conveyed his intended message with no gestures of his limbs and no alteration of his facial expression. Even that simplicity of manner was reminiscent of the great liberator of Iran. He was secretly pleased with the effect it had on listeners.

"That is enough for me, gentlemen. However, I will have to convince a nation of skeptics, perhaps a rather doubting world, of our full cooperation. My country's military is notoriously conservative, and it will take time from me to install more tractable officers. I will have to gain the cooperation of the Luddite conservative faction in our government and throughout our nation. I see them as the equivalent of the violent and intractable fundamentalists in your nations. I, therefore, propose that we move the formalities in cautious steps over a year's time. I will have a most formidable argument if, after a year, there is no violence coming from your side; and if my intelligence sources cease hearing messages that set their teeth on edge. In one year we can formalize this offer of yours that will be the equivalent of the scriptural 'beating the swords into plowshares and the spears into pruning hooks.'"

The Muslim leaders nodded their acquiescence and indicated their pleasure with the American leader for being a man of the Book.

"When shall we make the first announcement?" President Braithwaite asked.

"We came prepared to do so tomorrow. Can you mobilize your analysts in that time? I have taken the liberty to prepare a mutual statement. Your people can review it, and you can call an appropriate press conference at the White House."

The president took the proffered press release and examined it.

"This is perfect. I see no problems with the statement. I will run it past my people and—unless there is something unforeseen—we will stun the world tomorrow afternoon. In the meantime, where do you think you should stay? Do you wish to continue to be in my country incognito?"

"If we show up at our embassies, tongues will wag. I think it best that we accept your hospitality. Do you concur, *akh*?"

"I concur," the grand ayatollah replied in his practiced soft clerical voice.

"The presidential helicopter will take you to Camp David. I am sure you will enjoy the fresh air and accommodations while we prepare for this momentous occasion. I cannot tell you how grateful I am that you have taken this initiative."

"It is an idea whose time has come, Mr. President," said the king.

At three o'clock EST the following day, President Hollings Braithwaite of the United States, King Abdullah Said bin Saud of Saudi Arabia, and Grand Ayatollah Hussein Aliyy Bilal of Iran stood shoulder to shoulder in the Roosevelt room in the White House facing the glare of the media's lights. By previous agreement, the president made the announcement. Braithwaite considered the occasion important enough that he wore a handsome light grey suit, white shirt with presidential cufflinks, a subdued maroon tie, and spit polished black wingtip shoes. For most of his career, he had been a minor sartorial rebel, preferring turtle neck sweaters, sports jackets, and penny loafers even for official occasions. That had started a fairly persistent fashion trend since the president cut such a dashing figure with his movie-star good looks. On this occasion, he looked thoroughly presidential.

"My fellow Americans, friends and colleagues around the world," he began. "It is my pleasure to inform you that the king and the grand ayatollah and I have completed long and detailed negotiations regarding the achievement of peace in the Middle-East—peace in our time. These men, representing the united Muslim world, have unilaterally pledged their support to the orderly establishment of a Nation of Palestine and the recognition of the State of Israel. We unitedly pledge our good faith efforts to end hostilities in the Middle East and around the world. We will back away from war, and we call upon the nations of the world to give us their full support."

He smiled broadly and firmly shook each of the Muslim leaders' hands. By pre-arrangement, an orderly set of questions was accepted from selected media representatives in the attentive audience.

Elizabeth Rowan watched the news conference with amazement and a large dollop of doubt coupled with a tingle of hope—the same admixture of emotions shared by the one hundred twenty million other television viewers that afternoon.

"What hath God wrought?" she said out loud although she was sitting alone in her office in the Justice Building.

———————

While the American president spoke on television, his Secretary of Energy, Abraham Horowitz, signed the final documents to demand from foreign countries the immediate retrieval of the major portion of the more than nineteen tons of HEU shipped to fifty-one countries for use in their research reactors under the U.S. Atoms for Peace Program. To date less than 2,500 pounds of the highly enriched uranium had been retrieved from just twenty-two countries. The other thirty-nine recipient nations had not bothered to reply. Horowitz fretted over the simple math: it takes about 26 pounds of HEU to make an atomic bomb. The amount of HEU out of the control of the United States was enough to make 1,365 thermonuclear devices.

The Syrian government received one of Secretary Horowitz's formal letters. Foreign Minister Hafez al-Nassif showed the document to Prince Ahmed Wahhab ibn Saud. Together they read aloud the request that the HEU received by Syria could be returned to the United States for distribution to nations "with a proven record of nonproliferation to remove the danger from countries with the highest potential for diversion and the closest relationship with terrorists." The two men had a good laugh.

CHAPTER NINETEEN

NOVEMBER 11, 2009

The intercom speaker light flashed on in the attorney general's office. AG Rowan pushed the flashing red button.

"Yes, Abe, what is it?"

"Director Marques is requesting a face-to-face with you this morning."

"Must be important, some scandal brewing, I suspect."

"He is quite insistent, Madam Attorney General. I would say that it is most likely of some importance."

"So cancel the assistant AGs meeting…better, put it back for an hour. If it does involve something sensitive, we can start off on the right foot with the combined brains of the senior staff and avoid the near debacle surrounding the Hallweather case. See if the director can come right over. I hate to put off bad news."

"Maybe it will be something nice. Never can tell. It's best to think optimistically, Madam Attorney General. I always do."

"I know you do, Abe, and I admire you for it. But I am a realist—good news never comes by telephone."

Twenty minutes later, the director of the FBI was seated across from his nominal boss, Attorney General Elizabeth Rowan.

He knew she did not like small talk; so, he laid a heavy bound file on her desk and began. "I have four months of work here. We have been careful and ridiculously thorough about this."

She cocked an eyebrow.

"I'm getting there," he said. "We have a water-tight case for malfeasance, fraud, running a Ponzi scheme, criminal conspiracy, and participation in a continuing criminal enterprise against Clarence Maddox."

"Tell me you don't mean the Clarence Maddox who is the sitting vice-president of the United States."

Her face was grim.

"The same. I want you to listen to a tape made from a call to his office at the Naval Observatory residence. The rest you can peruse at your leisure. May I?"

"Sure. My day is ruined already."

Marques reached into his brief case and extracted a small hand held recording device and pressed 'play.'

The little machine produced a crystal clear recording:

"This is Lepke." "Look, Clarence; this is important, and besides, this is your secure line. You're safe. The feds—the FBI—were over at the distribution center this morning."

"Everything's covered and has been for the whole fifteen years we have been in business. So, what's the fuss today?"

"They made me get my attorney—you know, *our* attorney, if the truth were told—and meet with them and the assistant federal prosecutor and to produce all of our records. The federal prosecutor said point blank that I am a target for arrest, and they are preparing their case."

"But, I'm not involved, Phil—no paperwork or money leads to my door. I have to say that I think you are taking all of this too seriously."

"Yeah? And thanks for caring, my long-time friend. I made millions for you under the table while you were still the governor of Missouri. Maybe you don't recall, but it was me and my wife who set you up with the account in Vanuatu. And nobody—but nobody—can connect us; so, don't get self-defensive."

Rowan listened to the entire tape. She looked stunned.

"There's more. We got this Lepke guy to roll over for immunity, and Maddox's long-time heavy—the guy he called 'Tom' during the second call you heard—rolled even harder. We have more than fifteen years of records, cooked books, and CYA stuff kept by Lepke and Tom Falderman in case of a rainy day like this one. There's a ton of paper, but I selected some of the most incriminating for you to go over. It will be tough to keep a lid on this for much longer. I am convinced that the v.p. doesn't know anything yet."

"Take the day with me to go over this stuff, then, let's go see President Braithwaite."

"I blocked off the entire day. I'm yours. In addition, I have our techs and attorneys ready to come over and sit it to help. We have produced a short version for the president."

"Great, Leland. The Man doesn't like raw data all that much. Having a short block buster will be convincing and ought to save the lot of us all kinds of time. He can decide how to handle the political fallout and the press and all of that misery."

"How about getting Abe to get together a working lunch, and Ill get my crew."

"I'll make an appointment for you, your main investigator, and I to meet with the president at six tonight. I know he'll be in the Oval Office until at least then."

The justice and bureau officials worked efficiently at collating and highlighting the incriminating material. At five-fifteen, they were ready with a succinct damning summary and references to the even more incriminating raw data. The bureau's film people edited a shortened five minute version of a meeting between Lepke and Maddox and the night video of Tom Falderman picking up the documents from the garage floor of the Hickory Inn. They included a *res ipsa loquitor* [*Latin-the thing speaks for itself*] movie of Falderman's in depth confession including Special Agent Morrison's statement granting the accomplice immunity. Rowan had an arrest warrant including a search warrant prepared and a list of witnesses to be interviewed and deposed.

Rowan, Marques, and Terry Morrison, the lead investigator, were ushered into the Oval Office at precisely six p.m. The president bade them sit.

"What is this important matter, Madam Attorney General?"

"Director Marques and the bureau have completed a ten month investigation and a four month all-out effort to be certain of their case. They have produced a virtually incontestable case against Vice-President Clarence Maddox for racketeering, criminal conspiracy, fraud, and malfeasance in office. Here are the legal particulars."

She stood up and walked to the president's desk and handed him two sheets of Justice Department letter head paper.

"They will be filed tomorrow. We wanted you to have the opportunity to see the evidence before we do that."

The president's face blanched as he looked at the bullet points.

"I'm sure it is an open-shut-case, or you wouldn't be here. The ramifications of these charges can produce a constitutional crisis, I'm sure you know. I don't think I need to see the nitty-gritty details."

"With respect, Mr. President, the questions and controversies that will be stirred up will require that all of us have considerable knowledge of the evidence the bureau has collected. It is quite complete. If we have to go to court, every last detail will get aired while the man is still in office."

"What do you mean if?"

"Let's take an hour and go over the evidence including a taped telephone conversation and a couple of videos. They will lay out the crimes quite by themselves. We have prepared copies of the evidence including summaries for you."

She got up again and handed the frowning president a thin manila folder. He nodded his thanks. His face was grey. He looked stricken.

"May we play the tape first, sir?" Attorney General Rowan asked.

President Braithwaite waved with a defeated backhand gesture. As the lights dimmed in the projection room, he removed his Western sports jacket and rolled up the sleeves of his turtle neck sweater. The president was silent and listened intently even taking a few notes during the well orchestrated presentation over the next hour.

When Rowan indicated that the short version of the case of The United States v. Maddox was finished, he asked her, "Any suggestions about how to handle this legally? Politically? Every way?"

"That's a little out of my bailiwick, sir; but as the country's prosecutor and one with a memory of some U.S. history, I would advise a very early, very forthright, and very complete disclosure and a presidential recommendation—a firm statement, in fact—that the course of the law will be pursued without prejudice or favor."

"No chance that he could just resign for health reasons, and all of us could be spared the agony that is to come?"

"Mr. President, you did not even say such a thing. Director Marques, Special Agent Morrison, and I did not hear anything like that."

"Yes, yes. I know better. I have Nixon and Clinton to serve as the clear examples of what not to do. I wasn't serious about that suggestion. You know that. We can just forget that I said anything."

"About what, Mr. President?"

He gave her one of his award winning smiles and nodded his thanks.

"Back to my question. What do you suggest I do?"

"Let the federal agents do their duty, then confront him with the political reality. He can at least be spared the ignominy of impeachment by his own choice. If he cooperates, we can proceed with dispatch; and he can begin his sentence with as little public humiliation as possible. I will not recommend any form of leniency. The public would never permit it, and there is no excuse under the law."

"I have a refinement in your recommendation, Mrs. Rowan. Let's bring him to the Oval Office, arrest him here, and deal with the realities of law and politics in one fell swoop, to coin a phrase."

"Somehow, that all sounds simpler than I think it is going to be, Mr. President, but why not give it a try? Mr. Marques, can you assist with the arrest?"

"Sure. I'm just an old cop at heart. I haven't made a righteous collar on my own for thirty years. It would do my heart good."

"I'll get him."

The president pushed his secretary's signal.

"Yes, Mr. President?" Vilate Apflebaum's nasal voice sounded over the speaker phone.

"Please have Secretary O'Laughlin from State and Secretary Hewlet from Defense and the House and Senate majority and minority leaders brought here for a national emergency. Send whatever transportation is necessary. And, Vilate, get Vice-President Maddox on the line for me please."

In less than a minute, Clarence Maddox was on the line.

"Yes, Mr. President, I am at your service."

His voice and tone were slow and sonorous, a recurring source of minor irritation to the president who always thought it was a phony put-on for his constituency.

"Thank you, Mr. Vice-President. I need you to come to the Oval Office immediately. We have something of a situation on our hands."

"What is it, sir?"

"This is not one for the telephone, Clarence. And, please, don't let anyone know that you are coming here. I'll send a military vehicle for you."

"Oh, dear, Mr. President. It's that kind of thing. You can count on me. I know we have had our differences in the past and that you have seen fit to exclude me from national policy so far; but I will demonstrate to you that you have a valuable ally in me, Hollings, if I might be so familiar."

"I appreciate your willingness, Clarence. See you shortly. And, Clarence, come prepared for a long night."

"You bet, Mr. President. You can count on me."

The oval room rapidly filled with the senior government leaders. They sat with their backs to the bust of Churchill and anxiously waited for the President to tell them why they had been summoned. Only the vice-president was missing.

"Gentlemen and lady. I will make it clear to you why we are here in this extraordinary gathering very shortly. We are short one crucial member. Please be patient."

Ms. Apflebaum's familiar voice came over the speaker, "Mr. President, the vice-president is here. Do you want him to come in now?"

"Please, Vilate."

Maddox hurried in with none of his usual portly swagger. He was the very picture of earnestness.

"I hope I didn't cause any delay. I was in the shower when you called, had to make myself presentable."

"Good of you to come, Mr. Vice-President. We can get started. I think you know everyone here."

"I do."

He gave a puzzled look at the director of the FBI and the attorney general who seemed somehow out of place with this group of politicians.

"Good. Then we will have Director Marques start."

Marques stood up to his full lanky six feet five inches. He walked over to where the vice-president had ensconced himself, towering over the portly sweating African-American.

"Clarence Maddox," Marques said solemnly. "You are under arrest for malfeasance in office, fraud, wire fraud, racketeering, operation of a Ponzi scheme, criminal conspiracy, operation of an ongoing criminal enterprise, and theft of United States government property and property of the State of Missouri by deception. You have the right to remain silent. If you give up that right, anything you say can and will be used against you in a court of law. You have the right to have an attorney present at any time in the proceedings against you. If you cannot afford an attorney, one will be appointed for you at the People's expense. Do you understand these rights as I have recited them to you? Have you any questions regarding those rights?"

Vice-President Clarence Maddox was dumb-struck. He looked every bit as if he had been pole axed from behind. The usually eloquently profane and articulate politician and backroom political brawler was speechless. With the exception of the president, the attorney general, and the director of the FBI, everyone else in the room was too astonished and chagrined to utter a word. It was as if a prominent priest had dropped his pants and exposed himself in the middle of mass.

When the whirl of bewilderment began to clear, it first occurred to Maddox that this was some sort of extreme joke. Then, he decided that it was a pretext to set him up to force some political agenda he would have opposed with his last breath. He struggled for his composure. All eyes were on Director Marques, then on the president.

Maddox choked out, "What is the meaning of this outrage? If this is something...supposed to be...if this is a joke at my expense...I want, I mean, I demand to be let in on it. What *is* this?"

"I think we should hear from the attorney general, Clarence. It will be clear to you."

"Excuse me, Mr. President, but I am obliged by the law and by my office to require the arrested man to permit himself to be placed in handcuffs." Director Marques interjected and winced at the clumsy construction of his statement.

"Is that really necessary?" demanded the secretary of State. "I mean really. We all need an explanation, and we owe the vice-president his dignity."

"Mr. Secretary, I will let you be the judge of that after Attorney General Rowan explains the charges. In the meantime, Mr. Marques, feel free to do your duty," President Braithwaite said icily.

Marques offered his hand to Maddox who sullenly refused the help to rise from his chair. He swayed and almost toppled as he stood, and Marques had to steady him; so, the small gesture of defiance was muted. He was handcuffed with care to avoid the steel bracelets being applied too tightly.

President Braithwaite nodded to Elizabeth Rowan.

Attorney General Rowan said, "First of all I think everyone should sit down. This is going to take a while. And, gentlemen, please hold your questions until I finish. I think the summary of evidence we are about to present will be quite clear."

Maddox and Marques retook their chairs. Maddox's expressions and demeanors alternated among defiance, pathos, and intense concentration.

"What we have here," Rowan began, "is a litany of criminal conspiratorial activity and of overt criminal behavior unparalleled in government in recent years."

Maddox sputtered, "This is nuts. What are you talking about? Do you know who I am? Who do you think you are, you pipsqueak?"

"Be quiet, Clarence," the president said softly in a voice that pierced the blustering man to his marrow.

Maddox glowered but sat in stolid silence vigorously shaking his head as Mrs. Rowan began presenting her evidence. She purposefully presented the telephone tape and the videos first so that no one in the room could complain that there was any lack of clarity, certainty, or purpose on the part of the Department of Justice in this matter. The gathered governmental officials were wilted by the time she was done. Maddox—on the contrary—seemed to gather strength from somewhere. He looked proud, even steadily defiant. He refused to look down or to take his eyes away from the eyes of any one who looked his way.

When it was over, he shouted, "Stupid, trumped up lies. All lies. This is just another get-the-black-man stunt. Racism and a trumped up excuse for the moral and legal equivalence of a lynching as sure as if we were down there in Mississippi in the twenties."

His eyes were bulging. He was sweating, and the veins in his neck and forehead were bulging. His fury was written in etched lines on his scowling face. His blood pressure was skyrocketing.

"Let's reason together, Clarence," President Braithwaite said once the volcanic outburst waned.

"Like the Godfather said," Maddox snarled.

"As I said, there is some communication to be had between reasonable men."

"Ah, a deal. Now, I'm tuning in to your station."

"No deals, Mr. Maddox," Attorney General Rowan said with finality.

"But we can make this go down hard or easy," said the president.

"I'm all ears."

"Well, Clarence. You can suffer the prolonged misery and humiliation of an impeachment, a public trial, and a harsh sentence; or we can smooth the way for you and for us."

"Sounds like a deal to me," Maddox smiled.

His eyes remained hard and wild and did not enter into the smile.

"Only in a manner of speaking. The handwriting is on the wall, Clarence. You are going to be out of the vice-presidency, and you are going to prison. You can count on that. The 'deal', as you put it, is only that you can resign your office and retain your pension for a time; and you can plead guilty to all charges and spare yourself and your family and your people some of the pain of your public disgrace. At least, you can shorten your exposure. What do you say?"

"I say that this is a kangaroo court, a star chamber. You've got me found guilty before a trial; you've got the sentence all figured out. All that's left is to do the lynching. Is that about it?"

"Not at all. You will have due process like anyone else in the country. The charges are backed up by volumes of evidence. Resign the vice-presidency and plead guilty to the criminal charges, and the whole thing is over in a matter of a few days. You will be able to set your affairs in order. Maybe Justice or the state courts—wherever the jurisdiction finally lands—may take into account your cooperation."

"You will regret this Braithwaite. I know where all the Democratic skeletons are hidden and a good many Republican ones. I know who is having affairs, who is skimming from the government trough, and who has a felony or two to hide. I will bring down half the government before I'm through. This is personal, Hollings. You have treated me like a leper ever since we became running mates. But, I still have a lot of fight left in me. I'll get you."

"Mr. Maddox, I suggest that you keep silent as of this instant," Attorney General Rowan said with authority. "You just threatened the president of the United States, sir. That is a felony. You need to get a lawyer, and I can assure you that he or she will advise you not to speak again without advice. I will tell you this. The president just learned of this matter today. Your anger should be directed at me. I am responsible for the decisions made to date, and I will represent the government of the United States in all judicial proceedings and in all interaction with other judiciaries. Attacking the president is illogical, futile, and will only bring you problems and lose support for you from your historical allies."

She fixed her gaze on the black eyes of Maddox and left it there until he looked away.

"I...I'm sorry, Mr. President. I spoke in the heat of the moment. I am ruined. Please try to understand."

"Clarence. If you say no more, I will see to it that nothing comes of your outburst. I think it's time for the officers to escort you out. Follow Ms. Rowan's advice."

President Braithwaite looked to the entry hall to the Oval Office. Two FBI agents were standing patiently. The president looked over at the FBI director and nodded. Director Marques turned to the two special agents and beckoned them with a nod. They entered the office and assumed positions on each side of Maddox and led him away.

The president said, "A national catastrophe. Now what?"

It was obvious that he was speaking more to himself than to the others; so, they held their peace.

"All right, this meeting is over. We all need to get on with the work this will entail. Thank you for your efforts, I think."

Elizabeth gave the deeply concerned president a gentle and commiserating look, and he smiled wanly at her. Once again, she had handled an extraordinarily delicate situation with efficiency and due care. Once again, the president returned to his earliest impression that Elizabeth Rowan was a comer.

President Mohammed Yahya Farouk led the Egyptian delegation into the White House where they were met by an honor guard of White House Security. The four man delegation was escorted to the Oval Office. It was a grey, overhung day and snow clouds hovered close.

"Welcome, Mr. President," President Braithwaite said with enthusiasm.

It was the first lifting of the pall of gloom in his office since his vice-president had been ignominiously led out in shackles that morning. Seeing these men whom he considered his true friends, lightened his mood considerably.

"We hope that we find you well, Mr. President," President Farouk said.

"I have to tell you my friend; it has been a dismal day for the United States."

The Egyptians looked on raptly.

"You will be the first to get the news. It seems that our vice-president has been participating in a long history of serious criminal activity; and today, our law enforcement people arrested him. He will be impeached and convicted, and he will be found guilty in our criminal courts. The evidence against him is overwhelming. He does not have a leg to stand on."

"And what will be the effect on you politically, sir?"

"I wish I could say that it would not be all that bad since there is not a hint of the scandal touching me or my office. However, Vice-President Maddox did not take the criminal proceedings at all well. I'm afraid that he will work considerable mischief before his case is closed. I must tell you that it is a shame because our country was getting to be free of the divisiveness that plagued us when Bush was in power, and this will be a major setback."

"I, too, have profound regret that your administration should have such an evil descend upon it and for selfish motives. Personally, I hate to see my friend having difficulty, but my nation is so pleased with the new wind that blows from the White House, the new era of acceptance and toleration that you have created, that we will fear the worst."

"You needn't President Farouk. Nothing will change. The liberals are firmly in power, and we are every bit as strong in our allegiance to you this afternoon as we were this morning. You can still count on us. And I am most pleased at how well you have reigned in the freedom fighters. Real peace is within sight, and nothing must be allowed to get in the way of that."

"Indeed, Mr. President. The Egyptian, Iranian, and Arab world is as hopeful as you. We are in the process of settling our petty jealousies and envies. It seems that my own countrymen are the most difficult at present."

"In what way?"

"I am embarrassed to say, but many of our politicians feel that your country tilts towards Saudi Arabia as it once did towards Israel."

"You don't say. That seems a very hard construct to me. I am clearly surprised."

"It is sad, but true. My critics point to the glaring difference between our country's missile defenses and those of the Saudis. We have the same weaponry, including long range ICBMs, but they have quite a few more than we."

"Umm," President Braithwaite mused. "I thought that by granting even more military aid to you than we do to Israel, those concerns would be allayed."

"It may even seem a bit...how do you say? Silly. But to my countrymen, achieving at least parity with the Arabs is a crucial part of our history. Nothing makes an Egyptian bristle like being called an Arab, and nothing bores at our guts more than knowing that the Saudis and the Iraqis have oil riches as an almost capricious gift of Allah. Who can understand God's ways, eh?"

The thickset, hard-faced Egyptian leaned towards President Braithwaite, so that his body language conveyed the same intensity as his face.

"Who, indeed, my friend?" President Braithwaite commiserated, "I feel your pain, and I certainly do not want to be part of its cause. What can we do to assuage the feelings of your people?"

"The progressing détente between the Arabs and the Israelis has left us on the outside even though we were the first to recognize them. It is a small thing, but our national pride and our sense of being on a level playing ground with the Saudis could be accomplished, at least in the short term, by you providing us with the same level of security as the Saudis enjoy."

The president glanced over at his secretary of Defense who had been a quiet and thoughtful listener to this point.

Secretary Hewlett cleared his throat and received an affirmation by a presidential nod that it was his turn to speak. He had been in consultations with the Saudis and the Egyptians for a month, and there were no secrets about to be sprung on President Farouk.

"I believe we could even that gap between you and the Arabs, Mr. President. Certainly the government of Egypt has earned good favor from our government what with your long patience demonstrated with the Israelis and refusing to bow to pressure to break the fragile relationship. Perhaps our country has edged into an unrealized bias towards Saudi Arabia because of their position in the world's oil equation. I hope not, but I advise that we correct any perception of tilting away from our good friends."

"What do you suggest, Mr. Secretary?" The president asked.

"Well, for one thing, we could sell two LGM-118As to the Egyptian Defense Forces, Sir."

"Peacekeepers?"

"That was Reagan's name for them. They are no longer in production because of the huge cost. Congress—under wise liberal Democrat supervision—scrapped the project because the rail garrison system was unworkable and ghastly expensive. We produced somewhere over a hundred of them at a cost of $20 billion in 1998 dollars. They are literally just sitting around."

President Farouk's brow furrowed. He looked thoughtful and surprised that an idea had just come to him.

"I seem to recall that the Saudi to Egyptian differential is more like seven or eight such missiles. I hate to be indelicate, but I also recall that your government generously provided the Peacekeepers for an oil trade guarantee and without an exchange of money."

Farouk seemed genuinely hurt at having to bring up the subject of filthy lucre.

"My own information—checked recently as it turns out—is that the differential would only be four since two of the Saudi's Peacekeepers are inoperable for one reason or another. Would it be sufficient if we were to sell you those four at our cost, Mr. President?"

"I bow to your vaunted grasp of numbers, Mr. Secretary. However, my government would feel that the recent leaning towards the Arabs vis-à-vis the Egyptians would be narrowed beyond concern if you could grant them to us essentially gratis."

The Egyptian President's face, for all of its pugilistic toughness, was the picture of humble ingenuousness.

"How might that look to our conservative friends, to our business people, and to the Israelis, for that matter? We have domestic politics to consider just as you do, my friend," President Braithwaite said leaning towards his Egyptian counterpart expectantly.

"It could be done with a little craft, Mr. President," Farouk suggested. "We could easily construct a contract for you to sell us the missiles, and you accept deferred payment. We can promise you an opening in the cotton trade and a de facto tariff on our Egyptian cotton and electronics. That would translate into an increased number of U.S. jobs almost over night and a demonstrable lowering of the trade deficit for the United States versus Egypt. You can simply bury the payments for the missiles in one of your massive record archives that cost you more than a million dollars a day to maintain."

"What do you think, Mr. Secretary?" President Braithwaite asked Donlin Hewlett.

"It's workable and no more than we have done for the Israelis and what Clinton did for the Saudis just before the Iraqis attacked Kuwait. I think we should go ahead."

The president paused, deep in thought, for a moment.

He smiled and said, "President Farouk, I admire your single-minded concentration on what is best for your country. Since our paths are so intertwined, it is in our interest as well. We will make it happen. I cannot allow them to be fitted with nuclear warheads, Mr. Farouk; I'm sure you understand."

"Of course. The IAEA would never permit it, and we really don't want the responsibility for the nuclear weaponry. It is enough to have the rumor afloat and to have serious conventional explosives in place. We understand your concerns and will cooperate in every way."

Four LGM-118As were shipped to Cairo the following week under the most intense security and secrecy. Pakistani and Syrian scientists and technicians retrofitted Islamic nuclear MIRV warheads into the missile tubes over the next two weeks, and two of the missiles were flown to Tehran. Not even the pilots knew the WMD nature of the cargo they carried. Iranian, Saudi, and Egyptian relations were the best they had ever been starting that week.

Two days after the shipment of the ICBMs, Egyptian intelligence service operatives in Alexandria made a nighttime arrest of three Yemeni terrorists who had long been on the CIA's list of most wanted. The cooperation between the two intelligence services was the best in either service's memory. Fourteen days after the Egyptians received the missiles, the three Yemenis arrived in Guantanamo Bay, Cuba for incarceration looking considerably the worse for the wear. They had divulged a treasury of information for the CIA, and both services were insistent that torture was never involved.

CHAPTER TWENTY

NOVEMBER 24, 2009

The announcement by Attorney General Elizabeth Rowan on national television on November 1, that the sitting vice-president had been arrested and arraigned for malfeasance in office and white collar felonies had stunned the nation, and it was as if no other newsworthy event had occurred in the entire country for the past three quarters of a month. Maddox had been silent and absent from public view since, without even a token gesture of denial.

On the evening news for November 24, he made up for that lack of presence in spades. He agreed to an interview with Barbara Winchell—the diva of national interviewers—from his office. She had had to agree—albeit reluctantly—to give the vice-president the free reign of making a set of open ended, unedited remarks prior to her asking any questions.

Every television and radio outlet agreed enthusiastically to air the program. At the appointed prime-time hour, the HDTV cameras focused on Ms. Winchell with her blond good looks. Ms. Winchell had deliberately chosen to wear a subdued grey-green business suit to keep the focus of attention on the interviewee. She started the communication with the embattled vice-president.

Using agreed upon language, she said with her famous lisp and photogenic smile, "Thank you for agreeing to present your side of the controversy that swirls around you this month, Mr. Vice-President. It is a pleasure to be able to talk with you again, although, of course, I wish it were under more pleasant circumstances."

"Thank you, Barbara. Before I begin the interview, I wish to make a small change in the presentation."

He turned to his right and signaled to half a dozen men. They picked up their chairs and walked to the space behind Ms. Winchell and Vice-President Maddox and seated themselves. Ms. Winchell looked momentarily shocked and struggled to determine what she should say.

"Mr. Vice-President, this is a bit irregular, not what we agreed upon."

"I gather you don't like sudden negative surprises, don't think you deserve to be treated that way. Well, you can regard this small change as a token of what we African-Americans have suffered at the hands of the white establishment in this country all of these years. I am going to introduce these men to you, men who represent the black community that has rallied around me. These men, like the black communities they represent, are here to prevent a lynching."

"You don't trust me?" asked Ms. Winchell with obvious hurt.

"Neither you nor any of the white establishment. You are just a tool for my people tonight, like it or not."

Ms. Winchell frowned. She did not like it. She pursed her pink lipsticked full lips and considered her options.

Watching on the conference room television with her chief aids, Elizabeth Rowan said, "Make sure you get a dozen good copies of this program. It may well be evidence in our case against the man."

Maddox continued to speak as if Ms. Winchell were not there.

"I will introduce these men although many of them do not need any introduction, certainly in the African-American community. From my right to left we have the senior Senator from Vermont—the longest serving senator in Congress—Carl Aviard Washington. Next is the Reverend Hubert Humphrey Jones, pastor of the AME Church of Washington—the largest African American church in the country. To his left is a man you all know, the Reverend James J. Jackman. I need say nothing of the contribution this man has made to the betterment of all our citizens especially to his fellow oppressed African Americans. His record and his standing in the nation as the spiritual leader of the Diversity Coalition, and as an advisor to presidents and an ambassador of sanity to the world speak volumes for him. Finally, we have my good friend and advisor, Ibrahim Mohammed Dhul Fiqar. He speaks for the rising and unafraid black tide of Muslims in our country. He is, as his name indicates—the Sword of the Prophet."

"This is high-handed, Mr. Vice-President, after all we agreed upon," Ms. Winchell complained softly and politely, more worried that she had lost control of the interview than about anything Maddox might say.

She crossed and uncrossed her shapely legs and waggled her feet in the spike heeled shoes that matched her suit in an unconscious angry gesture that came across as nervousness. She caught herself and fought to appear unruffled and in control.

"Think I'm uppity, Missy? You ain't seen nothin' yet, as they say down South where many of my staunchest constituents live and suffer under whitey's thumb."

Knowing that she had lost control of the interview, Ms. Winchell sighed and gestured with her graceful long fingered right hand to Maddox to have his way.

Maddox continued, "I am the representative black man standing before the lynch mob. But—unlike the unfortunates who went before me—I will not go down quietly. I am falsely accused. I identify with my brothers languishing in prisons or being unjustly persecuted in the justice system on one level or another. I am accused, and I am the accuser. At the end of my remarks, I will present a folder to the members of the media that will give documentation and detail about the people I shall now accuse.

"In no particular order, the following whites flaunt the law and remain unpersecuted. I am innocent—a black sacrificial lamb—and I suffer."

Behind him, the four men murmured "Amen. Amen, brother. We shall overcome," in a soft chanting mantra.

"These crooks are but a few of the many possible examples. There's the fine Democratic Secretary of Transportation, Timothy Willows. He has a mistress, a black woman, who lives in his home state. He has convinced her that he was divorced from his overbearing wife and that it will take time for the adverse press of that divorce to die down before they can announce their own Las Vegas marriage. What she doesn't know is that the divorce has not been finalized. The senator from Idaho runs an illegal gambling syndicate. The governor of Mississippi, a Republican, takes kick-backs from the highway construction cartel in that state. The mayor of Chicago, also a Democrat, of course, accepted a bribe from the Garrison Group to push through a condemnation proceeding on that famous lakeside parcel; so, the Group can build yet another series of high rises. The president's mistress,—that MacIntosh woman—worked as a high-priced call girl in New York before becoming a stage actress."

Attorney General Rowan and her senior staffers listened intently with shaking heads as the vice-president skewered prominent politicians from the right and left indiscriminately. He talked non-stop for a full hour. Then he took a deep breath and abruptly stood up and strode out of the interview room flanked by his four confreres. Barbara Winchell simply shrugged her shoulders and bade the audience a good night. She knew that the latest ED drug ad that paid for that night of exciting television had to get in the last thirty second word.

Prince Ahmed ibn Wahhab Saud sat in the family quarters of the Riyadh Palace with King Abdullah Said ibn Saud and three hundred ranking princes and watched the broadcast on the BBC International with fascination as the American vice-president made a mighty effort to unravel the entire government of the country from city mayors to state governors to cabinet members and congressmen, even to include the harlot who lived outside of wedlock with the president. The king laughed and the princes followed suit. Soon, decorum was lost and bellies rolled and tears flowed down weathered Arab cheeks as the infection of the laughter spread.

Finally, the king got back his control and said, "Perhaps we will not have to defeat the fools at all; they will do it themselves."

No one in the hall disagreed, not even if their pandering manner before the king would have permitted it.

NOVEMBER 25, 2009

Clarence Maddox was hung over. He had a pounding bitemporal headache, a dry mouth, red and puffy eyes, and could not force his dehydrated brain to string thoughts together in a coordinated fashion. For some reason that he could not remember, he had agreed to meet with the congressional leadership when the speaker of the House called him at midnight the night before. He regretted his decision knowing that he was about to suffer yet another confrontation, and he was not up to it. It was seven o'clock in the morning, after all. Maddox did not think that any gentleman got up before ten.

His butler announced the delegation and quietly withdrew. Maddox had the somber faced delegation sit in the Naval Observatory vice-presidential residential conference room around a Honduran mahogany table so that every one could face every one else. He made them wait for half an hour while he fortified himself.

"Mr. Vice-President," the speaker said, "we are here to see if we can't put an end to the destruction that is happening to our government and to our country. Look around you. We have every one of the congressional leadership, Congress and Senate, Democrat and Republican. We could easily have had anyone we asked for from the executive. We seldom agree on anything with any unanimity, but we are all at heart ardent Americans and believers in our system."

"Get on with it and skip the sermon, Frank," Maddox grumped.

"I am doing just that, Mr. Vice-President. We saw your TV interview. Everybody saw it; and if they happened to be on Mars last night, the media has been replaying every juicy tidbit endlessly for their benefit. It's enough. Clarence, you have to go. You will just have to carry on your vendetta as a private citizen. We are here to tell you that either you resign right now with an announcement on the noon news, or we will impeach you on a fast track."

"It'll take you the better part of two years," Maddox said with a smirk.

"No it won't. Nobody slept last night. We are fully organized, and our count says that we have not just a plurality or a majority but a unanimous vote for impeachment in the House. Every senator is prepared to convict you. We have not run into a single dissenter. We can have the issue before a House committee tomorrow and into the main body in a week. We can hold a day's debate if you could even call it that and vote at the end of the day. The Senate can hear your arguments and those of any congressman or senator you can produce in a day. And nobody is going to let you filibuster. You will be out in less than two weeks, and not a dime of pension or the slightest support will be coming your way."

"The Black Caucus will support me, and you will have a huge race issue on your hands."

"No, sir, the Black Caucus sees you as the worst thing that has happened to their cause in a hundred years. They are solidly with us."

Maddox scanned the faces around the conference table. His eyes fixed on those of Carl Washington Aviard.

"*Et tu*, Carl?"

"Cooler and more practical heads have prevailed on me, Clarence. I have done some stupid things in my long life, but sitting behind you last night on that infernal program was the dumbest. You are a liability to our cause, the cause that our brothers, that the Reverend King, and thousands of others have fought for. I was weak last night, but in the clear light of day, I say; and will, if necessary, say to the country, that you have to go and right now."

Maddox for once hung his head.

The men and women around the conference table were silent, expectant.

"I need a deal from the attorney general. No jail time. I'll confess, name names, guide the courts to the pertinent documents, give up the bank accounts. But she has to guarantee that I don't go to jail."

"We have already spent half the night with the Justice Department and the FBI. Rowan is a lady of steel. She is not going to budge an iota. She doesn't have to because she has the best criminal case any of us have ever seen. There is no way to tempt her; she is the only person in Washington without political ambitions. She is as clean as they come; she can't be bribed or blackmailed. Elizabeth Leavitt Rowan is your worst nightmare; once she gets on a case she sees as righteous, she is unswervable. Forget it."

Maddox let out a long low sigh akin to a death rattle. His face contorted; and he fought for control, afraid he might break down in front of his peers, his enemies.

"So, this is what it comes down to, my *friends*," he hissed. "Full betrayal Washington style."

No one rebutted him. They waited. They seethed, but they waited.

An awkward period of two minutes without speech followed Maddox's last tortured utterance.

"I get to talk face to face with the heartless lady at Justice before I make my statement."

The delegation knew that they had won. They collectively held their breaths lest they somehow queer the follow through by Maddox.

"I'll arrange it," the speaker said.

"Good day, gentlemen and ladies. I'll likely not be seeing you again. I guess I should thank you for coming, but I can't bring myself to beg your forgiveness."

"Not necessary, Clarence. You are doing the right thing. That's enough."

He nodded to the others, and they all stood up to leave.

"We'll show ourselves out," said the speaker.

Maddox noted that no a single one of them offered his or her hand. His desolation was complete.

At ten sharp, Elizabeth Rowan arrived at the vice-presidential residence and was shown in to the Spartan office that every vice president had used for his real work for over a hundred years.

"I am prepared to work with you on your guilty plea and to make your next transition as swift and painless and as much out of the public eye as possible. I can offer you a choice of which prison you want to serve your sentence in, and I have considerable leeway about when you begin your sentence. I can have some leverage regarding how long the sentence will be; but the federal sentencing guidelines take up most of that, as you well know, Mr. Vice-President."

"No deal to keep me out of jail?"

"Not a chance, sir."

"I want to be able to handle my affairs, keep up a little business while I'm on the inside. That can't hurt anybody."

"Federal rules absolutely forbid any inmate from carrying on any business. And—just for your future reference—you will be allowed twelve thoroughly vetted visitors for the duration of your stay, no more. The books you read, the television you watch, the religious services you attend, your access to the public; and your use of the telephone are going to be subject to very strict rules. You are not going to be in control. The corrections officials will be. If you cooperate and settle in without getting a bad record and reputation while in prison, it will go easy. If not, you will find it a difficult time—it is not called 'doing hard time' for nothing.

"Break the rules in any serious way; and your time inside can increase; and your choice of where you do the time can be changed; and no one on the prosecution or defense side can alter that. I know something about prisons and about corrections officers. They don't care who you were. To them you will be just another con doing his time. Don't expect any favors or diminished status in prison based on who you once were."

"All right, short of suicide, I guess my only option is to give you full cooperation, that about it?"

"That's exactly it. Are you ready to get down to business?"

"All right. So, how about we talk about the proposed length of sentence first."

Rowan and Maddox were used to working with great efficiency when they had to. In thirty minutes they had agreed upon a ten year sentence with probable time inside about half of that followed by parole. He chose the Federal Penitentiary for Non-Violent Criminals in the Florence, Colorado complex. To Mrs. Rowan's surprise, Maddox elected to start his sentence a week after the formalities of arraignment and entering a guilty plea were over. He did not have the stomach for an appeal. He was an attorney and once had been a good one. He asked to represent himself. She took another half an hour to assist him in preparing for the speech announcing his resignation. At the end of the half hour, his composure suddenly broke; and he sobbed openly.

When he regained control, he requested, "Madam Attorney General, I just can't bring myself to make that appearance. Could you possibly get the president to make the announcement and to stick to the simple facts. I want to retain at least a shred of dignity."

"I'll do it. Now, you need to start getting your affairs in order."

Mrs. Rowan met with President Braithwaite at eleven fifteen. She brought him a suggested draft of his statement since the press conference was only forty-five minutes away. The government and the media had been spectacularly efficient that day.

The president sat in the Oval Office before the cameras to make the announcement. It was verbatim what the attorney general had written:

"My fellow Americans, it is my sad duty to inform you that, effective immediately, Vice-President Maddox resigns his office. I have his letter before me. He has been accused of and will plead guilty to felony charges related to his business activities over the past fifteen years. It will not be necessary to go through an impeachment process, and the judicial process will be very swift since Mr. Maddox has been fully cooperative. I wish to point out to you, my fellow Americans, that none of the criminal activities for which he is charged in any way compromised the integrity of the government. They are basically crimes of theft.

"I ask that you respect the privacy of this long-time servant of the people who has fallen afoul of our laws. No one is above the law, and justice will be swift and full. Allow your sympathy to extend to Mr. Maddox's wife and family. They are innocent and deserve elemental privacy. Thank you for your attention and good afternoon."

President Braithwaite stood up and walked out of the room. It had been stipulated before the broadcast that no questions would be taken.

———————

At two o'clock, Secretary of State O'Laughlin, Prince Khalid Abdurahman ibn Saud, Hafez al-Nassif, Sedegh Akbar Bazargan, and Jaffer Uday al-Samarrai, the foreign ministers of Saudi Arabia, Syria, Iran, and Iraq respectively, met with President Braithwaite in the Oval Office.

A butler served Egyptian coffee, Libyan sweet rolls, Moroccan candies, and sliced apples from Syria prepared by the assistant pastry chef with painstaking research and effort over the preceding four days. The gesture was not lost on the guests.

"I am delighted to meet with you. It is a significant occasion when such busy men as yourselves can come together to meet with your friends in the West," the president said after a polite interval.

"We bring good tidings, Mr. President," said Prince Khalid.

"All the more positive, sir. As you know, it has not been a stellar day around here." All six men smiled small rueful smiles.

"We are here to announce that our combined nations' intelligence and police services have arrested twelve ranking terrorists. Here are their names and dossiers," the prince said.

He handed a folder encased in a leather file holder made in the ancient leather works in Fez.

President Braithwaite rapidly perused the documents. The names of mid-level operatives from Abu Sayyaf, Hamas, Hezbollah, al Aksa Brigade, and al Qaeda were included. It was the single most significant coup in President Braithwaite's War on Terrorism. It was a full vindication of his policy of magnanimity towards the Arab world.

"This marks an important milestone in relations among our countries, gentlemen. How can we reciprocate?"

"We have offered a sincere olive branch from the whole of Islam. We ask that you officially call an end to the War on Terrorism and announce that the Bush administration's so-called Axis of Evil rhetoric be officially quashed."

"That's an easy one."

"We want your influence and in fact your pressure to get the Hindu entity to roll back its forces and embark on a peace effort with our brother nation, Pakistan. We ask you to force the Zionist Entity to dismantle the entirety of its obnoxious security fence. We, in turn, will do all in our power to prevent any incidents from over-zealous freedom fighters in those areas. We would like your administration to work with the godless ones in the PRC and in Russia to stop the persecution of the Xinjiang and Chechen Muslims. We will continue to root out extremists in our Muslim world, and we propose a joint effort with our intelligence services and yours to identify and expose injustices towards the world's Muslims wherever they may be found.

"Finally, we ask your indulgence in a sensitive matter. Three days ago your guided missile destroyer USS Decatur stopped a forty foot boat in the Gulf of Islam and allegedly seized two tons of hashish and arrested about a dozen men. This could cast a negative tilt of your already biased media against Islam because it suggests that al Qaeda has a link to criminal drug smugglers. We are trying our level best to present the Islamic world as peaceful and law abiding and the isolated actions of these alleged criminals undermines our progress. We would consider it a favor if your navy would release these men quietly into the hands of our authorities; so, we can deal with them out of the bright light of media scrutiny. Our reputation—even that of al Qaeda—is critical to the new world that we strive to achieve with your help."

"Mr. O'Laughlin, will you see to all of that? I want you to get with DCIA Davis and Daniel Ajami to work arm in arm with our friends. I will make it abundantly evident over the coming weeks that there is a new age in America, one that accords the great religion of Islam and the nations that flourish under its guidance full fellowship. The era of enmity is over."

O'Laughlin, Davis, and Ajami nodded.

"Thank you, Mr. President, we are greatly pleased to be witness to this era of enlightenment," Foreign Minister al-Nassif said, and his Muslim counterparts nodded their approval.

True to his word, the president and secretary of state conferred with Angelina Davis later that afternoon and approved the proposal by NSA Ajami to shift emphasis away from the Arab world and towards the concentration by the CIA on interdiction of the continuously growing Colombian cocaine trade, and upgraded efforts to undermine Indian control of Kashmir. The State Department was assigned to conduct missions to the Republic of China to hasten transfer of power to the PRC and to have Taiwan assume its correct place as an autonomous province on the same plan that worked so well in Hainan and Hong Kong. State was to threaten Israel if necessary to lower its inappropriate objections to a Palestinian State and to rid itself of the antiquarian vestiges of the anti-Muslim security apparatus. All charges against the alleged marijuana smugglers were dropped, and the dozen arrestees were turned over to Yemeni authorities. That event did not make the news.

The following day, Andrew McKnight, the press secretary, announced a Middle-East tour by the president to further what he described as the Braithwaite Doctrine. In his conferences and conversations with government officials, the president mounted an educational blitz to further what he came to regard as the seminal policy of his administration—the one that would ensure a lasting historical legacy.

CHAPTER TWENTY-ONE

NOVEMBER 29, 2009

Usama bin Laden lived a peaceful, secure, albeit somewhat mobile life in tribal controlled mountains of Pakistan. He was considered a valuable and honored guest so much so that he had been made a nonvoting member of the Pashtun tribal council. As such, he enjoyed considerable privilege under the second of the four laws of the Pashtunwali. This clause—called *melmastia*, or the rule of hospitality—expressly prohibits harming or disrespecting a recognized guest. That the al Qaeda leader regularly contributed considerable sums of money to the tribe probably did not hurt his standing.

bin Laden received a polite request from Prince Ahmed Wahhab ibn Saud transmitted through Pakistani Vice-President Walid Shamma Atallah who emphasized his own ties to the outlawed *Harkat ul-Mujahedeen Al-Almi* group affiliated with Usama. The verbal request was carried by Pakistani Air Force jets to Wana, capital city of South Waziristan Province, in wild Northwestern Pakistan on November 26th. The untamed province of Pakistan operates autonomously under tribal elder leadership with almost no interference or help from the Islamabad government. The province is huge, stretching from the Himalayas in the north to the deserts of Baluchistan in the south. The two thousand mile long border is a most forbidding place.

The chieftain of the Ahmedzai Wazir tribe personally drove to Usama's house in mountainous Kalotai village. The house was as featureless and windowless on the outside as any other in the extremely cautious region but was easily recognizable by the tall flag pole flying the red South Waziristan flag with the *Takbar* [*Akbar*] written on it. The writing on Usama's flag was in Arabic; the small flags of his neighbors were inscribed with Urdu characters. The chieftain never ceased to envy the sumptuous courtyard of Usama's house with the small ornate windows that only looked down into the opulence. The chieftain encountered the *wali* in the courtyard as he was disciplining his Hazara servant. Usama struck her across the face with the back of his hand knocking her backwards so that she almost fell. She kept her eyes resolutely down and did not react in the slightest to the hard blow.

bin Laden saw the chieftain and held his hands up in a gesture of minor despair.

"This Hazar—like all Shi'a women—does not know the sin of loud laughter. I cannot teach her."

The chieftain sighed in agreement, "Not like Pashtun women, not like decent women."

The prince's personal message—every syllable and word and emphasis memorized by the tribal elder—requested the esteemed leader of al Qaeda to hold all operations until further notice because of the delicacy and importance of negotiations with the Great Satan. Later in the day, bin Laden's lieutenant, Mahmoud Fasheh, the man charged with the responsibility for orchestrating operations in South East Asia, received his orders from the *wali* himself at bin Laden's comfortable home in the arid mountains. He flew the 225 miles northwest to the capital city of Islamabad on an air force jet then traveled first class on Air Pakistan to Mindanao, Philippines on the 27th. In the airport he met Dr. Benji Muhammad Gonzales, the leader of Abu Sayyaf.

"Greetings, brother," Fasheh said. "I have a message from the Great Leader directly to you."

"I am honored."

"First, I have a package for you."

He handed Gonzales his monthly allotment of funds for operations. Fasheh had done the same thing for the past thirty-seven months. The money originated from the Saudi charity organization, al-Haramain, and was as reliable as a Swiss clock.

"I have orders, brother. You are not to question the reasons. You are to cancel all operations immediately and until further notice. I am authorized to tell you that this is in relation to the peace proposals being negotiated between the Forces of God and the evil ones. Any questions?"

"I hate to do it. We have the Philippine army and their American Special Forces tied in knots. We have operations poised to go forward in a day to assist our finances. Can we get a stay on this, just for a week?"

"No. I have my orders, and you have yours. Allah's work—in His mysterious Way—requires this of us now. You are to be patient, and you are to order your followers to do the same. You will be held accountable for any mistakes."

"I will comply. I won't like it, brother; but I will obey. Send the Great Leader the greetings of his faithful servants in the Abu Sayyaf, please."

"I will do that. Good bye, Benji."

"Good bye, Mahmoud."

That evening, Gonzales met three of his assistants in the jungle near Mariveles.

He conveyed bin Laden's orders and gave his own with a threat, "You will not be involved in a single incident—even by accident—until I give the word. You will evaporate into the jungle until you are contacted. You will not survive if you disobey."

His assistants were offended by the order and the threat. They were sullen, but they nodded their acquiescence.

The following morning, the 11,000 ton Superferry 21 with 580 passengers and 168 crew members on its way out of the mouth of Manila Bay heading south to serve inter-island travel, was rocked by a series of tremendous explosions. The fuel tanks exploded turning the large ship in a huge crematorium. The Superferry sank with all hands in less than a minute. CNN received a recorded telephone message in which a spokesman for Abu Sayyaf claimed responsibility calling the action "another conspicuous victory for the Soldiers of Allah and the just cause of Islam."

CNN aired the story with the editorial comment that this was the first al Qaeda terrorist act since Hollis Braithwaite and the leaders of Saudi Arabia and Iran had pledged peace, and the president had made significant concessions to the Muslim nations. Every Philippine newspaper carried a headline with the general observation that this was the end of the uneasy détente with the terrorists and was no more than what the beleaguered Filipinos had expected. The *New York Times* headline read: "SOUTHERN PHILIPPINE FREEDOM FIGHTERS BREAK TRUCE". The front page story concentrated on the months of peace and speculated on what the Western nations had done to precipitate the attack which they labeled "an isolated incident, an aberration." *Al Jazeera* channel on Qatar TV described the incident as "a regrettable incident perpetrated by misguided zealots and not representative of the peace loving Muslims of the Philippine Islands."

The news anchor went on to communicate a video tape from Usama bin Laden that al Qaeda had ceased all hostile operations, and this incident was nothing more than an unauthorized action of a splinter group. The West should consider it as an aberrant event of no consequence and not disturb the blessed peace process now underway. The progressive magazine, the *Cornell Human Rights Watch*, *Al-Hayat*, the Arabic newspaper published in London, and *Ain-Al-Yaqeen* from the United States used almost identical language in their discussions of the incident.

Benji Muhammad Gonzales, M.D. ordered his personal bodyguard unit to kill every man and woman who had participated in the operation. The Abu Sayyad fighters were all dead before nightfall. Their heads were stuck on pikes in the center of the unit's camp and left there to rot and desiccate as a reminder of the fate of those who violate the discipline of the Islamic movement.

Gonzales walked to his clinic in Isabela town on Basilan Island. It was noon on a sweltering day. Dr. Gonzales was an archetypical middle-age Filipino— short, thin, brown, with strong wiry muscles—no different than a thousand other of the island's men. He was very fit and appeared ten years younger than his chronological age of fifty-one. It was part of his tradecraft to be part of the background, and he studiously cultivated the look. He had a natty thin black mustache and coal black hair that was as straight as young bamboo; it was covered with an old but functional Panama hat with a wide, sweat stained band that had once been several varieties of earth tone paisley. Except for the mustache, Gonzales was beardless without shaving. In fact—other than his mustache and scalp hair—he was all but hairless. He wore white tropical linen pants that he had picked up from the cleaners half an hour before, and already they were as limp and wrinkled as if he had rolled them into a ball before donning them. He had on his favorite white Jusi Barong with a Mandarin collar and decorations of Pechera embroidery.

As usual, indigent prospective patients were lined up in front of the run-down and none-too-clean store front clinic he ran between Abu Sayyaf operations. Everyone knew of his work for the al-Qaeda subordinate group and most of the island's people approved and actively shielded him from the investigators who poked around from time to time.

The Abu Sayyaf leader entered the sitting room where cooling fans made the area bearable. He walked directly into his office and sat at his desk to get through the logjam of paperwork that had accumulated since he was last there to perform his services as a physician. It seemed odd that none of the staff was present; but this being the Philippines, he was not overly surprised that the island's lassitude was in effect. He bent over his in-box and began to scribble clinical notes on the dozens of patient charts.

Without sound or the slightest warning, he felt a sudden jolting needle jab in the side of his neck. His medical training caused him briefly to admire the accuracy of the needle placement—Dr. Gonzales knew that his carotid artery had been penetrated. Before he could mount a reaction, he felt a warm sensation shoot up into his brain and then down into his chest. He stopped breathing instantly and toppled to the floor unable to move a muscle, but he was fully aware. He looked up into the hard face of his principle lieutenant who had served him faithfully in dozens of operations over twenty years. The face was impassive and patient.

In answer to the question Dr. Gonzales could not speak, the lieutenant said simply, "Curare."

It wasn't painful. He knew that he was not breathing, but he felt no physiological panic of suffocation, only the psychological distress of knowing that in about four minutes he would be dead. His heart began beating hard and fast as it was starved of oxygen, then it slowed precipitously to fifty per minute with powerful thrusting beats, then to thirty per minute with weak beats, then to ten per minute. Dr. Gonzales was no longer able to count. He was aware only of the impassive face of his murderer waiting and watching like a patient vulture. At five per minute darkness closed in; and after that, his rhythm was erratic. His brain was dead in the predicted four minutes post dosage, and his cardiac rhythm ceased altogether at the ten minute mark. The Abu Sayyaf assassin quietly turned and walked out of the back door of the clinic and had a smoke. He became invisible in the jungle before the nurses and the first patients entered the clinic to find the doctor dead

---

Six Yemeni Aulaqi tribal freedom fighters were released from their short imprisonment after repenting of their attempt to sell marijuana, according to Al Jazeera. The men vowed to keep the law and to respect the constitution of Yemen. They were freed with 1000 other men who repented. Judge Muhammad al-Bital announced that it was in accordance with God's will as part of a large amnesty during the holy month of Ramadan.

Raja Assi, age nineteen, was a Palestinian whose parents lived—if you could call their existence living—in a refuge camp in Nablus. He mounted the stairs of the Avia Hotel on Hahoresh Street in Yehud and walked empty handed all the way to the top floor, avoiding the crowded elevators. This was the first time he had ever been in a hotel. Raja wore standard issue Avia maintenance crew cover-alls given him by Palestinian brothers working for the hotel. He liked the cover-alls and intended to keep them since they were the best clothing he had ever worn. The young man was overly thin and none too healthy looking like almost all of the young men in his refugee camp. He had a pigeon chest, rotten teeth, and had lost one eye to skin leishmaniasis contracted from a sandfly vector in the camp. His skin was permanently scarred from the sores of the disease, and he had never fully recovered from the systemic effects that left him sickly and weak.

Raja followed the instructions from his Hezbollah superior and entered the first room on the opposite side of the stair entrance without knocking. He made his way through the empty hotel room into the bathroom. There he found a knotted rope dangling from the partly open trap door in the ceiling. Raja climbed up the rope and pulled himself into a crawl space and pulled the rope up after himself. Five meters into the crawl space he found a small heavy door that opened onto the roof.

It was dark. Raja was not permitted to use a flashlight, and he had to rely on the very precise instructions he had been given to find his way. It took him twenty minutes to move across thirty meters of roof to a large air-conditioning duct housing and to locate the weapon. Palestinians working at menial jobs in the hotel had painstakingly over weeks moved parts of the SAM-7 missile launcher and reassembled them on the roof. A blanket the exact same color of the roof surface had been placed over the launcher. Everyone in Raja's cell had done his or her job with precision. Raja reflected with pride on the great planning and efficiency of the operation; he was proud to be a freedom fighter for Allah. The thin young man fidgeted in his uncomfortable hiding place against the small unit on the roof. It was cold. and his old sweat suit and flip-flop sandals provided inadequate warmth.

He lamented that the Hezbollah leadership had not considered him worthy to be a holy martyr, but he was dimly aware that no martyrs had acted in the past several months. He took joy from his present assignment. It was dark, and he felt safe enough to heft his laser guided heat seeking SAM-7 launcher to his shoulder and to point it at the flight path the giant American 747 jet would take on its landing glide path just before first light that morning. He was not disturbed that he was hungry and weary. He was always hungry. The stress of the operation coupled with the young man's inherent lack of ease in new situations made him overly anxious and fatigued. Fortunately, the weapon did not require much work, and he could keep it steady; it weighed less than thirty-five pounds. He was ready.

Raja checked his digital watch again. It was time. He eased himself into position and aimed his weapon in the general direction of the flight path as he had practiced with his handler so many times. He heard the throaty rumble of the aircraft coming into Ben Gurion Airport from the north and immediately saw its running lights. It seemed so high and far away to Raja that he could not fathom how his missile could strike a blow at the Great Satan from such a distance. He marveled at the wonderful instrument Allah had created for him.

He pointed the launcher at a point two lengths in front of the aircraft so that his missile would not start out too far behind just as he had been taught. He satisfied himself of his aim in a few seconds and tripped the firing mechanism. The force of the rocket slammed him into the wall of his hiding place and almost rendered him unconscious. His nose was bleeding. He had to struggle to watch the missile follow unerringly towards the huge jet's hot exhaust. The leadership of Hezbollah had calculated the distance from Raja's hiding place to the plane to be less than four miles, well within the range of accuracy. It was unbearably exciting to watch the lethal little missile lock on to its target.

On board Delta Airlines flight 1080 from New York, the passengers were stirring in their seats preparatory to landing. The cockpit crew was in full activity mode to bring the aircraft into Ben Gurion International Airport twelve miles southeast of Tel Aviv both safely and comfortably. They were going to touch down exactly on time, and that would go well on their records. The cabin crew members had finished the last trash run and were buckled into their seats. Sharon Lesser, chief flight attendant, was about to start her memorized final landing spiel.

The pilot and co-pilot were tensely alert at this point in the flight both of them had made dozens of times. There were eighty thousand take-offs and landings a year from Sde Dov, Tel Aviv's overly busy local airport. Everything from business jets to hang gliders could be expected to enter unexpectedly into a jumbo jet's flight path. Military air traffic controllers had wanted for some time to close the air space to small craft traffic in the CTR [Controlled Technical Region] that encompassed the city and coastal region and a significant swath of the sea north of Tel Aviv to avoid the presumptive mid-air collision that had been avoided by acts of providence as much as by the work of the controllers. That had not been accomplished, and so everyone fretted every landing.

Sensors strategically located around the surface of the plane busily scanned the skies for five miles around looking for terrorist threats. One-tenth of the aircraft of the 6800 U.S. commercial jets were equipped with the costly security systems at an expense of $10 billion. Flight 1080 happened to be one of those aircraft protected by the newest and best system built by Raytheon. The entire protective system weighed less than three hundred pounds and fit in a pod the shape of a canoe on the belly of the airplane.

Captain Lorenzo Metelier fought his drowsiness and boredom from the long flight. He knew he needed to have all of his wits about him, but his brain felt sodden and slow. He always felt that way at the end of the long New York to Tel Aviv run. It was becoming more of an effort every flight, it seemed, to maintain his full attention for the critical landing phase. Metelier mused that he had reached the minimum retirement age and had enough years in; maybe it was time to hang it up. He was estranged from his wife, and she had custody of his two children. She was an ardent feminist who would not accept even child support from him. He could live a simple and uneventful life on his pension. The idea of retiring became more appealing every long-haul flight.

Co-pilot Reynolds was a thirty-two year old unmarried, cocky, former air force Top Gun jet fighter pilot. He chaffed at having to be second fiddle to a man who was past his prime and none too great a pilot at his best. Cliff was a ladies man—more accurately—a roué. The female flight attendants considered him something of a menace; but he never did anything out of line; and more than one of them succumbed to his charms. His plans at the end of the flight included an overnight date with Sharon Lesser. Reynolds was short but Alan Ladd handsome with wavy strawberry blond hair, chiseled features, and an expensive sun tan. He had his Delta uniforms custom made—a vain business expense—but a sure fire babe attracter. He had had his teeth done, and they were perfect—white, straight, and dazzling. He had green eyes that gleamed with sincerity, and a rich baritone voice that signaled to every woman he fancied that this was virility incarnate standing before her.

The security lights flashed on, and the radar warning receiver display demonstrated a hostile radar frequency which gave the approximate direction and type of threat—a SAM. Metelier look over at his co-pilot, Cliff Reynolds, who adjusted the sensor knobs.

"No malfunction, Lorenzo," Cliff reported. "The radar shows a bogie from the southeast. The security measures are being launched automatically."

The security equipment cost $750,000 per plane, and one fourth of the U.S. commercial aircraft fleet had been fitted with the costly devices that many in and out of government considered a waste of money. Delta had feared bankruptcy when the large airline company was forced to begin installing the systems. Flight 1080's system had been installed two weeks previously and never tested on that plane—too expensive.

Metelier pushed the intercom button, an automatic response from his years of endless training.

"Ladies and gentlemen, this is the captain. We are under attack by a missile; this is not a drill. Sit down, fasten your seat belts, and bend as far forward as possible. Put any articles you are using on the floor. Our security measures are in effect, and you will see flashes of light; you may hear some popping noises; and we will begin taking evasive measures now. It is going to be a bumpy ride."

While the passengers and the cabin crew gasped and hurried to comply, Metelier executed a rapid descent and a sharp turn to starboard. The cabin was filled with the noise of crashing crockery and utensils, books, and lap tops, and the wailing of the passengers' babies.

A laser beam flashed out of the security pod on the plane's belly and locked on to the SAM's optical system interfering with its electronic vision. The missile wobbled in its path but continued on its deadly course after a brief correction. Immediately, a flashing plume of heat generating material burst from the pod and was spread out well to the plane's left. The tissue paper thin metal disc fragments—coated with a chemical that ignited with contact to air—burst into thousands of tiny flames. The missile swerved to the left of the aircraft towards the dominant source of heat.

Metelier and Reynolds gritted their teeth and clenched their chair arms. It was going to be extremely close. The flight crew was white knuckled; and inside the passenger cabin, passengers began to scream as they saw the first red-hot bursts of light in the dark sky.

The missile locked onto the decoy heat source and headed for it with a vengeance. Metelier groaned.

"The decoys are too close to the plane. We're going to be hit."

Instinctively Reynolds put his head between his knees.

The missile's warhead was fully active. Contact with the heat source target would cause an explosion that would send lethal metal fragments out for a radius of four hundred yards. Even if the explosion were triggered by the decoys, the plane was going to take multiple serious shrapnel hits. Metelier gritted his teeth wondering whether his aircraft could make it down safely after those hits.

Suddenly, all of the tiny decoy fires and their awesome light show were extinguished. In the pitch black of the thin night sky, the SAM-7 missile's computer became confused. The missile passed through the area in the sky behind and above the plane where the decoys had only a second ago flashed a dazzling light and a white hot temperature. Now, there was no light; and the minus forty degree temperature of the stratosphere cooled the metallic bits to zero in that fragment of time. The missile did not explode. Its guidance system searched for a heat source and located the plane's exhaust. The deadly flying bomb made a long slow arc, reading the path of the airplane that was on its right and going down rapidly. The calculus built into its guidance system computed with minute exactness where the missile and the airplane would intersect and corrected for the new target location.

Metelier ordered Reynolds, "Make a hard turn to port and pull us up as much as this bird can do."

"But, Captain, that turns us into the missile's path. Did you mean to turn farther right?"

"Nope, we're going by the book. We don't have time to waste. Follow my orders."

"Aye, sir."

Reynolds had to use his considerable strength to hold the plane steady as it groaned and shuddered at the abrupt changes in directions. The passengers and cabin crew were heaving about and many of them were sick.

The missile had now reversed its direction and was speeding on its suicidal and homicidal mission towards the point where its electronic brain told it the hot exhaust would be.

Reynolds was sweating. Metelier watched the radar screen in fascinated horror as the blips of his airplane and that of the missile closed on each other. The aircraft responded at last and began to make a more acutely angled turn to the left. Two seconds later, the plane's altitude began to increase. The radar screen computed the time remaining to impact to be four seconds.

The missile's computer overrode its heat sensors in a last ditch effort to speed Allah's bullet into the heart of the Great Satan's device. Three seconds.

There was nothing more either pilot could do but to wait. Both of them closed their eyes, gritted their teeth and silently prayed for forgiveness for their past sins, a prudent thought as they were about to meet their Creator and Judge. Two seconds.

The missile hurtled past the rear of the airplane at a point one hundred feet below and two hundred feet to its right. One second. Zero seconds.

The badly confused missile was no longer able to adjust its trajectory because it did not have a lock on a source of heat. It careened out into the blackness on a wavering left-ward path until it ran out of fuel and fell harmlessly out of the sky and into the Mediterranean Sea.

CNN broke into its broadcast regarding the negotiations among politicians of all stripes over who would replace the disgraced Clarence Maddox as vice-president to announce that it had been confirmed by Israeli Defense Forces and FBI sources that an American jet liner had narrowly escaped disaster when it was attacked by a surface-to-air missile launched from Palestinian territory. No group had as yet claimed responsibility, and an investigation into the incident was continuing.

The following morning, *Al Hayat*, the London Arabic paper, the Cairo daily, *Akhbar al-Yawm*, the Saudi Arabian *Al-Madina*, the Tehran *Etelaat*, the Paris daily, *Libération*, and the German, *Der Spiegel*, all reported the incident expressing shock at the possible breach in the vaunted peace process. Each of them quoted press ministers of the Saudi government, the Iranian government, and the PLO who denied that any Muslim entity had launched the attack. The PLO spokesman stated emphatically that, "the peace-loving peoples who worship Allah and revere the Book of Books have taken the route of peace, turning the other cheek to the Zionist Entity's outlandish actions and accusations, and have ceased all actions of its freedom fighters until the Western powers can broker a peaceful solution. Our sources confirm that the Zionist Entity's Mossad service perpetrated this outrage. Your attention should be directed towards them and you should stop ignoring the evidence against them because of your Western bias."

The following day in Wisconsin, the *Madison Capital Times* headline quoted the PLO statement and gave equal credence to that theory versus the Muslim terrorist theory. In Beirut, *An Nahar* did not bother to consider the option that the Muslims might have been involved. *Etelaat* in Tehran, the *International Herald Tribune* in London, *Der Spiegel* in Germany, *Libération* in France, and the *San Francisco Chronicle* described the incident and raised the question of an accident as well as quoting the PLO.

New York Times political columnist, Irving Cohen, urged the leaders of the democracies to take a breath and wait before acting. It was crucial, he said, to investigate the core causes of this possible break in the self-imposed truce by the Islamists. The United States government was admonished to remain true to its liberal principles and to act in concert with the other Western governments and to have a United Nations resolution before considering any move that would be considered negative by the impoverished and beleaguered nations of the Middle-East.

King Abdullah and Grand Ayatollah Bilal made a conference call to President Braithwaite on the fully secured red phone network established among the principle nations of the peace process.

"Mr. President," King Abdullah said, "we are deeply grieved to learn of breaches in the peace process. We wish to assure you that the perpetrators were renegade Muslims who had no approval from any of our councils. We hope that you will regard these offenses as aberrations. We do freely admit that it is nonsense that the Zionist Entity had anything to do with the actions even though there is wide acceptance of that belief in the Muslim world."

"And, sir," broke in the grand ayatollah, "we wish to demonstrate to the world that we regret these occurrences and have taken serious steps to bring the criminals to justice. I will announce to the world as soon as we hang up that we have arrested the leader of Hezbollah and four of his top aides for the crimes, and we will deliver them and the evidence against them to you."

"The Saudi government has it on good authority that al Qaeda has executed the criminals who committed the monstrous attack on the Superferry in Manila harbor. We have the evidence, and it is being transmitted through channels to your CIA. We have been in contact with your new DCIA, Angelina Davis, so that she can rush the evidence to you. In addition, we have arrested the President of al-Haramain, the Saudi charity organization, for his complicity as the provider of funding for the Abu Sayyaf for this terrible crime. Our investigation reveals no other charity foundation officials to have been involved, and we are completely convinced that the Islamic freedom fighters of Abu Sayyaf were not involved except for those executed. As a gesture of supreme good will, al Qaeda has convinced the leader of Abu Sayyaf, Dr. Benji Muhammad Gonzales, and his three top aides, to surrender themselves to Philippine government officials. The surrender will be made through your marine contingent in Zamboanga."

"That is most gratifying, gentlemen…my friends," said the president. "We were, of course, shocked by the events, and will find it difficult to convince the arch conservative element in our country that you were not just acting true to form. Your call and the material actions you have taken can be brought before the media and will go a long way towards assuaging the doubts of the reactionaries in our government and abroad."

"What do you predict will be the effect on the peace process, Mr. President?" the grand ayatollah asked.

"And how can you demonstrate that you still believe that we are acting in all good faith?" the king asked.

"I have been mulling my response over as we have been talking, my friends. I believe it is time for a decisive token of our acceptance of the friendship among our nations. As soon as we have the criminals in our custody, I will announce an official end to the War on Terrorism. Henceforth, we will educate our citizens to the change that all of our nations will now regard the hunt for those who commit hate crimes, with the exception of those legitimate nationalists, to be a police and not a military effort. Will you agree to join with me in this change?"

"But, of course, Mr. President. We would be honored to follow your lead."

NOVEMBER 31, 2009

At seven o'clock pm, EDT, the president of the United States delivered an historical address on the four mainline channels and all of the cable and digital channels. He said:

"Ladies and gentlemen, my fellow countrymen, and indeed, my friends around the world, I am pleased to announce news that I am sure will be received well by all reasonable people. The criminals who broke the peaceful character of our rapidly and successfully progressing peace process were apprehended by the governments of the Muslim world and are now in our custody. They will be held in another country than the United States for further investigation and trial. This is a case of the exception proving the rule. We are working hand-in-glove with the governments of the Islamic nations and the swift arrest of these criminals is proof positive of the great change that has taken place.

"In response, I have ordered the following: First-we will process the release of the prisoners held since the Bush era in Guantanamo Bay, Cuba. They will be remanded into the custody of their respective countries for disposition. Second-we will cease from inconveniencing visitors from Middle-East and other heretofore suspect nations. Our countries are working out the process of lifting travel restrictions and the issuing of visas among us. Third-our government will no longer use the term Axis of Evil. We will begin swift rapprochement with all of the nations we have offended. Fourth-we will make the necessary apologies and concessions to our friends in France, Germany, and the United Nations. Fifth-the War on Terrorism is officially over. The entire world won that war as evidenced by the silenced guns, the veritable beating of swords into plowshares and spears into pruning hooks. In conjunction with Interpol and the police apparatuses of the family of nations we will treat all future negative events as criminal matters and will investigate, prosecute, and apply due judicial process to them.

"My friends, this is a new era. Let us join together and rejoice. I pledge that the United States will cease and desist from this time forward to interfere with the internal affairs of other nations. We are no longer the world's policeman. We are no longer regime changers or nation builders. However, we will offer the resources of our granaries and our charities to help our brothers and sisters in need around the world. I invite all of you within the range of my electronic communication to join with us in a new world order that honors peace, respect, and mutual cooperation.

"Good-night."

The president learned of the death of Dr. Benji Gonzales in the Philippines from DCIA Davis prior to his televised announcement. It was for the best since it saved the inevitable rehash of the news about Abu Sayyaf's violation of the de facto cease fire that would come about in a trial. The inaccuracy of his report to the world seemed to be of negligible importance.

The following morning, German Judge Rudolph Gabbler of the Hamburg High State Court, acting on the request of the Federal Criminal Office, ordered the immediate release of the eleven men and women being held in German prisons on charges of terrorist related activities for lack of evidence. German news media showed crowds flowing onto Berlin's *Kurfürstendamm Strassa* between *Uhlandstrassa* and *Adenauerplatz* with a view of the stores of Versace, Jil Sander, Gucci, and Sonia Rykiel. The young Germans were shouting and dancing in jubilation. Many of them carried placards reading, *"Danke, Gott für President Braithwaite"*.

The president of France went on national television to announce that the French government would immediately cancel the freeze on the assets of suspected terrorist organizations and their supporters and would release all political prisoners of Middle-East origin except for several particularly dangerous Israeli criminals taken in police actions. *Libération* printed as a lead story that the two terrorism suspects being held in French custody had repented to the satisfaction of the local Islamic leadership, and they were being released into the care and keeping of the Parisian mosques where they had been arrested.

With the stroke of a pen, the prisoners of Guantanamo Bay were released—all of them. The Defense Intelligence Agency's Joint Interagency Task Force for Counter-Terrorism and the Pentagon's Office of Special Operations and Low Intensity Conflict protested vociferously that all of these men were, "terrorists and will always be. It's as simple as that." It was to no avail.

Agents below DCIA Angelina Davis sent an unauthorized letter by courier to President Braithwaite that SatDef-10 intercepts recording Middle-East cell phone calls had revealed that traffic between the Iranian, Syrian, Egyptian, Saudi Arabian, and Libyan capitals and al Qaeda bases in northern Pakistan indicated that the peace was a ruse and that major plans for disastrous attacks on unnamed Western nations were well underway. The four agents who signed the letter were summarily fired.

That same afternoon Raja Assi returned to his home in the refugee camp in Nablus hungry and exhausted. He stepped inside the door of the shack, the place that his family was sad to call home, and was shot twice in the chest and once in the head at close range—the so-called Mozambique pattern. No suspects were ever identified.

Prince Ahmed Wahhab ibn Saud pulled down on the old-fashioned silk tasseled cord hanging near his desk. Almost immediately, Ali Abdullah Kaswari, his chief of security, and Said Mohammed Sisi, the Yemeni zealot who had served the cause so well for these many years, entered the room from behind a curtain.

"Brothers, our plans are succeeding beyond our best hopes. It is time for us to bring in Abdel Said Badr."

The veteran freedom fighters nodded and allowed the corners of their mouths to uplift slightly.

"I will get him, my prince," Kaswari said.

Prince ibn Said asked Kaswari for one more mission, "Send the Moroccans to Russia."

Kaswari and Sisi left immediately.

Abdel Said Badr was a missionary, a *tabligh*, trained in madrassas in Gaza and Kandahar. He received his formal *Qur'anic* education there and his more serious training in the Tarnak Farm training camp of al Qaeda, a 100 acre compound in the Afghanistan desert three miles south of the Kandahar airport. The *wali* actually lived there with one of his wives while Abdel was there, and it was the defining moment of his life to be able to see and hear the greatest man since The Prophet, may Allah bless him make his name revered. The main compound was encircled by a ten foot high crude mud-brick wall.

Inside were eighty small two-story mud structures; Abdel shared a room with fourteen other men, but whatever lack of privacy or inconveniences there might have been were nothing compared to the fact that Usama—the *wali*—lived in the very next house. Security there was integral with the terrain—miles of open sagebrush and sand desert that allowed a few lookouts to see any approaching threat from even afar off. Abdel was given the assignment to guard the drainage ditch near the wall on the airport side of the compound, a task he pursued with a singleness of purpose that both captured the attention of and amused the holy leader.

Abdel Said Badr's first assignment after leaving Tarnak Farm was to coordinate the traffic of heroin from Southern Afghanistan to the hideouts of Usama—the *wali*—in northwestern Pakistan. He was aided by the men of the Ahmedzai Wazir tribe and made fast friends with many of them, as much as the fiercely xenophobic and independent tribesmen would allow. Funds were drying up from the usual Saudi Arabian sources due to the difficulties imposed by the illegal invasion by the Americans. Badr was an integral part of the network that provided Usama bin Laden and his followers with $24,000,000 a year in heroin and enabled the Savior of Islam to continue his vital planning and work.

Afghanistan produces the vast majority of the world's illicit opium—the raw ingredient in heroin—and more than a million and a half Afghanis depend on opium farming, and therefore, on Usama bin Laden, for their livelihood. The entire industry that cycles around farmers, traffickers, and freedom fighters totals more than two and a third billion dollars a year. Usama, himself, had personally laid his large hand on Badr's shoulder and, in his soft voice, called the young missionary "one of God's best". It was the highlight of the pious twenty-one year old's life to date, and his faith was intensely enlivened. Abdel Said Badr, blessed by the man whom he considered to be next in importance after The Prophet, himself, may Allah's blessings be upon His Messenger, was the servant of the cause to the death.

Abdel was an energetic, vivacious person with a quick smile and an equally quick readiness to help. His full face beard was reddish brown and unruly like his hair. He looked more like a wild Scotsman in from the distant hills than a Muslim of fifteen generations heritage. He was modest and retiring by nature despite his outward friendliness. He never complained, and he tried to help his fellow freedom fighters to maintain their morale during the dark times. He was too small, had too high a voice, and his manners were too unsure and almost effeminate to be a leader, but his quick wit and native intelligence—coupled with his fanatical willingness to obey the leaders of his religion at every level—made him the ideal follower.

Prince ibn Saud had learned of the fine work done by Badr during a meeting with Usama and select members of the Council of the Leaders of Islam. The young man's intrepidity, cleverness, and dedication to the cause without being heedlessly reckless were all qualities the prince desired in a follower. It was an added bonus that Badr spoke passable English and could even pass for an Englishman with a little quality hair makeover. Without divulging too much, the prince asked Usama to allow Badr to leave his vital role in the Islamic freedom fighter-heroin linkage and to take a role as a missionary or *tabligh* for the religion and for al Qaeda. The Savior of Islam graciously accommodated his brother in arms, and Badr was transferred to Pemba, Tanzania.

Funding came from al Qaeda—originating in Saudi Arabia, Kuwait, and Pakistan. The money made a circuitous but efficient journey to the freedom fighters. A Liechtenstein based corporation called Galp International Trading Establishment—which is a wholly owned subsidiary of Portugal's principal oil Company—employs a law firm called Asat Trust. That trust is the financier of al-Qaeda through links to Al Taqwa—a group of financial entities all over the world controlled by the Muslim Brotherhood. The United States and United Nations designate Asat Trust as an al Qaeda financier.

With the security afforded by his al Qaeda funding, Abdel Said Badr moved freely about Tanzania speaking in a myriad of small mosques around the Zanzibar archipelago. He was sometimes invited by the older imams, but more often those men were suspicious of him and of the other *tabligh* who volunteered to spend forty days of each year preaching. Like the others, Badr wore traditional Pakistani clothing—a simple turban and tunic. He never once failed to perform his five daily *namaz* prayers. After speaking in the mosques to the faithful, Badr met with the young men, always in deep secrecy for fear of arrest by the police.

Wahhabi charities provided faxed textbooks extolling an extremist fundamentalism which Badr conveyed to the earnest young faithful by lamplight deep in the night. The endemic and recalcitrant poverty of East Africa produced a growing body of men who felt disenfranchised and were fertile soil for Badr's recruitment. He took pride in getting the desperate youngsters to join al Qaeda and made arrangements for them to be sent to schools in Pakistan and Afghanistan. By day the boys memorized and recited the *Qur'an*, and by night they learned by rote the Palestinian side of the Israeli/Palestinian conflict. They learned in secret to reject the gentle and pacifist brand of Islam—Sufism—which was popular in Zanzibar. They eventually learned to be killers; and for his part in that, Abdel Said Badr earned a name for himself among the men of the list (al Qaeda began in 1988 as the list of mujahedeen—one who wages jihad—fighting in Afghanistan. The name means "the list, or the base.")

Badr's young men went to Afghanistan and to Iraq to fight and to become martyrs, and East Africa contributed almost twenty-five percent of the foreign fighters there. Madrassas for girls also turned out zealots ready to become martyrs, but Abdel Said Badr had sworn to live a life of celibacy and had forsworn all contact with women. He was an intense young man.

During the afternoon of December first, Abdel assisted in an eye clinic in a tiny African island village, so small that neither the village nor the island had names. Abdel participated in the treatment of patients with old, stone hard cataracts. Only the area witch doctor had any medical knowledge, and he had long experience and was much sought after. While Abdel pinioned the arms of the patient, the witch doctor gave a well practiced one knuckle punch on the blind eyes. Frequently, the calcified lens of the eye would be dislodged, and the patient returned to possession of a distorted and shrunken vision of the world. Of course there were many failures, *masha'allah*. There was no time to treat women.

Ali Abdullah Kaswari and Said Mohammed Sisi hovered in the background of the clinic tent unnoticed and watched Badr at his work. They sat in the back row of the mosque while he gave a stirring, but non-inflammatory lesson on Islamic cleanliness. The young man passionately described how The Prophet, May God shine his mercy upon his Messenger, plucked his armpit and pubic hair and bathed twice a day. The two Council men remained in the shadows and followed Badr as he made his way in the dark to his rendezvous with prospective recruits in the secluded jungle. They observed with approval of the skillful way the young missionary cajoled and motivated the boys to join in the struggle. When the last man had faded back into the jungle, Kaswari and Sisi emerged from the dark and greeted Badr.

"*Masaa el-kheir, akh,* [Good evening, brother.] *Salam alekum.*"

Badr replied in kind, "*Wa alekum es salam.*"

"We come from the Leader of the Council and would have words with you."

"I am honored. Speak."

"The time has come for your great mission. Are you ready?"

"I have been from the beginning."

"Good. Forsake all you have here and come with us. We have a boat, and all arrangements are made for our journey back to the Leader."

Badr neither hesitated nor looked back.

The prince had a specific and critically important task for the earnest young practioner of the faith. The Leader of the Council of Leaders of Islam sent for six other *tablighs* over the next month.

It was very late on the last day of November. Everyone in the Senate-House committee wanted to be home and away from the endless wrangling. They all supposed that the country needed a vice-president, but they were openly wondering if perhaps the nation couldn't get along without one for the remainder of Braithwaite's first term. President Braithwaite could just appoint a person by his rights and responsibilities under the Constitution and submit the name for a vote by the House and Senate, but he and the entire government knew that that was impractical in the current hostile political environment.

He asked Congress to aid in the process after submitting a list of names that received an ice-cold response.

The Democratic majority proposed Governor Sam Pinkston of Vermont who was rejected as not only too liberal but because he was well known to have an inordinate amount of influence in the party apparatus. The moderate minority wing of the party was fearful of a tilt that far to the left. The House Republicans rejected a short list of eleven men and two women categorically. The Democrats knew this was payback for their intransigence in the nomination process for nearly a hundred federal judgeships during the Bush years. No liberal would permit the name of a conservative party member to be sent out to the floor. It was their turn to control the administration, and they meant to have the vice-presidency as a time-honored right. Braithwaite's people in the Senate and in the House mounted a brief—four day—filibuster of their respective appropriations bills to drive home their point: no conservatives or moderates need apply.

President Braithwaite despaired that the controversy would derail his programs.

In his frustration, he commented to his NSA Daniel Ajami, "Who cares who the vice-president is? The office has neither influence nor power. Yet, we are acting like the fate of the republic hangs on our getting the right person. I greatly fear that I will be a laughing stock of a president because I couldn't even get myself a vice-president, let alone the one I want."

"This'll pass, Mr. President," Ajami said. "You haven't a worry in the world about being any kind of laughing stock."

"Thank you, Daniel. I'm sure you're right, but it is galling nonetheless. Any ideas on how to hasten this process so we can get back to the work of governing the country?"

"There is a group called the Independent's Club…"

"I'm well aware of it, go on. I think you may be on to something."

"A few of them came to me and suggested that they could narrow the list to a confirmable two or three. They are consummate insiders and have never been known to leak to the press. They seem altogether sensible, and they know what party and what wing of the party is in power. Maybe we ought to give them a try."

"I'll run the idea past the congressional leaders. We have our working breakfast tomorrow morning. Thanks for always coming through, Daniel. I couldn't do without you."

"You flatter me, Mr. President, but thanks."

Between the grapefruit and the pancakes, President Braithwaite offered Ajami's suggestion to the leaders. They were lukewarm at first, but Cliff Assure pointed out that the country and certainly the administration could not afford to allow this Mexican stand-off to go on forever.

"We wouldn't necessarily be bound by their suggestion, though, Mr. President, would we?" the speaker of the House asked seriously.

"No, but it kind of gets us off the hook-like the base closing board might have done in Clinton's era. I like this organization. I think they are basically as apolitical as you can get in this town, and they are unfailingly practical and objective. I say, let's see if they can't break the log jam," the president suggested.

"I'll put it to our friends from the opposite side of the aisle. Frank, what would your people think about such a compromise?"

"It's as good as any suggestion so far," Senator Young of Ohio, the Minority Leader, said. "Let's give it a whirl."

"Anybody opposed?" The speaker asked and moved his eyes around the table in a polling look.

"Everybody's opposed," President Braithwaite said with a smile. "maybe that's the beauty of this scheme. Everybody's ox gets gored, and no one feels like anyone else gets an advantage. We can accept the choice and forget about him until election time."

The group grumped and griped over the problem and the proposed solution during coffee and sweet rolls, but in the end they all reluctantly agreed.

The Independents met in absolute secrecy for two weeks. Not a word went out to anyone despite promises and threats of punishment from the most powerful people in the country. On December 16, Lemuel Atherton, president of the Independents and head of the Home Security liaison with Canada and Mexico to finalize border security and NAFTA issues among the three countries, requested a joint meeting with the president, his cabinet, and the House and Senate leadership. The request was granted immediately.

At three thirty in the afternoon, the luminaries assembled in the cabinet room in the West Wing. President Braithwaite introduced the young man who was a virtual unknown and very nervous to be in the position of telling them who the next vice-president should be. But they had agreed to the arrangement; so, he moved directly ahead.

Lemuel Atherton started his argument, "Ladies and gentlemen, let me briefly tell you how we proceeded and what the final basis for our choice was. We obtained every name previously put before the joint committee from the House and Senate; we added the names of seven governors including ones from both parties; and we polled the major universities of the country. That gave us two hundred seven names. We vetted them through the FBI and reduced the number by close to half. There are a lot of hidden peccadillos out there."

The assemblage in the cabinet room chuckled.

"Then we evaluated the written statements by the remainder with the intention of weeding out the ones that were so extreme to the right or left that the opposite side of the aisle could never accept them. We considered age, but thought better of that. We looked at the advantages and disadvantages of race and gender and sexual preference. Last week we were down to eleven choices. We seemed as stuck as you were. Taking my prerogative as the chair, I directed our club members to go home and do nothing else until they had written one name on a sheet of paper. We had four names then. I told them that we would not leave the room that day and all of their agendae could wither on the vine until and unless we got one name to give you.

Finally, we got that name. I have here a discussion of all that went into the elimination process and the reasons for the suggestion we are making. We have taken the liberty of having him very thoroughly evaluated by the CIS and with FBI interviews. Basically, we think our man is harmless and respected, has no further political aspirations for himself, and is more than likely to accept a position of little stress or controversy for the remainder of his career. His age is such that he would probably be willing to step down for face saving health reasons at the end of this term and allow another person to take part in the bruising political campaign to come. He is a man that could be accepted by the public as president in the event—God forbid—of death or disability of President Braithwaite and would serve as a caretaker, much as did President Ford. If selected, he would be only the second black VP—a solid political coup for this president to so honor our fine African-American community once again—and there is considerable political cachet in that. Ladies and gentlemen, we offer as our suggestion for a new vice-president, Senator Carl Washington Aviard."

In the silence that followed his announcement, Atherton passed out the vinyl cover bound pages that he had promised. The front-sheet was marked TOP SECRET. No one opened his or her booklet. The members looked about questioningly, and then they began to discuss the choice. Braithwaite was pleased not only with the choice but to see that even the conservatives were not refusing to consider Aviard out of hand for all of his history of liberalism. A few other names were bandied about, but none seriously. Then the members began to thumb through their booklets with humming and haahing and whispering.

Cliff Assure was the first to speak aloud to the group. "I have to admit to a bias, but Senator Aviard is a great liberal in the truest sense of the term. He is a gentleman; he is African-American; and it wouldn't be a bad thing to have a bipartisan group nominate him and Congress put him in office. How about the non-liberals here? Can you live with him? I'd like to point out that if we can't agree to Aviard, then we are in for a long stretch without an agreement or a vice-president. The government will be mired in wrangling. Let's hear some opinions."

"I have a question," Senator Young said.

The liberals groaned quietly.

"Hang on," Senator Young said. "It's a nonpartisan kind of question. What about his health? He's eighty-three, as I recall. Is he up to this? Frankly put, is he going to survive two and a half years?"

Lemuel Atherton answered, "Senator Aviard is elderly, has high blood pressure controlled by medications, has had one minor heart attack and from time to time has mild congestive heart failure. We took that into consideration and decided that actuarially—at least—he should last out the first term."

President Braithwaite said, "He's acceptable to me. He is a fine old warhorse; he needs a rest; and I would like to think we could honor him in this way."

"Mr. President, said Secretary of State O'Laughlin, "I have polled the cabinet by cell phone while everyone was talking here, and we are in unanimous agreement to accept the nomination of Senator Aviard."

The president nodded and smiled carefully.

The other Democrats in the room either shrugged or nodded approvingly. All eyes turned to the Senate minority leader.

She screwed up her mouth in concentration before answering.

"I agree that he's harmless. That sways me. We Republicans have been treated shabbily by the Democrats in the judicial selection process, and it looks like we are headed in the same direction with our treatment of this president's nominees. Maybe this is a small breach in the walls that separate us, and we can actually be bipartisan on this choice. I would rather see a more middle-of-the-roader from the Democrat side; but Avaird's heart is in the right place; and I think he will be under the control of the president enough to hold down the most florid of his rhetoric. I'll go to work on my side of the aisle."

There was considerable grumbling throughout the Congressional and Senate office buildings for the next week while favorite choices of the rank and file were debated and eliminated and the pain borne with limited stoicism. Arms were twisted, threats made, and favors dispensed. At the end of the week, it was agreed to allow the matter to come to the floor of both houses. President Braithwaite made a formal nomination. A day of cursory debate followed; but the decision was already made; and everyone knew it. Only a simple majority of the House and Senate were required for the nomination to carry; but the House approved Aviard with only four negative votes and two abstentions; and the Senate had one negative vote. The senator from Vermont voted against him simply because she considered it undemocratic to have a vote by acclamation.

On December twenty-second Carl Washington Aviard was sworn in as vice-president in a dignified ceremony conducted by Justice Hidalgo of the Supreme Court on the steps of the Senate where Aviard had spent all of the good years of his life. He had agreed to abide by President Braithwaite's request that he accept a life of ceremonial obscurity. He was tired and happy not to have to strive. He was the perfect vice-president; everyone agreed; and everyone gave a sigh of relief that the ordeal was over.

CHAPTER TWENTY-TWO

DECEMBER, 2009

Abdelghani Labied, the leader, Mounir Binalshibh, Abderrazak el Motassadeq, Mohammed Jarrah, and Marwan Ramzi, the stalwarts of the Moroccan contingent of the Council flew by Aeroflot from Paris into Domodedovo International Airport. It was the middle of the night which contributed to their anonymity. They were escorted quickly to the regional air hangers where they boarded a 12 passenger Yak-40D salon charter flight to Ramenskoye Airport in Moscow Oblast, located 40 km southeast of Moscow and near the town of Ramenskoye/Zhukovsky where—by presidential decree—all charter and low-cost flights land. The greatest traffic occurs during the biennial MAKS Airshow and to accommodate the biennial Forum in Technologies in Machine Building. Despite its benign title, the forum is the largest arms bazaar in the world and operates by presidential decree from Vladimir Putin.

It was 0445 when the charter plane's doors opened. A blast of cold that only Russia—of all civilized nations—can offer, accosted the men from the desert; and they were ill prepared.

"Allah save us. We will freeze to death before we can accomplish His mission," Mounir complained.

He had barely made it to the tarmac before his beard began to develop a coat of frost.

"We will buy suitable foul weather gear as soon as the stores open in the morning, brother. Be patient until then," Abdelghani soothed.

A car was waiting, and its interior was as warm as a toaster oven, a blessed relief to the frozen men who were used to the heat of the Moroccan desert. They checked into the Na Teatralnoy Hotel under assumed names and slept like babies in the comfortable beds, a well-deserved rest after their arduous travel day.

They were scarcely prepared for the shear size of the bazaar and the immense crowds of serious arms sellers and purchasers already milling about in the grounds of the forum. More than 200 Russian companies were represented to present over 1000 military items. In all, over 20 companies and a host of free-lancers from 10 countries were attending the forum. Labied had a strict list from Prince ibn Saud which narrowed the decision making to a manageable degree. Despite the large crowds of dangerous looking people—and the distracting presence of several dozen Moscow prostitutes—the excellent organization of the bazaar made Labied and his men's searches and purchases quite efficient, a blessing from Allah on that frigid day.

The bazaar is a monopoly under the aegis of JSC Rosoboronexport, Russia's state weapons dealer—the sole state intermediary agency for Russia's exports/ imports of defense-related and dual use products, technologies, and services. It is charged with implementation of the policy of the State in the area of military-technical cooperation between Russia and foreign countries. The Rosoboronexport State Corporation is exclusively entitled to supply the international market the whole range of Russian armaments officially allowed for export, and the Russian government guarantees its support of Rosoboronexport in all export operations.

That has not always been an entirely smooth operation nor free of suspicion around the world during its fifty year history. On August 4, 2006, the Bush administration imposed sanctions on Rosoboronexport for supplying nuclear materials and equipment to Iran in violation of the United States Iran Nonproliferation Act of 2000. The Russian defense ministry countered and ignored Bush saying the move was nothing more than U.S. annoyance at arms sales to Venezuela and the insults to President Bush by Hugo Chavez at the U.N. Rosoboronexport was prohibited from doing business with the United States Federal Government from 2008 until 2010. The Bush administration then cancelled such sanctions in response to Russian support for a UN resolution concerning Iran's nuclear program. The new Braithwaite administration seemed to bend over backwards to accommodate Rosoboronexport and its expo in a broad gesture of friendship with its Russian ally. The new president went so far as to apologize to the Russian president in person for President Bush's boorishnes during his most recent state visit.

The Moroccans moved about from venue to venue rubbing shoulders with a remarkable assortment of thugs, arcane businessmen, generals, insurgents, gang bangers, clerics, and recognizable international Mafiosi. The five men recognized some of the more obvious seekers, but most were obscure. It was rather like a United Nations of Criminals—with an occasional legitimate arms dealer thrown into the mix for credibility. Represented on the grounds and in the building of the airport were: heads of the *Organizatsiya*—the Red Mafia—including Vyacheslav Petrovich Moglevich—"the Korean"—himself. There were Syrian Alawites, clerics from Iran, North Korean generals, Mexican drug lords from the Sinaloa, Beltrán Leyva—which was incorrectly believed to have been disbanded—and the Gulf, and Guadalajara Cartels.

As part of the intensive schooling required of his operatives by Prince ibn Saud, Labied recognized American gangs: Bloods, Crips, Outlaws, the Zerilli crime family—which is an American Mafia crime family based in Detroit, Michigan—the DeCavalcante crime family—which is considered to be one of the most active Italian-American crime families alongside the Five Families of New York. Such diverse criminal enterprises as the Chicago Outfit, Dixie mafia, and the Detroit Black Mafia Family roamed freely. Notorious motorcycle gangs as far reaching as the Canadian Grim Reapers, the Hangmen Motorcycle Club from Richmond, California, and the Pagans rubbed shoulders, maintaining an uneasy truce.

Because they were not part of the Faith or the Cause, Labied considered the lot of them to be little more than pirates, thugs, and miscreants—*Kaffirs* [unbelievers] all—The Moroccans spoke among themselves of the righteousness of their own cause in contradistinction to those criminals bent on gain while still recognizing the actual and potential benefit the posed for the Cause.

The faithful officers for the Cause recognized their co-religionists competing for the wares offered by the Russians: the Iraqi National Intelligence Service in the person of Saad al-Alusi—who, a week before Iraq's general election—was part of a cabal against whom were persisting allegations of vote buying and exorbitant handouts. The prince's Moroccans met Pakistan tribal lords, Hindu Kasmiri rebels, and Afghanistan military and Taliban—all their brothers in Islam—but misguided. They had to line up to haggle for purchases with the likes of the semi-psychotic MS-13, Aryan Brotherhood, Sicilian Cuntrera-Caruana family.

The attorney general of Mexico [Spanish: PGR—Logo Procuraduria General de la Republica] stated that LaFamilia Cartel was "exterminated" by mid-2011; but in the process, a splinter group—the Knights Templar Cartel—was formed. Labied had picked up that bit of intelligence in strategy meetings with gang bangers in Los Angeles when he had visited there to trade heroin for guns.

"The attorney general might think so, but those are La Familia," Labied observed to himself.

He also saw members of the Juarez, Los Zetas, and Tijuana Cartels who were all very much healthy and vigorous, contrary to reports in the news media. All of the gangs—by unwritten and unspoken concurrence—gave the other gangs a wide and peaceful berth.

There were more than a few officers of Iraq and Pakistan tribal lashkars [armies], and a defense minister from Zimbabwe. It was exhausting, and it soured all four men on their fellow religionists to say nothing of others who boasted of being freedom fighters but were not of the Faith and those who were nothing more than craven sociopathic criminals.

Prince ibn Saud's men started the three day task of obtaining their wish list of lethal toys—haggling, threatening, and pleading. They spent long hours during the evenings studying weapons specifications, condition of used ordinance, reliability of the sellers, and were exhausted and frustrated by the time their choices were made.

Part of the problem was that they were seeking huge numbers of armaments and ammunition and in absolute secrecy which bordered on an impossible combination. Finally, they put together $5B worth of material for shipment to the nations represented and controlled by members of the Council—men who could be relied upon to keep the secrets.

The Moroccans' final shipments from Russia included the Iskander ballistic missile system, a dozen used T-72 tanks, several hundred Grad rocket launchers, and RPGs for $2000 each, at which Labied was aghast.

He obtained contracts for an assorted weapons designed for a rapidly mobile force. There were: truck mounted rocket launchers, SAMS, M4 carbine grenade launcher with Beta C-Mag double Drum magazines—known in the trade as *Huevos de Toro* [Spanish for *Bull Testicles*]. They added crates of AK-104 assault rifles, "thermals"—heat seeking missiles—Colt AR-15 A3 Tactical Carbines, and Remington M24 NATO Sniper Rifles—enough for a dozen Muslim countries to defend themselves against the almost certain attacks by the Crusaders. Labied bought an assortment of night vision scopes—the best available—including PVS-22s, 27s, 7Ds, and 14s—all in mint condition and in quantities that would satisfy all of the Muslim nations and organizations committed to the cause.

The Moroccans found that small arms were plentiful and relatively cheap. Labied committed his resources to several hundred SACO Defense/Maremont Corporation M60E3 7.62x51mm belt fed machine guns, VK1-229B,/DD1-228 VK1-229B, and DD1-228 Colt M16A2 Rifles. Because the cost was so low, and his budget so forgiving, Labied ordered 5.56mm Colt machine guns with M203 40mm grenade launcher combination, Vector Arms Group Industries Vector Mini UZIs, 9mm submachine guns from an assortment of manufacturers, Heckler & Koch HKG3k 7.62 NATO (.308) push pin swing down registered receiver machine guns, Bazookas. That is the common name for a man-portable recoilless rocket antitank weapon—widely fielded by the US Army and usually referred to as "Stovepipes"—the poor man's artillery. Labied agreed on 500 M-106 mobile mortars which Armor fired 120 mm mortar rounds, and somehow made their way to Zhukovsky from 2nd Battalion, USA to Rosoboronexport.

Another coup for the cause came when Vladimir Novosky—the head of Rosoboronexport—offered them a weapon system so new and frightening that it had barely finished testing by the US. The Dragon Fire I system was designed to provide mobile fire support for expeditionary forces. The Muslim fighters were certainly going to meet that description. The Dragon Fire system utilized a 120mm rifled, recoiling, self-loading mortar that can fire rifled or smoothbore ammunition. The original system had a weight of 7,000 pounds, but the new version, Dragon Fire II weighed only 3,200 pounds, and was capable of deployment in towed, heliborne, and mounted versions.

This was ideal for the prince's plan to put rapidly mobile and highly adaptable forces into action to protect the Muslim homelands from any retaliations that could be mounted. Dragon Fire II was ridiculously expensive, but crucial; and the prince commanded a fortune for the effort larger than the defense departments of the majority of nations. Labied put aside his peasant's penuriousness and ordered 128 of them with an option for up to a thousand more if the need arose.

The prince had been adamant about explosives. Labied was not to haggle overmuch. The cause required huge amounts of high explosives, and Russia was the last remaining place to get the needed material in sufficient quantities. Labied met with Administrator Novosky in the airport's pavilion C a second time; and, after a prolonged discussion, the Rosoboronexport Company sold almost all of its currently available stocks and made such a huge profit that the company agreed to provide shipping in innocuous carriers and to hide the explosives as well as any world-class smuggler could. When the Muslim questioned the Russian about his boast regarding security, Novosky laughed.

"Where have you been? The Americans think you are all sweet and nice, and it would be a gross insult for them to look into any part of any ship bound for a Muslim country. Thank your Allah for His blessing. We will not be searched.

"*Thanks be to Allah, the all merciful and all wise...and to that nincompoop, Braithwaite fiddling in the Oval Office while the world is getting ready to burn,*" thought the Moroccan leader.

Tons of putty explosives including Semtex and C-4 [Czech Republic: Semtex-H (orange colored), Semtex 1A (red colored), NP10 (black colored)]; Russia: PVV-5A Plastic Explosive; Slovakia: CHEMEX (C4), TVAREX 4A, Danubit; Yugoslavia/Serbia: PP—01 (C4)] were invoiced to the large and growing shopping cart. The Moroccans received a discount because they purchased such a huge amount of the lethal high explosives.

Labied gave Novosky the list of names of the recipients and their exact addresses in the Muslim world and the time table for the arrival of the military ordinance. Being careful not to make an overt threat, Labied suggested that it would likely not go well for those involved should a failure occur or a leak to the Crusaders happen. Novosky knew better than to treat the flat statement as a joke. He nodded his understanding. It was no skin off his back to whom or to where the shipments went, and he was by his very nature closed-mouthed. He had just become a billionaire with the promise of more to come, and he was determined for his own greedy purposes to foster this major customer.

Labied, Mounir Binalshibh, Abderrazak el Motassadeq, Mohammed Jarrah, and Marwan Ramzi left Ramenskoye/Zhukovsky and flew—with four intermediate stops, plane changes, stopovers, and identity changes—to Damascus then to Tripoli, Lebanon to complete the final piece of business their mission required of them. A guide drove them to El-Mina [the harbor], a northern Mediterranean coastal city in Lebanon. El-Mina occupies the location of the ancient Phoenician city of Tripolis, and is Lebanon's second largest city. It is situated 5 km to the east of modern day Tripoli and serves as the harbor for the modern metropolis.

El-Mina is one of Lebanon's most demographically diverse cities and holds an assortment of different communities, of various sects, all of which are very territorial and reticent to admit strangers. Since the dress and dialects of strangers is distinctively different from those of the community where a stranger finds himself, he immediately becomes suspect. The religious diversity in Mina is—like everywhere else in Lebanon—of particular importance. In the country, and in the confines of Mina, populations are segregated on the basis of religious tradition. Tripoli is predominantly made up of Greek Orthodox Christians and Sunni Muslims, with small enclaves of Maronite Christians and Syriac Orthodox.

The city is also a regular destination for foreigners—most notably Mediterraneans—who tend to enjoy the diversity and richness of the city, and its unique atmosphere. Because of its coastal location, it is frequented by Mediterranean sailors, and many "Minawees"—as the locals call themselves—speak a Babel of different languages, including Greek, Italian, Spanish, French, and English. Almost all Lebanese speak or have some knowledge of Arabic and a smattering of Marathi, Hindi, and Mandarin among the shop keepers.

Among the city's advantages for Labied and his men are the facts that it teems with tourists: El-Mina is a regular destination for foreigners, most notably Mediterraneans. Because of its location, it always has its share of Mediterranean sailors from a host of countries. The manner of dress and speech is so broadly diverse almost nothing attracts the attention of the locals, most of whom are fishermen. This allowed the Moroccans to fit in without drawing attention. The second advantage is that it is a haven for pirates, gun smugglers, human traffickers, and drug dealers; so, the cruel faced Moroccan Arabs did not seem particularly out of place.

They were met by a hard looking Sunni Arab in a Range Rover and taken some distance up the coast until it became desolate and free of habitations. They were driven through winding dirt roads traversing sand dune hills to a nondescript restaurant that was part of a ramshackle assortment of ad hoc tin roof sheds. The driver did not speak, not even to ask their names. They, in turn, ventured nothing.

With a curt hand gesture to Labied and his men, the driver got out; and they remained in the vehicle. A few minutes later two powerful Arabs in black SWAT type outfits and brandishing AK-47s walked briskly up to the Range Rover.

"Get out," the more senior of the two ordered peremptorily.

The Moroccans alighted and were frisked very thoroughly. Had a man in a bar touched where the guard touched, Marwan Ramzi would have killed him on the spot and answered to Allah from the righteous act. With difficulty, he and the others endured the intrusions on their persons.

"Come," the guard ordered.

The five Moroccans and two guards marched into what looked like a decaying seafood restaurant and adjusted their eyes to the dimmer light of the interior. Abu Bakr Hussein watched them from his tall swivel chair seated behind a long cabinet with glass-front doors and shelves that would have been appropriate to a jewelry store but were filled to overflowing with guns that would have made the most easygoing NRA member wipe a tear of joy. Hussein wore an incongruous wife-beater shirt imprinted with a Budweiser logo and the company's marketing phrase: This Bud's For You. He was armed like Zapata—the Mexican bandito—with cross chest ammunition bandoleers from which hung six grenades and a Glock .40 on each side and huge ornate curved knife on the right hand side of his wide belt. Behind the heavily bearded and turbaned Sunni man was a series of heavy plate glass window/cabinet doors covered with fold-up heavy metal shutters. Hussein was in his early fifties and looked like a man who had spent long hours and days at sea or walking the desert. He was tanned and wrinkled, lean and wary.

"Welcome," he said, "sorry for the inconveniences, brothers. How may I be of service?

"*As-Salaamu-alaykum*, brother."

"*Wa alaikum assalaam*" [And upon you be peace.] said Hussein giving the appropriate reply. "May I offer you tea?"

"Please."

When the courtesies were over, Labied let Hussein—one of the Middle-East's largest gun dealers—know of his needs and of his ability to pay. Hussein knew better than to ask for what organization or for what purpose the materiel would be used. It was just business, and he did not care.

Labied eyed a particularly handsome weapon hanging across a gun rack formed by the horns of a deer. It was a Bushmaster Carbon 15, a matte-black semiautomatic rifle that looked like it should belong to a SWAT team. Labied liked the look.

He smiled, "Is the semiautomatic above your head for sale, brother?"

"Everything is for sale if we can agree on a price."

"Then, let us agree on a total price. We have need for quite a number of weapons."

He pulled a folded paper from the breast pocket of his utilitarian olive drab shirt.

With the obligatory ten minute period of haggling and intermittent sips of tea or sweet non-alcoholic juice, Hussein indicated that he had what the

Moroccans needed; and Labied agreed to the price. He had purposely appeared to be a hard bargainer, but desisted when he saw that Hussein was beginning to balk. In the end, Hussein guaranteed shipment to specified Muslim countries of thousands of automatic weapons in their original crates, Kevlar body armor and helmets, infantry boots, used uniforms without insignias, socks and underwear, communications equipment systems, sturdily built computers, field telephones, tons of grenades from assorted manufacturers and countries, and grenade launchers. Labied's negotiating produced a concession from Hussein to supply ten thousand machine pistols, again, from assorted manufacturers and countries at his cost. Hussein threw in the Bushmaster Carbon 15 semi-automatic gratis to Labied as a token of friendship and good business.

Hussein, Labied, Mounir, Abderrazak, Mohammed, and Marwan exchanged the obligatory three-cheek kiss when the business concluded.

Labied and Hussein said, at the same time, "*Shukran*" [thanks], and parted on excellent terms.

The Moroccans were driven to the Tripoli airport and once again took a long and circuitous set of flights back to Aleppo.

CHAPTER TWENTY-THREE

DECEMBER 31, 2009

Mordecai Narkiss, head of Mossad—and one of the least well known men in Israel outside those who needed to know—sat down to an informal lunch with four of his department chiefs. It was a light sweater day and comfortable enough to sit outside in the breezy patio of the restaurant. Narkiss never ate with subordinates unless he could do so outside where it was difficult to monitor his conversations and easy to find hostile listening devices. There were more than a dozen Mossad bodyguards around him, but the casual observer would not have been aware of any of them.

Narkiss—in particular—was a man whom a casual observer would pass over without remembering. He was of medium height, average build, medium weight, and had a bland, commonplace face with a rather pasty complexion. His hair was short, but not clipped short enough to mark him as military. He was clean shaven, wore no jewelry except for a simple gold wedding band, and customarily wore earth-tone collared pullover shirts with a pocket, casual cotton trousers, and utilitarian black lace shoes. He never wore any kind of a religious symbol. In habitus, facial appearance, and dress, Narkiss could not be pinned down as being of any particular ethnicity; his age was indeterminate; and his skin tones were just dark enough to render his race illusive. He was circumcised; but so were every Arab, Jewish, and nearly every other man in the region, even tourists. He had no tattoos or visible scars although his tough body was covered beneath his clothing with the results of stab wounds, gunshot scars, shrapnel marks, and lines of scars of cigarette burns—compliments of the associates in his line of work in Iran.

Not even his close associates knew where he lived, what he did when he was not at work—which was very seldom—if he had a wife or children or hobbies or friends. He never carried identification, credit cards, or bank checks—just cash.

Narkiss did not look tough. He looked like an accountant. He did not engage people in conversation whom he did not know. He never argued or appeared opinionated. He seldom made eye contact and seemed diffident and self-effacing. He never boasted, never discussed his profession, and generally was reticent even to amplify his cover as a purveyor of registered antiques. However, all of that was a sham—theater. Mordacai Narkiss was a PhD in military science, a black belt in Krav Maga, combat judo, and Tae Kwon Do; and he was a general in the commando forces of the Israeli Defense Forces. He had suffered more torture, killed more men face to face, and knew more secrets than almost any other man alive.

Neither Narkiss nor his men were religious Jews, and none of them paid attention to the ham finger rolls they were served. They all knew that it had to be something significant to bring them all together at such expense as a restaurant lunch from the already strained budget. Small talk flourished then dwindled away as the four lieutenants lost interest. They all wanted to know what was on the chief's mind.

He smiled, recognizing the suspense in their looks.

"I want to know your opinion about one of our agents and about the idea of risking his long time deep cover status. How many of you recognize the name of Ayoub Ibrahim Jadid?"

Two men flicked a finger up to indicate that they were aware of him.

"I'll tell you what we know," Narkiss said. "Job or Ayoub—as the Arabs prefer—is an Arab Christian, and officially a Syrian citizen. He was originally a citizen of the State of Israel and immigrated to Syria at our request; ostensibly, he was driven out by his intolerant orthodox neighbors in Haifa. He protested the destruction of a Palestinian friend's home—made the papers—and fell afoul of the law. He spent a few months in jail, then voluntarily left the country and was never heard of again here much to the dismay of his parents. He has not kept in contact with them. With a little help from us, Job received a superior education in Syria and Egypt, emerged as a computer engineer, and has a dual doctorate in computer business and networking administration. On his own, he got a job in the Syrian Ministry of Technology where he has maintained a sterling reputation and is considered a real comer in the Baath Party.

"Job has every credential to advance in the Arab world except for the one shortcoming: He is a Christian. Never mind that to all intents and purposes, he is a fervent Syrian. As a matter of fact, Job is about as much of a believing Christian as I am an Hasid.

"It has been put to him none too subtly that a conversion to Islam would further his career immeasurably."

The four men shifted uneasily in their chairs. For all their worldly appearance, each of them was uncomfortable with changing religions for career reasons even as a cover in their line of work. On a practical level it was dangerous. None of them said anything, but there was more studying of the bottoms of cups than was warranted by the beverage offerings.

Levi Harkabi asked Narkiss, "Who put it to him? Us or them?"

"Them."

"I feel a little better. You remember Eli Cohen."

Everybody remembered or knew about Eli Cohen. He was a national hero who lived as a Muslim businessman for two decades and provided the most valuable military information in the history of Israel, especially during the Six Day War. He paid with his life in 1967, and it took him days of torture to divulge all he knew to his former friends.

"I won't put sugar in your tea, Levi. This is as big an opportunity as Eli Cohen provided, and it is probably as dangerous. Whatever we do, I'll be responsible. That's why they pay me so much."

His subordinates smiled at him. Mossad pay was notoriously poor, and no one in the service did it for money.

"What are you going to do, have Job do?" asked Yahuda Grossman.

"Job is in a position with the Syrian government to be considered one of the country's leading experts in computer technology. Recently, he has had a couple of oblique questions about his interest in helping in the resistance against the intrusiveness of America. He talks with our man in Damascus who gets messages back and forth with me. These probings seem orchestrated but very subtle and tentative. He has the feeling that something big is afoot, but only a vague sense of it. I have come to trust his hunches.

"So, I have ordered him to make an oblique gesture. He is going to convert to Islam; and, in fact, has been studying under a mullah in the upscale Mazza district of Damascus. Any day now, he should have a formal but small and private ceremony. We'll see what comes of it. We will have to be patient."

JANUARY 12, 2010

Elizabeth Rowan agreed to be a figurehead patroness of the arts and made public appearances on behalf of the Saturday Morning at the National Theatre. She personally funded the Little Red Riding Hood classical theater puppet show that ran every Saturday in January and was co-chairperson of the fund drive for the Harriet Tubman and the Underground Railroad production that was to begin in February. Her limited extracurricular time was spent almost entirely at the theater on 1321 Pennsylvania Avenue.

In so doing, Elizabeth gained an additional expansion of her contact base and enjoyed the company of significant government officials' wives—women who became down to earth friends and co-workers in a worthy cause and introduced the attorney general into the closed society of the nation's capital. The contacts she engendered in her official capacity were becoming more personal and intimate; and she found herself in the enviable position of becoming a quiet private confidante of the most influential men and women in government, in foreign embassies, and with the nation's legal and judicial luminaries.

After Carl Washington Aviard was elevated to the vice-presidency and that traumatic period was over, a bipartisan delegation of Senate and House leaders, and the chief justice of the Supreme Court and the presiding judge of the Ninth Circuit requested a meeting with the attorney general to discuss a matter that they considered to be of vital importance. A measure of the regard they had for her came when the invitation tendered was for her to meet in the Georgetown home of the Senate majority leader. Her administrative assistant would not tell Elizabeth the purpose of the gathering, but he told her that the leaders insisted on casual dress because it was to be an informal meeting.

The butler admitted Mrs. Rowan and led her into the palatial dining room set with incongruously casual dinnerware. She had arrived at the appointed time and was, therefore, one of the earliest arrivals. Majority Leader Helen Clivener rose from her seat at the head of the table and walked briskly to Elizabeth and greeted her. Senator Clivener was about the same height, weight, and hair color as Elizabeth. Her smooth face was softer and more attractive; but absent the attorney general's scars and traumatic asymmetries, the two women could have been cousins. Helen had more refined features, a delicate nose which was the product of some careful work, and a softer figure. Elizabeth's form was more hard body and straight lines. The majority leader was wearing an expensive orange and white patterned cocktail dress that showed more than a little uplifted cleavage, quite a change from her modest business attire as seen by the media. She had once overtly championed a one payer national health insurance program that had been so poorly received that she had become a social recluse for three years. The new Helen—full of her old vivacity, wit, and intelligence—had come back like a Phoenix in the past year; and she radiated that charm in her greeting to the attorney general.

"Thanks for coming, Elizabeth. Is it all right if we dispense with titles and just use first names?"

She gave Elizabeth a full toothsome smile.

"It certainly is with me. It will take a little getting used to call you Helen."

"I get more done on an informal friend-to-friend basis. I think that's how the important things get done in this town. The glare of the limelight we all work under when we are in the public eye tends to produce a little more theater than substance, I'm afraid."

"I have avoided the public platform pretty much as a matter of policy my entire career, Helen, but I have had to admit on occasion that a little theater is necessary."

"Oh, speaking of that, how's your work with the National Theater coming?"

"Great. We could always use a little more money. We are still under funded for the Harriet Tubman production in February. I'm not all that good at fund raising, and somehow I let myself get roped into the responsibility for bringing in the money that makes or breaks the production. I am a worrier on the subject of money."

"I'll help. How much do you need?"

"At this point, somewhere in the neighborhood of a hundred thousand. We have most of what we need except for the final art and set work. The actors have been altogether generous or else we would have had to bow out long ago."

"I'll get you a check for fifty K myself, and before we go home this evening, I will arm twist the rest of these long time insiders into coming up with the rest. How's that?"

"Fantastic. It seems to me that they got the wrong woman to be in charge of the Saturday Theater program."

"Thanks, but no thanks. You are doing fine. Somebody would find my participation one more reason to attack me. I'll be content to contribute from arm's length. I've found that for politicians, at least, no good turn goes unpunished, as they say."

Elizabeth laughed.

"There's a lot to that. But, once in a while, we have to step up and do something anyway and just suck it up when the flack begins to fly."

The butler announced the arrival of the speaker of the House, the minority whip, vice-president Aviard, the chairman of the Senate Judiciary Committee, the counsel to the president, and the two eminent judges in rapid succession, all fashionably late.

In five minutes it was firmly established that the first-name-basis rule would be in force. The second rule was that there could be no talking shop during the meal; and the third rule was that from this moment forward, anyone who leaked information would be hanged, drawn, and quartered.

Elizabeth was not used to such wonderful food. She had eaten a lot of rubber chicken during her rise through the ranks, but she had never been able to afford such fare as this on her salary and invitations to gourmet dinners had been infrequent. They enjoyed cream of roasted garlic soup for starters, followed by the entrée of steak au Poivre, wild rice pilaf with chunks of Shitaki mushrooms, ginger asparagus, buttery pan rolls, and chocolate truffle mousse for dessert. Elizabeth declined the three courses of wine and endured a little razzing about being from Utah. She noted that Helen Clivener drank a couple of glasses too many, and the president's lawyer was a teetotaler like herself. It did not seem to matter much one way or the other which pleased Elizabeth because she was put off by the all-to-frequent references to her native state's peculiar liquor laws and the goody-two-shoes reputation of the state's dominant religion.

"Let's retire to the withdrawing room," Helen said and giggled.

"You're too fancy to have just a drawing room, Helen," Simon D. Morganthau, the minority whip said. "You are going to intimidate us."

"You don't get intimidated, Simon," Helen responded. "Anyhow, let's all get comfortable and look one another in the eye."

They assembled in a small but spectacularly appointed room. The ensemble of furniture stood on an antique Turkish Hereke carpet. Elizabeth sat on a luxuriously uncomfortable pre-1700 couch upholstered in hand made Genoa-velvet. She faced a handsome marble fireplace imported from a French chateau. The leaders sat on their English oak, Ming dynasty, and William and Mary lacquered armchairs around an Edward Colonna French art nouveau table. Helen reclined on an elbow rest Greek lounge. Elizabeth thought the eclectic character of the antique treasures was rather jangling to the nerves, but the room certainly outdid anything she had ever owned or would hope to own. The most jarring feature of the entire room was an odd painting by Marc Chagall of a woman holding a man on her shoulders while a purple angel flew over his head. There was no accounting for taste, she thought.

"I'll fall asleep if we don't get right to the point," Helen said. "We're here to explore an idea about achieving some sort of peace in the process of nominating and approving judicial nominations."

The minority whip said, "We have been flaying each other, tarnishing our reputations and that of the Congress, and have created an ongoing feud ever since Judge Bork was prevented from becoming a Supreme. We're not here to pick at old wounds; heaven knows that we have had too much of that over the years. Now, we are making the politics of judicial selection so venomous that good people are refusing to allow themselves to be considered. Nobody wants to be treated like a barbarian at the gates. We have got to compromise—a nice theory or platitude—but we have not been able to make the slightest headway in that direction. We are in a mean paralyzing stand-off. We are here to admit that Congress is unable to make the compromises necessary to allow this administration to have its reasonable choices and for the next administration to have its choices even if they are not of our own political persuasion. We need help, and we are humble enough to admit it."

"In here at least," Helen interjected.

There was a chuckle of acknowledgement of a truth spoken by the leaders.

"I'm listening," Elizabeth said. "What you are saying is common knowledge. What do you have in mind?"

"Look, we need an unbiased panel with some clout. We are willing to lobby our caucuses to go along with good choices, both from the legal competence point of view and from the political point of view. We need someone to head up a real committee to get us our judges. We have over two hundred empty seats and thousands of cases in back log."

"Mrs. Rowan…" the chief justice started to say.

"First names, sir," President Braithwaite's chief counsel prompted gently.

"Oh, yes. Elizabeth, we are impressed with your work at Justice. The whole government—and I dare say, the whole country—breathed easier at the way you handled the Hallweather case. Did you know that it is a case study at a number of law schools?"

"No, sir, I didn't. That's kind of frightening."

They all laughed.

"It's not my place to ask you; but I will tell you that we have done a quiet poll of the judiciary and the American Bar; and they are in agreement with the plan these congressional leaders are about to propose. We are all hoping that you will come aboard."

Helen said, "The proposal—in a nutshell—is that we formally appoint a committee to give us a practical list. We already have the American Bar competency ratings, but we need a group of respectable people who can tackle the political problem and present it to Congress in a persuasive way. It needs to be out of the hands of the administration and of the Congress in the initial phases, and the president's choices need to see the light of day with the sense of Congress being that these choices are the best we can do this go around. The members have to be convinced that, if they are the party not in executive power, they will get their chance next go-around.

"We want you to head the committee, Elizabeth. We want you to do your work without fanfare. Frankly, we can't think of anyone else with political savvy that doesn't also need the stroking of the public. We are all publicity addicts; it is our life's blood. We can't get elected without it; and for the past few years, most of our publicity has been bad when it comes to getting judges appointed," Speaker of the House, Frank Devlin said earnestly. "What do you say?"

Elizabeth thought a moment.

"It depends. Is this a blue ribbon panel to be put out before the voting public as a sop to their need to have the Congress do something about this unstoppable force meeting the immovable object? Also, who has the choice of how the committee is structured and who's on it? How willing are you to embrace the choices once you can agree on the process suggested by the committee, and how tightly can you control your followers?"

"All good questions. I, for one, would like to see you draft suggestions of how the selection process should work; and I have no problem with you finding the committee members. We can't abrogate our constitutional responsibility in this completely; so, we will have to give our approval at each of these two important first steps; and then we will still have to have the final say about whose name gets to the floor with the approval of the leadership. I don't foresee any particular problem with any of that with you in charge. If I am not misinformed, you are one of the few Washington insiders who isn't secretly running for president; and you have never espoused a partisan political stance. Is that accurate?" Helen said.

"It is. I sound like a pretty pale sort, but I assure you that I have opinions. I just don't have ambitions that require me to sell those ideas to the public at large or to establish a constituency. If you really want me to do this, I would like the powers you have offered. In return, I will assure you of as much objectivity as humans can attain in what has been demonstrated to be the ultimately painful subjective process. I want to work very much in the background. It suits me if your reference to me and my committee would be just something like the judiciary appointment research committee without naming names."

"Gentlemen? Ladies? Judges?" Helen asked and looked around the room at the powerful men and women who would be lending their significant influence to the project.

"Aye," said Frank Devlin. "Can we make it unanimous?"

It was. Elizabeth promised to have a working plan, and hopefully, a Committee selected, before the week was out. They toasted each other with champagne—with Elizabeth and Andy Purcell, the president's chief counsel, drinking ginger ale with equal ceremony.

———————

That same night in Aleppo, Prince ibn Saud met in deepest secrecy with his most important chosen operatives. He assigned each man and the one woman their specific tasks and introduced them to the technicians who would teach and train them in the refinements of the technology they would be employing and to the experts on trade-craft who would get them to their destinations safely and undetected when the time came. Only the prince knew when and where the final stroke would be made, and he was not ready to share with anyone.

The first task of the enlistees was for them to overcome their revulsion of all things American and to start to become more American than people who had lived in the accursed country for five generations. For the purposes of security, the trainees were divided into three cells to create some redundancy and to keep anyone from surmising the whole plan. For the foreseeable future these soldiers of Allah would belong body and soul to Prince Ahmed Wahhab ibn Saud.

CHAPTER TWENTY-FOUR

JANUARY 18, 2010

Attorney General Rowan held the last planning and defining session with the Judicial Nominations Committee. Her first task had been to select the members that would comprise the committee from planning to long term follow-up. That task required her to be on the phone for two full days and to secure the help of two appeals court judges, the president of the American Bar Association, the president of the American Trial Lawyers Association, and the district attorneys of Los Angeles, New York, and Dallas. Her work with prisons had brought her into contact with a large number of hard working and relatively unknown prosecutors and defense attorneys. She brought on board heads of the Senate judiciary committees of two previous administrations. She picked two of each. AG Rowan selected a forensic accountant, the deputy FBI director under the present administration and the previous one. She hired ten investigators from the private world, from big city police departments and district attorneys' offices.

Elizabeth presented the problem and the plan to four professors of political science—one each from Yale, Harvard, the University of Arizona, and the University of Kansas—with due care taken to make committee membership offers to liberals and conservatives on the far ends of the political spectrum and reserved two spots for well established moderates. She made the offer to two long time full tenured law school professors—one each from Stanford and Louisiana. Her final list for the committee as a whole included liberals and conservatives, Republicans and Democrats, Asians, African Americans,

Hispanics, and Caucasians, Christians, Jews, Hindus, and Muslims. The attorney general reserved the chairperson position for herself.

She spent an exhausting forty-eight hour period cajoling, persuading, promising, and threatening. In the end, she knew she had chosen well because no one refused the appointment to a committee that promised obscurity, no pay, long hours, and frustration. Every man and woman to whom she made the offer knew full well the extreme importance of the committee's task to the nation's future and was glad to be a part of it. The most important element in the persuasive process was Elizabeth Rowan herself. Not everyone liked her, but everyone trusted her.

The committee met four days later in a spartan utilitarian conference room on the 5th floor of the 9th Street FBI headquarters in the District—the Strategic Information Operations Division. They were provided with competent clerical help and with access to VICAP [Violent Crime Apprehension Program], CIS [Criminal Investigation Service], fifty states' and 750 major cities' criminal record data, and CIA satellite telephone surveillance data.

The committee members had been thinking about how they would proceed with the selection of judges if they were ever to be given the opportunity for most of their adult careers. They hammered out the criteria for selection in one long, rancorous,—but in the end—unanimous, day long session.

The foundation report of the committee was submitted to the bicameral Congressional, Judiciary, and Executive leaders who had directed its formation. The criteria included—on the legal side—requirements that the candidates be free of criminal and domestic violence convictions, known criminal or terrorist associations, or membership past or present in organizations listed on the FBI's ongoing list of subversive organizations. The candidates had to be American citizens greater than twenty-five years of age for some positions and thirty for others as specified. Each candidate had to be certified as competent—irrespective of political persuasion—by the American Bar and to have demonstrated a consistent record of judicial fairness.

It was easy to get all of the committee members to agree that the political questions that had bedeviled the previous selection process would be handled by a vote by all members of the committee with a simple majority carrying the vote for or against the candidate. They all knew that this vote would be the most difficult element of the selection process in practice.

The committee members insisted that a time frame for investigation and research on each candidate be established at three weeks and that the committee complete the vetting process with one additional week of debate and deliberation. Voting was to be accomplished in one day. The members agreed to submit to the application process for Top Secret clearance, and each member signed a bond declaring on pain of fine and imprisonment that they would not divulge to anyone the data and deliberations of the selection process or the names of the committee members.

Once the individual was selected, the name and pertinent data would be submitted simultaneously to the president, to the congressional leaders, and to the judicial system oversight selectees who would make the final decision. The name and relevant data were to be submitted on a form that included a caveat that the process of selection was as objective as could be achieved by well-intentioned Americans, and a veto for political gain by one side or the other would require the formation of an entirely new selection committee with no exceptions. Criminal sanctions were to be invoked in the case of any member of the committee divulging the Top Secret information or for accepting even the slightest favor from any person in or out of government that had any interest—however minor—in a particular judicial nomination.

On January 18, the report and proposals of the committee were submitted to the government leaders and were approved for action the following day, a measure of the concern shared by both parties and the entire judiciary over the heretofore flawed judicial selection process. On January 20, Elizabeth directed her committee to begin the formal process of evaluating the ten judgeship positions that had been vacant the longest or were listed as top priority by the congressional, executive branch, and judicial leaders.

President Braithwaite and British Prime Minister Chauncey Reed-Perkins released a joint communiqué timed for the evening news.

"Because of the unprecedented progress and cooperation between the leaders of the Islamic nations and the United States of America and the United Kingdom, we jointly announce that our Homeland Security alerts will be reduced to the green status—the first time in eight years. The most immediate consequence of this new status will be a discontinuation of the requirement that visitors from those countries must have a visitor's visa for travel in our countries for less than three months. Mandatory inspections of all aircraft from the Islamic countries will be discontinued. The costly practice of maintaining armed air marshal service on most flights will be studied, and we feel that we can reduce the inconvenience our security measures have been causing our people and our visitors.

"Productive meetings have been held and definite progress made in aviation safety with the help of our Muslim friends. We are pleased to announce that the list of those nations banned from British and American airspace will no longer include Albania, Sierra Leone, Equatorial Guinea, Gambia, Liberia, Tajikistan, Xinjiang, Chechnya, and the Democratic Republic of Congo's Central Air Express. U.S. Secretary of Transportation, Timothy Willows, and British Aviation Minister, Peter McTavish, along with those in charge of Homeland Security, will continue to monitor compliance with aviation safety standards."

That same evening in Tel Aviv, Mordecai Narkiss closeted with his chief deputies in his cramped Mossad office.

"I suppose you heard that the American big brothers and the Brits have lowered their security measures, especially those for aviation, drastically. I don't have to comment."

Levi Harkabi and Yahuda Grossman shook their heads.

"Job sent an encrypted message. He made a public conversion; there was a big celebration; and he had a visit from an enthusiast in that faith by the name of Saad Makram el-Deen, an Egyptian. Incidentally, with Job's signature, we were able to decrypt the message almost as fast as it came in. That could come in handy one day."

"el-Deen is an Egyptian terrorist on our long list of murderers approved by the PM for assassination," said Grossman flatly.

"The same. He spoke very carefully with Job, but when he finally got to the point—presuming that Job was a zealot like himself—he mentioned an organization of senior politicians and military officers and a shadowy leader whom no one knows about but is the real brains and brawn of the Islamic militant faction—an organization more wide-spread than al-Qaeda, better financed than the Saudis, and more ruthless than the 9-11 perpetrators. Now, all of this may be the same old excitable rhetoric from still another new jihadist organization; but Job—there on the ground—didn't think so. He is more inclined to think there is substance to the claims."

"Just what we need," said Harkabi.

"And just when the Mossad was becoming so sure that our friends and neighbors were leopards with changed spots," Grossman said sardonically.

That provoked a chorus of sardonic smiles.

"Job's message went on to tell us that he met with a scary looking killer-type, named Ali Abdullah Kaswari. Ever heard of him?"

The lieutenants' faces were blank.

"Me neither. Levi, get on it, will you?"

"As soon as we break up, Mordecai."

"Job was grilled for a couple of hours then driven home. The next day—Kaswari or whatever his real name is—called on Job during morning prayers, and he and Job were whisked away to meet a very shadowy guy that everyone called the prince. Job said the man was dressed like a Saudi and carried himself every bit like a prince. Every one they encountered treated the man with complete deference. This prince offered Job a position in his organization, gave him a set of chilling instructions that had more to do with maintaining secrecy than anything else, and asked him to think it over. He was cautioned that once in, there was no getting out. He was told rather cryptically that he would be lending his expertise to the most important movement in the history of Islam, and that the offer was especially significant because Job was only recently made a convert to the Holy Religion."

"And what did Job say?"

"He asked for a day to think it over. He is sure that he was tailed everywhere from the time he first met this Kaswari character until the next morning when he called the number the prince gave him on the disposable SIM technology cell phone he had been provided. In the meantime, he and I e-mailed in a peculiar code we worked out before he went to Syria. We use Arabic and speak in flowery messages about our mutual travels and drivel. He asked for and I gave him permission to join this group.

"When Job dialed the cell number he was given, the prince, himself, answered the cell phone and welcomed him. He gave Job a list of threats should he betray the organization and told our man with pride that no one had ever betrayed them. I got one more message telling me that he was going to Aleppo to the Council's operation center there. I haven't heard from him since and don't expect to unless there is something of real importance."

"I remember the stories about Eli Cohen. If I were a believer, I'd say a prayer for Job," said Yahuda ruefully. "If they suspect him, Job will have about as much chance as a pig farmer in Tehran."

"And I am afraid that the next prayer we say for Job will be the *Kaddish*," Levi added.

Ali Abdullah Kaswari, Said Mohammed Sisi, and Prince Ahmed Wahhab ibn Saud met with Nadim al-Kuwatly, the Syrian Council of Leaders of Islam deputy member with day-to-day responsibility for running the nuclear facility outside Aleppo. Al-Kuwatly was ideal for the job: He grew up in Hom; he was a nuclear physicist who received his doctorate in Cairo where he also joined *Gama'a al-Islamiyya*. He made his bones fighting with Dr. Ayman al-Zawahiri in Afghanistan—a man whom he considered to be the greatest surgeon in the world—a friend of God, who gave up his career for the righteous cause of Islamic resistance.

Dr. Al-Kuwatly did post graduate studies at Princeton University in the United States and astounded his Islamic colleagues with the incredibly free access he had to what they had considered top-secret American nuclear information. Before returning to his native Syria at the behest of the Council, al-Kuwatly engineered the theft and transfer of four hundred pounds of enriched uranium from the Numec Corporation in Apollo, Pennsylvania.

He had been assisted by the able Dr. Abrar A'mal Bint Farouk who had the complete trust of the Council and was still director of research at Numec and by Dr. Habeeba Junah, the Algerian nuclear physicist. Both of these women ranked high on the list of most trusted operatives in the organization by the prince despite their gender, and al-Kuwatly's association with them enhanced his already high standing. His standing was further enhanced by his hand-in-glove working relationship with A.Q. Khan—the hero of Pakistan's nuclear program and one of the forefathers of the Islamic bomb.

Hafiz al-Nassif, Foreign Minister of Syria, representing the Baath Party, attended the meeting as well. He spoke first.

"Greetings and congratulations, my brothers. You have done remarkable work in a short time. So far as I can tell, the secrecy has been complete. I take it from your summons, Prince ibn Saud, that you have a favorable report for us."

"I do. Dr. al-Kuwatly will summarize."

Al-Kuwatly stood up and cleared his throat. He had an uneven, annoying, squeaky voice; but everyone ignored this flaw. He turned on his lap-top and found the correct power-point program and supplemented his report with graphs, lists of materiel, and descriptions of the weapons now fully ready and those nearly so.

"Brothers, we are ready for the great day. We have fully operational thermonuclear devices and the intercontinental ballistic missiles and insulated ships to deliver them. We can provide more than a dozen limited devices—what the Western infidels so colorfully describe as 'dirty bombs.' We can ramp up production to allow us to produce more than twenty nuclear war heads a year capable of being dropped on target from airplanes. Of course, we would have to have control of the air in order to utilize these weapons. That is out of my area of expertise."

Al-Nassif asked, "I hate to ask such a question because it could well reflect poorly on all of the Islamic nations as well as the Council. But, do we have the necessary computer technology, communications facilities around the world, and maintenance people, equipment, and materials to sustain our effort once we send the first spear of God to pierce Great Satan?"

"I will answer that, Foreign Minister," said Prince ibn-Saud quietly.

No one made a sound as they waited for the Leader to inform them definitively.

"We have all of the things you mentioned and more. Perhaps our weakest link is in the area of computer technology, but we are rapidly catching up with the West. Just this morning, we were able to secure the services of the foremost expert in computer science in Syria to bring us up to speed, as the Americans say."

"Who is this expert? Do I know him," Nassif asked.

"Quite possible, Foreign Minister. His name is Ayoub Ibrahim Jadid. Until yesterday, he was employed by the Syrian government in the Ministry of Technology."

"Is he related to the martyr, Haji Muhammad Jadid?"

"His uncle."

"And the global satellite link-ups?"

"We have them. We were able to do atmospheric experiments with the Americans three years ago, and one of our people was an astronaut on that mission. He is a communications expert and; while his colleagues slept, he was able to provide us a link-up to several of their satellite systems. The Chinese—who will do anything for money—provided us with a direct link to their third satellite in orbit. We are fully operational."

"I am impressed. And when will the great day be? I am dying of curiosity. The feeling among our people is much as it must have been for The Prophet, may Allah shower his blessings on his Messenger, as he waited for the Message to unfold in the Cave on Mount Hira."

"*Akh*, security requires that only those who need to know can have access to that information. I am sure you understand," the prince said solicitously. "But, I can tell you that we are physically ready. The political timing requires patience. Allah wills that we wait for yet a short time."

"I will exercise patience, and I will continue our charade with the West. You will be amused to know that a speaker's bureau has been organized and is now touring Europe and the United States educating the public on the peaceful nature of Islam and of those of us who live in the shadow of The Prophet, may Allah the All-Powerful, continue to bless his Messenger."

————————

Vice-president Aviard listened to the eleven o'clock news and learned of the changes in aviation security for the first time. He muttered that he was so far out of the loop but did not really mind since he was growing accustomed to the quiet and relative stress free life he was leading as the vice-president. Avaird looked every bit the octogenarian he was that night. He once was a handsome young buck—he thought to himself—light enough to pass. A little hair straightener and the judicious use of a little makeup and he had passed for a short period in the immaturity and insecurity of his youth. He was brought to his senses by his father, a humble sharecropper with the wisdom of the Africans in his bones and the courage of Nate Turner in his heart. From the time he was twenty until the present moment, George Washington Aviard was a black man—now we have to be African-Americans, he thought to himself derisively—a Democrat, a liberal, and at least early on a civil rights firebrand.

A second wise man had reigned him in, made him train his good mind in a law school—Howard University Law School—and moved him into politics. Aviard, now an old man, had been a mayor, governor, congressman, and for more than fifty years, a Senator. His career was now capped by his being elevated to the vice-presidency. He was known for his persistence, his loyalty to the liberal cause, his civility with his opponents; and as a result, he had developed no real enemies. His knowledge of Senate protocol and history was second to no one. He had five blue serge suits, ten white shirts, and five red power ties. He did not wear sports or casual clothing, even in the privacy of his own home. Even now, at bedtime, he had not yet removed his signature clothing. His suits were always freshly cleaned and his shirts heavily starched and changed twice a day. He was a gentleman of the old school.

The vice-president had wrinkles on his wrinkles. His jowly face seemed to have a dour expression that was the fault of the laxity of age rather than an unpleasant disposition. He had small, half hooded, black eyes. He had worn his fine black hair long and combed straight back since he was fifteen and had had no reason to change the style now that he was a national figure. He rather liked his careworn face, but he was disappointed in the flabbiness of his physique that seemed to worsen by the day. He meant to get to the gym; he had had good intentions for sixty-five years but never quite got around to it. He yawned and noticed that he was fighting to stay awake.

His wife, Mildred, roused from her sleep beside him on the couch.

"Carl, shall I have the stewards bring you something before bed. I'm done in and will go to my room. Have them get me up at eight; I have a dentist appointment, and then I am off to see Sofronia and the children in Denver for the weekend."

"I'll tell them. I have some heartburn; so, I don't think I'll have anything. You?"

"No, I'm still one my diet—my fiftieth diet. When will I ever stop torturing myself?"

"Never. It's the American way."

They both laughed and gave each other an affectionate hug, all that remained of the passion they once had known in the early years of their marriage, sixty-two years ago.

The vice-president got his Filipino navy steward on the intercom and conveyed his wife's request for a wake-up.

"I am not feeling well, Manuel. Don't let anyone disturb me unless it's a national emergency. I need a good long rest. I'll get myself up and get my meals tomorrow. I'm declaring myself a short vacation."

Manuel said, "Good night, Mr. vice-president. I'm off for the weekend; so, I'll see you on Monday."

The portly vice-president showered and shaved and got into his best navy blue silk pajamas embossed with the insignia of his office. He belched and found it unpleasant, a pain moving beneath his breast bone and into the left side of his neck. He took a glass of water, and the pain went away. It was nothing; a little heart burn. Vice-President Aviard made a mental note to remind Manuel to cut down on the fat in his diet. That should get rid of this latest rash of heart-burn symptoms.

He threw back the brocade bedspread and lay down on the Sea Island cotton sheets embroidered with the crest of the Naval Observatory which were as cool and smooth as the best silk, and they were made in the U.S. His back was hurting; so, he stretched out his legs and interlaced his fingers across his chest. His discomfort died away. He closed his eyes and slipped into a peaceful dreamless sleep.

At two ten in the morning, a clot broke loose from his severely narrowed left coronary artery and lodged at the junction of the two main branches—the transverse and the descending—cutting off all blood flow to large portions of both the right and left ventricles. This triggered a sudden cardiac arrhythmia and an instantaneous cessation of the heart's pumping. Vice-President Carl Washington Aviard did not feel a thing. He was dead before the portions of the heart cut off from their blood supply could turn pale.

It was not until the third day, January 20th, that his body was discovered.

CHAPTER TWENTY-FIVE

JANUARY 30, 2010

President Braithwaite had been shocked and disturbed when he first heard of Aviard's passing. That feeling gave way to an unthinking anger at the old man for failing him, for generating another possible presidential crisis just when he thought all of that peripheral nonsense was behind him. The president became more rational on the subject as the days wore on, but still harbored a real concern about the choice of yet another vice-president. He was determined to avoid the acrimony that had surrounded Maddox's departure, and Aviard's selection. That determination led Braithwaite to a firm conclusion: the selection of the next vice-president was going to be swift, and he was going to be his most firm and presidential this time around. That motivated him to make a firm choice unencumbered by lists and committees.

The Thursday morning cabinet meeting agenda contained only one item—"Nomination of a new vice-president". That got the attention of the full cabinet, and every cabinet secretary was present and before time. President Braithwaite walked into the West Wing cabinet room at the stroke of eight. The cabinet members stood in respect, and The Man—as his cabinet secretaries and the Secret Service called him—took his seat in the middle of the long table that faced the door. He was a taller man than anyone else in the room and sat even taller in the president's chair that was three inches further off the floor and had a back that stood eight inches above the cabinet members' chair backs. The clerk gave the call to order.

"Ladies and gentlemen. I am sure that you remember the all too recent efforts to seat Vice-President Aviard. I will not have a long, drawn-out process, a divisive forum for every liberal and conservative who wants to advance his or her career or the political position of their party's favorite son or daughter. Therefore, I am going to make one nomination and send that name to the Senate."

He paused for effect. Their anticipation showed on the cabinet member's faces rather like children at Christmas.

"I propose the name of Attorney General Elizabeth Leavitt Rowan for nomination as the next vice-president."

The cabinet mulled over the choice. No one was particularly dismayed, but no one could muster any great enthusiasm.

"Well, let's hear your thoughts."

Secretary of State O'Laughlin—assuming his traditional right as the first cabinet member to offer his opinion—said, "Mr. President, it's a bit sudden. I must admit that her name would not have come to the top of the short list very quickly. Not mine, anyway. I certainly remember the Aviard process and am convinced we can do without a repeat of that. We were lucky to be able to get him in, and that choice proved to be perfect. I have to say that I am angry with Carl for leaving us too soon."

"Hear, hear."

"But, as I sit here and think about it, Mrs. Rowan seems like another ideal compromise choice. She is smart and free of scandal. She has a firm governmental background and is nobody's pushover. She is a team player as we all know from the Hallweather affair, the Maddox legal entanglements, and from her work on the Judicial Selection Committee. She can run a corporation and a governmental agency. She looks presentable, kind of motherly—a firm authoritarian mother. I have thought of little else this week and came up without a reasonable alternative to her. I'll support you, sir."

The secretaries of Defense, Homeland Security, Commerce, Labor, Transportation and Education all discussed other candidates and presented the political downside of Mrs. Rowan, a relative unknown outside the Beltway and from Utah—a state already lost to the conservatives. The secretary of Housing and Urban Development noted that whatever her politics were, the attorney general was well short of being a card carrying liberal. They argued among themselves and after half an hour nullified their several positions. One by one they came around and supported the president's choice.

Timothy Willows, Secretary of Transportation, said, "I certainly have no good alternatives. It is always said that the last great test in the selection of a vice-president should be whether or not he—or in this case, she—is of presidential timber since she will sit a heart beat away from the Office. I have mulled that over, and I guess she would be able to rise to the occasion, who knows?"

"Hardly a ringing endorsement from you, Timothy, or anyone else; but I have heard no real objections, either. Thank you, ladies and gentlemen. I will make the announcement for the national networks for their news coverage tonight. I am going to make it very brief. Please get on the phones and e-mails immediately after the broadcast and start selling her to the Congress. Get them to bring her name to the floor as soon as it is possible. Gerald Ford was named to replace Spiro T. Who in a matter of days, and Nixon's v-p problem disappeared from the scene. I very much want that to happen for this administration."

"Sir?" spoke up Secretary Willows.

"Yes, Mr. Secretary?"

"A detail. Have you talked to attorney general Rowan yet?"

"Not yet, but I will today. I would appreciate it if all of you would keep mum until I make the announcement."

There were unanimous nods of assent by the cabinet members.

President Braithwaite stood up, and his cabinet dutifully stood also as he walked briskly out of the cabinet room and down the hall to the Oval Office.

Ali Abdullah Kaswari and Said Mohammed Sisi gave final instructions to the six men and women chosen for the final coup against Satan and his minions. Abdel Said Badr glowed with pride from the knowledge that he was to be the instrument of the most important spear thrust into the belly of the beast.

Kaswari said, "This afternoon each of you will be given a packet with cover identification cards, round trip flight tickets, and details of your first contacts along your infiltration routes. Each person you meet will give you the next set of instructions and anything else you may need to smooth your movements. Each of these intermediaries will have very detailed and up-to-date information pertinent to your needs for that leg of the operation and no more. None of them will know anything beyond his or her small part. You are not to give them any additional information. You are all experts within the limits of your cover stories—remain absolutely true to the cover all of the time. That will protect you and the operation more than anything else."

"Any questions," Sisi asked.

"I have one," Naguib Eddin Moheiddin—the scarred Egyptian freedom fighter—said. "What shall we do if we are arrested before our mission is completed?"

Sisi's expressionless face did not alter as he replied, "First lie and stick to your lie. If you are kept in captivity, then die. I have two cyanide capsules for each of you. Before you leave today, our dentist will place a small capsule under a temporary tooth crown. You need only bite down hard on it, and you will no longer be subject to Satan's tortures. You can keep the second capsule as a back-up. I strongly doubt that it will ever be necessary to use the poison, however, because the Western police are weak and stupid. They want to believe Muslims in the current climate of détente. Keep calm, or as the Satanists say, 'keep your cool.'"

Col. Hosni Esmet Badr asked, "And after the missions are accomplished, if we are caught, shall we follow the same orders?"

"Yes," Kaswari broke in. "It will go better for you if you do."

Because he was fluent in French, Ayatollah Ali Velayati Mossedeq received his ticket for Paris. His fellow Iranian, Ayatollah Ali Mazdi Sedhavatal-Mudarasi was given his ticket for London. Col. Badr's flight was for Los Angeles; Yahha Mohammed Ali's was for Sydney; and Moheiddin's destination was Washington D.C. Abdel Said Badr's orders were for Caracas.

Attorney General Rowan arrived for her two o'clock meeting with the president two minutes ahead of the appointment time. Vilate Apfelbaum showed her to a comfortable chair in her office.

"Just be a minute, Madam Attorney General. The president is finishing with the first set of congressmen about the repeal of The Patriot Act."

The attorney general raised her eyebrows slightly but said nothing. It seemed premature to begin dismantling the nation's legal defenses at this point, but it was not her call.

A small red light flashed on Ms. Apflebaum's desk.

"The president will see you now. Please follow me."

Ms. Apflebaum rose quickly and began walking towards the Oval Office. AG Rowan had to trot to keep up.

"Attorney General Rowan, Mr. President," Ms Apflebaum announced.

"Come in, come in. I am very glad you could take time out from your tight schedule to see me on such short notice. Take a seat," President Braithwaite said, his face beaming and welcoming.

The president was wearing a burgundy turtle neck and a charcoal grey suit that set off his silvery hair well. It always bothered Elizabeth a little to have the president be in casual attire. It was silly she knew.

AG Rowan thought to herself about the summons, *"As if anyone would refuse a direct request from the President. And besides, what did the man who had no time to waste want with her?"*

"I know you are in the dark about why I asked you to meet me, Elizabeth. Okay if I use your first name?"

"Sure. And I am indeed in the dark."

"Have a mint?"

"No thanks."

He laughed.

"Ever the efficient nose-to-the-grindstone officer. I do like that about you. Doesn't tend to make you particularly colorful, but you get a lot of respect from that trait."

Elizabeth met his gaze and waited expectantly.

"Well, Elizabeth, this is it. I want you to agree to be my new vice-president. What do you say? Will you consider it?"

Elizabeth was truly speechless. Nothing could have prepared her for this offer. It was well beyond her girlhood or adult dreams and—she had to admit—not an office she coveted. She knew all about the inactivity and obscurity that attended the largely ceremonial position. Still…

The president arched a questioning eyebrow.

"I hardly know what to say, Mr. President."

"Say 'yes.'"

"Can I sleep on it?"

"I'd rather you didn't. I need to get this out of the way and let the government get on with governing. There will be something of a lag time even if you agree today."

"It is a shock. I am flattered and a bit overwhelmed, I must admit."

"Not turning coy on me, are you, Elizabeth?"

"I'm too old, too fat, and too gray to be coy, Mr. President. I presume you are serious and there must be some good reason for nominating me. I accept. I'm nervous; but if you want me, I will serve."

"I knew you would. I have had you vetted. Not a blemish. You are a shoe-in from that end. Incidentally, I used your judicial review system to check you out without your knowledge. I apologize for that, but it is a truly marvelous apparatus you have got going over there. You passed with flying colors even politically. I don't think we will have too much trouble in the House or Senate. Maybe you and I will have to do some smoozing for a while, but I am going to put the nomination on the fastest track I can.

"There is one area of concern, more mystery than concern. You are divorced, and there is nothing about that in print other than the pro forma announcements in the local Utah newspaper that you or your husband would no longer be responsible for each other's debts. The FBI investigators found a record that you had a child, but essentially nothing else is known. I know this is personal, but I have to know something about the situation. You understand. I can't have some enterprising investigative reporter finding some skeleton in your closet, and I can't be surprised. There is too much riding on the nomination."

"There's nothing sinister in my marital history—no adultery, no domestic violence. It was basically an amicable parting, and it was fundamentally over the death of our little girl. She was born with a rare skin and mucosal membrane disease called Epidermolysis Bullosa, Herlitz variety. It was evident within a day of her delivery. She developed terrible blistering sores around every orifice in her tiny body. They were horribly painful. Her skin was exquisitely sensitive to the slightest trauma. Soon she had great blisters—bullae—all over her skin and in every area of mucosa—nose and throat, g-i, g-u, and respiratory system. 85% of these kids die in the first year of life, and that is a blessing. Our little girl lived three years; she suffered every second of those three years through absolutely constant agony, bleeding, and sepsis.

"As if that were not bad enough, at the age of two, she developed skin cancer which is common in that disease. She had metastatic squamous cell carcinoma which was even more agonizing than her first two years of hell.

"My husband and I tried to work together on her care, but he just couldn't stand to see his baby suffer. I was left with all of the decisions and the active care. At the end, she developed generalized sepsis and pneumonia. I elected not to allow her to receive any more antibiotics or anything else to prolong her life. She died, and my husband blamed me. He held me responsible for the mutation that caused her disease, for the failure of her treatment, and ultimately decided that I was a cold-hearted monster for refusing any more medical treatment. Someone had to make the hard decisions, and it had to be me. My husband admitted that his attitude was unreasonable, but he could not shake it. Finally, our marriage was so eroded by our daughter's illness that we mutually agreed to separate and finally to divorce. He was in psychiatric treatment for several years after her death."

"And I take it that you were not."

Chapter Twenty-Five

"No, sir, I immersed myself in my work. I did what I had to do. I went on."

"No lasting effects, no scars of the psyche or the soul?"

"Oh, yes, there were both. I lost my religion for all practical purposes. I just could not accept a God that would let such a thing happen to a baby. Maybe that was irrational, but I could not shake it."

"I am terribly, terribly sorry, Elizabeth. Obviously, that is not germane to the nomination."

"It is deeply private, Mr. President. I have tucked it away somewhere in my core, and I do not let it come up unless it is absolutely necessary. It is the way I cope. I hope that that chapter can be left out during the nominating campaign. I won't refuse to accept or to serve on the basis of my personal problem, but I ask for your discretion."

"You will have it. I will do all I can to keep your pain out of the news."

"I appreciate that, sir."

Congratulations on the nomination."

"Thank you, Mr. President. Let me know what you want me to do."

At three o'clock that same afternoon, President Braithwaite met with the four ranking senators, two from each party.

"Thanks for coming by. I met with the House leaders a couple of hours ago, and we had a good exchange about the repeal of The Patriot Act that I have recommended. I'd like to hear your views."

"I'd like to have the chance to give the point of view of the liberals in your party, Mr. President, if I may?" Senator Cliff Assure said. "Okay with the rest of you?"

"Okay by me, "the majority leader said.

The others nodded.

The majority leader went on, "Senator Assure is the acknowledged expert on The Patriot Act."

"All right, Cliff. You have my undivided attention," said the president.

"First of all, the act covers too much—350 pages too much—in my estimation. It includes skyjacking, ship jacking, and now covers any act against an American abroad that can be construed as being an act of terrorism—by our definition—and without decent input by the foreign police, legal or judicial system. Secondly, one part of the act is the FISA or Foreign Intelligence Surveillance Act. It involves wiretaps without the subject's permission, the kind of thing we expressly forbid in our domestic criminal cases. The gist of the law is simplification—we can wiretap any communication device of the foreign subject without getting a new court order each time. U.S. prosecutors are sloppy and inefficient. They complain that it takes a week to get a new phone tap warrant. I say, let them prove their case just as they used to. The law was changed for criminals and not for terrorists, and the Act changed that. The prosecutors say the Act rectified a loophole for terrorists. I say that it is an overreaching and improper invasion of privacy for anyone who is surveilled. Every time we lose a right on the argument that it is for purposes of security, it stays lost. We need to get this one back.

"Thirdly, the Act provides police and prosecutors with the power to delay notification of the suspect that he or she is being investigated for terrorism. That is patently unfair and flies against the fairness doctrine that pervades the American way of justice. The Act gives broad powers to the government to follow money trails, to prevent flight, and to intimidate witnesses. What is really going on is the government has taken away the rights to privacy and to a decent defense in public. It is part of a kangaroo court type system. It has been abused severely, especially in the case of pursuing Muslim charities which it was supposed were funneling money to terrorists.

Take the investigation of the Holy Land Foundation with offices all around America whose officers have been imprisoned for allegedly supplying illegal funds to Palestinian Freedom Fighter groups, or the Safa Group working out of Herndon, Virginia. Their legitimate humanitarian work has been hamstrung by the pervasive investigative intrusions by the FBI and Homeland Security. These Arab-American citizens have appealed to our caucus on numerous occasions for relief. The same applies to Benevolence International Foundation, the Graduate School of Islamic and Social Sciences, the American Muslim Armed Forces and Veterans Affairs Council, the American Muslim Council, and the World Muslim League, all of which are active in the United States, or at least they were until our Gestapo shut them down.

"The civil rights of ordinary citizens are at risk, even their right to privacy when using library facilities. It is not the government's business what they are reading or what they research on-line. The proponents of the law say that the records being searched are the property of the library or of the hotel or the business and are not private. That is a patent dodge, a flim-flam, to get around the invasion of our people's constitutional right to privacy."

"Is that in the Constitution, Cliff?"

"The Supreme Court ruled that it was a constitutional right in Roe v. Wade even though it is not expressly spelled out in the document itself."

"And our conservative friends insist that Roe v. Wade was a classical example of legislative function being usurped by the judicial branch. Isn't that going to be an argument of some potency if we bring the Act before Congress for repeal?" the president asked.

"They had their turn in two terms by that Nazi, Bush. It is our turn now, Mr. President. Our answer is that our judges are only doing what we have always done, or certainly what we always need to have done—to make the Constitution adapt to the times."

"I'm satisfied. Of course you all know that. But, will it sell in that market of ideas we call the Congress?"

"With the Muslims calling a unilateral cease fire or even peace, we have little chance of losing the battle for repeal of The Patriot Act; and the broader issue of so-called judicial legislating is of serious disinterest to the American public. They sway with the breezes of change like palms in wind. This time they are going to sway in our direction because of the educational blitz we are mustering."

"We're a bit off the subject. Give me more ammunition to use to sell our proposal to get that fascist Act repealed."

"Oh, that's easy, Mr. President. Just keep saying the magic word, 'liberty.' That's what it is all about. That's what America has always been about. Even the Justice Department will admit that it has had and still retains a few U.S. attorneys who abuse their power for their own aggrandizement. The power they abuse belongs to the people; and what the people lose is their own individual privacy, in brief, their liberty. The U.S. attorneys control federal grand juries. Defendants going before the grand juries are not allowed to have defense attorneys and something like 98 percent of them get bound over for trial. They haven't got a chance."

"To take the Devil's Advocate position on your argument, Cliff, wouldn't that problem be largely done away with by simply instituting an adequate oversight provision in an updated law?"

"You can just forget that. The abuse is built in. And who watches the watchers? It is a Nazi plan, and the Nazis would be their own monitors. No sir, the solution is amputation, not a little elective fixit surgery. We have to get rid of The Patriot Act, and this is the best opportunity there will ever be. Terrorism went out with high button shoes, figuratively speaking. There isn't any international terrorism bugaboo any more. I'm not sure there ever was one. The attack on the Twin Towers all those years ago was nothing more or less than the act of a far right splinter group of the great religion of Islam. The real Islam is a peaceful religion, and the cool heads of the moderates have prevailed over the very small lunatic fringe of their people. The Patriot Act is outmoded and not needed. It only hurts Americans going about their lives not bothering anyone else. The Act has to go."

"Thanks, Cliff. Anyone else want to chime in?"

"No, sir," the other congressional leaders chorused.

"No defenders of the Act?"

"None here," Helen Clivener said.

"If there's nothing else, Mr. President, a couple of us have to get back to the Congress to save our citizens from the predatory companies and their conservative lackeys," Cliff Assure said with mock seriousness.

They all laughed.

"Lady and gentlemen, there is one more thing of some importance I wanted to bring before you, and I almost forgot. Tomorrow, I am going to submit the name of Attorney General Elizabeth Leavitt Rowan to fill the vice-presidential vacancy. If you have any powerful objections, I'd like to hear them. I would be gratified if her nomination could move through the process with alacrity."

Cliff Assure answered, "Mr. President, I much prefer that we have a bona fide liberal. This is one I personally will have to oppose, sir. No offense intended."

"Helen?"

"I remain a realist. Like Cliff, I want one of our people. But, we will have a terrible and prolonged fight in both houses for anyone who would be completely acceptable to our caucus. Frankly, I think the attorney general is pretty tame and innocuous. She will be in a protected seclusion, to be unkind about it. Like John Nance Garner said when he had to become the vice president, 'the job isn't worth a bucket of warm spit.' I presume you can control her, Mr. President?"

"I can. I have no illusions that she will be any kind of an asset. I will dump her for a more compatible running mate in the next election. She will just be a figurehead to fill the chair until then. It's pretty much the same arrangement as we had with Carl Aviard. She has essentially agreed to that. I don't see any political ambition in the woman; and therefore, Helen, I agree with you that she is innocuous and a noncontroversial choice. Will you help me, Madam Majority Leader?"

"Reluctantly, but yes, Mr. President."

"How about the rest?"

There were two reluctant but positive nods.

"What if you die or become incapacitated, Mr. President. All of a sudden this so-called 'innocuous' becomes president. She is not competent for the job; she has no backing; and she has no history. For all I know she could become the proverbial 500 pound Neo-Nazi conservative gorilla if—heaven forbid—she should succeed you," Senator Assure said worriedly.

"I am the fittest President in the history of the republic, Cliff. I have less fear of assassination than almost any president before me now that the terrorist threat has evaporated. You are a worry-wart, Cliff. Let's confine our concerns to the practical. The country will survive this little blip in the historical flow."

CHAPTER TWENTY-SIX

MARCH 3, 2010

Mossad Director Mordecai Narkiss received an e-mail communication from his agent, Dark Shadow, which, after decoding the encryption and interpreting the obscure references, read:

> Director, Mossad
> 3 March, 10
> Am new director of security nuclear facility Aleppo. Have been admitted to deputy membership in ultra secretive group—Council of Leaders of Islam—and am given access to information pertinent to my position related to their private nuc. program. Not certain, but appears nuclear devices ready including delivery systems. Plans closely guarded, but major. No possibility of receiving your reply.
> -Afflicted by God

Narkiss met his lieutenants, Levi Harkabi and Yahuda Grossman.

"I have a communiqué from Dark shadow. He is in thick with the thieves and was invited to join the group he alluded to before. Now, he has a name for us: The Council of Leaders of Islam. Levy, I want you to find out everything anybody knows about it. Sounds like a powerful organization, all the more so because it can keep secrets. Yahuda, Job thinks the head of it may be a Saudi prince. Get on that, okay?"

"Will do."

Yahuda Grossman was a man who stayed in the shadows and got things done. He was educated in universities in New York and Jerusalem, the Mossad training camp, and at The Farm—the CIA's training center, in rural Virginia. He knew everything there was to know about Islam and Judaism; he had a double PhD—in psychology and history. He had dedicated his life to counterterrorism, so much so, that he did not have a wife or children, any real friends in or out of the service; and he lived as an ascetic in a kibbutz. Grossman wore the clothing and fetlocks of an Orthodox Jew, and most who encountered him took him for a rabbi. He did not, however, believe a word of the Jewish religion or of any other intangible system of belief.

He was soft and plump. He had never excelled in hand-to-hand combat or in the use of weapons. He knew nothing of popular culture, the vibrant Israeli nightclub or cultural scene, or Israeli politics, business, or trade. He was not an artist, a cryptanalyst, a military strategist, or even a man of administrative ability. He was content to remain at his civil service level and had no ambitions or future plans. What he did know was vital to his country.

Yahuda could make computers do anything of which they were capable. He was a world-class hacker. He knew every detail about the people in Islamic terrorist organizations that could be known from personal interviews with field agents and detainees, computer traffic and written reports, from books, surveillance films, and recordings. He had a photographic, encyclopedic memory; and Mossad used him as a resource for almost everything the service needed to know about its enemies and its friends.

Yahuda, for all of his soft, almost effeminate mannerisms, was a relentless and ruthless interrogator. He was patient, cunning, and a chameleon. He could be anything to any man to get information. His parents had been murdered by suicide bombers sent by the al Aqsa Brigades. They were all the family he had; and as a consequence of their murder, there was nothing that Yahuda would not do to extract information. He obeyed the Mossad's rules, but sometimes the rules would be bent or warped when the occasion arose. If it was possible to find out more about the secretive prince or his organization, Yahuda Grossman was the man to find it.

Ayatollah Ali Velayati Mossedeq entered France from Tehran with a diplomatic passport in the name of Shahpur Ghotbzadeh, Second Deputy Trade Secretary. He brought with him eleven other men, bona fide trade deputies who were scheduled to operate an Iran trade booth in the International Trade and Travel Exposition in Lyon. They brought with them two dozen heavy crates of material for the exposition, all under diplomatic seal. No one in French customs bothered to open the crates. If an inspector had done so, he would have found posters, table decorations, brochures, special lighting and communications equipment, and one of the crates—a particularly heavy one—had specially prepared Iranian candy favors for distribution to exposition goers. The inspector would not have seen anything out of the ordinary in any of the crates, and all of the crates had successfully passed x-ray scrutiny.

One of the boxes had camera equipment and large stores of film in lead boxes, carefully labeled as such. It also had a lead lined bottom portion that held a torpedo shaped metal object, made of rather impure enriched uranium hexafluoride, weighing thirteen kilograms. Surrounding the uranium was a special heavy plastic wrapping in which a mixture of powdered cesium-137 and cobalt 60 was packed to effect widespread dispersal of intense radioactivity. Outside that layer was a full three inch thick encasement of Semtex A—94.3% PETN, 5.7% RDX plastique mixed with the antioxidant, n-octylpthalate, in a rubber binder. The Semtex A was military grade—similar to C-4—and only available from government sources ordinarily.

An al Qaeda operative had been placed in the Semtin Glass Works-Eastern Bohemian Chemical Works which enabled her to obtain all the necessary specialized plastique. The cesium 137 and cobalt 60 were stolen from a number of medical supply houses with ease. Attached to the explosive plastique material by det cord were several sticks of dynamite into which an electronic detonator wired to a blasting cap was affixed. All the simple electronics were attached to a rented—throw-away—cell phone.

Operation of the device was simplicity itself. All the operator had to do was to dial the cell phone's number from afar and know that the plastique and then the uranium, cobalt, and cesium mixture would explode within millionths of a second of one another. The explosion would act as a radiological dispersal device (RDD). All of the dirty bombs carried in by the prince's operatives were set to explode at the exact same moment around the world. They were of exactly the same construction—known to be reliable from the Council's tests.

The crates were loaded onto lorries and the men onto cheap buses under the careful eye of the Ayatollah, and they set out for Lyon. The Ayatollah checked the men into the down-on-its-luck Hotel Axotel Perrache in the heart of the city on 12 rue Marc Antoine Petit within a few steps of the TGV—high speed train—the metro, and the tram. The Ayatollah left his own name off the check-in list. Once the trade exposition members had left for their assigned rooms, Mossedeq returned to the lorry containing his special crate. He negotiated with the union representative who had ridden in one of the trucks' passenger seats, and shortly his crate was transferred to another lorry brought in from the local office, as is required by French labor law.

Ayatollah Mossedeq had his precious crate delivered to a faceless back street self-storage unit in Paris, and he was then driven to the Montparnasse area. Following his handler's directions, the ayatollah checked into the two star 42 room Avenir Hotel, located about a mile from the Eiffel Tower, a mile from the Montparnasse Major Train Station, and mere steps from the Convention Underground Station. His identity at the hotel was that of one Raul G. Ramirez, a Spanish traveling salesman. The ayatollah took quiet pride that he had been selected to avenge the affront to holy Islam that the greedy and arrogant French had perpetrated when they outlawed the legitimate wearing of religious scarves by school girls. It was time for them to pay. The following day, he had the all-important box removed from the self-storage facility and taken to the hotel's basement storage area by local members of an al Qaeda cell.

Mossedeq's countryman, Ayatollah Mazdi Sekhavatal-Muderasi, landed at Heathrow within fifteen minutes of Mossedeq's arrival at Orly. He traveled under an Israeli passport as David Ben Hodosh, a jewel merchant. Anticipating that British customs would be more thorough, Ayatollah Sekhavatal-Muderasi's handlers on the Council had prudently made arrangements for his special crate to arrive the previous day by air cargo on a different airline. That bit of prudence paid off because his personal luggage was thoroughly inspected including opening each suitcase while the cargo crate on the separate aircraft passed through without exciting any suspicion.

Sekhavatal-Muderasi checked in to the cheap Club Quarters St. Paul's hotel on Ludgate Street in the heart of The City, half a mile from Heathrow, half a mile from Waterloo Station, two miles from Fenchurch Street Railway Station, and six miles from London City Airport. By paying an excessive tip, he was able to have two porters lug his crate to his room without demurrer.

"My pewter collection for distribution to Harrods, Lillywhites, and the Benetton Megastore in Oxford Circus," he told the porters. "Are you interested in buying a nice ornate cake plate, perhaps?"

The two men snorted and let Sekhavatal-Muderasi know their disdain for such useless luxuries. "We're only working men, guv," one of them said.

After they left, the ayatollah perused his Cook's city map of London to determine his escape root when the time came. He planned to walk or drive the route the following day.

Abdel Said Badr arrived in Caracas, Venezuela in the late evening, one hour late. The heat in the inadequate airport suited Badr fine—he was a desert man. The attendant humidity was cloying and enervating. His passport was in the name of Rajah Arun, an Indian gem buyer. Unlike his Iranian counterparts, he was given no instructions about crates and was told only to take up residence in a rundown apartment building in barrio Fuerte Tiuna, a shanty town *urbanizacione* [suburb] where he—posing as Chilean, Roderigo Caraza—was to await further communication from the Council.

The ultimately precious box that was to accompany Badr rested at that moment in the hold of a nondescript freighter in the Port of La Guaira in Caracas Harbor. Said Mohammed Sisi was en route from Riyadh that same day to finalize arrangements for Badr and his elongated crate to make its way into the United States at the prescribed entry point at exactly the correct time and without interference from anyone.

Naguib Eddin Moheiddin flew into the John C. Munro Hamilton International Airport and checked through as Jameel Rabbo—a Palestinian rug merchant. He brought with him four heavy crates of exquisite hand woven carpets. In one of the crates was the same dirty bomb contraption that his two co-freedom fighters from Iran had brought in. Like them, he checked his luggage into a downtown hotel, under another alias; but unlike them, he was ensconced in the four star Sheraton on King Street. The hotel was chosen to be close to the row of rug merchants' shops to facilitate his cover. He took pains to store the precious crate containing his bomb where it would never be seen nor suspected-in a transients' luggage hold facility in the seedier part of Hamilton.

Col. Hosni Esmet Badr landed in the Garden City Victoria International Airport, caught the ferry from the island and took up short term residence on Burrard Street in Vancouver, British Columbia in the LeGrande Residence Hotel. His manner was so gruff and overbearing that no one bothered him about his luggage or the heavy crate that he so carefully tended. He carried a discardable cell phone identical to those carried by his fellow Council operatives. He did not settle into his hotel room until well past midnight. With his arrival, all of the key operatives were in place for the first phase of Operation Avenging the Crusades—as Prince ibn Saud had chosen to designate his long planned and meticulously guarded project to restore Islam to its rightful place as the government of the nations—on top.

Vilate Apflebaum escorted the director of the CIA, the director of the FBI, and the head of the CIA's Illicit Transactions Group into the Oval Office. The three chiefs had requested the audience with the president and were fitted into the last appointment slot of the day. Their faces were grave.

"Who is the spokesperson for this grim group?" the president asked.

"I am the primary, Mr. President," Leland Marques, the DFBI said.

"What is it?"

"We were informed that you and Secretary O'Laughlin are planning to drop the investigation and charges against the Safa Group and several other Islamic charities on the FBI's terrorist support list. We would like to give you some information to consider before you make that big step."

"I'll listen."

"I'll let the DCIA introduce our expert, sir."

DCIA Angelina Davis looked at the third member of the delegation.

"This is Dean Mathews, Mr. President. Even his name is listed as ultra secret—that's a category above Top Secret—so no more than five people know about him. He runs the CIA's Illicit Transactions Group. They trace terrorists, smugglers, and money launderers, all of whom are interconnected in the recent past history of perceptions of the workings of the terrorist world."

"It seems to me that the frequent use of the word, 'terrorist', is becoming a trifle hackneyed by overuse, Angelina. But do have Mr. Matthews go on."

"I'll give you my opinion when Mr. Mathews finishes. Go ahead, Dean."

"Sir, we have been investigating abroad, and the FBI has been carrying on the work domestically to track terrorists and their money trails and their support systems. American Islamic charities are second only to such front organizations in Saudi Arabia as the financial supporters of the terrorist networks—note the plural—al Qaeda, Hamas, Hezbollah, and the like. We have hard evidence on several American based groups that is definite enough for the FBI to make arrests and for the Justice Department to pursue prosecutions under The Patriot Act and the provisions of the Constitution's articles against treason.

"We hold the leaders of a number of these groups in custody and have frozen their assets. This has dramatically reduced the flow of funding from our country to the extremist murderers. Some of the groups on which we have the most undeniable evidence are: Benevolence International Foundation—an al Qaeda front—the Graduate School of Islamic and Social Sciences—a fund supplier for multiple terrorist groups—American Muslim Armed Forces and Veterans' Affairs

Council—an offshoot of Alamoudi's Libyan group with terrorist ties. The leader was arrested smuggling $350 thousand into Syria for use by Iraqi assassins.

"This group has infiltrated our armed forces and subverted the interrogations at Guantanamo Bay—a couple of our own Muslim clerics were arrested smuggling out classified material. An active investigation has targeted Day Al-Hijra Islamic Center in Falls Church, Virginia. Other organizations are the American Muslim Council and the World Muslim League whose top official—Wael Jailaidan—is one of the founders of and the current logistics chief of al Qaeda. That one is headquartered in Saudi Arabia and has an annual budget of $45 million. It has 36 open branch offices and is a major funder of Philippine terrorists. U.S. branch offices contribute significantly to Abu Sayyaf.

"The Riggs National Bank right here in D.C. is under active investigation for financing terrorism by what it calls 'diplomatic banking.' We are accumulating evidence that foreign investors, American Muslim charities, and major and minor companies, even individual well-to-do Arab-Americans with contacts in the Muslim underground have all made use of Riggs Bank to funnel money to Hamas, Hezbollah, and the Saudi charity fronts.

"The al-Haramain Foundation is also headquartered in Riyadh and makes some difficult to understand financial transactions with Riggs Bank via a bewildering series of holding companies and trusts with off-shore offices. It has an annual budget of a staggering $73 million with 50 branch offices. It has direct links to Egyptian terror groups and to Chechen rebels. The foundation has offices in ten countries and provides both money and arms to terrorists all over the world. In ten years al Qaeda received between $300 and $500 million from private phony charities.

"Even more widespread is the practice of funneling true charity money from the Zakat boxes by sympathetic mullahs to terrorist causes. Saudi charities have given well over $70 billion to spread Wahhabism world-wide. They build and support radical extremist mosques and schools. By 2002 they had built 1500 mosques, 201 Islamic centers, 2000 schools, and 202 colleges. Most of the officials of the Holy Land Foundation which funds Palestinian terrorists have had due process and are in prison.

"Our Illicit Transactions Group and the ODCI have seen no alteration in the funding schemes and the network that gets the money to the terrorist groups despite the public disavowal of terrorism, Mr. President. We have prepared an ultra secret dossier for your eyes only. We find the raw data compelling, and have added what we think are the minimal inescapable conclusions."

He handed the thick set of documents to the DCIA who stood and walked to the president's desk and handed him the body of work. He accepted it with a frown.

"Angelina, what's your take on all of this?"

The CIA group leader and the DFBI slumped in their seats.

"I have been over all of this with my esteemed colleagues here. I believe the data to be outmoded and exaggerated. They are the product of the John Ashcroft extremist era in the Justice Department and allowed to continue under AG Rowan. Historically, I think there was some fire amidst all the smoke, but I think that through the efforts of your enlightened administration our Islamic friends have gotten better control and have provided better direction for all of these funding organizations. You have given them some rope, and they have taken positive steps toward peace. Maybe the process is incomplete, but our Islamic friends are on top of the situation and are weeding out the few remaining extremists.

"It is high time we backed off from our aggressive and probably illegal approach, Mr. President. Take the Safa Group. In March, 2002 federal agents mounted a surprise raid on the organization's headquarters on Grove Street in Herndon. The agents confiscated computers and records, froze assets, and took religious and lay leaders into custody. The FBI's offices and the Justice Department have been flooded with protests by a variety of Muslim organizations all over our country and throughout the world. These organizations are widely regarded as legitimate charities and businesses, and our federal actions are seen as nothing more than dressed-up Nazism with blatant support for the illegal occupation of Palestine by Zionist extremists."

"Mr. President," DFBI Marques broke in. "We have evidence. Ms. Davis's argument is about feelings. On the part of the Muslims, these sort of feelings are self-serving if not outright collusion. We have evidentiary proof."

"Thank you, Ms. Davis. And Director Marquez, why don't you leave me your 'evidence' and I'll go over it. In the meantime, I don't want a word of this meeting to leave this room, understood?"

The DFBI started to protest but knew it was useless. The president did not like raw data—he saw it as a waste of his time to go over it. That was what his sworn deputies were for. Marques simply nodded his compliance like his two colleagues.

MARCH 4, 2004

CNN covered the news at five p.m. as soon as the last vote was passed in the House.

"We have been covering the vice-presidential nomination battle in the House all day. The vote is just now nearing its finale. As you no doubt know, Attorney General Rowan was a controversial choice—not because of her politics or from any scandal, but because she is so unknown. Our polls indicated that less than twenty-five percent of those polled knew that she was the attorney general. Only four percent could recall any other details of her career—that she was head of the Federal Prison System, before that the director of the most secure prison in the country, and before that a federal prosecutor. Let's look at the results as they come in."

The anchorman looked away to the House vote tally board as the numbers of nays and yeas continued to vacillate.

"It's still unclear whether or not the members of Congress will accept this nearly unknown woman whom many describe as inexperienced and unable to take a stand on issues confronting the country. This stems from her adamant refusal to grant interviews on political questions. The nearest this reporter has come to getting an answer is that Mrs. Rowan assured me that she supports the president. We could surmise that she is a liberal Democrat from that, but I don't think all the data is in on this quiet—and by most associates' observations—effective, middle level administrator."

The vote tally edged in Mrs. Rowan's favor with thirty-two votes left to be cast in the alphabetical order passing through the House members' names. Ayes and nays continued to be coming at about the same rate, but now the ayes outnumbered the nays by three.

"As you know, the Senate confirmed her by a vote of 49 to 51, a squeaker. The House vote is looking like it will be a photo finish as well This has to be a near record which is indicative of the deep interest Congress has. Every member of the Senate was present for the vote, and every single member of the House is on the floor today. I don't remember ever seeing perfect attendance before."

The vote was a tie with three votes left.

The speaker of the House called out, "Mr. Young?"

"Aye."

"Mr. Zelkoff?"

"Nay."

"Ms. Zybgniew?"

The representative from Chicago's Polish neighborhoods paused for full effect because she was well aware of the crucial character of her vote. She was somewhat torn having had a nasty run-in with the attorney general over a fraud case involving her chief contributor's work on the federal courthouse in her district. On the other hand, she could cast the vote that would put the first woman vice-president in office. It would be a stroke for the sisterhood that should transcend her petty grievance. Sofia Zybgniew was truly torn.

"Ms Zybgniew?"

"Aye."

The vote board showed 218 ayes to 217 nays. The gallery erupted in applause.

The CNN anchor said, "This is an historic day, ladies and gentlemen. We have all just seen the approval of the nomination of the first woman vice-president ratified by a thin majority of both houses of Congress. We have Jacob Stressor, professor of American History in our studio. Dr. Stressor, give us your expert knowledge on the historical underpinnings of this remarkable event."

Elizabeth muted the television and closed her eyes.

"What have I done? What have I gotten myself into?"

The CNN scene changed with a title of "Breaking News". Elizabeth absently clicked the mute button off and listened to the next news item.

"In other news today, President Braithwaite made three dramatic announcements at his news conference. We showed you this earlier this afternoon. For those of you who missed it, here is the president's brief announcement in full."

Braithwaite, sitting in the rose room and wearing a sporty lavender jacket and a pastel turtle neck, came on the screen. His makeup was better today—less obvious—thought Elizabeth. His hair had just been done and looked perfect. He was relaxed and smiling.

"My fellow Americans. It gives me great pleasure to announce that, as of today, the United States Transportation Security Authority—the TSA—will cease to function. The federal government will no longer manage aviation security throughout the civilian sector of our nation. As you know, Homeland Security has been on the green level of alert status for the past several months. We have been free of all terrorist attacks during that period, and our Muslim colleagues and friends continue to police the extremists among them. My only regret is that 43,000 people will no longer be employed by the government. I feel their pain. My administration will do everything we can to transfer the employees of the TSA to the private sector companies that will take over management in a phased-in process that will hand over responsibility in two months. Others we will try to relocate, and we will strive to retrain the remainder. Despite that note of concern, we should all regard this as a great step forward towards the establishment of lasting peace among equals.

"For the lasting benefit of our own people, this administration will today put the final nail in the coffin of the Matrix program. We deem it an unwarranted intrusion on the private information of our unsuspecting citizens. It would simplify the work of the government including in areas where citizens should expect privacy and would allow intrusions without a warrant. In short we regard the program as a neo-Nazi information gathering machination akin to the infamous 'enemies list' of Richard Nixon who was forced to resign from office because of such practices."

Elizabeth gritted her teeth because of all of the misrepresentations in the president's description of Matrix. Still—despite the usefulness to her office of the extensive data collected—she had her own qualms over the legality and the morality of such data retrieval. The president's televised speech continued.

"The next measure we have taken is to halt immediately the efforts by the Justice Department to investigate, arrest officers, or to interfere with the financial transactions of our Arab American charity organizations. My administration has studied the cases involved, which were carry overs from the previous administration. We find the actions of our government to be akin to those historical wrongs done to our Japanese-Americans during the Second World War, and to our African-American citizens throughout their long struggle with slavery and segregation.

"Specific cases include the actions taken to hinder and harass the Safa Group, also known as the SAAR Network, based in Herndon, Virginia. We find no evidence of wrong doing in the moving of an untraced twenty million dollars overseas. The accusations that this money was used to support foreign terrorists were never proved to our satisfaction. We therefore restore full rights to Safa Group and to all of the other fine humanitarian groups that our Arab American citizens have so charitably supported.

"Thank you, ladies and gentlemen, and good afternoon."

The former attorney general, now vice-president, was aghast. Her office had worked on those cases for two years and had what the prosecutors considered incontrovertible evidence of the criminal support for forces sworn to injure and destroy the United States. She realized that she had just witnessed how smoothly she had been maneuvered out of the loop; so, this travesty could be slipped by. In her new position she could never go public with her knowledge, and it would be futile for her to complain privately to the president or anyone else in his administration. She occupied the weakest place in that administration, and making a fuss would only alienate her and render her totally ineffective in anything else she would wish to accomplish. She gritted her teeth and fought back bitter tears of frustration. She knew that she had just had another lesson in the politics of Washington.

CHAPTER TWENTY-SEVEN

MARCH 8, 2010

Vice-President Rowan was invited to attend her first cabinet meeting. Donovan O'Laughlin took her aside and explained protocol.

"The meetings are conducted at the president's pleasure. No business is conducted until he comes into the room. When he does, we all stand. He sits; and we sit; and then usually he opens with a subject that concerns him. Sometimes he asks for a subject. The first person other than the president to speak is the Secretary of State whenever the president opens the forum for discussion. I would suggest that you follow the lead of the cabinet members and most of the time just hold your peace. The president hears discussion; then he makes the decision; and we go along with it even if we are in disagreement. The arrangement requires that the cabinet members and their subordinates be team players. Constitutionally, the vice-president is the ultimate team player because there is very little definition of the position that allows active involvement. Of course, you can be an advisor to the president, if he so desires; but you have to wait his pleasure. Do you have any questions, Madam Vice-President?"

"Will I be the one to run out and get coffee?" Elizabeth asked dead pan.

O'Laughlin laughed heartily.

"You have the main quality for survival as the vice-president. Don't lose your sense of humor, and you might even grow to like your position."

President Braithwaite took his larger raised seat in the cabinet room, and the members of the cabinet sat down. Elizabeth sat quietly, watching and learning.

"Ladies and gentlemen, welcome. It's a beautiful spring day. And that is a segue into the first item of business for today. I must say that I am glad to have something that isn't so globally complicated or serious to open with for a change. The evaporation of the War on Terrorism has made all of our jobs a lot more comfortable.

"And that observation is part of my segue. We need to establish a national day of unity in commemoration of the events of September 11, but to stay away from that day or even that basic time period. The day has become almost holy and is wholly serious. It is like stepping on the political third rail to inject anything light hearted into the period, like we were accidentally stepping on graves. And besides, 9/11 effectively excludes our Muslim friends. That is the last thing we want to do in a national holiday.

"I think we ought to have a major production in Washington during the period when the cherry blossoms come out—a real symbol of growth and renewal. We want to invite the whole world to the festival. It could be something like a celebration of peace. You remember the old Simon and Garfuncle song? If it's not too strange, I'd like to sing it for you; it goes something like this: 'Last night I had the strangest dream, I ever dreamed before. I dreamed the world had all agreed to put an end to war. I dreamed I saw a mighty room. The room was filled with men. And the paper they were signing said they'd never fight again. And when the papers all were signed and a million copies made, they all joined hands and bowed their heads and grateful prayers were prayed. And the people in the streets below were dancing round and round. And guns and swords and uniforms were scattered on the ground.'"

He had a fine baritone voice, obviously the product of long hours in training. His voice cracked slightly on the last line and tears welled up. Elizabeth thought that she still had much more to learn about this complex man.

"I think we can build a theme around that, perhaps for the first time in almost all of history. You know, someone once did a study of war in the world and determined that for all of recorded time, there have only been fourteen days of peace encompassing the entire world. We have a chance to change that which may never present itself again."

Elizabeth saw the glistening of tears on the president's cheeks, and she looked away out of courtesy.

"How about it? Any thoughts or suggestions?"

He turned to Secretary O'Laughlin.

"Mr. Secretary, what think you?"

"Mr. President, it is perhaps the loftiest idea in a century. I would hope that this concept, not just the trappings of the celebrations, would become the hallmark of your administration and would establish your place in history as the great peacemaker."

Elizabeth kept her face under control with a little effort. He was laying it on with a trowel.

"I recommend to the cabinet, and I think it should be quickly conveyed to the Congress and to the state houses that we get on with preparations—do it up in true Yankee style. One of the things we do best in our country is throwing parties. Might lift some of the gloom here and around the world. Let's invite everybody."

"I love your enthusiasm, Donovan. Anyone else?"

Every cabinet member dutifully followed suit. Each had a suggestion—how to deal with parking, what kind of security to employ, how to house the influx of party goers, who should be in charge, what entertainers would be appropriate and which ones were owed for their support during campaigns. The president was deeply pleased to see his idea taking wing.

"Maybe we can work in the biblical business about beating swords into plows or however it goes," suggested Donlin Hewlett, the Secretary of Defense, "or would that violate the separation clause?"

"That's quite a concession coming from you, Donlin," the president said.

The cabinet members smiled and chuckled a little.

"Do you remember the exact scripture on that, Madam Vice-President? *New Testament*, I presume," he asked Elizabeth who had been strictly obeying the secretary of State's admonition to keep quiet.

"And do you have anything else you'd like to add?"

"*Old Testament*, Mr. President. It is an interesting scripture. The text appears in almost exactly the same form in *Isaiah* and in *Micah*. I like the *Micah* version best. It's in the fourth chapter, third and fourth verses: 'And He shall judge among many people, and rebuke strong nations afar off; and they shall beat their swords into plowshares, and their spears into pruning hooks: nation shall not lift up a sword against nation, neither shall they learn war any more. But they shall sit every man under his vine and under his fig tree; and none shall make them afraid; for the mouth of the Lord of Hosts hath spoken it.'"

"I didn't know you were religious, Elizabeth. That was impressive."

"I keep my religion personal and out of my government involvement."

"Good choice. Now what are your thoughts on this celebration idea?"

"I'm all for it. I suggest that it is too large a project to have in just one city, even Washington. Perhaps it would be better if we launched a country wide series of activities on the order of the bicentennial celebration. It would give the people of the country a chance to show their innovation and to become involved in the process. We could make a broad effort to establish sister cities all around the world to include them in the planning and execution of the events with our cities."

Several of the cabinet members looked at their vice-president with new-found respect since the boost to the economy would be spread out over most of the country. The legislators would love the opportunity to announce their support, even their inspiration, for new income for their constituents.

The members were bidden to use the resources of their departments to make the first year's celebrations occur on April 16 to avoid any conflict with other holidays. The first two celebrations were to take place in Washington D.C. and Detroit with the national dignitaries shuttling between cities. Because of the serious problem of unemployment in Michigan, it was decided to have the president, a 9/11 fireman, the president of the Automobile Makers Union, Jesse Jackson, and Mullah Mohammed Sufti give the main speeches. By security protocol, the president and the vice-president would never attend the same celebrations.

President Braithwaite made the announcement to the media of the grand plan for the series of national celebrations with the rest of the world being invited to the party that would be spread out over several weeks and at a plentitude of venues. For the first time in nearly a decade, an idea coming from America was received with approbation.

The president's televised announcement was nowhere better received than in Aleppo, Syria at the compound housing the executives of the Council of the Leaders of Islam. Prince Ahmed Wahhab ibn Saud turned off his CNN World News broadcast and sent his aides with a personal summons to the entire Council. Even those not physically present were connected by e-mail. The prince's security concerns were such that he called for the personal services of Ayoub al-Qassam to ensure that there could be no possibility of a leak or interception to the Western intelligence services.

Ayoub signaled to the prince that security in the form of an XML encryption syntax using encrypted object cipher data as a base64 encoding was in place. Prince ibn Saud had insisted on having a working knowledge of the technology to prevent himself and his security team from being mystified by and thus vulnerable to the methods of the computer technologists involved in the operation. Technicians on twenty-five modems synchronized and signaled their readiness. The prince began his message that would be nothing but numerical gibberish to anyone receiving the e-mail message that did not have the proper key to decrypt the ciphertext.

"Brothers, our time table has been altered. Originally, we had hoped to honor The Prophet, blessed be his name, by launching our spear at the Great Satan on The Messenger's birthday, but we were insufficiently prepared. We were then ready to execute operation Avenging the Crusades in two days time, but the leaders of the Satanic Western world have given us a perfect opportunity. Our date will now be April 16. You will receive your orders and the information you need to know to carry them out at the appropriate time in advance. I hardly need caution you about the requirement for absolute secrecy nor Allah's penalties for betrayal—even inadvertent mistakes. We shall have zero tolerance. God has ordained nothing less in His great plan."

That terse message was all the Council members were to receive at that point, and the Prince abruptly terminated his speech. Ayoub sent a coded copy of the e-mail transmission through to the director of Mossad along with those going out to the freedom fighters and the national leaders who were in support of the great work. He found himself lightly sweating in the room kept cool for the computers. He had not dared to look about as he sent his message for fear of looking suspicious. He did not dare exhale in relief when he was done.

Mordecai Narkiss received Job's message as it was being printed. He frowned briefly and turned to Levi Harkabi.

"Get this decrypted and send an unedited copy to your friend in Langley and without comment. I don't need to tell you to say nothing about our source."

Levi asked, "Not to the DCIA?"

"To Angelina Davis? *Pal-eeease*."

Every ranking officer knew and shared their director's disdain for the radical Davis. All communications with the CIA had been on a personal agent-to-agent basis since her ascension to the directorship. It was cumbersome and well afield from standard protocol, but veterans in both camps would have it no other way.

Harkabi was not a cryptanalyst, but he was familiar enough with the look of obvious XML encryption to know where to go in the Mossad technology department. He was told that Job had taken the risk to include in cleartext his electronic secret decryption key signature—a series of numbers from a popular Israeli numerology study of the Kabala. The cryptanalyst set to work quickly to evaluate the apparently baffling encoded material. The original content had been compressed and wrapped in an XML compression syntax and then encrypting it, a device to render it more complicated and time consuming to decrypt, but once identified, it was a very rapidly decodable text.

In fifteen minutes, Jonah Silverstein—the cryptanalyst—found Harkabi and explained Job's methodology, "Simple, really. Kind of old fashioned, but probably chosen by your agent because his Arab friends are not as sophisticated as they think; and your agent—who calls himself 'Afflicted by God'—used this encryption device to make it easy for us. Good chap. He even let us have a C-to-English translator. It would have been deucedly difficult to decipher without his overt—and presumably very risky—help because he used a random number generator based on a true physical source of randomness that can't be predicted; I think he used the greater-than-128 bit true entropy from something like a semi-conductor device. He convinced his keepers that he had made an impenetrable code by adding a mandatory to implement algorithm using Key Transport with (CBC)—that's Cipher Block Chaining for you uninitiated—and with PKCS number 5 padding. He included Key Agreement with Diffie-Hellmen—old stuff—but looks impressive to the rag heads, I suspect. For future reference—since we have gone through this code successfully this time—it will be quite fast and simple to decipher future messages."

Anthony Pickering, CIA Special Assistant Director, was shown the message by the night duty officer. He pondered it and spoke of its content but not its source to his two deputies. They decided to await further developments and locked the message in Pickering's safe. The idea of sharing the information with the new DCIA never entered the conversation.

Pickering was a mousy appearing, but inwardly tough man. He had a high pitched squeaky voice that had been a serious detriment to getting girls when he was growing up but now was part of his cover—he hardly looked or sounded like a James Bond. He was short and thin, beginning to bald with a receding forehead hairline, and had a slight limp from the residua of boyhood

Legg-Calvé-Perthes disease. He was from the West and had been educated at the University of Montana both of which were considered significant negatives in his resume' by the eastern dominated State Department when he first applied for government work, but were not even considered when he was recruited out of college by the CIA. Pickering—a true believing Methodist—had, for some unknown reason, specialized in Judaism and the Hebrew language for his master's degree at Harvard, where he roomed with Levi Harkabi, and had studied in Jerusalem where he first encountered Yahuda Grossman.

The prince's message was received the same hour by the six Council agents-in-place. The handler for each of them ordered the men to pay for their residences for the next six months and to haggle for a reduced rate for the sake of appearances. None of them had been informed of the original date; so, April 16 did not come as any particular disappointment or frustration. It would only require an additional degree of patience. These were patient men.

President Braithwaite's reliable news outlets, CNN, NPR, The *San Francisco Chronicle*, The *Madison Capital Times*, The *Los Angeles Times*, The *National Review, Newsweek Magazine, Time Magazine*, and The *Legal Times* of the National Lawyers Guild and a score of other influential sources proclaimed his triumphant concept with such titles as "The Peace Party", "Real Peace from the Liberal Presidency", "Braithwaite, Candidate for Nobel Peace Prize?", and "Dramatic Results from Pres. Peace Proposal". Russia's ITAR-Tass news agency and state run TV—RTR declared, "Braithwaite Breaks Long U.S. Tradition and Seeks Peace". The general public supported the celebration—despite its requirement for a modest increase in taxes—by a huge margin—72% in the Gallup poll, 87% in the *Newsweek*, The *LA Times*, and The *NY Times* polls and 89% in the *Portland Oregonian* and The *Madison Capital Times*. The *Salt Lake Tribune*, FOXNews.com, NewsMax.com, and *Jane's Information Group* polls all reflected far less enthusiastic polling information but were roundly denounced as being of the 'sour grapes' conservative vintage by the dominant mainstream pundits.

CHAPTER TWENTY-EIGHT

APRIL 9, 2010

The cabinet meeting was lengthy despite there being only one subject on the agenda. Each cabinet member, beginning with the secretary of State, outlined his or her area of responsibility for the upcoming celebrations. Donovan O'Laughlin told the others about his successes with foreign governments. None of them refused to participate; even the French had agreed to send a delegation to each American celebration city that had established a sister city relationship with a French municipality, a total of twelve. The Muslim governments had been enthusiastic, well beyond the hopes of the State Department.

"Egypt, Saudi Arabia, and Syria will send a total of a hundred representatives each. The sister city idea was brilliant. They have taken to it like fish to water. Libya sees its attendance as the final step in its rehabilitation. Iran is looking forward to the opportunity to demonstrate its complete rapprochement with the West. Iraq's Islamic State government will come to Washington to convey its thanks to us for making it possible at last for Islam to rule their historically tortured land. I have taken steps to have the grand ayatollah address a session of Congress. He will speak on the third day of festivities here There will be a major Islamic nation dignitary speaking in every celebration city in the county. In all, we will see representatives of a billion and quarter Muslims during this miraculous détente event. 168 nations will send delegations."

"Well done, Mr. Secretary," the president said.

"I echo that, Donovan," the secretary of Commerce said, "just imagine the incredible uplift this series of events will represent for our business world, especially the tourism industry."

"Not that we would think of it in crass commercial terms," joked the secretary of Labor.

"No," said the president, "I rather think this is like what Buzz Aldrin said, 'this is one giant step for mankind.'"

She knew it was Neil Armstrong, but Elizabeth knew better than to correct the president. She maintained an uneasy silence. That she did not contribute was little noted and not remembered.

"The big kick-off is in Detroit. Are we all set?" asked President Braithwaite.

"I think everything is ready, sir. My committee has mobilized the entire city; we have FBI, ATF, state and local police standing by for security. We have a trainload of flowers coming in from Florida and Mexico. We have procured the Tiger stadium for the opening speech and have rented every major venue where a dance could be held in the entire city and its suburbs. We have the local tourism boards sprucing up every possible rental location and have made it mandatory that there be no price gouging. The area's churches are getting local citizens to open their houses for the incoming crowds. The problem of the homeless is still vexing, but we'll keep working on it. We are trucking in warehouses of food and drink. We are ready for the three million visitors—maybe four—and have done everything in our imagination and power to secure the full cooperation of the six and a half million citizens of Detroit and across the border in Windsor, Ontario," reported Steven Capelli, Secretary of HUD, who had been volunteered to head up the celebration overall.

"Superb, Steve. I presume the protocol and security list has been finalized for the attendance of the government officials," said the president.

"I'll have the list sent to everyone's office by this afternoon, Mr. President. In brief, you will head up the first day's activities in Detroit, the veep will be in charge in D.C., and you two will alternate every two days. Half of the cabinet will be in Detroit and half in D.C. We have asked Congress to portion the members out so that not all of them will be in Detroit the first day, but that was difficult. I think we will see an overabundance of legislators in your general vicinity on that momentous day."

"I didn't suppose that they could be repressed. It is the grandmother of all photo ops and schmoozing venues," the president laughed.

Abdel Said Badr received his orders from Ali Abdullah Kaswari personally. The two men left the Caracas *urbanizacione* of Fuerta Tuina and drove to the wharf in La Guaira port where the sleek 210 SuperSport Ski Nautique fast boat lay impatiently at anchor. It was midnight.

The two freedom fighters carted their few personal belongings and stowed them in the matching small built-in lockers amidships. Badr sat on the large tackle and cargo locker in the middle of the deck and watched as Kaswari started up the 330 horse power PCM engine and engaged the IB drive. He reassured himself that the gas tank was full. Badr looked around. He saw two fifty gallon drums of gasoline and the Coast Guard pack but no sign of the large container with the six thousand pound bomb that would serve the world of Islam as the instrument of the Avenging of the Crusades The young freedom fighter presumed that he and Kaswari would pick the box up somewhere along the Venezuelan coast where it had been hidden for security purposes.

"*Akh*, will it take us long to fetch our package?" Badr asked Kaswari.

To his surprise, the older man laughed, the first demonstration of a sense of humor he had ever seen from the prince's no-nonsense chief of security.

"You look, but you do not see, young *tabligh*." Kaswari said with pleased amusement.

Badr looked about and still he did not see. His facial expression further amused Kaswari.

"Our people are successful," Kaswari said. "If our camouflage fooled you, my *sadik*, [friend] then I think we have nothing to fear from the Venezuelan or Mexican or American coast guards."

Badr searched again. He got up and walked forward alongside the storage locker that occupied the center of the boat and peered into the tiny cabin. He opened the engine and double battery compartments. All he found were the standard equipment: bilge pump, Halon canisters, folded Bimini Top and rain guard, cd satellite ready system, spare parts for the AM/FM radio. Nothing.

"Come back and take your seat, my young brother. We must get underway. Incidentally, you are sitting on more explosives than were used on Hiroshima and Nagasaki."

He laughed heartily at Badr's incredulous face. Finally, the *tabligh* realized the cleverness of the hiding place.

"The boat was rebuilt to have this extra long tackle and gear locker. Our Avenger weapon fits in it like a hand in a glove. Our local al Qaeda brothers left just enough space at the top of the locker to place a few life jackets, lanterns, and foul weather gear. Unless a Coast Guardsman gets very curious and decides to be extra meticulous in his search, no one will ever be the wiser about our cargo," Kaswari explained and demonstrated the cleverly hidden locks and hinges for the top and sides.

It was obvious that the box contained inside could be removed and transferred in a matter of a few minutes with enough muscle. Now that he looked carefully, Badr was able to see that the sleek motorboat sat six or eight inches lower in the water than one would expect. He realized that he was going to have to hone his skills of observation.

Badr gave Kaswari a sheepish thumbs-up and smiled his appreciation for the remarkable job of hiding the precious cargo. Kaswari maneuvered the sleek fast power-boat away from La Guaira Wharf and through the maze of moored vessels which was made easy by the state-of-the-art hydraulic steering and SS prop. Kaswari was scrupulous about obeying speed limits in Caracas Harbor; but once in the open Caribbean, he streaked towards Puerto Caballo on the coast then headed due west past the Netherlands Antilles.

He steered a course north and west holding just above the Antilles and Aruba. When they were past the dangerous coastline of Colombia, they made one stop for a little rest and to take on fresh water on the Panama coast, then roared up the coast of the Gulf of Mexico past the shorelines of Costa Rica, Nicaragua, Honduras and Belize. The two spent the daylight hours holed up on the beach on the Yucatan Peninsula and at nightfall went on, keeping within a hundred miles of the Mexican coast until they pulled into Matamoros, just south of Brownsville, Texas. It was approaching first light. They pulled into the harbor, refueled, and went to ground until it was again dark enough to travel.

Using the excellent American Gulf charts, Kaswari thundered across the wide expanse of the Gulf. Badr was astounded at the magnitude of maritime traffic, even during the night.

"This body of water is one of the world's most concentrated areas of shipping. That fact is most helpful for us, my *sadik*," Kaswari told Badr. "We are but one of thousands of vessels, and the chances of being stopped by the American Coast Guard are miniscule. We are all but perfectly safe for now."

Badr nodded his gratitude to Allah, the Merciful.

"I have not been on the sea much, *Akh* Kaswari. I admit to some lack of comfort at the thought of so much water beneath us and the land so far away," he confessed. "And, I cannot swim."

"Do not worry your head, little brother, it would do you no good to swim. There is something like 12,000 feet of water beneath us and more miles than any man could swim to land. Relax and enjoy the ride."

Chapter Twenty-Eight

The western coast of Florida loomed before them at dawn.

"If I have read the charts correctly, we should be looking at Cape Coral or somewhere near there."

Badr strained his eyes to try and make out a city, but they were too far out.

"We will stay far enough off the coast to avoid curious eyes. I will have to slow down now for fear of bringing attention to us. Our people in Florida warned me that the DEA and the Coast Guard officers are on the lookout for fast boats like ours and to go fast is to act like a lightening rod to attract them."

At full light they slipped into a mangrove coastal swamp along the gulf border of the Everglades and rested fitfully due to the heat, humidity, and mosquitoes. They did not venture away from the tangled roots secluding them until it was pitch black out. Kaswari maintained absolute silence and used an infrared light to read his map.

During the long sweaty night, the two men and their precious cargo traveled across the open bay until they could glide silently into the Kemp Channel on the bayside landfall of Cudjoe Key. Kaswari fretted as he waited for a signal that had to come while it was still dark. An hour passed, and no signal light came. He cursed.

Badr whispered hoarsely, "There, *akh*; I see a flashing lantern."

Kaswari was instantly alert and wary.

"Where?"

"Just south of us. It's on the beach."

The light flashed on and off three times. Kaswari flashed his lantern once, waited for two seconds, then flashed three more times. He told Badr to get out of the boat and to carry his handgun with the safety off.

In five minutes, the two men sensed the presence of a group of three or four men. Kaswari and Badr lay down on the beach and watched. A green light flashed three times.

"The color of the religion," Kaswari said with a small sigh of relief. "We are among friends."

"Hsst," he whispered as loudly as he dared.

"*Allahu akbar*," whispered one of the men.

"*Allahu akbar, akh*," responded Kaswari.

The six men and exchanged cheek kisses and salutations.

"Where is the boat?" asked the al Qaeda officer in charge.

"A hundred meters north."

"Bring it here. The beach is level and firm, and we can put it on the truck."

Badr stayed with the al Qaeda men, and Kaswari fetched the boat. The night remained densely black due to the low overhang of dark clouds.

Kaswari moved the sleek speed boat into position, and the al Qaeda freedom fighters let down a ramp from the large truck. Two men attached lines from the motor winch attached to the truck, and the other four men guided the craft up the ramp and into the bowels of the truck. Two al Qaeda men took their places on pull down seat rests attached to the truck's cargo area walls. Kaswari ordered Badr to accompany them for the trip. All were armed with grenade launchers, Glock 40s, and M-16s.

Another of the American al Qaeda freedom fighters pulled himself into the driver's seat and spread out AAA highway maps in the middle. Kaswari sat in the passenger seat. The al Qaeda brother handed Kaswari and Badr each two genuine United States passports, part of the 400,000 blank passports missing and unaccounted for from countries all over the world. Interpol reported that only thirty-four nations—less than one fifth of the 181 member nations— had complied with the agency's request for information. Interpol could only identify 80,000 passports as even being missing. There was not the slightest chance of the passports now in Kaswari's and Badrs' hands being identified as counterfeit since verification required only that the customs officer punch in the number on the card.

The truck doors were shut and locked by the three remaining al Qaeda fighters who then walked quietly through the darkness to a parked car and drove away.

The truck with the speed boat and its lethal cargo and the single-minded soldiers of Allah pulled away from the beach, drove along Spanish Main Drive past the Venture Out development and onto Highway 1 headed north. At dawn they were on Alligator Alley—I-75—a few miles north of Pompano Beach.

Col. Hosni Esmet Badr paid the bill for his six day stay at the LeGrande Residence Hotel during the late evening of March 8. He made a mildly grumpy perfunctory complaint about the steepness of the bill and asked two or three detailed questions about the VAT and the British Columbia hotel guest tax. He paid for the following day and asked that his room not be disturbed until check-out time. Shortly after midnight, a knock came at the door.

The colonel peered through the peep hole and recognized his countryman, Anwar el Meshad.

Badr unlocked the bolt lock, and the two chain locks and admitted el Meshad. He patted the younger man down professionally.

"I apologize, *akh*; but in our business one cannot be too careful; and *marhaba, kaif halak.* [hello, how are you?] "

"No offense taken, my brother, *assalamu alaikum, wa rahmatullahi, wa barakatuhu.* [peace be upon you, and mercy and blessings]."

Col. Badr nodded. El Meshad had always been too flowery for his taste. Maybe the man was just currying favor all of the time, or maybe he was one of the pink ones.

"Are you ready to leave, Colonel?"

"Yes. I will need help with the box."

The two men carried the innocuous looking box with the dirty bomb inside down the rear exit stairs and onto the parking lot. El Meshad hurried over to an old Chevrolet truck with a California blue and yellow license plate and brought it to Badr and the box. They loaded the box into the pickup's bed and drove out of the residence hotel's parking lot. El Meshad drove, having had two weeks to memorize the route. He handed Col. Badr an envelope containing a U.S. passport and a set of work invoices for a Canadian and American liquor distribution service.

The old truck attracted no attention by itself, and the route the two freedom fighters took was slow but safe. They took the Cambie Street Bridge, headed east on 5th and on to Ontario Street all the way across town to the Fraser River area and past Queen Elizabeth park. They crossed Marine Drive and into an industrial area where the street became more like an alley. They turned east on Kent Avenue and drove all the way to the Vancouver city limits at Boundary Road. They bypassed most of Burnaby and worked their way along the New West Minster waterfront and into the downtown and over the Pattullo Bridge, then moved through the dark onto 110 Avenue, then to 108 Avenue and onto Whalley Ring Road allowing them to bypass busy downtown Surrey. They were making excellent time unimpeded by traffic when they turned left onto Fraser Highway. With a few side roads including two misturns, they were able to move smoothly onto Highway 15, the main artery leading to the border.

15 took them to Truck Crossing. Theirs' was the only car at the obscure U.S./Canadian border post. El Meshad dutifully stopped at the U.S. Customs kiosk. A uniformed officer approached the truck and peered in at el Meshad and Badr.

"Good morning, gentlemen," he said politely. "May I see your passports?"

The two men produced their phony passports with alacrity. The officer glanced at them and back at the documents' owners. He seemed satisfied.

"You are U.S. citizens?" he asked.

"Yes, sir," the two freedom fighters chorused their practiced lie.

"What was your business in Canada?"

"Delivering Olympia Beer to our outlets in Vancouver."

"Why California plates and not Washington?"

El Meshad laughed.

"This is our new old truck. The big delivery truck broke down, and we had to use one that belonged to a new employee on short notice."

"That accounts for the fresh paint job and signage."

"Yes, sir. We're a little embarrassed, but it had to do in a pinch."

The officer smiled.

"Got to get the beer through, even in the middle of the night, otherwise we might have an international crisis, eh?"

"That's about it, officer. Our boss is not an understanding kind of man. Doesn't think too much of Mexicans."

The border agent glanced at the passports again and saw that the names were Hispanic. That gibed with the comment about Mexicans. He handed the documents back to the men. They drove off in no hurry and turned out onto I-5. They planned to follow the interstate all the way to Los Angeles.

Naguib Eddin Moheiddin departed from the Sheraton Hotel on King Street in Hamilton, Ontario and out onto the QEW highway in plenty of time to put him at the U.S. Border Station facility at Niagara Falls during the pre-noon rush hour when the officers could be expected to be most busy and least vigilant. The large steamer trunk containing the dirty bomb had been removed from the transients' luggage hold facility during an unobtrusive visit two days previously and was safely packed into the center of a Jack Daniels whiskey delivery truck in such a way that even an overzealous border agent would have to remove hundreds of crates of breakable fifths of whiskey to see the box no matter what direction the search started. The box had been covered with cardboard sections to create the appearance of separate box fronts with Jack Daniels labels applied to each segment. The labels were real, having been stolen from the main plant in Lynchburg, Tennessee by an al Qaeda operative who worked in the packaging center. Muslims were preferred employees because they were unlikely to steal whiskey.

Moheiddin was sweating lightly as the customs officer approached his truck.

"Morning, Officer," the freedom fighter said. "Hot enough for ya?"

He had been taught the absurd phrase during his period of preparation and was surprised to see the officer's stern demeanor lighten as he heard the idiomatic speech characteristic of the jargon of the working class.

"Looks like summer awready," the officer replied.

Moheiddin was encouraged by his small success.

"It's a relief after the cold spring. It's been colder than a well digger's butt up north until just the last few days."

That was accurate and drew a knowing nod from the officer.

"May I see your ID, sir? Birth certificate or passport if you have one or the other."

Moheiddin made a small show of searching for his passport. He produced it, and the officer carefully examined it. Evidently, it passed muster because he gave the passport back to Moheiddin without comment.

"Mind pulling over to the inspection drive through, Mr. Muhammad?" the border agent asked politely.

For the briefest of moments Moheidden was confused. It took him a bit to remember that his passport and all of the truck's documentation were in the name of Ishmael Muhammad, resident of Sterling, Virginia.

His pause drew a curious look from the customs officer.

"Any problem, officer?" Moheidden managed.

"Just routine. You know about the big shindig they're having in the District next week. We're on special security alert. Every truck gets searched. Sorry for any inconvenience."

Moheidden masked his reaction to the disturbing alarm bell that went off in his head when he did not understand the agent's word, 'shindig.' In context, he told himself, it didn't matter, must mean celebration.

"Sure, anything to be sure our country's safe, officer. I live right there in Sterling. I sure don't want some terrorist hurting my family."

"Sterling? It's a small world. We're practically neighbors. I'm from McLean. You Muslim?"

"Yeah."

"You know the Hamads from there? They live on our same block. Good folks."

"'Fraid not. There's only a few million of us in the States."

He laughed.

The customs officer shared the joke with a broad self-deprecating smile.

"I know that's silly—I guess you get that all the time. I'm a Jehovah's Witness. I get the same kind of questions.

Moheiddin pulled into the second bay of the inspection station. A laundry service truck next to him had been completely unloaded, and a crew of agents was busily removing the truck's seats. Moheiddin began to feel very tense.

"Step out of the truck, sir. You'll find some coffee and doughnuts in the waiting room over there. I'm afraid this'll take a while.

Moheiddin did as he was told. He sat down on one of the uncomfortable metal folding chairs and feigned nonchalance while he tongued his false tooth with the cyanide capsule. He wondered what such a death would be like. He was sweating heavily now. He cursed himself for his lack of self-control—a lifelong flaw—but he was powerless to gain full control.

Four men in coveralls arduously removed heavy crates of jangling bottles and set them carefully aside on benches and on the ground until the available spaces were filled. Moheiddin could not hear what the men were saying, but he could tell by the shaking of their heads that they were not pleased with their task.

One of them—obviously the foreman—left the other three workers and walked over to the customs officer who was holding the documents from the truck's glove compartment. They spoke briefly, both pointed to the truck, and the foreman shook his head. The customs officer laughed and gestured for the foreman to return.

He talked to his fellow workers. They pushed aside the crates of bottles to make a space. Then they quickly removed the truck's seats. The customs officer went to the guard station and came out with a dog on a leash. The workers stepped aside and let the dog prowl all around the truck. They lifted it into the cab where it remained for a few minutes. It jumped back out onto the asphalt, and the officer put on its leash and returned it to the guard station. A moment later, he brought out a second dog, a German shepherd. The dog went through a similar exercise with the truck and was returned to the guard station.

The foreman directed his men, and they meticulously returned everything to its place inside the truck. The customs officer returned and made a brief inspection, signed a set of papers on his clip board, and handed a copy to the foreman.

The foreman walked to the waiting room and called out, "Mr. Muhammad, your truck's done. You want to come and give it the okay?"

Moheidden was rattled and could not quite understand the idiom the foreman used. He took the proffered inspection document and followed the workman back to the truck.

The two men stood awkwardly looking at the truck for a few minutes. Moheidden was unsure how he was supposed to respond, and he was getting more nervous.

"Okay?" the foreman asked, breaking the silence.

"Oh, yeah. Looks okay."

Moheidden was relieved finally to be able to catch on. He climbed back into the cab and was waved out of the inspection station. He entered a short line of trucks, presented his document when it came his turn, and drove out onto the QEW and over the bridge to US I-90. He drove all day and all night from Buffalo to Erie and followed I-79 to Morgantown and I-70 to D.C. He was too nervous to eat or to trust himself in a motel. He pulled into a vacant lot of a construction area situated adjacent to a Williamsburg Colonial house on Almey Court in Sterling, Virginia at four in the morning. He was shaking with exhaustion.

He walked warily to the house and knocked on the door. He waited tensely until a woman in a head scarf came to the door.

She asked nervously and groggily, "What brings you here, brother?"

It took Moheidden a moment.

"I come to avenge the crusades, sister."

The pass phrase required no learned rejoinder.

"Come in, come in. Do you want something to eat, or do you just want to get to bed?"

"I'll eat in the morning. Just show me a bed."

The woman's husband had roused himself by now and showed Moheidden to a guest bed room. It would have been unseeming for a woman to do so.

Director, Mossad
April 9, 1010

Message to large number Arabs. Big plans for April 16. No details. 6 special agents sent to several countries. None to Israel.
-Afflicted by God

Narkiss walked Dark Shadow's decrypted message himself to Levy Harkabi's office and directed him to send it to the CIA through the back door. Harkabi had it re-encrypted and sent to Langley to Anthony Pickering, CIA Special Assistant Director.

Narkiss was pleased with the work of his relatively recently promoted lieutenant. The young man seemed very much like the Mossad leader's own son, now off to university in Cambridge. Narkiss knew Harkabi's history intimately and trusted him as completely as he did any other man he had ever known. Above all else, Levy Harkabi could keep a secret.

Harkabi was thirty-two and a veteran of fifteen years of service to the Mossad. The handsome young man, as light skinned and fair haired a European as any Frenchman, Spaniard, or Portuguese, was also the scion of Jews with a genealogy that went back past Moses. He was not a sabra, a prickly pear, like his leader, not a native born Israeli. Harkabi—his birth name was Michael dePass Cardoso—came from a family that entered Spain in the 6th Century BCE after the destruction of the first temple.

The Moors crossed the Straits of Gibraltar and conquered the Iberian Peninsula. By 711 AD, there were no more openly Jewish communities left in Spain. The family Gottesman became the family Cardoso and quietly assumed the mantel of practicing Catholics despite the hardships entailed. It was better than being found out as a Jew—the Islamists tortured and killed the Jews. For the next seven hundred years, the Gottesmans—who ostensibly became the Cardosos—were outward humble Catholics and also secret faith keeping Jews. They spoke Ladino, the hybrid of medieval Spanish and Hebrew when the Moors were not around, and Arabic when they were. It was a difficult life—but with certain accommodations—tolerable.

The Cardosos were wary and bided their time when the Almohades conquered the Moors in wars from 1146 to 1172, when news came in 1197 that the Moors had been driven out of Lisbon and in 1212 when the Christian kings defeated the Almohades. They openly but unostentatiously practiced their Catholicism and in great secret kept alive the traditions of Judaism that bound them to the Chosen People over millennia. They joined the rejoicing crowds of Christians when Ferdinand drove the Moors out of Córdoba in 1236 and out of Seville in 1248, and when the Moors were finally driven out of Portugal in 1249. Life improved for the Cardosos; but they had a reputation of being a little less Catholic than their neighbors; and despite their professed great love for Santo Esterika and Santo Moises and never missing mass; they came under suspicion when the Inquisition began in 1479. They were among the fortunates who survived the terrible years but could no longer resist when the Jews and the converted Jews were finally driven out of Spain and to Portugal in 1495.

In Portugal, the Cardosos assimilated and flourished, more Catholic than the Pope. However, they continued to follow their old traditions—they married under the *huppah*, studied and practiced rituals from the Kabala, hung a rooster's head over the door where a birth would come, threw a silver coin in the baby's first bath water; at a funeral they threw away all the water in the house of the deceased, put a gold or silver coin in the mouth of the departed, depending on their economic status at the time, and gave it to a beggar; and the men did not shave for thirty days after the death of a relative.

Michael dePass Cardoso grew up keeping secrets. The family retired to their basement on Friday nights and lit candles in the darkened room, and he never mentioned it to his school mates. He became an accomplished thief and never divulged his activities or the identities of his young gang members even when he was subjected to the brutality of Portuguese police interrogators. When he was fifteen, he was recruited by the Mossad—more specifically, by Mordecai Narkiss. He was vulnerable to the wily spy because he was caught and punished for reading the Kabala in his religion class. The local rabbi heard about it and let the Israeli secret service know about the boy. Michael did small jobs for the service until he went to college—to Harvard—where he got a bachelors in history and was Anthony Pickering's roommate, to Stanford where he got an MBA, and to Yeshiva University where he got a doctorate in Jewish studies. He also began doing bigger things for Mossad.

The more he learned of the persecutions of the Jews, the more he volunteered. By the time he was twenty-five, he had graduated to being a frequent assassin for his service. In 2004, Michael killed the deputy ambassador of Egypt as he was passing information to Abu Nidal and barely missed killing the international terrorist. Nidal circulated Michael's picture, and Narkiss took his protégé to Israel. Michael dePass Cardoso became Levi Harkabi, a Jerusalem jewel merchant. He also became the best field espionage agent in the Mossad, able to pass for European or American, fluent in five languages, and exquisitely careful.

This time Pickering found a top secret clearance courier and had this message and the former one from the Mossad hand-delivered to DCIA Davis. She took the message, read it, rolled her eyes, and filed it in her safe. She would present it to the president in their weekly morning meeting on the eleventh. It was one of nearly a hundred such messages that had come her way in the past two weeks, and now she planned to deal with them all at once. She did not think it would be worth elevating the security level above green until the sixteenth as already planned, but she would leave that up to the president and the secretary of Homeland Security, that over reactive sycophant.

CHAPTER TWENTY-NINE

APRIL 14, 2010

The cabinet meeting was perfunctory. Protocol officers gave each secretary, the president and vice-president a packet containing their itineraries and speaking responsibilities for the week. Elizabeth Rowan was amused and somewhat put off at the obvious shunting to the side that characterized her assignments. There was no chance that she would upstage anyone, least of all the president. She was not fond of her job, but had adjusted to the life of relative ease and to being an adornment rather than a mover and a shaker. She knew it would not be forever; the president had told her so in clear prose. He would have a more politically useful running mate in the upcoming elections that he expected to win. He was unsure of his ground enough to be tilting toward a Southerner since the Southern Democrats had been becoming progressively disaffected in the past two decades and were deserting the party line and even the party itself in alarming numbers. It was nothing personal or even a reflection on any thing Elizabeth had done, or not done; it was just politics.

The vice-president was to speak at one in the afternoon at a gathering on the Mall. She was not even first speaker. The morning was to be a huge march for the minorities and a series of speeches by African-American, Asian-American, Hispanic-American, Native-American and Micronesian leaders. The afternoon would be a rousing celebration of American history and the announcement by the vice-president of the opening of the Freedom March Monument. She would follow the Reverend Jesse Jackson and the Ezekiel Baptist choir. She was to be free all morning and all afternoon after her speech, and then she was to attend a series of three grand galas featuring Hollywood glitterati, all personal friends of President Braithwaite. He would return on the second day to a series of balls and galas with specially invited big campaign donors. Although the next election was almost two years off, it was none too early to begin using his incumbency to further his next term.

Elizabeth Rowan decided to take the rest of the day off to practice her speech knowing that she would not be missed.

Angelina Davis and Anthony Pickering, her assistant from the CIA, Daniel Ajami, the NSA, Leland Marques, DFBI, Donald Pell Johnsen, Washington D.C. SAC, and his ASAC, Mort Crane, and Rupert Vernon, Secretary of Homeland Security, were ushered into the president's office to present the PDB. Davis had asked that the Presidential Daily Briefing be held an hour earlier than usual to be sure that everyone that mattered would be present; so, no one could blame her if her recommendation somehow led to a failure. She engineered the meeting carefully so that the latest so-called new terror threat would not be given overdue emphasis; the rapport with the administration's Arab friends had been cultivated too assiduously to bring offense now. She had been scrupulous in researching the recent traffic with people suspected of hostile intentions—excepting the French and Germans, of course—and found nothing to corroborate Pickering's message. The pipsqueak had stead-fastly refused to reveal his source—even to her—and she was very much put out by his insubordination.

Starting off the PDB, DCIA Davis read off a numbing array of National Security Administration intercepted messages, none of which had any speci-ficity. Most of them sounded pretty crack-pot. The White House National Security Council had paid them scant heed.

Then she said, "Mr. President, my special assistant," whom she noted with a perfunctory glance, "has received encoded information from an unnamed and uncorroborated source regarding a threat. I'll let him present the message."

Pickering presented the president with a copy of the Mossad message, but he had conspicuously blackened out the reference to the source. He read the message exactly as it had been received to the assemblage of National Security leaders otherwise.

"Big plans...six agents..." President Braithwaite mused. "What do the rest of you make of it?

"Who's the source, Anthony?" asked Leland Marques.

"Can't, Leland, sorry."

"I take it you respect your source's credibility pretty highly."

"I do."

The SAC and A-Sack shrugged.

"Not much to go on," Mr. President. "I don't see what we can do about it," said the SAC.

"I can't begin to emphasize enough the importance of my source, Mr. President. I am willing to risk my career on the message. This is real, important, and imminent. I strongly recommend that we go to orange at least or preferably change the agendae around in a wholesale fashion to confuse any terrorists."

"Madam Director, in future, I prefer to have the principles do the talking and not the assistants and deputies," the president said as if Pickering was not there.

Pickering shut up, put a look on his face about as revealing as a soda cracker, and vowed to bide his time.

"I apologize, Mr. President. Mr. Pickering won't be attending any more high level meetings."

Davis was livid. This was rank insubordination, and she would have his skin for this.

"Let's hear from Homeland Security. Rupert, what's your recommendation?"

"Well, Mr. President. I hate to think we would spoil our national celebration, but I do believe this is one of those moments that could come back to haunt us if we are wrong. I think we need to have Steve Capelli and the National Security Council and Homeland Security people get together and make some alterations. Better to be safe than sorry because in this case it could possibly be a big sorry."

"Anyone else buy that?" President Braithwaite asked, looking from eye to eye.

There was a thoughtful pause. Finally, all heads shook in the negative except for Secretary Vernon and Special CIA Assistant Pickering.

"I like this democracy stuff, especially when it goes my way. I am not going to work the nation or the world up into lather over another vague message which could well be nothing more than plans to attend our party. And while we're on the subject, I am going to do away with the federal no-fly list this afternoon and by the end of the week will dismantle the FBI TIPOFF, Special Interest Detainees, and Visas Condor Programs, all of which target unfairly twenty-six Muslim countries We will not permit funding of the provocative FBI MAXCAP 05 program for intelligence gathering. It has never yet received a functional level of funding, and we will not let it happen on our watch. My staff will be lobbying the legislators to do away with the top secret Foreign Intelligence Surveillance Court, a kangaroo setup if I ever heard of one. They average nearly 1700 warrants a year, mostly to snoop in the business of innocents, like the Hollywood and sports celebs who stump for me and for liberal causes. It's un-American.

"We are making ready a revision of PDD [Presidential Decision Directive] 39 drafted June 21, 1995 to permit and encourage the prosecution of so-called terrorists in their own countries and to do away entirely with the clauses that would enable the United States to induce the return of suspects to our country by force and without the cooperation of the host government. This we also regard as prejudicial towards our Arab friends, and we will foster peace by backing off from our heedlessly pugnacious stance. I have directed Secretary Donovan to communicate these changes to all fifty-seven countries of the Organization of the Islamic Conference. Their Islamic Conference of Foreign Ministers is meeting in Istanbul this week, and the secretary of State has been given the opportunity to address them. This change in U.S. policy will be his theme."

"Please, Mr. President…" Pickering blurted.

The president acted as if he did not hear the man.

Angelina Davis said brusquely without even looking over at Pickering, "leave."

Pickering dejectedly stood up and walked out.

He was not through, however. He made a quiet visit to the office of the editor of the *Intelligence Daily*, and requested that he include a message about the intelligence he had received. He had it placed on page three, the location for news about serious developments that was relatively obscure but meaningful for those who mattered. The *Intelligence Daily* is a compilation of raw data and discussions from the principles and the best thinkers and most important actors in the intelligence world. Anyone interested in the real thing, read their *Daily* from cover to cover every day.

Pickering then went to the CIA building, closed up his files in his desk, and left for home.

He walked into his house and said to his wife, Mary Anne and their two small children, "C'mon, we're going out to the coast for a little overnighter."

Angelina Davis was furious when she saw the *Daily* the following morning and could not get hold of Pickering the entire day. The man was a good field agent, and she half suspected that he was avoiding her on purpose. He was a valuable asset in the Company, but no leader could afford to keep a loose cannon like that one around. She wanted to be able to look him in the face when she fired him.

Chapter Twenty-Nine

APRIL 15, 2010

Naguib Eddin Moheidden awaked with a start, his heart racing. He had slept fitfully and was nervous and anxious. Although the woman served him a proper Muslim meal and did so with appropriate subservience, Moheidden snapped at her twice for trivial or maybe imagined offenses. Her husband took her into the kitchen and slapped her face and sent her to her room with no breakfast.

"What can you expect from a woman? The Great Satan corrupts our women. I can hardly wait to get back to Morocco where a man gets proper respect."

"Only in Fez, *akh*," observed Moheidden, "Casa Blanca is entirely corrupted by the West."

"Do you require assistance today?"

"No, I have a simple plan, set orders; and I require nothing in the way of assistance—it could draw attention to me."

"Then enjoy your breakfast. I will attend to my wife, and you can leave at your leisure."

"That would be best."

Moheidden hurried through his figs and picked at his steaming *fuul* and bread. He was too jumpy to have an appetite even for his staple fava beans. He did not trust the man of the house. Any man who let his woman insult a guest was suspect.

The freedom fighter was pleased to see that the men from the local al Qaeda cell had come in the night and had done their duty efficiently and quietly. Instead of the large liquor delivery truck, the vacant lot contained a dump truck. Faded letters on the driver's side door read, "District's Best Dirt Mover-Call for Budget Prices." The telephone number was illegible.

Moheiddin climbed onto the bed of the truck and saw several large cardboard boxes, all with the obvious appearance of trash. He found the key under the mat and started the engine which purred like a deep-throated cat. He loved working with men, dedicated men. They made his missions successful, and he knew that failure was not an option. Even the Americans used that phrase. The difference was that he meant it.

He followed his map into the heart of the District. It was overwhelmingly busy, like coming into Cairo's business center from his *Ein Shams* home district at rush hour. It turned out that the busyness was useful. Security people, some obviously only rent-a-cops, gave him no more than a cursory once over and went their harried way to the next vehicle, and the next, and the next.

Moheiddin wove his way to the Mall, turned north up 7th Street to E. and pulled into the commercial parking lot. He ignored the "Lot Full" sign and stopped at the attendant's booth.

A swarthy Egyptian man stepped out and looked at the dump truck carefully. "We're full. Didn't you see the sign?"

"I have come to avenge the crusades."

The Egyptian nodded. He had been expecting this exact vehicle.

"Follow me."

Moheiddin jerked forward. He was none too facile with the temperamental old truck's transmission with all of its double clutching and two gear shifts. It rattled him. The attendant directed Moheiddin to stop while he produced keys from his denim pocket and moved a pick-up truck out of a capacious parking space. He signaled Moheiddin to back into the spot. Moheiddin pulled forward and was at too acute of an angle and scraped the Mercedes on his left. He cursed and was ashamed when he saw the look of disdain on the Egyptian's face. It made him angry and upset. He was not doing well.

He backed up, pulled forward and looked out his window to back up. He had never actually backed any vehicle up, and, in fact, had had very little experience with driving. He jerked the car and killed the engine. He cursed. He tried again and killed the engine again. The attendant aggravated his sense of agitation by offering to park the truck for him. He raced the engine and ground the gears until the rotten old truck finally moved backwards. Too fast. He jammed his foot at the brake, but missed and hit the accelerator. The truck hurtled backwards and bashed in the side of the Mercedes and plowed on until the rear end of the Chevrolet in the next space was smashed in before he could regain his composure and move his foot to the brake. He was sweating and felt faint.

Forty-seven minutes prior to the events taking place in the 7th and E Street North parking lot, the Bank of America branch at 201 Pennsylvania Avenue SE had been held up, and all D.C. police were told to look for a swarthy man of medium build of either Hispanic or Arab ethnic background. Officer Elmer Foynston was on his third day on the job. He took seriously his duties to provide security during the large District celebration. His heart quickened with new purpose with the call to maintain a high index of suspicion for the bank robber, an unknown subject, who could not have escaped the area because of the grid-locked traffic. He scanned the crowds for men with the unsub's description and for anyone carrying a bag appropriate to the size required to hold the bank loot.

Foynston was pessimistic; this did not look like his day to shine after he had looked at several hundred party goers jockeying for position along parade routes and around celebration venues. He saw black people, Asian people, and white people until he felt that his vision was getting blurred. He had not seen a single Hispanic or Arab in the past hour; it was as if they had all gone to ground.

His attention was caught by a small disturbance taking place in the parking lot at the corner of 7th and E Streets. An old dump truck had obviously just banged into another car in the lot; and an Arab man—apparently the lot attendant—was gesticulating wildly to get the truck to pull into a parking space sensibly. As Officer Foynston turned to walk into the lot—muttering imprecations that his time was going to be frittered away in a meaningless traffic incident—he saw the truck jerk forward in two moves and; to his consternation, Foynston watched the truck intentionally ram into two cars in front of it. It had to be intentional; no one could be that bad of a driver.

He ran forward towards the accident scene. The truck driver ground the gears and appeared to be making a dogged attempt to back up. Foynston figured that the idiot was going to have another go at it.

He shouted, "You there, stop. Police! Stop!"

Foynston had a deep commanding voice, and it carried effectively. Inside the cab of the dump truck, Naguib Eddin Moheiddin abruptly jerked his head in the direction of the police officer's voice. He panicked. No matter what, he could not be caught with the bomb. The bomb could not be detonated until tomorrow, or it could destroy the entire world wide mission. The Council had drummed that fact into his head several thousand times. He had to get out of there and draw attention away from the dirty bomb reposing peacefully in the bed of the dump truck.

It never occurred to Moheiddin that he might simply call out to the officer and say, "Sorry officer, my brakes failed. I'm glad you came. I need help." Or something to that effect.

Moheiddin reacted from his guts. His long and painful days of training in Afghanistan and as a mujahideen—literally, one who wages jihad—clicked automatically into his wildly careening mind, and he reacted the only way he knew. He threw open the door of the truck and leaped to the ground, his feet in the firing stance. Without prior thought, his 9mm Sig Sauer pointed at the police officer's chest.

The uniformed police officer saw the truck door open, the man leap out, the firing stance, and the evil looking gun barrel staring at his chest. He knew he had to react and to do so with deadly force, but his training at the academy had conditioned him to look about to avoid collateral damage. It flitted through his mind to punch in a signal 13—"Assist Patrolman"—the highest priority radio call, which would cause all units to respond. There was no time.

It was only tenths of a second, but Moheiddin was unhampered by humanitarian considerations like the American police officer, and he fired three shots into DCPD Patrolman Elmer Foynston before the officer could unholster his firearm. The first two shots entered Foynston's chest and inch and a half apart, passed through his left lung and shattered his heart. The third shot caught the hapless policeman in the vertex of his skull as he pitched forward and drilled an expanding hole directly through the midline and into his brainstem where it pulverized an area three centimeters in diameter. Foynston was dead before he heard the shots, before he could feel fear or pain, and before he fell facedown on the asphalt of the parking lot. A pool of red-black blood spread around the black officer.

The Egyptian looked into the crazed eyes of the man from the dump truck and turned to run between two parked cars. A 9mm round caught him neatly in the occiput of his skull, and he pitched forward as if he were a straw man whose stuffing had all been suddenly removed.

Moheiddin ran south through the parking lots in the 7th and E block and the 7th and D block then zigzagged his way to the right and into the crowds meandering onto Pennsylvania Avenue. He pocketed his gun and forced himself to walk and to regain a facial expression of unconcern, but only with great force of will. He was approaching the Museum of Science and Technology by the time the first alarm went out that there had been a cop killing. The excited civilian who called 911 gave the wrong location—the police raced as rapidly as they could through the teeming thousands of tourists invading the streets to 7th and E Streets South. They lost more than forty minutes before they could analyze their situation and go to the correct location in the north of the District.

Officers placed yellow crime scene tape around the parking lot and called in DCPD Crime Scene Investigators and PERT—the FBI Physical Evidence Response Team. The D.C. detectives, FBI agents, and CSI agents concentrated on the downed officer and the hapless parking lot attendant. After more than an hour, CSI and PERT agents began painstakingly to examine the cab of the truck. They were interested to see if there was any evidence of alcohol use or on the far outside, if there was any hint that this truck had been driven by the desperate bank robber trying to make his escape. A quick once over of the truck bed revealed only trash. Two uniformed officers remained behind to keep looky-loos out of the crime scene while the CSI and PERT officers poked around, measured, dusted, and luminoled.

The detectives and some forty uniformed patrolmen and women fanned out to search for the killer or killers. They had no description, no motive, no clues. The detective lieutenant in charge of the DCPD contingent and the FBI special agent in charge of the investigation—in a rare show of cooperation—agreed as a working hypothesis to look for an Hispanic or Arab unsub as the perpetrator, possibly the bank robber, possibly just an EDP. They notified the VICAP [Violent Crime Apprehension Programs] office and a bulletin was dispatched to all police and security officers to that effect. The FBI Psychological Profile Unit began drafting the probable characteristics of an emotionally disturbed person. The senior officers ordered a dragnet.

By the time the first police footstep off the parking lot occurred, Moheiddin was crossing Virginia and 23rd into the park where he easily mingled with the crowds of hippies and became one of the 'dudes' enjoying the clouds of marijuana smoke and the views of topless drunk girls cavorting with clowns, jugglers, acrobats, street preachers, and Viet Nam War veteran attired wannabes. He disappeared.

Col. Hosni Esmet Badr and Anwar el-Meshad took three days to travel from Bellingham, Washington to Lancaster, California where the colonel holed up in the safe house to which he had been directed by the Council. El Meshad was taken to LAX and put on a flight to Cairo; his part in the Avenging the Crusades operation was completed. The house in Lancaster faced West Avenue L and then out into the windswept high desert. Badr felt at home in the locale and with the four devout men who occupied the house. This was California, and no one questioned the comings and goings of a group of men who came and went largely at night. This was the Antelope Valley where Edwards Air Force base is located and where a substantial portion of the population is employed in black-box aeronautical engineering facilities or by the United States government in jobs they do not talk about. Even juries are selected there by prosecutors and defense lawyers without being able to learn the place or type of employment of potential jurors—on the simple command of the courtroom judge, "You don't need to know that."

During the late evening of April 15—American tax day—Col.Badr drove out of the driveway of the safe house and onto Avenue L, past Stanley Park, and turned south on to the freeway, Highway 14. His vehicle was a non-descript slab-sided long white Dodge van that had no markings. The dirty bomb he transported was hidden in a front compartment separated from the cab and the rear portion of the bed of the truck by a partition that looked exactly like the original front of the bed. Only if one were to make actual or mental measurements could he recognize that there was a discrepancy of six feet between the outside and the inside dimensions. Looking from the rear of the truck into the cargo area one would see row upon row of dresses on clothes hangers, the very look intended for the truck's papers identifying it as a wholesale dress cleaning service.

The Egyptian colonel followed his very detailed map into the heart of downtown Los Angeles via the 110 Pasadena Freeway to Temple Street. A few blocks later, on his right, he came to the Civic Center and pulled into the vast parking lot. He took out his throwaway cell phone, dialed the number on his instructions and let it ring ten times and then hung up. He got out of the truck—ostensibly to stretch his legs—and walked to the nearest rubbish can and threw away the cell phone. Twenty minutes later a late model black Ford Mustang pulled along side the truck.

The man inside leaned out and asked Col. Badr, "Are you interested in avenging the crusades?"

"You have the right man."

"Here."

The Mustang driver handed Col. Badr an envelope embossed with the return address of the Sheraton Grande Hotel then drove out of the parking lot without further conversation. The envelope contained documentation permitting the driver, one Rafael Diaz-Perez, employee of the Actell Wholesale Cleaners Company, to deliver a load to the hotel and to park his truck overnight to enable early morning delivery of a load of hotel lady guests' dry cleaned dresses. The envelope also contained vouchers for the hotel's shuttle van and airline tickets to Canada.

Badr drove back north and west to Figueroa Street, turned left and entered the service entrance driveway of the hotel. He maneuvered his truck to the parking spaces near the loading dock. Badr admired the Council's choice of targets. The hotel, one of Sheraton's most luxurious, was situated in the Bunker Hill Gold Coast such that overhead walkways connected it to the Westin Bonaventure Hotel, the Crocker Center, the World Trade Center, Arco Plaza, Security Plaza, Union Plaza, and the Bunker Hill Condominiums. The bomb would take those places out and would severely damage the Los Angeles

Central Library on 5th Street, the Fashion Institute on Flower, LA City Hall on North Spring Street, and possibly Cigna Hospital further north and west on Temple Street. Major business centers, tourist destinations, government buildings, masses of civilians, and a major traffic hub would be destroyed, and the area made uninhabitable for the next fifty years. It was a good thing that Allah had inspired, Badr realized.

He walked to the back of the truck and opened it. It took about two minutes for the freedom fighter to push his way through the clothes to the false back. He undid a latch that looked like a hook for securing loads and opened a small entry door. He squirmed his way inside and opened the box with the bomb. In another minute he had set the bomb's timer for 0615 that day; it was now 0210 PST on April 16.

The freedom fighter exited the truck the way he had come in, padlocked the doors, and walked to the all-night attendant's booth.

"These are my papers. I'll be back early to unload. No problem with parking here, I'm told," he said to the young African-American man in the booth who was tuned to a deafening and mind numbing rap station.

"Nope, dude. You got the paper, you got the permission. See you come dawn."

Badr thanked him and walked around the corner of the hotel where he was out of sight and removed his coveralls. Underneath, he was dressed in an expensive custom tailored black suit with a red and blue power tie. The attendant had not noticed his incongruous brightly shined black wing-tip shoes. The gentleman freedom fighter walked the rest of the way around to the hotel's lobby. His timing was perfect. The airport shuttle was waiting for passengers. He showed his voucher and climbed aboard. Two more hotel guests got on, and the shuttle left precisely on time for the trip to LAX. They arrived at 0350, a few minutes early. Colonel Hosni Esmet Badr was on a United Flight to Toronto sixty minutes later with a connecting flight to Cairo.

APRIL 15, 2010

Abdel Said Badr and Ali Abdullah Kaswari took four days to drive the truck with their speed boat up the U.S. Eastern seaboard. Timing was critical. They had to be certain that the boat was docked in the pre-arranged berth on the Canadian side of the Detroit River estuary before midnight when the security curfew for the arrival of the U.S. president went into effect. They left their

Motel-6 in Syracuse, New York after the free continental breakfast of day-old doughnuts, Rice Crispies, and coffee from a packet. The trip on I-80 was slow due to the lines of boats headed for Buffalo where they expected to join the spectacular regatta planned for the following day to celebrate the peace festival inaugurated by President Braithwaite. The two men checked through Canadian Customs, obtained Canadian Maritime stamps, and walked out onto the launching ramp to wait their turn. The agent told them it would be at least an hour before their turn would come up.

Said Mohammed Sisi was waiting for them on the quay. He carefully avoided Arabic or Muslim gestures. The two freedom fighters recognized the athletic build and military posture of the Council security officer as he approached them. Sisi had short cropped black hair graying at the temples. His forehead hair line was receding markedly. He was handsome—like a wise guy is handsome—and he had a placid nut brown face. Unlike most of his countrymen, Sisi did not have a mustache or beard. He was a big man without any fat. He walked with the bowlegged swagger of a long time Judo or Jiu Jitsu artist; he was both. In the last Olympics he had taken a silver, losing only to the perennial champion, Junji Hashimoto of Japan. He was wearing a jaunty weekend sailing captain's hat with gold braid on the bill, a white Polo shirt with green stripes up the sides and across the pocket, cream colored flannel trousers, and blue no-slip deck shoes.

"Good morning, gentlemen," he said blandly. "I wonder if the day will come that the crusades will be avenged?"

He said it quietly and in a tone of voice that a passer-by could have mistaken for an inquiry about the day's shopping plans.

"It will be a great day for that soon, perhaps even tomorrow."

"I am instructed to take the truck and get rid of it. I will be in Toledo, Ohio at three o'clock in the morning. A brother will meet you at the berth in Windsor. You have exact directions to it, true?"

Badr and Kaswari nodded.

"He will take you to a safe house for a little rest. He will stay with you then will drive you from Windsor to Toledo. It is imperative that you are at the first Seven-Eleven parking lot no later than three-thirty tomorrow morning."

"How will we find you?" Kaswari asked.

"I know the car. I'll find you. We will drive separately to a little town called Piqua where we will join up. You do not need to know more than that."

Kaswari frowned, but Badr merely nodded in acquiescence with what he considered to be an order.

The three men frittered away the better part of a nervous hour then Kaswari and Badr left Sisi by the launch ramp and returned to their truck. Their number was only about ten away; so, they stayed in the truck. Per instructions from the customs officer, they left the vast parking lot and joined the line of five vehicles and their towed boats and inched their way down the ramp backwards. The other four trucks slid their boats off their trailers without incident and did so with admirable efficiency. Badr and Kaswari's truck occasioned some spectator interest since they were not towing a boat. Instead, their craft sat on top of the truck bed.

Kaswari backed into the oil slick filthy water enough to allow the large ramp to project out and into the water at sufficient depth. The hydraulic lift gently lowered the boat onto the ramp, and the winch allowed the fast boat to slide slowly into the water. Badr breathed a sigh of relief as he saw the critically valuable boat rock easily on the small eddies and waves. It sat eight inches deeper in the water than one might have predicted, otherwise there was no telltale evidence of the heavy torpedo-shaped object running the length of the middle of the speed boat. Sisi watched until the boat was successfully launched, then he walked to the truck and got into the driver's seat as Kaswari vacated it. Sisi pulled the truck up and out of the ramp, across the border and into the bright sunshine of the northern New York Spring day.

Badr and Kaswari clambered aboard the sleek vessel, making elaborate effort to avoid paying attention to the narrow box sitting amidships on the polished deck. An elderly man in gentlemanly sea captain costume complete with sun bronzed, deeply lined, cancer ready face called out to them from the quay.

"Hey, man, nice rig for launching. Where'd you get that set-up?"

"Miami, bro," Kaswari yelled back affably.

Badr turned his head to avoid being seen smiling. Kaswari had been practicing the dialect.

The fellow sailor pointed to his own boat slowly backing down the launch ramp on its trailer. A young man—presumably the old sea dog's son—was driving the brilliantly clean blood red Ford 150 Heritage. The older man continued to wave to the two Arabs as they slowly picked their way into the gathering regatta traffic.

"One more casualty for the list. The Satanists call them 'collateral damage' when they commit state sanctioned terrorism against our people," Badr said half angrily, half sadly.

A Canadian Coast Guard cutter wound its way through the now crowded launching area taking great care to remain on the north—Canadian—side of Lake Erie. A guardsman waved a friendly hand to Kaswari and Badr, and the two soldiers of God remembered to wave back. The cluster of boats thinned out as they pulled further away from the launch area, and they were able to make good time. Kaswari controlled the boat and was scrupulously careful to stay under the marine speed limit. Badr kept a low profile.

The two men entered the Detroit River from Lake Erie steering close to the Canadian side and began to see a remarkable collection of vessels. On an average day they might have expected to see at least one 600 foot ship going towards or away from them every three minutes. Today, the ships, large and small were passing two, three, and four abreast. As they slipped past Amhersburg and LaSalle, they encountered a continuous line of magnificent tall ships that were beginning to move into position for the regatta scheduled on the sixteenth immediately after the president's speech.

Kaswari and Badr watched the elegant vessels as they moved on up the river. The first tall sailing ship they saw was the *Soren Larsen*, a 140 foot brigantine. Next was the popular HMS *Rose*, a 179 foot schooner with 13,000 square foot of sail area and a 130 foot main mast. The vessel weighed 500 tons and sported 24 cannons. They saw the *Georg Stage* from Nyborg, Denmark and *The American Pride*, a 3 masted schooner with red sail that had come from Rainbow Harbor in Long Beach, California. An entirely black crew manned the Freedom Schooner *Amistad*. The crewmen and women shouted joyfully at every boat that passed them. The Amistad had a long banner stretched out along its side that read, 'Peace and Freedom, Today's the Day.'

Badr recognized the HMAV *Bounty*, the replica ship that he had seen in the movie, *Mutiny on the Bounty*. He pointed out to Kaswari the *Endeavor*, a ship rigged bark home ported in Sydney with 1511 square meters of sail area.

Kaswari was proud of his fund of historical lore.

He said, "That's the ship the Captain Cook sailed around the world in."

Badr had never heard of Captain Cook.

The panoply of shipping grandeur included the Fisherman's Schooner *J & B* from St. John's Harbor, Newfoundland, the *Kaisei*, a Japanese training ship, the *Gorch Fock* from Germany, the *Amerigo Vespucci* from Italy, the *Dar Mlodziezy* from Poland, the *Esprit* from Germany, the *Ice Maiden* from the United Kingdom, the *Zenobe Gramme* from Belgium, and the *Freelord* from the Czech Republic. There were dozens more that the two men could not determine their port of origin.

Badr said succinctly, "Filthy Western excess; these will be great targets."

Kaswari nodded in agreement and smiled malevolently.

The speedboat moved slowly through the logarithmically increasing marine traffic. They were making only five to ten knots up the 23 miles to their destination, the Riverside Marina on the quiet east side of Windsor, Ontario, south of Detroit. Of the 17 Canadian based marinas and more than 12,000 berthing slips along the busy river, the spot chosen for them was the location least apt to draw anyone's attention to them. It had been secured the day that President Braithwaite announced the schedule for the festivities in the U.S. The deep water marina looking out at the conservationist controlled Peche Island at the Detroit River entrance into Lake St. Clare is operated by the Windsor Port Authority, and the operators could not have been more cordial.

The entire operation had been so smooth from the time Badr and Kaswari left Caracas until they enjoyed watching the car plants, distilleries, chemical factories, salt mines, marinas and the sculptured gardens along the Detroit River waterfront that the two freedom fighters were relaxed, even joining in the bawdy sea going banter passing between boats. The 13 mile stretch of water of the Port of Windsor was crowded, but ship's courtesy made the going easy. Kaswari guided the speedboat into Riverside Marina, and the two men watched for slip 45. There are 127 transient boater slips in the marina, and number 45 was the only one remaining open. Kaswari backed in very carefully. It would not do to have an accident and draw attention to their boat.

Clarence Michelson, the Harbor Master, was waiting dockside when they pulled in. He extended his hand for the docking ropes. Kaswari tossed him the prow line, and Badr waited until the bow line was secured then tossed the gregarious and bluff Canadian the aft tie.

"Welcome, gentlemen. Come in and relax with a drink while we sort out your papers. How was the trip?"

"Grand," Kaswari said with a genuine smile. "Never had a hitch."

"Good. Now what'll you have?"

"Just a Coke for me," Kaswari said. "Gotta get my land legs back before I take any spirits."

"Same for me," said Badr, offended at the very idea of being offered an alcoholic beverage, but he knew that he should not expect better from the Godless ones.

Their papers passed muster without a blink. When Michelson left them alone at last, the two men hastily opened the large white box amidships, They were moving aside the life jackets and foul-weather gear packed over the Avenging the Crusades thermonuclear device when a voice from the dock startled them.

The two men whirled about.

A tall athletic officer in the easily recognized red tunic emblematic of Canada smiled affably and said, "Sorry, didn't mean to scare you. I'm Leftenant Carmichael from the RCMP. We're making routine security checks of the marinas and of the auto traffic. The customs people are a bit short-handed, you know, eh?"

Kaswari slid his hand into his front pocket and took the safety off his .40 Caliber Taurus pistol.

"May I have your permission to come aboard, gentlemen?"

"Sure," said Badr.

He extended his hand to help the policeman aboard the speedboat.

"Thank you, sir. Now, I'd like to give your craft a quick once-over for the record, if you don't mind."

It was obvious that he was going to inspect them whether they minded or not.

"No problem. Need any help?"

"No, thanks. I'll just be a minute."

He took out a pen and began to make notes on a yellow form on his small clip board. He opened the cabin cubby holes, checked the engine compartment superficially, and fiddled with the knobs on the dash.

"Nice little boat. I often wish that I could take up sailing, and this is the way to go—none of that old-fashioned hoisting canvas and all those other exhausting chores. But they're a sight to behold, are they not?"

"Yes, sir, they certainly are," Badr said.

Kaswari angled himself so that he was behind the RCMP officer all of the time. He had a grimly determined look.

"Mind if I look into this gear locker?"

"Go ahead."

In a cursory effort, the officer pushed aside the collection of scuba gear, fishing tackle, and safety equipment so neatly packed along the floor of the narrow rectangular box. He made a few notations on his yellow form.

"Warm under there; I guess an engine that big takes a bit of time to cool off."

"That it does, officer. The cooling system is pretty effective. No worries."

"All right then, you men have a good time in Canada, eh? Looks like a right proper party the yanks are throwing, and you have the best seat in the house for the regatta. I envy you. Good day to you now."

He stepped over the gunwales and onto the dock.

"Bye, now. See you around."

"Thanks, officer, we feel safer knowing you and the rest of the RCMP are on the job," said Badr.

"Pleasure. Just doing our jobs. But thanks for noticing."

He walked on down the dock way, a picture of solid Canadian efficiency and authority. Kaswari flicked the safety back on his gun and both freedom fighters loosed a small sigh of relief.

Hassan Tariq ibn Hanafi met them twenty minutes later.

"I have come to avenge the crusades," he said.

"Good. Let's get out of here. I have a nasty stress sweat stink in my armpits," said Kaswari.

"I would think so," Hanafi said. "I saw the mountie talking to you. I called on Allah to allow that little conversation to pass in peace; so, the main event could progress unhampered. I don't know what that may be, but I know that it is in the hands of Allah, the All Powerful."

"And that is all you need to know. You step back from the boat, and Abdel, you walk up towards Riverside Drive. I'll catch up."

Abdel and Hassan walked briskly away without looking back. Kaswari climbed into the gear box and fished around with his fingers until he found a switch. He flicked it on, and heard the satisfying metal clicks from all four sides. He lifted the port side handle of the false floor and moved it up; so, he could reach in. The digital keyboard was within reach.

Kaswari held up the false floor with his left hand and keyed in the necessary code with his right—2-8-3-6-4-3-8-4-3-2-7-8-7-2-3-3-7: AVENGE THE CRUSADES. An LED display came on. Date? It asked. Kaswari looked carefully at his chronometer and punched in 15042010. The LED then asked, Time? Kaswari had checked and rechecked the accuracy of his chronometer more than a dozen times. It was correct to half a second. He punched in 0915. The LED asked, 15042010, correct? Press 1 for yes and 2 for no. Kaswari punched in 1. The LED asked, 0915, correct? Press 1 for yes, and 2 for no. Kaswari again punched in 1. The LED asked, Are you sure? 1 for yes and 2 for no. Kaswari punched in 1 for the third time.

The LED now read, Verify with code. Kaswari punched in 2-8-3-6-4-3-8-4-3-2-7-8-7-2-3-3-7. again. The LED read, "Code Accepted. Fail safe with code every hour on the hour until one hour before final." 'Final' was a day away. The LED screen was blank now except for a small set of numbers reading down the time.

Kaswari was sweating lightly. He closed the false floor and secured the locks with the electronic switches. He rearranged the gear in the locker portion of the large box and closed and locked the multiple locks on the lid. He made one last inspection, satisfied himself, and hopped off the boat carrying his and Abdel Said Badr's small suitcases and trotted after Abdel and Hassan.

Hassan and Abdel were waiting beside a Canadian Ford Windstar-2007 van. The three men drove through the heavy traffic from 9000 Riverside Drive East to the Travelodge Hotel Windsor at 33 Riverside Drive East. It was after ten o'clock when they finally checked in. The hotel was located near the Detroit-Windsor tunnel, faced Dieppe Park, and was adjacent to Great Western Park on the edge of the Canadian city of 250,000. The tunnel was enormously busy, and was chosen for that very extreme activity. One common van more or less would not attract notice. More than 14 million vehicles and 8 thousand commercial ships and at least that many pleasure craft cross the Detroit River at that spot each year making it the busiest international border crossing in North America.

Kaswari was agitated. He did not want to remain a minute longer in the Windsor-Detroit area than he had to. He envisioned all manner of delays—security checks at the border by customs officials of both countries, car breakdowns, calamitous weather, and gridlocked traffic jams. He insisted that they clean up, eat, and get out. He grumbled when Hassan and Abdel reveled in the hot showers and doused themselves with the lotions and colognes supplied by the generous three star hotel.

The freedom fighters loaded into the Windstar and made their way into traffic at midnight. Kaswari's temper was short and easily provoked. His co-religionists quickly learned to keep quiet. It was two in the morning when their turn to cross the international border line finally arrived. Kaswari was frantic. The U.S. Customs and Border Guard officer was polite but firm. The men had to exit their vehicle for a brief but thorough inspection. Kaswari had thought of leaving his pistol under the front passenger seat, but had elected to keep it in his pocket. He gave a small "*alhamdulillah*" that he had made the correct decision. Allah's hand was everywhere in every detail of His great mission. Praise be unto Him.

When they were finally firmly locked into the bumper-to-bumper flow of south bound traffic on I-75 passing out of Detroit, Abdel Said Badr said, "We must find a *messjed* [mosque] and offer our thanks to Allah, the Merciful, as soon as we can."

Hassan replied, "We are not out of the clutches of the Great Satan yet. Be patient, *akh*."

It was three-ten in the morning when the Windstar passed into Toledo, and they saw the last of Lake Erie. That seemed like a good sign to all three men. They missed the first turn-off, and Hassan shouted that they had missed the Seven-Eleven. The three of them saw the convenience store as they passed it by on their right and a moment of panic ensued.

Kaswari said, "Don't get upset. This may be the Great Satan, but they can build roads. We'll just pull off at the next off-ramp and go back here. It will only be a few minutes."

He hoped he was right.

It was a mile. They made it into the nearly empty parking lot of the Seven-Eleven at three twenty-two a.m. A late model Chevy Blazer blinked its lights three times then turned and drove out of the parking lot.

"That's him," Badr said. "Let's go."

There were no other cars and no activity outside the small convenience store that was open all night. The Windstar followed the Blazer down I-75 to the little town of Piqua, Ohio. The Blazer pulled off the interstate and onto the frontage road and stopped in the shadow of a Budweiser Beer bill board. Said Mohammed Sisi got out and waved the Windstar down.

Hassan, Abdel, and Ali got out and walked over to Said.

"We have to keep moving. And we have to split up now. Abdel, you and Hassan head for Cincinnati. You have an eight o'clock plane to catch. Here's the tickets and information. You will be safe in Riyadh when the crusades are avenged. Take the Windstar. Hosni, my *akh*, you and I will have to drive like the desert wind to get to Indianapolis to catch an eight-thirty flight to Lisbon. We have a connecting flight on to Casa Blanca. We will all see each other in the new Islamic world, *inshallah*."

Hassan and Abdel drove back onto the freeway all the way to the Cincinnati International Airport and were there in more than sufficient time to make their flight. No one was leaving the area, and the influx of tourists and well-wishers coming into the mid-west hub was crushing. Hosni and Said made a hurried trip along I-70 and just made their flight out of Indianapolis, *alhamdulillah*.

CHAPTER THIRTY

APRIL 15, 2010

Detective Lieutenant Carl Bronsen and Special Agent Stephen Sondregger met on the steps of the Museum of History and Technology at six o'clock as agreed. They had been in cell phone contact all day and neither had come up with anything of substance. Their men had scoured the city north, east, south and west; they had talked to many hundreds of would be witnesses, wannabees, cranks, and people under the influence. No one had seen anything of the bank robber—or anyone who had promise that he might be the robber—despite dozens of absolutely positive identifications. They had raided two dozen buildings and gained nothing but frustration. They were back to zero, and their tempers were short and sharp.

Sondregger said, "Nada, zip, zero, nothing. Wasted a coupla thousand man hours that were needed in the security detail. So, any bright ideas, Bronsen?"

"Start over. Let's go back to the scene and see if CSI and PERT have anything."

Bronsen was a cop's cop—brawny, profane, short and thick of body. He had a pockmarked face, heavy brows, a perpetual stubble of beard, and his parents had not been able to afford dental braces. He was a staunch Catholic, sometimes bellicose in his defense of the faith of his father, grandfather, and great grand father, who had not been to mass or to confession in twenty-five years. He smoked cigars, drank whiskey chased with beer, and womanized whenever the opportunity arose. He watched sit-coms and any kind of ball game on the tube, never bothered to put the toilet seat down after urinating, and only went out after work to indulge his passion for NASCAR competitions.

The only music he listened to was country western, and he did not appreciate unkind comments about that musical genre. He was a stickler for rules, a loner, and lived in messy simplicity. He ate meat and potatoes and would never dream of eating quiche or any other froggie dish. He wore an American flag on his jacket shoulder as his only defiance of the rules. Today—like every other day on the job—he was wearing a blue blazer, khakis, a DCPD logo tie, and thick soled black brogans—a hold over from his beat cop days.

Sondregger was a dandy, a thinker, and over educated. He had two bachelor's degrees—one in political science and the other in accounting. He graduated five years previously from George Washington Law School with honors including law review. He liked classical music and jazz, never watched television, and was a patron of the Washington, D.C. ballet. He was gay and out of the closet. He was tough, hated crooks, and rules that interfered with collaring them. Sondregger was tall, lean, and had a reputation in the FBI that was widely known in the DCPD as well that he was a mean hombre and no one to mess with. Gay or not, no one gave him a hard time more than once. He had sandy hair kept very short because more than an inch long, it would not obey comb, brush, or Brilliantine. His face was smooth, round, freckled, and cherubic, belying his inner meanness. His only facial defect was a bulbous nose that he secretly intended to rectify with plastic surgery as soon as he could come up with enough spare cash. He had no bodily defects.

Despite their differences Sondregger got along well with Bronsen. One thing he liked about the D.C. detective was that the man had no prejudices against gays, Jews, Protestants, or persons of color—unless, of course, they were criminals. Sondregger worked the same way, and the two men worked together well. Unlike his DCPD counterpart's disdain for clothes, the FBI special agent wore a color coordinated beige suit that fit perfectly, a light pink cotton shirt, and beige and black club stripe tie. His marine cordovan wingtip shoes were perfectly shined every day by the bootblack who worked the sidewalk outside FBI headquarters. He wore a wedding band even though he had never married, and a pinky ring with a small diamond, just to provoke a comment that would allow him to administer a lesson against homophobia.

The bodies of the Egyptian with no identification and their own officer Elmer Foynston had been tagged, bagged, and removed. The bulk of the police effort at the scene had been to keep the general gawkers and the serious news people away. The efforts had not been entirely in vain. The CSI team had lost the toss and had to get into the back of the dump truck and to begin the tedious process of sifting and bagging the trash. The large truck bed had been nearly full of sacks of wet garbage, loose trash, and smashed down cardboard boxes. After a painstaking two hour effort, the CSI team made a most curious finding. A large rectangular box at the bottom of the truck bed with innocuous markings, ACME MACHINE PARTS, was found. The very heavy weight of the box was consistent with the painted lettering, but there were two oddities about the box. First of all, it was locked with a series of ingenious and high-tech security devices, and second of all, it was very warm.

The CSI team scrambled out without further contact with the box, called the Metro Bomb Squad and the Hazmat Team and sat down with the members of the PERT team to wait. The security situation in the city coupled with the infuriatingly snarled traffic congestion, prolonged the arrival of the specialist teams for over an hour.

The two squads haggled for ten minutes over who had responsibility before deciding that Hazmat should at least check for chemical presence or radio-activity. No chemicals were identified, and the Geiger counter readings were equivocal. The next decision was for the bomb squad to open the box with Hazmat standing by. Unable to open the locking system with the talent at hand and after an FBI lock specialist failed as well, the bomb squad crow-barred and cut off the top with an acetylene torch. What at first glance had appeared to be wood, was in fact high grade, case hardened cleverly painted steel outside. The second layer—inside the first—was two inch thick lead. That gave everyone a moment of deep pause. Hazmat took over after that. As the Hazmat team was gingerly lifting the lead top off the box, Lieutenant Bronsen and Special Agent Sondregger arrived. They showed their shields and walked across the parking lot to where the teams were milling about.

"What's up?" asked Sondregger.

"Looks pretty hinky," the special agent in charge of the scene replied grimly. "Maybe a bomb, even a nuc. Maybe some kind of hazmat. The Hazmat Team is in there now opening the lid on the big box that has been giving us the heebee-jeebees for the past two and a half hours."

"I need a look," said Sondregger.

"I wouldn't do that, sir, if I were you. No telling what we have. It looks like a serious thing in there."

Sondregger and Bronsen started climbing up on the truck despite the advice. Suddenly, the special agent in charge of the Hazmat Team yelled.

"Everybody off. This is some sort of big bomb. I think maybe a nuc, a dirty bomb."

The Metro Bomb Squad got on his phone immediately and called for back up.

"Get everybody out of here. Clear about six square blocks. We need all the help we can get," he shouted as soon as he was off the phone.

The Hazmat officer called in his reinforcements. By eight-thirty there was a robot bomb transporter and a Hazmat clear tent in place. The Hazmat officer reported that the crude looking bomb materials had a SIM technology cell phone attached. The CSI lieutenant remembered that a cell phone had been found lying half way between the dead cop and the dead Egyptian. He sent a beat cop to fetch it. A block and tackle suspended from a small crane was brought in and at eleven-thirty the box was out of the dump truck bed and secured in the largest bomb disposal unit in the city. It barely fit. Hazmat verified absolutely that the core substance of the bomb was intensely radioactive. What they had here was a dirty bomb, and every cop and agent was now as sober as men can be. The bomb squad members who had made initial contact with the device had been rushed to the closest hospitals. Two of them were already vomiting.

"So, whatta we do with this thing?" Sondregger asked Lieutenant Bronsen.

It seemed that everyone present—by unanimous tacit agreement—had elected Sondregger to be in charge. This was a case that could only bring pain to anyone whose name rose to the top responsibility.

Bronsen shrugged.

"At least let's haul it out to the middle of the Virginia countryside for the moment. Then let's kick it upstairs for a bigwig decision. When this hits the fan, we wanna be someplace taking orders, not giving them."

"It's chicken, but you're right. I'll call mine. You call yours."

In twenty minutes, the DFBI, ADFBI, the secretary of Defense, the secretary of Homeland Security, the NSA, and the president were rousted from their several parties and grouped in the Oval Office. The president's office and the perimeter of the White House were ringed by Secret Service agents. Vice-President Rowan was taken to an undisclosed location. All leaves were cancelled, and for the Secret Service it was DefCon 1.

"Give me the short version, Daniel," the president ordered.

"We have a verified dirty bomb from a parking lot in D.C., sir," Rupert Vernon interrupted, "It has been transported to rural central Virginia in an open area between Cumberland Plateau and New River. It was found in a parking lot on 7th and E north in an old dump truck. The perp was surprised by a D.C. cop while he was parking the truck. The perp—an unsub thus far—killed the cop and an Egyptian lot attendant before running off—just vanished. There were a couple of dozen spurious reports that he was Hispanic, or Arab, or Lebanese or black or white.

"At first it was thought that it was the same guy who robbed the B of A at 201 Pennsylvania, S.E. That hasn't panned out. We haven't got much to go on, but the FBI is tracking down a pair of discardable cell phones that they think may have been intended to set off the bomb's detonator. If it had gone off, it would have taken out a good four block area and damaged another four to six block square area. As it is, the thing is still radioactive as can be, and the FBI labs are working with their Hazmat Team to try and investigate it as evidence while still keeping the radioactivity damage to the participants to a minimum. There are now four known affected officers in hospitals and forty-seven more in quarantine. This is a colossal mess and has every appearance of a huge terrorist operation."

"By whom," the grim faced president asked pointedly.

"Unknown."

"Suspects?"

"Nothing worthy of the name, sir. Usual conventional wisdom is that it is al Qaeda or some other Arab terrorist group."

"Can't be," said the president. "They have been keeping the peace almost perfectly for more than a year and a half. Their own people are all over town. Their senior leaders have all assured us that they have all of the extremists under control As recently as yesterday—as you well know—the CIA gave us an all-clear signal."

Braithwaite prayed to the God in whom he had no belief that it could not be true.

DFBI Marques said, "We have teams out in the hinterlands looking into the domestic terror groups. Our main focus is the Separatist Homeland Republic—that's the homeland, as they call it, of a bunch of loonies called God's Covenant People who belong to a religious group they call the Church Militant. They're in western North Carolina where it is adjacent to eastern Tennessee and northern Georgia. It's remote and it's rugged country, part of southern Appalachia—highways 19, 28, and 141. I have been getting reports from our agents who've been looking around Murphy and Andrews, Texas and Franklin, Tennessee. Nothing much yet. I'll tell you, though—if you want to know—that there are government haters out there in our own country, all you have to do is to read their newspaper, the *Remnant Report.*"

"There are more of that ilk out there, true, Director?" asked President Braithwaite.

"Oh, yeah, plenty of them. The Minnesota Patriots Council, Aryan People's Republic, the Phineas Patriots, Mountaineer Militia, The Order, Army of God, Oklahoma Militia, Viper Militia, Odinists, you name it, there's a government hate group—usually acting in the name of God—around to preach the message."

"What about that report by, what's his name, from the CIA? The guy that Angelina Davis brought to the briefing?" asked Homeland Security Secretary Vernon.

"Wasn't that Dean Mathers from the illicit transport and smuggling unit of the CIA?"

"Him too, but no, the guy from just the other day. Remember, he got huffy," said ADFBI Braxton Nuttal.

Daniel Ajami snapped his fingers.

"Oh, yeah, that snotty upstart, Pickering. Anthony Pickering. Something about a major terrorist alert from some *undisclosed* source."

Ajami's acid comment was in a mocking but fairly accurate parody of Pickering's high pitched voice.

"And Angelina Davis is looking for him. He's gone missing for the better part the past two days," said Marques.

"And supposing he's right. The great work of the FBI has foiled the attempt, and it's over," said President Braithwaite whose face indicated that a considerable weight had just been lifted from him.

"And we have no real evidence, let alone proof, that this is a Muslim terrorist group. It could be any one of our own survivalists that we're looking into for all we know," said Marques. "Don't forget the Alfred P. Murrah Federal Building bombing in Oklahoma City in 1995."

Ajami and Nuttal nodded enthusiastically.

"All right, this is what we'll do," said President Braithwaite with authority. "We are going ahead with all of our plans. The only difference is that Homeland Security, the FBI, ATF, and CIA are going on full alert to see if there is anything else suspicious out there."

Ajami asked, "Do we consider upping the threat level to yellow, or maybe even orange?"

"I think we should," Homeland Security Secretary Rupert Vernon offered, "because the latest reports from the super secret U.S. surveillance network, Echelon, to the National Security Agency have indicated a stepped up chatter from the terrorists. This is confirmed as being from multiple sources, consistently threatening, and persistent; they seem to be planning something big."

"And I disagree, respectfully," Ajami said.

"The domestic political and international fallout would be a disaster if we did, Mr. President," said the DFBI. "Even as a cautious old cop, I think our evidence, even the traffic from Echelon, is flimsy. One swallow does not a summer make."

"I so want this Peace Celebration to be a success that I suppose that my judgment could be clouded. However, I have listened to the arguments and evidence, or rather the lack of it, and I am still inclined to keep a lid on it. We will not advance to yellow. Keep me posted, gentlemen, and let's get back to work. I will be on Air Force One at six tomorrow morning. Give me a briefing on anything you've got by then. You can patch through to the plane," the president said and clenched his jaw as if to punctuate his resolution.

APRIL 15, 2010

Yahha Mohammed Ali in Sydney, Ayatollah Ali Velayati Mossedeq in Paris, and Ayatollah Ali Mazdi Sekhavatal-Muderasi in London had virtually identical instructions and devices. The dirty bombs they secreted in their hotel rooms or storage facilities were rigged to be detonated by cell phone contact. Each of the men was instructed to update the length of their stay in their respective hotels for an additional five days beginning on April 15. The freedom fighters were instructed to leave the hotel and book flights for Cairo that night. None of them knew the telephone number that would detonate their bomb, but they were assured that they would be given final instructions when they landed in Egypt.

The two Iranian Hezbollah fighters on the Egyptair plane stretched their legs briefly before the seat-belt sign came on. They reluctantly gave the flight attendant their mini-bottles and chip bag trash and worked on waking up for the landing. Once on the ground, they walked swiftly through Terminal 1, sweating in the 34 degree Celsius heat, to get ahead of the crowd. As they proceeded through passport check, the customs officer handed each man an envelope. The letter inside contained an address on Sh. Muhammad Faird Street in the new city center of Maydan al-Tahrir near the Cairo Museum, and the instructions contained in the plain envelope told them to take an officially registered black and white cab there. The two ayatollahs arrived at the house, one that looked like every other dwelling within a mile square area except that it had a series of sophisticated antennae sprouting from its roof.

They entered the house without knocking and were met with the business ends of two Ingram 9mm M 10 submachine guns—room brooms—pointing at their chests.

"What business do you have here?" asked one of the two ski-masked gunmen quietly and politely, all the while keeping his right index finger on the trigger.

It took the Iranians a moment to know how to reply, and then Mossedeq exhaled and said, "We have come to avenge the crusades."

The guns lowered, and now the two guards affably escorted the men into a comfortable lounge and office in the rear of the house. Seated at the handsome teak desk in the northwest corner of the room was Muhammad Mohfouz, head of Sabfiya.

Mohfouz greeted the Hezbollah fighters with unfeigned enthusiasm. He walked to the tired men and embraced each of them and kissed each cheek.

"Here are your cell phones, your weapons in the final solution for avenging the crusades, *akhs*," he said. "Remember to discard them when you complete your mission."

The ayatollahs looked around the smoky room and were able to identify Yahha Mohammed Ali whom they recognized on sight.

"Greetings, comrades," Yahha said. "I am glad that you have returned safely."

The two Iranians nodded in greeting, and replied, *"shukran."* [thank you].

The Egyptian smiled effusively and said, "Welcome home, my friends. This is the first day of the new world. I am glad to share it with you."

"And we with you, old friend."

Mohfouz showed the newcomers the array of clocks on the east wall, the direction of Mecca. They were set for local time in Sydney, in London, in Paris, in Los Angeles, and in Detroit. In front of the clocks were seven prayer rugs. Mossedeq glanced at his watch which he had changed to Cairo time on the plane coming in and synchronized it with the wall clock for Paris, and Sekhavatal-Muderasi synchronized with London time. Shortly, each man would dial his cell phone and set off the apocalypse.

Abdel Said Badr and Hassan Tariq ibn Hanafi would be enroute to Riyadh, and Col. Hosni Esmet Badr and Said Mohammed Sisi would be in the air enroute to Lisbon from their airports in Ohio and Indiana when the time came to call their cell phone receiver in Windsor, Ontario. They luxuriated in the first class tilt-back seats as they waited.

Prince Ahmed Wahhab ibn Saud and ranking members or the Council of Leaders of Islam more than filled their last hours of waiting as they feverishly checked and rechecked every detail of the great Avenging the Crusades Operation. There was a prestigious gathering of the notables of the movement in Aleppo, and they watched the frenetic activity of the small army of technicians as they finished the last preparations before launch.

The prince was too involved to entertain, and none of the seasoned freedom fighters expected him to do so. A special theater viewing room was set up for the guests. In the room were Hafez al-Nassif, Foreign Minister of Syria, Walid Patel, Head of Jamaah Islamiyah, Mullah Ali Hussein Mercooi, Head of the Benevolent International Foundation headquartered in Columbus, Ohio, Hussein Habash, President of the Holy Land Foundation, largest Arab aid organization in the United States and one of the world's largest illegal contributors to Palestinian fighters. Walid Shamma Atallah, vice-president of Pakistan and his nephew, Awad Musa Ishteyyeh, the nominal owner of the Aleppo land where the huge nuclear plant and the ICBMs now stood occupied a separate area. Vice-president Atallah's son, Ikram Khalid Atallah, sat quietly beside his hard-faced father and his cousin surveyed the war room activity.

Imam Hadi Abolhassan Rajavi, Head of Hezbollah, was reading *The Great Virtue of Lowering the Gaze* by Imam ibn Qayyim al-Jawziyyah. Egyptian President Mohammed Yahya Farouk pondered the *Ayat al-Tathir*—the verse of purification—and a compilation of discussions on the *Ahul Bayat*. There were tables of light refreshments surrounded by such notables in the Council's fight for Islam as Yahha Mohammed Ali, Saad Makram el-Deen, and Mahmoud Fasbeh—Usama bin Laden's lieutenant responsible for al Qaeda operations in South East Asia. Khalid Atranik Ayoub—senior lieutenant of al Qaeda—kept himself aloof and was intently reading his pamphlet, *Shaving the Beard: A Modern Effeminacy*. The talk was subdued, but expectant. The men frequently checked their watches against the array of world times displayed on clocks on the far wall.

Security was oppressive and nothing was too picayune to escape the notice of the cadre of the uniformed officers entrusted with the safety and sanctity of Allah's work that was enfolding in the headquarters building and throughout the Council's Avenging the Crusades complex. Hand picked, highly trained, skilled soldiers, intensely loyal to the Council, patrolled every inch of the complex. They were in full battle dress and carried the latest and best communications equipment and arms. They were uniformly large men whose training had removed all humor or tendency to distraction. Inside the headquarters building, more than a dozen of them milled about freely among the technicians and the guests. No one and nothing was sacred or could be withheld from them.

Ayoub al Qassam and his fourteen computer security specialists moved about the vast computer driven complex scrutinizing terminals and console screens for any hint of an electronic leak or potential accidental communication outside the strictly curtailed list of those with a need and a right to know. With two hours to go to launch, Ayoub was fully aware of the exact nature of the mission and the exact time for launch of the Avenging the Crusades plan as it was to take place from the Aleppo base. He had been able to snoop enough as he passed computer after computer to deduce that the Aleppo portion of the action was only part of the plan. He knew—for example—that in-place bombs were scheduled to blow-up in Sydney and in Paris at the same time as the Aleppo missiles touched down on their targets. He had caught glimpses of Washington, D.C., Los Angeles, and Detroit on flickering screens, but it was unclear what was in store for those American cities.

Ayoub was exhausted as were his own squad of men from staring at computer screens and analyzing the reams of written and numbered data that were flashing by. He was annoyed by the constant companionship of one of the armed security guards. Ayoub was desperate to find a way to communicate with his superiors in the Mossad and had not had a moment to himself to be able to do that in the past two days that he had been fully awake, fully knowledgeable, and fully scrutinized.

Ayoub Ibrahim Jadid—a Christian Arab, or Job, as he preferred—the Dark Shadow or the one Afflicted by God—as he was known to Mossad—ruminated over whether he would ever use his real name again. For the safety of his life, he was Ayoub al Qassam, Syrian computer security expert working for the enemies of God and civilization as he saw it and was frustrated at his inability to do anything to help his native Israel and the great, good-hearted U.S.A.

Job was a slightly built man, looked studious and intense—not a man for action. That picture was all true. He was nervous even in polite society, and now he was stressed to near maximum. His thin sweaty face sported a full mustache that would be comparable to any Islamic counterpart; but his beard—though he had tried—was as thin and wispy as his hold on his recently acquired Muslim religion. He wore a Sunna green turban from Pakistan—a cloth ten and a half feet long by forty-three inches wide—and felt silly in it most of the time, but knew that it made him fit in comfortably with the men around him. He looked the part of an everyday Arab in his Yemeni dishadasha robe made of ultrasoft grey polyester over white cotton pajama pants.

Like most of his fellows, he gave into the vanity of having embroidery on the shoulders and neckline and a two button front closure covered with a decorative tasseled strip. The wide buttonless cuffs were ideal for performing *wudu* and *salat,* and Ayoub was able to work without excessive cloth interfering with his use of the computer keyboard

With one hundred fourteen minutes left in the countdown, Ayoub's small window of opportunity opened. His constant companion and guard, Wael Etamad, was a former Jordanian army sergeant and current thug whose sole education had been rote memorization of the *Qur'an* in a Wahhabi run madrassah followed by the strict regimen of the army and then that of the Council. He knew nothing about any electronic device and considered that computers were probably the work of Shaytan's angels. His only fault was a love of hot peppers. Lunch for the sergeant had been *fuul* with bread and a hard boiled egg served in the security officer's mess.

The sergeant found the food in the mess too bland for his taste and added his own Da' Bomb Ground Zero sauce, a gift from his imam when he left for Syria and the work of the Council. Da' Bomb—a mixture of pineapple juice, Habeñero peppers, lemon, and lime juice and a few minor spices—is the third hottest sauce in the world, rated 230,000 Scovilles—a measure of Capsaicin, the ingredient that makes peppers hot.

Islamic laws prevented the importation of *Naga Jolokia* from Assam, India—the world's hottest pepper—because India is polytheistic, and agricultural regulations forbad Mexico from bringing in Red Savina Habañero, the second hottest. Otherwise, Etamad would have had one of those as a gift.

One of his mates tasted a pinhead sized portion of the fiery liquid and washed his mouth with water for ten minutes. When Etamad taunted him for being a sissy, the squad dared Sergeant Etamad to put a tablespoonful on his *fuul.* The sergeant put two to show them, ate his simple meal with gusto, and controlled his facial expressions. Half an hour later, he became a prisoner of the toilet, and Ayoub was free from personal scrutiny for the next fifteen minutes.

Ayoub began to sweat profusely. He always gave himself away and knew that he could never be a truly effective spy. He was a poor liar in his estimation. He knew that he would cave in under torture. Nonetheless, he screwed up his courage, surreptitiously looking around him. He was seated at his master computer, one of four in the complex. No one paid him the least attention.

His computer was running the countdown sequence with intermittent automatic scans of all of the other computers. He was the watcher, and no one was watching the watcher. Ayoub drew in a jerky breath, typed in the top secret emergency only e-mail address for Mossad, and double clicked on send. The computer asked for the name of the file to send. Ayoub clicked on the choice for ALL. The computer screen remained as it had been, showing the countdown sequence—now 112 minutes—followed by a regular and annoying display of every other computer in the building. The only telltale indicator that his computer was electronically sending millions of bytes of information including scientific tables, drawings and photos, and chat conversations with freedom fighters from all over the world, was the tiny spinning tabulator icon in the lower right hand corner of the screen. Even that was rather innocuous since Ayoub was required to send and receive constant computer chatter as he went about his electronic surveillance work.

In ten minutes, the miracle of the internet had conveyed to the outside ninety-nine percent of all of the compressed files from the entire Avenging the Crusades operation starting from the first organization of the Council of the Leaders of Islam to the congratulatory e-mail exchanges between the most prominent men in the Islamic world typed in the last five minutes—absolutely damning criminal evidence. If only he could could get all of it to on time, if only they could act in time, if only…if only. He realized that the evidence would be seen by the world only after the inevitable Gog and Magog encounter had taken place. It was profoundly depressing.

Ayoub looked around again. No one was taking notice of him. Sweat—smelly fear and stress sweat—was running down his chest from his armpits. His eyes were becoming glazed, more with fear than with the intense concentration. Sergeant Etamad had not returned. Ayoub knew that he was all right for now. All past documents had been forwarded to Tel Aviv. Now, only the minute-to-minute communications were moving through. Ayoub was dumbfounded at the messages and the senders:

> My prince, *mabrouk* on the greatest feat accomplished by Islam since The Prophet, blessed be his name, subdued all of Arabia. My country is proud to serve. Our Egyptian ICBM is in perfect working order and will fire successfully at the appointed moment, 91 minutes from now. I speak as the president, the leader of Islam in my country, and for all of my countrymen. This is the end of the Great Satan. We will be proud to be the agents of death for Chicago.
> Mohammed Yahya Farouk,
> President of Egypt,
> and humble servant of Allah, the All Powerful.

Prince ibn Saud, I convey the well wishes of Grand Ayatollah Hussein Aliyy Bilal and the people of Iran. Not only will our Council strike a fatal blow to the degenerate West, but I rejoice in the contribution of Iran and the Iranian people to this cause that shall surely unite Shi'a and Sunni. Our great missile shall be the sword of Allah, the One God. We are synchronized with you by technology and in purpose. In 90 minutes, all of Iran and all of the world will know of what we have all done. *Bukra* will be a new day; the future belongs to Islam. May God guide your spears.
Muhammad Ali Hashemi,
President of Iran,
servant of Allah, the All Wise

My dear nephew, The entire Kingdom rejoices in your accomplishment. In 89 minutes the spears of God shall pierce the evil underbelly of Great Satan, and our nation will no longer have to maintain the charade of friendship or even civility with Great Satan or its minions. The plan to annihilate Little Satan is flawless, and we live to see the destructions as they happen on the miracle God has given us to see in the far distance. *Mabrouk.* The ICBMs of the Kingdom will unerringly strike a final blow to the degenerate cities of New York and Toronto. I echo the words of Grand Mufti Sheik Abu Sherif al-Sherif and of the entire Wahhabi family throughout the earth. Long Live Islam! This is the day of the One God.
King Abdullah Said ibn Saud,
Protector of the Faith.

Reply, to all Council of Leaders of Islam
My brothers. We are part of history and *bukra* we will be remembered with adoration by those who bask in the new world that we shall bring about. We dedicate Operation Avenging the Crusades to Allah and to his Holy Prophet, may God's blessings be upon the head of his Messenger forever. Thank you for your patience and contributions. Together we put Great Satan and his silly friends in the West to sleep. When they wake, it will be a world ruled by holy Islam.
Prince Ahmed Wahhab ibn Saud,
Chairman

It was dizzying to see the openly incriminating, even boastful messages from the presidents of Syria, Libya, Pakistan, Morocco, and Yemen. And Ayoub had lost track of time in his fascination. He looked to his right, all clear. He slowly felt the need to look to his left and he saw his guard, pale and wan, walking towards him from thirty yards away. Ayoub clicked on the stop forwarding icon and as calmly as possible stood up and walked towards the bathroom and his security guard, Wael Etamad.

There were now fifty-eight minutes to go before the apocalyptic moment. His only chance for survival was to be able to get out of the building and to put as much distance between himself and the security force of the Council. He knew that his treason would be discovered. It was only a question of whether it would be during the countdown or after the cataclysmic events of the next hour were completed, and the names and deeds of the heroes of Operation Avenging the Crusades were revealed for the glory of Islam and themselves. Ayoub realized fully that his name would be an accurate description of his fate when *his* heroic deeds were unveiled.

"You look ill, Sergeant," Ayoub said as he passed the security man.

"You do not look so well yourself, Mr. al Qassam."

"Something I ate," al Qassam said and walked on past.

Sergeant Etamad knew full well the need to hurry at such a time and did not even consider interfering with a mission as important as the one the computer specialist was about.

Ayoub was nervous—so nervous that he was shaking. He made his way through the labyrinthine hallways of the lower floor and approached the two guards lounging by the rear exit of the building.

"I need a little air, my friends. I'll take a little walk on the grounds and get back to my work," al Qassam said.

He held his laminated picture identification card hanging on the lanyard around his neck; so, the officers could more easily read it.

"We shouldn't," the superior of the two guards said, "but you look ill. No one will be hurt if you get a little air. But be quick about it."

They let him out, and Ayoub walked away as calmly as he could bear.

Sergeant Etamad looked at al Qassam's computer screen. In bold letters, the screen announced: SECURITY BREACH, UNAUTHORIZED RECIPIENT. ALERT. REPORT TO SECURITY.

Al Qassam was nowhere in sight. Etamad turned and ran towards the control room. He was duty bound to report the alert although he presumed it to be a computer glitch; the machines were constantly doing something wrong.

Prince Ahmed Wahhab ibn Saud saw Etamad rushing towards where he was sitting and at nearly the same time saw the message on his master computer screen. He quickly scanned the other masters, asked the computer, 'where?' and received an immediate answer, No.79351. A glance at his list of master computers indicated the new convert—al Qassam's—computer. He gasped. Etamad breathlessly reported the alert and that the man to whom he was assigned had gone to the toilet.

"For your sake, pray that that is all there is to it," the prince said with his obsidian eyes glinting in the bright lights of the control room.

There was retribution shining out of those eyes.

"Run to the toilet and find him. Bring him to me," the prince ordered calmly.

Etamad turned to leave. The rear of his trousers was stained.

"Wait. How is it that you lost track of al Qassam?"

"I had a case of the runs, sir. I was gone for just a moment."

"That is no excuse. Pray that you find him and that this is just a computer glitch. Your life and his depend on it."

Etamad was frantic. He swept through the bathroom slamming open the door of every stall resulting in a string of abusive epithets following him in his course. Al Qassam was nowhere. Sergeant Etamad inquired roughly of everyone he ran into. In a few moments, the sergeant was running headlong through the lower floor. He startled the lazing guards at the rear exit door.

"Al Qassam. Where is he?"

"He was sick. He is walking outside. Hasn't been gone but two minutes. What's the problem?"

"Traitor!" Etamad shouted looking out the window then clasping his head.

He was panic stricken.

"Open the door. One of you come with me. You, call the prince—extension 1111. Tell him where we are and get instructions."

Etamad and the senior guard bolted out of the door. There was no one to be seen on the grounds.

"Go left. I'll go right."

Etamad had enough sense to know that it was imperative to capture the traitor—probably a Zionist son of a monkey father and a pig mother—and to bring him to the prince; so, he could be made to talk. If al Qassam was dead, then so was Etamad; the quavering sergeant knew that. He had to be the one to find the tool of the State Terrorist Occupiers.

It was not to be. The senior guard who had gone to the left saw al Qassam walking briskly towards the fence.

He shouted, "Halt. Not another step"

Al Qassam acted as if he had not heard the command. He knew with perfect clarity that to be caught would mean prolonged torture. He was no Eli Cohen. He could not allow himself to be taken alive; so, he burst into a headlong dash for the fence. The fence was electrified with enough voltage to kill a man several times over upon contact. Al Qassam was well aware of that. Death by electrocution was infinitely more desirable than being brought back to the prince and his tender mercies.

"Stop, or I shoot," screamed the enraged guard.

Al Qassam knew that there was no escape, no future, no peace, no happiness for him. He would never hear his real name again, never wear real clothes. He told himself that maybe he would be remembered like Eli Cohen. He began to cry. He found himself foolishly saying his own *kaddish*. He did not feel the current of electricity that turned his body into char nor the ninety bullets that tore him apart as his corpse chattered from the electrocution on the unforgiving fence.

At the sound of the gunfire, Etamad abruptly turned and ran in time to see al Qassam's smoking charcolized body hanging on the fence, still jumping in a macabre *pas de morte*. With the same insight as his arch enemy, the sergeant knelt down and put his old friend—his Soviet Tokarev TT-33 pistol—in his mouth and pulled the trigger.

CHAPTER THIRTY-ONE

APRIL 16, 2010

The DFBI's call came to the president on board Air Force One at 0748 as the flying seat of executive government began its descent into Detroit International Airport.

"Yes, Leland?" The president asked.

"To this moment, we have no new information regarding the individual or organization responsible for the dirty bomb. We have two thousand agents and other police officers working exclusively on the case and will find the perpetrators, but I cannot give you that information yet. The nuclear material has been taken to safe storage."

"No evidence for or against an Islamic terrorist source?"

"None. The only suggestion is that the other man murdered at the parking lot looked to be an Arab and had no identification papers."

"Too thin to make anything out of that."

"Yes, sir. And we have no other leads and no more reason to believe right now that there is any more likelihood that there are any other planned attacks than at any other time."

"Keep me posted. We will go on with the show. It is worth a few jittery nerves to achieve real world peace in our time. I will not have this opportunity ruined for an unsupported theory."

"I understand, sir. Security is as tight as it can be. I am sure that we have had a close call on this one, and that's it. However, I do have to tell you that Percy Aquilara, Chief of the International Security Program at the Center for

Strategic and International Studies, believes this is likely to be only one part of a multi-pronged attack or is the first in a series. His advice for the U.S. and for the international guests is to postpone the celebrations, and completely change the printed schedule to disrupt any terrorist organization's planning."

"Does the Center have any information or evidence you don't have, Leland?"

"No, sir. Much of what they have comes from Interpol and from the FBI's Counterintelligence Service."

"So, they put two and two together and came up with five, then?"

"In a sense. This is largely a think tank, a research organization without authority. I must say that they are thorough and careful in my experience."

"Nevertheless, you still stand behind your bureau's assessment that this is more likely a renegade terrorist operation than a credible coordinated attack or part of a series?"

"All of the evidence available to us indicates no further activity."

"So, you recommend that I go ahead with the peace celebration plans."

"I think that overstates my position and my responsibility. I cannot offer you clear evidence of a conspiracy or that we are about to have a resurgence of terrorist activity. It would be the safest thing to cancel. Like the CIA, my oath is to protect the Constitution; I don't make political policy. It's your call, sir, of course."

"You can't sit on both sides of the fence, Mr. Director. I want your objectively based recommendation. Go ahead or cancel."

"Go ahead."

When he said it, DFBI Marquess had trepidations. However, he was sure that he was firmly grounded in the evidence.

"Thank you. Keep me posted."

"Yes, sir."

In his Tel Aviv office, Mordecai Narkiss was shocked. The most secret file in his computer was filling with page after page of encrypted material that could only have come from Dark Shadow. A few of the early pages were beginning to come through in the clear. It was obvious that the mass of information was going to be incredibly large; so, the head of Mossad linked four printers to handle the load. He called Yahuda Grossman and Levi Harkabi and had them bring their four most trusted subordinates and technicians along to the situation room.

His next call was to Prime Minister Avigador Haimovitz on the top security line.

"Mr. Prime Minister, this is Narkiss. We have a developing situation. I need you to trust me as you have never done before because we have no time to verify the information I am getting. I am asking you to put the entire armed forces of the country on full ready alert. Our agent in Syria is sending us thousands of documents about a nuclear program—the one we have discussed before, the Aleppo project. What is crucial is that it appears that an attack is about to be launched against the United States and probably Western Europe. We don't yet have confirmation that we are included; but given the scope of this operation, we can only presume so. I will send you everything as it comes in. Remember this comes at the cost of our best agent's life; of that I am certain. He is Job Ibrahim Jadid, and he is our new Eli Cohen."

"Thank you, Mordecai. I will do as you ask. Pray Jehovah protects us."

"I'm afraid I'm *Trefa* [unkosher]—just a Yom Kippur Jew—but I will join you this time, Mr. Prime Minister."

After he finished talking with the prime minister, Narkiss ordered Harkabi and Grossman to see to it that their protected source in the CIA received every word. The two men linked Narkiss's program to the prime minister's most secret e-mail server and abandoned anything that could slow down the process of getting the information to Anthony Pickering. They made no attempt to filter anything out or to protect their source. Without hearing the terrible news from a confirming source, everyone in the room knew that Job was dead. The best they could hope for was that the end had been quick.

Harkabi called Pickering's office directly. At Langley, it is easy to be connected to an individual. A call to a particular office—especially one as particular as Pickering's—would be politely deflected into the ether. There was no answer. Harkabi cursed.

He pressed his fingers into his temples trying to dredge up a name in the CIA that he could trust. His next call was to Dean Mathers, Head of the Illicit Transactions Group. Harkabi had met Mathers at a meeting in Paris where Pickering and he had found time to meet alone. Pickering had vouched for Mathers.

He left the room and went to his office where he opened his safe and rifled through the papers until he came to the five by six file card on which he had written—in his own personal code—the list of names and numbers of his key contacts in the friendly and unfriendly intelligence services around the world. It took a few minutes and a feat of memory since he had not consulted this list in many months. The computer was so much simpler, but Harkabi never trusted the machine the way he trusted his own tradecraft. He found Mathers's name and private number and called it.

The call came through on Mathers's updated Telcom 7 scrambler unit.

"How did you get this number?" was Mathers's greeting when he picked up the phone and heard Harkabi state his name.

"From Pickering."

"I don't believe it. Pickering never divulges anything to anyone."

"You and I met in Paris, in Pickering's room. Look, I haven't got time to chat. I have to send Pickering some incredible intelligence, and I have to do it right now. It is the most important information he, or you, and I will ever see. How do I get hold of him? He doesn't answer any of the numbers I have for him."

"How can I know that you are who you say you are?"

"Because I can tell you something for certain that you have only suspected. All of the peace bologna that has been going on for the past year was to lull all of us to sleep while my Semite brothers built a nuclear bomb and missile plant in Aleppo, Syria. I have information pouring into my computer that confirms that and the fact that a nuclear attack is going to take place in the next hour or two in your country. Only the documents will convince the people in the U.S. who matter. Let me send the material, and let it speak for itself. I don't want anything you have. I just want to give this material to you and hope that it isn't too late for you to do something."

"Send it to Pickering's e-mail address. What's the problem with that?"

"He's not there to get it. This can't sit overnight or until all of the parties are over. I'll send it, but I have to have your word that you will stand by his computer to receive it."

"I don't have his access code. If I fiddled with his computer, security would be on me in half a minute."

Harkabi despaired.

"Then you've got to get Pickering, or I've got to send it to you."

"My computer is in West Virginia and I don't know anybody else's codes. I'll find Pickering. Hold on. I'll do the best I can. You'd better not be jacking me around."

"This is no joke, no disinformation. My organization isn't into jokes. This is not about your career or your precious ego. This is about thermonuclear war and the remote possibility that you can find a way to stop it. Now stop wasting time."

Mathers hung up and muttered to himself that he was probably going to regret this as soon as he conveyed the message. However, there was a chilling ring of truth to the Mossad agent's tale. He called his friend, Anthony Pickering, on the throw away cell phone he was carrying while he evaded Angelina Davis and her security team. Mathers was the only person who knew about the phones and learned each day's new number.

"Tony, it's me."

"I take it this is important."

"I promised to use this number only in the most dire emergency, and I think that's what we have. I'll let you be the judge."

Mathers quickly filled Pickering in on the conversation he had just had with the Mossad agent.

He asked, "Is this guy on the up and up? Do you give credence to his claims? Do you want to receive his stuff?"

Pickering was a lawyer by education.

"Compound question, but I won't bother with niceties. The answers are yes, yes, and yes. I'll come right in, but in the mean time—and I'm already driving near the building—you get me uninterfered-with-clearance back into my office. My code word is Bestman. E-mail Harkabi.Moss.Landing@Telaviv. gov.net and get the info coming. You don't have anything else important today, Dean. I'm telling you this man is as straight as they come. If he says the third world war is about to start, I believe him. My credibility has been ruined by our esteemed Director, and I will need you to get through her and the White House cretins and to the president. Help me in this, my friend."

With DCIA Davis in Detroit, it was not very difficult to arrange for Pickering to get through the layers of security in the CIA building. The two men rushed to Pickering's office and began to print selected documents. The information was electrifying. The time frame was only a matter of minutes. Both Pickering and Mathers knew they were too late to stop a disaster if this was anything but a hoax; and each of them said a silent prayer that Harkabi was crazy or had the worst taste in humor in all history.

"Make a CD or two or whatever it takes, and let's get this to the president and everybody else that matters," urged Mathers.

Pickering was already inserting the first disc. In a few minutes they had filled three discs and had made two copies. Mathers called the FBI and was able to get through to Director Marques. Pickering called the DCIA on her secure line.

Marques told the two men to meet him at the White House, hung up his phone and made three calls: the first to the chairman of the Joint Chiefs of Staff, the second to the vice-president's office, and the third to the Senate office building in a search for any senator left out of the Detroit or Washington festivities. He gave his cell phone number and headed for the West Wing. While on the fly, he was able to brief Air Force General Houton Caruthers, the Chairman of the JCS. Caruthers agreed to meet at the White House because—as he said, if the information was true—the United States would need not only a new president, but most of a new government. The general stopped short of suggesting that the information would also usher in a war. He was put in his JCS seat by a very liberal administration, and not because he had any convictions that separated him from his commander-in-chief.

Senator Cliff Assure had been getting ready for his speech at the Lincoln Memorial when his aide informed him of the emergency. He caught Marques as he was passing through the White House security gate and was informed of the imminently grave situation. Vice-President Rowan's office informed the director that she was doing her swimming exercise in the White House lap pool. Someone would have to go after her personally. Presumptively, Marques called the Supreme Court, gave his name and demanded to speak to the Justice in residence for the day. He explained the situation to Justice Kim Prentiss Lathrop.

"Madam Justice, please meet us in the Oval Office as fast as you can get there. I'll send a car."

"I will be waiting in the lobby when your driver comes."

"And—if you can locate a copy—bring the exact wording for swearing in a new president. You will be a small part of history today, Justice Lathrop."

At the same time, Pickering's call to Angelina Davis was answered by her deputy.

"This is a secure line, go ahead."

"This is Pickering. I have to talk to the DCIA."

"I don't think she'll wish to have a conversation with you, Pickering. You're *persona non grata*. About the only communication she'll give you is to tell you you're fired."

"Thanks for sharing. However, Arthur, you and I don't have time to talk. I have a most secret, most urgent message for the director and the president. The emergency I am trying to tell them about is minutes away from happening. Move it and fire me or shoot me later!"

"Okay, it's your funeral."

Pickering had a two minute wait.

"Pickering?"

"Yes, ma'am."

"You have a lot of nerve calling me after dodging me for two days. You're fired. You don't get to quit. That's the whole of my message. Now get away from secure phones. I am going to have security escort you out of the building—I see where you're calling from—and they are going to hold you under house arrest until we sort out what you've been up to. I presume this is just another of your conspiracy theories, and the president is too busy for another crack pot message."

"Don't hang up, Dragon Lady."

"What did you call me, you pipsqueak?"

"I just wanted your attention. Listen to me. I have documentary evidence, CDs full of it, that there is going to be a nuclear attack on Detroit in the next few minutes. You have to tell the president and the Secret Service and get the main officials out of the area now while there is still the faintest hope."

"Get me the evidence."

"There isn't time. You know me. I have a perfect source in Mossad. This comes from them. Please, I have never failed you even though you don't like me. Please get the president out of there."

His voice betrayed the depths of his anxiety. It was unmistakable to her, and she knew him to have ice water for blood. This had to be for real.

"I will try. And if you are wrong, both of us will be on the bread line. I know I shouldn't trust you, but in the future I would be crucified if I let this warning pass. I am a hundred yards from the president and the nearest Secret Service agent, and there are half a million people between me and him. I'll move as fast as I can. If you are doing this to ruin me, remember that you will go to prison. All of my calls are recorded."

"There's no time for cya, Director."

She hung up and began hurrying towards the podium where the president was standing at the podium waiting to begin his speech. It was 7:01.

Security reported the deaths of al Qassam and Wael Etamad to Prince ibn Saud. He gritted his teeth and glared at the security officer who flinched.

The prince drew in a long slow breath to get control of himself and to try to think.

"It doesn't really matter," he said after a two second pause. "We have only fourteen minutes left. Nothing can interfere with Operation Avenging the Crusades now. Get me General al-Kuwatly."

The general arrived in a minute.

"The Occupiers know about our plan, even the time. We can expect an attack any second."

The Air Force general replied, "I will get the mobilization underway. This won't be any six day war."

He turned on his heel and rushed to his secure phone. The prince watched General al-Kuwatly as he yelled into the phone, gesticulating earnestly. The leader of the Council looked out the windows and saw the anti-missile defenses beginning to sprout out of their deep bunkers. He had done all that he could do. He tuned his hearing back into the countdown—thirteen minutes forty-seven seconds.

Director Marques called the president's military aide. The connection was execrable. He hoped that he had been able to convince the dubious aide that an attack was imminent. He hoped that he had been heard at all. He walked into the cabinet room and began issuing orders to staffers to find any cabinet members and any senators or congressmen they could round up.

"Where's the veep?" he demanded of a Secret Service agent.

"We've sent two agents to fetch her. They should be back any minute."

CHAPTER THIRTY-TWO

APRIL 16, 2010

Revel's *Bolero* was picking up tempo and volume with three minutes to go before the climactic final measures. Vice-President Rowan was sweating in the water as she pushed herself to keep up with the pulsating beat. Rowan always played *Bolero* when she did laps because the increasing tempo and throbbing beat stirred her on faster and faster towards the end of her two mile swim instead of her normal inclination to slow down and rest towards the end. Besides, she had read about the sexual overtones to the music as it approached its climactic finis, and it gave her a minor sense of naughtiness that she could not otherwise enjoy in her fish bowl existence as the vice-president—the ornament—as she viewed the office.

As she lifted her right arm and pulled it through the water, then lifted and pulled her left, she ran over her speech for the afternoon. At the president's insistence, she, like him, was to give a major address on world peace. He believed wholeheartedly that at last the time had come for real peace on earth, a veritable millennial state of international concord, harmony, and security. She—on the other hand—had to admit to herself that she was an ingrained skeptic—a cynic through and through. World peace seemed more to her like a beauty contestant's trite answer to what she wants most of all. But Vice-President Elizabeth Leavitt Rowan was a team player, and she planned to do her bit for king and country that day. Maybe she would break her hard and fast rule and have a stiff drink afterwards.

Rowan looked back over her shoulder to check the time. She was doing well, her pace improving by the month. It was 7:05; she had been swimming for forty-five minutes and had about twenty-five more laps to go. It pleased her that she was not yet tired. The vice-presidency might not be a powerful or even satisfying position, but she was enjoying the rest from her long legal career. She had to admit that the prospect of having a cushioning pension when her term ended was comforting. She guessed that she could go on like this for another two years or maybe even into a second Braithwaite administration if he would have her.

The president sat in rapt attention to the singers. He had never been so completely at peace. Success upon success was trailing him, and he was going to go down in history on a par with Washington and Lincoln. Perhaps future historians would elevate him even higher because he had been the great instrument of world peace as opposed to a successful architect of war. It was a trifle immodest of him to allow such thoughts to linger, but a man needed to feel truly successful at least once in his life. And his life was good, as good as it gets.

He had personally chosen the musical number that preceded him. It set the tone, and conveyed a profound message of acceptance of diversity, one of the cornerstones of his liberal administration and certainly one of the integral requirements of achieving peace. Wellesley College was honored to have their glee club give the opening musical peace. The dean of the venerable women's college had glowed with the same blush of pride as the president when the Governor of Michigan, Quentin Dastrup Fuller, introduced the Wellesley Lesbian and Feminist Choir.

"Last night I had the strangest dream,
I ever dreamed before…"

Braithwaite ran his speech over in his mind. It was a good one, a speech that should be remembered as emblematic of the great peace that was unfolding. He envisioned future children reciting portions of it to their classmates and proud parents. He chuckled at his hubris, but he *was* enjoying this day.

"…and the paper they were signing said, they'd never fight again.
And when the papers all were signed…"

The president looked over the massive crowd of whites and blacks, Americans and Muslims, men and women, old and young, at the jungle of wires and electronic equipment sending his message throughout the world. Kristy McNamara, his press secretary, had told him on the plane coming in that this broadcast would reach the largest audience in the history of the world. How fitting, he thought.

"...and guns and swords and uniforms
Were scattered on the ground."

Governor Fuller radiated one of his trademark full dental smiles and announced to the world, "Honored guests, visitors, my fellow citizens of the world, ladies and gentlemen, it is my profound honor to introduce the man who is responsible for this era of peace. I give you the president of the United States"

It was 7:05; he was five minutes late getting started; and President Braithwaite was a stickler for punctuality.

"Oh well," he thought, *"I'll go with the flow. It is too great a day to quibble."*

Thunderous applause roared from the immense crowd. Whistles and hoots and shouts of joy filled the air for a full five minutes before the president was able to begin. No one—including President Braithwaite or his Secret Service guardians—paid any heed to a well dressed African-American woman gesturing and shouting from the crowd and trying impolitely to push her way through.

"My friends from all over the world, my countrymen, thank you for being here. Never forget this momentous occasion. At the end of this week, I will meet in the United Nations with the heads of every sovereign country in the world. As in the words of the song by the Wellesley choir, we will sign papers agreeing never to fight again. At no moment in time has peace on the whole earth been so close at hand. It has taken great courage, immense work, tact, compromise, and a wellspring of good will on all sides to get to this point.

"I commit the United States to a course of peaceful co-existence, of friendly trade, of negotiation of differences with all the nations of the world. Our friends in the Islamic nations have done their part. In the recent Patterns of Global Terrorism Report, we have seen that there were only eight instances of international terrorism in the past twelve months compared to four hundred twenty-two the year before and three hundred eighty-six the year before that. All but two of this year's eight incidents occurred in Africa. To demonstrate that the promises my administration are making are based on a genuine commitment, this week, I will forward a Presidential Order to the atomic

Stockpile Stewardship Program managers through their responsible agency, the Department of Energy, via the National Security Administration to begin with all possible speed to dismantle the 10,000 nuclear weapons in our arsenal; I will order a measured but significant elimination of excess American Armed Forces and war ordnance.

"I will direct Homeland Security to dismantle the Transportation Security Administration and the multibillion dollar Visit border security system and will order that—effective by the time you enter our nation's airports—you and your loved ones will be able to say good-by at the gate and not in the sterile, even hostile, environment of a hallway by a set of security barriers. No longer will entrance be limited only to people with bona fide boarding cards.

"We will no longer permit racial profiling that singles out Muslims."

Enthusiastic clapping interrupted.

"Yesterday, I ordered our US Immigration and Customs Enforcement Agency, a Homeland Security Department—which we refer to as 'ICE'—to have its Compliance Enforcement Unit cease and desist from requiring visa checks on the honored guests coming to our country from the Muslim countries."

A spontaneous standing ovation followed Braithwaite's announcement. He could not have been more pleased. It was obvious that the timed agenda was going to be ignored. He did not care. He did not have a care in the world. It was the best day he could remember.

Angelina Davis looked frantically at her watch. 7: 12. If that idiot, Pickering, was right, something dreadful was about to happen in three minutes. She knew full well that even if she were able to get her message out, nothing could be done to save this crowd and her beloved president. She clung to the hope that Pickering was the dunderhead she believed he was and that there was no real threat. His hyperbolic announcement of the impending apocalypse was going to pass like all of history's other world's end predictions. Nevertheless, she continued her broken field run through the dense crowd with the burly Secret Serviceman doing the blocking. Their progress was exasperatingly slow, like swimming through molasses.

———————

The final countdown was announced. It was 7:13 on the Detroit clock, *Saga'a wa thalat'a'ashar*, the disconnected voice told the breathless crowd. Two minutes and counting. Prince ibn Saud tried to maintain his usual composure, but his heart was racing, and he feared that the men around him would detect this weakness.

There was a murmuring as the last minute countdown systems checks proceeded in an orderly and calm fashion. Thanks be to Allah for the passionless scientists and technologists who were making this great moment possible.

"*Sabin* [seventy]."

Ibn Saud glanced at the clocks. He looked around the room and saw flawless calm work. The ICBM project manager saw him looking and gave a thumbs up. The prince gave the man a rare smile.

"*Khamsin* [fifty]."

The master computers recorded the readiness status: systems-ready, rocket ignition computer-ready, directions and trajectory vectors-check. All systems ready.

The blast-off could be halted until five seconds to go. After that nothing could stop Allah's spear, and the crusades would be irrevocably revenged.

"*Talata* [three]."

———————

The nerve-wracked men and women waiting in the Oval Office watched spell bound as CNN showed the president making the greatest speech in history—the announcement that persisting world peace was at hand. Every mind in the room wondered at top internal volume whether they had acted precipitously and foolishly. But they had seen the evidence. They had had to act, hadn't they?

The president looked radiant; it was a beautiful day, and his audience was awed.

"But, it will take work, my friends," President Braithwaite continued, "and constant vigilance. I am a practical man; my nation is one of optimists, but also a land of pragmatists. We will do our part; we will reach out. I implore you to accept us, to talk with us, to exhaust all avenues of diplomacy and good will without resorting to violence or to the horrors of war."

The clock on his prompter read 0714; he was ten minutes behind; and that annoyed him; but he refused to let it show.

"And now, my friends…"

The television transmission became a shimmering grey blank.

Vice-President Rowan decided to swim two fast laps then to luxuriate in the presidential shower. She felt a bit tired, and her eyes burned from too much water and chlorine, but it was a good kind of tired. She looked forward to having her bottle of raspberry yogurt, her little reward for exercising.

She was on a never-ending stutteringly successful and unsuccessful diet. She laughed at herself for not having the strength of character to lose the weight and to keep it off.

Secret Service Agents Carter and Ramirez ran into the White House work out area and frantically looked around for the vice-president.

"I can hear her splashing. She's in the lap pool," Ramirez said.

They ran into the pool area. The time on the pool room clock read 7:14:59. Rowan's peaceful swim was about to end.

Twelve Israeli F/A-22 Raptor Stealthfighters, a top secret gift from the American $7 billion research and development effort, hurtled into the sky with their GPS guided computers locked onto Aleppo, Syria. After takeoff, the Raptors moved at a speed of Mach 1.8 without requiring an afterburner. The advanced aircraft do not appear on radar until it is too late for antiaircraft artillery to locate and lock on them. The Raptors were a direct and secret gift to the Israelis from the Bush Administration, and the Braithwaite administration was unaware of their existence outside the United States. The sleek, stealth-capable planes have low aerodynamic drag because their fuel tanks are largely internal and their two Pratt and Whitney F119-PW-100 engines provide 35,000 pounds of thrust—40% more than the F-15 they replaced.

The raptor is the best fighter other than for one the British Royal Navy was given a single engine version called the F-35 Joint Strike Force Fighter by Bush from the $5 billion American research and development effort. Raptors are equipped with two AIM-9 Sidewinders, six AIM-120C Advanced Medium-Range Air-to-Air Missiles (AMRAAM), one 20 mm Gatling gun, and two 1,000 pound Joint Direct Attack Munitions (JDAM) to provide cover for the three F-100 D jets with the better nuclear bombing capacity.

The Raptors' Integrated Avionics allow the F-22 pilots—one per plane—unprecedented and supremely efficient awareness of enemy forces by a fusion of on and off board information. The Raptors are altogether capable of protecting themselves as well as the F-100 Ds, for which the mission was dispatched. Four E-F-111 radar jamming aircraft led the attack group, widely spread out along the bee-line to Aleppo.

Close behind the Raptors came specially adapted F-16s whose task was SEAD—Suppression of Enemy Air Defenses. They began enticing the enemy to light up search and track radars, to prepare to launch SAMs, and to begin firing anti-aircraft guns. Once activated, the Syrian defenses were jammed by the sophisticated Israeli defensive aircraft.

"Seven minutes to target," Captain Eli Amnon Sarid announced to the wing pilots. "This is not a drill. The order comes from the PM and is a go unless rescinded."

Twenty-six pilots and co-pilots prayed that such an order would never come. The Israel Air Defense Ministry controllers joined in the silent prayer.

The Israeli air wing streaked up the Beka'a Valley of Lebanon. Beneath them lay the fertile plain of the valley 3000 feet above sea level and nestled between the Lebanon and Anti-Lebanon mountain ranges. At first blush, the aerial view of the long slender valley is a bucolic checkerboard of fields of grain and vegetables and fertile vineyards heavy with sweet fruit. Shepherds herd their sheep and goats among peaceful farms and villages. The two major towns are Chtaura and Zahle, commercial and tourism stops between Beirut and Damascus. Closer inspection from the Israeli air wing's high vantage point allowed them to locate fascinating ancient ruins such as Anjar and Baalbek.

More ominously, and of no less fascination, are the fields of cotton and poppies for the heroin trade. Uppermost in the minds of the Israelis, however, were the terrorist training camps of Hezbollah, Abu Nidal, and al Qaeda operating in the open and with impunity that dot the valley from top to bottom. The AAA capability of the camps was the predominant concern in the fighter/bomber wing at the moment, and the eyes of technicians strained over radar screens to see if they had been detected. The Israelis in their Raptors passed over the sleeping Beka'a Valley without registering a blip of activity and heaved a collective sigh of relief that nothing from the pastoral but military hotbed would interfere with their mission. The follow-up F-16s took care of the resistance as it appeared.

Prince ibn Saud's lips finished the count with the control room engineer's disembodied voice.

"*Triein, wahid, sifr*. Ignition."

In toto, fourteen LGM-118A Peacekeeper ICBM missiles, each with MIRV nuclear capability, blasted with a deafening and blinding roar and explosion out of ground silos in Aleppo, Egypt, Iran, and from the dedicated site in the Ar-Rab' al-Khali in Saudi Arabia with precision of synchronism at the nano-second level. They streaked with tails of white fire into the stratosphere for targets half a world away. The total destructive power exceeded the weapons that leveled Hiroshima and Nagasaki by nearly 10,000 times.

At the first deafening blast, Prince Ahmed, tears of joy streaming down his leathery face, cried, "*La ilaha illa 'l-Lah, wa Muhammadan rasula l-Lah* [There is no God but God, and Muhammad is the Messenger of God], may peace be upon him. Israfil, the angel, has sounded the trumpet announcing the end of the decadent Western world."

Someone shouted over the din to the Prince, "*Mabrouk, mabrouk!*" [Congratulations]

Beneath the cacophony of the missiles' blastoffs, the room murmured with fervent recitals of the *shahadah* by the faithful.

The Libyan representative to the Council cried out, "*Bism 'l-lahi allahu akbar,* [in the name of God] look what we have done."

"Prince, you have accomplished a *coup de maître*! [master blow]," the representative of the Algerian Salafist Group for Call and Combat exulted.

Reports from all four locations came in instantaneously. The attack had been launched without even a microscopic flaw, *alhamdulillah*. Jubilation erupted in the control room. There were shouts praising Allah, The Prophet, blessed be his name, the holy martyrs, and the Council of Islamic Leaders. The communal ecstasy in the room approached mutual simultaneous orgasm.

CHAPTER THIRTY-THREE

APRIL 16, 2010, 0715:00 EDT, 1115:00 ZULU (GMT)

President Hollings Braithwaite drew in a breath before entering the last paragraph of his prepared speech to the waiting world. CNN, Fox, ABC, CBS, NBC, BBC, Al Arabiya, and al Jazeera for their hundreds of millions of viewers showed his image, broadcast his last words, "And now my friends…" and recorded his last breath as a sigh.

At slip 45 in the Riverside Marina on the Windsor, Ontario side of the Detroit River, the luminous dial in the hidden box on the obscure boat read, "Pre-ignition". Inside the box an electronic hum mingled with a series of soft clicks. The fire-control computer unit activated. The LED flashed, "Pre-ignition phase two". There was a ten second interval; then the LED counted down the last ten seconds. The entire LED lit up and glowed, "Zero", then "Ignition" at the same instant as the president's sigh.

Immediately, a quantity of high energy Semtex A explosive—with its high percentage composition of PETN—was detonated around a pit of enriched uranium to start off a chain reaction nuclear fission device which in turn caused the fusion of hydrogen and helium into heavy elements releasing stupendous amounts of energy and the greatest explosion in the history of the the world. In a few nanoseconds, a sixty megaton hydrogen bomb explosion erupted which was exponentially greater than the approximately ten kiloton fission bomb with the equivalent of 12,500 tons of TNT that leveled Hiroshima. A one megaton hydrogen bomb, detonated on land would be eighty times the blast of the explosion that occurred in 1945, and the explosion emanating from slip 45 reached 5000 megatons.

First came the stupendous thermal radiation—mostly soft x-ray—creating a fireball visible for three hundred miles. It was like the exhalation of a dragon. Thirty percent of the bomb's total energy was concentrated in that portion of the explosion. Nearly nine million people were dead before they heard the blast; most of them died without even having the immense million degree heat and sun intensity light register on their senses. The heat was so great that a mass fire was created that caused earthquake proof buildings to melt; streets and cars and presidential podiums to be vaporized—literally turned to radioactive dust; and every building for more than six miles went up in an instantaneous conflagration.

There were two components of the explosion itself which constituted sixty percent of the total energy of the thermonuclear device: the shock wave wall of pressure that expanded outward symmetrically from the detonation and the monster hurricane wind that was generated by the blast. The blast followed the heat ball by nanoseconds. Everything not burned or carried away by the heat and pressure of the heat wave was blown into atoms or pulverized by 40 psi, 1000 mile an hour, static overpressure. Dynamic pressure winds pushed, tumbled, and tore every object in their paths and rendered Greater Detroit, Wayne County, and Southern Ontario a formless nuclear ash desert. The ninth largest city in the United States disappeared.

A mushroom shaped cloud of earth and the debris rendered radioactive that which once was Detroit now rocketed into the sky and topped out at three miles. The radiation in the mushroom was the equivalent of tens of millions of kilograms of radium. It was twenty-two miles in diameter at its base. Birds in flight, people celebrating peace, animals in their burrows, insects in their hiding places—everything was dead, gone from the planet.

Most of the radioactive ash fell directly back on Wayne County and Windsor, Ontario in drifts a foot thick and settled in heavy lethal accumulations on the area of the fire ball, the area of the blast, the area of the fire contagion, and for a distance of a ten mile perimeter around the area of absolute and relative physical destruction. A 3,000 Rem [Roentgen equivalent man] radiation dose that rained down upon the area thirty miles away from the blast center was much more that the recognized lethal dose.

For ninety miles a lethal dose was spread with death coming within fourteen days on the living beings exposed to the insidious dust. Extensive internal nerve, digestive tract, white blood cell damage, and hair loss occurred at 160 miles. Lesser amounts spread for thousands of square miles forever contaminating the earth. A minority of the radioactive material stayed aloft and entered the stratosphere where it would remain for decades. Seventy percent of all living things in that penumbra area were dead within an hour from asphyxiation and direct contact with hot nuclear poison. Twenty percent more died in two weeks; and of the remaining, all but three or four percent would be mortally wounded with immediate or with longer term effects— burns, cancers, eroded gastrointestinal tracts, destroyed bone marrows, blindness, wrecked auto-immune systems, nonfunctioning thyroids, and not least, with psychiatric meltdown.

World-wide fallout and the harm it was to do over the long-term was guaranteed by the accumulation of long-lived radioisotopes—strontium-90 and cesium-137—in the earth, in foods and in bodies. The only factor that saved the United States from a more wide-spread deposition of the fallout was that it was a cloudless, day with a light breeze that formed the mushroom cloud into a narrower and longer plume. Most of the survivors were left with little but nightmares and reproductive monstrosities.

Simultaneously, dirty bombs—also referred to as area denial weapons and RDDs, of much less ferocity—exploded in the Avenir Hotel in Paris, the Club Quarters St. Paul Hotel on Ludgate Street in London, at the Sheraton Grande Hotel on Figueroa Street in Los Angeles and from a self-storage lock-up in Sydney. Each bomb devastated a mile radius area and deposited ionizing radioactive dust in every tiny crevice remaining in the rubble. Neutrons—like microscopic bunker-busting missiles—penetrated all solid objects with ease. The ground was contaminated down a foot deep in places making the metro centers of five major cities of the world uninhabitable for decades. In sum—over a ten second period of blast and initial fire followed by a series of spreading fires unprecedented since the incendiary raids on German cities during the Second World War—a mind boggling degree of damage had befallen three continents.

In London, severe damage occurred at Heathrow Airport, Waterloo Station, Fenchurch St. Railway Station, and most of the major business area of The City. In Paris, the Montparnasse area was totally wrecked with irreparable damage to the Eiffel Tower, the Montparnasse Train Station, the Convention Underground Station and to the major streets, sewer systems, telephone land line systems, businesses, restaurants, and hotels large and small that had thrived in the district just seconds before. Sydney's core business district was rendered unapproachable.

Los Angeles lost the Bunker Hill Gold Coast including the Westin Bonaventure Hotel, the Crocker Center, the World Trade Center, the Arco Plaza, Security Plaza, Union Plaza, Bunker Hill Condominiums, the Los Angeles Central Library, the Fashion Institute, and Los Angeles City Hall. Some of the heaviest traveled and most crucial transportation routes were turned into craters; buildings were leveled or made unsafe for future occupancy; local, state, national, and international business was disrupted. It was eventually estimated in London, Paris, Sydney, and Los Angeles that three and a quarter million people lost their lives; three hundred thousand jobs were lost or disrupted for a prolonged period of recovery; and the cost of the damage caused by the dirty bombs alone was estimated to be five hundred twelve billion dollars.

And that devastation paled in comparison to the horrific losses caused by the Windsor/Detroit thermonuclear explosion. For practical purposes there was no more Detroit—no automobile manufacturers, no vital shipping lanes, no link with Canada as there had once been, no Cobo Conference and Exhibition Center, Joe Louis Arena, Comerica Park, Pontiac Silverdome, DTE Music Theater, Meadowbrook, Palace of Auburn Hills, or Ford Field. Forty-six thousand businesses, eleven hundred churches, two thousand schools and universities, twenty-eight thousand restaurants—all gone. One hundred eighty-two of the world's most elegant tall ships that had been lined up in front of the Riverside Marina on the Detroit River became known only to history. What had once been a vital, bustling metropolis with parks and arts, theater, scandals, triumphs, sports giants, and a manufacturing mecca was gone.

All the people—their hopes, aspirations, fears, and futures—gone. The bomb created a crater lake where the Detroit River had once been that made a single huge body of water out of Lake Erie and Lake St. Clair. The instantaneous cataclysmic changes resulted in a tidal wave thirty feet high that scoured the banks of Erie and St. Clair and spread the carnage four miles inland. Huge numbers of buildings and everything that was not secured to bedrock were sucked back into the crater when the waters retracted. The final level of the lakes was lowered three feet.

In all, two decades later, the cost of that holocaust alone—not including the horrifying damage in the cities attacked by the dirty bombs—was six and a half trillion dollars, eleven million lives, and the extinguishment of the City of Detroit and Wayne County, Michigan. From the epicenter of the blast outward to a radius of ten miles there was not a stone still laying upon a stone, no streets recognizable as such, and not a flicker of activity. For another ten miles out, it was utter devastation with portions of walls still standing like ghost monuments to what once had been there; and now was a landscape of grey white dust—a formless desert. The next ten miles out looked like Dresden after the World War II fire bombing raids, and that—relatively speaking— was the fortunate area. Occasional casts of what were once people stood in place like the men who gazed into the eyes of the Medusa. The crusades had been avenged. There was a silence in the whole land.

CHAPTER THIRTY-FOUR

APRIL 16, 2010, 0716 EDT, 0116 Syrian Daylight Time

A lowly computer specialist in the control center was the first to see the incoming air force which seemed to materialize from nowhere. The planes were unchallenged. The air defenses of Syria including the Aleppo Military Air Field, had failed to detect them.

He pointed towards the south west and started to shout, but no sound was heard from him. His attempted outcry was cutoff by a medium level thermonuclear device released by one of the Israeli Air Force F-100D Supersaber Jets. The bomb's combined fireball, superheated gases, enormous blast effects, and demolishing impact force obliterated the Islamic bomb plant, ICBM launching sites, palatial estates on the grounds, and a significant portion of ancient Aleppo—the place where Abraham milked his grey cow, hence the correct name, *Halab Al-Shahba.*

The IDF air wing scattered according to pre-planned routes and escaped the holocaust without serious damage to any plane or crew member. One intrepid F-22, visually sighting an ICBM's fiery tail, abruptly throttled to full speed and aimed itself almost vertically into the sky on a direct course with the ICBM in early flight. The pilot computer fix-sighted on the missile and—in an apparently futile gesture—fired two of his AIM-9 Sidewinders. The air-to-air missiles unerringly locked themselves onto the huge burning tail of the ICBM and by a small miracle caught and scratched one LGM-118A Peacekeeper ICBM over Aleppo. The resulting impact was enough to set off a chain reaction nuclear explosion that consumed the missile and one of it's Avenging the Crusades partner ICBMs, the F 100-D that had scored the lucky hit, one of the F-22 Raptors, and all of the rest of Aleppo. A crater four hundred feet deep covered the entire area occupied for five thousand years by Syrians and their forebears.

Aleppo—the second largest Syrian city and the nation's center of commerce with three million diverse inhabitants—had been one of the oldest cities on earth—continuously occupied since 3000 B.C.E. The city had been home to Arabs, Turks, Armenians, Russians, and a few Jews the day the bombs fell. The venerable capital with its 13th century acropolis Citadel, Christian churches, mosques, regular schools, and *Qur'anic* medrassas, or Old Schools, venerated tombs, Turkish Hammam baths, souks, twenty-first century markets and business centers, air force and army bases, and all of its citizens and visitors were gone. The marvelous ancient and modern architecture—Baroque, Neo-classical, Norman, Islamic, and Oriental, including even a few Chinese pagodas—was erased.

The Israeli wing commander, Capt. Eli Amnon Sarid, saw the heroic attempt of the F-22 Raptor that scored the hit and died in the effort.

He heard the last words of the doomed pilot, "*Visgadal viyiskadishy, shimay Rabbah.*" [Hebrew-May His name be celebrated and sanctified.].

He cursed, holding himself responsible.

"*Meshuggenah!*" Capt. Sarid said, whether he meant that the pilot or he was crazy was unclear even to himself.

He had no time to ruminate on such irrelevancies as guilt, however. His radio contact informed him that Damascus had scrambled what appeared to be an entire air force and rather than heading northwest towards Capt. Sarid's attackers, the Syrians were about to cross the Golan Heights for Israel.

Sarid blanched.

"Nucs," he said to his wing pilots. "Let's go after them. Stay close."

The Israelis faced a most formidable opponent. The Syrian Air Force—*Al Quwwat al-Jawwiyaal as-Souriya*—was the largest in the Middle East. Most of the equipment and air craft in the air force came from Russia and today; the Israelis would face new Sukhoi Su-27s, MIG-25, M Versions, and MIG 29 SMTs. The generous American government had provided a few F-15 Eagle's, F4 G Wild Weasels, and F-111 Fighter Bombers, which were exceptional military aircraft; and they were piloted by well-trained pilots and crews by Middle-East standards. Most were trained in the old Soviet Union and successor Russia, many in British Flight Schools; and after Hollings Braithwaite became president of the United States, some had once again started to be trained in the United States. The Syrian Air Force was dedicated, brave, and cool under fire. They had substantial and sustaining *esprit d' corps*. The vaunted Su-22 squadrons—677 and 685—considered themselves to be unbeatable; and the Su-24 squadrons with thirty planes—each one more sophisticated and deadly than the 22s—scoffed at their brethren.

And they were all no match for the small stealth armada that came out of nowhere from above and behind them or for the sophisticated antiair-craft home defenses of the Israeli state. The Syrian radar systems—including Russian TU-126 Moss AWACS, sophisticated though they were—and their maneuverability and fighting capabilities—which were beyond the imagina-tion of an air force commander in 2008—were no match for the Raptors that dropped out of the sky with the Syrians as prey. In a fierce dog-fight that lasted less than fourteen minutes, every Syrian airplane—including the entirety of Navy Squadron 618—exploded or crashed in a fiery melt of metal on Israeli occupied territory. In desperation, the Syrians sent fleets of Navy Ka25 attack helicopters which never had a chance. One hundred fifty seven of them littered the green hilly countryside and adjacent desert floor.

The frightened men in the Internal Security Military headquarters in Mukhabarat decided to put every asset into this effort to save their home-land. No longer were they pursuing an offensive attack; the question now was whether the Syrian nation or its people could survive this day. They launched ASMs, AT-2, AS-7,9,10,11,12, and 14 and HOT missiles and reserve fighter planes from Military Air Fields around the country. Everything available from Abu-Dhur, Blay, Damascus, Damascus's Al Mazzah, Day az Zawr, Hamah, Khalkhalah and half a dozen other bases was sent into the fray and perished. Only T-4 on the pipeline was held in reserve in case of a final solution battle following a failure of a land attack by Syria and its friends. It was no longer unthinkable that another 1967 or Six-Day War could happen.

No Israeli kibbutzes, towns, synagogues or civilians were hit; no Israeli airmen or planes died; and no nuclear bombs were exploded in the short, fierce and uneven battle. Israel once again owned the sky. The Kibbutznicks watching from below cheered and sang *Am Yisrael Chai [The Nation of Israel Lives]*.

While the dog-fight took place over the Golan Heights and Israel's soil, the ICBMs from Aleppo—minus two—Saudi Arabia, Iran, and Egypt main-tained their supersonic course towards the heart of the Great Satan. These MIRV [Multiple independently targetable reentry vehicle] capable nuclear weapons were enough to emasculate the United States and to thrust the God cursed country into a century or more of pathetic weakness. Once the multiple warheads found their marks, there would not be enough left of the Great Satan's power to mount a defense. These spears of God would usher in the millennium, the Islamic millennium; the *Yawm al-Qiyamah, Yawm al-Din,* the Day of Judgment was at hand.

———————

"Madam Vice-President, we need you to come with us now," the senior Secret Service officer said a little breathlessly having run the last fifty yards to catch the vice-president as she tapped the end of the pool completing her lap.

Vice-President Rowan was startled and put off by having been so totally taken by surprise. She had been focused on the last passionate strains of Bolero and on keeping an accurate count of the number of laps she was adding to her score.

She shook the water from her hair and face and asked, "What's up?"

"A national emergency. Taking place right now," Agent Carter said gravely. Nothing in his face suggested that he was exaggerating.

Agent Ramirez's cell phone signaled two beeps.

"Ramirez," she said.

Ramirez listened then closed her phone and put it into her blouse pocket. She had something of a dazed look.

"What?" asked Carter.

"Not now and not here. Let's get the CINC to her office."

The significance of what Ramirez just said was missed by Vice-President Rowan, but not on Carter.

"Oh," he said with a deflated tone.

"Ma'am, please towel off and dress as quickly as you can. Your presence really is required in the Oval Office as quickly as you possibly can."

"I'll help you, ma'am," offered Agent Ramirez.

"I've had a lot of years of practice, Agent Ramirez," said Rowan glancing at the agent's name tag. "I can dress myself. I'll just be a minute, and I'll take care of it alone."

"Sorry, ma'am, my orders are to accompany you all the time. Sorry for any inconvenience."

Vice-President Rowan detected a change in status, and it made her uneasy. She stepped around a corner in the dressing room, nodded towards the shower, and caught a definite negative head shake from Ramirez. She slicked back her hair and threw on her simple business suit.

"Ready," she said.

"Thanks for hurrying, ma'am. Let's go."

Rowan and Ramirez reappeared from around the corner of the shower and dressing room and met a squad of heavily armed men and women in SWAT uniforms, the elite Presidential Secret Service action squad.

"This way, ma'am," said Carter, and the vice-president and her newly formed entourage moved briskly across to the West Wing, down the hall, turned to the left, and entered the Oval Office.

The president's office—arguably the most important room in the history of the world—was a place of shock and gloom. Men and women stood mute before the room's television sets and marveled at the images of unimaginable destruction that were displayed. CNN's intrepid reporters were already flying about the periphery of the bomb sites—risking life and bone marrow—and sending back sketchy reports of what had happened.

As Elizabeth Rowan walked into the room, everyone turned and looked at her. An unspoken command caused the people in the room to part and offer an unhindered pathway to the executive desk.

"Tell me, what is going on?" she requested.

The television set now showed footage from Al Jeezra Channel/Qatar. There was an hysterical celebration erupting in every Muslim country in the Middle-East. Flashes of exultant Egyptians, defiant Palestinians, mocking Iranians, jubilant Libyans, and of Pakistanis tearing down the United States flag at the embassy in Islamabad were now on display. It was the largest party ever thrown; it was entirely spontaneous, and seemingly every Muslim in the world had been invited. The festival of passion and mood of deliverance in the world of Islam contrasted completely with the previous ten minute summary of the horrors of thermonuclear devastation in the West.

Senator Cliff Assure said sadly, "Somebody bombed us. Bombed and destroyed Detroit and Los Angeles. It is unthinkable, unimaginable. We are at a loss about who or why,"

"I beg to differ, ma'am. I am Anthony Pickering, Special Assistant Director of the Central Intelligence Agency; and, so far as I know right now, the senior remaining officer. I hold proof positive that an evil combination from the Muslim world has collaborated to set off nuclear devices in the most cowardly stab in the back in the world's history. We can only guess at the losses, but it would be conservative to estimate anything less than ten million lives and hundreds of billons, maybe trillions, of dollars of financial loss. Our country has been devastated; and with all due respect to Senator Assure and his liberal friends, there is not a scintilla of doubt about who the perpetrators are."

"I'm waiting to see the evidence," Assure said. "You and your cronies are ever prompt to place the blame on our Muslim friends."

Dean Mathews said, "I've seen the evidence. There is no doubt, ma'am."

"I hate to say, it, but I see no doubt. We have been the victims of a criminal attack and almost certainly on the part of nations we trusted—Egypt, Iran, Syria, Libya, Saudi Arabia, and Pakistan. Saudi Arabia and Pakistan, our real friends for decades. I cannot believe what the evidence is telling me, but neither can I doubt it. We must gather a council and decide our next move," said General Houton Caruthers, Chairman of the JCS.

"This is a lot of dithering, if I can take such a liberty to say so, ma'am," blurted Anthony Pickering. "It is clear what happened, and it is clear what must be done."

"Let's not be hasty," Senator Assure said.

"That's right, Justice Lathrop interrupted. "There is the small matter of the presidential succession. Is there anyone here that doubts that the president is dead?"

All heads shook a unanimous no answer.

"We need to appoint a president pursuant to the Constitution. The vice-president is among us, alive and competent. Let us have a legal commander-in-chief and head of the executive branch before we debate further."

She was right, and the acting presidential secretary produced a Bible. Tears were streaming down her face because she had been part of President Braithwaite's—former President Braithwaite's—loyal staff for two decades.

Justice Lathrop took the Bible and walked over by Vice-President Rowan. A White House photographer moved in to record the occasion.

"Madam Vice-President, please place your left hand on the Bible and raise your right hand to the square."

Elizabeth Rowan did so rather robotically. It was all happening so fast that it might have been the stuff of a dream—a nightmare—were she not certain of the reality of the room and the situation.

"Please repeat after me. I, Elizabeth Leavitt Rowan, do solemnly swear and affirm…"

"I, Elizabeth Leavitt Rowan, do solemnly swear and affirm…"

"that I will faithfully execute the office of President of the United States…"

"that I will faithfully execute the office of President of the United States…"

Elizabeth drew in a deep breathe and seemed to enliven; she no longer functioned as a living robot, but was now becoming fully involved.

"and I will to the best of my ability, preserve, protect and defend the Constitution of the United States."

"and I will to the best of my ability, preserve, protect and defend the Constitution of the United States," She drew in a breath for control and added, "so help me God."

"Madam President, what would you have us do?" requested DFBI Marques deferentially. The mantle had fallen on a new president.

"I appreciate you all being here. I have some questions, and I will have some presidential directives. First, Mr. Marques, Mr. Pickering, and Mr. Mathers, do you each stake the reputation of your organizations and your personal careers on the information you have given us here today?"

"Yes, Madam President, we do," they said nearly in unison.

"Second, and this is for General Caruthers. Are we capable of striking the perpetrators of these colossal atrocities with ICBMs?"

"Yes, Madam President, but…"

"Before any 'buts', I have a third question. How long will it take to launch the ICBMs and to mobilize an aerial strike force followed by a naval invasion?"

"Once the discussions are complete and all principals are on board in the decision process, a little less than half an hour to reprogram the ICBM force and launch it. The air strike force could be ready to leave as a second wave in three hours, four at tops. The navy can set sail this afternoon theoretically."

He was about to say more, but President Rowan held up her hand for quiet.

"I see that the president's—the former president's—personal counsel is waiting in the hallway. Would you ask Mr. Goodman to step in? I need a lawyer," President Rowan said, having seen President Braithwaite's counsel standing outside the room with a small crowd of deferential government leaders. "I'm sorry, I don't know your name."

The question was directed to the acting presidential secretary.

"Abigail Young," the secretary answered blushing from the sudden attention.

"Thank you, Ms. Young."

Shortly three men walked in: Andy Purcell, Lead Counsel for the President, John Y. Goodman, and Terence Long, Executive Branch senior attorneys.

"Yes, Madam President," said Mr. Goodman. "How can we be of service?"

"Right now, answer me a question."

"We'll try."

"Do I have the authority to order a responsive strike on the nations that have attacked us?"

"Most assuredly, ma'am. The War Powers Act expressly grants such power to use the military for up to ninety days without prior authorization. History, current law, and the Constitution all affirm that right and responsibility.

The president can commit troops abroad and can authorize military action without declaring war. Nothing in the Constitution limits the president's military power. Congress was granted power to declare war, not to *make* war. That right and responsibility lies with the president, ma'am. Then attorney general and later supreme court justice, Robert Jackson, stated flatly that the president 'has supreme command' of the United States military and may, on his or her decision alone, order the military to duty for the defense of the nation which duty is the sworn oath of the president.

"Presidents have so ordered the military in the approximately two hundred instances of U.S. use of force beyond our borders. Recent examples include Truman ordering troops into Korea, Kennedy's naval blockade of Cuba, Carter's attempted hostage rescue in Iran, Reagan's attack in Grenada to rescue American citizens, Clinton's order of military action in Kosovo when Europe dithered, and Bush's launch of military strikes and sustained offensives in Afghanistan and Iraq in pursuance of the War on Terrorism. There is good law and ample precedent to grant authority to the sitting president to launch our military in defense of our nation."

"Thank you. Here is my first order. General Caruthers, you are hereby ordered to commence a military attack including immediate use of nuclear weapons on the nations of Iran, Saudi Arabia, Egypt, Libya, Pakistan...Have I left anyone out?"

"Syria, Madam President," Anthony Pickering said quickly.

"And Syria."

General Caruthers stood stock still as if his feet were nailed to the floor. He was obviously summoning up his courage for a reply.

"No, ma'am, I will not do that."

"Do I understand correctly, General? Are you refusing a direct lawful order from your commander-in-chief?"

"I don't consider you the commander-in-chief yet. You are totally unseasoned and not fit for this office. We cannot start World War III without due consideration. Such a response as you are contemplating ordering is unthinkable until we learn more, until we consult with our European allies and have a consensus."

"I am not contemplating, sir. I am ordering. I will repeat the order. General Caruthers, in your capacity as the chairman of the Joint Chiefs of Staff of the armed forces of the United States, I hereby order you to launch a responsive full military strike forthwith against the nations and territory of Iran, Libya, Syria, Egypt, Pakistan, and Saudi Arabia. Will you comply with this order?"

General Caruthers face was contorted. He had never refused to obey or disobeyed a military order in his entire thirty year career.

"I refuse," he said simply.

"For the formal third and last time. General Caruthers, in your capacity as the chairman of the Joint Chiefs of Staff of the armed forces of the United States, I hereby order you to launch a responsive full military strike including the use of nuclear weapons against the nations and territories of Iran, Libya, Syria, Egypt, Pakistan, and Saudi Arabia. Will you comply with this lawful order from your commander-in-chief?"

This time there was no hesitation.

"No, madam, I will not. I consider it an unlawful order."

"Then, General Caruthers, you are hereby and immediately relieved of your command."

"I resign. I will take my thirty and spend the rest of my life—beginning today—exposing you and this folly."

"No, sir, you will do neither. You are fired with all of the consequences that implies. Further, we are about to enter a war, and you are not to be allowed to aid and abet our enemies with treasonous transmissions to them. Sergeant, place the general under arrest and escort him to the Marine Brig under guard. He is to be treated with full respect of his former office; but he is not to be permitted to speak to anyone; and I mean anyone. Is that clear?"

Her order was directed to the two marine guards stationed at the door into the Oval Office.

The marine gulped and snapped to attention.

"Yes, Madam President. General Caruthers, will you come with us peacefully?"

"Of course, you idiot. Mrs. Rowan, you will regret this. I guarantee it."

"Remove the general."

The two marines walked the general out of the Oval Office. Their places at the door were taken by two more marines.

The new president's face had locked into a grim set.

"Abigail, step outside and find out where the next highest ranking officer is and get him in here as fast as it is humanly possible."

"Yes, ma'am."

"Lieutenant General, Hoyt Prescott, Madam President," Ms. Young announced after less than half a minute's delay.

"General Prescott, I'm surprised and pleased to have you here. I remember you from the old days of the Independent's Club get togethers. Congratulations on your appointment to the Joint Chiefs."

"And my congratulations to you, Madam President."

"Thank you, I think."

She lifted the corners of her mouth in a slight smile. She was glad to have a familiar face in the room, and that of a man whose judgment she highly respected.

Prescott was all spit and polish; and even in this crisis, his uniform was perfectly creased and the Windsor knot of his regulation tie was exactly in the midline. He was a tall, broad shouldered, bluff man not given to much talk. He had a strong face with deeply etched lines in his forehead and around his eyes from long hours in the desert sun squinting at yet another horizon for the approach of an enemy. He had good even teeth and smiled often. He was a man who concentrated on getting things done, not on explanations. He did not suffer fools easily, and he knew that the new president didn't either. He liked that in her.

"Are you the *ranking* officer?"

"So far as I can determine, General Caruthers and I were the only members of the JCS to survive the attacks. I guess that I am the acting chairman now."

"Did you hear my orders to General Caruthers and his response?"

"Yes, ma'am, I admit that I did."

"I so order you. Do I need to repeat the order or any part of it?"

"No need to repeat the order, Madam President. I serve under your command. I will carry out your orders."

"Thank you, General Prescott. I will nominate you for your fourth star today. Now, there's no more time to spare. Get on with your assignment, and God be with you."

General Prescott saluted sharply, did a smart about face, pleased that he didn't wobble after all of these years, and walked out of the room. He went immediately to the Pentagon, crafted a message to all United States military units to establish a new SIOP—Single Integrated Operational Plan—and when it met his requirements, had it sent it TOP-SECRET-SPECAT: Special Category—for immediate implementation against the nations named in the president's direct order. The messages were sent with a KWR-37 NSA cryptographic machine. General Prescott ordered that the encrypted messages be sent to every Department of Defense department head via AUTOSEVOCOM—Automatic Secure Voice Communications System—the world wide near immediate network, with security devices installed to protect its transmissions. Further protection was afforded by the use of the KY-8 voice scrambling machine that turned the speaker's transmission into a nearly unintelligible Donald Duck voice.

In the Oval Office, the new president turned her attention to the civilian authorities.

"Abigail, please have the congressional leaders in the hall escorted in. All of them."

Ms. Young stood aside for Helen Clivener, the majority leader of the Senate, Frank Devlin, the speaker of the House, and Simon Morganthau, the minority whip.

"Thank you for being here. I am most gratified that for any of the reasons there were that none of you were taken in the attacks."

It was heartfelt and was received in the same spirit.

"I, as president, have a formal request for the Congress. I am asking that you prepare a Declaration of War on the nations of Syria, Egypt, Iran, Libya, Pakistan and Saudi Arabia."

"Madam President, I am sorry to interrupt, but our quick evaluation of the evidence indicates that Morocco, Yemen, the Sudan, and separatist terrorists in Chechnya, the Xinjiang Province of China, and the Southern Philippines have all made contributions to this series of attacks in one form and to one degree or another."

"Mr. Pickering, will you and Mr. Mathers accompany the congressional leadership and assist them with a review of the evidence to help with the determination of how the Declaration of War should be framed and against whom?"

"With pleasure, Madam President, with pleasure."

Cliff Assure marched up to the president and stood overly close, almost threateningly so. Secret Service Officer Clark—in a knee-jerk response—took two steps forward and thrust his muscular arm between them.

"Easy, sir," Clark said.

Assure stepped back a pace.

"The Congress cannot prepare or vote on a declaration of war, Madam President. The majority of both houses are dead. We cannot mount a quorum and will not be able to do so for many months."

There was a note of triumph in the voice of the liberal senator from Nevada.

"There you're wrong, Senator Assure. The Congressional Emergency Act of 2004 allows the Congress to appoint successors immediately upon the deaths of more than 100 congressional representatives and/or senators in a short period of time. The act was passed to deal with just such a situation as this one."

Assure had been certain that the vapid colorless vice-president, who had just been elevated to the presidency by a stroke of calamity, would be ignorant of that provision. He had hoped to be able to delay and to marshal the liberals against her ghastly plans.

"I'll have to concede that, Madam President, but it will take weeks, maybe months. The Congress can't act swiftly; it's one of the legislative branches best features."

"Cliff, we'll see about that," said Senator Morganthau. "If I were a betting man, I would put my money on the probability that we can have a declaration passed by midnight tonight."

"Senator Morganthau, I am going to call the heads of the involved nations today before our attack is accomplished. I would deeply appreciate it if you could have it done by 1700 today."

"Madam President, we will give it our all," Morganthau said.

Cliff Assure stood by Helen Clivener, and both of them gritted their teeth.

"Over my dead body," muttered Senator Clivener.

The members of Congress left.

"Please send in the cabinet members, Abigail. If the secretary is missing, have the office find the ranking substitute. The substitute in each case is to be named the acting secretary."

"I'll take care of it."

Homeland Secretary, Rupert Vernon, and Deputy Secretary of State Gadi ben Elazar were ushered in.

"Thank you for coming, gentlemen."

"Congratulations on your appointment, Madam President," Vernon said for both of the cabinet members.

"Mr. ben Elazar, is Secretary O'Laughlin dead?"

"I'm afraid so."

"Are you willing to serve the new administration? I believe you understand what that entails."

"A war cabinet."

"Exactly."

"Yes, Madam President. I am a dyed in the wool liberal and a former Israeli; but I am first, last and always a loyal American. I believe in the decision and will serve with enthusiasm."

"Excellent. Surround yourself with like-minded people. We don't have time to debate. It is time posthumous to do something. What I want you to do is to see to the protection of our embassies and our representatives all over the world. Place them on war footing. Evacuate all nonessential personnel from everywhere at risk and as fast as it can be accomplished. Hereafter, I intend that we shall lose as few more Americans as is humanly possible. That is going to be the first article of faith—a veritable shibboleth of my administration—and we will act preemptively as needed to accomplish that end.

"As the second order of business, I want you to inform every nation on the globe of what has happened to us and to our allies and let them know that we are going to war. We expect their cooperation and will remember in perpetuity those who came forward to help, those who chose to sit on the fence, and those who opposed us. Use your initiative and your office to get the international business underway. You are the acting secretary of State as of this moment. In that capacity, I want you to see to it that we have an acting cabinet in place by the end of this day."

Acting Secretary ben Elazar nodded his acceptance. He figured that the orders from his president were more than he would be able to accomplish; but, then, everything the government and indeed, the American people would be called upon to do after this grievous wound would be beyond their capacity. As in the era of the Great Depression, the great world wars, and the accomplishments of a people who proved themselves to be the most magnanimous in all of history, Americans would rise to the occasion.

CHAPTER THIRTY-FIVE

APRIL 16, 2010, 0742, EDT

The president's military aide-de-camp, Lieutenant Commander, Scott Parkinson, requested permission to speak with the president.

"Yes, Scott," President Rowan said as the trim young naval officer entered the Oval Office.

At LCDR Parkinson's request, all others had been asked to leave the room.

"Madam President, I am the bearer of bad news from General Prescott—confirmed bad news."

"I am amazed that there can be any more bad news left in the world today, but go ahead."

"We have certain identification of eleven ICBMS on course towards CONUS and one en route to Hawaii, presumably Pearl Harbor. We presume them to be nuclear, armed with MIRV capability. They originated in Southwest Asia."

"I don't even need to ask the result of them successfully blowing up in the continental United States or Hawaii. So, I'll ask with more hope than expectation: can we stop them?"

"It's statistical. The bottom line is we are not likely to stop them all."

"So, we can expect another Detroit or even several."

"Yes, Madam President, I'm afraid that's so, and that's the best case scenario."

"It would be nice to sit down and have a good cry and wait for the inevitable, Commander. However, keep me apprised of the situation."

"Yes, ma'am."

General Hoyt Prescott watched the trails of the offensive ICBMS on the Situation Room radar displays as they lengthened their arcs and drew inexorably closer to the United States.

"How long before they are close enough to make impact?" he asked Col. Robert Stephens, Chief of Missile Defense for the JCS.

"An hour, two at the outside."

"Give me an update on NORAD."

"NORAD and USNORTHCOM are scrambling as we speak, sir. The Alaska site is effective against East Asia; we were prepared for an attack from China, but not for an attack from Iran, Iraq, Syria, the Saudis—our long-time friends—and the like. So, our earliest interdiction site is not going to do the job. North Warning System has provided good surveillance but will be too late for a defense. Of fifteen long range radar sites, eleven are in Canada and are online and ready; and fighter aircraft are moving off their bases already. We are confident of interdiction from Alaska to Newfoundland."

"How about the National Missile Defense System?"

"In motion, but not fully ready yet. Patriot Advanced Capability—PAC in military speak, and Theater High Altitude Air Defense or THAAD, might interdict but it will be close."

Prescott smiled.

"The space military programs we're not supposed to have."

"And won't be ready until 2020."

"I was not aware that the Space Based Platform and Space Operation Vehicles were ready yet."

"With respect—sir, until today—you didn't need to know. And until right now, you didn't need to know that the Space Lasers have been tested and are operational. We'll see whether or not they are practical in an hour or so."

"Anything else I need to know?"

"Maybe that the US/Soviet ABM treaty of 1972 obligated us and them to have no more than two long range, high power ABMs. In December, 2001, after the monsters perpetrated 9/11, we mutually abrogated the treaty. Maybe it won't come as a surprise that we have a few more ABMs than our allotment of two. The Soviets agreed since we had become such pals. We are up and running in Phase III of Ballistic Missile Defense plan—BMD."

"Are we going to be ready in time?"

"I certainly hope so, General Prescott. If not, you and I won't have jobs."

"You and I won't have a country. Anyway, Col. Stephens, I'm keeping you from your more important work. Get out there and make somebody hurry."

"Yes, sir."

After LCDR Parkinson left the president, Rupert Vernon, Secretary of Homeland Defense, came to the Oval Office for his turn to brief the president and to receive orders. He was impressed with her decisiveness and felt too overwhelmed with his own areas of responsibility to have time to worry about the morality of the firing of weapons of mass destruction that was about to take place by the fledgling president.

"Have a seat, Secretary Vernon. I appreciate your patience. I can assure that your agency's role is the most important one in the whole equation to me, but I had to get the rest of it underway. I have to count on you to mobilize FEMA and every professional and volunteer asset we have in the entire United States. Feel free to ask, to beg, to threaten. Don't be shy about asking help from Canada or Mexico or from Central and South America. It will be revealing how they respond, and we will remember."

"Homeland Security is already working on all of that feverishly. All four FEMA disaster and counterterrorism teams have been mobilized and are trying to find ways and means. I have to tell you, Madam President, the response from the citizens has been nothing short of marvelous. I'm proud to be an American."

"Me, too. Practically speaking, how can we cope with the colossal scope of this disaster?"

"That is the main reason I've come to see you this early. You know that we have disaster plans, libraries full of them. I'll tell you what's not in those plans. You are familiar with the concept of triage in contained disaster—a doctor or nurse sorts out the salvageable, treatable, and the hopeless patients and with hearts of steel, the medical staffs begin to work on the first two and sadly lets those beyond hope die in peace and without using up precious resources."

"I'm following you, Mr. Secretary. Spell it out."

"We need a national triage. We cannot cover it all. We will look like cold blooded robots, but we have to do very little for Detroit. Do what we can for the treatable injured; and for now, leave the people terribly injured and beyond hope to the mercy of morphine and kind volunteers. We can't begin to do any search and rescue; we'll have to leave that to the locals. Frankly, there is not much left to search in. Sadly, we need to let the fires burn themselves out. I don't have the clout—the authority—to allocate resources on such a stupendous level and to order that the minimum be done for Wayne County. I don't have the moxie to say no to the Canadians, either."

"I understand. What do you need me to do?"

"I'll have a presidential order drafted which will spell out the triage plan. It will have to come from you."

"And for that and a few other reasons coming out of this day, I will be considered the most heartless human being in history. Cliff Assure already told me that I was about to be responsible for more murders than Hitler and Mao Tze Tung put together. Please get the document to me before eleven."

"Yes, ma'am. I don't envy your position, but I'm with you."

"Thanks."

The red button on the president's console flashed.

"I'm summoned. Keep me posted, Mr. Secretary.

Rupert Vernon passed LCDR Parkinson in the entryway of the Oval Office.

Abigail Young leaned in the doorway and said, "Commander Parkinson has an urgent update, ma'am."

"Ah, my good news man. Come in Commander."

"I have firm news at least. We have launched cruise missiles and ICBMS with MIRVs, all with fixed targets—the capitals of the world of Islam. You can cause those multi-billion dollar weapons to self-destruct anytime in the next one and a half hours, then the mission cannot be altered."

"I understand."

"JCS has ordered the immediate takeoff of our B1-B, B-2A bombers, and even some of the older B-52Hs all with multiple thermonuclear devices at their disposal. That will take half a day. The navy has Tridents in the Indian Ocean and the Mediterranean and two in the Gulf of Hormuz. They can be ready to fire in two hours and can wage this entire war by themselves."

"I need to do something before they fire. Give me forty-five minutes. Then have General Prescott call me, and I will give the final orders."

"Very well, Madam President. I'll be in my office when you need me."

The red light flashed again.

"Send him in, Abigail."

President Rowan had asked that the acting press secretary, Andrew McKnight, have an appointment as soon as her military situation briefing was complete.

McKnight was a big man—a body builder with a commanding presence—and a strong mellifluous voice. He had wavy brown hair, dimples in his cheeks, and maintained a suntan year round. He was a good, conservative dresser and looked like a *GQ* model in his favorite dark suits. He had been a reporter for the *New York Times*, then for CNN where he had achieved respect at a young age—no mean feat in that highly competitive world. Andrew was the son of a Baptist preacher, but had lapsed his faith. He studied journalism and evolution at U.C. Berkeley where he initially bought into the whole liberal scene, but after some experience in the real world, his faith in American liberalism had also lapsed. He had neglected to emphasize that when he sought a position with the Braithwaite administration.

"Good morning, Madam President. Congratulations are in order even in these ghastly times."

"Thank you, Andrew. Do you mind working for me?"

"I'm honored, Madam President. I am an American, and my country is in crisis. We don't need critics or shirkers right now. History will give us the time later."

"Great, because, you are going to have to be the voice of this administration—at least until the horrific amount of work dies down—and we once again have the luxury of pondering and planning for what we can say and do that will meet all of the demands of politics and war and reconstruction. I am going to tell you something. I intend to be brutally transparent about the entire situation with the American people. Right now, I am going to tell you that there are eleven ICBMs en route to our country. We have defenses, but we cannot be sure they will be successful; and it is frankly unlikely that all of the missiles will be interdicted.

McKnight emitted a strained gasp. He paled.

"I want you to call an immediate press conference and give the general situation to the press and the people. Arrange for me to address the nation in two hours. I will give them an honest status report and an outline of our plans of defense and offense. I don't want to think about the details. You do that, okay?"

"Yes, ma'am, I'll get right on it."

"Andrew, we are not going to have the luxury of distilling everything you say. You are going to have great latitude in handling your job. I want you to be briefed on everything, and you can communicate anything not classified to the media. I need to count on your wisdom and discretion. Get all the help you need."

McKnight left, and President Rowan summoned Abigail Young.

"Abigail, you're doing a great job. It's been a baptism by fire for you as well as for me. I count on you even though this is your first day as the secretary."

"It's nice of you to notice, Madam President. You are so busy."

"Indeed. Here's what I need you to do. Arrange a conference call to the leaders of France, England, Germany, Australia, Japan, the People's Republic, and Israel. I want that to happen in less than an hour. I am only going to talk to them for about ten minutes. Right after that, say in an hour and a half, I want you to have me on another conference call. This time we'll have a chat with the leaders of Iran, Pakistan, Egypt, Libya, Saudi Arabia, and Syria."

Ms. Young scribbled furiously on her steno pad.

"Got all of that?"

"Yes, ma'am. I presume you want to keep this secret and not to have the recipients of your call informed of the exact subject material beforehand."

"In absolute terms. I have a couple of surprises, and timing is everything."

CHAPTER THIRTY-SIX

APRIL 16, 3:38 p.m., Israeli Daylight Time

The Egyptian attack commenced with a dual air and land offensive coordinated with the land approach by the Syrian Army. The Syrians—though chagrined by their air force losses—were emboldened by the sheer mass of the Egyptian forces committed to the battle and by the Islamic zeal that had been instilled in the massive Egyptian army. That had boosted the morale of the Syrian troops. Although Israel had gained air superiority due to their special relationship with the duplicitous Americans, the great Syrian Army was intact and ready to avenge the fatherland.

Mordecai Narkiss, Yahuda Grossman, and Levi Harkabi watched the reports from their live agents along Israel's borders and the radar images detailing the two-front attack. Although no one in the Israeli Defense Forces situation room acted frightened or excited, there was a palpable undercurrent of amazement and a consensus of unspoken great fear as the onslaught pincer advanced.

Narkiss maintained an open connection with the Prime Minister, Avigador Haimovitz, in Tel Aviv.

"Mr. Prime Minister, we have the first reports from our agents on the border. They are confirmed by the Defense Forces. Egypt has launched more than a hundred SAMs of all types, probably the bulk of their arsenal in the theory that our defenses will be overwhelmed by having to deal with them all at once. Our people in Egypt and the border people indicate that they are throwing old Soviet SA-2s, from near the border; but they are too far out of range to do anything. The more modern SA-2s updated by the Brits and the

Tayir as Sabah SA-2s made by the Egyptians themselves, are going to be more effective. They are moving SA-6s on their tracked vehicles to use in a second wave it appears. Their air force is as yet uncommitted."

"What about the Syrians?"

"They'll keep for a little while, Prime Minister. Their air power is now nil, and they are just moving down through Lebanese territory. We need to concentrate on the Egyptians first."

"Do our anti-missile defenses appear up to the task, Mordecai?"

"That's not my area of expertise, Prime Minister, but General Gur tells me that he is confident."

"He's always confident, Mordecai. He's a glass half full person. What do *you* think?"

"I believe that we can weather the first attack from the air with minimal damage, but I am concerned about their ability to send in another wave. I don't think this is all they have."

"They would be stupid to put all of their eggs in one basket as the Americans are fond of saying."

"Our Arrow ABMs are ready, Mr. Prime Minister. It was an enormous drain on the treasury and on our relations with Big Brother, but this is the day of reckoning about whether the cost was worth it. In the next five minutes we'll see."

"I'll be waiting, Mordecai. Let me know. I will have to address the nation very soon, but I want to be able to give them some hope in my message."

"Yes, sir. You will know what I know."

Dispatches were pouring in. Army, Air Force and Naval Forces were waiting commands, and General Gur fretted over the moment to give the go signals.

"Range?" he asked again.

The long suffering radar technologist replied without sighing, "Thirty kilometers from the Negev and closing rapidly."

General Gur turned to his second in command and said quietly, "Fire the Arrows."

Major General Leibowitz passed the order on down the line, which took twelve seconds. The War Room monitors lit up. The missile defense system of the State of Israel was fully activated, and almost every anxious citizen of the country was able to see at least one of the anti-ballistic missiles rear up and fire.

General Gur then ordered, "Scramble air defenses."

It was done, and a fleet of fighters, AWACS, and attack helicopters lifted off in the direction of the Sinai and Egypt.

"What about the Syrian advance, General?" asked Leibowitz.

"They can wait. We have to neutralize the Egyptian air threat first. With that under control, we can fight the land battles with confidence."

"Do you have something of an estimate of casualties, General?"

"Ours or theirs?"

"Ours. At this juncture, theirs don't count. This is the battle of Armageddon, and I have the full okay from the P.M. and the Knesset to use any and everything we've got, including nucs."

That was something of an overstatement, but Gur was not a man of half measures. He knew he could convince the prime minister.

He went on, "The Amis have been hit by a devastating thermonuclear device and have pulled out all the stops. They are not going to 'be the voice of reason and compromise' this time around."

"Are we ready for a nuclear retaliation? I mean, are we as a people ready? I know the weapons and the delivery systems are ready."

"It was always going to come to this. Everyone for the past—what is it, sixty-three years? from Ben Gurion and Golda Meir to the present moment—has known that this day would come. We have fought six wars, been through a dozen peace plans, filled libraries with plans and theories; and all of them put together are inconclusive. This is it. Unless some fool ties one of Israel's arms behind her back and forces us not to use what we have and accepts defeat and slavery or annihilation, we will have a decisive battle today and tomorrow. Get me a battle field plan for Egypt: so, I can see their forces. Once they bunch up enough; and we know they will, we are going to let fly our tactical nuclear battle field weapons."

The general's face was set. He seemed to feel all sixty-three years of fear, suspense, terror, and murder at the hands of Israel's neighbors. He knew that the Muslim world would never allow a different culture and religion in its heart land unless they were so weak that they could not resist the reality of Israel. He prayed to the god in whom he did not believe to keep the politicians from halting the doomsday plan.

Reports from the missile battle began pouring in over the computers. Arrow ABMs were killing short and long range ballistic missiles, including the most up to date multialtitude I-Hawk SAMs from the United States, Soviet SA-2 and Sa 3 short range SAMs fired at the Israeli planes and Egyptian Arrow ABMs themselves. The skies belonged to the Israelis and their superior weaponry. The only issue was whose number of missiles would be greatest in the end? Over the course of a seven minute missile-to-missile encounter, the

Israeli Arrows performed flawlessly. The screens cleared, and no missiles were noted on the radar screens. No new missiles were being launched from Egypt, and what few had penetrated Israeli air space lay in shattered ruin in the Negev Desert south of Qezoit. No Israeli lives had been lost thus far.

Gur asked Leibowitz, "What's the status of our Arrow supply?"

"Seventeen left, General. Appears to be more than enough."

"Right now it does, Leibowitz, but we'll make that judgment after we make them truly desperate."

A lieutenant handed Gur a message: "Both Syrian and Egyptian armies advancing and are within twenty minutes of our borders."

"Update me on the concentrations, Leibowitz."

"Looks like they have concentrated in a narrow wedge intent on breaking through our defenses at two defined points and not all along either border. Each army is larger than ours by almost triple."

"It would appear that we won't be able to outnumber them; so, my friend, Leibowitz, what shall we do? Conventional? Protracted intense fighting with the loss of upwards of half of our brave young men and women? Or nucs?"

"I'm glad it's your call, General."

"I'll have one last word with the P.M. before giving the order," Gur said.

"He's coming on the line, general."

Avigador Haimovitz's well known gravely voice came on the line.

"Sir, Gur here."

"Change in the situation?

"Yes and for the better."

Gur gave him a quick report.

"What happens if we wait?" the prime minister asked.

"I think they will gouge a hole into our midsection from two approaches, then they'll fan out to do the most possible damage to the widest and most vulnerable areas."

"Can we beat them in a conventional war, like we did as soon as our nation was established in 1948 and the Arab League declared war, and in the Six Day War in 1967, and the Yom Kippur War in 1973, and in 1982 when we drove the PLO out of Lebanon?"

The P.M. paused, and Gur readied his answer.

"I think we can probably win but not as before. They are much better prepared and have been working on this for many years. They have more men, better equipment, and better plans. They will be more successful, and that means serious losses for us. The war will be protracted—weeks or even a couple of years or more. We will see several hundred thousand Israelis killed and wounded at a minimum. The property and military losses will be staggering even as we are the nominal winners. I do not think we will be a viable trading nation for another thirty, maybe fifty years. If we lose—and even the weakness from fighting a conventional war with Egypt and Syria may hasten a defeat at the hands of emboldened Muslim nations beyond Egypt and Syria—there will be genocide."

The prime minister interjected, "I have been in contact with the new American President, Elizabeth Rowan. She seems tough and resolved; but her country has been grievously hurt; and there is little she can do right now. We are on our own."

"It's 1947 only worse, Prime Minister. Frankly, we are treated as pariahs by most of the world already. I don't think much will change in that regard if we do defend ourselves fully. The Muslims hate us period. They do not understand talk or negotiation or compromise. They do understand action—force. We must make them unable to attack us—at least make Egypt and Syria unable. The political fallout is your department, but you are tough. At Notre Dame—in the U.S. where I did my undergraduate work—there is a sign over the locker room door as the athletes exit. It says, 'When the going gets tough, the tough get going.' When all is said and done, Prime Minister Haimovitz, I think the world—the new world order after this war—will respect you and the nation for being tough when it was required. I think that's enough speech making for me, today."

The prime minister sighed.

"Time's wasting, he said, "Order the tactical field nuclear attacks on the Egyptian and Syrian armies."

"Can I have that written?" Mr. Prime Minister. "I mean no disrespect, but I am a military man in a nation in which the military is subordinate to civilian authority."

"Is a fax good enough, given the times?"

"Perfectly."

Gur called Leibowitz to his side.

"Order the field commanders to use all—I emphasize the word 'all'—means necessary to preserve the nation. We cannot lose this war, the war that will be finished before the end of this day. Tell them to use nuclear weapons against the men and equipment of Egypt and Syria as a pre-emptive strike. Anyone who refuses to do so will be automatically relieved of his or her command. Any questions?"

"No, sir. I am in full agreement and will get this new phase of the battle underway."

The forward units of the Syrian offensive were coming in force to the Lebanon side of the Golan Heights. Israeli artillery pounded them with limited success. The onslaught of the Syrian Muslim Army included nearly 100,000 troops, 5400 tanks—most of which were Soviet built T-72s upgraded by the markedly improved Syrian armament industry—a world class mechanized cavalry, and one of the largest and most mobile artillery divisions in the world.

Forward observers reported into the Israeli War Room.

Mordecai Narkiss was designated to accept the information for the intelligence services and worked literally side by side with General Leibowitz in the cramped but secure location in Tel Aviv.

The two men received the message simultaneously: we can hold only another half an hour and then we will be over run. We are not enough to stop them. To this point we have had only 11 KIA and another 8 wounded. Shall we retreat and fight at a new line or stay and die to buy the rest of the forces time?"

The commander was known to both of them as an extraordinarily brave man. He was also a pragmatist asking a practical question, not a cowardly one.

Leibowitz sent back: wait ten minutes then retreat into *Yisrael*—and as the word means—God will preserve.

As the messages were moving through cyberspace, Israeli Raptor 22s and F100-Ds roared out of invisibility and carpeted the advancing Syrian army with field tactical nuclear bombs. It was over in three minutes. The Israeli forces were at sufficient distance to witness the sudden disappearance of the army that had only moments before threatened the sparse border protectors with annihilation. It was an awesome sight, as if the hand of God had swallowed up the army of Pharaoh a second time.

The level of destruction and death seen by the Israelis was so stupendous that they were quiet. It was not a time for exultation—rather a time to question—what hath God wrought?"

The field commander from his vantage point on the Golan Heights read General Gur's message about retreating. He sent a question in his message back to the War Room: No more Syrian Army. What should we do now?"

Gur told them to stay for an hour then to come down from the Golan Heights via intact Highway 789 to the Kursi Junction with 92 and from Hamat Gader down Highway 98 to 92 and muster at Kibbutz Ein Gev and wait in the area of the kibbutz and Kfar Haruv. They were needed at the Egyptian front.

The small army moved swiftly and efficiently and was waiting when the troop transports and towing vehicles arrived an hour and thirty minutes later. In three hours they were advancing south through the Negev Desert towards the Sinai and their rendezvous with the vaunted Egyptian Army.

The anti-missile attack by Israel had decimated the missile capacity of the Egyptian military, but the air force and advancing army itself was virtually unscathed at 0700 Israeli time. The Egyptians had crossed into Israel all along the Sinai/Negev border from Egypt's Bl'r Lahfān, Abā 'Ulaylah, 'Ayn al Quṣayman, Al Kuntillah and Tābā from north to south and into southern Israel's Elat by the Gulf of Aqaba to the border city of Qezoit in the north. Except for forty-one SA-6 tracked vehicle SAMs, sixty-eight French Crotale SAM launchers held in reserve, and two *Amun* Skyguard gun-missile-radar systems that integrated twin 23 mm guns with Sparrow and Egyptian *Ayn as Saqr* SAMs, the Egyptians had no more missiles to put into the air; and every time one of them was fired it was extinguished by Israeli counter fire.

The two armies were not in range for the one-sided artillery duel being carried out by the Egyptians to be effective. Not a single Israeli combatant had been injured, and the sparsity of the civilian population in the Negev had kept them from even accidental harm from an errant missile.

The air war commenced as the Egyptian Army maneuvered itself into positions that were at once defensible and mobile. The high command had decreed an offensive posture and a dedicated attack as soon as the air battle engaged IDF aircraft sufficiently to divert them from entering into an attack on the Egyptian Air Force.

The air battle took place over An Nakhl, Egypt near the middle of the Sinai Desert to the rear of the advancing land army. The Egyptian air corps would have preferred to have advanced to at least the middle of the Negev, but they were comfortable with the place Allah had willed for the fight.

The Egyptian commitment was truly massive. In keeping with the war plan of a single overwhelming full force attack, they had put in the air 80 American multimission F-16s and 51 F-4Es, 32 French Mirage 2000s, 145 older model Russian MIGs—that had been refurbished with advanced electronics, new radar systems, modern jamming equipment, and a full complement of Sidewinder and Matra A-A missiles—237 late model MIG Interceptors, and 175 combat helicopters. Allah had willed that nothing be held back, and Air

Force Headquarters in Heliopolis near Cairo had bowed to Allah's will, *Allah alim* [Allah knows best]

On land, the two Egyptian SSM regiments permanently assigned to the Sinai consisting of a thousand men each moved rapidly into position in a pincer around the southeast and southwest approaches to Qazoit. The besieging force was overwhelming for Qazoit—four armored divisions, six mechanized infantry, two ground pounder infantry, Republican Guard Armored, and two heavy mortar divisions The impressive attack force knew of the ignominious defeat of the missile units thus far and were dedicated to the preservation of Islam's Holy Egypt. The regiments—however—were largely manned by poorly educated fanatical fundamentalists who had been instructed by their mullahs to join the units closest to the illegal Zionist Entity. They operated under a controlled blood lust and were ready to exact a slaughter of the Little Satan town comparable to that of The Prophet, may Allah bless his name.

In the 7th Century A.D., a Jewish tribe, Banū Qurayzah, compacted with the Muslims of Medina under Muhammad to defend against the marauding Meccans. The Muslims were humiliated in the battle of Uhūd and barely escaped occupation of Medina by the Quraysh tribe from Mecca. The fickle Jews—contrary to their pact with The Prophet—refused to bide by their mutual protection agreement and worse, ridiculed the Muslims' fighting ability. The Prophet had the Qurayzah taken into custody, and had judgment passed on them. It was decreed that all fighting men should be executed. A price of survival was offered: convert to Islam or die. Only four converted, and the rest were slaughtered. It was the end of active resistance by Jews in Arabia and has stood as a momentous historical event in the hearts of right minded Muslims.

Col. Abraham Jacob Rosenstein, IDF Air Force—leading the Raptor squadron at 40,000 feet above the desert floor—received the message from BARCAP pilots protecting the border that an attack force was coming at Israel from the south and west.

He radioed Air Force Command, gave his call sign, and announced, "We are at angels 40 and preparing to dive."

"May Jehovah guide you," came the reply from the OOD, an Orthodox Jew.

The incredible aerial armada of Egypt advancing from the Sinai did not see the F/A-22 Raptors diving down on them at supersonic speed and with no afterburners in evidence. Israeli EF-111 Jamming Aircraft had interfered with what little radar or sensory visibility the Egyptians had. The sleek black planes—made up of more than a million integrated parts—were flying and shooting among the Egyptian attackers like hawks on a flock of sparrows. Before the Egyptians could organize an offensive, the Raptors, with their superior air combat maneuvering—jinking—and greater energy for greater speed, were dropping the Egyptian air planes from the sky in a one-sided skeet shoot. As soon as the Egyptian AWACS got a fix on a Raptor, it was gone, or the AWACS was shot out of the sky. In seven minutes the Egyptian Air Force was radar blind.

"It's a fur ball," screamed an Egyptian pilot as he looked confusedly into what appeared to him to be a chaos of a dogfight.

The IDF raptor pilots were intensely trained to be able to cope with a myriad of incoming information. His avionics provided wide-angle HUD screens mounted above the cockpit that continually projected critical flight, target, and weapons information. The pilot did not even need to look down at his gauges to know that his weaponry had been effective.

He would sometimes call in a report to command, "Bandit splashed," but most of them were too busy to talk.

In the ten minutes after the battle was engaged, the Egyptians had lost every MIG, half of the Mirage 2000s and F-16s and three quarters of the attack helicopters. The ground below was dotted with smoke plumes, twisted metal, and a few recognizable Egyptian corpses. One Raptor and two Israeli F-16s had been downed with only one pilot surviving.

The Raptors returned home to refit and refuel for the next conflict when it arose. The IDF air attack was then carried on by their U.S. made F-15C Eagles. The Eagles, under the guidance of the Israeli pilots, were formidable weapons. They were equipped with Air Intercept radar, and APG-70 capability to allow locking on small targets during high G-force maneuvers. The Egyptian air force scarcely existed at this point, and their ground weapons were no match for the F-15s' defensive counter measures—the Northrop ALQ-135 (v), Loral ALR-56C radio warning receivers.

Almost at will, the Eagles poured devastation down upon the hapless runt army of Egypt with their GE M-61 Vulcan 6 barreled rotary 20mm cannons. Death came at a rate of 940 rounds in 9.4 seconds with an assortment of PGU-28 armor piercing shells, explosive fragmentation rounds, and HEI (High Explosive Incendiary) ammunition. The end for Egyptians was also wrought by a sophisticated array of AGM missiles. The Optempo of the intense IDF attack completely overwhelmed the enemy's ability to respond, and the Weapons System Officers—WSOs, or "wizzos"—on the Eagles were hard put to keep up their pace—their killing pace.

The Egyptians saw too late the value of conducting an orderly retreat of their meager remaining air defenses to fight the final contest in defense of their home territory. Israeli Air Force attackers surrounded them in the air. The bemused Egyptians had no idea where the enemy was until a Wild Weasel, HARM (High Speed Anti-Radiation radar guided Missile), or AIM-9B or 9L (Aerial Intercept Missile) heat seeking missile approached them from an Israeli aircraft. Once the Israeli planes came into view, the Egyptians were harassed by standard short range—2.6 mile—AAMs.

The dwindling force of Egyptian aerial defenders was decimated. They began to lose all discipline; some rammed into fellow Egyptian planes; some crashed into the ground because of disorientation or from empty air fuel tanks; and not a few committed suicide. Only a handful of intact fighter craft and support planes was able to turn tail and to run for Cairo and ignominy.

Tel Aviv was fully informed of the mounting victory. The staff officers ordered the F-15C Eagles to disengage and to move northwest towards Qazoit. They were joined by the refueled F/A 22 Raptors. The first strike force was to swing around the ground forces and to approach them from the north. They required four minutes to make the journey.

In accordance with traditional Muslim form, the Jewish elders of Qazoit were offered a surrender of sorts by the Egyptian general who was unaware of the outcome of the air battle. The conditions were that all fighting age men would lay down their arms and submit to group execution. Their women, children, and elderly would convert to Islam immediately and would submit peacefully to forced march into the Sinai to a concentration camp that would be built there for them.

Rabbi Issar ben Rabinowicz spoke for the beleaguered Qazoitians.

"Never," the little bantam rooster of a man said. "Move in closer; so, we can kill you."

Egyptian Lieutenant General Ahmed Heikel Nagy asked again, "This is the last offer. Submit to our terms or be annihilated."

"Come and take us," returned Rabbi Rabinowicz's answer.

"Commence..." General Nagy was about to say, "firing," but his attention was diverted to a staccato of explosions occurring on his right flank, then from the northern perimeter of his army, and then from the area south and west of the city of Qazoit.

"General," his intelligence officer shouted above the thunderous noise, "the Zionist Entity is attacking from the air. We have had no prior warning. Our British radar system failed us. I'm sorry."

"You will be more sorry, Captain," the general responded with harsh malevolence in his voice.

He rushed to his bewildered officers and tried to organize them.

"The IDF seems to be attacking mostly from the south and west. Move our left flank to this side—north and east of the city—" he pointed on the map, "and we will make a stand here. We cannot survive as scattered as we are. We must regroup and make an orderly stand against the accursed Israeli Defense Forces."

The subordinate officers hurriedly contacted their underlings east of Qazoit and rallied them for the push to the right. Qazoit itself was ignored. The army made excellent progress and within fifteen minutes, most of the functional units had gathered with the western section of the army and were engaged in the process of forming a defensive perimeter. The Israeli planes were raining death down on the Egyptians from the northwest, and the land bound soldiers swung away from the worst of the barrage and headed southwest on the eastern side of Qazoit.

Allah seemed to be with them because the Israeli air attack was dying down. General Nagy attributed the lessening barrage to the diminution in the IDF's ammunition. It was a dictum that had been drummed into him since he received his commission that Israel's weakness as a small nation was that its resources of men and ammunition would run out early if a massive strike were to be mounted by God's warrior nations. He breathed a small sigh of relief that at least one of the things he had learned at the academy had proved to be correct. In the short space allotted him, General Nagy was able to move the great bulk of his forces around Qazoit and to collect them on the east. He was most grateful to Allah that discipline had been maintained and that his men had been granted enough surcease to be able to form up their units in an orderly fashion. They were looking like professional Egyptian soldiers once more.

The War Room in Tel Aviv radioed the National Guard officers inside the beleaguered city of Qazoit:

"Send every man to the edges of the town and fire everything you have out at the Egyptians now."

Rabbi Rabinowicz grabbed up his M-16 A and called to his men in the synagogue to follow him to the west city wall.

The unexpected fire from the city hastened the movement of the frightened Egyptian fighters to gather in the defensive perimeter on the east of the city. For safety—both in numbers and position—the army began to swing south and west towards the main body of the Egyptian offensive coming up from Elat and Yotvata.

The main body of the Egyptian Sinai force was seven miles from Qazoit when F-22 Raptors protecting F-100 Ds swooped in and dropped a single bomb the size of a celebratory loaf for an *Eid al-Fitr* festival over the concentration of soldiers. The nuclear device exploded in the air above the accumulated army and killed nearly everything in a two mile radius. There were three hundred eight survivors of the blast who watched their comrades perish in a holocaust under a mushroom shaped cloud.

General Nagy and his entire staff were dead. One officer in the whole regiment remained alive, and he was wounded so severely that he could not give directions. Like other men whose bodies were burned, limbs blown off, and lungs scorched, that officer was abandoned on the field as the remainder of the regiment ran towards Elat—every man for himself.

Tel Aviv radioed the all clear to Qazoit and had the air force return to rearm and refuel. The two wings of the IDF ground force began moving as rapidly as possible in the direction of Elat and the main body of the Egyptian Army. Every military and civilian vehicle that could be found was commandeered for the rapid advance. It was a land version of Dunkirk, except that the IDF was headed *into* the fray. The principal occupation of the Israeli officers at this point was to keep the advance orderly.

The first of the Qazoit area Egyptian military refugees began streaming into the main army's established territory over the next hour. The uncontrolled admittance of the panicked and distraught Egyptian soldiers caused a mounting alarm among the rank and file who witnessed them filing into their midst like zombies just risen from unhallowed graves, still covered with white dust, many of them screaming from burns, many with lost limbs and faces. The effect was stunning on the once proud and disciplined Egyptians.

The incoming refugees reported the disaster of Qazoit in frantic and immoderate terms. Their excitement was contagious, even among the officers. It took half an hour for the staff officers to form a cohesive plan, the same plan that the Qazoit contingent had formulated an hour earlier because it came out of the same training manual and because communications had broken down. The army was spread out in now indefensible separate units. The officers hurried to regroup and to set up a defensive core that could concentrate fire power to use against the IDF army that was on the rapid march and against the air force that was waiting out there somewhere in the heavens to attack. Stragglers who were felt to be deserters were shot on the spot as an object lesson.

The seething mass of ill-disciplined Egyptian soldiers murmured among themselves about the men at Qazoit having heard the trump of Israfil. For them, Israfil's end-of-the-world trumpeting was a death knell, not a triumphant signal. Evidently, the Jews had not heard Gabriel's trump. The men waited, fidgeted, and cowered behind equipment and sand dunes. Many of them ignored their weapons. They were more prepared for flight than fight.

"They're coming," announced a loud speaker. "Every man do his duty for God and for Egypt. We shall be triumphant."

Most of the soldiers grunted their disbelief. Morale was at an acute all time low.

A steady throb of cannon fire from M-119 105 mm howitzers—the most popular artillery piece in the world—and from large light weight M-195 howitzers came from the north and west with their thump, thump, thump and soon anti-tank laser guided copperhead projectiles and HE M483 anti-personnel/armor piercing shells began bursting in the desert and taking out some Egyptian tanks and a smattering of men.

There was a pause—a readjustment of distance—and then deadly accurate shelling began in earnest. Through the smoke and dust plumes, the first Israeli tanks could now be seen in the far distance. The IDF tanks formed an ominous crescent on the north and began shelling the concentrated Egyptian forces at will with ghastly results. Explosions tore men and machines into ghoulish pieces. The Egyptian will to fight—fragile at the onset—began to evaporate. There were stirrings in the foxholes, and here and there an officer was seen beating a recruit with a swagger stick; and once in a while came the report of an officer's pistol as he dispatched a would-be deserter.

As the tension among the troops mounted to near hysteria, the first F-100 D flew in at low altitude and dropped a small cigar shaped bomb over the center of the quavering military force. A second and a third plane swept in dropping their bombs over the right and left flanks. The three explosions detonated in the air within four seconds of each other. The Egyptian army; organized as such—ceased to exist in a matter of seconds. In the aftermath, nine military vehicles remained functional and fewer than a thousand men were alive and well enough to turn and run headlong into the desert back towards Egypt and safety. They looked back at the huge mushroom shaped cloud that had coalesced from the three tactical field nuclear bombs. They needed no further encouragement beyond that sight and their awful memories to flee—every man for himself.

IDF field commanders radioed Tel Aviv for CONOPS guidance to pass on to their subordinate units.

The concept of operations message came back from command, "Pursue. No prisoners. No surrenders. Take out cities on your way."

One hundred miles from Cairo, the last remnants of the once massive Egyptian army perished from the arms of the IDF, from exhaustion and thirst, and from suicide. The rout was complete. Egypt would not be able to mount a military offensive for the next fifty years even if no more attacks were to follow.

The Egyptians had lost over a thousand M 60 A3 American battle tanks, fifteen hundred Soviet T-54, 55, and 62 tanks refitted with 105 mm howitzers, diesel engines, fire control systems, and powerful new external armor. None of the fourteen hundred M-113 A2 personnel carriers from America survived, and fewer than fifty of the eleven hundred refitted Soviet BTR 50s and OT-62s and five hundred Fahds—manufactured in Egypt from a German design—were able to limp back to the capital city where panicked citizens hijacked them in an orgy of looting. Seventy-eight remaining survivors of the original nine hundred combat vehicles met the same fate. Eleven out of the more than eight hundred planes made it back intact. Upon landing the pilots were executed for cowardice by members of the *Salafiya*.

Of one hundred thousand regular troops and thirty thousand reservists who were sent into the desert to fight the Avenging the Crusades Operation, only twenty-two thousand survived to make it back to the cities of Egypt where they added to the looting marauding ranks spreading panic, rape, and pillage. The Egyptian Armed Forces left thirty-eight thousand men suffering and dying on the battle field to become martyrs for Allah and food for ravens. It would take weeks to clean up the carnage, and the rusted hulks of battle wagons and plane parts would serve for decades as a reminder of the last great war.

Thirty-seven Israeli armed forces personnel and Israeli civilians died and another twenty-two were injured badly enough to warrant hospitalization. Four IDF planes were lost; two tanks were killed, and an artillery battery was blown up as the result of collateral fire. A formal investigation into that unfortunate error was mounted three days later. The nation went into formal mourning for the heroic dead who were honored with the creation of a Martyr's Park on the grounds of the Holocaust Museum.

CHAPTER THIRTY-SEVEN

APRIL 16, 0842, EDT

General Prescott watched the array of radar screens and computer global position simulators with fascination as the eleven ICBM trails from the Middle-East converged on the seven hundred twenty-two ICBM trails leaving the United States in the opposite direction. The points of convergence had the appearance of impending impacts; although, of course, the general was well aware of the wide distances separating the opposing nuclear missiles.

As they drew closer and closer to the point of crossing, Gen. Prescott turned to his J-3, Lt. Col. Bradley Canon—the operations officer—and to the JCS Chief of Missile Defense, Col. Robert Stephens, who were seated in the swivel chairs on either side of him and said, "They're passing each other, unseeing—a *dos-à-dos.*"

"*Un dos-à-dos en a pas de mort,*" said Lt. Col. Canon.

The three men nodded grimly.

"Indeed, passing back to back in a dance of death," mused Gen. Prescott.

"When can we hit them, Colonel?" Canon asked Col. Stephens.

"We need enough separation…" he gestured to the radar screen array, "between our dancers to be sure that we don't shoot down our own."

"It's pretty dicey, seems to me. If we give too much time and space, we not only miss our ICBMs; but we also miss theirs."

"And we'll err on the side of shooting too soon, Col. Canon," Gen. Prescott broke in. "In fact, we are about ready, are we not, Col. Stephens?"

"Five more minutes. Technically, five minutes, twenty-one seconds and counting. It will be complicated because we are going to throw everything we've got at them and that involves multiple services and systems. And we are going to try some things that have never before been fired. It ought to be interesting."

"The highest stakes poker game in history," said Lt. Col. Canon. "The future of civilization rides on what we do. We won't get a second card draw or a time out. And we can't bluff."

Col. Stephens left to check on the progress of the hastily assembled anti-ICBM defenses, some of which were so ultra secret that he was the only one in the room authorized to know about them. He returned almost five minutes later.

"Keep your eyes on the screens, gentlemen. It is going to be quite a show." He checked his watch.

"Thirty-two seconds for the first salvo."

The half minute passed then the screens lit up.

Col. Stephens spoke into a head mounted speaker phone connected to the president. The men sitting next to him were able to hear first hand the moment to moment commentary.

"Yes, ma'am, we have fired the first protective screen. The first ABMs are designed to disable the electronics for detonation of the Arabs' nuclear warheads. We don't have to make direct contact, but we have to pass very close to the enemy ICBM. The screen will show a small bright flash, but the enemy weapon will continue on its way. There goes one, two, looks like we at least were good enough shots to put our ABMs on target. I may have missed one or two there."

There was a two minute pause in his running dialogue, and nothing seemed to be happening on the screens.

Then a very bright spot appeared in the lower left hand corner of the radar array and the radars began to show a very rapidly moving trail aimed in the direction of the enemy ICBMs. There were two more then another five.

"Spartan's, ma'am. These ABMs of ours accelerate to Mach 10 in less than five seconds of flight resulting in 100gs of force. They carry a low kiloton war head for in-atmosphere interception. Their range is in the hundreds of miles. The first five were shot in series from CANR."

"What is CANR, Colonel?" asked the president.

"Canadian NORAD, ma'am. Their headquarters are in Winnipeg and at the Canadian Air Defense Sector in North Bay, Ontario. The plan is for the Canadians to fire a series of Spartans to take out the enemy missiles from the rear. Let me direct your attention to your screens. A bright light will be a direct hit and a kill."

"Won't that set off an atmospheric hydrogen bomb explosion, as destructive as if the ICBM and its warhead had made it to its target, Colonel?"

"No, ma'am. That would be extraordinarily unlikely. The symmetry of the explosion around the critical plutonium core would not occur. The explosions we are going to see are going to be strictly from our own ABMs, and they will occur over vast reaches of unoccupied Canadian barren land."

"It can't happen too soon."

"Amen to that, ma'am. Any moment now."

They watched with morbid fascination as the fast moving streaks of light representing the Spartans closed in on the Islamic ICBMs. One of the Spartans flew widely past its target, then another, and then a third. There was palpable disappointment in the Situation Room. Then three almost simultaneous bright flashes lit up the screens, momentarily blotting out the myriad of light trails.

"Three more down. I think we can consider those confirmed. We can't be so sure about the first set that may or may not have been disabled. We will attack them again."

There was a shift to the right on the screen array.

"We are now in CONR—Continental NORAD," announced Lt. Col. Canon. "There are three sectors, and it looks like we have bogeys headed to all three. The West Air Defense Sector is based at McCord Air Force Base in Washington, the Northeast is based in Rome, New York, and the Southeast is based at Tyndall AFB in Florida. The ABMs should start firing off right now."

On cue, the bright flashes began lighting up different sections of the radar displays.

"Everyone is in the action," Col. Stephens said.

The hot streaks moved with incredible speed across the screens, far faster than the signature markings from the enemy ICBMs. In two minutes there were two hits and three misses.

Gen. Prescott and Col. Stephens cursed.

"Those three are the bogey men. We have two last gasps here, ma'am, neither weapon has ever been fired in anger."

"Space based?" the president queried.

"Yes, ma'am. We've got several options, and we're going to fire them all, no reserves."

"And you're sure they don't have more to shoot at us?"

"I am. They would have done so by now if they had anything left. From our intelligence from the IDF, it appears that the basic Islamic attack plan was to hurl everything they had in one gigantic and final attack."

"I see."

At the War Situation Room, General Prescott ordered Airman First Class, Edgar Firman, to give the order to the satellite controlling the Defense Space Platform to launch.

"Aye, sir."

Firman turned to the men on his right and his left and said, "On my count of three, squirt the bird."

The signal to the satellite shot through space at the speed of light.

On the United States Department of Defense Space Platform fifty thousand feet above CONUS [the continental United States] the first of the final doomsday weapons was unleashed from the stratosphere above Kansas. The Space Operation Vehicle—or Rutan's SpaceShipOne, after the inventor—was dropped directly from a hatch in the floor of the platform and immediately began a supersonic climb to sixty miles above the earth. Its two pilots were largely there to bring the space vehicle back to the platform after firing their nuclear warhead missiles. The vehicle's on-board computer was program locked onto the Aleppo launched ICBM that had penetrated furthest into CONUS.

With the missile in electronic sight, the Rutan plummeted out of the sky at speeds approaching Mach 6. The gravitational forces were enormous, and both pilots were temporarily and mercifully unconscious. They awakened in time to watch the dials and screens of their cockpit energize into action mode as they approached firing range from the target. The on-board computer began talking to them.

"Five thousand yards and closing. Missiles armed."

The pilots could do little except be spectators.

Three seconds later the computer announced, "One thousand yards. Target locked. Launch sequence underway."

A target screen showed a hot tailed prey species fixed in the cross hairs. The computer counted.

"Fiver, four, three, two, one, zero. Fire one."

The Rutan shuddered and bucked as the nuclear missile was fired. The screen illuminated with a bright flash that persisted for three seconds. By the time the screen cleared, there was no evidence of the bogey. The pilots were at the point of contact and could visualize debris dropping out of the sky. They radioed their success and arced back upwards to their space station platform.

A voice radio contact brought unexpected orders.

"Second bogey, may be in range. GPS latitude, longitude, altitude and trajectory coordinates are being fed into your system. Give it a try."

The arc the pilots had been making was subtly adapted. The target was honing in on Chicago in a forty-five degree angle. The Rutan's computer estimated that the bogey would be directly over the city in eleven minutes. It also estimated that the ETA of the Rutan to within firing range would be ten minutes—a very close-call subject to the possibility of computer error.

They flew at Mach 3, nowhere near as fast as they had done when they first dropped from sixty miles above. They were not going to make it. That meant that Chicago was going to be another Detroit.

"We are too late," Col. Spetzler radioed. "Do something else, now."

The two pilots had no idea what that 'something else' could be. It seemed too late for land based ABMs to be effective. They felt sick.

Two Spartans were fired, and indeed, they were too late. One locked onto the ICBM outside of firing range with only twenty seconds to spare, and the other missed altogether. The officers and enlisted people in the Situation Room held their collective breaths and counted off the seconds.

At twelve seconds before the calculated time of aerial detonation of the ICBM over the megalopolis of Chicago, a new weapon came on line, one that only Col. Stephens had been designated as one who needed to know.

Phase III of the Ballistic Missile Defense Program (BMD) was the creation of a space-based laser weapon, the SBIRS (Space Based Infrared System) capable of interception operations from the reaches of outer space. The program was rejected in open Congress as being too costly and put on hold for a possible completion date of 2020. The American public never knew about the program, and Congress quickly went on to other things. The military lobbied for funds for weapon systems that could be used in smaller more mobile war situations, and all but a handful believed that Phase III was a piece of history.

However, in fact, the colossal sums of money required for research and development were pried out of secret sources, funneled through the Department of Agriculture—unbeknown to the secretary and his senior officers. The system was completed in 2008 at the end of the Bush 43 administration and tested in 2009 without telling the sitting anti-war liberal president, Hollings Braithwaite.

With twelve seconds left in the terrible timetable, a burst of white hot light accelerated from space. In less than a second, the Islamic ICBM on an errand of mass destruction to Chicago melted over Saskatchewan and dropped harmlessly into the field of a radical Doukhobor. The farmer was a man whose entire adult life had been spent in opposition to Russian and then Canadian civil authority. He was a contrarian when it came to the establishment of churches by the Canadian government and enjoyed causing consternation among the faithful of Canada's religious folk and irritation of the government was not at home that day. Debris fell in several thousand spots and caused burns a foot deep, but otherwise no harm.

The usually irritatingly calm Col. Stephens stood up and hooted as the radar screens and witness messages confirmed the strike. His response was infectious and even taciturn Gen. Prescott let out a whoop.

Their elation was premature. The last two Islamic ICBMs—complete with their MIRV weaponry—were still unscathed and on target closing in on the San Francisco Bay area and Dallas/Fort Worth.

"How long," groaned Prescott.

"Under a minute," sighed the deeply worried Col. Stephens.

A bolt of laser energy evaporated the nuclear missile that had been intent on the annihilation of the Dallas metropolitan area. The Fairmont Hotel on Akard Street in downtown Dallas was directly in the line of fire of the laser and caught an edge of the white hot beam and was impacted by several chunks of near molten metal from the destroyed ICBM. The hotel's upper four floors caught fire resulting in the deaths of two hundred twelve guests and staff and serious injury to seventy-two others. There was no nuclear holocaust and no blast damage. It was a sad thing but not a Detroit level catastrophe.

In the Oval Office, President Rowan wiped a bead of sweat from her forehead, and General Prescott in the Situation Room continued to suffer near panic. There was one more fully operational Islamic nuclear ICBM closing in on San Francisco. Unless something happened immediately, it looked as if the bomb would burst over the roof of the St. Francis Hotel. Prescott's heart was racing. His aide, Lt. Col. Canon, found himself holding his breath.

A laser strike flashed from the heavens. Missed. A nanosecond later a second one was fired and missed. The experimental weapon had done well to make two hits, but it was now nonfunctional, a computer glitch.

Seven seconds and ticking on the ICBM's LED display. That put the missile almost directly over San Francisco. The missile was out of range of the land launched Spartans, space launched RutanSpaceShipOne, and the space-based lasers were temporarily inoperable.

Six seconds.

3200 kilometers west of San Francisco in the Pacific Ocean, the nuclear submarine, USS *Abraham Lincoln*, en route to the Middle-East received an urgent message to surface and if possible to intercept the last of the ICBMs. At twenty-seven seconds before the ballistic missile was due to explode and to wipe out the city by the sea, Captain Napolini ordered the firing of its sea-based interceptor ABM. The two missiles collided with three seconds to spare, but the *Abraham Lincoln's* ABM either failed to detonate as programmed, or the strike was inadequate to precipitate the explosion. The impact, however, occurred near the tail of the huge ICBM deflecting it towards the ocean.

Two seconds.

One second.

The missile pierced the ocean's surface and was under thirty feet of water at zero.

No explosion.

The ABM's contact with the enemy ICBM caused a severe jarring of the delicate electronic connections of the ICBM and resulted in a malfunction, quite literally at the last second. The only concern was for the future contamination of the beautiful blue ocean off the rough coast of Northern California.

Col. Stephens pointed out an ICBM on track for Miami and another headed for San Diego.

"Those are the two that were hit by the ABMs early on and should have had their electronics ruined and won't be able to detonate."

"And we can't get them with one of the incredible weapons we have been seeing today, and be sure, Colonel?" asked the president.

"No, ma'am, we knew from the get-go that we would not be able to kill every single one. We had to make choices at the end, and these two had to be left."

"Pray that you're right, Colonel," President Rowan said with a note of pleading in her voice.

He could not see her sitting at her desk in the Oval Office with her fingers crossed.

"I have prayed a direct line to the Creator all morning, ma'am. I just hope He is hearing."

The two ICBMs went off the radar screens at about the same time.

The watchers in the Situation Room and in the Oval Office made the same conclusion: the nuclear bombs had hit their targets and no more transmissions were possible.

They were wrong. The missile headed for Miami was knocked off course by its near contact with the American Spartan ABM over Canada enough to cause it to land in the Atlantic Ocean midway between Key West and Cuba. The ICBM bound for San Diego had its MIRV warheads programmed to strike Fort Ord, Phoenix, and Denver. None of the detonator coordinates were available over the missile's computer to instruct it to fire the multiple warheads or for the warheads to explode. The missile with all of its components stuck nose first in a table grape orchard in Imperial Valley. Aside from the transitory terror experienced by the illegal Mexican seasonal workers picking grapes in a nearby orchard and the destruction of twenty-one fruit laden plants, no damage was done.

President Elizabeth Rowan dropped her head in relief when General Prescott and Col. Stephens assured her that the ICBM attacks were done. She had lived half a lifetime during that excruciatingly tense sky wars battle.

"I was told there was one ICBM headed for Hawaii, General. What became of that one?" President Rowan asked.

"We must have gotten it in the early splashes, ma'am," the General said.

At least there was no evidence of a missile track headed across the Pacific.

"A marvelous thing, Madam President," said Acting Secretary of State Gadi ben Elazar.

The emotionally drained president nodded her head.

She took a big breath, as if it were her first of the day, and said, "Somehow, you made me think of what Daniel Webster said at the dedication of the Bunker Hill Monument in 1841. He had just commented on what a remarkable—or to use your words—'marvelous' thing the people fighting at Bunker Hill had done and on the sacrifices made there. He said, 'Thank God! I—I *also*—am an American."

"Yes, ma'am, I guess that sums it up for all of us and for all Americans today."

CHAPTER THIRTY-EIGHT

APRIL 16, 2010, 0952, EDT

Abigail Young passed a written message to President Rowan:

"The acting president of Egypt is on the hotline. Demands to speak to you. The president of Syria called earlier and demands an immediate call."

The president pressed the intercom button. Ms. Young answered immediately. President Rowan formed a small wry smile. "*Magic,*" she thought.

"Yes, Madam President?"

"Have a regular secretary—and by that I mean an administrative assistant not a cabinet member—return the call and courteously inform the two leaders that I am busy and that I will call them in a conference call at twelve noon sharp today. Also, make sure we are up and running on the series of conference calls I asked Andrew McKnight to arrange."

"Already done. Press Secretary McKnight assures me that you need only say the word, and you will be connected. However, he suggests that you hold off on your address to the nation until twelve thirty when the networks can be fully up and running. Also, he believes that there will be a formal declaration of war by then, and you can announce it to the public."

"*Magic,*" the president said to herself again.

"Then let's get the prime ministers or presidents of England, Australia, France, Germany, Italy, Belgium, Russia, and the PRC on the line as soon as possible. Buzz me when you have them all. Have Mr. McKnight inform them in general about what has just taken place here and that I will only be able to convey an official message from the United States in this call. I will talk with each of them in due time."

"Yes, ma'am."

It was fifteen minutes later when Abigail buzzed the president.

"Ready?" President Rowan asked.

"Everyone is waiting on the integrated hot line, Madam President. Pick up a phone and speak, and you are communicating with all of the leaders."

The president lifted her receiver and said, "Greetings, my friends. It would be inappropriate to say, 'good morning.' I will cut to the chase immediately. We were attacked with a major thermonuclear bomb this morning which devastated our industrial city of Detroit, killing and maiming millions of our citizens and our guests from around the world. We were then attacked by half a score of ICBMs, all of which have been neutralized without causing significant additional damage.

"A dirty bomb exploded in the heart of one of the major business districts in Los Angeles causing terrible and as yet incompletely assessed damage. An attempt to set one off in Washington, D.C. was thwarted. I know that similar bombs have destroyed sections of London, Sydney, and Paris with similar terrible destruction to that in Los Angeles. German counterintelligence forces intercepted a dirty bomb being brought in by train and headed for Bonn. That excellent piece of work probably saved Germany a similar fate.

"I congratulate Germany; and I tell each of you and through you, the citizens of Australia, France, and England that we understand and fully appreciate your losses; and we mourn along with your survivors.

"I am in possession of indisputable documentary evidence obtained at the cost of martyrdom that these outrageous acts of war were perpetrated by the nations of Egypt, Syria, Pakistan, Libya, Iran, and the terrorist organizations they support. Note that I am careful not to say crimes. Our response will not be about crimes, and it will not be by police or a judiciary. This is war. Our Congress is even now discussing a formal Declaration of War against the hostiles, and I expect to have that document in my hands before noon. The wrath of our nation—even the most generous among us—has been ignited. The costs to those who did these terrible things will be terrible beyond their most excruciating imaginations.

"I hereby inform you that the United States of America has launched ICBMs with MIRV nuclear warheads targeted on the major cities of the nations I listed. Those nuclear devices should reach their destinations in less than an hour. Your actions today and in the near future will be duly recorded here whether you elect to be friend or foe. I tell you this: do not interfere. If you do, you will be treated as an enemy nation with all that implies. You may stand aside; we will remember; but we will not attack you. You may elect to help us; we will remember for all time and will count you as friends.

"Thank you for your time and attention. I am—as you might imagine—overwhelmingly busy with our national security effort. When it is possible, I will be back in contact with you individually. Please do not feel slighted. Until then, good-by."

Before she could put down her receiver, the German Chancellor blurted, "*Sie sind herzlos.*" *[You are heartless.].*

The president was about to hang-up on the German, but decided on a brief reply.

"Mr. Chancellor, the ones who did this will think, '*Ich bin der Teufel selbst.*'" [I am the devil, himself.].

She put down her receiver and took a breath. She was going to have to get out of her habit of holding her breath if she was going to get through this.

"The secretary of Homeland Security, Madam President," Ms Young announced.

President Rowan gestured from her desk for Secretary Vernon to come into the Oval Office.

"Have a seat, Rupert, you look tired."

On his best day, the rotund Secretary of Homeland Security looked out of shape. Today, he was sweaty and appeared to be out of breath as if he had had to climb several flights of stairs to get to the president's office. His grey flannel suit was rumpled, and he had forgotten to do tighten his yellow polka dot tie. His shirt front had been hastily and asymmetrically tucked into his trousers. His face was flushed and anxious.

"I am, and my day has scarcely begun. I'll give you a quick report and get back to work."

"Go ahead."

"FEMA groups have just barely started working in Los Angeles and in Michigan. There is no Detroit. Our most pressing effort right now is to organize evacuation from the irradiated areas, and that is an enormity. I asked Acting Secretary of Defense Perry Ralston—I think you know him—to call out the Guard to help in the evacuation. I hope that meets with your approval."

"I like your initiative, Rupert. The allocation of our armed forces is a tough decision; and I concur, but only on a temporary basis until as many people as possible are safe and some semblance of order can be achieved for their sustenance. Unfortunately, we are going to war—a war on the order of WWII—and the soldiers will be needed abroad."

"Mr. Ralston and I discussed that thoroughly. I think we can get the people moved into the heartland and to unaffected areas in less than two days. I have my people networking the telephones with state organizations, and they will take the most active role in setting up temporary tent cities and in providing food. The major medical centers all over the country have volunteered their services. There is not a doctor or nurse or hospital that is off duty or working just at usual capacity this day.

"I regret to inform you that we will be very limited in our ability to perform search and rescue operations in the areas irradiated by the bombs. Practically speaking that could only increase the number of casualties. We will appear cold—even heartless—Madam President, but it is only what is absolutely necessary. As it is, thousands of corpses will have to be buried in mass graves and right away to prevent an epidemic. Thousands—maybe hundreds of thousands—of sick people will not make it.

"Our medical resources are so strained that we will have to triage many of the injured to a morphine injection and a comfortable death who—in another situation—might well survive. We have a cut-off: if death appears imminent or would occur even with treatment, they will have to go without definitive care. If they require surgery that would take more than three hours, they will not be able to receive it. For every one of them—each with a limited chance of treatment even with surgery—there are hundreds more who can live after short operations."

"I understand," the sober faced president said.

"I am ashamed as an American to report that looting is becoming a major problem in the bombed cities. Worse, there are people in unaffected cities who are taking advantage of the temporary chaos and involvement of law enforcement in other areas to riot and plunder. It appears that sleeper cells of Islamic fundamentalist organizations have become active and are causing widespread destruction—bombs, train derailments, kidnapping of officials, and feeding on the hysteria of otherwise law-abiding Muslims to join with them in a end-of-the-world *jihad*. Homeland Security is in constant contact with law enforcement at all levels all over the country; and none of us has a decent handle on who among the eight million U.S. Muslims is involved in organized or random terrorism; and who remains a loyal American. I think we will be in a state of anarchy in much of the country in another day."

The president blanched and fought back tears of sadness, anger, and frustration.

She said with fierce determination, "That is the worst news I have received this terrible day. Let me tell you this. As long as I remain president, anarchy will not prevail. Looting will not be tolerated. We will work together as Americans. I am now going to give the first of the two most difficult orders I will have to issue today and then a third one that may be more palatable.

"First, I hereby direct you to put into motion a Presidential Order declaring martial law and the suspension of habeas corpus throughout the United States and its territories. You are directed to have National Guard and police officials shoot looters on sight."

She paused briefly to scan Vernon's expression. It was calm, perhaps relieved.

"Our scant remaining resources will not stretch to accommodate the detention of masses of criminals; so, we have to get a harsh message out immediately that looting and the like will not be tolerated. Make certain that the public is informed by every means possible—by signs, on TV and radio, from pulpits and community gatherings. Get the media and the Faith Based Network to help.

"Second—and this will make my name an historical hiss and a byword as the Bible says, I officially direct you, under the provisions of the newly installed status of martial law to evacuate all Muslims: all Arab, Egyptian, and Iranian citizens and non-citizens, including students and their families. Move them—by force—if necessary, to concentration camps in the deserts of New Mexico, Arizona, and Utah. Make it happen as fast as is possible.

"Try and gain their cooperation as much as you can. Let them know that, unfortunately, too many of their ranks have acted in a hostile way towards our country; too many of them have contributed their time, talents, and their resources to terrorist causes both knowingly and unknowingly to permit them to move freely in the United States for the time being. Assure them—if you can—that this is temporary and in as brief a time as is possible, we will adjudicate individual cases and get them back to their homes and restore all of their former properties and rights. Let them know that we realize that this inconvenience will be misdirected in many cases but to maintain their faith in America. We will make it as right as we can when we can, but it will take time. This will have to be their way to contribute to the war effort.

"While you're at it, let's organize an army of volunteers to keep records about this huge misplacement of people. Get all the secretaries, computer whizzes, accountants, and underemployed lawyers to get the necessary information. They can prepare cases against me, only not now.

"I just realized that I don't have a chief of staff here in the White House. I am going to get McDonald Pearson over at the Judicial Selection Committee to come on board. Help him get started on the volunteer army idea—people to carry out the mass movement of our citizens, people to do the clerk jobs of government, people to direct traffic, teach schools in concentration camps, and as many other things as you can think of."

"This'll take a minute or two, Madam President. I'll get started."

"Thanks, Rupert. Get back to me later in the day."

"Yes, Madam President. And, just as an aside, I wouldn't have your job for all of Midas's fortune."

As soon as Rupert Vernon left, President Rowan called Abigail and had her get McDonald Pearson, the President of the American Red Cross, Malcolm Wright, the Head of United Way, and the grand mullah of Washington's main mosque scheduled for meetings before the end of the day. First though, she directed Abigail to call Chauncey Reed-Perkins, Prime Minister of England.

"Mr. Prime Minister, I hope I did not give you any offense by being abrupt in the earlier call."

"Not at all, Madam President. I regret the circumstances, but allow me to offer my congratulations at your appointment to the office of the presidency. I wouldn't wish the job on my worst enemy, but I do wish you God Speed."

"Thank you, Mr. Prime Minister. Unfortunately, your long and trusted friendship with us has undoubtedly endangered your nation and your people throughout the world beyond the attack that has already occurred. I am asking you to have Great Britain declare war formally and to launch an air attack on the hostile nations. I am holding off on sending troops as much as possible because I do not want another American life lost, and I trust that you will feel the same way about your citizens in and out of uniform.

"Of course. I'm frankly glad that we can finally take off the gloves and get to it without all of the pussyfooting around about coalitions, worrying about how we'll be perceived; or, silliest of all, having to negotiate with the terrorists as if they were sovereigns."

"Also," the president said, "I think we both should round up the Muslim dissidents for the short term and keep them from becoming any more of a fifth column than they already may be."

"We have already begun the process, Madam President. Incidentally, the late President Braithwaite and I were on a first name basis. Would you consider a similar cordial arrangement?"

"I need someone with whom I can be on a first name basis. Please call me Elizabeth."

"My first name is Chauncey, but I have hated the name since public school. Sounds sissy. All of my friends call me 'C.'"

"Let's keep in touch, 'C.' I'll direct our military people to coordinate with the British. I am going to keep our communications free of secrets. America needs to trust you completely, and I am going to set that into motion."

"Thank you, Elizabeth. I wish you and all of your people the protection of the Almighty in this darkest hour."

Next, President Rowan was put on the line with Amos Ben-Tov, Deputy Prime Minister of Israel.

"Mr. Deputy Prime Minister, this is Elizabeth Rowan. Please bring me up to date on your ongoing conflict."

"Let me say, first of all, that Prime Minister Haimovitz regrets that he cannot speak with you himself right now. He is waist deep in our hot conflict and can't get away from the moment-to-moment problems that threaten our existence."

"I certainly understand. We are headed into the same level of activity."

Ben-Tov gave Rowan the details of the Israeli/Arab conflict fully but succinctly. He added something that President Rowan did not know.

"The Palestinians have risen up en masse and are attacking the Israeli settlements and our border positions with an arsenal well beyond anything our intelligence services had predicted that they possessed. We have killed some ninety suicide bombers and are fully engaged with a fanatical and organized small army. They are better organized than we thought them to be. We have excellent evidence that the weapons being used against us came originally from Russia, from their Ramenskoye Arms Bazaar; that will be an issue to deal with another day. While we have effectively done away with the Syrians and the Egyptians, our country's security is threatened, and we presume that the Iranians will follow the PLO and all of its offshoots and associates on the presumption that we are seriously weakened.

"I know that the United States has tried to maintain at least a strong measure of balance in its treatment of Israel and Palestine and your presidents have put pressure on our leaders to hold back in our responses to the atrocities committed by the Muslims. We have always done so in the past; but now, I am asking your indulgence. We must attack fully, or we stand in danger of falling."

"Mr. Ben-Tov, our country is at war. We consider your country an ally being attacked by elements of the same belligerent coalition. We will not stand in your way in the slightest. Do what you must. When we have done what we must to protect ourselves; if you need us, we will assist in your military efforts as much as we can."

"Thank you, Madam President. That is the best news we have heard since 1948."

"Good by, Mr. Deputy Prime Minister."

"Good bye, Madam President."

Her next two calls were from the presidents of the Peoples' Republic of China and Russia. Their requests were similar to those of the prime minister of Israel. Each nation had an insurgency that threatened the security of their country, and they wanted assurance that the United States would not interfere as they tended to their long overdue business.

President Rowan gave them that assurance and asked in return that neither nation take advantage of the current emergency situation to encroach on the sphere of interest of the United States or of each other. The two men agreed, and further agreed to maintain open communications.

The president of Russia smiled as he put down his receiver, then he finished the dregs of the iced Moskovskaya vodka in his crystal tumbler. He took a last drag on his Trud cigarette, a nasty holdover from the Soviet Union era. He felt a twinge of guilt if he lit up his favorite American cigarette, Lucky Strike; so, most of the time, he suffered the bad taste of the product of the *Rodina*.

Using the extraordinary power vested in the presidency by the Russian constitution, he made a single secure telephone call to Marshall Dimitri Ivanovich Rodchenko, commander of the Russian military machine that had been champing at the bit for years to return to the rogue province since the fiasco presided over by Boris Yeltsin in his abortive effort to punish the Chechens.

"Finish the Chechens," the president said.

Chairman Chou Heng Po of the Peoples' Republic of China pressed a button on the console array on his desk.

"Yes, Chairman?" came the voice of the general in command of the largest land army in the world.

"Proceed against Xinjiang. Do what is necessary."

Within the hour, the Red Army moved in force into Xinjiang and began what could only be described as an ethnic cleansing. The inadequate insurgent forces were no match for the mighty land and air attack, now unfettered by American political opposition that came as a total surprise to the rebellious province. Ujimamadi Rahman and Islam Yasyn and the hotel in which they were eating dinner were demolished in an artillery attack that decimated Hotan at the same time as an air attack devastated the capital city of UrUmqi with its partisan Uighurs and its loyal Han Chinese population.

The chairman of the party regretted that such losses of true citizens of the nation had to be borne by the country, but it was for the greater good. In two weeks, the Autonomous Region of Xinjiang was under the firm hand of the Red Army; and the process of eliminating the dissidents in the population was underway with ferocity reminiscent of the liquidation of dissidents after Mao Tse Tung inaugurated the PRC.

The pacification of the insurgency in Chechnya started with Marshall Rodchenko's reception of his telephoned orders and took a month; but with the full force of the Russian Armed Forces engaged in the series of attacks, it was only a matter of time. The Russian losses were heavy; but the Russian people—well known for their Stoicism—did not even regret that the cost was heavy. The reduction of Grozny to a noncombatant city was more than worth the terrible cost. The nationalist or terrorist group—depending on one's perspective—the Riyadus Salakhin Reconnaissance and Sabotage Battalion of Chechen Martyrs, Muhammad Khattab and Abdul-Bari, and six thousand of their al Qaeda and other Muslim brethren were subjected to being hanged in public. They were stripped naked, beards and heads shaved, and smeared with pigs' blood before being executed. Their families, the young and old, male and female, were shot; and their homes and offices were bulldozed to the ground. The Chechen insurgency was eradicated. The Russians did everything but salt the ground.

Sixteen Arab children, boys and girls aged seven to thirteen, were apprehended within Israeli territory or at its borders with the Palestinian Authority territory. They were all wearing martyr's belts—explosives strapped to their torsos in a fitted vest—that were placed on them by the leaders of Hamas, Hezbollah, the al Aqsa Martyrs' Brigades, and al Qaeda. Each child carried a martyr's letter promising the child the blessings of Allah in paradise and the parents the sum of $20,000 and an honored place in the new, Jew free, Palestinian state. None of them was able to detonate his or her explosive vests and after being divested of the lethal garment, the children were locked in detention.

As the bewildered children were being rounded up at the borders, the Palestinian prisoners in Hadariam prison north of Tel Aviv announced a hunger strike. They would starve to death with the world's communications media in full attendance if the State of Israel did not relinquish control of the Occupied Territories. Prime Minister Avigador Haimovitz received a telephone message from the warden.

He listened politely, then replied tersely, "They are grown men capable of making their own decisions. They elect to be martyrs. Allow them that privilege. We are too busy to force feed men with whom we cannot reason. Keep the press away. Let them die in privacy."

The mullahs of Judea and Samaria—or Palestine, as the world's liberal press dubbed the region—working closely with the leaders of the terrorist organizations, had planned for this day for many months. This was to be the culmination of the intifada that began twenty-three years earlier. The beginnings were relatively minor and were the work of many of the same mullahs who made false charges of atrocities by Israelis.

The date of the beginning was December 6, 1987. An Israeli citizen was stabbed to death on a shopping trip in Gaza City. The following day, four Arab-Palestinians from the Gaza Jebaliya refugee camp were killed in an automobile accident; and mullahs spread the rumor that they were killed by Israelis as revenge for the stabbing. Three days after the stabbing and two days after the unrelated traffic accident, a seventeen year old Palestinian was killed by an IDF soldier after he threw a Molotov cocktail at an army patrol unit. Through the next week the mullahs led Arab youths in rock-throwing, road blocking, gas bombing, and tire burning incidents. By December 12, six Arab-Palestinians were killed and thirty more were wounded.

The mullahs circulated rumors that the young Arabs had been taken to an army hospital and murdered, that the Khan Yunis reservoir had been poisoned, and that a series of Israeli atrocities had been committed. United Nations officials investigated and found all of the rumors to be unfounded, but that made no difference.

In the next four years alone, 3,600 gasoline bomb attacks, 100 hand grenade attacks, and 600 aggravated assaults with guns and assorted explosives occurred, fomented by the mullahs who capitalized on the culture of hate they had so carefully nurtured. By 1992, more than 1000 Palestinian Arabs had been killed. After that, the number of attacks became so frequent that an accurate count was all but impossible to tally. The PLO took full advantage of the escalating violence to send out death squads to remove the Arabs who allegedly collaborated with Israel. The squads stabbed, shot, bludgeoned with axes, clubbed, and burned to death 118 of their own people. The PLO's own investigation determined that 116 of them were innocent of the charges alleged; they were granted status of Martyrs of the Palestinian Revolution.

Reports of the latest uprising continued to pour into the PM's office. At the same time as the children entered the territory of Israel proper with their lethal martyrs' belts, screaming, taunting, rock throwing teenagers and younger children, women, and old men filled the streets of Gaza City and Hebron in pre-arranged riots described later by news media as a "spontaneous uprising". The mullahs had informed the excitable zealot populace that the Syrian and Egyptian combined attacks earlier that morning had successfully carried the battle for Allah against Little Satan, and all that remained to be done for Allah's minions to triumph was to come forth in righteous rebellion. The mullahs did not tell the crowds of vulnerable worshippers that they would serve as the vanguard and shield for the fighters with real weapons who would be hiding behind them.

There were a few shots in the direction of the phalanx of IDF soldiers. The Israelis stood their ground protected by tanks and fired an occasional well aimed shot in return. A grenade launcher was fired from amongst the Palestinian hordes. The explosive fell short, and none of the Israelis were injured. That grenade was a signal. As soon as it exploded, the milling crowd began running at the Israeli lines screaming their joy at becoming martyrs. From behind them, light weapon fire began; and two IDF soldiers fell, one dead and one with a leg wound.

Then, from roof tops and obscure alleys rocket salvos from Nasser 3s made by the Popular Resistance Communities began to rain lethal shrapnel towards the Israeli defenses. The new rockets fired ordnance weighing eight pounds that exploded in air spewing explosives and shrapnel—an improvement over their earlier generation homemade Qassam rockets. The Israel forces were well protected behind their tanks and military vehicles and were spared serious injury, but the huge crowds friendly to the freedom fighters firing the rockets absorbed most of the casualties.

The IDF opened fire into the crowd with machine guns, rockets and tank rounds. The result was the worst carnage since the intifada started in 1987. Severed limbs, torsos, and indecipherable parts littered the scorched and pocked ground. The freedom fighters began squeezing off rounds from their shoulder fired rocket launchers from their hiding places above the rapidly diminishing crowd. The wounded were screaming; children wandered in a daze; men used women as shields; and savage blasphemies came from the mouths of religious men on both sides.

The IDF called in air support; and this time—unlike ever before—the attack aircraft did not hold back and did not remain content to make a surgical strike. Conventional bombs and rockets rained down hellfire on the innocent and guilty alike in the hapless towns and villages of old Judea and Samaria. In thirty minutes, there was no further resistance. Nearly one hundred thousand Palestinian rioters and their partners in violence—the PLO, Hamas, Hezbollah, al Aqsa Brigades, and every other freedom fighter organization—had lost all but a handful of their leaders and members. Effectively they were finished. The towns and villages of the Palestinians lost upwards of three-quarters of their buildings. Two Israelis were killed in the brief struggle. The Israeli/Palestinian conflict was all but over except for a few skirmishes initiated by die-hard fundamentalist Islamic religious zealots.

———————

At ten fifteen, Abigail told the president that the leaders of Egypt and Syria were both calling. This time they were polite and conciliatory. President Rowan gave her secretary the same reply as before:

"Have the same secretary inform them again that I am busy, but that I will address them at noon EDT."

CHAPTER THIRTY-NINE

APRIL 16, 2010, 11:55 a.m., EDT

Shortly before the president's scheduled call to the leaders of the aggressor nations, McDonald Pearson, the new chief of staff, ushered the leaders of Congress into the Oval Office.

"Please have a seat. What do you have for me?" the president asked.

She was beginning to show wear from her stressful morning.

"We have the Declaration of War just passed by the new Congress. We took the option of appointing legislative members from the states and from the staffs of the deceased law makers to achieve a legal quorum. The ink is still wet on the parchment. The vote was not close; only one senator voted against the resolution," said the Majority Leader, Helen Clivener.

"Let me guess—Cliff Assure?"

"You're psychic, Madam President," smiled the speaker.

"Thank you for making the trip personally. You might like to listen in to my next conversation."

The leaders nodded their interest.

"Mac, is the conference call ready?"

"It is. We have the current heads of government of Syria, Egypt, Iran, Pakistan, Libya, and Saudi Arabia waiting. For your information, there are thirty-one seconds left before noon exactly," he said to the assembled government officials.

"In the interests of precision we'll keep them waiting another half a minute," said the president.

Abigail held a marine chronometer and mouthed the seconds. She held up ten fingers when ten seconds remained, and ticked them off down to one and pointed at the president.

President Rowan started to speak on the stroke of noon.

"I am Elizabeth Leavitt Rowan, the new president of the United States, and I have a message for you…"

She was interrupted by the king of Saudi Arabia, "Madam President, let me offer the profound condolences of the Saudi government…"

President Rowan was not going to have any of it.

"Be quiet and listen. I am about to give you a message, and I am not here to receive information."

No one had ever spoken to King Abdullah Said ibn Saud disrespectfully, not even when he was a child. He was shocked, and the same degree of shock was transmitted to the leaders of Syria, Egypt, Iran, Libya, and Pakistan who were hanging on their separate lines.

"This is the message of the president and people of the United States. At 0715 Eastern Daylight Time today, April 16, 2010, a thermonuclear device exploded and destroyed Detroit. Los Angeles was the victim of a so-called dirty bomb as were the cities of Sydney, Paris, and London. More than twelve million people, citizens of nearly one hundred ninety countries, were murdered in those attacks. The president of the United States and several score of our most senior officials were killed. The financial cost is inestimable at present. In addition, twelve intercontinental ballistics missiles with nuclear warheads were launched against us. They were neutralized.

"This monstrous action was planned, supported with material and technological expertise, and executed from your countries and with your knowledge. We are in possession of a mountain of documentary evidence which no one could deny that implicates each of you directly. Accordingly, we, the people of the United States, through the Congress, hereby declare war against your nations. In the next fifteen minutes, you will feel the righteous wrath of America. The skies over your cities will light up with our reply to your treacherous infamy, and your civilizations will be obliterated from the earth. I am finished."

She put down her receiver and did not hear the sputterings and imprecations from the deeply shaken Islamic national leaders.

The majority leader shook her head.

"Madam President," she said, "Senator Assure asked me to have your office send him your evidence of the guilt of the Muslims; preferably, he wants you to call him."

President Rowan looked at Helen Clivener. It was obvious that she was far from convinced that the evidence warranted the nuclear response.

The president said, by way of answer, "The Romans had a truism: *Vox audita perit; litera scripta manet*—literally, the spoken word perishes; the written word remains. Frankly, I am not going to give fuel to the coming liberal spin that my administration and the U.S. Armed Forces acted precipitously or in any way inappropriately. Let it be known that I did not answer Senator Assure's request. Rather, I am having a thoroughly documented written history of this attack on us prepared and will release it to the entire world when it is finished."

Helen Clivener made no reply, but her facial expression indicated her displeasure.

President Rowan retired to her quarters for the next half an hour following her conference call to the Muslim leaders. She needed to stiffen her resolve and to tighten her focus. The President picked up her well thumbed copy of The *Complete Works of Shakespeare* and turned to a highlighted page in *King Henry*, Act III, Scene I: Before the battle at Harfleur:

"Once more into the breach, dear friends, once more. Or close the wall up with our English dead! In peace there's nothing so becomes a man as modest stillness and humility; but when the blast of war blows in our ears, then imitate the action of the tiger; stiffen the sinews, summon up the blood; disguise fair nature with hard favor'd rage. Then lend the eye a terrible aspect...

"Be copy now to men of grosser blood, and teach them how to war...show us here the mettle of your pasture; let us swear that you are worth your breeding which I doubt not...The game's afoot. Follow your spirit..."

She closed her eyes and concentrated on the details of what she would say to a shocked and demoralized nation. She was clear eyed, and her jaw was clenched when Andrew McKnight came to fetch her.

The press secretary escorted President Rowan to the Map Room where the networks were set up for her broadcast to the nation.

"We have three minutes before you're on, Madam President. Want to close your eyes for a moment?"

"I'll get into my chair and do just that, thanks Andrew. Run interference for me."

With thirty seconds to go, McKnight gently awakened the tired president and two makeup artists quickly made her look less like a zombie.

The media pool director announced, "Ten seconds. Silence on the set."

He pointed at the president and counted down with his fingers. At twelve-thirty on the dot, Elizabeth Rowan rose to the occasion of the most important speech she would ever give.

She glanced at the teleprompter and began, "Today, the sixteenth of April, 2010—a day that will be etched in the hearts and minds of Americans forever—our nation suffered the single worst betrayal and attack ever committed on a people. An atomic bomb hundreds of times greater in destructive power than the ones that destroyed Hiroshima and Nagasaki exploded and annihilated Detroit and nearby Windsor, Ontario, Canada. Smaller but still terrible devices caused great harm in Los Angeles, England, France, and Australia. More than twelve million people are dead, hundreds of thousands more are dreadfully injured. Our president and many of the senior members of our government were among those who perished. It will be some time before a total of the awful devastation can be established, but it is not difficult to conceive a loss of trillions of dollars.

"Every resource—public and private, civilian and military, paid and volunteer—that exists in the United States and from its friends such as Canada and England is being mustered into the enormous emergency effort. Please be patient as an injured nation works to search and to save and then to rebuild. We will need to mount a huge effort to re-establish an elected government and to achieve order. Because of the magnitude of the calamity and because—I regret to inform you—looting has become a serious impediment, I have declared a state of martial law effective immediately.

"We know beyond a shadow of a doubt the identities of those who attacked us and have more than ample documentation to prove it. That evidence will be released to the world as soon as it is physically possible to do so. Acting as the commander-in-chief of the armed forces and in accordance with my oath to protect and defend the Constitution and the American people, I have ordered counter military measures. The dreadful American engine of war has been unleashed on the perpetrators. They consider us to be a paper tiger; they are wrong. The sleeping giant—America—is now awake. I assure you that—dreadful as the attack on us was—we are not acting out of vengeance or wrath; and our actions are not that of a police agency. We are responding to war and are legitimately defending ourselves. It is past time that this great scourge of Islamic fundamentalist terrorism be eradicated from the earth forever. That is the reason for our response. We will not only persist, but we will prevail. In time we will heal, and we will do it in safety.

"Good afternoon, ladies and gentlemen, friends and neighbors, my fellow countrymen, my brothers and sisters. God bless and keep you and the United States of America and give you the strength to carry the great burdens that have been foisted upon you. Please pray for me and for the country."

The television cameras panned away. President Rowan stood and walked directly back to the Oval Office and returned to work.

———————

Less than a minute after President Rowan's speech—of which Bara'ah Noor Abtahi was not aware since she did not know about television—properly covered by her abaya, and with appropriate eyes down demeanor, the eighteen year old mother deposited her four children at the Hezbollah madrassah. She paused for a moment to hear the familiar chant of the children: "Death to Great Satan; Death to Little Satan; Death to the decadent West; Death to the nonhuman Jews; Death to Americans; Death to Polytheists."

It was a comfort to Bara'ah that she had given over the education of her precious little ones to the care and keeping of the Imams who knew best the will of God. Her husband was a soldier in the Army of God, and it left him but little time to provide the necessities of life. His contribution to Allah's cause was too important for him to be concerned with such mundane matters. Bara'ah and her husband kept a poster on each wall of their humble home bearing the photograph of a young man or young woman from the neighborhood dressed in a martyr's belt.

There was almost no sound from the cigar shaped object that swept into her peripheral vision as she gazed heavenward contemplating the time when her own sons and daughters could be considered for holy martyrdom. She was briefly aware of a sudden great rushing of wind and caught a nanosecond's sight of a fireball more brilliant than the sun. Neither she, nor her children, nor any citizen of her home city of Isfahan, felt pain as they vanished into the atmosphere as micro atomic fragments.

King Abdullah Said ibn Saud was troubled by the calm deliberateness he saw in the new American president. He had watched the woman's speech to the American people on Al Jezeera Television. He had been affronted the by peremptory manner she used with him on the telephone, but he wrote that off as the unworthy actions of a woman and a Westerner—who could expect more from those barbarians? The threats she had made did not seem credible, but you never knew with the Americans. He had learned that from his older friends, the Soviets. The Americans were naïve people who were capable of incredible barbarity under circumstances important to them, and he did not entirely underestimate them.

However, King ibn Saud was at his core a pragmatist, and he knew how severely the Great Satan had been injured by the Spear of God. Little Satan could be dealt with later even though the country peopled by the spawn of pigs and monkeys held a temporary upper hand. It was the Americans who needed to be removed from the equation, and he besought Allah to come to the aid of his chosen people.

The electronically amplified voice of the muezzin called from the minaret. That was unusual since it was not time for prayer. King ibn Saud strained to understand the broadcast words—not a call to prayer, but some sort of warning, most of the transmission unclear. The King made out 'tawari' [emergencies] and the ending of the muezzin's message, 'aakhir kalaam' [my last word].

An air raid klaxon sounded, the first one in King ibn Saud's memory. He stepped to the palace window and looked out. The last thing he saw was a hurricane bearing down on his home. Before he could form a thought, there was a flicker of a moment's vision of the sun engulfing his city, his home, and himself. Riyadh was gone.

Sallem el-Meishi—a Bedouin camel trader—made his way to the camel market in the desert outskirts of Tripoli. He was riding the most beautiful and the most wonderful of all his camels. The animal was a sleek tawny male with erect posture and proud eye and was the swiftest of the swift. He would net Sallem a fine purse in the races as he had done for two years running, and he would be a fine advertisement for the string of camels Sallem had so carefully bred and nurtured.

Sallem had another occupation, a sort of seasonal career. The proud Bedu was a fighter for Allah in the al Qaeda movement of the *wali*, Usama. The middle-aged Libyan Bedouin had been well trained in the Beka'a Valley by the people of the list and had done his part in Afghanistan against the god-less ones, in Iraq against the lackey's of the Great Satan, and in the Zionist Entity against the enemies of The Prophet, may Allah bless his name. Being a freedom fighter was a part-time job, one that el-Meishi was careful to keep separate from his life of making money in his lucrative and satisfying camel breeding, herding, and trading business. Another advantage of keeping his business life separate from his participation in the holy jihad with Usama's blessed army was that for a large portion of the year, he was safe from reprisal from the Zionist Entity state terrorists and from the devilish Americans. Not that he had anything to fear from the great talkers—the toothless eunuchs from the West. But…still, it was always better to be safe.

That was Sallem el-Meishi's last coherent thought. An American cruise missile with MIRV capability detonated over the decaying old U.S. Embassy on Mohamed Thabit Street in the center of the Tripoli. The building was evacuated in 1979 with such haste that the Americans had to leave the colors behind, and the flag now lay in a dirty heap at the bottom of the flag pole. The Embassy was sacked and burned by Muslim extremists in that year. Across from the dilapidated building stood a billboard with large Arabic letters that could still be read clearly-"The People are with Our Leader in Challenging America".

Within the epicenter of the blast was the upscale Gargarsh neighborhood with its classy stores selling the latest clothes and the best electronics and Tripoli's only 5-star hotel—the Corinthia Bab Africa—and Al Fateh University where 42 Americans were arrested and detained for being Christians. Also included was the Sea Breeze Golf Course adjacent to the former Wheelus Air Force base expropriated from the Americans when the U.S. Military was driven out by the Great Leader. A short distance to the south in Rabta sat the chemical factory that made mustard gas by the ton.

The wind, fireball, and blast that evaporated Tripoli and its 2.2 million inhabitants also removed the great camel market in its path. The camel trader and soldier of God became one with the universe along with everyone he cared about.

Seventy-five miles to the east, the Roman ruins of Leptis Magna were leveled thus ruining a hundred years of archeological work. The second missile from the MIRV exploded dead center over Benghazi's Garyounis University, the Port on the Mediterranean, and the Souq al-Jareeda. Libya's second largest city, the main population center of Cyrenaica, was founded in the 7th Century by Greeks. Benghazi was small enough that nothing recognizable remained of the half million people, its history, or the city's structures in the aftermath.

Although she led a life of privilege owing to the fact that President Assad was her cousin, Kulus Murjanah Assad was a diligent student at Damascus University. Like everyone on campus that day, she had heard the American president's idle threats on CNN Asia and had laughed along with them when the students stridently mocked the old lady with the crooked nose in the White House. They all knew that America was finished because of the great

ICBMs that had been proudly launched from their own country as the Spears of God. The missiles now were openly called that. Islam had triumphed as the imams had said would happen all along. It was the end of the world, and they had but to wait for Gabriel's trump; then they would be swept up into paradise and to lives of ease and pleasure singing Allah's praises. Kulus could not have been prouder.

On a more prosaic level, Kulus went back to the chemistry lab and began to weigh her unknown for the day on the new electronic Metler scale. She had to do better than the other students because of the high status of her family. She had to be able to defend her position as a first tier student achieved on her own merits. Her ambition was to become one of the few Syrian female chemical engineers, and she had absolutely no interest in politics. Like all of her countrymen and women, Kulus was scrupulous in her avoidance of even a hint of criticism of her illustrious grand uncle—the late president—and her cousin, the current head of state.

The LED letters lit up as the final weight of her lump of grey-green unknown chemical—now free of its sulfite contaminate—appeared.

The laboratory room lit up like a refiner's fire, and Kulus and her aspirations and her insecurities were extinguished along with the whole of greater Damascus and all of its history, tradition, and culture. All that remained of the attractive scarved young woman was a tracing of ash in the form of the general contours of her incinerated body on what had once been the laboratory floor.

The official limousine pulled up to the door of his office on Aga Khan Road Shalimar in the lush semi-tropical business and government section of Islamabad near the Marriott Islamabad Hotel eight minutes after U.S. President Rowan finished her threatening speech. Pakistani Vice-President Walid Shamma Atallah walked briskly up to the ornate door leading onto the Islamabad street. His two bodyguards opened the door and peered out, and—seeing no threat—walked onto the quiet street. One of them remained at the office building door, and the other took his place of vigilance by the limousine's rear door. There no signs of an assassin or of an overzealous countryman. The guard by the door nodded, and the other guard opened the door for the vice-president. He hurried behind his guard and slipped into the open door of his car.

The driver drove rapidly through busy streets clogged with bicycles, motorized rickshaws huffing poisonous acrid blue smoke, and pedestrians completely heedless of the dangerous traffic. The smells wafting from the maze of narrow lanes and alleys and the combined cacophony of *Pashtu*, *Qawali*, and *Hindi* music annoyed the vice-president; so, he rolled up the windows of the limousine and removed himself from the discomfiture of smelling or hearing the lowly among his countrymen. He read a day old *New York Times*, and the morning's *Sindh Today*, *Daily Khabrain Pakistan*, the largest Urdu language newspaper, and the national *PakTribune*. None of them carried the news of the catastrophe befalling his beloved country, and with the darkened windows raised he was able to avoid having to look at the nascent strawberry fields, the kabob stalls, and sweet shops that represented the Third World character of most of his country. He despised the bearded vendors with teeth stained green with *naswar* selling religious trinkets, lamp shades made of animal skins, amateurishly embroidered shawls, and the ubiquitous gaudy carpets, woven by tribal women, that fell apart with a year's use.

The driver wound his way aggressively and efficiently through the labyrinthine unnamed streets to the air force base section of Islamabad-Rawalpindi International Airport where the official vehicle was ushered in without having to pause at the manned gate. The limousine pulled to the VIP hanger, and again the guards exited first and surveyed the area of the hanger for potential threats. They saw none. Atallah got out and walked briskly towards the army's U.S Marine AV 8B II Harrier, gift of the trusting American fools. The flight plan was for Atallah to join Usama in Wana in South Waziristan Province. The only variance in arrangements with any usual flight arranged for the vice-president was that the flight crew and Atallah's guards from the time he entered the short range vertical take-off and landing air craft would be provided by members of *Harkat ul-Mujahedeen Al-Almi*. Atallah felt safer with these freedom fighters than with regular air force personnel during this perilous escape.

The vice-president stepped into the air craft, took his plush seat, and buckled his seat and shoulder belts. As he always did when he was about to fly in his beloved country, Atallah began to mouth the words to the national anthem: "Blessed by the sacred land, happy be the bounteous realm symbol of high resolve, Land of Pakistan". He looked out at the tarmac filled with U.S. provided fighter planes, mostly older F-4G Wild Weasels and converted trainers, the AT-37 Dragon Flies, and the old reliable Iranian F-4Ds refitted with computer based Dive Toss bomb release system, E-3A AWACS, C-130s and OH-58C Kiowa attack helicopters.

If the Americans did choose to attack Pakistan as threatened, his air force could make a credible show of defense, since he was certain of the innate reticence on the part of the Americans to use their ultimate weapons. Certainly the Pakistani Armed Forces could provide him time to get to safety in the mountains. He heaved a sigh of relief as the Harrier's 23,000 pound thrust engines roared into life. Atallah closed his eyes to rest during takeoff.

Then, the world ended in a cataclysmic mushroom cloud that blasted the capital city of Pakistan into pieces of debris, none of which was as large as a mustard seed, and hurtled them into the stratosphere. Atallah and his plane, the air base and everything in it, the capital city, and three quarters of a million lives were changed to atomic particle size in less than an instant.

The crowd of Alexandria University students gravitated quickly to the location of the latest violent disturbance in the city. Word of mouth spread that army deserters plundering the sacred artifacts in the venerated Abu El Abbas al-Mursi Mosque had been captured by police just south of the suq district. There were murmurs of sacrilege and of ultimate disrespect to The Prophet, may Allah's blessings be upon the *Rasuli*, by the military cowards. The hapless looters were caught holding the sacred *Qur'an* believed to have been used by the last of the right thinking Caliphs and were now kneeling trembling in the clutter of the construction site where they had attempted to hide.

The four men kept their heads bowed in ultimate submission. In front and on each side of them was a growing throng of vengeful screaming students and women from the nearby neighborhood. Behind them stood an unfinished cinder brick wall, propped up by two by four struts because the side supports were not yet in place and the contractor—to save money—had placed only the bare bones minimum of reinforcement bar.

One properly bearded young man in cleric garb—although he was actually a computer science major at the university—organized an impromptu trial. He and two young women—with their heads properly covered with *hajibs* [headscarves]—found witnesses to the crime and the deserters flight into hiding, and commandeered one older gentleman onlooker to be the requisite defense attorney. The computer science major assumed the roles of prosecutor and *kady* [judge]. The crowd and the organizers did not feel it either practical or necessary to call a jury.

The student judge raised his hands for quiet.

"First witness to the crime against Allah and His Holy Prophet, blessed be his name."

An angry *hajibi* marched proudly over the construction rubble and stood in front of the taciturn crowd.

Chapter Thirty-Nine

"As you love Allah, will you give us only the truth, *akh*?"

"Of course. I saw these blasphemers touch then actually take away the Sacred Recitation once used by Abu Bakr himself—the first of the *al-khulafa al-rashidin* [rightly guided caliphs]."

"What else?"

"They ran from the mosque when Believers saw them and gave chase."

"Did you see where they went or what they did with the holy relics?"

"No."

"I will call the next witness."

A grizzled old man, then two university religion students, gave brief testimony about the flight to avoid capture of the vicious criminals still in their tattered army uniforms. The evidence was damning.

Without having ever spoken to his cowering clients, the hastily commandeered defense attorney—an elderly man in a shiny and shabby black business suit and wearing a red velveteen fez—tentatively stepped out before the angry crowd. Their looks told him that his life was in jeopardy for defending these miscreants. However, his duty before God and by the Sharia required that he be brave and carry out his religious obligation lest the trial be nothing more than a kangaroo court. His sense of justice and his love for his religion overrode his trepidations. He would stand blameless before the Seat of Judgment of *al Ilah,* the *Khairy* [beneficent] and *Rahman* [most merciful].

"My clients admit their guilt and repent. They throw themselves upon the mercy of the court and of these people," the defense attorney said and waved his hand around the ever growing and restive crowd.

He had never spoken to the defendants.

One of the defendants, knees throbbing from pressure against the rocks on the ground, looked up in surprise at the news that he had confessed, repented, and had begged for mercy. The other three men were too cowed even to raise their heads at the statements from a man they had never heard of, let alone met or talked with.

The student judge turned dramatically to the crowd. He enjoyed his moment of fame.

"What say you, Muslims, guilty or not guilty?"

"GUILTY! screamed the crowd that now numbered in the tens of thousands.

Many of them did not even know the nature of the offenses charged and had not been able to catch a glimpse of the criminal blasphemers.

"GUILTY! GUILTY!" they chanted.

"The court, acting under the Sharia finds you guilty," the self-appointed *kady* intoned solemnly. "The Prophet, blessed is his name, said in the Hadith, 'He, who has no loyalty, has no faith, and he who lacks fidelity, lacks religion.'"

The snarling crowd advanced towards the disloyal blasphemers. The *haris* [student guards] held them back with increasing difficulty.

"In the name of Allah and his Holy Prophet and the Sharia, I pronounce sentence. You shall die by stoning."

The four men groaned quietly, two of them more from the injuries suffered in the beating they had received when they were captured than from emotional distress emanating from the ominous sentence.

The *kady* and *haris* dragged each of the condemned men to the approximate middle of the rickety cinder block wall. He gestured to two strong men in the roiling crowd. They stepped to the two by four supports of the wall and removed them. The *kady* then addressed the crowd.

He raised his arms for quiet and said, "Brothers, step behind the stone wall and carry out the sentence."

Dozens, then hundreds of men rushed to get into position behind the wall and out of sight of the cowering and whimpering former soldiers. A little girl was trampled to death in the stampede to get a place of honor on the wall.

"Proceed!" shouted the *kady*.

There was a collective grunt of effort from behind the wall, then it tottered. The blocks scraped against each other and began to loosen. There was a mighty shout, and the wall was disrupted from its concrete foundations. Its tons of man-made stones crashed down on the defendants in proper execution of the sentence of God. The four men were crushed to death. The massive crowd cheered and surged forward to jump up and down on the stones where they thought the condemned men lay hidden. It took ten minutes for the crowd to vent its full fury and for calm to return.

An imam from the nearby *gamei* [mosque] looked heavenward and began to give thanks to Allah, the Just, for the correctness of the way He had directed his Believers. As he did, the heavens above opened with apocalyptic light and for the slightest fraction of a second, the massive crowd believed that they had ushered in the end of the world.

In a sense, they had done just that. Alexandria, Egypt, the second largest metropolis in the nation, the Bride and Pearl of the Mediterranean—from the lighthouse on the island of Pharos in the Rasel-Tin [Cape of Figs] to the lake harbor with all its four and a half million people, its magnificent historical buildings, universities, madrassahs, mosques, business and government buildings, streets, factories, homes, gardens, and secret hiding places for fundamentalist freedom fighters was blown to bits; and the bits were scattered beneath the mushroom shaped cloud for a distance of fifteen miles around the Al Iskindavryah Governate.

CHAPTER FORTY

APRIL 16, 2010, 10:10 p.m., SYRIAN TIME

In the Mediterranean at a point off the Syrian coast 35°10' longitude and 35°33' latitude, the massive LA-class nuclear powered USS *City of Corpus Christi* submarine received a direct AUTOVON [Automatic Voice Network] telephone message routed through AUTODIN [Automatic Digital Information Message System]. In compliance with the orders from the CNO [Chief of Naval Operations] the awesome war machine rose out of the ocean like a silent black avenger. At the beginning of the war the previous day, the *Corpus Christi* and its sister ships of the 5th Fleet, Middle-East had been on a peaceful cruise to show the colors in Middle-Eastern ports. Now, the battle ready ship whose crew wore the E-ready patch, turned slightly more nose in to the coast.

The crew of 140 concentrated on a single task—the firing of its Tomahawk cruise missiles with atomic warheads. The quiet underwater ship was cold, and the crewmen were wearing heavy mittens. The final check and count-down were completed. One by one, the twenty-five extremely accurate missiles were launched from the twelve underwater launch tubes. Each launch produced a small shudder and a slight shift of the hull in the water. Three hundred miles north, the USS *Springville* carried out identical procedures. The USS *San Juan* fired from two hundred fifty miles south of the *Corpus Christi's* position.

Lying beneath three hundred feet of water in the Persian Gulf, the Los Angeles class USS *Augusta* slipped silently to the dark surface of the narrow water way and fired its complement of Trident 3 missiles. Three other subs rose within a few miles of each other and fired simultaneously. The U.S. submarines—headquartered in Manama, Bahrain—were protected by Aircraft Carrier Battle Groups including an Amphibious Ready Group, reconnaissance aircraft, logistics vessels, maritime patrol, and surface combatant ships. Effectively, the 5th Fleet had cordoned off all waters leading to and from the Middle-East Muslim combatant nations. The submarines fired at will, and there was no return fire.

Aden, Yemen was attacked by the USS *Boise* from its vantage point in the Gulf of Aden. The accuracy of the long range missiles was nothing short of phenomenal. After two hours, the offending Pakistani cities of Karachi, Islamabad, Quetta, Multan, Lahore, Bhopal, and Rawalpindi were all but obliterated. The military bases in the region of those cities were rendered inoperable. Fewer that fifty airplanes remained in condition to defend Pakistan.

The Syrian cities of Homs, Hama, and the major port of Latakia were reduced to smoldering ruins. Saudi Arabia lost Jiddah and Dhahran with its massive oil industry—the headquarters of Saudi Aramco and thirty thousand British and American petroleum technologists. Mecca and Medina with their sacred shrines and relics were reduced to atomic fragments. The Transarabian Pipeline crossing from al-Hasa in the eastern province was destroyed for five hundred miles.

Iran lost Tehran, Tabriz, Dezful, Bandar, Khomeini, Abadan, Khorramshahr, the Kharg Island oil port, Mashad, Qom, and Kermanshah. The Iranian air force had only three hundred planes left operable in the entire country, civilian or military, and no way to communicate with any of them. The great air force of Iran was only a shadow of the powerful force that once supported the dependent totalitarian regime of Syria and threatened its other Sunni and Israeli neighbors. The vaunted power of the Revolutionary Guards and the mighty military machine created since Grand Ayatollah Khomeini had enabled it to be belligerent in international relations. The power and the belligerence were no more. In less than a day of warfare with the mighty American military machine the pitiful Pakistani armed forces and all of their materiel of war were dust.

———————

At five o'clock EDT in the afternoon of the dreadful long day, General Hoyt Prescott called the president.

"Madam President, we have had peace feelers from most of the countries we have attacked. I have referred them to State. Since I had to brief you anyway, they suggested that you could give me any pertinent orders about the offers."

"Thank you Gen. Prescott. I presume that you chose your words carefully. You said 'peace' not surrender.' Was that deliberate?"

"Yes, ma'am. They have not even approached the idea of surrender yet."

"Ignore them and have State do the same."

"Roger that, ma'am. The next area of information is to tell you that we have destroyed almost every large city in the Islamic Middle-East. Your CIA briefer will have a detailed report for you tomorrow morning. Things are happening pretty fast."

"Military casualties?"

"Not one. Not a single member of our armed forces has been wounded or killed. We haven't even had an accident."

"That's the most gratifying thing I have heard today. Keep up the good work, General."

"Ma'am, I would be less than candid if I did not let you know that there have been American civilians killed. Our expatriate community in the Middle-East has been decimated. I can't give you a number."

The president was somber. She shook her head. No good news could come without being tempered by worse news.

"I knew it would happen, but it still is very painful. I am responsible for untold misery. I will never forgive myself even though I know it had to be done, and these innocent collateral victims were inevitable," she said softly.

The general thought it best not to amplify.

"I'll let you know if anything new develops. As we speak, the ground war is starting, but it is going to be far more a mopping up operation from the air than an infantry engagement."

"That is the plan. I don't want to lose a single man in this Third World War if we can possibly do it. Good-bye, General."

"Good-bye, Madam President."

President Rowan was suddenly overcome with sleepiness. She put her head on her desk and took a forty minute power nap.

Abigail Young looked in on the exhausted president and decided that her news could wait.

When the president opened her eyes, it took her a few moments to orient. The place looked exactly like the Oval Office of movie fame, but what was she—the ordinary woman from Utah—doing there? Finally her head cleared, and she was able to get back to work.

Abigail rapped on the door jam, and President Rowan looked up and smiled at her.

"Abigail, your job is to keep me from having periods of narcolepsy."

"Sorry, ma'am, I just couldn't bear to wake you up. The acting secretary of State needs to see you."

"Show him in."

Gadi ben Elazar walked in and took a seat. He looked haggard.

"What's going on, Mr. Secretary?"

"We have had positive communications including condolences from most of the members of the United Nations except the Muslim countries, of course. Notable by their absence are communications from France, Germany, Spain, and Belgium. No one has indicated any outright opposition. The countries subjected to our attacks seem to have pretty much lost communication with the outside world. We had those peace feelers that Gen. Prescott conveyed to you but nothing else. In practical fact, I think there are really no functioning governments in those countries. The usual anti-American media diatribes are being seen in England, France, Germany, Austria, the Netherlands, most of Africa, New Zealand, and Australia."

"Who can we count on?"

"The Brits, of course. The conservative main line media are solidly behind us as are the vast majority of government figures. Australia, New Zealand, Korea, Japan, the P.I., India, and Portugal have declared themselves formally."

"How about here in the U.S.?"

"I have been up to my lower lip in alligators the whole day, ma'am. I'll leave that assessment to the Fat Boys Incorporated and to Rupert Vernon."

"Thanks for holding things together, Gadi. I'd like to ask you a broad question. Where do you think we will stand among nations when this dies down?"

"Well, that is a huge and complicated question. First of all, it does not look like this war is going to last much longer. In the short run, I think we will be pariahs. Mid-term, there will probably be mixed reactions and dialogues about us. Long term, I think we will either be the world's absolute dictator, or we will shrink back into a decidedly more isolated and diminished position. If that is the result, the United States will have a far less powerful influence."

"Perhaps that would not be all bad, given the turmoil of the past ten or so years," the president mused.

"Maybe not. It will take a while to determine the right course, I think."

"Thanks for coming in, Gadi. Keep up your good work. Try to get some rest."

"I will. Good day, Madam President."

APRIL 17, 2010, 1:00 a.m., IRANIAN TIME

The major nuclear attack from both sides was over. The suffering of the populace in the areas struck by the nuclear *Götterdammerung* was like nothing the world had ever seen. And the vicious close at hand battles were about to begin.

Lieutenant General Ayatollah Ali Hassan Sekhavat—the Secretary General of the all-powerful Council of Guardians—sat with his hands folded in his lap, his face impassive as befitted both his religious and his military rank. He watched the army gathering amidst plumes of dust outside his capacious and luxurious command tent. He was one of the few men in the country who was privy to the full information on how much damage the Great Satan had done in the nuclear attacks. He also knew about Iran's involvement in the ICBM launches against the United States, but he only knew what he had been told about the impact those Islamic missiles had had on the enemy. Grand Ayatollah Hussein Aliyy Bilal himself and Sedegh Akbar Bazargan, the Foreign Minister, had both personally assured the military cleric that Great Satan was on its knees.

To prevent any further damage from another—but of course, weak—attack, the general worked feverishly to shore up Iran's defenses. He had been traveling in his personal plane from the time it was safe to do so after the nuclear bombs had struck. He was partially successful. The remnants of the army from the entire command were converging on the main base near Kashan on the edge of the Dasht-i Kavir [Salt Desert]. The site was well chosen because it was still shrouded in the smoke and dust that had spread from the bombing of nearby Isfahan, and it allowed rapid maneuverability in the open desert. It had been a struggle, but the bulk of the remaining armed forces with almost every military asset left in the country were en route to Kashan. The army was well armed from the Iranian stockpiles of weaponry from the Russian arms bazaar, and the men were primed to fight.

Gen. Ayatollah Sekhavat knew full well that the grand ayatollah had made a daring and dangerous decision. The great leader of the Shi'a and of the nation had obviously been inspired by Allah, himself, when he decreed that the defenses of the cities were to be withdrawn to Kashan. The option was more prosaic than that because it was clear to the remaining officers that the feeble garrisons in the devastated cities would be no deterrent to an invasion.

The enemy would find that the cities could be taken as easily as one plucks a chicken. The hope was that the easy entrance into the populated—or one time populated—areas would breed complacence and an erroneous perception that Iran's armed forces were either destroyed or dispersed. Great Satan and its lap-dog—Little Satan—would prove to be ripe pickings when the right moment came. Events had spiraled out of control so fast that Gen. Ayatollah Sekhavat expected what attack there was to be to come soon.

His plan was simple: if the Satanic hordes brought the battle to him, Sekhavat was prepared to hurl everything the Army of Islam had left on the outnumbered enemy in a surprise pre-emptive strike. If the enemy elected to take the remaining cities first, all the better. He would divide into four or five groups of rapidly mobile attackers and strike at the backs of the invaders. The buyers of arms for the Avenging the Crusades mission had been inspired at Rosoboronexport when they provisioned a facile and rapidly mobile fighting force throughout the nations of Believers.

Sekhavat got up from his easy chair and walked to the opening in the front of the tent.

"Omar," he called. "Get out the word that there is to be no unnecessary movement of the vehicles. Petrol is too limited and precious."

Master Sergeant Omar al-Shehhi snapped sharply to attention.

"Yes, sir. Consider it done."

The hastily regrouped Iranian army did not have long to wait for the arrival of its enemy for the final organized battle of the war that was now less than one day old. American C-130s landed on now abandoned airstrips in Saudi Arabia, Iran, and Syria during the late afternoon of the 16th and disgorged rapid deployment mobile battalions. Great cargo ships began arriving in the mid evening and set up supply centers in Libya, Egypt, Afghanistan, and Iraq, unopposed. By midnight of the first day of the ground war, the fundamentals of air and land assault were in place if still less than perfectly organized. The sea was controlled by the U.S. Middle-East 5th Fleet now supplemented by the Mediterranean 6th Fleet with its sixty-five ships, four hundred aircraft, and seventy-five thousand Navy and Marine Corps servicemen and women. Blunt messages had been sent to Germany and France to stay back—since they were not with America in its doomsday war, it would not be wise for them to probe into the waters of the conflict.

The United States Air Force commanded the skies just as the Navy controlled the oceans. No supplies entered the belligerent nations from the sky or the sea; and more moderate Muslim countries including Iraq, Turkey, and

Jordan patrolled their own borders to ensure that nothing was smuggled in by land. No one needed to tell them that it was not a time to test the patience of the American juggernaut.

Reconnaissance flights and satellite intelligence detailed the exodus of the Iranian military from the cities and their gathering in the Dasht-i Kavir. The scanty human intelligence available indicated that a final great battle with the barren land as the massive killing ground was planned by the die-hard Iranians. The Iranian generals perceived the last defense as being akin to the merciless struggle for existence that had characterized the last battles with the invading Iraqis under Saddam Hussein twenty years earlier. As the desperation of that time had required, so did this struggle demand extraordinary sacrifices—the conscription of boys of ten, many of whom were to enter the final apocalyptic battle unarmed and for the first time, women and girls were enlisted. All of the ready soldiers and neophytes had been obliged to find their own weapons; but they were—to a man and woman, boy and girl—ready for martyrdom or triumph.

American and British infrared satellite and air camera images located the spread out distributions of the Iranian defense force, and unmanned drones with IIR—infrared imaging electro-optical devices that were capable of imaging small differences in temperature—confirmed the sightings down to a few feet of precision. The surveillance drones patrolled at 15,000 feet and were able to stay aloft for over twenty hours. They were capable of detecting movement from fifteen miles above, read a license plate, view and record the occupants of a vehicle, and detect weapons. The drones weighed 1,000 pounds, had a wing span of thirty-five feet, and flew at one hundred miles per hour. Pilots on the ground controlled some of the unmanned aircraft, and others were pre-programmed. Each aircraft cost the taxpayers of the United States $2 million. The U.S. drones were on emergency loan from the U.S. Border Patrol Service by request of Homeland Security, and others—Hermes 450s—were loaned by the Israeli Defense Forces.

Air Force Lieutenant General Patrick Davis, complying gladly with the orders of the secretary of Defense and the president, ordered the first sorties under his command to be undertaken by BI-B Lancer bombers and B2s with the Conventional Munitions Upgrade Program including Tactical Munitions Dispensers for wider dispersion range. The huge bombers also employed the JDAM-Joint Direct Attack Munitions Systems using a NAVSTAR GPS mission computer and wiring connections to the bomb bay for high speed MIL-STD-1760 data base to transfer information to smart bombs as needed.

By 0110 the first bombing raids were passing over Kashan, led by EF-111 Raven "Spark 'Vark" Jamming aircraft, followed by the B1-Bs and B2s diving in from 50,000 feet at a speed of 550 knots and starting to lay down a grid-iron pattern of bombing—sixteen bombs per plane. The purpose of the initial raid was to remove belligerent personnel. GPS guided CBU-871 89/97 cluster bomb units and their thousands of contained bomblets were dropped all around the terrified combatants on the ground. The attack was far from a scatter-gun approach. The bombers' APQ-164 radar employed thirteen different modes of detection for ground mapping, navigation, and all-weather terrain following to permit low altitude flight and precise weapons targeting.

It was impossible to escape the hailstorm of steel balls and shrapnel coming at the scattering ground combatants from every direction. Men, women, children, the elderly, professional disciplined soldiers, and conscripted unfortunates were shredded and dismembered in a ghastly giant grinder effect. By 0125 when the B2s and B1-Bs left the theater, fewer than a thousand belligerents remained standing. For them, the worst was yet to come.

Gen. Davis ordered the bombers back to their makeshift bases and revetments for refueling and preventative maintenance and then sent AGM-69 Short-Range Attack Missiles with GPS guidance systems and F-111A Raven Tank Killers and F-117A-10 Close Air Support and Tank Killer planes that surgically demolished every remaining enemy vehicle and incinerated the vehicle's drivers, passengers, and those hiding near the vehicles. All of this death and destruction came upon the Iranians from the dark of night which added an increased quality of psychological horror.

Davis waited until first light to drop in troops. The few hundred Iranian fanatics with guns positioned themselves behind sand dunes, in bomb pockets, and behind burned out tanks and waited for the last stand. Imams harangued them and promised them all of the joys of paradise—their own seventy-five houris—if they would but fight to the end in Allah's cause. Those exhortations were the only effective catalyst to continue for some; the others were too weary to move on or to desert. They simply awaited the inevitable.

The huge reborn C5 Galaxy military cargo planes protected by digital avionics, composite material propellers, and a guard of one hundred F-15 Eagles and A-10s landed and opened their giant rear hatches. 61 ton M1A1 Abrams tanks with their composite shape-charge resistant armor and 105mm main guns, M270 Multiple Launch Rocket System, and BGM-71 TOW anti-tank missile field artillery, APCs, M-119 105 mm Howitzers and M-198 Lightweight Howitzers that fired antitank mines, laser-guided explosive projectiles, and a few dozen superbly trained marines rolled off the transports and onto the hardpack salt floor.

The marines began to advance behind the massively armored tanks on a search and destroy mission designed to remove every last vestige of an organized Iranian military machine. It was already hot, and the marines were sweating under their Kevlar vests and heavy burdens of guns and ammunition. None of them griped about the protective armor. Morale was at an all-time high because the word had come down to every officer and grunt that the president and the secretary of Defense had ordered the planners to avoid any operation that was likely to inflict American casualties.

When a foolhardy Iranian gunman opened fire, the response came with a call to surface artillery to place a well-aimed laser-guided HE Anti-personnel armor round or a Copperhead antitank round from the 155mm Howitzers or to AH-64A Apache attack helicopters and their missiles. It was overkill by anyone's criteria, but it was eminently satisfying. The occasional terrorist who stood up to launch an RPG-7V explosive was picked off the old-fashioned way—by a marine sharp shooter.

The mop-up operation was declared complete at 0800 with capture of seven women and children who raced over a sand dune throwing rocks at nearby American troops. Only one of the seven, a woman of sixty-eight who was hampered by her abaya, was killed by the surprised marines. The rest were driven to Kashan and unceremoniously dumped on a major thoroughfare of the empty city.

With the complete neutralization of the organized Iranian defense force, Gen. Davis radioed his superior. Gen. Lyman T. Cowley.

"Lyman. Mission accomplished. The Iranian military is no more so far as our intelligence can determine. We expect nothing more than sporadic guerilla incidents from here on out."

"Job well done, Pat. Bring your people back to their bases and give them a rest. The army will start the dirty work in the cities or what's left of the cities."

"Good hunting."

Confident in his subordinate's work and his message, Gen. Cowley radioed his infantry commanders to proceed as ordered. Small mobile attack forces moved to the outskirts of cities and towns. A dozen units at a time were deployed with the same simple plan. At the periphery of the populated center—those destroyed by the nuclear attack and those left relatively unscathed—the psy-ops teams called out in Farsi, Kurdish, Turkic, Urdu, and

Arabic for the immediate surrender of all citizens, males first. Every male was ordered to march out with any weapon he possessed held high about his head.

The loudspeaker message was repeated with leaflet drops. The message was repeated three times over a thirty minute period. Any men who complied were hurriedly disarmed; the arms stacked on a small mountain of arms and explosives; and the men were taken away in troop convoys. Women and children came out by the thousands, but only a few hundred men—of all ages—surrendered.

The women and children were taken to an open area and surrounded with army machine gunners where they were searched thoroughly and left to stand or sit in the sun. After thirty minutes, the armed patrols advanced onto the streets of the town or city with much the same unit strength as had been used on the ground at the battle of Kashan. From time to time, a gun shot or grenade or rocket would be launched from a hiding place, most often a sacred shrine or particularly revered mosque.

The Shiite Fundamentalist gunmen presumed that the old rules were in effect: Stupid Americans would be stymied by the convention that the Islamic places of veneration and worship would be protected at all costs, and those places could continue to be useful hiding places for fighters and armaments. However, the rules of engagement had changed since the atomic bombs ruined two U.S. cities. The American infantrymen—instead of engaging in sporadic small gun battles and in exercising great care to protect the religious edifices—simply backed off and called in air and artillery support. After about an hour of this type of response, the Iranian hold-outs began communicating to one another that the old ways of the Americans were no longer extant.

The sensible killers marched out of their mosque and shrine hiding places with their weapons in plain sight over their heads, released their women shields, and knelt on the ground where they were picked up and driven to the hastily constructed razor wire enclosures outside of the town.

The fanatical hold-out would-be martyrs became actual martyrs to the heavy explosives raining from the air and from ground cannon until finally town by town and city by city the message was conveyed even without American or British troops being present. The problem for the occupying force eventually became the logistical one of coping with the thousands of refugees and surrenderees. Nothing about the ruined city bore evidence that it had once been a bustling Muslim metropolis.

Shortly after 1600 on the 16th, Gen. Cowley received enough mission completion reports to be able to convey the message of victory to that point in time to the secretary of Defense and the JCS. President Rowan received the message at 1800 after the information was confirmed by Army, Navy, and Air Force Intelligence and by the CIA. She was having a light supper with the concerned representatives from Central and South America.

The president conveyed the message as she received it then added, "Ladies and gentlemen—my hemispheral friends—you can see that we are pressed, and you can also see that we do not have time to debate fine points over our actions. Please bring out any terrorists and turn them over to us. We will handle their disposition, and you will never have to be concerned about them. But let me make this clear. We will not tolerate the death or wounding of even one more American by a terrorist no matter where or why or how. We will hold the nation responsible in which any such an outrage occurs. Our long-suffering patience is at an end. Do yourselves a favor and get rid of the sources of trouble in your countries.

"Now, enjoy your lunch."

There was not a doubter in the room. After a particularly nice cinnamon tinged flan dessert, the leaders of every American state found his or her way to a telephone and gave orders that would result in the apprehension of the people on the list of subversives and terrorists that the United States had given them in months past; and they had heretofore ignored.

Egypt had no army, navy, or air force left for practical purposes. Gen. Matt Sollinger's search and destroy units made up of SEAL teams, Army Rangers, Marine Recon squads, and British SAS teams all linked with IDF commandos to make a rapid deployment invasion of the country; town by town. Unlike Iran, the Egyptians knew they were beaten; and the coalition forces met almost no resistance; the Egyptians' primal interest now was the avoidance of starvation. The embedded news people wryly commented that it was clear to them that no one in the country had ever been in the military, ever joined a fundamentalist—let alone a terrorist—organization, and no one had ever heard of al Qaeda, the Salafiya, or even the Muslim Brotherhood.

The principle problem in pacifying Egypt was in dealing with the huge populations of scattered country people—the *fellahin*—that theoretically needed to be detained. By evening, the Western forces knew they could never bring in enough guards; so, they elected to allow the obvious noncombatants to return to town and kept only the young and middle-aged men. From those—over three days—the warders confiscated a football stadium full of weaponry which was destroyed in a series of huge explosive detonations. During the course of the search, destroy, and detain missions, some fifty-five thousand extremists who preferred martyrdom in combat to the ignominy of defeat and living under the control of the Great Satan, were granted their wishes, most by explosions from artillery, bombs and missiles. The American and British ground troops kept their distance and were used largely for intelligence reporting—where was the latest group of martyrs hiding and from where were they shooting? The remaining townspeople were left to bury the dead which—for the time being—was the number one occupation in the country. Casualties on the West's side were one SAS sergeant, two American Rangers killed and an IDF captain wounded in the leg by an AK-47 round.

Gen. Sollinger's teams and those of Gen. Davis were allowed three hours of R and R before they were flown to Riyadh where they joined the search, destroy, and detain action already underway under the overall command of Lieutenant General Sir Arthur Fitzpatrick of the Scots Guards, 1st Battalion—the elite unit stationed in Wellington Barracks in Central London. The Guards unit specialized in combat in arid and desert environments. For the past year—during the liberals' giveaway program for the Islamic Fundamentalist terrorists—the battalion had suffered the ignominy of service as a fire fighting brigade in London.

The nuclear decimation of the cities of Saudi Arabia prior to the coalition's central command allowing Western troops to set foot on the Kingdom's ground had been considerably more complete than in the rest of the Arab countries because of the fear by the JCS and the Pentagon that the well-trained and well armed Kingdom would mount a much more effective defense. In the south, it was not difficult to effect pacification; but the remains of a still formidable army and air force persisted in the north above the transnational railroad line running between Al Hufuf in the east and Yanbu'al Bahr airfield on the coast of the Red Sea.

The elderly Scottish General had no more intention of losing men than did his superiors in the American and British commands. He called in every asset in the theater to attack the stronghold northern region because he knew that there were enough Saudi F-15 Eagles, Block 25 F-16C Fighting Falcons, F-106s, F-111F Aardvark Tank Killers, F-100D Super Sabers, F-110Fs, Mirage F-1s and US Marine Harriers to defend against almost any invasion from almost any country for some time.

But today, the United States was not almost any country. The victimized American nation had brought every conceivable asset from half way across the globe into the fray, and the world was about to witness the greatest air battle of all time.

The Saudis kept to a limited airspace but one that permitted the maneuverability they needed. No one in the Saudi command or piloting a Saudi fighter had the slightest underestimation of their formidable opponents. On the other hand, because they were well trained—mostly in the United States—and thoroughly disciplined; none of them considered their erstwhile American friends—now avowed enemies—to be invincible either. The Saudi fighters trembled with anticipation. Maybe they would die, but it would be an exciting exercise in tactics nonetheless.

Ever unpredictable, the Americans and British first sent in Boeing Dragon Eye backpackable X-45 robotic aircraft by the hundreds. The small unmanned planes were wired so that one man could control several of the aircraft, and for the man on the ground it was like having a huge radio controlled model plane. To a man, the experience was exhilarating—all the more because it was safe. The very presence of the small, difficult to detect erratically swooping, diving, and climbing unmanned craft was confusing and disruptive to the individual Saudi dog-fighters' defense plans. The American aircraft moved about erratically and without establishing any pattern the Saudis could identify and intercept, began releasing inert global positioning system-guided 250 pound tactical nuclear bombs on the widespread land army. One third of the X-45s were fitted with down-sized versions of Slammer-AIM-120A AMRAAMs—the quickest, fastest, smartest—and most lethal of the United States' arsenal of air-to-air missiles.

Use of the X-45s had been heavily debated in the War Situation Room at the Pentagon and with the president during the late afternoon of April 16 because of the $12 million price tag per robot. President Rowan had asked only one question.

"Give me an estimate of the number of American and British lives that will be saved by using these expensive little monsters."

Gen. Vladislov Kosinski, USAF, of the JCS, had answered promptly, "Upwards of 750 to a 1000 pilots and that many more on the ground when any land attack commences."

That had been all that President Rowan had needed to hear.

"Use them. Make sure that you expend those $12 million packages at the right place and in the right time."

Gen. Sir Fitzpatrick determined that if ever there was to be the right place and time, this was it. He and his staff were more than gratified with the outcome of their calculated decision. Twenty percent of aircraft the Saudis had in the air when the X-45s appeared were downed and more than half of the land vehicles including APCs, tanks, and HMMVs—gifts of the previously kind and generous Americans—were taken out of commission. The intelligence services monitoring the battlefield estimated that a third to half of all enemy ground troops were KIA or were out of commission by the time the robots were guided to their home base. A total of fifteen X-45s were lost in the action.

Approximately twenty minutes of combat had elapsed; and in contrast to the heavy Saudi losses, no American or British armed serviceman or woman had been injured or killed. While the Saudis were still reeling from their initial beating, the Scots Guards General signaled the air force to launch an all out attack on the remaining airborne Saudi planes. The United States had given the formerly friendly Saudis a generous gift of four F/A-22 Raptors, and the now enemy Saudis were counting on the surprise effect of encountering these stealthy and versatile attack jets would have on the foolishly generous American idiots. *Al Arabiya* TV was jubilantly heralding final victory at 0217, Saudi time, based on the possession of the incredible secret fighting machines by the Kingdom.

The final attack commenced at 0218 Saudi time with the U.S. Command launching one hundred tri-service standoff attack missiles [TSSAMs] with totally unnerving effect on the ground forces. The missiles, fired from more than 180 nm away were stealthy, extremely accurate and—like the X-45s—extremely expensive. They so disrupted command and control and mobile defense systems that the Saudi air traffic controllers and ground forces were useless to the air fighters. The enormous cost of the TSSAMs was justified on this one day.

USAF E-3A AWACS with all of the best and most sophisticated airborne warning and control systems available to any air force in the world flanked the American manned aircraft attack. The Saudis had E-3As, but they did not have the updates of the American planes that made the Saudi AWACS with the same militarized version of the Boeing 707-320 B commercial airframe obsolete in comparison. Airborne surveillance, command and control, functions in a fully mobile, highly survivable, aircraft with a fully outfitted C2 platform was the general characteristic sought by air forces all over the world.

The sophisticated and extremely costly American updates included more powerful CFM-56 engines with thrust exceeding 21,000 pounds so that the Americans could climb to higher altitudes and extend the horizon of its radar observation significantly. The information distribution system was upgraded to the TADIL-J antennae—a GPS Satellite system—to locate the

AWACS anywhere on the globe. Another upgrade included the HAVE Quick A-NETS secure anti-jam UHF radio contact. The Saudis did not have the American look-down quick-reaction surveillance APY 1,2 radar that can distinguish among airborne, land, or sea targets simultaneously over all types of terrain even at low altitudes and can read effectively a 360 degree view for 200 miles. The APY 1,2 radar can detect smaller and stealthier targets than the Saudis counterpart apparatus. This new radar had extremely sensitive IFF [Identify Friend or Foe] capability.

The nerve center of the improved American AWACS—not available on the enemy aircraft—was the new IBM CC2-E multiprocessing command and control computer. The American AWACS units versus the Saudi version was like a rapid thinking contest between a genius level computer PhD and a high school drop out level diesel mechanic's helper.

The American/British attack burst into the plumes of dust and ashes that covered the far flung desert battlefield. Out of the lightly cloudy sky thousands of feet above the unsuspecting Saudis, three hundred VRML 3-D model F/A-22 Raptors—the version the Americans had reserved for their own Military, and had flown all the way from Nellis AFB in Las Vegas for the occasion—dived on their prey like Peregrine falcons on pigeons. For all the conventional Raptors' sophistication, they were nowhere near a match for the latest American fighters.

The VRML 3-Ds hurtled out of the heavens killing Saudi planes two at a time before veering away to safety. Before any Saudi F-18, F-15 Eagle, or Raptor could respond to an attack the American was either gone or had sent a lethal smart-bomb missile into the nearly defenseless Saudi. Two VRML-3Ds got the same signal from one of the AWACS on the periphery, and they attacked a Saudi Raptor at the same time.

They realized the mistake too late and flew into each other at speeds in excess of Mach 1. The Saudi Raptor was so close to the resulting explosion that all three sophisticated fighters were consumed in the accident. Those two American planes were the only casualties of the aerial dogfight. The much vaunted Saudi Arabian Air Force with all of its remarkably sophisticated equipment was destroyed. The pilots and their ground crews were brave and technically efficient. They were the pride of the Islamic world, and they were no match for the now fully engaged Americans and their stalwart comrades, the British.

Psy-ops teams papered the huge battlefield with Arabic leaflets demanding immediate surrender. Fighters remaining alive were ordered to march to Hā'il

Airbase in the Jabel Shammar and to stack their arms. They were then to form ranks in a sitting position and to await the coalition ground forces. Those who complied would be released to safety, and those who resisted would die. The bedraggled former army limped its way to the desolate town and airbase. The once proud Saudi army was beaten and had no means of collective defense.

The Americans and British dogged their footsteps from the air. The forced march without food or drink took two days. The daytime temperatures were 120 degrees, and the nights were in the thirties. Exposure, dehydration, inadequate nourishment, and untreated war wounds took a frightful toll. Men died and were left in the sand by their comrades who had no energy to spare. The Saudis were too exhausted even to hate any longer.

CHAPTER FORTY-ONE

APRIL 16, 10:10 p.m. EDT

Elizabeth Rowan—who had been president of the United States for thirteen—hours, felt that it had been more like the duration of Franklin Delano Roosevelt's three administrations. She knew that she was beyond the capacity for careful thinking, and she should no longer make the kind of decisions that had been required of her during that hellish day.

She buzzed Abigail Young and her Chief of Staff, McDonald Pearson, into the Oval Office.

"We need a new crew. I want you two to brief replacements for the night."

Pearson opened his mouth to protest, and the president held up her hand to stop him.

"I am too tired to make decent decisions, and you are too tired to sift information and to give it to me succinctly and carefully. I am going to bed, and I want the two of you to do the same. Instruct the night OOD to awaken me only if there is something that no one else can take care of."

"We need a new V-P."

"Tomorrow."

"We have a political firestorm mounting in the country, and there needs to be some hard decisions made."

"Tomorrow."

Pearson's adrenaline fueled brain was having a very hard time letting go.

He finally recognized that all of it would keep, and he said, "Then, good night, Madam President, Abigail."

"Good night," said the president and Abigail.

President Rowan found the family bed that President Braithwaite had shared with his significant other, Darlene MacIntosh—the beautiful late ice queen Darlene MacIntosh—when the sophisticate chose to grace the White House. Rowan dropped onto the bed spread without making even a gesture towards turning down the sheets. It had not occurred to her to call a butler. She did notice and was pleased to find most of her personal things had been brought over to the White House residence from the Naval Observatory sometime that day. It was nice to have at least some small familiar thing in her life on that strange day. She slept the sleep of the just.

President Rowan was awakened by a maid at six and was disoriented and grumpy. She apologized to the frightened girl and had a hurried shower, dressed in a grey business suit and pastel lavender blouse, and got the steward to bring her a simple bowl of steaming oatmeal and fresh orange juice. Thus fortified, she made her way into the hall where two serious Secret Service agents flanked her as she went to the Oval Office and her second day as president.

The faithfuls, Abigail and McDonald Pearson, were there to greet her along with her military aide-de-camp, LCDR Scot Parkinson.

Pearson said, "We have good news and bad news. Which do you want first?"

"The bad. Let's get it over with."

Pearson nodded to LCDR Parkinson.

"Madam President, our military victories have happened so fast and are so overwhelming that we are faced with a refugee problem like nothing ever seen before. Not only are the problems logistically incredible, but the national and foreign press are howling. The *Nation* and the *New York Times* are calling for your impeachment, and this is only your second day in office. CNN has been running videos of the pathetic Saudi army stragglers since three o'clock in the morning. The French are demanding that we do something. I need to convey a response from the military, and Secretary Ralston and Secretary ben Elazar asked me to brief them on your decision for civvie street. They asked that we convey their apologies for not being here, but they are engaged elsewhere and thought you'd understand."

"I fully appreciate how busy everyone is. I have given some thought to the refugee problem. Maybe someday when it is perfectly safe, the French, or the Germans, or the Austrians, or the Canadians will decide to help. That someday will have to be after this war is over. I am adamant about no more Americans being hurt or killed. I grieve for the refugees, but I cannot spare the manpower or the money to help them. We must prosecute this war until the Muslim fanatics are unable to continue for the short term or for the long term. I'm sorry; and you can say so to the people who need to know; but I am not going to offer services for these people in the foreseeable future. We will have serious difficulty being able to provide the services our own extremely injured people need.

"Ordinarily, I don't go on about what I think; but rather, I let my actions speak for themselves. But here goes; and, Abigail, you might as well take notes so that those with the need to know will have guidelines as to how I intend to proceed and why. Over the past thirty or forty years of atrocities committed by the Islamic fundamentalist terrorists, no amount of persuasion, diplomacy, placement of economic sanctions, making examples of, police investigations, arrests, trials, or convictions, or limited, cautiously well directed military action has been effective. The policy of appeasement and of pandering to those people because of some misguided enchantment with the value of diversity at any cost resulted in the devastation of our innocent nation on April 16. Our generosity and humanitarianism over and above our forbearance with the acts of war against us, the other Western nations, and Israel resulted only in more hatred and disdain.

"They consider us to be weak and stupid. They doubt our resolve; and I must say, with good reason. That has come to an end. It is now time to effect a lasting change. This action in which we are involved is a war, not an exposé, a political or diplomatic exercise, or a police activity. It is not about a crime, or achieving justice, or making a threat, or even about exacting retribution or teaching a lesson, or making an example. We are going to render those monsters incapable of mounting an action against us, not just to make them afraid, or convince them to be persuaded, but completely unable.

"President James A Garfield put it in proper perspective when he said, 'For mere vengeance I would do nothing. This nation is too great to look for mere revenge. But for the security of the future I would do everything.' I have adopted that concept as my strategy. This war is a cold and calculated effort on our part to destroy and to render wholly incapable those who would destroy us simply because we are Americans or Israelis or British. We have had decades of hand-wringing, listening to the smoke-and-mirror dissembling of the PLO and other terrorist groups, and endless appeasing talk. It is time posthumous to do something definitive and final.

"Now, to the problem at hand, the plight of the refugees. Mary Renault, in her brilliant book about Alexander the Great's childhood, *Fire From Heaven,* described a situation something like the question before us. King Philip,

Alexander's father, in order to take the great city of Olynthos without blood-shed, paid a huge price in gold to city leaders. They, however, considered that Philip was not, in fact, all that strong; and they reneged and haggled more over the price. Philip offered them an ultimatum: join his political coalition or see their city destroyed. The men of the city voted to hold out. So—despite having paid a more than fair price—Philip was obliged to take the city by force and to lose many good Macedonians in the process.

"His response was to defeat the city, to enslave the men and attractive girls, and to send the rest of the citizens south to seek what comfort they could find from their friends, the Athenians. The citizens of Olynthos making their way under the lash, starving, with weeping women and children, and looking like the cities that Greeks had defeated, became the objects of pity of Greeks along their trail of tears. The Greeks in the cities the Olynthosnians passed begged Philip to relent and to release them and to give them help. Mary Renault told of Philip's response: 'It brought a millennial message. This is defeat; avoid it.'"

Her listeners were silent and thoughtful. They looked at the new president's stone face and knew for an unequivocal certainty that the unassuming little women was in dead earnest and beyond persuasion on the matter of all things to do with her sworn oath to protect Americans.

LCDR Parkinson went on to the second of his 'bad news' reports.

"We have lost twenty-two lives, eleven airplanes including drones, three Abrams tanks, and seventeen other military vehicles."

"Abigail, I want to know whatever possible about the killed and injured individuals. I will write a personal note to each of their families. Would you get someone to find a transcript of that famous letter that Abraham Lincoln sent to the mother who lost five sons in the Civil War? I think it was five, anyway," President Rowan asked.

"Yes, ma'am."

"That about it for the bad news, Commander?"

"Yes. Are you ready for the good news?"

"It would be a nice change. Please do go ahead."

"The nuclear attack is over. The heavy bombing raids are done. We will be continuing the policy of fairly mass bombing in areas where there is even minor gunfire resistance. We are already seeing the fruits of that policy. The remaining leaders of many cities in Iran, Saudi Arabia, Syria, and even Pakistan are arresting the known terrorists in their regions and are requesting instructions on how to get them to us. They do not want them remaining in their towns, and they don't want us to think there is any possibility that they are hiding terrorists."

"But, you still have a ways to go."

"Of course. General Prescott estimates that the easy part of rounding up terrorists will take about two weeks. Secretary Ralston has made arrangements for transfer of the worst of them to Gitmo."

Ralston nodded.

"The last ditch hold-outs will take longer—probably a month or two, maybe a year."

"And you are to convey my orders that the war is not over until those hold-outs are eliminated. We are not going to have another Iraq guerilla stand-off situation that drags on and on."

"Yes, ma'am."

At eight, the full cabinet as it was presently constituted, the JCS, CIA, the State Department, and Homeland Security met in the Oval Office and gave the president the most up-to-date briefing they could scrabble together.

Rupert Vernon from Homeland Security spoke first.

"Madam President, as you might imagine, we are a long ways from making martial law a fact or in stopping looting although we are making progress. We have established a truly remarkable telephone network, and the volunteer program is gaining steam even at this early point. I think we will be functioning nearly normally in terms of communications, border protection, record keeping, and in FEMA operations by the end of the week. In the irradiated areas there is not that much we can do yet."

"What do you need?" Rowan asked.

"The National Guard."

"That's a tall order, given that there's a war on, Rupert," interrupted Perry Ralston, the Acting Secretary of Defense.

"Perry, I know that Defense always wants to have layers of back-up; but being realistic, how crucial is the Guard to the war plans?"

"Let Gen. Prescott field that one, if you don't mind, Madam President."

Prescott leaned forward with a thoughtful look on his face.

"It is premature to say so, but it looks like the overwhelming shock and awe that we brought to bear with our attack force has been a successful decision. We are meeting literally no resistance now, although we haven't been on the ground for long yet. I'd say it is reasonable to project that we are not going to have to use a large contingent of troops in Muslim stan. Maybe we could compromise. What would you say, Rupert, if you took half of the reservists and deployed them and left the other half in reserve for call up when the DOD needs them?"

"And I would have to relinquish my troops when you need them back no matter how badly they are needed?"

"That's about it, Rupert. It's a whole lot better than nothing which is what you have at the present."

"True," Vernon said, "and I'll live with it. Maybe the jerks and criminals out there will buy into the help America concept before we face a crisis over the choices in deployment of the National Guard."

"Stranger things have happened, I suppose," Ralston agreed.

"We have made the best progress, surprisingly enough—and I'm embarrassed to say—in the relocation of our Muslim-American citizens. They grumbled some about the unfairness, but there seems to be a majority that are chagrined about what their co-religionists did and are sick of the record of the past thirty years. Today was a clarifying moment; many of them faced the fact that Islam has taken a wrong turn; and they are determined to take their religion back from the fundamentalist murderers. That has translated into a patriotic spirit that has helped a great deal in getting cooperation in moving them to camps. We are scrambling to get the wherewithal to make those camps a reality. We need the legislature to get us enough emergency money that we can feed, clothe, and house these largely decent people properly. That's about all I have, Madam President."

The president nodded then turned to her left and asked Cecil C. Carpenter, "Triple C, give us a capsule account of how business has been affected by the war."

"That's easy," the secretary of Commerce said. "The Dow, the Nasdaq, the S&P, and all the rest, domestic and foreign, are so far down that trading was suspended before opening this morning. All regular air, rail, and truck traffic has been halted until we can be sure that the attacks are over. Somewhere in the neighborhood of half a million people are stranded somewhere they don't want to be. Nobody bought or sold a house today. Retailers around the country have essentially called a holiday since no one darkens the doors of their stores. The unemployment rate today must be somewhere in the neighborhood of thirty percent and could get worse if we don't demonstrate that our country is winning. Maybe you need to give another talk to the country. Meaning no disrespect, but hopefully you could inject some positive items in with all of the doom and gloom. Our quickie prediction for the GDP this year is that it will flatline; the deficit will climb to a record high; and our international credit rating will go down to an historic low and will stay there until business starts up again."

"And—other than that—we seem to be doing fine, I take it," the president said with a soda cracker expression.

The men and women in the room laughed. It felt good to have a bit of levity in a decidedly unfunny world.

"I have a political question for anyone and everyone," the president said. "Tell me how this administration is perceived. Any idea what the approval rating is?"

"You don't want to know, Madam President," said Gadi ben Elazar.

"I do, as a matter of fact."

ben Elazar shrugged.

"Gallup, ABC, CBS, and NBC have all run polls. Basically, nobody knows who you are; eighty percent disapprove of what you've done so far. The near consensus is that you are a monster, but they're glad you're our monster. They blame you for the riots, for the dead people in the bombings, for the maltreatment of the Arab-Americans, for the near nuclear winter conditions in the atmosphere, for the deprivation of their rights under your martial law decree, and for the inefficiencies in the delivery of emergency, social, and health services. Almost no one gives you a pass for hunger, loss of the Eastern states' electric grid, and for the difficulties in getting goods from the stores."

"Otherwise, they seem to approve of my program, then, it would appear."

The cabinet room resounded with a short but cathartic laughter.

"Did I mention that your approval rating is 25%?"

"Not exactly, but thanks for sharing."

President Rowan smiled with her face but not with her eyes. There was a lifetime of world weariness in those eyes that had come in the course of one day.

"Perry, General Prescott?" she asked, "What about casualties?"

"I'm glad to contribute a positive note. Thus far, since the actual attack on CONUS, we still have only lost twenty-two servicemen and women and have fourteen seriously wounded. That can't continue—especially after we get our army troops on the ground—but it is great for the time being."

"General Prescott, I want that to continue as long and as completely as possible. In wars past—especially when we have engaged the Muslims—we have tiptoed around their apparently innocent populations, avoided hitting their mosques and shrines while they hole up in them and launch their offensives from their sacred buildings, and have refrained from pushing an all out attack to avoid appearing offensive in the eyes of our European friends. We lose troops while we work at rebuilding the countries damaged by war and by their kleptocratic governments. I am now speaking as the president and the commander-in-chief of the armed forces. Do not make any of these mistakes in your prosecution of this war. Do not waste American lives on such frivolous concerns as the sanctity of some building. Use air power and arms length weaponry as much as possible even though collateral damage occurs. I repeat: I do not want any more Americans to die or to suffer. It is time for the fundamentalists who fomented all of this to suffer. They prize martyrdom so highly; I am in favor of helping them to achieve it."

"That's music to a general's ears, ma'am. We won't do anything unnecessary to inflict pain and loss on the Muslim people; but unfortunately, they have been placed in harm's way; and many of them will suffer. Many of them already are suffering. The events of the last twenty-four hours have exceeded in one day what the world lost in its two great wars during their entire combined durations. And it will get worse. Thank you for being with us and for us, Madam President."

President Rowan nodded.

"Please, everyone—a week from now—have a report for us on the progress of getting a new, duly elected government. Let's get back to doing the people's work."

The next appointment was with the Senate and House Liberal Caucus leaders. The spokesman was the new caucus leader, Senator Cliff Assure of Nevada. Senators David Christensen of Minnesota, Sharon Holme of Colorado, Helen Clivener of Washington, Carol Amman of Oregon and Daniel Yamamoto of Hawaii accompanied him. The House leaders included the Acting Speaker, Pedro Rodriguez of East Los Angeles, Danny O'Brien of South Chicago, Abraham Levy of Carmel, Mary O'Reilly Yablonski of Montpelier, and Alphonse Dagnall of South Philadelphia.

"Thank you for coming. You requested the meeting, Senator Assure. What can I do for you?"

"I know you're busy, what with blowing up the world and all; so, I'll come right to the point."

He paused to see what affect his deliberately provocative and disrespectful tone would produce. The president had an expression no more animated than the Sphinx.

"First, you were not elected; and you should resign. We can appoint an interim president until elections can be held. Failing that, we will launch impeachment proceedings against you. Second, you and your military thugs have destroyed quite enough of the Arab world—you know, those people who a week ago were our friends, *those* Arabs. Third, we demand that—in your remaining few acts—you do a few decent things. We expect you to order an emergency relief program for the war-ravaged areas. Instead of killing them, we should be donating blood. Instead of fighting the unfortunate Muslims, we are going to launch a war against PID."

The president doubted that Assure meant 'pelvic inflammatory disease'; so, she cast him a querying glance.

"Poverty, ignorance and disease," he snapped, his voice raised half a decibel louder than necessary as if he were speaking to a mentally deficient student.

Even his liberal cohorts winced at the overt display of disrespect to the presidency.

There was a pause. During the pause, the president completed the notes she was taking as his angry message was transmitted. When Sen. Assure did not fill the empty auditory space, President Rowan spoke.

"Correct me if I miss any of your points. I will respond to each of them individually, Senator Assure. First, drawing up articles of impeachment and passing them through Congress is a House of Representatives prerogative. I will cooperate as requested by the House. However—until it is necessary for me to do that—I will keep on with the people's work. Second, and the one thing I will not tolerate in this office is an insult to our brave military men and women who are behaving in a most professional way. They are not 'thugs' and don't ever use such pejoratives about them in this building again."

Her eyes emitted fire.

"Directly to your demand that we cease military action—the answer is no. We have not finished guaranteeing that Americans like you are safe to make your First Amendment comments. The third request that we take care of the refugees—the answer is no. We have nothing left to help those people— the majority of whom contributed to the fundamentalist terrorism cause— because we are in deep trouble trying to assist our own people during the emergency let alone even considering reconstruction of our own country. Our past generosity resulted only in exacerbating the hatred on the part of the recipients."

The president locked eyes with the Nevada senator and paused long enough to allow him to protest or rebut. He fumed, rolled his eyes, and gritted his teeth; but he kept quiet.

"Now, if you don't have anything further, I will—as you suggested—get back to doing 'a few decent things.' Those will all come under the umbrella of defending and protecting the Constitution as I have sworn to do. Incidentally, my oath does not include a responsibility to the rest of the world who decide to attack us."

"I have a few more things, *Liz*," Assure snapped.

"That's enough, Cliff," Helen Clivener stood and interjected.

She glared at the red faced demagogue.

"You are speaking to the President of the United States. I disagree with her, but I will not stand by and listen to you shout her down with insults. You apologize this instant; or you will leave; and we will have a new caucus leader."

Senator Clivener looked at her liberal colleagues for affirmation, and their nods gave her what she needed. The consensus among the liberal enemies of the president but supporters of the presidency was not lost on Sen. Assure. He abruptly stood up and left the Oval Office.

Sen. Clivener apologized; the other liberals mumbled something about being appalled and sorry for the display; but all of them added *soto voce* amendments that the core problems were not over; and they were going to support Sen. Assure's initiatives.

Next, the president welcomed Homeland Security Secretary Vernon and three bearded men in Muslim kaftans.

"Have a seat, gentlemen," President Rowan offered. "Coffee?"

"Thank you, yes, Madam President," the eldest of the three Muslims said.

The steward served them, and they were quiet as they sipped the scalding aromatic liquid. Each person was given coffee prepared exactly as he or she preferred it, a nicety of the remarkable fact gathering service of the State Department and the White House culinary staff.

When the cups and saucers were removed, President Rowan asked, "Now, what can I do for you?"

"Madam President, this is an ad hoc committee of concerned American Muslims. They wish to have you consider the subject of the transportation of the Muslims away from their homes. They have worked out a plan that I think has merit. I would appreciate it if you would give them a hearing, Madam President," Secretary Vernon asked.

"Of course. Do you have a spokesman?"

The eldest leaned forward and said, "I am Mullah Omar Elmenyawi, and this is Imam Ali Ruhani of the Shi'a. On my right is Khalid Mikdadi, a private citizen originally of Saudi origin. We have come to tell you that we are loyal Americans first, Muslims second, and that we personally have had no involvement with the terrorist elements that have attacked our country. We have voluntarily moved where we were asked to go, an inhospitable place called Barstow. We do not complain. However, we possess knowledge of persons who are loyal Americans and some perhaps useful information that could lead our FBI to the apprehension of those who bring shame and sorrow upon us and our peaceful religion."

"I appreciate that you would come to see me, Mullah. I am truly sorry personally, and apologize for the United States that you have been obliged to make such sacrifices. I have spent some time in Barstow, and you don't need to tell me more. More importantly, I believe what you say. Have you a plan whereby we can get you back to your homes, businesses, and mosques and also be assured that your neighbors and the country will be safe? I will be completely candid. There are a substantial number of your American Muslim adherents who have contributed to terrorist causes under the guise of Muslim charities. Your people have contributed more than any other country except Saudi Arabia to the terrorists, in fact.

"I am charged with protecting Americans. I want that protection to extend to you, but I need insurance. If American Muslims go home in large numbers; and then there is some atrocity committed in the name of your God and your religion; it will be all but impossible to treat Islam any differently than the country had to deal with the communist party after the fifties. That may not be altogether fair, but it is reality."

"We understand. As you said, Madam President, we don't especially like it, but we will adjust. Yes, we have a plan to present to you. Please consider that we are sincere in presenting it to you, and we wish to have a consideration in return."

"Go ahead. I welcome your ideas."

"Our people chafe at being considered disloyal just because we are Muslims in much the same way as the Japanese-Americans did during the Second World War. Like them, we wish to be given the opportunity to prove ourselves. This is what we offer: we will conduct our own thorough investigations and will turn over suspects to the FBI and to Homeland Security with all the evidence we can find. On the other hand, we also want the opportunity to give you evidence about individuals that are true Americans; and when you have that evidence to your satisfaction, it would only be fair to release them."

"I have no problem with the essentials of your plan, Mullah. It will take time, because the people of the United States—you included—need to be as sure as possible that we are safe. Furthermore, the people need to trust that their government will not treat any of the problems lightly. Here's what I propose in general: you select from all over the country a board of some dozen ranking Arab-Americans or Muslims of any origin whom you consider to be above reproach. Bring to the FBI every possible fragment of information—good or bad about them—and have them agree to submit to a vetting process akin to that required of individuals who apply for top secret security status. Once that board is constituted, you can make appointments of lieutenants who will hire subordinates to do the actual work. Prepare a dossier on each individual; and when you are convinced that you have someone who should be released, submit it to the FBI; and I will order that they expedite their investigation. It will be cumbersome and slow at first; but once the machinery is in place, I think we can get most of your people home in a year, maybe less. Will you work with me?"

"That is fair, Madam President. It is good to bargain with someone who has her eyes wide open. Ours is a people of hagglers. Once we strike a bargain, we keep it. I ask you point blank. Will you keep your end of the bargain? Our people would be gravely injured as Americans if you were to fail us."

"That is a fair question and one worth asking. I will pledge my personal word and my guarantee as president of the United States. However, I cannot guarantee anything if I am not allowed to stay in office. There is a threat to impeach me. I may run for election in 2012 and lose. I suppose I could die while in office. In any of those scenarios I would be unable to fulfill the promises of today. I promise you, sir, as long as I have breath and can act in authority, the bargain will be kept."

"That is all a man can ask. May I shake your hand, Madam President?"

"It will seal our bargain."

To the chagrin and amusement of Abigail Young, Andrew McKnight, MacDonald Pearson, and Rupert Vernon who stood as witnesses, Mullah Elmenyawi spat on his palm and offered his hand to the president. She did not appear to mind, spat on her own hand, and shook the old man's right hand with vigor.

"Mr. Secretary, will you find people to work with these gentlemen? Make it a priority. In all of our interests, it would be great to resolve this status in less than a year. In the meantime, perhaps you can get some of the regional charitable organizations to work with you as well to help relieve as much of the suffering as possible."

"It will be my pleasure, Madam President."

CHAPTER FORTY-TWO

APRIL 17, 2010, 4:34 a.m., ISRAELI TIME

IDF Lt. David Levy and his eleven man fighting squad and two man vehicle operating crew slowly drove their armored personnel carrier along the buffer zone military road that encircled the southern Gaza Strip city of Rafah, with its population of about 100,000 rabidly anti-Israeli Palestinians. The area was kept under constant military surveillance because it served as a conduit for smuggling arms across the border with Egypt's Sinai. The pre-dawn shadows were inspected by the constantly wary IDF troops who jumped at every stray cat or dog that moved and caressed the triggers on their M-249 mounted machine guns. The number of incidents from the Palestinians had increased logarithmically over the past twenty-four hours since the nuclear war began.

Suddenly, the relative calm was fractured with the firing of a dozen volleys from an RPG-7v. The Israeli APC M-113—the Zelda—made a hard left and bumped across the open space off the road. The driver sped to the wall of the nearest dwelling and hid as best he could in the shadows of the low mud brick apartment building. The TOW anti-tank missile launcher, the turreted 25 mm automatic cannon, and the mounted M-249s were all pointed at the hostile neighborhood. Screams came from the neighborhood of "*Itbach al-yahud*!" [Murder the Jews!] and "*Thawra, thawra hat al nasr*!" [Revolution until victory!] The voices of men, women, and children were in the chorus of strident hate music.

"Taking fire from Tel al-Sultan neighborhood," Levy radioed. "Request back-up and orders to proceed."

Static crackled on the radio for a second then Col. Benjamin Cohen answered, "Pull back as far and as fast as possible. Do not engage. Give us better co-ordinates."

Levy turned to Sergeant Gottesman. Without verbal communication, the sergeant set to work. Shortly, he gave GPS figures down to two feet accuracy.

"I'm guessing on exactly which building, but I think I'm right." Sergeant Gottesman told his lieutenant.

"Close enough for government work, as the Americans say," Lt. Levy said.

He reported the co-ordinates and had the driver back away as fast as they could. They heard the rattle of machine guns trying to find them, but nothing came anywhere near them. In a minute they were on the road and out of range of enemy fire. As they hurried along the dusty utilitarian road, they were passed by an Israeli Merkava or "Chariot" tank. It moved across the buffer open zone and drove directly through a house in the Rafah neighborhood demolishing the building without slowing the tank's progress. Levy's APC was out of sight of the tank when he and his men heard the heavy thump, thump, thump of tank rounds going off. The early dawn sky was lit up with the incandescent shelling. Whole buildings came down, and the area was clouded with acrid smoke.

Two Israeli Lockheed Martin no frills Block 52 F-16C Viper fighters swooped in and fired racks of Sidewinder missiles and dropped Mk 82 general purpose bombs from their wing pylons that leveled two full blocks of the refugee camp parallel to the buffer road in a spectacular series bombing. The fighters made a second run laying a carpet of fire and explosion from AGM-65 Maverick and AGM HARM 85 missiles and 20 mm shell fire from their M-61s. In five minutes from the time the RPG-7v rockets were fired by the insurgents, the battle was over; two-thirds of the camp was a pile of rocks and two hundred dazed and shell shocked people appeared out of the smoke and gloom to make the familiar trudge to safer areas. Their houses, mosques, and madrassahs were gone—twenty-two thousand of them were now homeless.

Soon there was a long line of dust covered refugees limping their way to the next town, also called Rafah, for some reason. They received a lukewarm welcome from local homeowners already overcrowded with survivors of the previous day's and night's combat. Many of the citizens of Rafah were beginning to question the utility of continuing the struggle against Little Satan. It was all well and good to talk of martyrdom and the glories of God that awaited them and to speculate on the future of a Muslim world unhampered by the presence of *kaffirs*, but it took little imagination to realize that there was not going to be a Muslim world at all if this kept up. Some of them were refusing to take in fighters for fear of reprisal. The Israeli message that further resistance was not worth the terrible cost was sifting into the Arab community.

Shortly after the action in Rafah, rockets were fired from the Gaza border at the Israeli town of Sderot. The IDF response was the same as in the Rafah refugee camp—destruction of the perpetrators.

By eight fifteen, a total of eighty-one separate incidents in Palestinian territory had converted the previously precarious peace of two days before into a renewal of frank war. That war was decidedly one-sided, and Palestinian fighters left after the recent major IDF thrusts were being killed by the scores along with a terrible toll of collaterals including children. A few brave imams were openly advocating a unilateral cessation of hostilities by the Palestinians before it was too late. No Israeli had been killed or wounded in the past eighteen hours.

Imam Haji Farouk sent a neatly typed note to the Israeli government stating that the Palestinians would declare an immediate cease fire and would send representatives to a peace conference as soon as one could be arranged. He listed two conditions: All Israelis were to be removed from the West Bank and the Golan Heights was to be turned over to the Palestinians as a precondition to the cease fires. No one in the Israeli government had ever heard of the Haji and no one among the Palestinians seemed to know who he was either.

IDF Lt. David Levy's platoon was handed the message; and, acting as the Israeli government, Lt. Levy penned an immediate reply.

- No.
- There is no such "people" as the Palestinians. Jews were the original Palestinians and the few—some 228,000—Arabs who were present in the area at the time of Israel's creation were then and are now are the same as all other Arabs in the region. They were there by resettlement no farther back than 1882. 75% of the Arabs of Palestine are either immigrants themselves or descendants of people who immigrated in over the past 100 years. Those Arabs who left their homes and dispersed outside the boundaries of Israel did so at the orders of the Transjordanian Army in large part, not by the Israelis.
- Henceforth, the area referred to by the army of the Kingdom of Transjordan and the five other Arab armies who invaded the Jewish state of Israel on the first day of its existence as the "West Bank"

has been returned to its original names—Judea and Samaria—thereby doing away with the myth of the "West Bank".

- The 400 square mile plateau called the "Golan Heights" was part of Syria as determined by the British-French agreement and that was to be temporary until it reverted to its final status as part of the Jewish National Homeland as defined in the Balfour Declaration. That area was captured and is controlled by the state of Israel as a result of an unprovoked attack by Syria—the so-called Six Day War—which ended in another defeat of the Arab armies—there being no such thing as a "Palestinian" army.

David Levy, Lt., Israel Defense Forces

At eleven o'clock in the morning the same day, the runt army of Saudi Arabians struggled its way into Al Gazzālah in the northern desert. It was evident that they would not be able to go on. Men were dying and being left all along the way. Jackals and ravens fed on the corpses, and none of the men had the strength to stop them. Following the orders of their Wahhabi mullahs, almost none of the men had dropped their weapons or the bandoliers of ammunition they carried strapped around their chests.

The senior Mullah, Abdurahman bin Abdullah al-Wahhab al Shaykh gathered the fighters still able to stand upright, about a thousand in number.

"Brothers, you are still valiant freedom fighters, and together we will finally defeat the infidels and Jewish Occupiers who are the offspring of pig mothers and monkey fathers. We must keep our sacred faith, remember our vows, and go underground with the expectation of rising on a new day to emasculate the followers of the Great and the Little Satans.

"I will negotiate a peace with the infidels in order for us to survive and to carry on. You must do everything in your power to keep your weapons even though they demand that we give them up. We will turn in a small number of our guns as a token, eat their bread and meat, and bleed the beast for all we can obtain then; we will fade away into the desert before they know what we were about. They are blind donkeys, and we will show them our superiority once again. Remember that we have the exclusive favor of the One God, the Beneficent Allah. He will bring us to final victory despite the present temporary setback. He will honor the martyrs.

"*Allahu Akbar!*"

The response from the exhausted and dehydrated men was feeble but unanimous. Imam al-Wahhab was gratified. He sent a note to the enemy commander, the one who wore a skirt like a woman, explaining the Saudi position and willingness to negotiate. The imam demanded a meeting of men to arrange a peaceful parting of the ways of equals. Specifically, to Gen. Sir Arthur Fitzpatrick, the soldier-cleric outlined a meeting plan. The American/British force was to place 1000 men on the desert floor meeting place to stand face to face with the 1000 Saudi fighters. The Saudis would lay down their arms in an orderly fashion while facing similarly unarmed Americans and British. The Saudis would then be fed and clothed by the opposite army, and would find their own ways back to their homes to live in peace.

Gen. Sir Fitzpatrick smiled at the arrogant tone of the imam's request for terms.

"There are no terms," he told Col. Sanchez. "We will be happy to meet and collect their arms. Every American and Brit will keep a firm hold on his weapon. We have no food to give these fanatics. Convey all of that and arrange the meeting."

Sanchez left out some of the more colorful portions of what Fitzpatrick had said and in the fluent Arabic he learned at Fort Ord, arranged the meeting for the following morning. Nothing was written. The 1000 well dressed, well fed, amply armed victors marched out of their air conditioned fighting vehicles and formed up in good order four abreast The column marched directly towards the ragtag defeated army in an impressive show of military order and power. A fife and drum corps played *Yankee Doodle*. When they were fifty yards in front of the defeated enemy soldiers and religious officers, the column split into two and marched at the double around the flanks of the enemy 1000 until the miserable remnant was surrounded.

From the troop trucks came the horrendously loud blaring of the heavy metal group AC/DC's pounding lyrics:

I'm rolling thunder, pouring rain
I'm coming on like a hurricane
My lightning's flashing across the sky
You're only young, but you're gonna die
I won't take no prisoners won't spare no lives
Nobody's putting up a fight
I got my bell I'm gonna take you to hell
I'm gonna get ya, Satan get ya
α&θ
Hells bells
Hells bells, you got me ringing

Hells bells, my temperature's high
Hells bells

The Satanic song was repeated in Arabic for the benefit of those of the remnant Saudi army who did not know English. The effect of the dark threatening music was nearly stupefying to the exhausted and dispirited Arabs. They changed from proud to inappropriately hostile to defeated. The coalition force took ten minutes to set up defensive emplacements and held their weapons in the crooks of their arms with the same stiff state of readiness as had characterized their march. When they stopped their movements, the music faded away.

Sr. Master Sergeant, Terence Y. Jones barked, "Ready, sir!"

British Captain Barkley Atcheson and American Marine Captain Amos Rothman exited their vehicles and walked smartly across the uneven sand to where Imam al-Wahhab al Shaykh was standing with his two minor clerical aides.

Capt. Atcheson snapped a salute and, in his exaggeratedly clipped Etonian accent asked, "*Hai tatakalum Al Engleaziah?*"

"Of course, I do," snorted the imam.

He presumed that the ignorant American infidel did not speak the language of God; so, he did not deign to inquire of the other coalition soldiers.

"We are the representatives of the coalition army. This is Captain Rothman. Our mission is to collect your arms so that you can disperse and return to your homes. I am ordered to inform you that not a single one of you will be allowed to leave until every weapon is piled in the center of this meeting ground. Once that is completed, you will be allowed to leave in groups not exceeding four in number. Have you any questions?"

"Where is your general? I demand to be treated with respect and to meet the commanding officer," the imam said haughtily.

He was gravely insulted, not only that the ranking officer had not appeared, but also because the quiet American marine was so obviously Jewish. Rothman's name tag was over sized and displayed a Star of David before his rank. He had a prominent nose, a thin studious face, thick glasses, and black hair. He was the stereotypical Jewish man. May God curse that race.

"The general declines. You will treat with us," Atcheson said flatly.

Imam al-Wahhab turned to his left to get the reaction of his subordinate. As he did, a large explosion took place in the rear of the Arab ranks. One of the soldiers—a recruit from a Riyadh Wahhab madrassah—who saw this as a last chance to prove himself worthy of the legion of martyrs who had preceded him, had strung three garlands of grenades around his chest and hid them under his loose desert robes. He had been standing at attention with his knees locked when he fainted. His finger was locked on the wire that connected all of the firing pins. When he fell, he gave a spasmodic jerk and set off the entire string. The zealot and fifty of his comrades where shredded by the explosion.

Arab soldiers with their weapons secreted under their clothing who were standing peripheral to the carnage made the logical assumption—the soldiers of the Great Satan had started a slaughter of the defenseless Muslims just as the Christian Crusaders of the twelfth century had done. They were men, and no man would stand by and allow himself to be slaughtered like a sheep.

"*Allahu akbar!*" screamed one of the men.

A hundred Arabs swiftly pulled out their hidden weapons and turned them in the direction of the surrounding Americans and British. Before the stunned coalition troops could react, seven of them were dead; and another eleven were wounded. Eighteen Saudis were cut down as collateral damage by the wild firing of their comrades.

The disciplined American and British troops opened fire at the core of the insurgent fire distributing a withering cross-fire pattern from right to left in a systematic and relentless order. The mass of Arabs—enlivened by the last great fight—began a disorderly fusillade at random, killing many of their comrades and wounding six more coalition soldiers encircling the Arabs. Imam al-Wahhab reached under his filthy robe and drew out a 9mm hand gun. His reflexes were slow. Capt. Rothman shot the man twice in the chest and once in the head from a distance of five feet. Capt. Atcheson dispatched the imam's two aides.

The American/British troops systematically raked the hysterical Arab fighters who were dropping like scythed wheat from the controlled machine gun fire. The air was filled with the shrieks of the dying and wounded and the steady staccato cacophony of the now one-sided gun fire. In seventeen seconds it was over. No more coalition soldiers were lost, but only twenty-two of the one thousand Arabs remained alive and only fourteen of them were unwounded. The rest were critical and were beyond help.

The two coalition captains held up their hands for cease-fire and sent men to examine the fallen bodies. One of the captains waved to the truck drivers, and Hells Bells blared again. It was a fitting accompaniment to carnage. The fourteen relatively unscathed fanatics were stunned by the horror around them. They knew that the army was no more—that Saudi Arabia was no more—and they presumed that their God had abandoned them. And things were about to get worse.

Capt. Atcheson ordered the remaining fourteen to be fed and clothed.

When the bewildered and defeated but now satiated men were done with their meals and had had time to admire their new camo fatigues, Capt. Atchison ordered, "Put all but one of them on cargo flights, half to Damascus and half to Tehran. Let them tell their stories there."

The semi-hysterical men were dropped off as ordered and immediately began telling their wild tale of defeat, betrayal, and humiliation to the already devastated survivors of Damascus and Tehran. In each city there were enough religious police left alive to execute the lying defeatists. It was necessary for the executions to be done by the sword because there were not sufficient guns and ammunition to use that method. The swordsmen were inexperienced and multiple attempts were necessary to complete the sentences. The fourteen soldiers were dispatched one by one and had to stand by in a mute state of shock as their turn approached.

Capt. Acheson radioed for two back hoes to be flown to the site. The pilot and crew brought along three 50 gallon barrels of rendered pork fat. Six 100 meter long, eight feet deep trenches were dug in parallel rows in a north-south orientation. The enemy bodies were dumped into the trenches in haphazard piles, none facing Mecca. The pork grease was poured over the rapidly decaying bodies, and dirt was plowed over them. The lone surviving Saudi watched in horror. The smell of the pig fat was too much; he vomited until he fainted. The allies pulled away from the now unexciting desert scene. The survivor was left to his own devices to get back to where he could tell his story.

The fate of the Saudi army did not make the local or international news.

CHAPTER FORTY-THREE

APRIL 21, 2010, 9:00 EDT

President Rowan had given three national media addresses on the course of the war, but had not had to face the questions of the free press until today. This was her first true press conference, and she dreaded the impending experience. However, she was rested and was sure she had a firm command of the facts. She and Andrew McKnight had gone over and over the potential questions. Her face and hair were done up better than usual and considerably better than she did them herself. Her fitted charcoal gray business suit was set off with a business card size American flag on the left breast pocket. She wore a light pink silk blouse with a single strand of small pearls around her neck. The president felt a little off-balance in heels taller than her regular shoes, but she had to admit that the effect was just the right touch.

The press secretary looked her way. She nodded.

"Ladies and gentlemen, please stand for the president of the United States."

The room was as full as it could be arranged for the national and international press. There was even a grade school newspaper reporter in attendance with a notebook, pencil, and serious expression. Some ten reporters conspicuously remained in their seats.

McKnight frowned and shook his head, then said calmly, "Please take your seats."

"Good morning, ladies and gentlemen of the media," President Rowan said. "I'll start with a short comment then open for questions."

"Skip the face-saving commentary. Let's get to the hard questions," shouted the reporter for the *Legal Times*.

He was dressed in a tie-dye shirt over unwashed denims. His blond hair was dirty and done up in dread-locks. He wore sandals made from used rubber tires. He waved his arm to get her attention.

Andrew McKnight stood up and said curtly, "This is the president of the United States. You will show proper respect, or you will be escorted from the room. Those of you who did not stand for President Rowan may not agree with her or her policies, but you were asked to show respect for the presidency. Behave yourselves."

President Rowan smiled indulgently at Andrew and gestured with her head that she would handle it. The *Legal Times* journalist took the hint finally and sat down.

"I will give a short commentary. As of an hour ago, the coalition forces have completed major offensive operations. Our military personnel are no longer encountering resistance of any significance, and we are moving town by town and city by city to ascertain whether or not there are any remaining cells of terrorists that threaten us. Our policy is that no more Americans than absolutely necessary will lose their lives; enough of us have perished already at the hands of the Muslim fundamentalist terrorists and their supporting organizations and nations. Our military and central intelligence people are now reporting that municipalities, provincial leaders, and common citizens are bringing forth terrorists that are still hiding among them. They are also yielding up weapons at a rate that is taxing the capacity of the people in our military who are responsible for collecting and destroying them. I do not know how long the process will take, but our best estimates are that it will be weeks, not months or years.

"Within our nation, the emergency and volunteer groups have joined together in a massive search and rescue effort. Unfortunately, the damage and carnage from the thermonuclear attacks were so absolute that most of the search and rescue phase is over; and we are beginning a reconstruction phase to get traffic moving, support services into place, and business back up and running. We will start nonemergency public sector transportation and private trucking, air traffic, and allow our railroads to get back into operation today.

"Now, your questions."

Up went a forest of hands and an indecipherable bedlam of voices, raised and gesticulating arms, banging on chairs and stamping of angry feet. The president waited calmly until the clamor subsided.

Somehow the unruly journalists quieted and allowed one polite hand to be raised.

"That's Mary Cagney from the *Madison Capital Times*. Skip her for now, Madam President," Andrew whispered.

President Rowan laughed and said, "Go ahead Ms. Cagney."

"Mary Cagney from Wisconsin—*Madison Capital Times*, Ms Rowan."

There was a soft hum of murmuring.

President Rowan looked Cagney directly in the eyes and waited. Cagney dropped her eyes first.

"Madam President, reports from the Middle-East indicate a slaughter, a holocaust visited on the helpless Muslim people. What do you have to say to such charges?"

"Let's be straight here. The world has had a holocaust. That is when the Nazis murdered six million Jews in cold blood and about that many more Gypsies, homosexuals, retarded people, Poles, Russians, and Germans who dared to speak the truth. Our attack in the Middle-East was a direct straight-forward defensive response to the vicious nuclear attack on ourselves, the British, the French, and the Australians. I am sure you are well aware that ICBMs with MIRV nuclear warheads were also fired at us and would have taken our country back into the stone age. I take full responsibility. I ordered the response, and I stand by the fact that it was necessary to do so to save Americans and the Constitution which I swore an oath to defend. It is regret-table that innocents had to die. Have you been to what was once Detroit? You can see the slaughter of innocents up close and personal in your own country. I repeat, Ms. Cagney, *your* own country."

"Garret Phillips, *San Francisco Chronicle*. Madam President, do you sleep at night knowing that you have killed more people than Hitler, Mao Tse Tung, and Stalin put together?"

"Yes."

The president pointed at a handsome African-American man on the third row who had been waiting politely with his hand raised.

He stood and asked, "President Rowan, I am Meriweather Atwood Brown from the *Chicago Sun Times*."

"I'm familiar with your work. It seems thoughtful and objective."

"Thank you, Madam President. I have a question on a different tack. My sources inform me that you have ordered the attorney general to investi-gate and then to arrest the officers of the Tides Foundation. Is that because they have such a long and loud record of opposition to war—this war being no exception."

"No, sir. To do so would be akin to having a Nixonian enemies list. The Tides Foundation exercises its First Amendment rights regularly. They have come under investigation because it is alleged that their Action Center has had a heavy communications traffic with the leaders of the terrorist organizations that attacked us, and it is further alleged that their Democratic Justice Fund has been active in easing restrictions on Muslims including specifically requested waivers for individuals known to be terrorists by the FBI during the recent past administration.

"There is evidence enough to allege that that fund directly supports the Council for American-Islamic Relations—a group with close ties to Hamas. Finally, there is evidence that is more than suggestive to allege that the Tides Foundation actively supports the National Lawyers Guild and that organization has had one of its attorneys arrested for materially helping a client— Sheikh Omar Abdel Rahman—communicate with terror cells in Egypt. You may recall that the Sheikh was the master mind of the 1993 WTC bombing. There is suspicion and mounting evidence alleging more involvement with terrorist organizations. I will repeat myself, Mr. Brown, I have sworn an oath to protect the Constitution, and I consider these people to be a potential and possibly an actual threat."

The acting secretary of State walked quietly up behind the president and whispered to her. She nodded almost imperceptively to him.

"I can take one more question, then I must leave."

"Ivan Peterson, Madam President, *New York Times*. You say you are responsible. Your decisions seem so rash. Wouldn't it have been better to have waited, consulted the United Nations, the EU, NATO, our French and German allies, gotten a consensus? Couldn't we have used diplomatic means, negotiations, maybe even sanctions before embarking on this genocidal war?"

"Mr. Peterson, I informed all of those you mentioned, but the decision to act was mine. It was not a time to dither or debate or delay. I believed then; and I still do, based on indisputable evidence, that our nation was under a preemptive strike attack intended to destroy us completely. I acted. I did so on the same basis that Tom Paine suggested just before the patriots responded to unbearable actions by the British tyrants. He said, 'If there must be trouble, let it be in my day that my children may live in peace.'

And I'll tell you this, I intend to continue to mount our defense because I also believe what Samuel Adams had to say in that same revolutionary war era, 'The liberties of our country, the freedom of our civil constitution, are worth defending against all hazards, and it is our *duty* to defend them against all attacks.' There are those among us who appear to believe that their First Amendment rights give them an obligation to attack and demean everything their representative government does or stands for. Heroes have died to give such critics that right, but the "anti" press should take time to reflect on the damage they do to that cause."

More hands went up; this time in respectful and thoughtful silence. The president waved pleasantly to the assembled media reporters, turned and followed Gadi ben Elazar out of the room.

"What is it, Gadi?" she asked when they were out of earshot.

"The president of Indonesia needs an immediate call. He says his countrymen are getting ready to riot and agitators plan to behead every Christian in the country because they have been fed rumors that we are about to attack Indonesia."

"That's all we need is for the horrors of this war to spread still further. Let's get back to him as fast as we can."

"Her."

"Oh, dear, I am so woefully under prepared for all of this. Give me the particulars as we walk, Gadi. I don't want to insult the lady by accident."

ben Elazar helped President Rowan with her pronunciation of the unfamiliar name and gave her a few pointers of protocol.

The red phone in the Oval Office was connected to Jakarta, and the panicky voice of the Indonesian president came on the line almost immediately.

"What can I do for you, Madam President?"

"Please, Madam President, tell me, do we expect an atomic bomb attack even this very day?"

"No, Madam President. Our two countries have had a long and friendly relationship. Our information over those years indicates that your country has maintained a moderate stance in the Muslim world, and your government is a voice of reason in an inflamed area. Yours is the largest Muslim country in the world and therefore exerts considerable influence for peace. We have no desire to attack you and no desire to do so.

"However, I have to tell you, that our country was attacked by Islamic extremists who operated with the connivance of national governments to which our country turned a blind eye in times past. The United States can no longer afford to do so. I will be perfectly frank, Madam President. Your government is run through with terrorist sympathizers. You have been at best lukewarm in your pursuit to uncover and prosecute the terrorist organization, Jemaah Islamiyah. We would rest easier if you and your police and armed forces were to arrest and detain the known terrorists in your country. We would consider it a major demonstration of solidarity with our efforts to eradicate violent terrorism if you would deliver these murderers and warmongers to us for disposition."

"I understand, President Rowan. I want to be able to give our excited people something concrete. Would you please invite our ambassador to the White House and with full press coverage hand him a formal letter of agreement. Specify that you guarantee by the honor of your country that you will not attack and in return, our ambassador will publicly guarantee for my government that we will deliver any and all terrorists we can find and arrest?"

"I will do that today, but Madam President; this cannot be a token measure. It must cut widely and deeply into Jemaah Islamiyah. We will hold you, your government, and your people responsible if you fail and if terrorism comes out of your country to affect us or the British or the Israelis. That will be made crystal clear in the letter. I will say now what I have said from the beginning of this dreadful war. If any individual, organization, or nation supports the murderers who attacked the United States—even after the fact—we will respond in a way that will leave no one in that grouping *able* to attack again."

"That is acceptable to us. We can use this with our frightened people. They will understand the harsh bargain I had to make and will help us in their own interests. Thank you for communicating with me."

"It was my pleasure. I wish you well in your efforts. Please keep us informed."

President Rowan put down the receiver. ben Elazar smiled his approval.

"You have another call. The French foreign minister is on the second line. Seems he wants France to be a part of the action after all."

"Hmmh," Rowan said.

She pushed the speaker phone button.

"Madam President, it is a great pleasure to have the opportunity to speak with you and to reaffirm the long friendship between our two countries. I am Pierre de Gastogne-la Croix. My president has just today appointed me foreign minister."

"And what may I do for you, Mr. Foreign Minister?"

"Ah, no, Madam President, it is what our country can do for you. We share the common experience of having been attacked by terrorists, and we offer our services to help in your efforts from this point forward."

"In what form would this 'help' come and; to be fully candid, what would you expect in return?"

"My government has directed me to offer the services of France toward rebuilding the infrastructure of the war-torn Middle-East nations including our businesses, military personnel for security, and our governmental servants for administration."

"What would your military provide in the way of security, Monsieur la Croix?"

"We would be happy to render major buildings—even industries—secure."

"And, I take it that you would not be participating in the present combat." La Croix paused from the briefest of moments.

"That is substantially correct."

"Could you give me an example of a building or industry that would be the beneficiary of the generous French offer?"

"Well…, for one, we would be willing to watch over the petroleum industry of Saudi Arabia, or even Iran or Iraq."

Gadi ben Elazar, listening to the conversation on the speaker phone rolled his eyes and pantomimed putting his finger down his throat to elicit gagging. President Rowan stifled a laugh and covered it with a cough.

"The area of former Iraq has some one hundred billion barrels of oil reserves, and Saudi Arabia has considerably more than that. I suppose it is possible that there is a profit to be made. However—we could expect—in the present terrible circumstances that France would be altruistic toward the world community, no?"

"Well…, Madam President…, the usually articulate La Croix stammered.

The president went on, "To the second half of my question. What would your nation expect in return for all of this generosity, sir?"

"Madam President, we French would take an altruistic approach—no territory, no reparations, no power. Rather, we will gladly assist in the rebuilding of the petroleum producing industry and guide it into successful business directions that will benefit the severely depressed Middle-Eastern economies."

The president turned her head and pinched herself; so, the French foreign minister would not hear her snicker.

"As you can well imagine, Mr. Foreign Minister," she said, "it is too preliminary in the struggle to be making concrete plans for the future. Secretary ben Elazar will get back to you when the dust settles sufficiently."

There was a disappointed pause at the French end of the line.

"Thank you, Madam President; I will convey your message to President du Plessy. We will await your communication."

When it was certain that de Gastogne la-Croix was no longer on the line, the President and Gadi had a cathartic laugh.

"What hubris," the acting secretary of State said finally. "Now that we have a moment to think of it, how do you think we should handle the oil question?"

"I have given it some thought. Actually, a few years ago when I was in the Independents Club, we tackled this very possibility. We pretty unanimously decided that the petroleum industry of the world—but at the very least of the Middle-East—should be internationalized. Maybe we should create a cartel along the lines of the DeBeers Diamond Cartel. A governing body would supervise production and distribution. The profits which would be kept within reason would create jobs in the supplier countries, and pump revenue into the national coffers. Those profits would not be on the obscene level that OPEC created. And—more importantly—the profits would be spread out so that the poor and underprivileged would get a real share."

"I like the idea. Where do the French fit into that scheme"

"They, like the Germans, would be spectators."

Gadi laughed.

"I really favor having the British run that show and not us. I think we should begin a stepwise phase out of our involvement in affairs in that part of the world. Would you get with the Departments of Energy, Commerce, and State and get the ball rolling. The more I think of it, the more I believe this is a golden opportunity to get the work done from the ground up. Get me a feasibility report by two weeks from today, Gadi."

"I will, Madam President," he said.

President Rowan fielded calls from the leaders of Morocco and Turkey with much the same conversation as she had held with Indonesia. She ended each call with a requirement that the country deliver its terrorists. The president emphasized the long and fruitful friendly relationships with the countries and left each foreign president with the iron-fist-in-a-velvet-glove pointed suggestion that their terrorists be delivered up in the next few weeks and not just the low level operatives.

"Mr. President," she told the Turk, "you have been soft on your Islamic Great Eastern Raiders Front for years. That organization is nothing more than a frank al Qaeda cell. I understand your delicate position with the Islamist party nipping constantly at your heels. However, the world has changed. Islamic parties no longer wield the political power they did a week ago. Terrorists get no compromises or special favors any more. I am going to tell you what I have told every other caller on this subject: If you cannot rid yourself of the terrorists, we will come in and help you. We will no longer tolerate the threat they pose to the world."

Admiral Gordon Y. Chang, commander of the Naval Forces of the People's Republic of China, spoke quietly to Captain Jong Fat Lee, and the captain gave the orders to have the fleet command anti-aircraft carrier point its bow east towards Quemoy and Taiwan. An armada of seventy-eight capital ships followed on the calm East China Sea. The PRC Air Force began flying provocative sorties ever closer to and then into the Republic of China's air space.

Chairman Chou Heng Po, seated in his office in Beijing, nodded to his assistant, who handed him the hot-line telephone to the island province.

"Good morning, Mr. President. It is a fine day. What is it that I can do for you?"

"Your armed forces are provoking us again, as if this would come as news to you. Before there is a tragic miscalculation, we demand that you back away, and stop your incursions. We are not blind or feeble minded; we see your naval force."

"I am glad of that, Mr. Hang. Then we can dispense with frivolous diplomatic beating around the bush. Today is the day you knew was coming. This is the day that China takes control of its off shore island province. The People's Republic has been patient for three-quarters of a century, and our patience has finally worn out."

"We will fight you to the death—on the sea, in the air, and on every foot of our homeland. The losses will be most terrible on both sides," President Hang cried excitedly.

Party Chairman Chou remained aggravatingly calm. The eighty-three year old veteran of fifty years of political infighting had not survived by being emotional. He was a steely pragmatist although his frail elderly frame belied the steel within. He was wrinkled; he wheezed; and for some anachronistic reason, he clung to his habit of wearing colorless Mao jackets. He had once been five foot seven inches tall; now, the ravages of his poorly nourished youth and his old age osteoporosis had robbed him of two inches. He sat with one leg up on an ottoman to nurse thrombophlebitis.

"It does not have to be that way, my countryman. We could effect a smooth and painless transition together without bloodshed or reprisal. I will make you three guarantees. If you will welcome us instead of fighting us, we will leave you and most of your party members in their places in government. We will not damage your magnificent shrines and museums, your government buildings or military establishment. Finally, we will not interfere with and in fact will encourage your profit based economy. We will give you fifty years to make the full transition to governance by the Peoples' Republic."

"We will not be brow beaten or black mailed, Chairman Chou. We have the United States at our side. Are you ready to take on the Americans as well as us? Maybe even the British since they do as they are bidden by the Americans."

"I have no desire to brow beat you, my friend. I want us to work together peacefully and profitably for all our Chinese people. I believe that you have miscalculated in one respect. Perhaps you should give the new American president a call and see what their intentions are before you make any unfortunate and irrevocable decisions. I will be in my office for another two and a half hours. I will be happy to take your call. In the meantime, the Red Army and Navy and Air Force are under my orders to continue to your area. They have been directed to commence hostilities once they cross your twelve mile territorial sea line. Once they do, all of my guarantees are null and void. We will be especially unsympathetic towards governmental officials who put up the resistance that results in the death of Chinese people and destruction of Chinese property."

The chairman hung up abruptly as President Hang began his reply to the bellicose pronouncement from the leader of the most populous nation in the world.

Hang—sitting on pins and needles in his ornate office—gave no more than a moment's thought, then requested a direct call to the new American president. It took a few moments to get her full name for the Republic of China's president.

President Rowan was in conference with the JCS, the DOD officials, and secretary of Defense Ralston when the call came through. The agenda of the meeting was largely completed; so, President Rowan took the call.

"Good morning, Mr. President. What occasions the pleasure of this communication?"

"War, Madam President. The PRC is on its way to the Republic of China in force. Chairman Chou as issued an ultimatum to us. An ultimatum! He says he will bomb us or govern us and let most of our institutions remain. I told him we could count on our steadfast American friends and that the costs to him of an attack would be prohibitive. Madam, I am convinced that Chairman Chou is not bluffing. I have never known him to do so, as a matter of fact."

"President Hang, the world order has changed dramatically in the last few days. The United States is in a war that is depleting our resources at an alarming rate. Our military machine is spread far too thin already, and the PRC knows that full well. My main hope is that they will not increase tensions in Korea or Japan or Southeast Asia. They have assured me that this will not happen, but they required that we not interfere with their operations in Xinjiang. Can you imagine their response if we interfered in the union of your island and China? It can't be lost on either one of us that the U.S., the PRC, and you made an agreement to allow the union to take place peacefully. They are taking advantage of the currently unsettled world situation; and I don't care for that; but you and I both knew that this day had to come. They just made it come about unilaterally."

"Will you help us or not?"

"No. I cannot. We do not have the resources to open another front. The PRC is no Syria or Iran. I suggest that you save your country and your people by bending with this wind. What you have is worthless if you are dead."

"Then, I must bow to the inevitable."

"Good bye, Mr. President."

President Hang gnashed his teeth and screwed up his face in unimaginable pain. He contemplated suicide and letting others face this ultimate disgrace. He knew that would be cowardly, and he was a brave man. He called Admiral Ho.

"Admiral, where are they?"

"Seventeen miles out. We cannot fight them without nuclear weapons. Shall I ready them?"

"No, Admiral. I order you to turn back and stay within five miles of our coast line."

"For what purpose, sir?"

"I must have some room to negotiate. My orders must be obeyed to the letter and to the minute. Otherwise, we stand to lose all."

"I understand the order and will comply."

Admiral Ho was neither pleased nor proud of the order, but he did understand. So, this was the inevitable and dreaded day. He shrugged and did as he was ordered. When he conveyed those orders down the line, he made it understood that he would brook no resistance.

The next call made by President Hang was even more painful.

"Derek?"

"Yes, Mr. President?"

"In a very few minutes I am going to turn this island over to the Chairman of the Chinese Communist Party. I have no reasonable alternative choice. Our only other option is impossible—the destruction of all we have built all of these years. I am asking you as chairman of the party to get the message out to our people and even to the opposition. This is the time, if ever there was one, for us to be united to be able to bear the unbearable. Will you do what I ask?"

"Yes, Mr. President. You know that I have long favored a step by step union with the mainland, and I have no opposition to doing it immediately, given the circumstances. I will have trouble with the conservative wing, and you may even have to exert force. Are you ready to do that?"

"I see no other choice. We must do everything in our power to have our beloved homeland survive and even to thrive. I cannot allow a few old men and women to dominate this process. There is no time."

Derek Chun hung up and started a telephone blitz.

President Hang called Chairman Chou.

"We will give you what you ask. Will you allow us to save face by propagating the fiction that this hand over was secretly negotiated over months and that we are welcoming you with open arms and in the spirit of brotherhood?"

"But of course. We will remain outside the twelve mile boundary until you can set up placards and appropriate signage. Do not attempt to trick me, President Chou. The results would be catastrophic for you and your country."

Within the boundaries of the State of Israel, quiet prevailed; not the quiet of peace, but there was a kind of exhausted calm on the part of the ordinary Arab and Jewish citizens. That is why the explosions that shattered the morning's sense of ease were so disturbing, even to the Arabs. They had—for the most part—come to grips with the idea that survival and peace were better than the decades of nerve-wracking violence and uncertainty. Rocket fire and machine gun bursts coupled with the usual hate-Israel, hate-Jews rhetoric blasted out of the large Jabaliya and Kalandia refuge camps, known Hamas strongholds, aimed at the passing IDF patrols on opposite sides of the camp.

It was the ill fortune of Lt. David Levy once again to be the leader of the patrol that served as the lightening rod to draw the Palestinian fire.

"Sergeant Gottesman, call in the position, and we will move out of the area. The shooters have to be stupid, crazy, or suicidal. The brass will level the camp, and there will be no more non Israeli Arabs left in the country inside a week. Those fools had to know that."

"You credit them with too much of a thought process, sir. This is what has gone on since 1948 and without let-up since the intifada started in '87. The fundamentalist zealots don't care a whit about anyone else in their quest for martyrdom. It's like a drug. Well, they're finally going to get their wish."

Gottesman radioed the command post while the three vehicle patrol made a sharp right turn into the relative shelter of the west side of a mosque in the Brazil neighborhood. In fifteen seconds, six IDF jets streaked into view and systematically carpet bombed the refugee camp in a gridiron pattern. There was no attempt at making surgical strikes, or in any way sparing buildings or people. The responses in the past several days were directed at people who would not learn; and now, extermination was the only aim. That aim was accomplished with awe inspiring efficiency. Buildings, automobiles, donkey carts, trucks, and religious shrines were turned to rubble. The shrieks and cries of the wounded and dying punctuated the short intervals between explosions. Thirty seconds later, there were no more planes and no more explosions. The human cries now dominated the audible sensory input. Minutes later, zombies covered with blood and dust shambled out of the ruins and began walking aimlessly to the west away from the Israeli border.

Unlike previous times when the IDF units pulled back to await yet another round of outrage followed by seven-fold retaliation, a large ground force moved forward over the now ephemeral border. Tanks, APCs, troop trucks, and columns of marching men all came out of the dust clouds and began entering the destroyed villages, towns, and cities of the Palestinian enclave. Over ten thousand armed citizens of the twenty-one stubborn island Israel settlements in Gaza and four in Judea and Samaria joined in the search and capture march. The men and women of the IDF and the settlements moved with grim determination from house to house and from rubble pile to adjacent crater or rubble pile rousting survivors. There was not a shot or shout or protest of resistance from the beaten refugees. Like the refugees from Olynthos, after the city was conquered by Philip of Macedon, they had grasped the millennial message; this is defeat.

The bombardment continued on into the night. Lockheed Martin AAQ-13/14 LANTIRNs [Low Altitude Navigation and Targeting Infrared] for night sorties with Terrain following Radar [TFR] capability made the night runs almost like day attacks. The Palestinian hold outs were systematically pounded into dust, both men and buildings.

During the night and into the next morning, disheveled and terrified Arabs began walking out of their homes and neighborhoods and villages toward the west as they were being driven by the inexorable conquering force close at their heels. The families joined small groups of neighbors and in turn these groups united with crowds of weeping but otherwise quiet refugees. The crowds became hordes as the erstwhile Palestinians began marching out of Beit Lahia, Beit Hanoun, Dura al Qara village, what was left of al Bureij and Nafah refugee camps in the Gaza Strip, Nablus, Ramallah, Bethlehem and Gaza City. They poured out of Jebaliya—nearly 100,000 of them—in a few hours depopulating the Palestinian's largest refugee camp, the most densely populated place on earth.

They were driven by fear. Fear of being machine gunned, fear of being run over by the IDF vehicles, fear of being clubbed by the Israeli soldiers who now formed a column on each side of the stumbling rabble. The ominous presence of AH-64 A Apache helicopter gun ships hovering close overhead and IMI Negev light machine guns riding incongruously in the back of pick-up trucks menacing the marchers added to the Stygian quality of the scene. The only possessions accompanying the walking lost were those things they could carry on their backs and most of those things were abandoned along the pot holed and treacherous roadways.

There were no gun shots; no one was crushed by an Israeli military vehicle; and no person was clubbed or otherwise molested by the grim faced young men and women in Israeli uniforms. The angry Israeli settlers were kept at bay by the military and soon; they too, marched in an orderly fashion keeping their Uzis, IMI Margals and Tavors, Galili's, and A-Ks trimmed. No one in the column of refugees even considered trying to escape or make an unauthorized turn to the right or left. No one had the energy, and there was no place to go.

The walking damned were hungry, thirsty, and tired; many were injured; but on they went until they were herded into large shoving and shouting groups at the water's edge. They cursed each other, fought and kicked at one another, robbed the weakest and most vulnerable. Their world had become a Hobbesian state, a jungle where every man and woman was an enemy to every other man and woman. The many and the strong preyed on the few and the weak. Some of those began to die.

At first it was hardly noticeable, then the huge mob became aware of an inexorable push toward the sea. Their bodies pressed ever closer to each other and the stink of unclean bodies and of fear was stultifying. The westerly most ranks began to step into the water because they could no longer resist the crush of the crowd. It dawned on the people closest to the Mediterranean what the Israeli plan was: they were going to be forced into the sea and as a people to drown and be forgotten. Grown men began to cry; women and children screamed. A few more of them were forced into the water. Some of them were now up to their waists and looked as resigned as captured Chinese rebels marching without hope to their beheadings.

Imam Haji Farouq was near the eastern border of the horde, the line of bodies nearest the Israeli military machine. He recognized with dreadful clarity what was happening and looked around wildly for a way out. He saw none.

Then, he happened upon a face he recognized among the Israeli soldiers. Lt. David Levy was sitting impassively on the front of an Abrams tank whose gun was pointing directly at the imam.

Farouq was a brave man. He turned away from the mob being pressed into the sea and walked determinedly towards Levy.

"You," he shouted. "Levy!"

Lt. Levy looked in the direction of the shout and recognized the once arrogant and defiant imam. He gestured to the cleric to approach the tank.

When Farouq was close enough so the two men could talk, Levy held up his hand to stop him.

"What is it, Imam Farouq?" he asked in a flat and uncaring tone.

"This is inhuman. This is the holocaust except this time the Jews are the Nazis. You must not do this. The Jewish people will never forgive themselves. Stop this!"

"What alternative do you offer, Imam?"

That stopped the cleric. He tried to calm himself to think. He was joined by three other religious leaders, men with a history of being more moderate. He had refused to recognize their authority or to listen to their advice during the years of the intifada; now, he desperately turned to them for the solution to the apparent genocide taking place to his rear.

The three ranking Muslims and Imam Farouq leaned their heads together and launched into an animated discussion.

Sergeant Gottesman gestured to his platoon to center their weapons on the clerics in case their response was a suicidal one. Lt. Levy seemed unconcerned as did the several IDF officers who were now monitoring the situation. It was a surreal scene of genteel debate in a swirling maelstrom of pushing and shoving and cursing and pointing weapons around them.

Farouq appeared to be the spokesman for the small group of Muslims. He faced the Israelis.

"We have an alternative. We will convince our people to leave, to go into the Sinai—which, after all—is not so far from here. We will promise never to fight you again. You will not push us into the sea. That is all we ask. Let us go. Let there at last be peace. For us it is the peace of the defeated, but it is survival. What do you say, Levy?"

"I am not the officer in charge."

"And I am not the Grand Mufti; but we are men, and we can do something. I will convince our people. All you have to do is to use one of your magical communications devices and the answer—perhaps even the authority—can be yours."

"How do I know that we can trust you, Muslim?"

"We have nothing left but to do this thing. How about a show of mercy, Jew?"

"I can only try, Imam Farouq. I will do that."

"I will begin this minute," Farouq said, "Please get your military machine to stop here. Give me half an hour, just half an hour. I will return if I still have breath, and we can learn of each other's success."

The four mullahs hurried into the seething crowd and began shouting their message of bitter hope. Given the alternative of being pressed into ocean or being killed by the awful implements of war behind them, a ground swell of grudging acceptance began to spread.

Levy watched with amusement. He gave a thumbs up to his fellow officers who passed the signal on down the line.

Levy radioed Col. Rabinowitz. "Sir, they have made the suggestion. I believe they will march into the Sinai just as the P.M. predicted. Maybe it's premature, but I think we've won."

Col Rabinowitz answered, "And none too soon. I was afraid we would have to back off before we had a drowning. Good work, Lieutenant. Go ahead and continue to represent Israel. You've done a good job so far."

He laughed, partly at the elaborate macabre joke that was playing out and partly in relief.

It was forty minutes before the four mullahs were able to fight their way back to Levy's tank.

"What did you learn, Lieutenant?"

"I have orders to wheel about and face south, Imam. It all depends on you now."

"I need to stand on top of your tank."

"Sergeant, help the cleric up."

Farouq clambered aboard and made his way to stand on the top of the turret. Gottesman held his hand to steady him. The imam shouted in his deep baritone voice that somehow carried over the tumult. He gave his message in Arabic half a dozen times before the great mass of people finally grew silent. Their stunned expressions indicated that they understood their Hobbesian choice—submit to the dreadful will of their new sovereign or perish in short order at the whim of that sovereign.

A murmur passed through the crowd. The IDF officers and men understood the one word that carried over the soft murmur of voices—*na'am* [yes]. Some said, *mish momken* [impossible], but they were drowned out.

The four mullahs were joined by another hundred who moved to the new front of the multitude. They urged their co-religionists along, and shortly the massive collection of rudderless humanity heeled to the left and swung south. They marched the few miles in a few hours and began spilling over the Egyptian border. When the last child crossed the border, the IDF guards allowed them to fall where they were and to rest.

"We perish of thirst and hunger, Lt. Levy," remonstrated Imam Farouq.

"I have nothing for you. You will have to make do in the desert. You are people of the desert. You will find a way."

"Many will die."

"Sadly, yes, but this you brought on yourselves. Tomorrow you will be moved thirty miles into Egypt and left to your own devices. We will be quit of each other then."

Levy's face radiated as much feeling as a stone. The years of enduring murders and destruction within his harried little country had left him cold towards the perpetrators. He had used up all of his emotions when his beloved little three year old daughter and his wife were blown up on a day-care center bus ride. There was nothing left for the murderers he now looked down upon.

"Can we not at least talk, Levy?"

"We can, but my orders are final; and they come from the highest source in our nation—the Israeli people."

"I will not ask more, but I would like to know why you—you personally—hate us so? We are of the same Semite blood, after all."

"I will tell you, Imam. I don't hate you. My fellow citizens have never preached hatred towards you, but we have had to protect ourselves everyday since 1948 from you and the likes of you. The atrocities have been going on since the history between our peoples began. I know that you can recite every response by Israelis and know only the pain that came from those responses. You do not even have the objectivity to look upon our actions as responses.

"So, I will tell you; and you can carry this with you and perhaps use what I tell you when you attempt an explanation of why you are in a state of misery out there in the desert. In the eighth century Idris I wiped out a large number of helpless Jewish communities. The Jews of Fez endured a massacre during the eleventh century and again in the fifteenth century. On that occasion only eleven Jews out of thousands survived. There were similar massacres of Jews by Muslim neighbors in Basra in 1776, Algiers in 1805, again in 1815 and still again in 1830, in Marrakesh in 1880, and in Mosstaganem in 1897.

"In each of those atrocities, the Jews—people just minding their own business—suffered extortion, seizure of their property, destruction of their houses, businesses, synagogues, even their tombs—all by Muslims. In fact such treatment was the regular rule for the Jews living under Muslim rule. April 4, 1918, during the Nabi Musa Muslim festival in Jerusalem, Jews—

and most of them old men, women, and children—were beaten to death, burned alive, and stoned. Their homes and stores were looted. In August 1929 a pogrom run by Muslims in Jerusalem, Hebron, and Safed caused the deaths of 100 Jews.

"During 1941 and 1942, the Grand Mufti of Jerusalem, Haj Amin, helped create the Muslim SS units in Yugoslavia and became a close friend of Adolf Eichman. As a reward for his services, he was given the privilege of being taken to Auschwitz to see for himself the thoroughness of the work of extermination in progress. He laughed in glee and gloated over the mass murder of the Jews. In June, 1941, 400 Jews were murdered in Baghdad, and their property looted and destroyed. On May 30, 1972, 24 of us were murdered in cold blood in the Lod Airport Massacre. On September 11, 1972, 11 of the most cherished of our young people were murdered when they went to Munich to participate in the Olympic Games.

"And...most significant to me, one of your martyrs murdered my beautiful little girl and the love of my life, my good wife, Miriam, who never hurt anyone in all of their lives. There is not a single soldier out there," he pointed behind him at the assembled Israeli army, "who has not suffered such a loss just because his family member was a Jew."

Levy turned and walked away leaving the Muslim mullah to chew on his words.

CHAPTER FORTY-FOUR

APRIL 30, 2010

Congress worked with singleness of purpose to reconstitute itself and had filled slightly over three-fourths of the vacant seats in the House and all but five seats in the Senate with full members replacing the acting members. The majority and minority leaders reported that accomplishment to the president along with the further success of having eight of the seventeen governors who were killed being replaced by emergency elections.

Senator Clivener said, "Madam President, we expect that it will be six months before we return to a full complement of elected officials, and the appointees requiring confirmation will take up to a year, I'm afraid."

"We need the four members of the Supreme Court replaced, Senator. Partisan politics aside, the country cannot go on without that vital arm up to its constitutional strength."

"Our caucus will never sit by and let you railroad in a bunch of red-neck conservative Luddites, Madam President. I'm sure you know that."

"I'm not sure I know any Luddites, myself, Helen. What objective evidence do you have that I am a political conservative of the Michigan Militia stripe, anyway?"

"I guess I am just making a presumption, but your conduct of the war wasn't exactly the way Bill Clinton would have handled it."

"I'll easily grant you that. We would still be feeling their pain and looking for root causes. I have a proposition for you—a fair one—I think."

"I'm ready to listen, at least."

"The people of the United States need to have an intact and functioning Supreme Court *tout de suite*. We just don't have time to fumble through *Martindale Hubble*."

Senator Clivener nodded her agreement that the government and the people had to have a method quicker than thumbing through the national registry of attorneys. She indicated her willingness to listen.

"We have a Judicial Selection Committee in place with the concurrence of both parties—even the far left and the far right—that was established during the Braithwaite administration, a rather liberal administration at that. The purpose was to relieve the logjam of appointees and to avoid the colossal waste of legislative time in partisan posturing over the choices. I propose that we resurrect that committee and get them to come up with a balanced Supreme Court and go on to get us good people at the lower levels in the judiciary. I am perfectly willing to require a political litmus test—no extremists of either persuasion be considered. Those who get to the nomination stage will be qualified and as moderate as is possible. That will give the future a fifteen to twenty year head start on rational judicial performance. After that, we will probably get back to the pre-Braithwaite status quo that was so abhorrent. At least we will have a chance at rationality during these crisis years."

"We will take the suggestion to our caucuses. I doubt that there will be much serious conflict over that idea. You could have mounted a fight for a stacked court of your own political people—whoever they may—but you didn't. That is a plus that I will take back to the liberals. That I promise," said Helen Clivener.

"Any other pressing items, Helen?" the president asked, knowing full well that impeachment proceedings were well under way, but that the press of other business in the House and the obstacles placed in the way of progress of that unpleasant scenario by the conservatives in the House Judiciary Committee had so far prevented the issue from coming to a committee vote.

"I gather that you are not one for pussy footing, President Rowan; so, I will give it to you straight. Cliff Assure tells me that the House liberals have the votes to bring the matter of impeachment to the floor of the House. It is only a matter of time. You can stall the matter by refusing to give us the details of the decision making prior to and during the war, but you won't be able to hold it off forever. You will be impeached in the House before your term of office is up."

"Not to be argumentative, Helen, but my sources tell me that the votes are not there even to get it out of committee. All of that is speculation, however. I will give you any record from the executive branch that does not compromise the war effort. I will never willingly allow a single piece of information to leave the administration that will result in the death of a single American soldier. I have one observation. Your people pandered to the communists before and during the Cold War and succeeded in rallying public opinion during the Vietnam War to injure the war effort and turn a military victory into a political defeat. Maybe you should have a close look at your motives against me and against this war before you use your not inconsiderable influence to weaken the resolve of Americans."

"You are challenging my patriotism, Madam President," Clivener huffed, her face red. "Just because I happen to have a difference of opinion on the issues. That is unpardonable."

"And a hackneyed and obfuscating argument, Helen. There is nothing personal. Your First Amendment rights remain intact. All I suggest is that you consider carefully what an attack on the commander-in-chief right now would mean to the country and especially to the armed forces."

"We'll have a new president and chief officer, and the public will hardly blink an eye."

"Any possibility that I am looking at that potential new choice?"

"Don't keep impugning my motives, President Rowan. As a matter of fact, Cliff Assure seems to be the more likely candidate with me as veep. I haven't made up my mind."

"I hold no ill will against you, Helen. In the meantime, please work with me on these nonpartisan, American issues. Together we have a country to run. The impeachment business will take care of itself, and the chips will fall where they may. Until then let's keep on the track of winning the war, getting out of the Middle-East, and rebuilding the country and its economy."

"We have an agreement on that, Madam President."

Gen. Prescott presented his daily report to the president.

"There is no more war, per se, Madam President. We are now dealing with an immediate problem of what to do with the armies of detainees being brought to us by every city, political party, religious group, and government, such as they are, in the Middle-East. There is no more room in Guantanamo. No one has the least enthusiasm about putting up a prison in CONUS. I need some help in finding a place for these former terrorists. Incidentally, we are not having a bit of trouble with them. They are a beaten lot. However, we will have to corral them soon; or we will have trouble. We are ignoring the refugees; even if our country had not suffered its own terrible and costly losses, we would be unable to cope in any meaningful way with the glut of displaced, hungry, dispirited people who lack just about everything."

"I have given this some thought, General. I will contact Carlos Sanchez over at the Bureau of Prisons and will get him to make a prison system for the less violent of these men near the complex in Florence, Colorado. I want you to make some sort of assignment of capacity to do us harm, and we'll take the least terrible of them and hold them in Florence. I will dispatch the wardens and administrators of the Federal Penitentiaries in Purgatory, Arizona, Marion, Illinois and Leavenworth, Kansas to find a spot in the Sinai where we can keep the really bad actors. I'll put a fire under them; so, we can get the situation under control as rapidly as possible. It will not be a choice for the vanquished countries. This will be another example of what defeat looks like."

"Thank you, Madam President. The only other item, I guess, is that we will need to load the prisoners onto some of the big naval vessels returning home. I will get the sorting done and have the ships fitted out as floating brigs. We will have eight, maybe ten helicopter carriers, half a dozen fighter carriers, including the *Nimitz* and the *Forrestal*, and the battleships *Iowa* and *New Jersey* coming back by the middle of May. The air force is sending home a couple of C-5 Galaxy cargo planes, one C-17, and several C-130 model Js. We can handcuff quite a few of them to wall clips to get them back to CONUS."

"I get asked every day more than once; so, I have to ask you. When do you think we can withdraw?"

"That is now more of a political question than a simple military one, ma'am. We can leave tomorrow morning, and the Arab world will not be a threat on any large scale for years to come. We would leave America haters, and they would find suppliers. The French are still around, and they want to participate in reconstruction. That means getting at the oil to pay for weapons."

"The world press wouldn't like you for saying such things, General, but you do bring up a very real concern. We have to stay until we can have adequate assurance that the rabid fundamentalists cannot rebuild a terror machine. I will make that concern the number one topic on this week's cabinet agenda. I'll get back to you on the answer to the question I posed. Your problem is to secure the oil reserves for us and the rest of the world and to be quiet about it."

MAY 5, 2010

All but two members of the new cabinet had been approved by the Senate, and all of the new officers were becoming comfortable in their positions. The two unconfirmed members of the cabinet—Education and Treasury— had acting secretaries in place. The mood had lightened enough in the inner circles to permit the occasional bit of levity, and the cabinet's work was progressing more smoothly as a result of the relaxation of the sense of continuous emergency status.

"It is good to see you all," President Rowan said and looked around the room at her hand picked counselors. "I have your summary reports and have made copies for every one. Please take the time to read them, because today, I want us to brainstorm about a matter of the utmost importance in the effort to end this war and to allow us to withdraw. The secretary of State will outline the problem and State's proposed solution."

Gadi ben Elazar walked to the far wall and pulled down a multicolored map of the traditional countries of the Middle-East as their borders were defined prior to April 16. The map had a series of transparencies rolled up above the main map.

"The issue is this," he began. "We have a major and a minor problem to solve before we can leave the military theater or even really begin to do so. The major problem is how to extract ourselves without leaving a vacuum that will be filled by terrorists who right now may be latent, or expatriate to the countries with which we have just fought a war. We need to leave functioning governments, but we cannot permit the potential for regaining power that would eventually threaten us. The Arab way is for a strong man to emerge from the military officers and to claw and murder his way to the top. He becomes a tyrant, abuses his people, establishes a standard kleptocracy, and begins to build a secret terrorist organization to attack us. We need to prevent that historically repetitive cycle."

"You don't think that the military loss they have just suffered will persuade them to back away from confrontation and from the sponsorship of terrorism?" Secretary of Transportation, Timothy Willows asked Elazar.

"I don't think so. Certainly not for any length of time. No, we have to have a plan that will materially interfere with what the nascent strong man wants to do no matter how brutal and cold hearted he may be. With the president's blessing, we at State have developed a plan. Needs some tweaking and surveying, but we feel strongly that we are on the right track. First, take a look at the old map—the map of a month or so ago."

He pointed to the large letters of the country names on the colorful map. Then, he dropped the first transparency over the colored map. New borders were shown. The projected new countries being shown were far smaller than the original ones. There were no names, just numbers.

"The idea is to break up the countries now while they are no longer functional and create boundaries of new, smaller, more ethnically homogeneous nations. In some instances, and for a variety of reasons, some of the countries will be larger even than they are now.

"First, consider Israel, Turkey, and Palestine."

Elazar used his laser pointer to outline new boundaries. Israel's borders now included the entire Beka'a valley and the fertile southern one third of Syria to a point just above Damascus and most of the southern half of the Sinai. Turkey's new territory took in the fertile northern valley segment of Syria including the area once occupied by Aleppo.

"In the interests of lasting peace, we have come to a compromise with the Turks," Elazar said. "They get northern Syria, a border that has been disputed forever. In return, they give up a portion of their southern and eastern territory to form a new nation of Kurdistan. The northern portion of Iran and Iraq will join this portion of Syria and be included with the present country of Kurdistan to the north to form the large, rather arid country that will have a sparse but homogeneous population. The Kurds, in return, have agreed to a long term peace pact with the Turks. Further, they and the Turks have agreed to have the United Nations monitor the peace process in perpetuity. Iraq stayed out of the war and agreed to the new boundaries in return for obtaining the oil rich northern one-third of Saudi Arabia."

"And, presumably, the old antagonisms over oil continue with this new arrangements, isn't that about it, Gadi?" asked Steven Capelli, Secretary of HUD.

Capelli had survived the nuclear attack in Detroit only because he came down with a severe case of gastroenteritis the day before the peace celebration and had been hospitalized in D.C. when the bomb exploded.

"I'll get to that. Matters are complicated, but we certainly have no intention of ignoring the issues surrounding oil," answered Elazar.

He drew the red line of light from his pointer from the Iraqi border city of Jabal Unayzah, where Jordan, Iraq, and Saudi Arabia joined, and across to Mecca.

"This is the proposed new border of Jordan."

He then drew a line a quick line from Medina to Qatar.

"Above this is Iraq except that Kuwait takes this eastern section down to Qatar. Because Qatar, Bahrain, and the United Arab Emirates supplied conduits and safe passage for terrorists but did not participate in the war, their territories remain unchanged."

The red light outlined Yemen. The transparency showed four divisions.

"Historical Yemen is no more, and these four divisions roughly represent ancient tribal areas that will now become sovereign states. Look over here at Egypt."

The transparency showed another four divisions.

"Here, in the area of Cairo, the borders extend to the Sinai portion of the Palestinian territory. It is a small but rich agricultural area, or will be again once the radioactivity subsides. The other three divisions are new countries. Note that the Sudan is similarly divided. The southern half is to be a Christian and black African Muslim enclave to halt the fratricidal conflicts with the northern Muslims. Libya is divided in half with the western portion going to Algeria who, in turn, gives up a segment of their eastern territory to Morocco to end the prolonged dispute over that bit of desert."

The secretary of State paused for a sip of Perrier.

"Eastern Iran down to where it borders with Pakistan goes to Afghanistan which was helpful to us during the war. They provided landing fields and launching areas for our invasions. Iraq gets the southern one-third of Iran; Iran itself occupies the middle third of what was once its territory."

The cabinet members pondered what they were seeing.

"Any questions?"

"Oil," said Steven Capelli.

"Right. We are going to internationalize oil reserves, drilling, and refining in the entire new Middle-East. We have been in negotiations with the British to run the program. American, British, and Venezuelan companies will provide the expertise at a modest profit. The French aren't happy about it, but President Rowan made that an absolute."

"Score one for the president," said Rupert Vernon.

"I wanted to have the distribution of oil changed from a capricious dictatorship reaping obscene profits for a few to a new system where legitimate business practices prevail. The Middle-Eastern countries—now quite a larger number than before—are benefited by having their citizens be the major work force, one that is paid decently. The United Nations will provide security. They had to be argued into doing so, but the perceived benefits of getting us out of the region made it worth almost any sacrifice to them," said the president.

"Do all of these new countries form their own constitutions and governments? What do we do about the inevitable fundamentalist Islamic state that will appear? Are you building in safeguards against the military dictatorships that the region seems to spawn at the drop of a hat?" asked Devlin Prince, the new attorney general.

"All good questions. Roughly, we will supply a standardized constitution and leave the details up to the new countries to work out under our watchful eye. The new constitutions will include provisions prohibiting Islam from being part of the government or the judicial system. There will be a built-in absolute separation of mosque and state. We are at a new beginning stage with one real advantage. The militaries of these countries are almost nonexistent. Their constitutions will include a Japanese-like restriction to a purely defensive military with only short range, non nuclear weapons. Light arms will be permitted only for a small defensive force and for police. The public will have no rights to bear arms of any kind; the prohibition against guns will be run on the Singapore model with severe penalties for possession of a firearm of any description at any time. Same goes for drug possession because drug trafficking has figured so importantly in the financing of Islamic terrorism."

"I'd guess all of this will take a few days to implement," said Perry Ralston, Secretary of Defense, dryly.

"It will be a gradual process that will take all the rest of this administration and that presumes that President Rowan gets elected for two terms."

"What do you see the more or less final role of the United States in the region and in the world for that matter, Gadi?" asked Ralston.

"I'll field that question, Perry," the president said. "We are going to get out of the world policeman role. We are going to get out of the relatively recent role of world welfare provider. The United Nations, Europe, most of Africa, and all of the Middle-East except Israel have long had a schizophrenic relationship with us. They want our money and military protection, but they don't want us to have any voice in the use of that money or military force. We are going to change all of that as one of my administrations's overriding policies. We are in serious economic straits as a result of the attack on us and what we had to expend for the war effort. Until things change significantly, we will suspend payments to the United Nations; we will stop the hemorrhaging foreign aid policy."

"That include Israel?" Vernon asked.

"Yes. Their defense needs should be miniscule now in comparison to pre-April 16, and they will have a rich agricultural section added to their territory. They are marvelously efficient farmers, and they will make a success of feeding themselves and running their economy without further help from us. In general—in this brave new world—we will become honest traders and brokers and will do business as business with foreign countries without the previously omnipresent political ramifications. I know that's somewhat naive, but it will be more of a principle than it was in times past."

"What about the terrorist prisoners—both short and long term? That's a real Homeland Security thorn and will undoubtedly be a major problem for the new nations and for our self-protective foreign policy," asked the Homeland secretary.

"I asked Carlos Sanchez to come today to brief us on his progress. You all know that he's the director of the Federal Bureau of Corrections. I have to say that I had my misgivings about that appointment, made when I was attorney general, but he has blossomed in his job. I think he has done small wonders in the brief time he has had to work on the problem."

She signaled the guard, and he opened the cabinet room door for Sanchez. The strikingly handsome Latino—dressed to the nines in a black suit, pink shirt and same color tie—strode confidently into the room.

"Thank you for coming, Mr. Sanchez," President Rowan said. "You have the floor. Tell us about the new world of prisons."

"Thank you, Madam President. At the president's direction and under the supervision of the FBI, CIA, Homeland Security, and the Departments of Justice and Interior, we have developed a plan and have begun the first phase of it. We will have long term maximum security prison additions in the Federal prison camp in Yankton, South Dakota, U.S. Penitentiaries and Correctional Institutions in Florence, Colorado, Littleton, Phoenix, Bastrop, Big Spring, and Seagoville, Texas, Terminal Island, California and Marion, Illinois.

"We will build modern secure correction centers outside our national borders as a foreign aid measure, then turn over operation to the countries in which those prisoners are now held. We will provide appropriate planning and education for the locals in Palestine, the new Iranian, Syrian, Pakistani, and Libyan entities. Right now, every one of these prisons will be heavily guarded hard wire cage construction like the situation in Guantanamo. This is labor intensive and expensive. In the future, and as fast as possible, we will build secure buildings to house these terrorists. Most of them, I presume, will be lifers. I can't see them getting back out on the street to foment a new round of fundamentalist terrorism."

"How about the judicial process?" the director of the FBI asked looking around the room.

"Mr. Prince?" the president queried.

The recently confirmed attorney general interlocked his fingers and cracked them, a nervous habit.

"The process is not going to meet with the approval of the liberals. We are going to hold expedited public trials of groups of terrorists based on the seriousness of the charges against them. Most of them will be in the serious category unfortunately. The trials will be military tribunals—the only way to get through them in our lifetimes. If found guilty, they will be assigned to one of Mr. Sanchez's new prisons. We are ruling out capital punishment—too inflammatory. For those convicted who get life, the solution is simple. They are housed in the prisons with only the necessary provisions. Those getting shorter terms will be more of a problem. The general plan is to have them serve their terms then to release them somewhere that they have never lived before, but all in the general Middle-East area. We will stagger releases so that only a few at a time have to be absorbed by the communities. We will monitor them with the same strict regimen that we use for sex offenders in this country."

"When will all of this get under way, Devlin?" asked DFBI Marquess.

"End of next month."

"How long do you project that it will take?"

"Three, maybe four years."

"Boy, talk about full employment for lawyers," Emil Cranston, secretary of Labor—who had replaced the late Michael Hinton—said with a sardonic laugh.

"Look at it this way. The U.S. will have a housekeeping sort of involvement for the next five to six years then we can largely be disentangled from the Middle-East and from the rest of the world. Our relationships, responsibilities, and risks will all be simplified and hopefully reduced in scope. It is worth it for us to do the work now and relieve the burdens of those who take our places and for the next generation or two."

"Thank you for coming, Mr. Sanchez," the president said.

He took that as his cue to exit, gave a small courtly bow, and left.

"And thanks to all of you for your great work. Keep the formal and informal reports coming in."

With that the meeting adjourned.

CHAPTER FORTY-FIVE

AUGUST, 2012

The Republican National Convention was held in Las Vegas for security reasons. Like the Democratic Convention in New Orleans in June, the National Guard was activated to provide security, and that protection included land and air components. Cliff Assure won the Democratic nomination for president with Helen Clivener given the vice-presidential nod only after a near record thirty-nine ballots. Elizabeth Rowan was the Republican candidate by acclimation since the Republicans had no serious candidate to consider taking her place and no reason to risk changing horses at this point in time. The impeachment proceedings against her were still stalled in committee, and that status did not appear to be likely to change before November.

On the third evening of the convention, President Rowan announced her vice-presidential running mate thus ending the only suspense in a fairly lackluster convention. Sophronia Tellerman had been reluctant to run or to do anything in politics. She rightly pointed out to the president that she lacked recognition by the public, was the wrong color for American politics, and a Catholic which would alienate half the voters. She had the opposite point of view regarding the role of government vis-à-vis the individual held by most of the people of her race; and she was an Intellectual—an analytical, studious, uncharismatic logistician—who would be trying to gain election in a world where appearance trumped accomplishment.

"And you would make a fine president should the need fall on you. That is the first criterion. I expect you to be a real help in running the government, Sophy, and not a figurehead."

"And not a token, I trust," Dr. Tellerman said, only partly in jest.

"Vice-presidential candidates have regularly been chosen at least in part for their vote getting potential and for their capability in leading the hard-nosed portion of the fight; so, the candidate for president can appear to be above the fray. I am perfectly unabashed about using your race, your religion, your contacts in the corporate and university world, and all of your time and talents to get us elected and our unfinished job completed," President Rowan told her.

Dr. Tellerman had finally acquiesced, and the ticket was considered a solid one even though it was unprecedented in American history—two women and one of them an African-American.

Near the end of the third evening, the crowd was as enthusiastic as it could be with the efforts of the floor managers. Vice-presidential candidate Tellerman rose to give her acceptance speech with her husband of twenty years and their three children at her side. The glowing sheen of her beautiful ebony face was set off with a close to the scalp hairdo and by her shimmering full length white gown. She was slender and tall—five feet eleven inches—patrician, and commanding in appearance.

"My fellow Republicans, my fellow countrymen of all parties and persuasions, I am honored and humbled by having been given this opportunity to serve by the woman whom I consider to be the greatest leader in our country's history. I am proud to accept the nomination to be party's choice for the vice-presidency."

The delegates cheered uproariously. The media cameras focused on Dr. Tellerman's face, a happy, earnest, committed face. She smiled her dazzling smile, even bright white teeth contrasting with the rich dark color of her skin.

"We have been thrust into a war by nations who hate us for what we are more than what we do. We have borne the worst of the pain and sacrifice. It would be a great waste not to finish this work. I pledge all that I can offer to get President Rowan elected so that nothing such as happened on April 16 can ever happen again. This is a message of hope and striving. We do not hold out enmity to any one. However, we will not allow ourselves to be ambushed again. With President Rowan in office, we have the best chance to protect ourselves, to rebuild, to ensure our future in an uncertain and frightening world."

The delegates drowned out the vice-presidential candidate with their enthusiastic applause. It took several minutes for the tumult to subside. She finished with a flourish that the media later described as the best speech by a running mate in their memories.

It was the president's turn. The crowd cheered, then quieted. President Rowan waited patiently for full quiet. She was beginning to grey at the temples; she was losing the battle of middle age spread. After looking at the remarkable bright face and dramatic outfit of her running mate, she felt as dowdy as Queen Elizabeth in her purple-grey business suit with her trademark flag pin on the lapel. There were a few wrinkles in her face, and she now needed more makeup to prevent her from looking tired. The president stiffened her resolve and began her speech.

"My fellow Americans, we are in the late stages of a short and terrible war. The cost has been more $3.5 trillion dollars for the war alone, to say nothing of the monetary cost of the destruction visited upon us on April 16. We may well see a cost approaching twelve trillion dollars before this is over. The loss of life—both American and those lost in the countries against which we have waged war—is incalculable. The changes that have come upon the world and that have affected our place in the world are profound and evolving rapidly.

"We must complete this work. We must not allow the cynics and critics and appeasers among us to bear sway. We cannot allow another attack on our country. That is why I gave the orders for war and to prosecute that war to the point that our enemies are no longer capable of mounting another attack. It seems only common sense to me that we should protect ourselves. However, it is also part of international law. UNSCR 1373 holds that the counter terrorism conventions and protocols and inherent rights under international law of individual and collective self-defense confirm the legitimacy of the international community to eradicate terrorism. Elect me president and Dr. Sophronia Tellerman vice-president, and we will continue to campaign to afford our people the right to peace and security and prosperity and will make every effort possible to ensure those rights to our posterity."

The delegates gave the president a standing ovation. She had appeared tired at the beginning; but now, she was imbued with a new strength. The delegates in the hall and the viewers throughout the country and the world were aware of the change. Her supporters were encouraged and her detractors disheartened by the strength and confidence the unelected president demonstrated.

"We are the greatest nation in the history of the world. We will defeat our enemies. We will rebuild our great country. We will heal the wounds inflicted upon us. But we will never forget what happened on April 16. We must not forget. We will grieve and commemorate, build monuments, and pen tributes for the next hundred or a thousand years. We will not forget.

"We cannot let nay-sayers and appeasers gain control. We cannot have the weak rule our democratic country. Weakness breeds contempt from our enemies, and we have had enough of that. Help us, please."

Her short speech was followed by another standing ovation. The orchestra played the "*Star Spangled Banner*", and the audience sang in unison.

NOVEMBER 12, 2012

The members of the liberal caucus finally overcame the last of the obstacles put in the way of a committee vote by the conservative bloc. The House Judiciary Committee was called to order by Rep. Ivan Patterson, Dem. California, at eight o'clock on a blustery cold day. He had heard all of the arguments for waiting until after the elections to allow an atmosphere of fairness. He had successfully argued that he was not holding the vote to embarrass the candidate, but to impeach the president; and it was past time to deal with the issue forthrightly. It was not lost on him that President Rowan's approval ratings had dipped from her high of 83% during the first days of the war to only 48% after the media announced that the committee's vote to allow the impeachment proceedings to advance to a floor vote would be held today.

"We are here to vote, ladies and gentlemen, not to politic or posture or debate. We agreed in our last session to hold the vote this morning, and that is all we are going to do. The clerk will read the names of the committee members and each may respond with an aye, a nay, or an abstention."

The clerk began reading the names, and the nation watched as their television screens slowly tallied the count. There were twenty-one members of the committee including the chairman. Eight had publicly committed to an aye vote for moving the measure to the floor; ten had gone public with their intention to vote against the measure. Leland Y. Potter of Delaware, Sanford Watkins of Wyoming, and Alice Johanneson of Michigan had steadfastly refused to allow the public to know their thinking. The tension was evident in the nearly strident way that each vote, aye or nay, was voiced.

"Andrew Jacobsen."

"Nay."

"Alice Johanneson."

"Aye."

Sitting with her immediate staff in the Oval Office, President Rowan winced. The clerk's unemotional voice continued to proceed down the list of the committee members. The votes were all as expected.

"Leland Y. Potter."

"Aye."

That was unexpected, and the president and her confidants gasped quietly. They had never been sure of the Delaware representative's true leanings until now.

Rupert Vernon turned to McDonald Pearson and whispered, "Doesn't look good, Mac. Unless we have an unexpected switch in our favor, we are headed for a floor fight."

"Which we might win, or we might then win the Senate fight after that, but we will lose the presidency even if we win in both houses."

He looked grim.

The clerk was moving through the Ws with no surprises.

"Sanford Watkins."

"Nay."

"We're still in the hole. Pray for a change of heart," whispered Vernon.

The television cameras panned in on Rep Young of Utah. A staffer handed her a note and stepped back. The Representative looked briefly at the note then returned her attention to the proceedings.

"Constance Wyman."

"Aye."

"Donald Yepes."

"Nay."

"LaPreal Young."

Rep. Young seemed to be having a conflict. She paused for a moment.

"Nay," she said firmly.

The observers in the Oval Office and around the country were stunned. Rep Young had been one of President Rowan's most virulent enemies since the day Rowan was sworn in as president. Elizabeth Rowan was dumbstruck. It appeared that her most bitter personal enemy had saved her. The enmity was a petty thing that went back to their high school days when Rowan had beaten out Young for the valedictorian position. LaPreal Carlisle Young was convinced at the time by a teacher that Elizabeth Leavitt had beaten her out because the principal was in a summer business with Elizabeth's father. They had both married, had successful business and legal careers, and had climbed the difficult political ladders to their present middle-aged pinnacles. Still, Young was ready to believe every piece of gossip that suggested that Rowan had somehow gotten each position in her career from undue influence. On several occasions, Rowan had tried to reason with her enemy but was soundly rebuffed each time. The president had presumed that her fate might well be determined by her girlhood rival, but could not have dreamt that it would be in a positive way.

"Richard Zantell."

"Aye."

"Emmanuel Zegron."

"Nay."

President Rowan blinked in almost unbelieving relief and looked around the office at the still tense members of her staff.

"Congratulations, Madam President," said MacDonald Pearson. "Now we can get on with the work of the election without this terrible distraction."

"I am all for that recommendation," and here she scanned the room, "to get back to work. I, on the other hand, am going to the residence, get into bed, assume the fetal position, and turn the electric blanket up to nine. Then, I will watch the evening's news, and if they say it's over, I'll come out and put up my dukes and get back to punching."

The laughter in the room relieved the tension. Everyone shook the president's hand. She responded with real affection to each of these, her greatest supporters.

The next morning, after confirming that there would be no impeachment procedure, President Rowan called LaPreal Young at home.

"Representative Young, will you take a call from the president?" the White House operator asked.

"Of course. Thank you."

"Representative Young, this is Elizabeth Rowan. I wanted to thank you personally for saving my behind. I know that there have been ill feelings between us for altogether too long a time. I am curious as to why you didn't take this golden opportunity to do me the greatest harm that has ever been available to you. Perhaps we could get together and talk. I am saddened that our relationship—that should have been so positive—has been so bad."

"I have always been a spoiled brat, Madam President. I was never really convinced of that or able to admit it until I got the note yesterday. I'm sure you've seen the news. They replayed the scene of me and my note ad nauseum. Well, it was as life changing as it seemed to be. It was from my mother.

I'll read it to you, but I hope you won't feel the need to spread it any further than between us."

"Of course, I won't, LaPreal. You don't mind if I call you by your first name, do you?"

"I'm flattered. I might just slip and call you Liz, like I did before the stupid graduation day."

"Maybe we could be friends after all, LaPreal. I'd like to be Liz again."

"I'll keep it to our private conversations and consider it a privilege. Anyway, my mother's note said, 'You foolish girl. You have earned every thing you have, and you have begrudged Elizabeth Leavitt every thing she has ever gotten. You are envious, and it is wrong of you. Principle Lane did not even make the decision about who was to be the valedictorian. First of all, Liz's grades got her there. She beat you out by two 'A's. It was close enough that a committee of students and teachers voted. She got twenty-one votes and you got five. I never told you that to spare you. I thought you would get over such silliness. Now, you are about to do real harm to someone who never harmed you and for nothing. And, I know that you know your constituents are 100%—I mean 100%—in favor of keeping Elizabeth Leavitt Rowan as president. We are afraid of that crazy man from Nevada. He'll sell us out to the United Nations. Now, you go and do what's right.'"

"And Mom's always right," laughed President Rowan.

"Mine is, anyway," said Rep. Young with a sigh. "I'm sorry, Liz. I am truly sorry. Please forgive me. I will try to make it up to you. I have been a fool, and I admit it."

"You're forgiven. I would love to have us Utah girls defeat the gentiles arrayed against us."

"I haven't heard that expression for a long time. Count me in for help in these last days of the campaign. I'll do my best to undo my mistakes."

"It takes a big man to admit a mistake, my friend. Thanks."

"Good by, Liz."

"Good by, LaPreal."

President Rowan set down the receiver and shook her head. It was a crazy world when such trivialities could have such momentous import. Maybe that was the explanation for the evolution of the world's current problem. She vowed to pay closer attention to details in the future. She told MacDonald Pearson and no one else about the details of her talk with Representative Young. To her surprise, he broke out into a long and hearty laugh. She looked at him quizzically.

"What?" she asked slightly testily sensing that there was something behind that display of mirth.

"I'm sorry, but you are going to have to admit how little you know about politics; or you will get into trouble. You need me. Gantry Lomax, the staffer who gave your new friend, Ms. Young, the note, told me what was in it."

"And what was *really* in it?"

"The gist was this: Michael Phillip Horner from the Utah Chemical zillionaire Horners sent the note. He happens to be a big fan and a considerable contributor of yours and Ms. Young's. He told Rep. Young in no uncertain terms that she would either vote against the articles of impeachment being brought to the House floor, or she would never see a dime of his money again. Lomax told me that the speaker added an addendum. This, Lomax remembered verbatim: 'If you vote against the president I will see to it that your next assignment is to chair the harbors and rivers pollution committee.'"

"You are definitely right about my political naiveté, Mac. I am going to depend on you to get me through this Washington labyrinth; so, we can get something worthwhile done here."

CHAPTER FORTY-SIX

THE FIRST TUESDAY IN NOVEMBER, 2012, ELEVEN-FIFTY, P.M., EST

Mac and Andrew sat with their eyes fixed on the three television sets in the Oval Office somehow keeping track of all of the three regular networks, CNN, FoxNews, and MSNBC with clever slight-of-hand channel changer finger movements. All of the stations had been predicting victory for President Rowan for over two and a half hours. She, Abigail Young, and Sophronia Tellerman had gone to bed half an hour ago. Gadi ben Elazar, Perry Ralston, Henry Magleby, the campaign manager, and Timothy Willows were pacing, still too nervous to sit and too much the skeptics to admit success.

The operator put a call through to the office, and MacDonald Pearson took it. He listened for a moment then put the phone down angrily.

"What?" asked Perry.

"Cliff Assure's campaign manager just read a canned message to me stating that his candidate conceded the election but would not be available to talk to anyone in our camp," Gadi answered.

"'Life is like licking honey off a thorn', Josh Billings used to say," said Timothy. "Let's just enjoy the honey."

"You're right. Should we inform the president?" Henry asked.

"Nay, good news can keep until morning. She's bushed," Perry answered.

"Okay," said Mac, "I think we can call it a day. CNN made it 58% for the president and Dr. Tellerman. Maybe not a landslide, but pretty respectable."

Timothy poured each of them a flute of good champagne.

"Good work everyone," he said. "The president doesn't drink, and it would be a shame to let good stuff like this go to waste Like the old song says, 'Do drink it up, you know it won't keep.'"

They all laughed giddily and knew that they had been at the election watch too long.

All over the United States and around the world, people awakened to a brief statement that Elizabeth Rowan and Sophronia Tellerman had been elected president and vice-president. The news was otherwise dominated by Cliff Assure, Helen Clivener, and a panel of the editors of The *Legal Times*, The *Nation*, The *New York Times*, The *San Francisco Chronicle*, The *Madison Capital Times*, The *Progressive Magazine* from Cornell, and the *Human Rights Watch*. The panel included the pastor of the Ebenezer Baptist Church and two leaders of the Rainbow Coalition. Cliff Assure and Helen Clivener dominated the conversation with Warren Crondell, the retired dean of the *WorldNews* team.

"We will formally request an investigation into irregularities in the Florida, Wisconsin, California, and Vermont election procedures. We have reason to belief that there has been out-and-out voter fraud and further, we will present evidence that key Democratic voter groups were systematically excluded, including Democrat servicemen and women, elderly retirees, African-Americans from Broward and Miami-Dade in Florida and on the South side of Chicago. We are confident that the election will be overturned.

"Much as we hate to indicate it; but the American people have a right to know; the human rights violations in the Middle-East are so heinous that an international commission will meet this week in The Hague to launch a formal investigation leading to war crimes and crimes against humanity charges against the usurper president."

CNN lined up each of the panel members and elicited a short, somewhat duplicating statement from each of them.

Pastor Lemuel Heffnen made a challenge.

"The good book talks of the 'Prince of Peace'; please look at *Isaiah 9 and 6* and *the Gospel of Saint Luke 2 and 14*. Jesus demanded 'on earth peace, good will toward men.' We are a Christian nation, and our unelected president—one foisted upon us like a plague of the devil—has violated every tenet of the teachings of the Prince of Peace. She did it for the oil over there. She did it for the filthy lucre. She must be called to the tribunal to answer for her unChristian behavior, for murder!"

Crondell, abandoning any pretense of objectivity, said that, "this woman must be brought to justice before an international tribunal so that we can once again join the company of nations untainted by the tyrant who has acted with malice aforethought to cause murder and wanton destruction. Our place at the table of nations is at stake, and our future depends on legal action. We cannot control the masses of Americans who seethe to rise up. Mrs. Rowan, step down. Resign the presidency and allow the office to regain its honor."

Andrew McKnight sipped coffee over a Spartan breakfast of Wheaties and fruit with the president and MacDonald Pearson as they watched the broadcast.

"I'm no historian, but I would be willing to bet that that is the worst post-election loser performance in the history of the country," said Andrew.

The president nodded thoughtfully.

"You have yet to make your gracious acceptance speech, Madam President. What do you want to do?"

"I am going to speak at two if you can arrange it. I'll barely touch on this silly panel's liberal zealot diatribe then I am going to give a foretaste of what we expect to do in this new administration. Don't get too upset. This will pass. No one is going to get anywhere with criminal allegations. Even the Hague would have to come and get me to force a trial there. I can't see them getting a visitors' visa for that purpose," the president said.

She looked well rested and loaded for bear.

At noon, Abigail Young brought in the twelve ranking members of the American Islamic Leadership Council and introduced each of them to the president.

"Thank you for taking the time to come by and see me, gentlemen. I especially appreciate that you requested the meeting. It is time we talked."

"When you instituted the security measure of having our seven million American Muslims moved to concentration camps, you made the general promise that we would be repatriated into mainstream society as soon as possible. We understood that to mean that the police and justice department forces of the United States would investigate us and our institutions and would separate the wheat from the chaff. When that process was completed, we would not only be allowed to return to our homes and our businesses, but would be vigorously defended as Americans," Omar Fahd Rabbo, the group's president and spokesman, said.

"That is my purpose in dealing with the Muslim-American people in a nutshell, sir," the president said.

"We have no dispute with your purpose or the measures you have taken. We can only hope that you are a person of your word, and this is not a political expediency that could constitute—in a minor way—a pogrom. We are proud Americans, and we want to be able to take our place with the reputation as being loyal Americans.

"We offered our services. Through the organizations that exist in our mosques, we have information that led to the conviction of those among us who have betrayed our religion and our chosen nation. We have performed citizens' arrests of more than eight thousand individuals and have seized the records and computers of three dozen companies and phony charity and humanitarian organizations. They are being held in designated detention centers in each of the concentration camps. I was happy to supply the exact information to the FBI counterterrorism people and to have our men assist in getting these criminals into Justice Department custody."

"That will materially speed the repatriation process, Mr. Rabbo."

"Our organization has a further suggestion, one that could begin the process in a way that would likely be acceptable to the traumatized American public. We have spent our time in custody productively. We have interviewed our young men and have developed an extensive list of men who could enter military training immediately to serve wherever they are called. Almost all of them speak Arabic—a skill we hear is quite lacking among government and military personnel—and would be of some use in the present emergency and in future relations with the Arab nations. We respectfully suggest that you consider the formation of a Muslim-American battalion similar to the Japanese-American troops in World War II who lost so many men in our nation's cause and who were so highly decorated and like the historical Mormon Battalion. In all three instances, despised and displaced peoples were given the opportunity to serve and to earn their honorable place in our society."

"And, if that were to happen and to have a positive outcome?"

"Each of the Muslim-American soldiers and their nuclear families would be automatically restored to their full American rights; the battalion's performance would be given wide and frequent praise from the government leading to a change in perception by the public of the Muslim people in our country. This would allow the repatriation of some of our most prominent religious, business, professional, and education leaders who would not be likely to be considered a threat. The public would then be more ready to accept the government's vetting of the bulk of the individuals left in custody."

"That is an excellent outline of a workable plan. How long do you think all of this is likely to take?"

"We believe in the fairness of our country. We firmly believe that, with cooperation, every criminal can be in custody and every good Muslim-American citizen can be back home and restored to full rights within two years."

"If, in fact, you honor your end, I will do everything in my power to make it happen and sooner, Mr. Rabbo. I know you are aware that some thirty-two percent of the detainees have already returned home, largely due to the cooperation of your community."

When the American Muslim delegation left, President Rowan asked to have Secretary Elazar come to the office.

"Good morning, Gadi," the president said warmly.

"Good morning, to you, Madam President. How can I be of service?"

"Having the Muslim Council delegation here gave me a couple of ideas. I hope—first of all that you will approve of them—and second that you will want to carry them out promptly."

"I'll do my best."

"I would like to find a Muslim Arab-American who works in the State Department in a rather junior position and probably one that is over qualified for that position. I want to propose to him or her—and I prefer a her—that she be our senior negotiator with the new Muslim country leaders who will come to us eventually for recognition. I want the new leaders to meet a very lowly secretary, and while they may not be informed of the fact, she should be given very senior authority in the decision making process subject to your final say."

"I like the idea, and I know just the woman. I would have argued for her even if you had recommended someone else. Her name is Sofia Rabbo, daughter of Omar Fahd Rabbo, head of the American Islamic Leadership Council."

"Good, I respect her father. Let's get her on board today. I know you have had feelers."

"Only from the old countries. They haven't even heard of our proposed realignment of the Middle-East. The old guard is not going to receive that information positively."

"No. And, I have to admit that that is part of what convinces me of the correctness of our realignment. New blood, new ideas, new appreciation of the value of denouncing and renouncing terrorism."

NOVEMBER 7, 2012, 2:00 p.m. EST

"Five, four, three, two, one…" The producer pointed at the president and silently mouthed "zero."

The network cameras panned in on the president seated at her desk in the Oval Office.

"My fellow Americans. The election is over; and the people have chosen my administration and presumably, my policies, to guide the nation for the next four years. The question of impeachment is behind us. The vicious war is now becoming history while the new world that has resulted is just being formed. My administration will follow a policy of cautious and judicious withdrawal back to our borders; and we will—as soon as it is safe—concentrate all of our nation's energies and resources to the end of rebuilding our nation. We will leave to the other nations of the United Nations and the economically powerful G8—Group of 8 industrialized nations—to contribute to the reconstruction of the Middle-East as they see fit.

"We have had no help from the EU except for our deeply rooted partnership with the British and the Australians, and we will maintain an amicable but restrained relationship with those who chose not to join us.

"I, like you, watched the performance of my recent opponent in the election process. I regret that he has refused us the courtesy of a public concession and the people the peace of moving on without rancor. I will not debate the senator or his council. I will leave his accusations to the judgment of the people and the election review board. However, since that council introduced the subject of religion into the equation, to suggest that I should have sought peace as Jesus would have done, I will make one defensive comment. I will quote a religious leader, J. Reuben Clark, Jr. who spoke in 1939 on the eve of Hitler's invasions. 'Christ did proclaim a peace—the peace of everlasting righteousness which is the eternal and mortal enemy of sin. Between righteousness and sin, in whatever form, there can only be unceasing war, whether in one man, among the people, or between nations in armed conflict. This war is the sword of Christ; whatever its form this war cannot end until sin is crushed, and Christ brings all flesh under his dominion.'

"My fellow Americans, in the decade or two before April 16, the world actively sought to excuse an escalating series of travesties against America, Israel, democracy, and freedom of choice and expression. Many apologized for murders, for vicious tyrannies, for crimes against mankind, for the mutilation and brutal subjugation of women, and for the grossest of religious intolerance. This policy of appeasement may have been employed for genuine liberal sentiments that hoped that good will and persuasion would win out in the end or for the purpose of keeping up the flow of Middle-Eastern oil, or to encourage business and trade. Whatever the case, the policy was a failure—a predictable one—since appeasing extortionists, bullies, and bigots has never worked and never can.

"I will state the philosophy that has guided me as I have led the country. There are absolutes and among them are life, liberty, and the pursuit of happiness for us and for our friends. One guiding principle for which we fought was stated succinctly by a former Israeli Prime Minister, Ariel Sharon, 'The Jews, too, have a right to live.' There are negative absolutes as well. American jurisprudence recognizes a principle stated in legal Latin that some things are: *mala in se*—evil in themselves.

"Murder—including honor killings and in the form of acts of terrorism in the name of the religion—is unacceptable no matter what the culture. Vile treatment of women including mutilating them, making them criminally responsible for having been the victim of rape, preventing them from owning property, denying them the right to vote or to hold office, denying them decent modern medical care because they cannot be examined by a physician, or making them move about in a suffocating heavy shroud in the heat of the desert, are evils that must stop. The practice of suttee must never again be permitted.

"The idea that one may only have a set of beliefs that corresponds to that of the man in power or the religion that dominates is evil and must cease. We have fought a great war, one that was visited upon us without our choice and without provocation. We will pursue the results of that war to the end that fundamentalist terrorism and all that it entails is eradicated now and forever from the earth."

The president sipped from a cup of water.

"I hold no personal enmity for Muslims in general or the religion of Islam. Neither do I have regrets for having acted in our nation's defense against Muslims. Our intelligence information estimates that somewhere in the neighborhood of 200 million of the slightly more than a billion Muslims in the world actively or indirectly but knowingly, supported the terrorist program. That corresponds roughly to the number of people killed in those Muslim countries in this war. The new Islam—the religion that supplanted legitimate Islam in the past thirty to forty years—may well no longer exist. Recognize that that region of the world has had millennia of recurrent cataclysmic conflicts, some of which essentially eradicated established civilizations and cultures and were supplanted by new cultures, even new systems of writing. The autochthonous peoples lived on, embracing the new ideas and leaders, and there was precious little mourning at the changes wrought. I am convinced that the removal of fundamentalist Islamic terrorism as a takeover religion will not be mourned and will not be long remembered.

"Today, I spoke at length with the American Islamic Leadership Council. Together, we have devised a plan to rehabilitate the good and loyal American citizens who are Muslim to their rightful place in their country. I ask that you give them and your government every courtesy and acceptance as they are cleared for return to their homes and businesses.

"Also, we will begin the long process of establishing legal governments in the Middle-East. We welcome all governments of jurisdictions that are to be determined, which unite with the society of nations in fostering democracy, the rule of law, and the rejection of religious dominated ruling systems that would deny fundamental rights to some or many of their citizens.

"As our generation and the generations to come wrestle with core problems, one must be paramount. We, The People of the World, must unitedly do all in our power to prevent another war like the one we have just suffered and whose effects will haunt us for generations. Albert Einstein described the sophistication of wars in which we have engaged, but described the final great war this way: 'I know not with what weapons World *War* III will be fought, but World *War* IV will be fought with sticks and stones.' Let us prevent that with all of our energies.

"Finally, now that the worst brutality of the war appears to be over and the recent election is behind us, let us unite to build a stronger America. Let us work together, even those of you who campaigned against me. I hold no malice towards any of you. It is the American way to fight hard in a bipartisan election and then to unite as Americans behind the winner. I ask that of you. Good day, my friends, my fellow Americans."

When the microphones were securely off, the president made an aside comment to her trusted advisor, MacDonald Pearson, "You know, Mac, we will now be part of a ruined world and will only be able lay claim to a pyrrhic victory. I reluctantly envision our new world as did Ezekial in his vision: (*Ezekial 37:1*) "The hand of the LORD was on me, and he brought me out by the Spirit of the LORD and set me in the middle of a valley; it was full of bones. He led me back and forth among them, and I saw a great many bones on the floor of the valley, bones that were very dry."

Chapter Forty-Six

NOVEMBER 31, 2012

A delegation of self-appointed leaders of Egypt, Syria, Saudi Arabia, Libya, Iran, and Yemen—mostly expatriates of their countries who missed the American attacks—bypassed Sophia Rabbo and badgered Gadi ben Elazar until he threw up his hands and asked the president to give a definitive and final answer to them.

The president smiled at his frustration and had Elazar bring the six men to the West Wing conference room.

"Hereafter, every country's emissaries, and *only* those from the newly demarcated nations, will go through Sofia Rabbo first. I want them to get the message fully and finally. This is the new world that they inherited from their vicious bigoted fundamentalist terrorist predecessors. They will have to live with it. I will make that clear to these men who have come here today. Make a recording of my communication with them that they can take back to their constituencies and provide it to future applicants from the old countries."

"With pleasure, Madam President. I hope I haven't failed you by being too soft."

"It's the liberal in you, Gadi. Forget about it."

He rolled his eyes and smiled at her.

The nine well-dressed emissaries filed into the conference room and took their places around the polished oak conference table.

"The president's time is limited. Present your case succinctly. As we agreed in the hallway, only one of you will speak for the group," the secretary of State told the delegation.

The Saudi Arabian served as spokesman.

"I am Prince Faisal Walid ibn Talal, descendant of the Hashemite kings and The Prophet's lineage, may Allah shine his blessings upon his Messenger. I speak for the nations represented here to demand that each state be re-established as it was before the unfortunate events of April 16. All international law and custom and normalcy require it."

President Rowan's expression was bland. She made direct eye contact with each man and let him know that what she was about to say was meant for him.

"Thank you for coming. I am going to give you a short message that will be a reply to your request and will serve as a final notice to anyone who might come to me with a similar demand, as you phrased it.

"The United States—as the victor in this vicious war you started—will not ever permit the reconstitution of the original countries that attacked us. We will not be a party to another country that threatens and bullies its neighbors, whose human rights policies such as institutional use of torture to obtain confessions for criminal and political offenses, are nothing short of demonic, and whose history of inbred and deeply perpetuated intolerance is anything like yours.

"I will be specific in answering you, Mr. Talal. Saudi Arabia has abominable record—amputation for theft, public beheadings, nothing remotely reminiscent of democracy such as the right to vote, flagrant intolerance for all other religions, exportation of terrorism, the corruption of children with textbooks that preach hatred and misconceptions and a perverted definition of the noble concept of jihad. Your country and your faith—using the Sharia as your judicial code—does not recognize adoption and as a result abandons orphans to the streets, often to be molested, to starve, to suffer, and to die uncared for.

"You had institutional slavery until 1962 and quietly fostered it in Africa for three decades thereafter. You caused or allowed the most atrocious mutilations of women and the deprivation of the most fundamental rights of your daughters, sisters, wives, and mothers. You expropriated virtually all of the riches that poured into your country leaving your citizens near beggars at the table. You used and betrayed us, decent people who assumed that you were friends. I could provide a litany of similar offenses against every one of the countries represented here by you men. Suffice it that we—the people of the United States—will not allow your vile regimes to start again. A sea change has occurred, and you are going to be witness to it.

"Hopefully, the changes will include an alleviation of ignorance that produces laws such as one in Lebanon that allows men to have sex with animals so long as the animals are female and making the act of having sexual relations with a male animal punishable by death. Or the Muslim inspired law in Bahrain that allows a male doctor to examine a woman's genitals legally, but he is prohibited from looking directly at them during the examination. The law was modified by religious jurists to permit him to view her parts in a mirror. Undertakers are banned from viewing the genitalia of a corpse. The genitals must be covered by a brick or a piece of wood at all times. In Muslim Indonesia, the penalty for masturbation is decapitation.

"The world will be a better place without such institutionalized ignorance and cruelty. Now, get out of my sight."

The shocked and chagrined Arabs, who had never heard such things divulged out loud, were promptly ushered out of the Oval Office and were given copies of the president's unflinchingly harsh statement. No delegation ever again presented itself with a similar request in the West Wing.

CHAPTER FORTY-SEVEN
EPILOGUE

APRIL 16, 2066

In the final chapter of his book, *A History of World War III- The Gog and Magog Conflict*, released on the fiftieth anniversary of the attack on Detroit, Professor Emeritus of History from Harvard, Harley Bedford Clivener, penned his conclusions. The chapter is quoted here in full:

It is rather early to make an historical conclusion about events only some fifty years in the past, and time and more study may well render them premature and incomplete. However, much of the foregoing material has been obtained from people still living, and many of them will not be with us for even another decade. I have been scrupulous in presenting facts, reconstructing situations, and giving both sides of controversies. My staff and I had train car loads of original documents with which to work, comparable in scope to the raw data available to William L. Shirer when he undertook the monumental project of writing *The Rise and Fall of the Third Reich*. Now, it is time for the author to present a summation and to make an effort to draw conclusions despite the limitations. I admit to being a liberal and to having come from a long line of liberals; and, therefore, I may have an unconscious bias; but I will try in this summary to set that bias aside and to present the history of World War III—popularly known as the Battle of Armageddon or the Gog and Magog War—as the factual information best justifies.

The beginnings of the war—like all wars—were more complicated than a simple construction would suggest. Please refer back to chapters one through three for details. The best date to assign as the beginning of the process that led to the World War III was midnight on May 14, 1948, the day that Israel was created by the United Nations. Israel was attacked by the TransJordanian Arab Army, the combined might of the Arab world surrounding the tiny nascent country that same day. Arabs living in Palestine were ordered out by the advancing Arab military machine—and not by the Israelis, which is a popular and inaccurate myth—and most of them went to Jordan. Jews were driven out of those same attacking Arab countries, their property and possessions stolen, and many were killed. Many of them found their way to Israel bringing with them the gall of bitterness.

Israel won the war and established itself; but no real peace was achieved and a legacy of bitterness, frustration, and hatred persisted among the Arabs. They refused to recognize Israel, took upon themselves as a cause, the concept that the displaced Arabs—the so-called Palestinians—had been driven out by the malicious Jews of Israel. In fact, Jordan eventually drove the hapless refugee Palestinian Arabs out of their country and created a diaspora with only a portion of those displaced persons filtering back into their previous region of residence. The United States of America tilted towards Israel in its dealings with the Middle-East and thereby earned the persisting enmity of the Arabs.

Two more wars were fought, each beginning with a sneak attack by Arabs and each ending in failure and humiliation for the Arabs. Hatred for Israel and for America became more intense and widespread and entrenched. The Palestinian cause took on a Holy Grail quest character and came to dominate all interactions with the West. Unable to win militarily, the Arabs, Egyptians, and Iranians used terrorism as a tool, committing hundreds of atrocities against Jews. Israelis responded with reprisal measures of seven to as much as a hundred fold intensity. America continued to arm both sides of the controversy and conflict but supported Israel disproportionately. In 1987 a jihad movement—the intifada—was started, and then Americans and other westerners were targeted as never before.

In 1992 Iraq—under its then dictator—Saddam Hussein, invaded Kuwait and threatened nearby Saudi Arabia. A coalition of Western nations led by the United States rushed to battle with Saddam and imposed a humiliating defeat. However, the dictator was not killed or removed from office and became something of an Arab icon. He was eventually captured and hanged. A fundamentalist zealot, the immensely wealthy Usama bin Laden—operating from within Afghanistan—collected fundamentalist Islamic terrorists for training in Afghanistan and created a world wide terrorist organization called al Qaeda.

Al Qaeda was responsible for a number of atrocities against the United States. Two attacks on the World Trade Center in New York City, the first in 1973 and a second devastating surprise attack in September, 2001 that demolished the twin towers of one of the world's most important business centers and killed more than 3000 people finally galvanized the United States into an action called the War on Terrorism. Please refer to Chapter Two for a more complete listing of attacks on the United States.

Unable to make progress against their powerful enemy, the Islamic fundamentalist terrorists secretly joined together in an elaborate plan to mollify, and to pacify the West and to lull the United States into the notion that the Arab world had changed to a peaceful and affable monolithic society. As the West progressively let down its defenses, the Arab plotters patiently developed the capacity to create nuclear bombs. The president of the United States—so taken with the prospects for peace—turned a blind eye and a deaf ear to any reports that conflicted with his much more palatable "peace in our time" policy—the so-called "Braithwaite Doctrine". He arranged for a huge celebration of the new peace and invited the world to come to the United States to join the American people in the realization of their dreams for lasting peace with the Muslims and everyone else.

On April 16, 2010 at seven-fifteen in the morning—without provocation—the Islamic plot against the Western world reached its culmination. A thermonuclear device exploded in the Detroit River, and at the same moment, radiation dispersal devices were exploded in Los Angeles, Sydney, Paris, and London. A dozen ICBMs with multiple warheads were launched from Aleppo, Syria, from the desert near Cairo, from the Empty Quarter of Saudi Arabia, and from Iran, all directed at the United States. All of the missiles were intercepted and destroyed by the antimissile defenses of America. The United States declared war on the involved nations including Libya that very day and launched a brief, overwhelming, and earth changing nuclear attack. Israel fought Syria, Iran, Egypt, and the Palestinians and drove them all out of her territory and to near annihilation.

The costs of World War III, which lasted less than ten days, were these: American deaths including those from the late effects of radiation were 12 million. Islamic nation deaths, including deaths due to the late effects of radiation, amounted to more than 200 million, a figure coincidently that closely approximates the number of people who supported the terrorist effort to one degree or another. By comparison, World War II resulted in some forty million deaths. 163 nations lost citizens in the initial attack, in the resulting war, and to pestilence, disease, starvation, and lawlessness following the war.

In financial terms, the United States of America alone lost more than twelve trillion dollars; France, England, and Australia lost approximately fifteen billion dollars each. The financial losses of the Muslim countries are incalculable for they lost everything. One economist estimated that the cost of rebuilding the war devastated areas would be on the order of four trillion dollars. However, no such rebuilding effort ever took place. Oil—once the life's blood of the leaders of the terrorist nations—has, since the war, been internationalized and has ceased to be a factor of bellicosity. The entire world shares in the earth's bounty with no one individual, family, ruling junta, or nation garnering great riches from exploitation of the precious natural resource from the earth where we all live.

Sociologically, the losses for the nations that perpetrated the war resulted in the near extinction of their Islamic way of life; and certainly, all vestiges of modern Islam in those countries have been lost. There remain only a fraction of the original numbers of believers, most of them now old and dying away. Careful studies at Harvard and Yale estimate that fewer than five million Muslims of the eight billion human beings on earth will carry on the religion by the end of the century. The young have all but abandoned the faith, having lost all confidence in their religious leaders and in the future of the religion. Before the war, the Muslim Middle-East boasted large bustling cities, magnificent libraries, remarkable historic sites preserving the reminders of civilizations of millennial antiquity, and a bursting pride in the accomplishments of Islam. All of that was casualty to the Gog and Magog War.

World War III resulted in one of the greatest geographical reshufflings in all of the world's history. Israel, Iraq, Morocco, and Turkey gained substantial land mass; the formerly great nations of Egypt, Syria, Libya, Iran, and Yemen exist only in history books; not even their names persist in any present country. More than fifty new nations have filled in their locations—none of them fundamentalist Islamic, none of them an Islamic state per se, and none of them with more than five million people, or a GDP of more than ten million dollars a year; and none of them with a military establishment with offensive capabilities. Not a single one of them can launch a missile that can fly beyond its borders.

Natural groupings of peoples prevails as never before; there is a nation of Kurds, a fact considered impossible before the war. The principle endeavors of all of these new nations is the accumulation of enough food and water for their inhabitants, most of whom live on a level comparable to that seen in the sixth century.

All but a tiny fraction of the prisoners of war have died, and the rest have returned to their former areas in ignominy or worse. There has not been a war since 2010, and acts of terrorism throughout the world can be counted on the fingers of one hand each year. They are dealt with as police problems and as often as not by vigilante justice on the part of local citizens who either remember the costs of terrorism or have had the lessons passed on to them by their parents or grandparents.

The West achieved peace at the expense of a policy of isolation on the part of the United States—a policy strongly encouraged by nations around the world and by the desires of the American public. With America no longer the trading partner it was before the war, the EU, OAS, and Middle-Eastern mercantile nations have entered into what can best be described as ennui—a prolonged global recession—that has only begun to show signs of lifting in the past five years. The United States has entirely abrogated its role as the world's policeman, moral judge, and financial benefactor. Like Great Britain after the cataclysm of World War II which lost its empire and its standing, the United States has become only one among affluent countries—not the first among them.

Ten years after the war, great divisions became frank schisms in America as elsewhere. Initially, Canada and Mexico approached the victors of World War III with various proposals of union. In the end, all of the proposals were soundly rejected by the nations themselves or by their electorates. Canada finally voted to allow Quebec to become an independent French speaking nation. The new nation failed financially, and has become a protectorate of France and by so doing has imposed a crippling financial burden on its new mother country. In harmony with the general preference for like people to join together with each other politically, most of the northern half of Canada achieved nationhood as Nunavik, a home for indigenous peoples. Without Canadian subsidies, Nunavik has largely returned to a primitive subsistence hunter-gatherer pre-historic way of life. Eastern and Western Canadian provinces are politically, religiously, and socially at opposite poles; and commissions in each section of the remaining country are at work preparing arguments and plans for and against separation. Separation appears more likely than not to take place.

De facto secessions from the union of states that existed before the war are now extant in America. California has split into northern and southern halves that have each applied for formal secession from the union along with Alaska and Hawaii, and a coalition of Utah and Idaho as the State of Deseret. The southern quarters of Southern California, Arizona, New Mexico, Texas, and the southern half of Colorado have indicated their intention to form a new—more congenial nation—with the Mexican states of Baja California, Sonora, Chihuahua, Coahuila, Nuevo Leon, and Tamaulipas. Approval has been given in full by Mexico, and by the U.S. Senate for the creation of the new Hispanic nation, which will be called Republica del Norte.

The Southern states that failed in their original bid to secede from the union more than 200 years previously are now once again seriously pursuing that aim with every prospect of making a peaceful transition this time around. The Middle-Western States are undecided and therefore uncommitted about how they will align themselves, whether as one independent state or as several separate entities or whether to unite with the Northeast. The strong conservative streak in the traditional Mid-West is at odds with the long standing liberal persuasion that permeates the East.

At present, the Mid-Westerners appear to be moving toward independence. The only segment of the once great nation that has stated a strong intention to retain the title, United States of America, is a runt segment of the Northeastern states. The dissolution of the American union will likely be complete in the next ten years to twenty years with a loose federation coming into existence among the several new nations being completed.

The Russian federation is dividing into small nations on ethnic or religious lines. Throughout the world, similar reductions in the size of great nations are being accomplished by peaceful means. Apparently, the concept of "great nation" or dominating power has lost its savor with sober reflection on the costs of the inevitable war—the Gog and Magog conflict—that now is part of history.

By a process of social evolution on the part of the rest of the nations of the world, the People's Republic of China has become the largest, most populous, and most powerful nation in the world. Art, trade, the center of military research and power, language dominance, and educational opportunity have all gravitated to the nominally communist country. The PRC has moderated its stance on political, social, and religious diversity, and that has further encouraged a movement of the world's thinkers, traders—and much to the chagrin of the long-time leadership of China—also dissidents. Mandarin is steadily becoming the language of commerce, education, and diplomacy. Unlike the predecessor great power nations of England, France, Germany, and the United States, the PRC appears to be content with a premier role in the world while eschewing hegemony and military adventurism. Theirs has been a strong voice and hand to quell violent actions among nations before war has been started.

What place in history is occupied by the men and women who played pivotal roles in the great conflict?

Prince Ahmed Wahhab ibn Saud—the planner and catalyst of Operation Avenging the Crusades, as he named his colossal attack on the West—was hoist by his own petard. He perished along with his grand ideas of a millennial world ruled by a strict Islamic theocracy in the early minutes of the war. The presidents of Iran, Syria, Libya, Yemen, and Egypt are all documented to have died in the counterattack by the United States.

The prime minister of Great Britain, Chauncey Reed-Perkins, was ousted from membership in the Labor Party after receiving a no-confidence vote from the British public a year after the war began and before the period of reconstruction had been fully begun.

Strictly speaking, there were no great generals on either side. The attacks were so sudden; and the conflict so brief, that no individual stood out. No British or American military notable to date has written a history or has entered into active public discourse on the war.

The American detractors and opponents of the war, particularly Senator Cliff Assure of Nevada, and the then senator from the State of Washington, Helen Clivener, became political opponents of each other in the Democratic primaries for the office of president in 2020. Clivener was elected—and in an unprecedented move—appointed Assure to the Supreme Court bench where he served until his death in 2038. President Clivener served two terms and after that was appointed the ambassador to the Court of St. James and then to the United Nations during the brief interlude when the United States resumed active membership in the world organization.

Clivener was responsible for establishing final Middle-Eastern national boundaries and functioning governments in nearly fifty countries while serving as secretary of State under her old nemesis, President Elizabeth Rowan during her third term—more accurately, 2½ terms. While president, Clivener was responsible for instituting a national health service, strict gun registration, control, and confiscation, abolition of the death penalty—and for good or ill—presided over the beginning of the end of the American union. She died in 2041 at the age of 92 while still actively serving as president of Yale University. As an aside, the powerful liberal figure was my grandmother.

And what of the central figure, Elizabeth Leavitt Rowan—the apolitical retiring mid-level governmental functionary who—by a combination of rather incredible fortuitous events was thrust into the position of ultimate decision, power, and responsibility? President Rowan served two and a half terms as president of the United States, the maximum allowed by the Constitution. The people of the United States were then and are even now—some fifty years later—nearly evenly divided as to whether Rowan was a good, even great president, a woman of steely nerve in the tradition of Washington and Lincoln, who did what had to be done and made the world a better and safer place. Or was she a monster—an avenging devil responsible for loss of American liberties, status of the United States among the family of nations, and for state terrorism and mass murder on a level never before imagined, even when compared to earlier historical figures: Hitler, Stalin, and Mao Tze Tung.

Rowan retired to self-imposed obscurity. She never wrote her memoirs or a book or even an article on her role in the great war or in the reshaping of the world that occurred afterwards although she was surely the central figure. She died July 7, 2022 at the age of 79 in her home in the mountains of Utah. Her funeral was attended by only a handful of her staunch friends and supporters from the war period and a few old friends from her home town. There was no national funeral ceremony such as was accorded the liberal, John F. Kennedy, or the conservative, Ronald Reagan, or even an official acknowledgment of her passing other than that the nation's flags were flown at half mast for a week. She was buried without fanfare in a plot in her small town cemetery with a grave stone that gave only her name and the dates of her birth and death. President Rowan will likely remain an enigmatic and controversial figure throughout history as the world rests from the apocalyptic events over which she presided.

DECEMBER 12, 2067

Four Arabs sat in the outdoor section of the neat little café looking at the sunset descending over the Eiffel Tower Memorial. They had each come from a different section of Paris by a different mode of transportation. They had arrived separately from each other and had initially taken separate tables. As the busy evening trade began gathering, they casually gravitated to the same table and; had anyone cared to observe, they engaged in quiet, apparently unexciting dialogue with one another.

The eldest, a man known to the others as Ibraham Wahhab, spoke in hushed tones in Arabic. It had been only five years since the French had permitted Arabs to return to French soil; so, almost no one else in the country beyond his three companions understood his language.

"Brothers," he said, "we are the last true believers. It is up to us to bring our faith back to life. We can only do that by making a statement that our brothers scattered throughout the world can understand. We must not betray ourselves with silly public messages, nor should we take credit for our actions. It is time to put the plan into effect. We now have the means to sting Jewry and the countries that kowtow to those sons of dogs. Each of us will carry one small bomb to a decadent Western country and will explode it on their day of memory—April 16—next year. It will do no real physical damage but the psychological effect will be considerable. And…the message will be there: 'we are back.'"

The four men huddled in a planning session, each seeing a new world vision and the resurrection of his Holy Religion.

-END-

Synopsis of Carl Douglass' The Vulture and the Phoenix

Sheep Dog and the Wolf: A Story of Terrorism and Response, and the Sheep Dogs Who Protect, tells about Hunter Caulfield--a man who had long since shaken off his extraordinary past—but is drawn back in with a vengeance when his family encounters terrorists and is annihilated. He is no longer a spectator of inhumanity; it is now personal. Hunter had been in the nefarious CIA Phoenix program during the 'police action' in Vietnam, and had learned a dangerous skill set. His old buddy, now the assistant DCIA, recruits him to be a Sheep Dog—a man who protects the rest of us, the sheep. Hunter undergoes an educational and training ordeal at the CIA's "Farm" training center in Virginia in preparation for his new role.

The U.S. tries diplomacy, bellicosity, threats, embargoes, and a police approach to terrorist devils-incarnate, but none of them works. The president cannot reasonably launch another Iraq or Afghanistan without more harm coming to America. The American public is growing ever more restive. Senior diplomats, military officers, and the administration need a new approach, a new weapon. Sheep Dog is that weapon--an assassin who is a nearly perfectly crafted hunter and killer; a man who can work alone, and who can be disavowed and denied in a moment by a whim of the president.

Hunter—the Sheep Dog—is more than successful; he becomes dangerous. The leaders of the Middle-East became alarmed and threatening toward the American administration. Iran comes to hold the crucial leverage: Israel attacked and destroyed Iran's nuclear production facilities, and Iran presented President Tom Storebridge with an ultimatum. The American government can comply with its demands, including eliminating with maximum prejudice the individual or group whom the Iranian secret service has dubbed "The Shadow", or Iran would launch an all-out nuclear attack on little Israel. Although it is painful to sacrifice an intelligence officer who is serving loyally and with distinction, the decision was quite simple. Storebridge orders the killing of Sheep Dog.

Sheep Dog, however, requires a lot of killing. The American assassin's response to being betrayed is predictable: he became the devil himself. An enormous amount of hand-wringing and regret on the part of his erstwhile friends and fellow warriors follows in the wake of Sheep Dog's cold anger. Neither emotional angst nor efforts to fight back avail the administration or the agency the slightest modicum of success. Hunter Caulfield relentlessly comes for them.

Sheep Dog and the Wolf author, Carl Douglass, is a former neurosurgeon turned successful author who writes with gripping realism. That realism comes from his long exposure to the rigors of the world's most competitive profession and from the camaraderie with men and women he regards as the best story-tellers in the world. Douglass enjoys his now tranquil life of world traveling, medical humanitarian efforts, teaching and writing. He shares those interests with his good wife.